PRAISE FOR JOEY W. HILL'S VAMP

Bound by the Vampire Queen

"Such an emotionally charged tale and so unique . . . Readers will become spellbound as they are taken deeper into this gripping tale one page at a time . . . Truly a wondrous adventure . . . I am looking forward to reading Hill's next endeavor, as she continues to enthrall and surprise me."

—*Risqué Reviews*

Vampire Instinct

"Erotic writing at its best."

—*RT Book Reviews*

"Has everything you would want in an erotic romance . . . I highly recommend this book. [It] takes the reader on an emotional roller coaster along with the cha...

: *Romance Reviews*

"I LOVED th...   ...or writes beautifully and she ...   . . . I can't wait to read what happens next."

—*ParaNormal Romance*

"Grabs the reader's attention on page one and takes the reader on a rollercoaster ride of plot twists and turns and emotional highs and lows through the entire book . . . I highly recommend *Vampire Instinct* and that you keep a box of tissues handy."

—*TwoLips Reviews*

continued . . .

Vampire Trinity

"Only Joey W. Hill can make me yearn for blood and fangs."
— *Romance Junkies*

"One amazingly phenomenal sexy novel that will keep the pages turning, your imagination running, your dreams carnally vivid and your partner very happy." — *Bitten by Books*

"Joey W. Hill impresses me with every word she writes."
— *Joyfully Reviewed*

"Ms. Hill is a talented writer with a style that can only be deemed exclusively hers . . . All of the books in this series are ardently poignant romances at their finest." — *Risqué Reviews*

Vampire Mistress

"Keep a fan and a glass of ice water handy; this one will raise your temperature." — *RT Book Reviews*

"The Vampire Queen novels are more than a reader ever needs to indulge in a world where connection with the characters is amazingly intense and all-consuming, leaving you very, very satisfied." — *Fresh Fiction*

Beloved Vampire

"Lock the door, turn off the television and hide the phone before starting this book, because it's impossible to put down! . . . The story is full of action, intrigue, danger, history and sexual tension . . . This is definitely a keeper!" — *RT Book Reviews*

"This has to be the best vampire novel I've read in a very long time! Joey W. Hill has outdone herself . . . [I] couldn't put it down and didn't want it to end." — *ParaNormal Romance*

A Vampire's Claim

"Had me in its thrall. Joey W. Hill pulled me in and didn't let me go."
—*Joyfully Reviewed*

"So ardent with action and sex you won't remember to breathe . . . Another stunning installment in her vampire series." —*TwoLips Reviews*

"A great vampire romance . . . [An] enticing, invigorating thriller."
—*The Best Reviews*

The Mark of the Vampire Queen

"Superb . . . This is erotica at its best with lots of sizzle and a love that is truly sacrificial. Joey W. Hill continues to grow as a stunning storyteller."
—*A Romance Review*

"Packs a powerful punch." —*TwoLips Reviews*

"Hill never ceases to amaze us . . . She keeps you riveted to your seat and leaves you longing for more with each sentence." —*Night Owl Reviews*

"Fans of erotic romantic fantasy will relish [it]." —*The Best Reviews*

The Vampire Queen's Servant

"Should come with a warning: intensely sexy, sensual story that will hold you hostage until the final word is read. The story line is fresh and unique, complete with a twist." —*RT Book Reviews*

"Hot, kinky, sweating, hard-pounding, oh-my-god-is-it-hot-in-here-or-is-it-just-me sex . . . So compelling it just grabs you deep inside."
—*TwoLips Reviews*

continued . . .

MORE PRAISE FOR THE NOVELS OF JOEY W. HILL

"Everything Joey W. Hill writes just rocks my world."   —Jaci Burton

"Sweet yet erotic . . . will linger in your heart long after the story is over."
—*Sensual Romance Reviews*

"One of the finest, most erotic love stories I've ever read. Reading this book was a physical experience because it pushes through every other plane until you feel it in your marrow."
—Shelby Reed, author of *Holiday Inn*

"The perfect blend of suspense and romance."   —*The Road to Romance*

"Wonderful . . . The sex is hot, very HOT, [and] more than a little kinky . . . Erotic romance that touches the heart and mind as well as the libido."
—*Scribes World*

"A beautifully told story of true love, magic and strength . . . a wondrous tale . . . A must-read."   —*Romance Junkies*

"A passionate, poignant tale . . . the sex was emotional and charged with meaning . . . yet another must-read story from the ever-talented Joey W. Hill."   —*Just Erotic Romance Reviews*

"This is not only a keeper but one you will want to run out and tell your friends about."   —*Fallen Angel Reviews*

"Not for the closed-minded. And it's definitely not for those who like their erotica soft."   —*A Romance Review*

Taken by a Vampire

Joey W. Hill

HEAT BOOKS
New York

THE BERKLEY PUBLISHING GROUP
Published by the Penguin Group
Penguin Group (USA) Inc.
375 Hudson Street, New York, New York 10014, USA

USA | Canada | UK | Ireland | Australia | New Zealand | India | South Africa | China

Penguin Books Ltd., Registered Offices: 80 Strand, London WC2R 0RL, England
For more information about the Penguin Group, visit penguin.com.

HEAT and the HEAT design are trademarks of Penguin Group (USA) Inc.

Library of Congress Cataloging-in-Publication Data

Hill, Joey W.
Taken by a Vampire / Joey W. Hill. — Heat trade paperback edition.
pages cm
ISBN 978-0-425-26067-8
1. Vampires—Fiction.   2. Erotic fiction.   3. Occult fiction.   I. Title.
PS3608.I4343T35   2013
813'.6—dc23
2012046048

PUBLISHING HISTORY
Heat trade paperback edition / May 2013

PRINTED IN THE UNITED STATES OF AMERICA

10 9 8 7 6 5 4 3 2

Cover art by Don Sipley.
Cover design by George Long.

Acknowledgments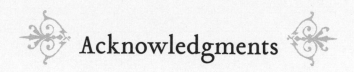

I'd love to have nothing but hours and hours to research the characters and events in my books. Since deadline demands usually discourage such leisurely pursuits, I'm always so grateful for my readers, fellow authors and other experts who jump in and help me out when I need fast, specific answers to improve the authenticity of my work.

As a result, Evan's Jewish roots and Niall's Scottish background/dialect have been improved tremendously by those resources. I give my great thanks to Rachel, Brittany and Paulina for their dedicated efforts in this regard. I also thank Trixie for her offer of backup help. An author can never have too many resources at her fingertips.

The provocative tattoo scene between Evan and Niall allowed me to learn a great deal more about this art form. Geoff, who patiently fielded all my follow-up questions, has probably never had an un-tattooed person so interested in his process! My thanks to him and Ferg both for letting me observe for several hours at the 2012 Authors After Dark conference. It was a very educational and entertaining experience. Thanks also to Mindy for sitting with me and offering quiet insights—you were wonderful company, girl!

Any errors in the book are entirely mine and likely due to this author's woeful propensity to get carried away with foreign vernacular and her romantic imaginings.

Finally, my usual huge thanks to my critique partners and the Berkley editorial staff and cover art department, for making all my work so much better.

1

SHE'D betrayed her Master. In the vampire world, there was no greater crime a servant could commit. She should be overwhelmed by her failure, but she was numb. What did anything matter, once a decision was made that was the end of everything? Her feelings since that moment had been out of reach, faces at the top of a well, staring down at her silent, prolonged drowning.

She was cold, but that was immaterial. Her needs had always been secondary to her Master's. A simple issue of being cold wouldn't interfere with her respectful silence, the straightness of her back as she sat on her knees in the empty hallway. There was a chair here, but she hadn't been told she could use it. A tapestry hung on the wall before her, a depiction of Hell, monsters with gaping mouths, staring eyes.

Lady Lyssa, the new head of the Vampire Council, planned to move their headquarters out of this grim Berlin castle. But there was other business to finish first, and Alanna was part of that. The only reason she was still alive was because they'd hoped to track her Master through her blood connection to him. When Lord Stephen had plotted the murder of the Council's primary assassin as part of a larger conspiracy to increase the influence of made vampires, he'd become a fugitive. He'd have killed her before he fled, but escape had been a higher priority.

That didn't guarantee her safety, not that she'd ever had any hope of that. Once he'd found a safe hole, he'd begun tearing her apart. It was the only practical choice, really. He had no ally loyal enough to risk the Council's wrath by taking her life. So he'd destroy her from the inside. A fully marked servant had no defense against her Master's invasion. He could reach into her soul, torment and break the mind of his bloodbound human minion.

She wondered if whoever had created that tapestry had endured such an experience. If so, the terrified eyes and gaping mouths belonged to people the artist had loved, or different, twisted versions of his own soul, put through unspeakable horrors. Time had no meaning in the face of such mental agony.

The tapestry dominated her field of vision, but she wouldn't alter the correct alignment of her eyes straight ahead. However, the gooseflesh caused by the chilly hall prickled in reaction as she stared at the wash of bloodred fibers that dissolved, became blood itself, trickling down over the scene.

She supposed it had been exhausting to Stephen, maintaining the energy to keep her spinning on her axis so the Council couldn't draw a bead on him, send their assassin to end him. That he hated her for her betrayal, would kill her for punishment as well as self-preservation, was certain. But overall it wasn't personal. The soul torment had been to preserve his hiding place. He had no feelings for her. A human servant was a valuable tool until she wasn't. Stephen had made that clear, long ago.

Lord Belizar, the Council head when Stephen's treachery had come to light, had harshly commanded her to stay alive, to endure. His thunderous Russian baritone had penetrated the nightmares, and her training had done the rest. She was an Inherited Servant. She would obey, would serve with every ounce of will she had.

Before she'd been conceived, she'd been promised to the InhServ program. The intense indoctrination had begun at age six, the last time she'd sat at a table with her birth family. Her parents taught her to kneel behind her father's chair and wait silently while they ate dinner, talked to their other children and each other. It had been confusing, but when she understood she was being prepared for the great honor of serving a vampire, she'd embraced the idea. Her one desire, her one goal in life, had been to exceed even the high expectations of that honor.

Yet, in the end, she'd come to this.

Lord Brian, the Council scientist and doctor, had experimented with a variety of blockers, things that would stop Stephen's interference with her mind, but each one failed. As Stephen's torment of her mind persisted for weeks, Lord Belizar's command wasn't enough to override her Master's power over her soul. She had to be strapped down to keep her from taking her own life, because Stephen was doing everything in his power to make her do just that.

"I will find a way to block him, Alanna. But you must help me. You must hold on."

When he said that, Lord Brian didn't know he looked like a giant spider to her, with snapping mandibles and hairy legs reaching for her, but even as she was screaming and writhing against her bonds, soiling herself with her fear, the inexorable command penetrated.

There was a gentle firmness in Lord Brian's directive that made her want to try harder, keep struggling, though she didn't know why it bolstered her will more than Lord Belizar's harsh, impersonal command. There was no room in her mind for asking such questions. She did hear snippets of conversation, voices in the storm.

Could try more aggressive methods . . . but it will kill her. Only one shot, and if it doesn't work, we lose our chance.

They should do it. She was useless otherwise. She couldn't keep her Master from unbalancing her mind long enough for them to get a fix on him. If they could pin the butterfly to the board and, in those few moments while her wings were still twitching, get a bead on him, then her last act would be one of service.

"Please . . ." She must have said something to that effect, because it was the only time she remembered Lord Brian touching her, a brief whisper of fingertips over her forehead that Stephen turned into worms crawling into her eyes, sending her screaming down another blood-soaked tunnel. But then something else had happened. Even now, she didn't know whether her mind had created something to help her obey the Council's will, or if it had been real. Since Lord Brian's blockers had started to work, she'd had difficulty parsing the reality from the nightmares she'd experienced during those terrible days.

She'd been too exhausted to fight anymore, deaf and dumb to everything but those hallucinations. The significant thing had happened while she was staring at a group of rats, perched on her ripped-open belly, feeding on her exposed insides. Blood on their muzzles.

Dead . . . better off dead . . . kill yourself. Serve your Master. Make up for your betrayal. It's the only way to make it right.

"I never paint dreams or nightmares. I paint my own reality." The calm, confident tone brought the rats to an abrupt stop. They stood on their haunches, looked through the wall of flames surrounding her. "That's a quote from Frida Kahlo. Easy, *yekirati*. We'll see what pictures we can paint together."

She couldn't see anything, but that voice . . . A vampire male for certain, but just like Lord Brian's voice, his had something . . . *more* to it. Something that made her want to please, to obey, and not just because of her natural desire to serve, honed by her training. His hand settled on her abdomen. Long, elegant fingers, pale skin. Ragged nails, rough cuticles. Odd. Most vampires had well-manicured hands.

The rats fizzled away into scattered ash, her flesh reknitting over her concave stomach. Her ribs protruded over it like the lip of a cave. They'd tried feeding her, but everything came up. Only steel through the heart could kill a third-mark servant . . . or beheading, which killed pretty much everything, so she could be a skeleton with skin stretched over it and endure to serve.

Those fingers whispered over her flesh, distracting her. When they disappeared from her view, she drew an unhappy breath, but they returned covered in paint, which they started to swirl across her flesh. He'd meant it quite literally. He was painting a picture. This was obviously another hallucination, which meant Stephen would turn it into something horrid, but she'd take the respite. She wanted to hear that voice again. But a servant didn't ask for anything.

The figment of her imagination created a sky across her stomach. Blue, green, a touch of rose. The muted red and orange he'd applied first became a hazy sunrise. His touch soothed. She didn't want it to go away, but she was at her Master's mercy. She'd betrayed him once, but she would resist him no other way. She would honor her training that much.

An abrupt sting in her arm told her something new was flowing through her veins. Lord Brian, perhaps trying something different. But she kept staring at those fingers. More details were coming into focus. The new male wore a ring, a heavy pewter band with markings on it. As he drew his hand away, he grazed her bound one. She managed to latch on to the middle finger that bore the ring and tried to make sense of it, like a blind person reading Braille. He stilled, letting her hold on to him with that awkward, weak grasp. A servant didn't touch a vampire unless invited, but this wasn't real, so it didn't matter.

"Time is a great healer. That is what the ring says, in Hebrew. My ancestral language, so to speak."

His voice was thoroughly masculine. It seemed absurd to call a man's voice masculine, but Stephen's hadn't struck her that way. She thought of the Edgar Rice Burroughs story, where the hero described a trusted brother-in-arms as "fully male," meaning he had all the best qualities a man could have. So perhaps it wasn't so absurd.

He had no definable accent, typical of a well-traveled vampire with a few centuries in age, but she'd guess American. Whatever Lord Brian had injected seemed to be clearing her mind. Her body twitched, then went into a rigid, muscle-grinding spasm. She clamped down on that ring finger as her other hand convulsed, fingers jerking into a splayed, spiderlike rigor. Her thighs strained, pressing her hips hard into the table, her neck arching. A cry struggled free of her throat, crossed an inert tongue, dry lips.

"Easy . . . dinnae fash yourself, lass." Another new voice, Scottish, came from directly above her. Though he had a different accent, this man had a tone like the other man's. Gentle, irrefutable command that told her she should do her best to obey—once she determined what *fashing* was and why she shouldn't do it—and that obeying their will was a port in the storm. A shelter.

She was looking up into tawny brown eyes. Dark brown hair was carelessly pulled back from his strong-featured face. He was a big man, towering over her like a concerned oak. If she put her slim hand on his jaw, she expected it would look like a child's in comparison. When he put his hands on her head, cupping her ears, her jaw, it emphasized his size.

Her lashes brushed her cheeks as she looked downward again. The hazy sun painted on her abdomen now shone on a green meadow dotted with white flowers, all of it smeared and dreamlike, like an Impressionist painting. The man with the ring tugged the sheet down as he decorated her mons, the tops of her thighs, expanding the meadow over the terrain of her naked body.

Even in this state her body was trained to respond to a vampire's touch. An unbidden tear rolled out her right eye, sliding along her temple. The Scot caught it on his thumb, made another reassuring noise. He bent, brushed his lips across her strapped-down forehead. It told her he was this vampire's servant, for no vampire would ever act with such tender sentiment, especially not in front of Lord Brian. But he didn't seem like any servant she knew. Stephen was obviously still playing with her mind, her own broken dreams weaving among his vicissitudes like creeper vines in a crumbling castle wall.

"Alanna, tell me what you feel."

She never refused a vampire's command, but Lord Brian asked her a question she'd never been asked. She couldn't remember when she'd stopped thinking about it, or if she'd ever thought about it at all. Service was above ego, above individual need and want. There were only the Master's feelings and needs. Yet she'd spent the past . . . she really didn't know how long it had been anymore . . . resisting Stephen's screaming command for her to die, to take her own life. Because Lord Belizar had told her no, Lord Brian had told her no. She refused to be a total failure. Perhaps she did have a will of her own, which meant she'd never been as good a servant as she'd thought.

"Alanna. Tell him how you feel." The painter was giving her the command now. He pressed down on the wet paint, his thumb making slow, easy passes over her pubic bone, charging the nerves at the tops of her thighs. He gave her the command as if she belonged to him personally. Did he understand that had been the biggest loss to her? For the first time in so many years, she didn't belong to someone. Cut out of the circle, no longer a part of anything.

"Do I need to tell you twice?"

"No, Master." When the unplanned response rasped from her lips, the two sets of fingers stilled. Yes, she'd only called Stephen that, but it felt right. Maybe more right than it had with him, ever. That also didn't make sense, but her mind and soul were broken. Sanity and logic were beyond her grasp.

She was too tired to dissect anything. She didn't spend much time on such things even on a good day, and this was certainly not a good day.

"I feel . . ." Searching the scarred battlefield of her mind and soul, she latched on to the word that meant the end of her usefulness.

"Abandoned. He's gone."

~

Lord Brian had at last found a chemical combination that blocked the nightmares, but it also blocked Stephen's access to her. She didn't understand why they'd bothered to keep her alive after that. She'd proven too weak to resist his dismemberment of her soul, the scrambling of her mind. As long as she was taking those injections, they couldn't use her to pinpoint his location.

However, during the weeks of her illness and months of recuperation, remarkable changes had occurred. The Vampire Council was now under new leadership. Lady Lyssa, last of the vampire royals, had staged a coup and knocked Lord Belizar from his position as head of the Council. She'd killed the only other made vampire on the Council, Lady Barbra, and installed Lady Daniela from the Australian territories to take her place.

Soon after Alanna had been moved to a regular bed to be fed and assigned a daily exercise regimen to recover atrophied muscle, Lady Lyssa had visited her. Alanna had struggled to leave the bed, go to her knees, but the vampire queen had forbidden it.

"You will preserve your strength." Those cool jade eyes assessed her state, kept her pinned in place. "I command you to regain your health. I will determine what to do with you shortly."

So now, at last, "shortly" had come. As she waited outside Council chambers, in this cold, silent hallway, Alanna couldn't hear what was going on behind the solid doors. She should be able to hear the occasional murmur caused by a raised voice, which was why this hallway was kept clear during Council sessions. However, the blocker had a devastating side effect. The exceptional strength, speed and senses that came with being a third mark were neutralized. For the first time since she'd become Stephen's third mark, at age sixteen, she felt merely human.

Lady Lyssa's command to "regain your health" was the second hardest thing that had ever been demanded of her, but the queen was the closest thing to a Master she had now, however temporal that would be.

Alanna recalled the fingers on her stomach, the vampire attached to them commanding her to answer Lord Brian. She also thought about the Scot's soothing tone. He'd spoken often while she was being painted by his Master. His accent was like music, the way he dragged out the vowels in some places, made them dense and strong in others. *Fiiinal . . . Book* was *buek . . . Certainly* was *cairtenly.* And the wonderful rolling *rs . . .*

The effectiveness of the blocker had brought on exhaustion and desolation, sending her into unconsciousness. When she woke, they hadn't been there, and there was no paint on her body. She'd looked thoroughly for any trace of it, and found nothing. During the days that followed, where she remained mute unless Lord Brian needed an answer to a question, she realized the men touching her had been some strange mental defense against Stephen's torment. But it felt more real than the most hideous nightmare he'd sent her, and since what made the nightmares so awful was how *very* real they felt, that was saying something.

"Alanna?"

She lifted her head to see Jacob, Lady Lyssa's servant, standing in the doorway. She hadn't heard the heavy portal open. Exhorting herself to focus, be attentive as she should, she slid her weight to the balls of her feet and tried to rise gracefully in one motion. It worked, but the effort was phenomenal. She was still so weak.

Offering assistance to any InhServ was a deep insult to them. Requiring help was a mark of shame. But the broad-shouldered Irishman with steady midnight blue eyes was an odd sort, not the usual kind of servant. One never knew what he might do.

She stepped into the chamber. The dimly lit oval room with stone walls, iron chandelier and crescent-shaped table elevated on a platform was as intimidating as it was intended to be. Even the floor-length velvet tablecloth was the color of dried blood. It was easy to imagine black-cloaked Inquisitioners here, staring down upon hapless souls.

She'd expected to face the whole Council. Instead, only Lady Lyssa was present.

The oldest living vampire was a master at that eerie stillness that could make her almost invisible, except for the itchy feeling suggesting a predator was watching. Correctly realizing she didn't need any props to make her more scary, the queen had the head Council chair positioned on the flagstone floor, not on the raised dais behind the table. An empty chair faced her, several paces away.

Alanna knelt, keeping the proscribed distance from a Council vampire. "I'm here to serve, my lady. What is your will for me?"

"You are aware of the dilemma your existence presents, Alanna. What do you think we should do with you?"

Even without looking up, she felt the weight of those jade green eyes boring into her. Lady Lyssa was barely over five feet. The porcelain skin and sharp nails, the long black hair she often kept clipped over one shoulder, enhanced her beauty, but they also reinforced how striking and untouchable she was. Except to Jacob, who stood behind her chair now.

An InhServ, when requested to respond, only offered opinions on how something should best be done to serve her Master's interests. So Alanna framed her answer accordingly.

"I am a liability, because I cannot help you find my Master. He might use my mind to determine what your plans are, if I am kept in proximity to Council. I submit to your judgment and willingly sacrifice my life."

"The treatment Brian found blocks Lord Stephen's hold on your mind. The pain as well?"

Alanna flushed, her knuckles pressing hard into the cold flagstone. "Yes. I am too weak to bear the pain he inflicts on me when the blocker is not present. It blinds me to his location. I apologize for my failure."

"You are apologizing that your will is not strong enough to overcome your Master's?"

Alanna shook her head. "Forgive me, my lady. It's clear I am not worthy of my training. I await your judgment."

Please, just get it over with. Let this end.

Instead, she stiffened as a male hand closed on her elbow.

"You will permit Jacob to assist you."

She couldn't refuse the queen's order, but her shame was nigh unbearable as Jacob lifted her into the empty chair. She'd become stiff, sitting on her knees. He put a woman's cloak over her shoulders, a ruby-colored thick fabric that smelled like cloves. Had it come from Lady Lyssa's chair? It had retained some of the body heat of the previous occupant, so it could be no other's.

Pushed into a paradigm she couldn't comprehend, she looked up at Jacob blankly.

"You're shivering," he said. "Your skin is ice-cold."

Why would that matter? Staring at him, she registered he was handsome, not unusual for a servant, but there was a directness to his midnight blue eyes, the way he touched a woman, that suggested a knight of medieval times. It gave him a unique appeal, but what made him truly exceptional was how he used that quality to serve his lady. The relationship between him and Lady Lyssa, the last Queen of the Far East Clan, was barely whispered about even among servants—because of how forbidden it was.

He'd declared his love for her, but a servant was permitted to have that level of feeling for his Mistress. Alanna had never felt love toward Stephen, but dedication, loyalty and devotion were what he demanded. No, what was shocking was that Lady Lyssa had reciprocated Jacob's feelings. Not just in private, where such a thing *might* rarely happen, and, if it did, a wise servant never spoke of it. The Queen had declared it before the whole Council.

A vampire falling in love with his or her servant was almost as taboo as revealing the existence of vampires to the human world. Vampires were superior beings, regarding their servants at best as treasured pets, but pets all the same. Love suggested some type of . . . equal footing, at least on an emotional level. Unthinkable.

Even so, Alanna suspected Lady Lyssa's idea of love was still a different concept than Jacob's. However, the queen had delayed the business which had brought Alanna before her, allowing her servant the time to lift her from the floor, get her settled and comfortable, even speak to her. When he left Alanna's side, moving to stand behind his lady's chair again, Alanna dared a quick glance. Lady Lyssa showed no disapproval. Nor did she seem less queenlike for it.

"Lord Brian has told me that if a more powerful vampire than Lord Stephen third-marks you, there is a possibility we can override Lord Stephen's hold *and* track him. He also feels that would permanently break your mind. Though it was not his intent that you overhear that information, my understanding is that you did, and immediately volunteered to submit to such treatment."

"When Lord Stephen is brought to justice, my life will end, my lady. My sanity does not seem of great importance during that temporary period. If I cannot help you, it's best to remove me from the equation." The cape's warmth helped her straighten further, though she kept her eyes downcast.

"I have a different alternative in mind," Lyssa said, after a weighted pause. "You met Evan. Do you remember?"

Alanna struggled with the change of subject. "No, my lady."

"When Lord Brian was testing the blocking serum, he and his servant helped calm you. He's an artist. His servant, Niall, is Scottish."

She almost forgot herself and lifted her head. Instead, she tightened her fingers around one another. Just an inconsequential bit of memory, suddenly so significant to her. A piece of reality Stephen hadn't been able to twist into a nightmare.

"Though your mind is blocked, your importance to him is such that Stephen might use other methods to find you. So we will use the rabbit to flush the wolf a different way. One that poses less risk to you, but perhaps not so much less that it insults your InhServ protocol."

She didn't know what to make of that remark. Sarcasm? Sympathy? Straight fact? Fortunately, Lady Lyssa wasn't requesting a response.

"Evan is a made vampire, one with no political standing. Part of the fabric of our society rather than an outstanding marker upon it." Rather than condescension, Lyssa's tone suggested amused irony. "He has an incurable case of wanderlust but, as luck will have it, the next few months he plans to be in the southern region of the United States, which is where I will be moving Council headquarters once I conclude matters here. You are being put in his care until the situation with Stephen alters. Evan will second-mark you, for Brian believes Evan's strength and age, less than Stephen's, will make that possible without damage. Evan agreed to Lord Daegan taking his blood as a sire so that he can communicate with him as needed, a conduit to your mind and location."

No vampire allowed another vampire to take their blood, not if they could prevent it. It was done by overlords and Region Masters to ensure the loyalties of the vampires within their territories, or by vampires forcibly imposing dominance on weaker ones. What little she knew of Evan didn't seem to fit that assessment, but it didn't matter. The decision was out of her hands.

She hadn't imagined serving another vampire. No one of political stature would want her again, and an InhServ was too integrated into the upper echelon to be used anywhere else. Lady Lyssa uttering Lord Daegan's name in her presence was a prime example. Only the Council members and their servants—and of course Lord Stephen had been on the Council—knew Daegan was the Council assassin, dispatching vampires who broke the laws of their volatile world. She'd been in his presence rarely herself, but he exuded exactly what he was. The top predator in a world of predators, perhaps only surpassed by Lady Lyssa herself, and Alanna wouldn't be putting money on the winner of that combat.

In short, Alanna knew as much about vampire politics and etiquette as the queen. But it was a moot point. When Stephen was apprehended, he would be executed. As soon as a vampire died, blocker or no, his fully marked servant died with him.

Was the burden of dealing with her, putting him in Stephen's path, a punishment for Evan? A debt he owed to the Council?

"Niall will arrive Friday to escort you to him. Until you receive any further direction from the Council, you serve Evan as a servant should. Obey him as you would obey me, in all things."

"Yes, my lady." The command of any vampire was law, as long as that command didn't conflict with orders from the servant's Master or Mistress. Even their will could be overridden if the command was issued by a higher-ranking vampire, though the servant could expect punishment for it by her vampire later. Stephen had done so severely, once or twice, when she'd obeyed the directive of a Council member who outranked him. He hadn't expected her to disobey the Council member, any more than she'd been surprised to endure his ire and abused ego over it. Being the outlet for his anger was part of her responsibilities.

Pushing away any tension she had over serving a vampire again, she accepted her charge. She was to treat Evan as her Master, even though he would withhold the vital third mark that would bind her irrevocably to him, and she would be bait for Stephen, her true Master. It made her tired and sad.

If a servant was allowed preferences—and she wasn't—she would have preferred death.

2

THERE wouldn't be much to pack. Stephen's household items had been seized by the Council, and most of the items she'd brought to the castle before everything transpired were gone, stolen while she was in the infirmary. However, upon her return from the meeting with Lady Lyssa, she found everything else had been taken. Apparently, the small corps of InhServ in permanent residence with the Council were sending one last message. Since it would be three days before Niall came for her, and she didn't want her new Master's representative to find her unprepared, she quietly approached the household staff, offering to help out with their duties in exchange for a couple of changes of clothes and basic toiletries. Hairbrush, toothbrush, makeup. Feminine products, since her health had improved enough for her monthly courses to resume.

Within a few hours of that discussion, a knock at her door revealed Jacob. Glancing at the sign that had been tacked there by the InhServs, his mouth tightened, his blue eyes getting cold, making it clear his Mistress wasn't the only one with a dangerous side. When he reached for it, she lifted a hand.

"Please don't. It's better to leave it."

After a close study of her expression, he nodded. Stepping inside the room, he put down an armload of packages and store bags. "These contain the items you requested from the staff."

She couldn't have been more mortified if Lady Lyssa herself had delivered them. "I didn't—"

"No, you didn't. But you should have." He touched her face, drawing her gaze up to him. "If you need anything further like this, Alanna, you'll come to me or Victor and let us know. Don't let me find out otherwise."

Victor, Belizar's servant, had run the castle before Lyssa took the Council head's position by force. In that interesting way servants had, Victor and Jacob had overlooked their vampires' differences and worked together to keep things running efficiently.

"I didn't intend to cause you any additional work. If there's anything I can do . . ."

"You won't be helping the household staff." Picking up her hand, he examined the thinness of her wrists. "If you need something to keep you occupied, I'll give you desk work. There's plenty of correspondence. God knows, both Victor and I hate doing it."

Jacob had been the only one to touch her since . . . Evan and Niall. She didn't want him to let go of her hand. The strength and gentleness of his touch, the mild but unmistakable sternness of his voice, awakened a craving in her so strong she almost swayed on her feet. Drawing her dignity around her, even if it was a tattered cloak, she steadied herself.

"Thank you. Anything you need, I will be happy to do."

~

Over the next three days, he'd kept her busy as promised, though she suspected it was more of his unexpected kindness than a real need for her assistance. But today that came to an end. She was preparing to join her new Master. Even if the main purpose of her placement was to draw Stephen out of hiding, perhaps she'd prove to be of true use to Evan. While drawing out Stephen was a use, she wasn't certain how functional that was to Evan's needs, except as a way to be rid of her sooner.

She'd become a burden.

When she was done packing, she sat on her bed, the suitcase before her. Her mind stepped back into that painting on her flesh. The hazy sun, the small dots of white flowers . . . the casually possessive graze of fingers over her sex. It was the only thing worth remembering any- more. That and Adam. But thinking about Adam was still too painful, because it connected to everything else.

She'd had four other siblings. Three considered her an oddity in their world of school, sports, making friends. Dating. But Adam was her twin. On his eighth birthday he'd asked for only one gift. To be enlisted in the preenrollment training with her. Her parents had re- fused, not wanting to lose both their firstborns, but Adam persevered, appealing directly to the InhServ rep who made monthly visits to check on her progress. All she'd had to do was see the two of them side by side, red-haired, fair-skinned twins, and Adam's will persevered.

Alanna was considered exceptional by the trainers. Hungering for the ability to serve and do everything needed for a vampire Master or Mistress, she had no resistance to full submission, no need to deter- mine her own sexuality or any other preferences. Those decisions be- longed to her Master or Mistress.

Though the vampire world was dominated by born vampires, the Council advanced a handful of made ones who demonstrated enough power and Machiavellian traits to warrant notice. As such, they often assigned an InhServ to a made vampire who met their qualifications for the privilege. Alanna's job had been not only to serve Stephen, but to give him insight into the politics and culture of the born vampire world, to help him adapt to their ways. Since she was only sixteen, it was an unprecedented honor to her.

It wasn't natural to Adam like it was to her, but he'd been assigned to a well-placed Mistress, a born vampire who was an overlord of a territory in Spain.

And now he was dead.

That was why she'd done it, gone to Lord Brian when she'd learned of Lord Stephen's deceit against the Council. Her own selfish pain for Adam. A servant accepted that a Master's or Mistress's sins were their own. There was no need to make a decision between right and wrong. The Master's will was the only compass. She lived to serve him in every way, regardless of what kind of person he was. The point was the service.

It had been a moment of unforgivable weakness, a purely emo- tional decision. Adam had loved her so much he became an InhServ with her. Even knowing they wouldn't share the same household, he'd chosen to share the same life she did, the same world. Her Master had refused to allow her to grieve him, had even forced her to . . .

Refusing to go any further with that, Alanna began a meditation discipline, intended to center and focus her mind. Whether a mockery or not, her training had become the puppet strings that kept her moving.

A knock on the door interrupted it. It was Debra, bringing her several months' worth of blocking treatment. Lord Brian had made it clear she must take them religiously. If that wall fell, Stephen could not only set upon her mind and soul again; he might tear her apart if he detected the challenge of a second-marking from Evan.

As Debra emphasized those instructions again, Alanna nodded. "I understand. Can you tell me anything useful about my service to . . . my new Master?" She'd never served a vampire without the title of lord, and she didn't know Evan's last name, so she went with the honorific. "Did he . . . paint on me?"

"Yes, he did," Debra said. "At that point, Lord Brian was willing to attempt anything that might salvage your mind, no matter the scientific merits."

She wasn't sure how to respond to that. "And Niall is Scottish?"

"Yes. He's a forceful personality, for a servant. Much like Jacob." Debra's serious eyes twinkled. "A definite alpha."

Alanna remembered Niall's large hands on her face, the way he'd spoken to her. She'd responded as if his words were commands, so perhaps Debra was right about that.

"You calmed under their touch, when not even our strongest tranquilizers had an effect. It influenced Lady Lyssa's decision about their custody."

Debra's expression changed, that inward look when a servant was receiving a communication from her vampire. It filled Alanna with envy. The emptiness of her soul and the solitary state of her mind were a daily ache, even if the last time a vampire had been there it had been to shred them. "My lord Brian is coming," Debra said. "He has Lord Daegan with him."

Alanna wanted to know more about Niall and Evan, but that would have to wait. She'd seen Lord Daegan only briefly at a couple of Council meetings. His anonymity was necessary to do the Council's bidding, so he wasn't a regular visitor at the castle. As he slid into her room, she noted the tall, dark-eyed vampire's purposeful way of moving, the emotionless countenance that suggested he could decapitate or stake one of his brethren with the ease of breathing.

Sliding from her chair, she went to her knees in automatic deference, a graceful fold of motion.

"None of that, now. He'll get delusions of grandeur, expect that bullshit out of me."

Gideon, Daegan's servant, put his hand under her arm, brought her back to her feet. The strength of his grip, tempered by the fact that he was handling a woman, was familiar. Even if she didn't glance up into the same midnight blue eyes, she would have known Jacob was his brother. Gideon had a harder, rougher look, but the steady attention that could fluster a woman was the same.

Jacob and Gideon were not like her and Adam. They hadn't become servants at the same time, nor for the same motives and circumstances. Gideon had been an exceptionally successful vampire hunter, slated for death by the Vampire Council. He'd been part of the team who'd set explosives at the previous Vampire Gathering, where Adam and his Mistress had been killed.

She'd wanted to hate him, but the world was more complicated than that. Ironically, he was the first who understood and acknowledged her grief over her brother's death. In a surprising twist of fate, he now had two vampire Masters, Lord Daegan and Anwyn. Anwyn was still a fledgling by vampire standards, but she'd been a Mistress and owner of a BDSM club as a human, so her direct look and air of dominance had made her a complement to the vampire world from the beginning. She stood at the door, watching the proceedings silently, but Alanna could feel Gideon's connection to her and Daegan like a three-pointed star, shining painfully bright.

Drawing her hand away from Gideon, Alanna stood alone. Her job was service, not to be comforted. It was forgivable, their lack of understanding, because he, Jacob and Debra were Randoms, those who'd come to their vampires by happenstance and choice, not selected from birth as she'd been. However, that didn't absolve her of the requirement to courteously rebuff such gestures. That was what set an InhServ apart, made them the elite in the servant ranks.

It's a charade, all of it.

She was too tired to block the thought.

"While Lord Daegan is not going to mark you, Alanna, he is going to taste your blood."

While she didn't require an explanation, Gideon added, "It's similar to giving a bloodhound a piece of clothing. He can pick up your scent easier later if needed."

She nodded. She'd kept her eyes down and now sensed the three men exchanging glances with Debra. Whatever they were communicating apparently did not delay what they intended, for Gideon's hands were on her shoulders, steadying her as Lord Daegan swept her hair away from her neck. As she automatically tilted her head toward Gideon, giving his Master access to the artery, her chin brushed both men's fingers. Daegan's hands overlapped Gideon's on either side. It was an interesting intimacy, because she picked up reassurance in it.

Stephen had certainly never cared to reassure her when he marked other servants, for he had a household of second-marks. Perhaps the vampire assassin was not as emotionally detached as he always seemed. Flicking her gaze up to Gideon's face, she saw he had his eyes on the vampire. From his intent focus, she was sure they'd locked gazes, something she never did with a vampire. Some vampire–servant relationships were different.

"If anything starts to feel wrong, or you're in pain, he wants you to tell us." Gideon shifted his attention to her. "That's an order. Got it?"

She was surrounded by exceptionally authoritative servants of late. Jacob, Gideon . . . Niall. That dynamic wasn't uncommon in male vampire–male servant pairings, but it was for female vampire–male servant bonds. Another reason Lady Lyssa and Jacob were an anomaly.

"Yes, my lord." She directed the response to the vampire. "But I can bear pain. I've no wish to inconvenience you any more than I have already."

She sensed another exchange between the men. As Daegan's fingers tightened over Gideon's, a warning, she saw the servant bite back some comment, a flash in his blue eyes, though his temper didn't seem directed at her or his Master.

"It's important that we not disrupt the blocker, Alanna," Lord Brian said. "Remember, physical or emotional stress can weaken its effect. Protecting your health and state of mind is how you can best serve us now."

"Yes, my lord." Daegan's breath was on her neck, fangs unsheathing, such that she anticipated the pain as he sank into her flesh. However, the discomfort was less than expected, for he didn't go as deep as a vampire went for a feeding. Of course. Lord Brian was monitoring her reaction; it was a clinical situation. To them, there was no intimacy in this exchange, no sexual significance to a deep penetration of fangs. But Lord Daegan's body was powerful and warm behind her, Gideon's hands against her flesh solid and real. Her body stirred to it, as it always did when she was serving a Master.

Not wanting to embarrass herself, she shifted into a meditative state, while staying tuned in to her surroundings. She'd stood behind Stephen at meetings for hours that way. Motionless and unobtrusive, until the vampires would turn their attention to entertainment, the highly politicized, sexual games she would perform with others at her Master's direction.

Twelve servants . . . Her mind got trapped in the memory of that fateful dinner party after Adam's death. A dozen closed in on her, took her down to the floor at the end, overcome by their lust, goaded by their Masters and Mistresses, until there was a screaming in her head she bit through her tongue to hold back. She blindly followed what was expected of her . . . her every orifice penetrated, her mouth working over cock after cock, tasting her own blood, each climax feeling like her heart was being torn from her chest, a betrayal so deep . . .

"Shhh . . ." Gideon's lips brushed her cheek, taking away a tear as his Master finished, licked over the puncture wounds to coagulate the blood. Five minutes had passed without her even noticing. So much for staying tuned in to her surroundings.

"I'm all right," she said, every muscle tightening up.

"Yes, you are." Daegan ran a hand over her hair, a brief stroke down her back, flummoxing her. Had the assassin himself just reassured her? There was something to his tone, as if he'd learned something from tasting her blood. Something that had earned his approval.

"I won't be far, Alanna," he said. "Follow Lady Lyssa and Evan's direction, and you'll be fine."

Of course she'd follow their direction. But she responded as she should. "Yes, my lord."

When Daegan captured Stephen and the Council executed him, she would die, because a fully-marked servant's life force was linked to her Master's. But that wasn't the end of it, was it? Servants were bound to their vampires in the afterlife, so she'd be with Stephen wherever he went, forever despised by him, forever a failure.

After they all left, she was back to waiting with her single suitcase. She touched that part of her cheek that Gideon's mouth had touched, felt again the pressure of the male hands holding her up.

Realizing what she was doing, she stiffened as if the whip of the InhServ trainer had snapped across her shoulders. She was unacceptably unfocused. Dedication and duty were the two sides of the InhServ knife, both required to stay sharp. The InhServ discipline protocols would serve that purpose. Punishment, deprivation, reflection.

She'd already packed her scourge, else she would have beaten herself bloody, but there were other ways to remind herself. Rising, she found the small bag of uncooked rice she'd left in the nightstand. Putting a towel on the floor, she spread the rice over it and then knelt. It dug into her knees, her calves. She had an hour before Niall was scheduled to come get her. The pain would drive away anything but what was required of her.

～

Niall paused briefly on the Inherited Servants' corridor. The small rooms reminded him of monk's cells, each one with the bare minimum in furnishings, no pictures on the walls. It was a wholly different servant culture he knew little about, for all his three centuries as a vampire's servant. Evan didn't really run in the highbrow circles that included InhServs.

He did know they were an elite guard within the servant ranks, with a severe code when one of them fell short. Kind of overkill, to his way of thinking, given that most vampires were swift to hand out punishment when their servants erred. It further pissed him off to learn from the housekeeping staff that the rest of the InhServs had shunned her since her betrayal of Stephen. Even so, it was still unexpected to see the red *S* sign on her door. Painted in blood, a scent he recognized right off.

He remembered her writhing in pain, her eyes locked on nightmares no one else could see. Stephen had inflicted the torment on her to protect his worthless hide. Evan had taught him well enough to keep such thoughts to himself among other vampires, but it didn't mean he'd take leave of his own code of right and wrong.

When he knocked, she called out to enter in a cultured voice, all soft and fine. He expected she had a bonny singing voice. She rose from the straight-backed chair where she'd been waiting for him behind one suitcase. The room was otherwise sterile, the bed made military-drum tight, the closet door open, showing it empty. She had her long, dark red hair clipped back, the strands falling all the way to her waist in a wealth of curls. He knew she had eyes dark and expressive as a deer's, though of course they were lowered right now, the automatic deference she showed to everyone. She had the delicate fragility of a Fae sprite in her face, her willowy, beautiful body enhanced by the travel clothes of tailored brown skirt and formfitting buttercream sweater. The pair of heeled boots that came to just below her knee suited the chill Berlin weather.

He hadn't seen her since they'd helped Lord Brian in his infirmary, so it was something to see her all put together like this, not sweating and out of her head, screaming and afraid. Brian said she'd stayed alive because she'd been commanded to do so. But Niall remembered the way her lips had curled back, revealing the rage inside the fear. Even if she wasn't aware of it, there might be more to it than that.

Catching the scent of blood again, he narrowed his eyes. Before he zeroed in on the trash can, she explained, anticipating his question. "A punishment exercise. It broke the skin, but no worse than shaving cuts. You needn't worry about the car seats."

Oh, well, aye, that was my main concern. He held back the caustic response, remembering Evan's admonition. *Don't mock her training. Inherited Servants are very different from servants that come to a vampire from . . . more random methods.*

Evan had changed the subject then, because the memories associated with Niall's "random" fate as his servant weren't all pleasant, such that they both tended to leave that subject alone. More convenient for all concerned.

Get her here, and we'll worry about the rest. That had been Evan's primary directive. Time to get on with it, then.

She picked up the suitcase, but it was heavy for her, a reminder that the blocker gave her a human woman's strength, not a third mark's. In a world of fanged predators, it was a serious handicap. Humans connected with the vampire world were marked, not just to protect the secrets of that world, but to prevent a vampire's mild flash of temper from breaking his servant's neck.

"I'll get that."

"I'll carry it."

"Nae while I'm here." When he closed his hand over hers, she stiffened like a startled deer, dropping the case on his foot.

"My apologies," she said stiffly. "I'm not accustomed to another servant touching me when a vampire isn't present to order it."

"No worries, lass. My foot's hard as my heid. Almost." Giving her flushed cheeks a casual scrutiny, he thought there was more to her startled reaction than that. "Is that a forbidden thing, then?"

"Yes. Incidental brushes of contact can lead to other things, given how attuned servants are to the carnal appetites of their Masters and Mistresses. A Master or Mistress requires that all desire be centered or channeled through their orders, not the feelings or desires of the servant. It's important for the servant to keep their focus at all times on their Master or Mistress."

Niall blinked. "That's a mouthful, lass. So you're saying ye dinnae trust yourself to touch me."

When her gaze snapped up, he gave her a charming smile, in spite of her haunted look that twisted his heart. "There you are. Lass, I dinnae know a thing about Inherited Servants. My run-o'-the-mill servant skills are shabby enough. But you've no need to worry about my manners. They're rough, but I wouldnae force myself on an unwilling woman. You're safe with me."

She shook her head. "I'm not afraid of that. InhServs follow a strict code of conduct. It's necessary for us to maintain the quality of our service. There's no reason you should know about it, and I shouldn't have reacted that way. I really can carry my case."

"Why would a lady want to do that when she has a big clumsy bear like myself tae do it? I have to be useful somehow. Let's get out o' this damp hellhole."

Her brows lifted, but she nodded. When he gestured to the door, she hesitated. Niall realized she wasn't used to preceding anyone out a door.

"Go on," he encouraged. "I want to keep you in sight. Otherwise, I might thump ye with this wee case. Plus," he added, "a man enjoys watching the way a lass walks."

She pressed her lips together. Evan had thought it would be easier for Niall to bring her home alone, give her time to talk servant-to-servant. Niall was starting to think she'd be more at ease with the vampire, where every word was a gospel command, a safe structure.

"Has your Master sent any instructions for me?" she asked, under-scoring it.

"To follow my direction as if it's his own. If I tell ye to eat a triple-scoop chocolate fudge sundae and take a good long nap on the flight, that's what you better have. He gets pretty worked up if we dinnae follow his instructions."

He thought he saw something in the doe brown eyes—a flash of impatience or temper—but then it was replaced with resignation. A numbness he didn't like. "Whatever your Master wills, I will follow. I am here to serve. You do not have to expend any effort toward my well-being."

Surely the lass knew he was teasing her? Or had she thought he was mocking her?

Setting down the case, Niall saw her brief flash of alarm when he didn't react as he was sure she'd hoped, taking the lead, getting her to the plane, no more conversation required. Instead, he moved to the trash can. Poking around, he saw the rice wrapped in a cloth. As she'd said, the cuts had been minor, the cloth marked with only a few drops of blood. "How'd they get blood for their sign?"

When she didn't respond, he lifted his head, fixed his gaze on her. "You'll want to answer me, lass," he said.

Those lashes swept down, telling him she knew a command when she heard it. But it took her another second to get it out. "The first night I was back from the infirmary, they came in at dawn, cut my arm, made me draw the S. It is expected in such a situation."

When he crossed the room and clasped her wrist, he could feel her fighting not to move. He pushed up the sweater sleeve and suppressed an oath. Had they used a bloody rusty steak knife? The jagged cut had been made over another mark, a fleur-de-lis enclosed in a circle of Latin script he couldn't make out because of the wound. At some point the tattoo must have been infused with her Master's blood to make it permanent, kept fresh with periodic re-inking. Evan did it to Niall's own tattoos every so often; otherwise Niall's third mark would re-knit skin, mar the design.

"What's this writing? Beneath it?"

"My InhServ mark. The fleur-de-lis is enclosed by the motto *Forever Bound; Blood, Body and Soul.*"

Her voice was flat, though he expected at one time she'd explained it with reverence or even pride. Dropping to one knee, he eased up the hem of her skirt. Her knees and calves were raw and abraded from the sharp bits, but the few cuts were minor, as she said. Not like her arm. The blocker Lord Brian was giving her was likely impeding her third-mark ability to heal any wound quickly, but perhaps when Evan second-marked her, it would help.

Niall wrapped his fingers around her leg above her knee, noting how his rough, tanned fingers looked against that supple, silken flesh. Christ, she was a beauty, but she seemed more fragile now than when she'd been screaming and raging, Stephen doing his best to break her mind.

By walking on eggshells, he was making it worse. *Well, hell with it.* Evan always said he had more intuition than brains.

"Our Master doesnae like a servant hurting herself without his say so," he said brusquely. "Ye haven't earned a punishment from him; dinnae do this to yourself again. Aye?"

She became paler, as if she'd been chastised severely. Damn it all. Gripping her shoulders from his kneeling position, a fairly easy thing given his height, he gave her a little shake. "Can you tell stories? Sing a bit?"

"I'm trained in all the cultural arts. Yes."

"Guid. It's a long flight, *muirnín.* Perhaps ye could tell me a story or two to put us down for a nap, so the jet lag willnae catch us. It's not an order," he added gently. "Just an idea to keep us both busy. I know this is bloody awkward for you. If you'd rather read a book or be silent as a stone, that's fine."

"It would be my pleasure to tell you stories."

Apparently giving her something to do settled her. Poor lass was a duck out of water and trying to paddle her way through sand.

"All right, then. If ye run out of tales to tell, I ha' drinking songs from every country Evan and I have visited. And I bray like a mule. They're bawdy songs, mostly about beautiful, big-breasted women and their highly unlikely encounters with sweaty sailors. The pilot will crash the plane to shut me up."

Not a hint of a smile in her sad eyes. Niall wondered if Evan had made a decision out of his depth, but she'd stilled under his touch, called him Master. He had that unexpected way about him, Evan did, though Niall didn't spend a lot of time dwelling on it. He also remembered how Alanna had looked up at him. Even in her delirium, Niall had seen fire, need, courage. Yearning.

He'd wager good money she hadn't flinched from his touch because of some bullshit InhServ rule. She'd remembered the infirmary, how she had responded to their touch, and had been startled to feel that same reaction now.

Testing it, he put a firm hand to the small of her back as he guided her out the door. Another ripple went through her lovely body, warming his palm against her.

Nothing for it. First a plane trip, then they'd see where the day took them.

~

When she'd told him she was "trained in the cultural arts," he hadn't realized what that meant. After he settled them into the private plane and told her he'd have his story now, it was like putting a quarter into a mannequin. She flipped from detached silence into a vivid tale of the Otherworld travels of Thomas, the famous Scottish bard who reputedly became a favorite of the Fae queen.

Complete with voices and expressive gestures, Alanna gave him an excellent version of one of Thomas's adventures in the monarch's service. Her mesmerizing narration, coupled with the lass's exceptional beauty, had him damn near speechless. Even their flight attendant was a wide-eyed listening child, her hands resting motionless on the beverage tray she'd been organizing when Alanna started.

Yet when Alanna was done, the lass settled back into her seat and folded her hands, unresponsive to the appreciation he and the attendant expressed. "Do you wish another?" she asked. His quarter paid for the story, no more, no less. Though he should listen to Evan's advice and let the lass be, leaving her stewing in her own head didn't sit well.

"How about I do one instead, give your throat a rest?"

He'd noticed her getting hoarse, was merely being courteous, but when a muscle jumped next to her right eye he realized he'd reminded her of the human limitations a third mark didn't have.

"Don't fret, *muirnín*. Having Evan's second mark might boost your strength."

"Dinnae fash myself?"

He smiled. "You remember that, do ye?"

She seemed flustered by his pleasure. "Your accent isn't that thick all the time."

"No. After all these years, I can put it on or off like a *bauchle*." He winked. "Old shoe. Though Evan claims I'll pull it out of my arse and speak full Scottish when I get crabbit. Which, since he's usually the cause of my ill temper, is his own fault if he can't understand what I'm saying."

"You . . . get angry at your Master?" Her eyes widened, a charming effect with the long lashes. He wondered if she realized how enchanting she was to watch.

"Well, he's a right git sometime." He wanted her to smile back at him, but so far that was a lost cause. He'd keep trying, though, because he expected a smile on that face would make a lad's heart stop. "More a Sassenach than a Scot term, but that's the advantage of being a world traveler. You can mash the languages together. All right, then, no more putting it off. Since you gave me such a pretty tale, I'm going tae give you a romantic one. Brace yourself, because I'm going tae sing it."

She probably had the wisdom to object, but before she could, he'd already put his own quarter in, so to speak. Instead of the bawdy song he'd promised, he sang her the ballad of Tam Lin. Because his singing voice actually did make a bear's indigestion sound like birdsong, he gave her and the flight attendant respites, adding his own commentary in between the verses.

" '*Why pu's thou the rose, Janet, And why breaks thou the wand? Or why comes thou to Carterhaugh, Withoutten my command?*'

"And being a saucy wench with her own mind," he added, "because aren't they all? She replies . . .

" '*Carterhaugh, it is my ain, My daddie gave it me; I'll come and gang by Carterhaugh, And ask no leave at thee.*'"

The attractive flight attendant gave him a smile. Another time, he'd have taken advantage of it, but his first duty was to his charge. Plus, Alanna was intriguing enough to have his full attention. She noted the woman's interest, though, and cataloged his response. Most servants didn't miss such details, part self-preservation, part anticipation of their vampire's need for intel, but it was obvious to him that she took it to a higher level, her attention honed razor sharp.

According to Brian, her dedication to her training was what had saved her. Stephen had expected resistance to his invasion, and she hadn't obliged him. She'd fought to stay alive, but she hadn't fought what he was doing to her, and that had preserved her mind, like wheat-grass bending down before a storm wind. But it had taken a hard battering, as if she'd been hanging onto a cliff edge, stoically enduring a maniac stomping on her fingers, refusing to let go as he crushed her bones with steel-toed boots.

She'd obeyed the laws of pure servitude, believing that her Master had the right to do as he would with her, except that a higher power—in the form of the Council—had trumped his claim on the one issue of her staying alive. It showed a remarkable will, for a lass who claimed to have none of her own.

When he finished the ballad, her lips curved politely. "Thank you. I need to take my medication now. Will you excuse me?"

"Would you like me to do the injection? I've a gentle hand for it."

She paused, already half rising. It was clear she wanted an escape from scrutiny, but her face went back to that mask. "You don't need to trouble yourself. I can do it."

"No trouble for me. But if you prefer to do it, that's fine."

Sitting back down, she opened the case Lord Brian had given to her and proferred it to him in that same distantly courteous manner. She didn't in fact prefer him to do it; she was erring on the side of what his desires might be.

Leaning forward in his seat, splaying his knees to accommodate her closed ones, Niall put his hands on hers on the case, closed and latched it again. "*Muirnín*, take a little time without me gawping at you. There's a small sitting area beyond the lavatory, a couch. Have a nap or whatever ye desire. It's fine by me."

Her eyes frosted, but she rose like a wooden mannequin. Swearing softly, he caught her waist and rose. "Okay, now I've insulted ye. You're going to have to tell me what it is I've done wrong so I dinnae keep doing it."

"It's nothing you're doing wrong." Frustration crossed her face.

"My actions are making you think I need . . . comfort. Care. Reassurance. That's something an Inherited Servant never requires."

"So what's making you so mad? That you're makin' me think that, or that ye *do* need those things?"

She paled, even as she became more rigid. "I serve your Master now, Niall. Is this a question he requires answered?"

She'd gone to being pissy. Was that an improvement? Niall wasn't sure if they were in range of Evan's mind, but that question was quickly answered.

Are you children already fighting? Tell her I want her to do as you instructed. She's not required to engage you further.

I didnae . . .

Niall, if you tapped her with a pencil, she'd shatter into a thousand pieces. You're fucking with her paradigm, and she's not yet strong enough for that. Leave her be.

I think she's stronger than you think.

Steel is strong once it's tempered. Put pressure on it before then and you'll ruin it.

Alanna's brown eyes lifted to Niall's in question. "He says he wants you to take your injection and rest in the back until we land," Niall said grudgingly. "That's all."

"It's my pleasure to obey." Sliding her hand from Niall's grasp, she disappeared behind the curtain with her case.

He should listen to Evan. If he didn't, the vampire would take a strip out of his hide, but it wouldn't be the first time. His hide was pretty tough, all in all. After ten minutes, Niall followed her. She was sitting by a window, but until she placed her fingertips on the glass, he wasn't sure if she was seeing any of the view. She made a circular motion as if following a bird winging its way through the sky, or tracing the clouds chasing them. Her lips moved, words without sound.

Servants weren't like made vampires. If third-marked before age thirty, they didn't stay the age of their marking, but matured until they reached thirty. The aging process stopped there, give or take a few years. He knew she'd become a servant at sixteen and was only twenty-nine years old now. However, at the moment, her brown eyes looked ten times that age.

Laying her forehead on the glass, she closed them, but kept her palm on the glass as if reluctant to lose the contact. He could stay motionless for quite some time, a skill all servants seemed to have, since even he'd had to endure some of those interminable vampire get-togethers Evan couldn't avoid. So he continued to watch over her.

Her breath evened out, her fingers drifting down the window and into her lap, her shoulders dropping. Debra had brought him up to speed on the treatment side effects, which included a short period of fatigue directly after injection. Between that and the excitement of the day, he expected she was overwhelmed. She no longer had third-mark strength, after all. It was going to take a while for him to remember that, but probably not as long as it would if she'd been a he.

You going to be pissed if I engage her now?

Would it matter? I know what you're thinking, neshama.

The fact that Evan used the Hebrew endearment said he hadn't pushed it too far. Or Evan was engrossed in a project and would chastise later. Either way, Niall would take the opening.

Sliding his arms under her back and thighs, he lifted her, concerned by how light she was. He was going to have the stewardess make her that ice cream sundae for certain. For now, he'd put her on the couch, get her a blanket so she could be more comfortable. Hopefully she wouldn't be one of those who got out of sorts because her hair got mussed. He could well imagine those thick red locks in disarray. Her hair fell to her hips, and he'd love to see it brushing her sweet, naked arse.

Stop being a rutting beast, he reminded himself. Christ, she was cold. Instead of going to the couch, he sat back down in the chair, cradling her in his lap. Her cheek lay on his chest, her hands coiled in her lap. He kept one hand on her hip, holding her there, but put his other hand up on the window. He copied the movement as he remembered it, and he'd been correct. It was like she'd been following the up and down soaring flight of a bird, keeping pace with the plane.

"Our Master . . . Debra said he's an artist?"

She didn't move at all, but it was obvious she'd been awake as soon as he'd touched her. She might not be a warrior, but over a decade of being an Inherited Servant meant he couldn't sneak up on her. She'd let him pick her up without complaint, though. Maybe she thought Evan was okay with it.

"Aye. He's ae o' a kind. Paint's still his favorite medium, but now he does photography, sculpting, metalwork, whatever interests him. He doesnae stay any one place too long. Never has."

"How can I be a good servant to him?"

Such a simple, direct question. One he'd never asked himself, not in three hundred years. Niall shifted. "Cannae say. I'm no prize in that department, but he keeps me around. Gives him a dog to kick without me actually being one. He likes dogs."

She was staring at him as if he'd spoken gibberish. When she immediately dropped her gaze at his attention, he touched her chin. "I'm not a vampire. You can look at me. Make faces, blow raspberries, whatever pleases ye."

"You are his representative. An Inherited Servant treats all with deference."

"Well, I'd appreciate it if ye didnae. I like your eyes. I like seeing your eyes," he amended, in case she started worrying about the whole manners thing again.

She studied him. "How long have you been with him?"

She seemed okay being where she was, but he wouldn't call her relaxed. She was a nice lapful, her arse soft, and she smelled exotic, some light scent he couldn't place. He wrapped the hair spilling over his knuckles around them, gentle-like and casual. "Since the early 1700s."

As she digested that, her gaze sharpened. "So you are . . ."

"Just over three hundred." He drew his finger across his throat. "The usual servant life span. From what I ken, it happens fairly sudden. One day the clock will just stop ticking, but until then I have all my faculties. A bonny deal, if you compare it to getting all creaky and gray, limp-dicked. Sorry. Shouldn't have said that."

She pressed her lips together. "I'm not offended. Have the two of you traveled without female companionship for all those years? Does your Master not . . . ?"

"Aye, he likes women well enough. 'Tis the artist thing. The issue isn't male or female for him, but what 'engages him artistically.' That's how he puts it. He likes a man for a servant because we're nae very complicated." He shrugged. Hell, he couldn't say what it was about him that had "artistically engaged" Evan for nearly three centuries, but there it was. As for him . . . well, there was no expiration on a debt of honor.

He nodded toward the window. "What were you doing, the bird thing?"

She looked startled, then uncomfortable, so he waved a hand. "You dinnae have to tell me. I was spying, something Evan told me not to do."

Alanna arched a brow. "Are you in the habit of disobeying your Master?"

"Chronically, according to him. Of course, he's very fond o' the single tail, probably because using it properly is artistically engaging as well. You've no need to worrit on that yourself. Never seen him beat a woman. Well, a guid spanking turns him on now and then, particularly if the lass has a fine, soft—"

Niall. Really?

Just making sure you were paying attention.

You will wish I wasn't paying such close attention when you land.

She was giving him that three-headed dog look again, but then Evan startled him. *Kiss her, Niall. I want to see how she reacts.*

Didnae ye just say, about tempered steel and all?

Do it. Don't say anything to warn her.

Niall didn't have any problem with the kiss, but he didn't want to scare her. Tightening his hand on her hair, a reassurance rather than an attack, he moved his hand up her back, feeling the thin strap of bra beneath the sweater, hooking his thumb there as he eased her toward his face. A variety of expressions crossed her brown eyes. Alarm, recognition, determination . . . decision.

She caught him in the chin with the heel of her hand in a blow so smart it snapped his teeth together on his tongue. She surged out of his lap, stomping on his thinly shod foot with her booted heel, likely breaking two of his toes. In a blink, she was holding the syringe she'd used like a dagger.

"Lord Brian says this treatment is not pleasant if it's not tailored to your DNA. You are disobeying and disgracing your Master. He deserves better from his servant. He did not authorize any sexual congress between us, you said so."

He was a capable fighter, but he hadn't expected the same of her. Her jaw was set, the hand clutching the syringe not even shaking.

Evan's chuckle was grating enough that Niall envisioned breaking several of the skinny painter's limbs. *She just took care of your punishment for me.*

Niall ignored that. "He did. Authorize the kiss, that is."

"Oh." Digesting that statement, she set the syringe aside. "I'm trained to repel unsanctioned advances. My apologies."

"None needed. I should have warned you." *But I listened to my* "Master," *like a damned idiot.* "So why did you let me pick you up?"

"I sensed your intent was to move me, which I assumed might be our Master's will. When you sat down, I thought he might be using you to help him experience what I am like physically. You did not seem . . . erotically involved. At that moment."

"Lass, you're a strange one. But you've got a braw punch." As he wiped the blood off his chin with the back of his hand, she moved to the lavatory. Bemused, he watched her return with a wet paper towel. When she stepped up to him to apply it to his mouth, she didn't hesitate, despite the fact that he had a foot of height and a hundred pounds on her.

"How did you know the kiss wasn't motivated by his desire to experience you?"

"Because it felt more impulsive. Like your desire. I misjudged. I apologize to him for that. I will learn quickly, I promise. Does he still wish you to kiss me?"

With her face so neutral, she might have been asking him if Evan wanted a plate of broccoli. But he took a closer look. Tension hummed just below the surface, her body anticipating, needing . . . something.

Niall took the paper towel from her hand. *Well, O Lord and Master? Do you want to kiss her?*

Now *my wants matter? I expect you already know the answer.*

Yes, which is why I'm denying you. Tell her no.

Niall turned to drop the towel on the sink. Then he swung back, caught her by the waist, twisting her to the wall with her arm behind her back. Using his knee thrust high between her thighs to keep her pinned, he held her with easy strength. As she struggled, trying to figure out ways to throw him, he stayed alert to any signs of distress. There were none. When she deduced he was making a point, not an attack, she stilled, submitting to his dominance in the matter. It sent a healthy surge of blood to his cock, but he put that aside.

"Evan and I are not quite what ye expect in a vampire–servant pairing," he said against her perfect ear, taking a nice breath of that haunting scent. "You'll come tae no harm at our hands. But you try something like that against me again, I'll turn you over my knee, no matter what price I pay for it. I'm not a docile man, and I'm near three centuries your senior, lass."

"My intent is to serve your Master, not to disrespect you."

"Hmm. He said no to the kiss. For now." Which of course meant now he was thinking about it far more than he should.

But while her breath had shortened, her emotions seemed blank. Maybe Evan *had* really stepped in it with this one. Yet when nothing else had eased her suffering, the two of them had been able to do so. Some things a man did, not because they were wise, but because they were the honorable thing.

It was a philosophy that had determined most of the forks in Niall's life, and he didn't see that changing anytime soon. Especially if it involved a fascinating lass.

3

Aᴸᴬɴɴᴀ wasn't sure what to feel. She'd never experienced a servant like Niall, or the type of Master that Evan seemed to be to him. Something about their interactions, experienced through the one-sided communication of Niall, reminded her of the way Adam had related to his friends, before he'd departed with her for the InhServ program. Another difference between her and her brother; he'd had friends, had maintained those connections as long as he possibly could, while her focus had always been on her future.

Though she'd been oblivious to their attentions, his friends had been intrigued by her looks, much as Niall was. Adam had been protective of her, and not only because he was her brother. A female or male Inherited Servant came to the in-house training program an untouched virgin, never even romantically kissed. She expected that had presented more difficulties for Adam than it had for her, but he'd never complained about it.

Once the private plane landed at the airport in Asheville, North Carolina, Niall guided her to a battered Range Rover and took the wheel. As they drove through town, a postcard blue-green mountain range as its backdrop, she saw it was not a large city at all, not compared to Berlin. In short order, they were off the main highway and winding up smaller roads, headed deeper into the mountains. Despite the fall season, the sun was warm, so he kept the windows down. She wrapped her hair into a twist on the back of her head to keep it out of her eyes, and inhaled the scent of trees, water, mountains and sunshine. The rolling landscape and increasing solitude were a very different experience from the past few weeks, one she didn't mind at all.

He'd said little after the kiss incident. She didn't sense he was closed to conversation, just waiting for her to initiate it if she desired. Her main question, how best to serve his Master, had received such a hard-to-interpret reply, she wasn't sure where to go from there. She'd have to figure it out as she went, which might not be a bad thing, having her mind occupied by that instead of when the life would be choked from her, her heart seizing in her chest because Stephen's had been staked.

She tried not to dwell on such a thing, because of the fear it could incite. Not of death, but of that afterlife reunion with Stephen. Her temples pounded, a warning of the headache that could come if she thought of him too much, even with the blocker. Lord Brian had explained Stephen's invasion into her mind had caused such trauma to her body that it would protect her if she turned her thoughts toward him. She was glad to have a sanctioned excuse not to think of her Master.

"Do you like music?"

She turned her head, holding back the few shorter wisps of hair that had escaped the bun and were dancing in the breeze. "If you'd like to play some, I don't object."

"Not what I asked, *muirnín*." His direct look reminded her of what he'd said in her room. How he'd said it. *You'll want to answer me.* Before she could stop herself, she'd shifted her gaze downward, as she might when a vampire addressed her.

"I . . . I haven't thought about it."

A slight tap of the chin, a reminder, and she lifted her attention to him. "Better." He smiled, but that intent look kept her attention. "You mean you don't listen to music for your own enjoyment?"

"I listen to whatever my Master wishes to play. I'm trained to dance in a variety of styles for his pleasure. I can also sing."

"Okay." He pushed the player between them. "Scroll through and find something that strikes your fancy. One song."

She picked up the device, studied the list of songs. "Are these your favorites?"

"Playlists I've put together, aye."

"All right, then." She chose the shuffle option and hit play, so that the player chose the first song. He gave her a look, but he didn't say anything further. The song was country bluegrass, a male band that filled the vehicle with music that fit their surroundings well. With the windows down, she adjusted the volume upward. When she did that, she won a grin. It made her feel a little better, though she couldn't explain why. Reaching across the seat, he squeezed her hand briefly, then returned to driving, humming the song while she gazed at him, mystified both by the touch and the situation.

Each road they turned up became rougher, steeper, until they were bumping along on what seemed little more than a deer path. The trees closed in on either side, such that Niall raised her window, the leafy branches passing along the glass rather than slapping her during their passage. Just when she was certain he was going to have to produce an axe to get them any farther, they emerged into a small clearing. To one side was a log cabin built into the side of the hill, a necessary anchor given that the front yard had only enough level ground for a grouping of Adirondack chairs and a picnic table before it began to slope down dramatically, drawing the gaze in that direction.

Niall backed the vehicle into a spot obviously carved out for it next to the cabin, which gave Alanna the opportunity to stare at that overwhelming view. The slope was dotted with yellow wildflowers with black centers that danced at the touch of the wind. The hill disappeared into a forested gorge, enough daylight left that the sunlight gleamed on the golds, yellows, rust reds and countless greens, an artist's mixed palette, forming the foreground for the mountain range behind, dark green hills giving way to blue-green ones. Beyond that, layers of hazy blue rocky formations rose into the sky, wisps of white clouds draped over them like silken spider webs. It was a view that kept the mind engaged and the tongue silent.

When she realized Niall had cut the engine, she looked toward him.

"Evan calls this the Atheist Test. Says if you look at the view and don't believe in a higher power, no other miracle will change your mind."

Not knowing what to say to that, she simply nodded and then

forced herself to evaluate her surroundings more practically. Another vehicle, a sturdy SUV that looked like it had been decommissioned from the military, was parked on the other side of the cabin. There was a well, but now that Niall had opened his door, holding it there with a braced foot, she could also hear the rush of water, possibly a stream beyond the cusp of the hill on the west side of the property. Lifting her gaze to the steep grade above the cabin, she saw several cameras on tripods. They were loosely protected by a plastic tent, the flap tied back from the picture-taking end. Niall scowled.

"Idiot," he muttered. He exited the vehicle, his size making it rock. Before she realized his intent, he was at her door, opening it for her. She wasn't used to that, nor how he offered a hand so she could more easily step down from the Range Rover's greater height.

"You're lucky it didn't rain today," he muttered. "That plastic wouldn't have held against a stiff breeze. You'd have fried your arse, getting out here to rescue the equipment."

Because she'd spent most of her life around servants, she knew when one was speaking to his Master internally, though it was the first time she'd heard one be that rude. She waited, hand still clasped in his because he'd not yet let go. She didn't take it as an impropriety, given that his mind was obviously engaged, so she had the opportunity to observe his fingers were strong and warm, his palm rough. She wanted to run her touch over it, feel the grooved lines. She quelled the inappropriate response.

"He said it didnae smell like rain today." Niall snorted, giving Alanna an eye roll. "Aye, ye remember Seattle?" Dropping her hand, he circled around back, retrieving her suitcase. "Come on, he's inside."

She eyed the size of the cabin. "Where does he protect himself from the sun?"

"The back bedroom is inside the hill itself, but during daylight, that's only adequate for early morning or just after sunset. The root cellar is below the house and accessible through the kitchen. It's been modernized enough that there's indoor plumbing, and electricity comes from a generator, but for the most part it's a pioneer experience. The place is a couple hundred years old."

"This is your . . . home?"

"A step down for you, princess?"

His narrowed look flustered her. "No. I didn't mean it like that at all. I apologize. I'm accustomed to vampires who require more of their accommodations."

"Aye, he's not one of those. That's all he requires." Niall nodded toward the view. "As long as he can see the next great wonder, he could sleep in a hole in the ground. As for me, I just need a guid meal, so he keeps me fed. We all have our priorities."

She followed him to the door, her cheeks pink at the idea he'd thought she was complaining. She didn't know how to rectify such an unprecedented assumption.

"We've been here a couple o' weeks," he continued. "No telling when Evan'll move on, but that should make it bloody hard for Stephen to sneak up on us. If he resorts to spy work, he won't get very far. Evan willnae use cell phones, and these auld trucks don't have GPS chips."

"But I thought they want . . . him to find me." She stumbled over the pronoun. After referring to him as "my lord" for so long, she had trouble calling him merely Stephen. She also couldn't call him Master. Though technically he still was, she couldn't make herself do it, no matter how much it underscored her failure as a servant. "My purpose is to be bait."

Niall stopped, such that she almost bumped into him. When he turned, that stern set of his lips was back, giving her the impression she'd offended him somehow.

"I'm sorry," she said, though she questioned why she was apologizing to a servant.

"So you should be, *muirnín*. Ye have value beyond bait, and you should remember that. Making it more difficult for Stephen to find you provides more opportunities to flush him out. A man on a long treasure hunt makes more mistakes than one on a short one."

The logic was sound, but the first part had her confused. What value?

After feeling nothing for so long, it was odd to feel unsettled, uncertain. Serving a vampire who lived inside a mountain with a big Scot who was entirely unpredictable in his behavior was like finding herself on Mars. That quick hand squeeze in the Rover came back to her, and she had an unprecedented urge to take his hand again, as she had taken Adam's when they first came to the InhServ program together. She'd been the one to drive them toward the goal, but at that momentous transition, Adam had made her feel protected, his hand sure and strong on hers.

When Niall gestured her forward, she squashed the moment of weakness, squaring her shoulders. She was taught to be prepared for anything. She was about to meet her new Master, and no matter how temporary that was, she would serve him as if she would do so for the rest of her life. Which, in this case, was likely true.

Evan was supposed to give her two marks. Would he do it tonight or wait?

It was not her place to wonder such things. As she stepped into the cabin, she found that it wasn't dark and gloomy as she expected. Things were clean and smelled like the mountains and forest. Though it was small, there appeared to be several rooms. A main sitting area with a kitchen. A bedroom was visible through an open door. Stepping into the hallway, she saw the open door to the back bedroom, a bathroom dividing it from the other bedroom. The beds had handmade quilts in fall colors and pillows with earth-tone cases. Dried wildflowers and a few mountain prints provided comforting touches to the décor. As she turned back toward the main room, she saw the knotty pine log walls were a pale golden color that added light to what was coming in through the windows. A bookcase had a mountain scene carved in the molding piece overlapping the top shelf. A wooden black bear stood next to the shelf, black eyes steady upon her.

"Stay still a moment, lass." Closing the door, Niall moved to do the same to the windows. In addition to curtains, they had interior shutters. Once he closed both, it put the cabin in darkness, shutting out the midday sun. As a third mark, she could see in the dark, but with the blocker she was blinded, explaining Niall's order. A match was struck, the sulfur hitting her nostrils before he lit a lantern on the kitchen table, filling the room with shadows. "He does a lot o' black-and-white photography, prefers to develop it rather than relying on digital media. That's what he's doing now, so we cannae let any light down. It's better for him as well."

Moving the oval braided rug on the kitchen floor, Niall revealed the door to the cellar. When he lifted it, his forearm was bathed in a reddish light coming up from the room below. She also sensed the presence of her new Master. At least that was one thing the blocker had not taken away from her—a servant's ability to detect a vampire nearby.

Setting the injection case on the table, she followed Niall's direction to go down the ladder ahead of him. She couldn't see much more than red light and shadows, but as she started to descend, a pair of hands touched her legs. A shiver ran from that contact point up her thighs. She remembered those long, strong fingers far better than she'd expected. Though Debra had confirmed the two males had been there, that they weren't a dream, she didn't know if the painting, the way those hands had made her feel, had been true, or something she'd enhanced, an oasis constructed by her mind to survive Stephen's punishing invasion. She had that answer now.

Those hands slid from her calves to her thighs with easy intimacy, because of course she was his to touch, right? His hands had a different strength than Niall's, but were no less reassuring as they brushed over her hips, closed on her waist, ensuring she made it safely to the floor. Understanding the peculiarities of Randoms, she'd managed their kindnesses accordingly. But she had no clue how to take such a gesture from a vampire. It seemed very . . . human. Evan was a made vampire, but then so was Stephen, and many of his acquaintances. None of them would have assisted a servant in such a way.

Turning away from the ladder, she faced her new Master. She was five four, so she estimated his height at six feet when she did a quick glance upward. Evan didn't have Niall's height or breadth—she didn't imagine many men did—but his shoulders were broad, despite a rangy body type, lean and knotted. He had the decided features of a handsome Jewish man—straight slash cheekbones, his mouth a firm, thin line, his straight nose the dividing marker for wide-spaced eyes that were gray and deep-set, with dark fine brows to complement the straight fall of hair over them. She suspected the charisma he emanated had been there before he was turned, but the vampire blood only enhanced it.

She was wrong. She *had* seen his face at some point, because she remembered his eyes. How long had they stayed at her bedside? The painting, the touch of Niall's hands on her face . . . it had seemed to go on a long time. Hell's minions had been howling at the door, but they'd been unable to get through while Evan and Niall were there.

"Just as impossibly beautiful as I expected," Evan murmured. Without permission, her body swayed toward his, recalling that voice.

He put a hand on her shoulder. "Though a little dizzy. Niall didn't feed you."

"No, he did, Master. My apologies. I . . ." It wasn't dizziness, not that kind. They'd been *real*. It made the memory something far more significant to her, and she wasn't sure how to process that. She was so outside her normal milieu, it made their reality almost more fantastic than when she thought them a hallucination.

He touched a loose lock of her hair. The dark red color, with shimmers of gold throughout, had always drawn attention. She had to fight the urge to turn into that touch. InhServs could show pleasure when the time was appropriate, but this didn't feel like that time. He'd think her a fool. "Was your trip a pleasant experience?" he asked. "I expect the opportunity to put Niall back on his heels was the best part."

She blinked. "Yes . . . I mean, the trip was fine, Master."

Evan chuckled. Brushing her cheek with his fingertips, he kept his other hand on her waist, but it didn't feel like a casual touch. He was learning her, and she was vibrating beneath the attention. The flicker in those heavy-lidded eyes showed his awareness of it, but she kept her gaze on his throat. A servant didn't meet a vampire's gaze unless she had permission. Even if the vampire had gray eyes that reminded her of that still, floating place after the nightmares had receded.

His regard was different from that of other vampires, however. It was a full exploration, as if he was trying to see below the skin and muscle, the architecture of bone, to determine what emotions and experiences radiating from her soul made her face look like it did. It was disconcerting, but she stayed still.

Glimpsing him through her lashes, she realized he'd been turned young, perhaps when he was no more than twenty-one or twenty-two. But four hundred years of life and that innate charisma tempered his youthful appearance, even as the combination made him look even more preternatural. He wouldn't ever blend in among humans easily.

"Evan Samuel Miller is my full name. When I was born, it was Eitan ben Samuel, so you might see some correspondence from older friends—much older friends—with that name on the address. I Anglicized it after my father's death. Bad luck while he's living. Old superstition, but then, I am old." Evan flashed teeth at her, a bare hint of

fang, and his hand on her waist tightened. "Four hundred and something . . . Since I turned two hundred, I only track the numbers that
end with two zeros."

She blinked, nodded, because that seemed the appropriate response.

"I spend a great deal of time around humans, compared to other
vampires, so you'll call me Evan," he added. Then he tipped up her
chin, capturing her in that gaze. "When it's time to call me Master,
you'll know it."

"Yes, Mas— Evan."

"Good." Releasing her, he turned back to his task, but she noticed
he took his support away gradually, making sure she was firm on her
feet. She wasn't, but she managed to stand upright regardless, shifting
away from the ladder so Niall could join them when he desired to do
so. The scent of the chemical bath was distinct but not unpleasant. The
dim light glimmered across the series of trays in which photo paper
floated, shapes slowly coming into focus. Stepping forward to study
one, Evan reached for a pair of tongs, using them to transfer the picture into a different tray. "Has Niall given you the information you
need?"

Panic tripped through her chest. Had she missed a step? "Sir?"

Evan glanced toward the ladder. Niall was now leaning against it,
the trapdoor closed above him. She hadn't even heard him come down.
He moved like a scout for an invading army, even more silently than
she was used to third marks moving. His eyes were darker in the dim
light, the broad planes of his face even more rugged. "She didn't have
any questions, except how best to serve you."

"I'm sure Niall told you he was not the best source for that." Evan
studied the contents of another tray, checked his watch. "Another minute or two," he mused. Then he looked toward her again. "He didn't tell
you what he said, did he? The first time I called our view the Atheist
Test?"

She looked at Niall, then back at Evan. "No, sir."

"All it proves is God likes to pick up a paintbrush," Niall said. "Just
like Evan, He may not be guid for much else than pretty pictures."

Though she was astounded by the disrespect, Evan bared his fangs
at his servant, a feral smile. "But you didn't refute the theory. Whether
you think He's an inept deity or not, you don't deny His presence in
your life."

"No more than I deny when there's a thorn stuck in my arse," Niall said mildly.

Evan lifted a brow, but shifted his attention back to Alanna. "You are an exceptionally intelligent woman, Alanna. A very accomplished one. I'm certain you realize we are a far cry from what you've known. Much of your training may not apply here. Plus the circumstances are somewhat different."

The tray at the far end of the table had caught his attention. As he shifted to stand before it, he fell silent, studying what was coming into form there. He braced his knuckles on the table and picked up another set of tongs, swishing the paper in the bath. When Alanna looked toward Niall, hoping for some cue, Niall put a finger to his lips, indicating she should wait. She could do that. She was exceptionally good at waiting.

"I'm charged to keep you on the outer fringes of Stephen's radar, while the Council hunts that *benzona*." Evan at last spoke, setting aside the tongs, though he kept his gaze on the picture. "While you are to behave as my servant, it's a temporary situation. The place for your beauty and talents is not among the peasantry, but available to vampires far more ambitious than I. My job is to keep you safe until that happens."

She was caught up in determining what a *benzona* was—from the slight edge in his voice, something not complimentary—and the flow of his voice. It reminded her of a classical guitar piece, the melody interspersed with deeper bass tones. However, his last sentence broke her out of the dangerous reverie. Surely he realized once Stephen was caught, he would be executed, and she would die with him? Lord Brian's blocker didn't change that. However, since her personal fate did not require mention, she remained silent.

"So here it is. I don't require much. Help Niall with the tasks he performs for me, and let us know if you notice anything that indicates Stephen's presence." Evan turned, his piercing eyes suddenly upon her. "I do understand certain things about Inherited Servants, Alanna. As you regain your strength, your need to be of ultimate service will grow. Even if you think it will hasten Stephen's capture to forgo it, you *will* take the blocking serum Lord Brian gave you. If you put yourself at that kind of risk, you are disobeying me, and I will not be pleasant about it."

She nodded. "Yes, Mas— sir. Evan." *Damn it.* A simple thing like a name shouldn't be giving her this much trouble.

"If you have any questions, you can ask Niall or me, if I'm available to answer," he continued. "They told you that I'll be giving you the first and second marks?"

"Yes, sir."

"Brian was certain they wouldn't cause you ill effects, but we'll do the first mark now, and the second one later tonight. I want some spacing to be sure it doesn't upset your system."

"I'm sure I can handle them both right now, sir, if it's more convenient for you. I am quite recovered."

"Well, just to be sure, we're doing it my way." Picking up a cloth, he wiped his hands on it, took a sniff at the results. "Oh, that's terrible. Hold on." Going to the sink, he washed them more thoroughly, using the soap there. Noticing the paper towels were at the end of the counter, she picked them up, brought them to Evan such that they were handy when he finished washing his hands. The soap had a fragrant citrus scent.

The vampire gave her a sweeping glance that held her in place and spread warmth over her skin. As he bent his head to pull a few towels off the roll, the straight strands of hair over his forehead caught her attention, the way the ends teased his slim black brows. "Thank you."

A thank-you from a vampire? No vampire thanked a human. It didn't matter what rank they possessed. Then she realized she'd committed a grave faux pas herself. She'd done something for Evan before looking for verbal cues from Niall, his fully marked servant.

Glancing quickly toward him, she was relieved to find the Scot unperturbed. However, there was a different quality to his regard. On the plane he'd been genial, attentive, but now she was aware of how alone she was with the two males.

It was a ridiculous thought, given that a vampire could do anything he wished to her, whether in the presence of his servant or the entire vampire populace. Her nervousness wasn't fear, not exactly. She didn't know how to classify the unfamiliar emotions coursing through her as Evan took the towel roll from her hands. The cellar seemed smaller, a dark, intimate den within the earth, far away from anything else.

The vampire surprised her by bending and sliding one arm behind her legs, the other around her back to lift her in his arms. Her arm landed on his neck, her hand on his shoulder. Though all vampires were stronger than humans, something about the angularity of his frame made the ease with which he lifted her unexpected.

It was barely a step to Niall. Her quick look at him through lowered lashes must have conveyed her curiosity, because Evan looked quietly amused. "I wanted to see what kind of armful you are. As you can guess, I have little occasion or desire to scoop Niall up in my arms."

When he put her down, she was so close to Niall she was leaning against him. The servant put an arm around her waist. With his hips propped on the ladder step, his legs stretched out on either side of her, she found his thigh the best resting place for her hand. Beneath the utilitarian cargo pants, he was hard muscle. On the plane, when he'd retaliated against her strike, he'd controlled her easily with that power, holding her like an egg inside a grip she couldn't break.

Evan lifted her other hand, his thumb sweeping over her pulse, registering the increase in the beat. She was trained to respond sexually to a vampire's touch, as long as it was her Master's will. Yet it had been months since she'd been required to respond. Even after the blocker started working, she was in the monastic solitude of her room, or the central garden, the only place at the Berlin castle that received much sun.

Arousal was more than training, however. It was also an instinct, when the stimulus was right. She wasn't afraid of her ability to respond; she was worried about her ability to channel it properly. Her pulse was definitely tripping as Evan kept his thumb gliding over it, his eyes tracking her expression, her elevated breathing. When Niall slid her hair over her left shoulder, freeing the strands from their wide silver clip, the vampire watched the red curls tumble down over her breast. Now Niall's breath was on the right side of her neck. As his lips settled there, gooseflesh spread out from the point of contact. She hadn't been touched in months. *Months.*

The body was anatomically designed to experience pleasure. It was never to be resisted in a vampire's presence, unless they ordered that as a form of torment, because vampires relished seeing their servants surrender sexual control at their command.

But Evan's simple touch roused something different than that. In

Stephen's service, she had no trouble channeling her responses to his requirements. Yet she'd noticed servants outside his household who experienced orgasms with tears, looks of clinging adoration toward their Master or Mistress, impulsive acts of devotion in the aftermath.

InhServs were taught that "natural" servants were much less disciplined, so such emotional reactions were to be expected from them. It was not a failing, but a sign of why an Inherited Servant was a cut above. No InhServ would say that outright, because it suggested ego, but it was generally understood. Then she'd seen Adam with his Mistress. He'd pressed a fervent kiss to her foot, rubbed his cheek there as she touched his hair . . .

Why was she thinking about something like that now? What was Evan expecting, looking at her the way he was? Was she supposed to be doing something she wasn't? The best InhServ anticipated her vampire's need before he had to tell her. She'd been one of the best, but now she had no frame of reference.

Niall's mouth opened, a heated moistness on her throat that tightened her nipples, drew in her breath. An electrical current ran between that contact and Evan's thumb stroking her pulse, a current branching out, building a response in her lower belly, her thighs. She was dampening because she was supposed to respond that way, because he would require her to be wet if he wished to take her or have Niall take her, but it felt . . . She was afraid.

No. She was never afraid, not of this. But they were making her feel something different from what she was used to feeling.

"Shhh . . . you're tensing, *muirnín.*" When Niall ran his hand down the arm she had propped on his thigh, she realized she was gripping him with tense fingers. It horrified her. He covered them, interlaced them with his own. "Let's change this up a bit, aye? He's a voyeur, and ye need to get lost in your heid."

Sliding down the side zipper of her skirt, he moved their linked hands under the waistband. Touching the lace band of her panties, he traced the soft skin, then pushed farther beneath the silky fabric, guiding her fingers over her smooth mound, the tender petals beneath. She swallowed as he tapped her clit, then slid his middle finger below it, teasing wetness. "There ye go. Lie your head on my shoulder, close your eyes. Pleasure yourself, lass."

She flicked her glance up to Evan, saw his slight nod, the intentness of his face, the firm set of his mouth. He brought her hand up to it, teased the palm with his lips, tasting her.

His fingers were truly extraordinary. Elegant but capable, like the hands of a master artisan, or a tree spirit. She remembered a card Adam had sent her, showing a male dryad coming to life, the branches of his tree becoming arms, wrapping around the body of a human woman. She was kissing his face, evolving through the bark, a powerful, graceful spirit that shared life with the tree. Evan's hands reminded her of that. He also smelled like the forest.

The hard enamel of his fang slid over the pad of her index finger, a reminder that she'd been told to do something for them. Stephen had rarely commanded her to masturbate before him, but Niall's hand was sliding between her fingers. The roughness of his skin was a friction that created another indrawn breath, a shuddering lift of her bosom under his appreciative gaze, if the near growl he made was any indication. She began to massage her clit, a tiny noise catching in her throat.

"Head on my shoulder."

She obeyed, closing her eyes. The darkness intensified the aroma of developer chemicals, mixing with the earthy underground. Niall and Evan bore the scent of the earth as well, the mountains, the trees. It was new to her, people who didn't smell of the civilized world. Houses, cleansers, paint, furniture upholstery, shower products from fancy salons.

His thighs steadying her with their bracket around her hips, Niall cupped her breast through the stretched fabric of the yellow sweater. As he explored the curve, stroking with his knuckles, the nipple stiffened, begged for touch through the thin stuff of her bra.

"Keep stroking yourself, lass."

She'd almost forgotten, a little lost under their caresses. Teasing her clit, she dipped her fingers into herself and rubbed the moisture on the outside, giving herself lubrication. Her hips lifted at the stimulation, and her other hand curled in Evan's grip, a reaction of pleasure. It made her fingers brush that sharp slash of cheekbone.

He'd moved his mouth from her fingers down to her palm, and the hair that had caught her attention earlier now feathered over her knuckles, a pleasant sensation. Her fingertips brushed his eyebrow.

His fangs teased her pulse, once, twice, and then he punctured flesh, the pain drawing her up in an arch toward him, a shudder passing through her as his tongue swirled over the area, his lips sealing down as he began to taste her. She stiffened as a burning sensation rippled up her arm, the geographical locator, the first mark. It hurt more than expected, as if her body was fighting any mark other than her original Master's.

"All right, then?" Niall had registered it. Evan stilled. His mouth remained on her, but his gaze flickered up to her face, seeing everything. She gave a quick nod, breathed through it, realizing with each deep inhalation her body was sinking deeper into the hollows and planes of Niall's. Evan's gaze met his servant's, some unspoken communication. As his attention returned to her arm, Niall's fingers slid between hers on her clit, helping with the slow massage as she managed that pain. His skilled touch helped lessen it. In fact, a slow detonation of sensation started through her pussy and lower belly.

"She's fair wet." Niall's voice was a rumble through his chest, vibrating against her shoulder blades. Would Evan take her now, since her body was ready for him? Niall's body was ready as well, his hard organ pushing against her buttocks through the restriction of the cargo pants. Perhaps her new Master would want her on her knees, servicing him. Some vampires liked drawing it out that way, keeping their servants wanting, the power and anticipation even more arousing to them than the sex itself.

An icy cold blade sliced through the heated pain in her arm, and she twitched, a hard spasm. In that one instant, she understood how hot glass could crack if immersed in cold water too suddenly. Both men stopped, Evan withdrawing now that the mark was done, holding pressure on the dual puncture with his thumb. "Alanna? Talk to us. What's happening?"

"I'm . . . fine. It just hurts for a while . . . but it will pass. I can take care of your needs, Master. Lord Evan. I mean Evan."

Everything seemed to be reminding her how far she'd slipped in her discipline, her focus. Causing Evan to stop twice to check on her was the equivalent of two reprimands. But she'd improve.

When he released her arm, she brought it in to her body, pressing it against her to help relieve the throbbing. She could sense Evan watching her, far too closely. *Please don't say anything. Don't make me more ashamed than I already am.*

"Right now I need to focus on the rest of these pictures," he said at length. "The timing of the development is critical. Niall will take you upstairs and put you to bed to rest after your trip."

Her well-being shouldn't be his concern, but before she could manage a courteously worded demur, he tapped her cheek firmly, bringing her attention back to him. "Trust me, you'll need the rest. We have a hike planned for tonight. Do you have hiking shoes?"

"No, sir." She wasn't sure how she could have anticipated needing any, but at the moment every question was revealing her shortcomings.

"Bugger, I forgot about that," Niall grumbled. "I'll get some from the general supply store while she's sleeping."

Evan nodded, gave her a half smile. "He told you he knew nothing about being a proper servant. You may have to teach him a thing or two, Alanna."

"Aye, and then I'll have to find a proper nancy vampire to do all that crap for. Ye should be in bed yourself. Way past your bedtime."

"I can stay up quite a bit later here. The age of the mountain helps."

Niall shifted behind her. Realizing she was still leaning against him, she straightened, stood on her own two feet. When he did the same, taking his hips off the ladder, he was still pressed close behind her, Evan right in front. While her arm was throbbing, other parts of her were as well, used to being offered to a vampire whenever he desired her, fed from her.

Because of her mixed response, the men were reining themselves back. She wanted to scream, but throwing a tantrum wasn't in the repertoire of proper InhServ responses, was it?

Touching Alanna's cheek with his knuckles, Evan bent, put his lips to her forehead. "If you wish to accompany Niall and pick up a few things for yourself, you may."

Then he turned away to his trays, his head bent attentively over them.

Niall gave Alanna a wry smile. Their vampire Master was done with them for now. Alanna was grateful for the Scot's steadying touch as she made her way back up. A roiling stomach, the sensation of prickling lava and icy frost coursing through her arm, as well as the stricken feeling in her chest, weren't conducive to good balance.

Before Niall dropped the trap door that would hide Evan from her sight, she looked back down once more at the vampire studying his pictures. His gray eyes were intent, long fingers moving the images under their wavering layer of pungent fluid.

She was a ship cut adrift, not sure if she was headed into a storm or calm seas. Not knowing, not being prepared, that was the worst part. If she was an InhServ worth anything, she would figure it out. Soon.

4

SHE'D vaguely remembered passing the general store at the bottom of the mountain, but hadn't recognized it as a store. The large building had a rusty tin roof and gravel parking lot, surrounded by clumps of scrub. While the inventory inside was organized, there had been no attempt made to create eye-catching displays. Clothes were stacked on tables or hung up on a clothesline over them. Shoes were filed along another wall. Every available space was crammed full of foodstuffs, tools, deer corn, firearms, and over-the-counter medicines. By the cash register was a large bin of colorful hard candy. The interior smelled of old pine, the walls marked with sap like hardened candle wax.

Niall picked out her hiking shoes, loosened the lacings and put them on a bench made from a split log. The grain had a dull luster, polished by a variety of backsides. "Try these on, see if they're a fair fit."

As she took a seat and slipped off her boots, the proprietor ambled over. Given their surroundings, she'd expected a grizzled mountain man, but he was a fit male in his forties, with a clean-shaven face and receding hairline, evident by his close-cropped hairstyle. From the flag displayed behind the register, proudly stating *Semper Fi*, she deduced he'd been in the Marine Corps.

"Your friend going to be staying with you long, Niall?" he asked, eyeing her with friendly curiosity.

"Depends on how long it takes for law enforcement to track her. Kidnapping a female and bringing her up here to cook and clean for us isnae as easy as it used to be."

"Yeah, damn it all. Howard Keel made it look so easy."

"Which reminds me. Ye still have your movie section?"

"Sure do. Including several copies of *Seven Brides for Seven Brothers*."

Niall gave Alanna a grin. "Throw one in the pile, Henry. She can use it as research. See what mountain life's really like."

"Yeah, that'll help." The man snorted, gave Alanna a second appreciative look. "Might have to come up and see how she's doing."

"And I might have to tell Elaine you dinnae have enough to do about the house. That woman will shoot ye in the gut if you stray. Let the coyotes finish you off."

"You make her sound far more merciful than she is." Henry nodded to Alanna. "How are those fitting, ma'am?"

"Very well." She stood up, rocking on her feet. She'd never worn such a shoe. Though heavy and clunky, it would obviously be useful for moving through heavy forest terrain.

"Add in some Band-Aids. The lass will have blisters, those first couple hikes."

As Henry moved back toward his register, Niall pointed to a shelf stuffed full of books. "There's a few left at the cabin, but ye might pick up a few of those as well. Nae always much to do 'til Evan's up."

"Does he like having books read to him?"

"He's never asked me to do it, and he taught me to read far better than I kenned at the time. But I was thinking about your own leisure time."

Alanna dismissed that idea, but she did check out the shelves. She found one on area plants, an old one about painting landscapes, and another about Scots history. When she brought them to the counter and placed them next to Niall's purchases, he grunted. "Those dinnae look like pleasure reading."

"These will expand my knowledge of the area and Evan's paintings."

He glanced at the book of Scots history. "At least that one's a work of romantic fiction."

Alanna had kept the shoes on, wanting to get used to their feel. Now she rocked back and forth on her toes and the balls of her feet again. Niall gave her an amused look, gaze sweeping over the contrast of the bulky shoes with the feminine sweater and snug skirt. Taking the supple brown dress boots from her, he had Henry pack those in the empty box for the hiking shoes. He'd also had her choose several pairs of cargo pants like his, shorts and some long-sleeved T-shirts. When she'd balked at the expense to her Master, he'd overruled her, sensibly pointing out that her few casual clothes were suited for in-house chores, not trekking up rocky mountainsides with swarms of bugs and jutting branches that could tear thin, loose clothing. After another glance at her pale skin, Niall also added in sunblock.

Henry made an approving noise. "You'll think you don't need it, miss, because of how cool it'll get at night, but the sun still shines hot on some days."

He handed her a Hershey bar from a big glass jar kept in front of a fan to keep it cool in the non-air-conditioned building. There was a big woodstove in the center suggesting he heated up the store as needed during the snowy months. "Don't fret," he added. "If Niall did kidnap you, I expect a whole troop of male relatives will be coming to string him up in no time. In the meantime, you need help, just let me know. He's no worse than wrestling a bear barehanded, and I've done that plenty of times."

Niall scoffed. "Aye. Yet mention his wife and he turns pale and runs like a long-eared *coineanach*."

"Shows I'm a man with good sense." Henry laughed. "Rather than a thickheaded Scot. You all have a good day, now."

Niall took up their bags, Alanna managing to snag one to help. Outside the store, she noticed a row of carved bears like the ones next to the bookcase. "Does Henry make those?"

"Aye, he's a chain saw carver. Loves it. I'll run ye out to his place if we've enough time here. Eagles, life-sized elk, even dragons and people. Better than a museum. So, do you have male relatives?"

She'd like to see all those carvings, but wondered if she should assure him there was no need to take her places, entertain her. Instead, she answered his question. "I had siblings and biological parents, but when you enter into the InhServ program, they cease to exist. So I have no family. However, I expect they're still living."

"Biological parents?" Niall looked puzzled.

"Yes." She was patient, knowing most servants knew little about

InhServs. "I was not permitted to call my parents familiar names, like Mother or Father, or even John and Stella. They were sir or ma'am, Mistress or Master."

Anticipating him, she reached the Rover first, opened her own door. "You don't have to wait on me, Niall. I'm here to serve, not to be taken care of. It's going to be dinnertime soon. Does Evan like to join us, or do we prepare food just for us?" While vampires couldn't eat food in the same quantities as servants, most liked to sample for taste and texture, and she assumed Evan would be the same.

Niall shrugged. "I always make a little extra, but ye already saw it. If he gets caught up in what he's doing, hours pass before he'll notice anything." He slid into the driver's side. Fishing in the bag, he tossed the sunscreen in her lap. "Go ahead and put some of that on your face. I'll be happy to put it anywhere you can't reach."

"I can handle it myself," she said evenly. His flirting confused her, but it was an even trade, because she could tell her family situation had baffled him. Randoms didn't understand. On Day One, InhServs were told they weren't human. They didn't have family, friends or human experiences. She was a vampire's servant, the sum total of her identity.

It was an honor like no other.

∽

She put her belongings away in the dresser of the guest room. Niall said he wouldn't need her until the dinner preparations, so she curled up on the sofa in the living room to read the book about plants. After handling some tasks outside, he ended up at the kitchen table, repairing what appeared to be some type of small engine.

He'd said little throughout the rest of the afternoon, giving her room with her own thoughts. Silence with him was surprisingly comfortable. She'd enjoyed pausing in her reading to watch him work oil into the gears, troubleshoot the engine. He had his hair tied back on his shoulders, his tawny gaze steady on his task. He handled the small machine parts with capable grace.

When he'd noted her curiosity, he'd invited her to come over and learn how it was done. A good teacher, he explained what he was doing, letting her adjust one of the gears under his direction. When it worked as it should, she felt a welcome sense of accomplishment that made the lines around his eyes crinkle at her obvious pleasure.

Mechanical skills had not been required of her, since Stephen had an extensive household, but any new skill could be useful. Even if she wouldn't be around long to use it.

Apparently, there was no way to silence that cynical, terrifying voice in the back of her head.

Fortunately, it was time to prepare for dinner. Midafternoon, he'd had her take a frozen venison stew out of the freezer to thaw. Now he rose to start cooking, putting his project and tools away in a crate and stowing them in a corner. He told her to set the table.

She started that immediately after wiping the grease, oil and dirt from the table. She suspected he had deduced she would if he didn't. His wink at her confirmed it. Typical male.

Ignoring him, she put out three place settings, but she could feel his regard. When she took up an extra set of napkins and began folding them, his curiosity drew him back to the table.

He slid into a chair next to her, making it creak with his bulk. "What are you doing?"

"Origami. This is something I did when preparing Lord Stephen's table. His guests seemed to enjoy it."

As the bird of paradise took shape, a relatively simple design, she handed the next napkin to him. "If you like, you can fold with me, follow the pattern."

He shook his head. Remembering his mechanical aptitude with the engine parts, she suspected he could pick up the skill quickly enough based on sight alone.

When she finished, she placed the bird in the middle of Evan's empty plate. "Do we have candles? A tablecloth?"

"Probably somewhere. It's a rental cabin."

She found a few stubby votives in the cabinets, a vinyl oval tablecloth in decent condition, printed with a pattern of cream-colored transparent leaves, and a silver plate. Bringing them back to the table, she removed the settings to the sideboard and put the cloth down, leaning over the table to smooth it. Her gaze was on her work, but she was well aware of Niall's attention as she stretched across the table, her position emphasizing the roundness of hip and buttock.

Indulging such personal pleasures was not necessarily against the rules; she'd stolen more than one glance at him as well this afternoon. The open throat of his shirt, revealing the burnished curl of dark chest hair, the stretch of the cargo pants over haunch and thigh as he knelt to check something on the woodstove. The shrug of broad shoulders as he answered her questions. The way those tawny brown eyes watched her, trying to figure her out as much as she was him.

It was normal for servants to measure each other, getting familiar with what they might be required to touch in ways far more intimate. Evan hadn't indicated whether he would enjoy performances by his two servants, the way it happened at vampire gatherings, but a servant must always be prepared. The idea made her feel unusually flustered. Perhaps it was the different surroundings, the situation. Plus, Niall's regard could be . . . intense.

She made herself ignore it, creating a centerpiece with the silver plate and the stubby votives. When Niall went back to the stew, she slipped out the cabin door to hunt up some of the wildflowers she'd seen there. Retrieving a short blade from her pants pocket, since she'd changed into the clothes Niall said would be most suitable for hiking tonight, she flicked it open, cut the stems cleanly. She brought them in and arranged them in a couple of water glasses among the votives. It made an appropriate and attractive centerpiece for their mountain surroundings.

Finding matches, she lit the candles. As she did, Niall came to retrieve the cups. He moved back so she could pass between him and the table to reach the votives on the other side, but when she did, he put his hands lightly on her hips. She tensed, not sure of his intent, but it was a simple caress as he moved past.

The heat of his hands went right through her clothes. It made her think of that impending second mark, and how aroused the two men had been earlier in the evening. Her mind and body were anticipating, which she expected, but the butterflies were a surprise. Not unpleasant, but somewhat disconcerting.

Niall poured two cups of water, a glass of wine for her. "When I started out with him, I wasnae sure what he wanted, either. Beyond the obvious: blood and sex."

It was as if he'd read her mind, but she took it in stride. "Blood and sex are primitive, essential needs," she agreed, "but they're the least important and easiest things we give to our Master. Vampires desire much more than that. A sense of the servant's soul, resting fully in their hand, to do with as they will. The servant's complete submission to that idea. Their unconditional devotion to the vampire's care. That is what they seek."

Niall raised a brow. "All that, then? Not every vampire is alike."

"Not in the ways they approach it, perhaps. But that desire is what makes them vampire, and what draws us to them as servants. Weren't you drawn to your Master?"

"It wasnae really like that for us. It was necessity. A debt owed." He brought the wine and water to the table. While she'd been working on the wildflowers, she saw he'd made an attempt at the origami. As she lifted the mangled napkin, he snorted. "I've better luck with engines."

"It's like any new skill. Once you figure out the way of it, practice, it becomes easy. Or easier," she amended, examining the results of his efforts. "If you sit down, I can show you how to do it again and guide your hands. It's easier to learn that way."

When he complied, she leaned over him with a new paper napkin, pressing close to guide his hands. However, his shoulders were too broad and arms too long for her to capably guide him. So she came around to his front, perched on his knee with a very practical air that made him smile, especially when she guided his arms around her and then aligned her own on the outside of them. "It starts with a skinny rectangle, then it's just all about shapes and creases. And freeing the wings."

～

Niall was sure she was right, that it was easy, but it was difficult to pay close attention with her sitting on his thigh. She'd already made it clear that everything she did was at Evan's behest. However, her comfort with being so physically intimate with another servant—and so detached about it—was distracting. Especially when combined with how responsive she was to sexual stimulation. Whether a trained reaction or not, she became aroused at his and Evan's touches as if she was meant to be theirs. It made him feel like a bear with a honeycomb held just out of reach.

However, even if he pushed that tree over to get the honey, she wasn't his or anybody else's to use, no matter that she seemed to think she was. Her attitude toward her family still had him reeling.

"Was it hard for your mother and father, to treat their wee bairn as a servant?"

Finished with the origami, she rose to retrieve the plates. When she brought them back to the table, she correctly put the one with far more stew poured over rice in front of him. She lifted a delicate shoulder. The T-shirt she was wearing was snug enough to create nice creases between her breasts, coaxing a male to trace them.

"They were prepared for it, long before I was born. It was far more difficult for my mother when Adam, my twin, decided to go with me and the InhServ accepted his petition." She put her napkin in her lap, unfolded it. "The day we left, she held on to Adam so hard my father had to pry her fingers from the car door, keep her away from it as we drove off."

She straightened, lips tightening. "There was no need for her to grieve. It was a great honor to be chosen, and they were compensated. They can live well for the rest of their lives, send all the rest of their children to college."

"Except you." Christ, it was like she was brainwashed.

"My training exceeds that of most college educations in the required subject areas." She gave him an intelligent, shrewd look, not the vacant stare of an indoctrinated drone. That almost made it worse. "What I am shouldn't distress you, Niall, because it certainly doesn't me. I embraced being a servant fully, with no regrets. Didn't you?"

Something in his expression must have alerted her, for she stopped. "My apologies. That's a very personal thing. I wasn't trying to pry."

"I started it." Truth, but he still couldn't help the ugly twist in his gut. He nodded toward the centerpiece. She'd taken a discarded magazine, cut strips out of colorful ads and turned them into decorative curlicues around the glasses holding the flowers and votives. "This is pretty, but not necessary. Even if he had showed for dinner."

"It's important for a servant to make her vampire's home inviting for him at all times," she said, Miss Emily Post of the vampire world. "Even if he doesn't come to dinner, everything is prepared as if he will be there. So when and if he comes, he knows his needs have been uppermost in the servant's mind."

"He's not a bloody Council vampire."

"He doesn't have to be." She looked genuinely puzzled. "It's part of the core tenets of our service to any vampire."

"Fine." He scooped up stew, shoveled a bite in his mouth, chewed, staring at those flickering candles. Then he picked up the origami bird perched next to his water glass and crumpled it, wiping his mouth on the paper.

"I'm no vampire. I don't need that kind of nonsense." Picking up his plate and water, he left her there, shoving open the screen door with his foot. He'd eat out there, where there was more air to breathe.

Alanna folded her hands in her lap to conceal their tremor, not sure how to react. Staring at Niall's broad back as he took a seat at the picnic table, she felt like she needed to say she was sorry, but she wasn't sure for what. It wasn't about him or her. All the settings needed to look properly prepared. What was wrong with that?

Despite the fact that her stomach now had a cold ball inside of it, she ate her stew. He'd reduced the wild game taste with a good marinade, but she could already imagine different herbs or mushrooms that might add to it. If she set some of her own stew aside, she could experiment with it. When he was in an improved mood, or when she came to know him somewhat better, she could make her suggestions then.

The cleaned and dressed kills in the refrigerator told her Niall was a capable subsistence hunter in their mountain environment, but, like many carnivorous males, he obviously didn't see much need for anything beyond meat and potatoes. Henry's store had a produce stand with locally grown vegetables and fruits. She could supplement and expand the menu, offer different tastes and textures, which might also bring Evan to the table more often.

Perhaps she was treating Evan like the type of vampire he wasn't, but she had to be useful. If not, she would go mad.

Right after his meal, Niall came in to dump the plate in the sink and mentioned checking on something for Evan. He said he would be back by sunset. He didn't invite her to come. Feeling shunned, and wanting to quell the self-serving feeling, Alanna put Evan's unused place setting away, and washed the dishes she and Niall had used. Changing out of the soft shirt she wore for dinner, she put on her new long-sleeved tee over her cargo pants and braided her hair into a thick tail. Then she sat back down with her plant book.

Perhaps she'd eaten too much stew, because she found her eyelids drooping, the day catching up with her. As she struggled to keep reading, she realized she missed Niall's company.

A touch on her shoulder woke her instantly, but Niall's fingers tightened before she could jump up. "It's all right, lass. You dozed off for a bit. We're getting ready to go, and I wanted ye to have time to wake up. Feel like putting together some provisions for us?"

"Yes, certainly." She flushed as she scrambled to her feet, the book dropping from her lap. It was full dark outside, suggesting she'd done more than nod off. As Niall retrieved the book, he gave her an appraising look. "If your clothes didn't have the smell of Henry's store, you'd pass for a seasoned hiker. Put water in your backpack, as well as the Band-Aids and a snack or two. You might take a couple o' books to pass the time. If Evan doesnae need us, I'll take ye for a hike."

She was even more disconcerted to see Evan leaning against the kitchen counter. He was wearing fitted cargo pants similar to Niall's, and a button-down shirt. The cotton fabric was relaxed enough that the open neckline showed a generous line of his chest. He gave her an absent nod, his mind obviously already on the subject matter ahead and the camera equipment he was checking.

Once she packed the backpack, she stayed out of the way. She wasn't a fluttering bird when she didn't know what to do. Instead, she noted how Niall arranged the equipment in a much larger pack, going through a mental checklist to ensure he had everything needed. Evan did something similar, rechecking the items that would be most important to him. Though she picked up that there was some urgency to arriving at a certain time at their destination, Evan could get lost in whatever he was doing, whether it was studying some earlier films, considering lens options or thinking about choices of lighting. However, Niall anticipated him, keeping the vampire moving with prodding comments and of course having everything ready when Evan finally closed his case and latched it.

In her experience, an undercurrent of deference always existed between vampire and servant. It might be taught, like with an InhServ, but it was also something instinctual, something in the respective natures of the human and vampire that created that sense of servant and Master. With Niall and Evan, it was more elusive. The two men were well-synced, though, so familiar with each other their movements seemed choreographed. When Niall placed something in the pack and Evan reached under his arm for another lens, Niall automatically shifted to give him room. Evan noted something about the schedule while Niall shrugged in response, without glancing his way.

It was . . . intriguing. A puzzle. So intriguing she almost missed her own cue. They'd gone out into the yard, and now Niall was looking for her. "Alanna? Time to go."

There was impatience in his tone, as if he expected to have to pull her away from flower gathering or some such female nonsense. When she came out promptly, his brow smoothed, however. He put her in the passenger seat while Evan took the back, where he started scribbling some notes and calculations on a pad he had spread open on the seat. Niall put the vehicle in gear, and they were headed up the mountain in the moonlight.

The road was still a deer path, so Niall moved at a crawl over the bumpy terrain, paying attention to the faint ruts that marked the road, twisting and turning through the trees. When they passed through sudden openings, she glimpsed the mountain view before the trees closed in once more. She studied the patterns of the leaves that slid along the glass, reaching up to follow them with her fingertips. On one of them she saw a green bug of some kind, valiantly continuing to chew on his evening meal even as it rippled across the surface of the window. Looking ahead, she caught the flash of red in a deer's eyes as the doe lifted her head then moved out of the track without hurry. A moment later, Alanna drew in a breath as a stag bounded out of the trees, touched down directly in front of the Rover's grill, and then, with one leap, cleared the foliage on the other side and disappeared again.

"Wow," she breathed. Niall gave her a sidelong glance and a half smile, then returned his attention to the road.

"I'm sorry," he said. "I was an arse."

She shook her head, denying the need for the apology, but it made something loosen in her chest, especially when he reached out, touched her knee. Glancing behind her, she saw Evan still writing. It reminded her of Lord Brian's preoccupation with his research, how often Debra handled communication because he was deep in his head. "Don't be fooled," Niall advised. "He doesn't miss anything."

"No, I don't," Evan said, not looking up. "You acting like an ass is such a common occurrence, I didn't figure it required any comment on my part."

Niall shifted gears, making the Rover jump and rev with a brief spurt of gas. Alanna saw Evan lift his pencil a mere second before it happened, preventing a jagged slash across his paper, then he calmly went back to scribbling. "I think you just underscored my point."

"*Numpty.*" Niall snorted.

"Best you can do? *Noshech kariot.*"

"That part's mostly your fault, isn't it? *Och, weel, you wur brocht up mair refainit than me then.*" Niall nodded out the window. "Look, Alanna."

She jerked her astounded attention to the front again, in time to see a possum scurrying across their path. It paused, baring its yellowed teeth in a hiss, then continued across.

"During the birthing season, she might have a wee one or two clinging to her, if they're not inclined to ride in her pouch. The bairns are cute as kittens. The adults are almost as cantankerous as I am." Seeing her blank look, he grinned. "*Numpty* is the Scots term for idiot. He called me a pillow biter in Hebrew. I think you can figure out the rest."

She wasn't sure she could.

A few moments later, Niall turned off into another small clearing, this one ringed with trees that hid the mountain view. "We hike from here," he advised.

The men donned the two large backpacks holding the equipment, Niall refusing to let her carry anything but the small pack with snacks and her chosen book. "You'll have enough to do, keeping pace," he promised, and he was right.

She realized she should bring up the rear, so she wouldn't delay the men, but Niall took that position, the two of them flanking her. Determined not to be a burden, she pushed herself to keep up with their longer legs. However, the steep grade began to take its toll within a couple of miles. As a servant, she'd maintained a strict workout and diet regimen to stay in excellent shape, but she hadn't had time to restore her strength properly, even by human standards.

Never in her life had a complaint passed her lips, and today wasn't going to be the first time. She tried to focus on her surroundings, how the forest canopy occasionally thinned enough to show her the moon, or a glimpse of the mountains off the steep decline to her left. It was as if they were traveling through a woodland tunnel, granted the occasional window of the world outside of it.

There were all sorts of sounds. Niall told her the short grunts or gusts were deer, and they had to stay cautious of them during rutting season, which was almost upon them. A chittering noise turned out to be a pair of raccoons climbing a nearby tree. Pointing, he showed her the shadows of their movements along the bark. The moonlight was sufficient to light the way of a vampire and third mark; she understood better now why they were having her walk between them, because though the light wouldn't have been enough for her in that regard, it was enough to stay aligned with their track. She wanted that second mark. It might augment her strength, and it would definitely help her night vision. As well as her sensitivity to temperature.

As the night deepened, it also cooled. She'd worn only the pants and serviceable long-sleeved T-shirt, because the men were in similar outfits. With the exertion of keeping up, it wasn't a present concern. But she reminded herself it wouldn't matter anyway. She'd been cold plenty of times.

Stumbling, she caught herself on a branch, wrapped in a thorny vine that jabbed her hand. *Smilax bona-nox.* Saw greenbrier. She recognized it from her book. Unfortunately, when she started to draw back, she realized she'd stepped into the patch of it growing up from the base of the sapling, such that it dug its barbs into her pants leg and tangled over her foot. A whole thicket of it came up with her when she tried to pull away, which also incited a small army of bugs to swarm around her. The branch had swayed under her shift of weight, and now the vine there had trapped her hand.

She started to yank free, but Niall caught her arm. "Be still, *muirnín*. The barbs'll tear your skin." The moonlight flashed over the switchblade he pulled out to free her legs with several efficient cuts. Then he straightened and did the same for her arm. As he did so, he slid his fingers along her forearm. "Ye could do some intriguing things with this, keeping a lass still while pleasuring her, hmm? Or watch her get so wild under tongue and hands that she doesnae mind the bite of thorns so much."

Her reaction to that was involuntary and immediate, her breath shortening and skin tingling beneath his hold. Currently held by his command to be still, and by the light prick of the thorns, she was aware of how close he stood to her, the lazy survey of those tawny eyes, acknowledging her helplessness and her reaction to being at his mercy. And not him alone.

Evan had retraced his steps, and now pressed up behind her, his fingers replacing Niall's around her forearm to hold it steady as Niall finished cutting her loose. "An intriguing thought. Fortunately, plenty of this grows close to the cabin as well." The vampire surveyed her arm, which had two jagged scratches.

"I apologize, sir," she said. "I'm not familiar with hiking. No need for me to slow you down. I'll catch up."

"If I wanted to use my vampire speed, I'd be there about an hour before both of you, wouldn't I?" Giving her an inscrutable look, he bent to put his mouth on her arm, sucking on the two gashes, his tongue swirling over her flesh. She wanted to lean back into him, but that was seeking intimacy, closeness, and Stephen had never welcomed that, pushing her away and teaching her to remain still. The way Evan touched her made her wonder if he felt differently about it. Figuring the blocker and Stephen's torment had distorted her perspective, she played it safe, remaining upright. However, the longer Evan's mouth rested on her skin, the more she wanted to be closer, follow his movement with a complementary response.

Evan lifted his head, sparing her the embarrassment of such impropriety. "Even on a schedule," he said, "it's never just about getting where we're going. What's along the way may end up being more important." He fingered the thorny vine. "The birds love the berries on these. Look through there. Can you see the tree, its leaves?"

He leaned past the greenbrier, his elegant hand passing unscathed through the vines, like a forest spirit in truth. When he caught a slim branch of the tree he'd indicated, he pulled it down with a gentle grip, showing her the unusual leaf shape. Niall provided a small flashlight, augmenting her vision. "The leaves look like teapots, don't they? In the spring, they have clusters of berries that look like tiny pumpkins, no bigger than a child's marble."

When he nodded that it was okay, she touched the leaves, feeling the smooth shapes. "If you're studying the plant life here, you should take leaf samples, make yourself a journal to document them, figure out the ones you're not sure about."

Preparing such a journal would be useful . . . and it interested her. She thought of supplementing the samples with some sketches of the trees, and then regretted she hadn't brought one of her composition books with her, because she'd bought a couple at the store to take notes about her duties.

"I'm sorry, sir. I should have brought—"

"If I want an apology from you, Alanna, I'll tell you."

"Yes, sir." She bit back the additional apology, but the direct order infused her with a sudden, welcome calm, despite bugs, thorny vines and aching feet, back and legs.

He nodded. "Not to contradict myself, but we are trying to reach our destination ahead of the moon's current track. We're going to pick up the pace. Can you manage it?"

She didn't lie about things that could inconvenience her Master, but she would have preferred to cut out her tongue rather than say it. "No, sir. But I can wait here until you return."

"No. You're only carrying the one mark right now. I won't be able to hear you if there's a problem."

"You were going to take care of the second mark when you got up," Niall reminded him. "You just pissed away your time as usual."

"I didn't forget," Evan said, unconcerned. "Timing is important. I'd rather not treat her second mark like one of your beef jerky breaks."

"Artists." Niall rolled his eyes at Alanna. "Everything is a bloody production."

"Whereas a practical Scot calls the Mona Lisa a homely lass with a dodgy smile."

"I'm not wrong about that. I can carry her, if you can carry the gear. Or vice versa."

Alanna was starting to digest the astounding fact that this was normal conversation between them. "That's not necessary," she interjected hastily. "Since you've given me the first mark, sir, I can sense where you are, if you'll open your mind to allow that. I can follow and catch up to you both."

"She weighs no more than a brace of quail," Niall pointed out. He shot her a grin and spoke in broad Scots. "Guid things come in sma bulk."

Evan shrugged. "Very well." Taking the second pack from Niall, he shook his head at her. "It's no inconvenience for him, Alanna. He's very suited to being a beast of burden. I'm fairly certain he was an ox in a previous life."

"I probably ended up jamming one of my horns up some vampire's arse, too," Niall replied. He dropped to a knee. "Jump on, *muirnín*. If you wrap your arms and legs around me, I'll be able to 'experience the journey' all the better."

Evan had shouldered the gear, was already proceeding up the trail. They'd completely ignored her opinion in the matter. She should be used to that, but it rankled all the same, given the circumstances. Regardless, she obeyed, bending to put her arms around Niall's shoulders. As he rose to his feet, he gave her a hitch to secure her legs, crossing them over his abdomen and clasping her ankles. He also adjusted her arms so instead of pressing against his windpipe, her forearms crossed his sternum, her cheek pressed against the side of his head, his hair teasing her face.

"I willnae rattle your teeth, but let me know if ye get uncomfortable."

She was as likely to do that as she was to saw off one of her fingers, but she merely nodded against his jaw. She felt the pull of a smile and then he was moving, his legs eating up the ground in a steady trot she never could have matched. Even as a third mark, she would have had to run to keep up. As the grade became steeper, his speed increased accordingly, the Scot not winded by the pace or terrain.

When they were cutting her loose from the vines, she'd resisted the desire to lean into Evan's body. She didn't have to resist this time. For one thing, Niall was a servant, but for another, the position required her to hold on tight, which pressed her breasts into his broad back, her inner thighs spread to accommodate his hips, her calves over his groin. His pace provided a stimulating friction that had her fantasizing about him putting her down on the forest floor, using those vines to secure her. The thorns would be a delicious prick of pain as he spread her for his Master, her thighs pushed down farther by their bodies as they each took their turn, lying upon her, naked, hard and wanting, her pussy wet and ready to serve them.

There had been times Stephen took her while feeding. Though it had been merely a functional release for him, she always responded with excitement and pleasure, even if her mind sometimes escaped, going to a place where he responded to her emotionally during the sex, in a way he never truly did. He didn't mind her fantasizing in such a way, as long as the fantasy was about him and achieved the desired result.

She didn't need the fantasy to be aroused now. The need for touch, connection, was sharp as a vampire's fang. As she held on to Niall, she had to bite down on a moan as the impact of his swift pace and the rocky terrain created a repetitive bump against her clit.

When at last he came to a stop, she estimated they'd covered several miles in less than a half hour. Her breath was unsteady, her palms damp against his chest. In the not-so-casual insertion of his thumb beneath her clasped hands, the intimate rub against the damn creases of her palm, he acknowledged the arousal she was sure he could scent.

"Look up," he said. "This is our first stop. The one where the moon's track is important."

Reluctantly shifting her grip to his shoulders, she tilted her head back. The clearing was so small the tree branches laced together around it. The moon was directly in the center of their circle, a halo of yellow-white light radiating out from the white pearl.

"Like a moon goddess in a circle of ancient witches, reaching up with bony fingers to adore her." Evan was behind her. "Lean all the way back and let go, Alanna. Keep your eyes on the moon."

Tightening her thighs over Niall's hips, she obeyed. Compliance had long ago made the issue of trust irrelevant. As she dropped her head back, she let go of the Scot's shoulders. A short drop of her upper body through space, and then she was at a forty-five degree angle. Niall held her ankles locked securely around his body as Evan's palm supported her between her shoulder blades. "Lift your hand," the vampire said. "Toward the moon."

He'd sent a command to Niall, because the servant turned inside the grasp of her legs. As his groin rubbed against hers from the movement, her body contracted in reaction. His large hands rested on her thighs as her ankles crossed over the rise of his buttocks.

"Alanna."

She jerked her hand up, obeying Evan's command. The vampire intercepted it, catching her wrist, stroking it, soothing her, and then eased her hand upward along the track he wanted before he let her go.

As her fingers reached toward that full sphere, Niall's met them. His forefinger crossed her middle finger, his ring finger crooking around her smallest one. The branches formed the backdrop, the moon casting different types of light against pale skin, tanned skin, the gray-toned bark.

"There. Keep them still." She heard the camera clicking from below and realized Evan was crouching beneath them, working the camera one-handed as he kept the bracing hand on her back. "Now, move your fingers with Niall's however you like. Just keep them inside the moon's sphere."

Complying, she saw their fingers were becoming part of the tapestry of the tree branches. When the pictures were developed, she wondered if it would be hard to distinguish what part was human hands, and what digits belonged to the trees, reality concealed by the twist and turns of the shadows, the light breeze moving those thinner branches, the haze of the moon's aura behind it all.

Move your fingers with Niall's however you like . . . She started in a functional way, a predictable pattern, not certain what Evan was seeking, but Niall slowed her pace, made it a more random, sensual dance, like that of the trees. His fingers slid under and over hers, tracing her knuckles, the tender flesh between. The wind moving the branches became something different, spirits dancing for the moon, a dance in which they were also a part.

Niall's thumb slid down the center of her palm, gliding over her wrist pulse, then went back up, following her straightening fingertips, exercising enough pressure her fingers uncurled and responded to the strength of his, like the branches giving way before the breeze. Her thighs constricted further on his waist, his hips, responding to his hardening cock with a rhythmic undulation. It felt natural, like part of the dance, and Niall's other hand pressed into her hip, underscoring it.

Evan set aside his camera to free her hair. He combed out the braid, putting her in a state of bliss at the stroking caress. When the hip-length tresses came loose, they drifted to the forest floor, the weight of it pulling her head back so her throat arched. She wanted to look at him, but kept her eyes on the moon, her lips parted with pleasure.

Niall met her fingertips in a tent shape, sliding back down between the crevices, clasping her hand, holding that unified shape, an octagonal space between their palms through which the light of the moon funneled, spreading its glow on what should be the dark side of their grip. The camera clicked again, Evan's other hand leaving her briefly, but then it was back, the camera silent.

When Evan gripped a handful of her hair, twisting it in a closed fist so she felt the tug on her scalp, her eyes closed. As his fangs brushed her throat, she let out a little sigh of air. Her pulse pounded, an invitation. A plea he must hear.

Though Niall had goaded Evan about his misuse of time, she'd also detected an amused acceptance she now understood. The vampire might not respect a schedule, but his value of timing, if it was always like this, made up for it.

Since Stephen, she hadn't realized how cold and lifeless she'd been inside, preparing to be a corpse. She'd been afraid to let in warmth or light, because fear of death would come with it. It was better to go ahead and make her mind believe she was already dead.

Evan wouldn't allow her to be cold and lifeless. The two males felt . . . immersed in her responses. As Evan caressed the tender joining skin between her fingers and won a soft moan from her lips, Niall's eyes flickered. Evan laid his other hand on her heart, fingers firm over the curve of her breast, her heartbeat increasing beneath his touch as he brushed his lips along her throat, teased her with his tongue, his breath.

He was touching her purely for his enjoyment, yes, but he wanted something from her . . . something more than a measurable physical response. Something more spontaneous, less trained. If she thought about what that was, anxiety could invade this moment, freeze her under their touch. Since she was certain that wouldn't be what he desired, she tried not to think.

She was clutching Niall's fingers, then releasing them, then stretching her own fingers out, a rhythmic cycle, an articulation of what they were making her feel inside. Had Evan been taking pictures of that as well, and she'd been too involved to notice?

It didn't matter. Staring up at that moon, seeing the interplay of all the pieces of the picture, she wondered if what Evan had orchestrated was like what divine powers did, bringing together certain elements to see what kind of magic they produced, for their own wonder and delight.

Evan bit down, fangs piercing her artery. She cried out, clasping Niall's fingers hard, then they were sliding free again, twisting . . . It was a tangled dance against a moon that became even brighter with the rush of emotion through her chest. She would once again have the mind of another in her head, that empty, cold area filled with something new. It wouldn't be the third mark, but she'd take it, the closest she'd get to that feeling she'd missed so much.

The flutter of the leaves and slim branches that had joined the silhouettes of their hands, brushing and caressing those shadows, was too far up for contact, but she felt so connected to them that the movement of the wind over her skin felt like their touch.

As Evan released the second mark into her vein, she stiffened despite her best attempt not to do so. This one hurt even worse. She clutched Niall's hand again, trying not to fight the pain. She wanted to embrace it, let it course through her. It was the best moment she'd had in a while.

Bring me back to life . . . you healed me . . . broken pieces . . . It was a song she'd heard once, on the music player of the gardener at the Berlin castle. The song had a Latin rhythm, soft guitar strands. The voice of the male singer was yearning, rough. In need.

Your touch makes me whole again . . .

She'd rarely spoken during those days she sat in the garden. But she'd asked the gardener the name of the song.

"Stitch by Stitch." Appropriate. She was a broken doll, being stitched back together again, and the needle's puncture hurt.

"Easy. There we go, lass. Easy." The earlier mark was a burn, like a flame too close. This was like holding her arm again a hot stove, only the fire was scorching her skin from inside her veins. She gasped, struggling through it as Evan eased his touch on her hair. His thumb massaged the occipital bone, and when Niall's hand closed over her wrist, that restraint, the stimulation to two erogenous zones, counterbalanced the agony, giving her something to combat it.

I would have liked you to only feel pleasure from that. I'm sorry, Alanna.

Pain . . . demand. Please. The natural response of her body to a Master's demand came to her defense, to bear whatever a vampire needed her to bear. His apology wasn't what she needed, and the plea was in her mind before she thought about the presumption of making it. But his fingers stilled for only a breath before he dug his fingers into her hair, drawing her head back, pulling against her scalp. "Let it flow through, Alanna," he said, low and steady, those gray eyes dominating her vision. Dominating her, period. "Accept me as your Master."

Niall captured both of her wrists, now crossed over her chest. His knuckles brushed the cleft between her breasts, and she arched into the strength of his hands. Had Evan spoken to the Scot directly, told him to increase the sense of restraint, or had he simply known? Somehow, she suspected the latter.

A relieved breath escaped her, even though it was thready, overcome by the pain. "Thank you, sir."

It seemed to take the pain far longer to ebb this time, but agony was like that. She'd been at a vampire dinner once where they'd subjected the servants to a pain endurance test, and then asked the servant to guess how much time had passed while the pain was inflicted upon them. The one who guessed closest won a special prize for his Master or Mistress, a pretty silver goblet offered by the host. She'd won, because she'd counted every second off in her head, refusing to lose track, even through the application of the brands to the bottoms of her feet. They had healed in almost the same amount of time, the benefit of the third mark.

Opening her eyes, she saw Niall's intent brown eyes, the set line of his jaw. His thumbs passed over her pulse again, making her lips part anew, the muscles in her thighs tremble.

All right, then, muirnín?

Evan had given his servant a direct line to her mind, at least for this moment, and knowing they were both there, that she was no longer alone in her head, was so overwhelming, she couldn't speak, even as thought. She started trembling, her fingers curling over Niall's, still holding her wrists.

It's all right, yekirati. *Shhh. We're here.*

Evan's voice now. Never in her entire life had a vampire comforted her. Thanked her. Apologized to her. Evan had done all three in less than a day.

"So I require a great deal of training from my InhServ to meet proper standards?"

"No, sir . . . I could never . . ." Then she saw the gray eyes crinkling at the corners, though a serious cast remained to his features.

"That's your job, isn't it? Teaching a made vampire how to act more like a born vampire?"

Yes, but even when providing the most subtle guidance to Stephen, she did so from a kneeling position, her head bowed, always making it clear she was an instrument. A gift, like money or a title, that would help him ascend in the ranks of the vampires. At no time was the gift to appear superior to the one to whom she'd been given. In the end, she'd certainly not been a gift to Lord Stephen.

"I'm here to serve you however you require, Master." He'd said she'd know when to call him that. She saw the dark brows knitting, lips firming in a way that made her want to touch his face, even if she'd never dream of doing that without being commanded.

Evan returned her to a vertical position, guiding her to put her arms around Niall's shoulders again, only she was face-to-face with the Scot this time. As he guided her legs back to the ground he held on to her, because her legs were shaking. One large hand cupped her face, pressing her cheek to his shoulder as Evan redid her hair in a loose braid.

"'And whenever a woman grows her hair, it is a glory to her, because her hair is given to her in place of a covering.' In short, a veil to show her respect to God, to her Master." The vampire stroked the shorter tendrils behind her ears, lingering on the delicate shell shape. Alanna stayed still, thinking she could remain like this forever. Their bodies and hands touching her, their voices in her mind. It was the safest she'd ever felt, in a world where she'd never thought to ask for sanctuary.

When she was at last steady enough for Niall to ease his hold, let her stand on her own two feet, Evan was squatting on his heels nearby, the thin fabric of the cargos pulling attractively across his thighs. He was checking the shots on the screen of the camera. His notebook was open on the ground, and he was making some other notations.

"We have a little farther to go," Niall told her, his hand on the small of her back. "But it's just a couple hundred yards. Since he's done the timed shot, we can set an easier pace. Do you feel up to walking?"

She felt like flying. So she nodded.

5

Their destination was a rocky ledge, with tufts of silver-limned grass spiking from the overlapping stones. The trees fell back, no longer a thatched net above. Now she was beneath a wide black sky, illuminated by plentiful stars scattered in so many patterns, it would take a lifetime to draw all the pictures they created.

Niall bade her take a seat on one of the flat rocks and watch how he set up Evan's equipment. While she accepted that as a useful course of action, she wondered if he'd done it because she still looked like a good breeze could send her off the cliff.

She assumed Evan intended to photograph the surroundings here as well, and he did take some shots as Niall was unloading the backpacks, but then she saw the servant setting up two easels, stretching canvas over pegged frames. A folding table came next, with brushes, assorted tubes of paint, palette, rags, a bottle of water.

Fishing out his pocketknife, Niall used the corkscrew to open a bottle of red wine, sitting it on the table with a stack of plastic cups. The vampires she knew would have packed wineglasses and an expensive cheese and fruit tray.

"Too uncouth?" Evan lifted his head from his camera.

Never knowing when he was listening—the one disconcerting thing about having a vampire in her mind.

"Only one?" His handsome mouth curved.

"Of course not, my l—" She stopped. "Sir."

Niall chuckled. Done with his tasks, he flopped down next to her, leaning back on his elbows, propping one giant hiking boot atop the other. She guessed he wore a size thirteen, since his foot looked twice as broad and long as hers. "Most times, he uses the cups to clean his brushes and chugs the wine straight from the bottle. Does anything about him say his lairdship?"

"His ownership of me . . . and you," she said stiffly. "It demands respect and honor. Service."

"I knew slave owners in my time. Some of them needed to have their testicles hacked off and their throats cut. In that order." Removing an apple from the pack she'd brought, Niall cut a slice, offering it to her. "Want a bite?"

Evan appeared to be involved in his paints. Even so, Niall's blatant rudeness shocked her.

"No. Our Master isn't that type of vampire. Why would you say such a horrible, disrespectful thing?"

Niall stopped chewing. His suddenly cool expression made her color rise in contrast. She'd just asserted she knew far more about Evan than his three-hundred-year-old servant and, even worse, criticized Niall's service to him.

I don't need a champion, Alanna. Though I thank you for the thought.

If her cheeks could burn hotter, she was sure they would. When she lowered her gaze with a nod, she hoped the ground would swallow her. She didn't know how to deal with a servant who didn't act like a servant at all. Even so, Evan's lack of reaction to it made her wonder. Stephen would have had any servant with half that insolence whipped until blood ran down their backs.

"Alanna."

She lifted her confused eyes to the vampire. She sincerely hoped he wasn't going to say that thought out loud. She'd never thought of having to guard her thoughts from what a servant might think of her.

"Evan," the vampire said. "Say my name."

"Evan." She managed it, though it felt clumsy, wrong. "Sir."

At Niall's snort, she quelled sudden anger, an unexpected emotion for her.

"My apologies. Evan." She said it carefully, like a foreign language, and it was. "I'm accustomed to referring to all vampires as my lord."

"Because all of them were." Evan nodded, unperturbed. "Born vampires, territory overlords, or Region Masters. It's understandable. I don't mind if you slip. Just keep correcting yourself." His tone became dry. "The more time you spend around me, the easier it will get. As Niall pointed out, the differences will be quite obvious."

He *was* different. But it wasn't because he was ill-mannered, unrefined. It was something hard to define, something that held her attention, like the puzzle of how to best serve him. That challenge, such a change from what she'd known, made her cautiously like the difference.

A strange thought. She hadn't thought about liking or disliking things in quite a while. That path was best pushed aside. The best way to do that was to perform some task for her new Master, yet at the moment she saw nothing to hand.

Niall had left her side. Finished with his apple, he headed farther down the rocky grade, apparently to toss the core off the ledge for the wildlife. The Scot turned his head at her regard, gave her a wink that reassured her that his offense with her comment was short-lived. She let out a sigh of relief, just as his knee went out from beneath him and he lost his footing.

As he skidded down the precipitous grade, the distance was so short there was no time to cry out. He went right over it, in a shower of dirt and rock. She jumped to her feet with a cry, spinning to look at Evan. The vampire was mixing his paints, not the least bit concerned his full servant had toppled off the edge of a mountain. Her eyes narrowed. Looking back toward the cliff edge, she saw Niall's fingers appear, digits curving over the stone lip.

"A wee bit of help, lass?"

She told herself he was fine, but it looked so dire, that deep gorge just beyond the rock edge. Imagining his feet dangling free over a yawning drop, the sharp pines and firs ready to catch him in their teeth, she quickened her step. Of course, with her diminished strength, she wouldn't be able to do much if he truly needed help. Since Evan appeared to have no plans to leave his work in progress, Niall might have to hang there for a while.

She knelt on the ledge carefully by Niall's hands and leaned out, fully expecting to see him dangling. Instead there was a generous shelf of rock jutting out below that one. He stood on that, his fingers curled on the rock. He was leaning, not hanging from it.

"I like the way ye look when you hurry, lass," he noted. "You've a lovely shape."

"Why would you do that?" she demanded. As she straightened, she did her best to step on those fingers, but he moved them, anticipating her.

"If you want to push him off for real, Alanna, that's fine with me," Evan noted. He had the palette in hand, was dabbing some color on the canvas, considering it critically.

"Without my usual strength, I need the element of surprise," she responded. When she gave Niall a condemning look, he chuckled.

"She's serious, Evan."

"So am I." The vampire shifted to study the canvas from another angle. Alanna couldn't help but notice how the pants creased attractively over his groin, displaying what was there. It cooled her irritation with Niall, yet heated other parts of her.

Evan glanced up, giving her an appraising glance that increased that heat. "I now have a new servant who treats me with proper deference and respect. She also has a gorgeous body and miles of lovely hair. Why do I need your ugly face and poor manners?"

"Because ye need a pack mule. Remember?" Hauling himself back up on the ledge, Niall planted his backside there, feet dangling. He gave the bemused Alanna a wink. "You have to be hungry after that marking. How about a light supper while Evan works?"

～

They ate their picnic at that same spot. Niall was pleased when Alanna sat next to him, slim legs and new hiking shoes dangling over open space. As he cut up another apple and gave her the lion's share of it, she gave him the bulk of the sandwiches, though he coaxed her to eat two before she insisted she was stuffed.

It was absorbing to watch her, and not only because of the expected things. Her training controlled everything. No wasted gestures, such that she had an exceptional stillness to her, almost like a vampire. No fidgeting or shifting. Even when she blinked, it seemed a deliberate movement, the feather of the dark lashes pressing along her cheek before the rich brown irises were revealed again.

He'd compare her to an automaton, except there was so much vibrating beneath her skin, a chaotic emotional and sexual energy. It spun a fascinating net, drawing the casual observer closer, waiting for any move she made, any word she spoke.

When he'd apologized to her in the Rover, telling her he'd been an arse, Evan had echoed it in his mind. *Yes, you were. Don't take out your anger with me or the way the vampire world is on her,* neshama. *If you need a fight, I am right here. Always.*

Always. What was it she'd said? *A full sense of the servant's soul, resting in their hand, to do with as they will. The servant's complete submission to that idea. Their unconditional devotion to the vampire's care. That is what they seek.*

Her words had taken him back. Had it been 1754? He didn't remember dates all that well anymore. They'd been on a hilltop overlooking Florence, the city bathed in moonlight, much like this. The vampire was working on a stark black-and-white landscape, not the usual thing for artists at that time. But Evan had been experimenting with those haunting contrasts even then . . .

~

"Ye want me to describe what?"

Evan gestured to the tree line. "I need you to describe the way the light hits the trees at sunrise. What it looks like, every detail that seems important. How it makes you feel. What it smells like, what it makes you want to do."

Niall drew his gaze away from the nighttime view of Florence. It was so different from Scotland, everything warm, prosperous and colorful, the town full of intellectuals and laughing children. Earlier that evening they'd been at Ponte Vecchio. Evan had wanted to see the Pasquino, a sculpture of Menelaus supporting the body of Patroclus. While Niall found it heroic and romantic, Evan explained it was based on a fragment of an ancient Roman sculpture. That fragment was simply a headless warrior the archaeologists had deduced had been supporting the body of a fallen comrade, because the shards remaining showed his hand upon a piece of the torso.

The spirit endures through the physical, no matter how time has de-cayed the original vision. It still inspires statues like this, an echo.

Niall turned his attention back to the pair of rabbits he was clean-ing. He intended to prepare them for dinner, have them with the bread they'd bought in the last town. The baker's wife had a generous bosom, gleaming like a pair of butter-glazed loaves, thanks to the perspiration caused by her ovens. He'd wanted to taste the damp salt on them, but he'd stopped at his imaginings. He didn't dally with what belonged to another man.

"Pay attention, lazy servant." Evan drew him out of the pleasant recollection. "Tell me how sunlight hits a tree."

"How does that help you know how to paint it?" Niall's tone was deeply suspicious, such that Evan laughed at him.

"Trust me, it does. You're a hands-on man. You'll understand it more after you see it. When the sun comes up tomorrow, think about it. Make notes. Practice your writing."

Like most Scottish lads, Niall had learned his Latin and letters, but it hadn't stuck that well, since he'd had little use for it before he met Evan. The vampire had tutored him, though, helping him improve such that now he could handle functional correspondence.

"I dinnae have to wait. I've seen the sunrise every day since I was old enough to help my da. It falls the same way that moonlight you're looking at does it. Except, there's more brightness. The greenness of the leaves, they melt with the gold summat, so you get both colors."

He paused, thinking it through a bit deeper. "Ye start to see the outline of the trees, gradual-like. They're dark against the dark, and then ye notice they're becoming more defined, the sky a soft gray, like a cheetie's fur."

In the beginning, he'd been self-conscious about giving such de-scriptions, but then he'd learned Evan was evaluating his described emotional response to help paint the picture, not make Niall more vulnerable. That was when he'd become more confident with it, though Evan had embarrassed him by saying he'd finally found the poet in his soul.

"Ye feel a sense o' sadness, because there's always that in the gray predawn light. Your chest gets tight, and there's a hitch in your wame, like something's about to be lost, or something that was lost is so close ye might be able to touch it, there on that dividing point between light and dark. Then the colors start to change. It's different every day. This morning 'twas a blue with some rose mixed in, and the rose took over, washing over to blue, blending with it so it shimmered like pearl. Then comes the fire. The streaks of clouds, the hints of light t'come. You can feel the heat, and ye know God's given you another day to do His work."

Evan's gaze was fixed on him, so still it made Niall shift uncomfortably.

"One day," the vampire said, "I expect there will be a way to capture an image on paper with a machine, so it replicates it exactly. But even so, it won't show what you just described."

Niall shrugged. "I described it as ye asked. If you want sonnets or science, you've chosen the wrong man to ask."

"You mistake me. No machine will ever be able to show an image the way the soul sees it. And that's the picture an artist seeks."

"Most artists I know are seeking coin. Hoping for fat commissions from titled lords."

"So I'm not an artist?" Evan arched a brow, emphasizing those patrician features, the straight nose and high cheekbones. Ach, but the man needed a broken nose or a scar to make his face less . . . distracting.

"Not the usual kind." Niall cleared his throat. "For one thing, ye came to Scotland to paint landscapes. Most of the English look at Scotland in horror and flee back to their estates with their smooth green gardens."

Evan smiled. "I'm not English, remember? If I do it right, the subject itself infuses the brush with life, from the first contact with the canvas. That connection makes all the difference. And I didn't initially come to Scotland to paint landscapes. I came to see the Book of Kells."

"Aye, so you said. Fascinated because they used thousands o' wee dots to form a letter. I've seen thousands o' ants carry grains of sand to make their house, keep the rain out and the food in. That seems far more practical than wasting all that effort on a letter of the alphabet."

"Pict barbarian."

"You said the Picts had admirable methods o' stone carving."

"Uncouth Viking, then."

Niall snorted, but left the rabbits, coming to Evan's side to see what he was doing with the information he'd given him. Of course, he was probably mulling it for a future painting. There was no way to predict how the vampire's mind worked, unless unpredictability itself could be considered predictable.

Evan was painting a tree, a hardy Caledonian pinewood as he'd seen it in Scotland, but he'd painted it against the picturesque spires, domes and bridges of Florence. Even though he'd done the picture in grays and whites, somehow he'd captured the sense of bright daylight over the city. But as the eye traveled up the hill toward the misplaced tree, the sky became more turbulent, the tree an angular soldier standing alone from all the rest. Out of place, yet enduring, strong.

Niall had found a disconcerting kind of peace, watching Evan work. There was no denying or describing it. Fortunately, Evan asked plenty of questions about light and trees and such, but he never asked Niall what he thought of a painting. The one time he'd volunteered a comment, it had been about a commissioned portrait of an Italian noblewoman and her two ratlike dogs. He'd told Evan it was nice. Evan had just arched that fine brow, offered a neutral sound and gone back to it.

Now, though, Evan's fingers had stilled. The vampire's attention was on him. Niall didn't look toward him, keeping his eyes on the canvas. When Evan touched his face, he quivered. He knew he was that tree, out of place, yet captured on that canvas by the truths that Evan saw.

"What do you see in it?" Niall asked gruffly.

Evan's touch moved to his jaw, guided his face toward him. Niall was startled to find the vampire's face so close to his own. While he was a couple of inches taller than Evan, and looked a decade older, the male had a way of making it clear who was the more imposing of the two, on every level.

Niall made a noise, an uncertain resistance. Evan closed the distance, bringing his mouth to his. Coaxing Niall's stiff lips open, he teased his tongue with his own, tightening his fingers on his neck even more, letting him feel their strength. Evan had the ability to bruise and force, but now it was reined back. Instead, he shifted a step closer and let his other hand slide to Niall's back, take a firm hold of the stuff of his shirt, twist with the deepening pleasure of the kiss. That twist constricted into a tight fist when Niall exploded into life, kissing him back.

He finally let himself feel it, get lost in it. For the first time in his life, he could steep himself in another man's desire. As a result, it felt much like the sunrise he'd described. An unfolding moment of possibilities, stretching out before them.

Evan threaded his hand into his servant's hair, taking a firm hold as he explored him thoroughly with tongue and fangs, obviously enjoying the taste of him against that dark tapestry of trees waiting for the kiss of dawn.

Waiting for the possibilities of God's work, for the sadness of endings. For the ephemeral and yet eternal nature of it all. That's what affects your wame, neshama. *The forest will be here long after both of us, but this moment will be part of the impressions that linger here, that an artist will sense, even if he hasn't witnessed it firsthand. Our passion will guide the brush.*

"You asked what I see," Evan murmured, at last pulling back. Niall realized he was gripping the male's shoulder in one hand, a lifeline. "I see your soul, Niall. That is what I see."

It was their first kiss.

∾

So aye, he kent well what Alanna was saying. Vampires had a peculiar obsession with the human soul, particularly their servant's.

The first time Evan had seen a camera, a huge piece of machinery with a cover in the back, Niall had thought the vampire was going to dismantle it right there to figure it out. It still surprised him when Evan experienced the same wonder at a new invention that a human would have. He expected vampires to reach the point where nothing seemed new or different, but that never happened with Evan. In fact, Niall was far more likely to react with jaded cynicism than his Master.

Coming back to their present-day surroundings, Niall saw Alanna leaning back on her arms, tilting her face up to the moonlight. *The spirit endures through the physical, no matter how time has decayed and destroyed the original vision.* Reaching out, he touched her bare throat. When she stilled, registering the questing nature of his caress, he stroked down that graceful line to her sternum, tracing the curve of her right breast under her rib cage. He remembered how he'd quivered under Evan's touch, understood when she did so now. He'd grown up since then, and understood even better the feeling that swelled in his chest in response to it, the desire to take what she was unconsciously offering. Instead he rose, leaning over her. He caught a brief glimpse of the deep brown eyes, the dark rings around the irises that made them even more compelling, before he brushed his lips over her forehead and straightened. Pressing his hand into her shoulder, he left her, seeking a higher spot to take a nap. The fragrance of her skin, her hair, would be pleasant company in his dreams.

$\sim$

Alanna turned to watch Niall go, her skin still tingling along the track his fingers had made. When he stretched out on the grassy knoll to the left of Evan, forming the center point of a narrow triangle of space between the three of them, she shifted her attention to Evan. The vampire didn't react to his servant's familiarity with her. However, she agreed with Niall's warning. There was something about Evan, even when he wasn't looking in her direction or Niall's, that made her certain the vampire was aware of every move and thought they had.

Niall's sexual caress made her feel uncomfortable, but only because she wasn't sure how to classify it. She sighed. What did it matter? Even now Lord Daegan was hunting Stephen. She could be in the middle of deciphering her precious structure and rules, and drop dead. Her heart did a funny jump, as if she could feel it getting ready to explode in her chest, supposedly what happened when a vampire Master was staked. She knew better than to think about this.

Alanna, do you paint?

She looked toward the vampire. "I can sketch. I was taught the basic arts."

Come up here then.

She rose, moving up the slope. Following a compulsion, she deviated from her track enough to stop where Niall reclined. As she stepped over him, he cracked his eyelids and gave her an absent half smile. Bending, she studiously brushed away a cadre of bread crumbs caught in the stubble of his hard jaw. Satisfied, she straightened, leaving him with a curious look on his face as she quickened her pace to make up for the delay.

Evan was using quick brushstrokes on the clean canvas to mock up a subject. As she came to stand beside him, she saw a rough but excellent rendering of Niall's profile. The one the vampire had pulled off the easel and propped at its base was a study of the sky, nothing but moonlight and stars. As she bent to take a closer look, she saw the shadows of the mountains and something else . . . something in flight above them. Perhaps a bird, dragon . . . or even a man, arms flung out against the darkness.

Evan drew her attention to the upper canvas. "I started the face, and thought you might want to fill in the details, draw out the torso."

She hesitated. "For what purpose . . . Evan?"

"I'd like to see you do it." He proffered the brush.

Taking it, she considered Niall. Whether by the direction of his Master or some other reason, he was propped on his elbows, but still in a half doze.

She was tempted to respond to the command as she would any other task, focused primarily on precision and response time, being ready for the next order. Yet when Evan painted or took pictures, he took time before pressing the button, or making the first slash of paint. He was reaching for something else, something deeper.

You're on to it, Alanna. Keep following that.

She gave a slight nod. Despite Evan's teasing, Niall was far from ugly. No vampire's servant was ugly, and they didn't age. Even so, there was a weathered, rugged look to Niall's face, lines that gave it depth. She could see the trained focus of a scout's eyes, even now when they seemed deceptively unfocused and lazy. His mouth had a capable intent to it that made a woman think of his possibilities as both protector and lover. The solid jawline complemented it. He was power, strength, steadiness . . . and stillness. He'd teased her, tried to play with her. The laugh lines around his mouth and eyes said it wasn't artifice, but there was something else that became obvious when his face was at rest like this. Something deep . . . painful . . . magnetic.

His gaze shifted then, focusing on her face, and it clicked. They were both servants, both knowing what that meant. He *knew* all about the hunger and need, the inarticulate wanting . . . the sorrow and disappointment. The rage.

As surprising as that was, what startled her was realizing she was more like him than she was like the other Inherited Servants. None of them had understood, sympathized or cared. That wasn't their job, though, so that wasn't supposed to bother her.

She'd stepped back, clutching the brush hard against her chest. When Evan's hands settled on her shoulders, she almost wrenched away. Recalling herself in time, she went wooden, holding it all in. Evan's hands withdrew, leaving her standing on her own, all that energy pulsing around her. "I . . . ah . . ."

"Take a few breaths. When you're ready, paint."

She wanted to put slashes of red, black, brown on that canvas. A reflection of something else, not someone's face. The colors of a soul.

"If that's what you see . . ." Evan shifted behind her once more. When he touched her waist, a gentle pressure, she found herself doing as she'd wanted to do before. She leaned into his body as he closed his hand over hers. Lifting it with the brush toward the rough rendering of Niall's face, she knew she couldn't do it. Her hand was trembling, fingers clutched hard on the wooden stem.

"You're overthinking it. Take your mind out of the equation. If you were a portrait artist working on commission, it wouldn't matter. Most patrons don't want you to paint their soul. They want you to get rid of those unsightly pounds, the wart on their nose, the blemishes."

She drew a shaky breath at the warmth of his tone. His body was also warm. Warm and solid behind hers, his other hand sliding around her waist to hold her more firmly against him, make it clear he wanted her to lean, to press her backside against him. "See that hump of a nose, broken one too many times? The patron would want that straightened . . ."

"This patron wants it documented. You were responsible for one of those breaks, after all," Niall commented.

"You had it coming."

"That's what all the wife-beaters say."

She drew in a breath as Evan, ignoring him, bent to kiss her throat, nudging past the braid. His tongue traced her major artery as her blood pressure ramped up. Her fingers tightened on the brush. "All the lines around his eyes would be gone," Evan continued, breath heated on her skin. "You'd leave or create ones that make him look serene and wise, handsome. We do the best with what we've been given, and the good thing about painting is you can take artistic license."

She steadied, pulled from the storm by the calm, matter-of-fact explanation. When her gaze went back to Niall, the Scot crossed his eyes.

Her lips twitched. He saw it, his own curving, eyes warming to enhance all that character in his face. It told her everything was okay. She was allowed to feel whatever she was feeling.

She couldn't trust such an unlikely message. The very fact the thought had crossed her mind was enough to knock the floor out of her world. Her feelings weren't safe at all. That's how she'd arrived at this point, wasn't it?

"I don't want to ruin what you've already started." She recognized the desperate tone in her voice, struggled to dispel it.

"It's just a practice canvas. Here, look." Evan took the brush, made a smiley face in one corner, then turned it into a vampire cartoon face with slashed downward eyebrows and two points jutting from the curved mouth for fangs. *Paint whatever you like. It doesn't have to be Niall.*

Shifting away from her, Evan picked up his other in-process canvas and started to work on it on the other easel, leaving her to her own devices. In the meantime, Niall sat up. Taking out a whittling knife, he began to shape a fallen branch. She blanched, realizing he was sharpening it into a wooden stake. As always, Evan seemed unconcerned. They really were an odd pair.

Testing the brush's movement, she executed a smooth glide along the side of the canvas, below the smiley face. Evan had offered a second palette and a selection of tubed colors. She mixed some muted earth tones, experimented to come up with crimson and different shades of blue. Using a toothpick-sized brush, she dotted dark blue in the depths of the brown eyes Evan had created for Niall. Using her fingers and earth tones, she sketched out Niall's reclining body, giving more definition to the braced arms, the long thighs.

Though he wore a T-shirt, she left that out, intrigued by the body beneath it that she'd not yet seen. If Evan had done a quick rendering of the body as he had the face, he would have known by touch and instinct how the broad back and shoulders curved, how the line of thigh connected to hip and buttock. But she could explore, based on her own eyesight, her own instincts, remembering the press of Niall's body behind hers during the second marking.

She filled in a brown-tinted flesh tone, making him darker than he was, but scratching across it with nails and toothpick to create different textures, an abstract interpretation. When Evan touched Niall, did he imagine the smooth curves and ridges of muscles in paint?

She gave him longer hair, dark strands tangling down his back. She imagined him in kilt and hunting gear, traversing the craggy terrain of Scotland. He'd have scars from before he was a servant, but they might be faded by now.

Vampires might talk about things that had happened to them five hundred years ago, but an amenable servant would answer questions about that time period, providing fascinating specifics. She recalled making breakfast for a visiting Random one morning and learning about his life with his Mistress in Russia prior to the Bolshevik Revolution. Another time, she'd had the opportunity to talk to one who'd been in the industrial North with her Master during the American Civil War. Those discussions were a chance most human historians, unaware of vampires or their servants, would sell their souls to get.

As educated as many vampires were, most didn't pursue scholarly endeavors. For example, Lord Brian's scientific efforts had only been lauded in recent decades by the Vampire Council. As such, vampires didn't maintain detailed histories. Was it because immortals didn't feel the need to leave a record when they might be around forever, or at least far beyond when such a thing would matter to them?

Since Stephen had had so many second-marked servants, she'd often had to initiate useful activity for herself. She'd started documenting some of the things she learned, thinking it might be useful to him, the history of different vampires with whom he'd interacted politically. She supposed the Vampire Council had confiscated her handwritten logs when they ransacked his home for any clues to his whereabouts.

She'd sketched out Niall's lower torso bare, massaging the paint into thigh and buttock, but now she added a dark kilt, one that slid up to his thighs as he sat in his bent-legged position. The knife driven into the ground next to him said he was ready for defense or dinner. His fingers lay light and ready on it, like how they felt on her skin.

It was rough, but her sketch practice had served her well. As she studied it, she realized Evan was standing there again, looking at her work.

"Not too bad," he said, with an approval that warmed her. "If you enjoy it, you can continue painting while you're here, whenever you wish."

At this time of night, his gray irises were like the silhouettes of the mountains, illuminated by the moon and stars. "Thank you, sir. I won't let it interfere with my assigned duties. Whatever they will be."

He cocked his head. "Was that a push to give you duties?"

She bit her lip. "I am here to serve you, however you need, sir. I merely want you to be certain of my willingness to do so."

"It's bugging the hell out of her that you havenae given her a detailed list. That was her very polite way of nagging you for one." By now, Niall had broken the branch and whittled it into three sharp stakes.

Her lips tightened. "It's my duty to serve," she said. "Not to be insolent."

"You're right. That's my job."

Obviously. She bit back the word before it crossed her lips, but from Niall's bland look, that touch of coolness again, he'd caught it. Why did she keep responding to him like this? Yes, he was mocking everything she was, but that shouldn't matter. She knew better than this.

"My apologies." She nodded toward Niall stiffly, then Evan. "I was not intending to insult your servant, sir. Or you."

Evan touched her chin, drawing her gaze back to him. "I haven't given you any specific duties beyond supporting Niall's efforts because I expect you'll see where and how you might be useful even better than I would. Trust me; if I need something specific from you, you'll know it. Like right now. Take off your clothes."

Despite the fact that his words brought the confusion in her head to an abrupt stop, he maintained the same relaxed tone. That bare hesitation was all she allowed herself before she obeyed, reaching for the hem of her shirt and pulling it over her head, the braid falling loose against her bare back and bra strap, teasing the waistband of her trousers.

"Stop." Evan tapped her shoulder with the tip of his brush. It was cool and damp from his last cleaning of it. "Move out in front of the canvas, toward that patch of grass where Niall is. Then I want you to take your time removing the rest. Do it as it feels right."

"Do you wish a striptease, Master? I am trained for that."

"No. Focus on the view, the moon and stars. The night air, the sounds. Not me. I'm not here. Neither is Niall."

Uncertain, she shifted to the spot he wanted, her hand resting on the slim belt of the cargo pants, fiddling with the button. He'd gone silent, giving her time to think over his words. Lifting her arms, she pulled the braid loose, began to unravel it. She dropped to one knee to do it, bowing her head as she combed the strands with her fingers. She'd liked how it felt when he did that, so it seemed a good way to find the track of what he was seeking.

Most women feel a primal connection to the moon, if they give themselves the time and exposure to feel it. Feel its light on your bare back, every exposed inch of your flesh. Feel the elements around you, the trees, the breeze, the temperature. The aroma of the forest. It's all around you, like the paint that creates a full picture.

"You can paint the wind? The smells?" She whispered it.

"If I do it right, yes. The mind creates the picture, with all the senses at its command. In the end, everything is visual, even with your eyes closed. I'm going to be silent now. Take your time with it, and when it feels right to you, remove your clothes the way the elements direct you."

~

Niall knew exactly which words had stumped her. *When it feels right to you.* Whenever Evan tried to get her to act on her own desires, that tension returned to her shoulders.

When the vampire shifted his gaze to Niall, he anticipated what he wanted, no thoughts needed. He removed his shirt, dropped it over a rock. As he crossed the ground, he knew she could hear him coming, for her head tilted, eyes still closed. Standing behind her, he touched the curve of her spine, bringing her to her feet. He slid his fingers into the spaces between her rigid ones, lifting her arms out to her sides. It brought their bodies into alignment, his chest and upper abdomen against her shoulder blades.

"Use my hands and body for balance. Feel the wind, sway like the trees do. He likes to watch the human form meld with the natural one. That's what he's ordering ye to do."

Her shoulders immediately eased.

That's cheating, Niall.

We have to help her get started. She doesnae ken how to make a choice that belongs to her.

She does. She did. For one key, fateful moment.

Aye. Look how that turned out for her.

He knew Evan wasn't really pissed that he'd helped her out; it was why he'd wanted Niall to go to her. She'd begun to sway, and was using him for balance, her fingers curled over his straightened ones, her shoulders brushing his chest, her hair teasing his stomach, blowing against his thighs. Lord God, she was beautiful. Like some lovely Fae spirit, so fragile and elusive. Not even real.

But that wasn't a beauty thing. It was as if her spirit was already half gone . . . or had never been called fully into her body. Perhaps she was a changeling, only she was pure sweetness, not a drop of evil to her. Her tongue could be sharp on occasion, but that was a woman's way. That sharpness had surprised her far more than it had him.

Her arms dropped, elbows bending so she could slide her hands over her stomach. Niall unhooked the lacy bra she was wearing, stroking the straps off her shoulders. When he dropped it to the side, she straightened, stepped away from him. As she did, she lifted her arms the way she had when their hands were laced in the forest, only now she reached up alone to cup the moon in her palms.

✸

As Niall stayed in her shadow, Evan watched them both. The Scot was one of the most graceful men he'd ever known, a fact made even more entrancing by how big and powerful he was. Guided by the touch of his hand on her bare waist, she molded her body back into the lines of his like a trusted dance partner. Opening her trousers, he slid them off her hips with her underwear, leaving all those pale curves exposed to the moonlight and their mutual male pleasure.

Niall left the garments gathered over her hiking shoes, so now she was like one of the slender trees Evan had photographed, the shoes and clothes keeping her rooted in place, contrasting with the slim beauty of the torso and limbs rising above them. She swayed against her pinioned state, caught in her own erotic response. Niall backed off a few feet, dropping to a knee to watch her. Evan snapped a couple of shots, knowing he could do a great deal with the expression on his servant's face as well as Alanna's profile when she finally turned to look at Niall. The wind lifted her hair off her shoulders, rippling it across her back. Even with his second mark, she was cold, a shiver rippling along her skin, but other parts of her were warm. And about to get warmer.

"You were rude to my servant," Evan said.

Alanna's head rose. A languorous movement, showing her sensual immersion, but as Evan's words settled into her mind, she straightened, despite the clothes hampering her legs. Her head dipped down again, her hands going to her sides. A cultured and highly trained servant responding to his command, she was part of the power of the Vampire Council, those who knew nothing of quiet mountains and a moonlit gleam on a woman's skin. Their loss, and he wasn't in a mood to share. At least not with them.

"Niall will punish you on my behalf while I watch."

"Yes, Master. I apologize. To you and Niall." It had bothered her, the way she'd treated Niall, and she wanted to make amends. But he also picked up an undercurrent of anxiety.

The second mark gave him access to her thoughts, the snarl of emotions there. While punishment and pleasure were bonded in the vampire world, and she was fully capable of integrating them, the damaged part of her remembered Stephen's torment, his idea of punishment.

Sexual sadism was part of both human and vampire races. Vampires tended to indulge it a little too enthusiastically at times, whereas humans tried to suppress and deny it. Most servants had a built-in facility for embracing the vampire version of it, but what Stephen had inflicted on her was equal to the seven levels of Hell. Rather than giving him a reason to back away from punishment, however, it was the most important reason Evan had to remind her of the type of pain that she would welcome. His servant had his own tastes for inflicting sexual punishment, the kind a woman like Alanna would be helpless to resist, the pleasure absorbing her as much as that moon miasma.

"Niall." He spoke aloud when the Scot didn't move. The man's cock had leaped at Evan's decision, but he wasn't sure of the timing. Even without direct access to her mind, Niall was picking up on the same warning signs as Evan. His honorable servant.

Do it. Trust me.

Niall went to her. In one fluid movement, he went to one knee again, bending her over it so her palms were flat on the ground, her hiking shoes digging into the earth on the other side to hold her balance, body tented over his thigh. The pants at her ankles, the sweet, vulnerable curves of her ass and the pink folds revealed by the tear-shaped opening between her thighs, created a memorable picture, one that hardened his own cock.

Niall was very good at spanking women. It never failed to arouse Evan to watch him do it, but more importantly this time, it should push Alanna past the lock she'd put on her own desires. Another vampire might scoff, reminding him that she'd been trained to let herself go for pleasure. But what Evan saw was a show pony, one who would run if commanded to gallop, but she never forgot where the fence was, modifying speed and direction to stay within that boundary. He wanted her caught up in the euphoria, running full tilt at that fence. He and Niall would help her soar over it.

It was the key difference between InhServs and a servant like Niall, and why Evan would always prefer the latter. InhServs were for those with ambition, and he was sure they did their jobs wonderfully. But unlocking passions Niall had suppressed for so long, helping him discover those he'd never even suspected existed within him, giving him free rein to explore anything that interested him . . . Rousing him to a fight, enjoying the plethora of emotions and passion that tangled between commands and service, anger and passion . . . That was what made having a servant such a deep, damn pleasure.

Evan sensed it in Alanna, like a masterpiece waiting to happen. He just had to figure out which colors, which approach and medium to use.

Niall wrapped his hand in her hair, pulling on it to hold her head down, even as he kept his forearm pressed against her upper body. He wouldn't let her fall, but he was making sure the position felt precarious, exposed. "How many?"

"Until I say stop. Alanna, count them off."

"Yes, Master." Her voice was even, precise. Her mind was in the same state. She knew how to handle this. There was little performance to it, because the visual was what stimulated a vampire. She was only required to experience it as he desired.

As he desired . . . Evan frowned, nodded to Niall.

Niall's large hands were the key to his effective technique. He would sweep up from beneath and hit the widest part of the buttock with an effective smack that would resound through all the nerve endings between pussy and ass, up through the lower belly, even making the nipples tingle. Evan shifted position so that he saw the pink tips harden from that first stroke. She let out a small gasp, her fingers digging into the earth.

Niall alternated sides. *Thwack. Thwack.* Her breath started to labor, because he knew how to make it hurt as well. However, between hits, he would rub both buttocks, kneading firmly to make her shudder, writhe, then force herself to stillness when he hit again, a reproof for her movement.

"Legs spread out more, lass. Your Master wants to see your pussy cream."

Niall didn't help her, not obviously, for that awkward wriggle was part of the punishment. Then he was at it again. Evan's nostrils flared, taking in her arousal. Trained to please, to perform . . . Her mind was doing something different, though, something unexpected. Her head dropped lower to the ground, and the gasps became harsher. She wasn't rising up to Niall's hand; she was bearing down, as if she was trying to grip his leg with her body, hold on to an anchor in a world that was starting to spin too fast.

Her arousal was building so fast, already stoked from the earlier marking, the way they'd touched her but not allowed her a release. That spin was uncontrolled, a hazy, disorienting world.

Evan's eyes narrowed, watching her come apart. Her pussy was wet and getting wetter, but her fingers were in tight balls on the ground, her hair falling forward over her face. Her breathing was hitching in her throat, close to a sob. Niall hit her twice more, but his servant was keyed into it as well.

Something's wrong.

Yes. Bring her to climax. Hard and fast. Give her no choice, no time to think. Let's see if we can bring it to a head.

Three more flat-handed strokes, her white buttocks now rosy with his handprints, and then Niall stroked through her wet folds, three fingers pushing into her pussy like a cock, working and teasing the walls within as his thumb found her clit. He clamped down on it, squeezed and worried it. Alanna's cry broke forth as if it had ripped a strip from her heart.

"Noooo . . . no, please . . ."

Evan was sure she wasn't even aware of what she was saying as the climax tore through her, her body well used to obeying skilled physical manipulation. But the heart and soul couldn't be trained, and they'd been sorely treated, too fragile to handle an assault like this. As the climax shuddered through her, her forehead was pressed to the earth next to her closed fists. He knew she was crying, trying to hide it, her mind a maelstrom of things she couldn't understand. She'd been tortured by her former Master, was facing the possibility of death with every breath she took, trying to understand her new Master and his servant in ways far beyond her depth . . .

She couldn't hold a lock on her emotions in the face of a powerful orgasm. Confused and frightened, she rode a tide of harsh emotional response that blasted through the wall of her training. The aftermath left her aching, throbbing with need. All alone.

I truly am ruined. Broken. Dark emptiness closed over her mind.

Niall had turned her in his arms, was trying to cradle her, but Evan wasn't surprised to see her struggling to get out of his arms.

Let her go, Niall. She needs to breathe.

He didn't want to do it, his arms reflexively tightening. *Niall.*

With an oath, Niall let her go, though it wasn't from his sharp directive. The Scot knew Evan was right.

Stumbling a few feet away, she fell hard to her knees because the pants still hobbled her. Bending over, she folded her arms across her stomach, began to heave.

Niall . . .

The Scot was already there, scooping her hair out of her face as she retched into the grass. She put shaking fingers down, tenting them to hold herself when it was done. She was shivering, her eyes glassy, lips wet with her stomach's refusal to accept any of this.

"I apologize, Master," she gasped. "I . . . will do better."

In her mind, he saw she had no idea how she was going to manage it. It was just the only thing she knew to say.

Don't comfort her, Niall. That will make it worse. He opened the link between the two servants' minds so his hardheaded servant could see it. She was like glass. The least pressure was going to break her. *There will be time to comfort later.*

"You didn't displease me, Alanna," Evan said evenly. When her head came up, brown eyes staring at him, he nodded, let her see it in his calm expression. "Put your clothes back on. We'll be heading back to the cabin within the next hour."

6

I'M *coming for you. We will go to Hell together.*

Alanna woke, heart pounding. Since she didn't hear the echo of a scream, she'd bitten down on it before it could escape. Even with the blocker, the nightmares still came. The InhServs had mocked her, beaten her when she woke them with the cries. So great was her crime against their purpose, they probably would have done Stephen's will for him, staked her with metal, if the Council hadn't forbidden it.

Sitting up, she drew steadying breaths. *One . . . in, out. Two . . . in, out.*

She hadn't been asleep long. Through the window of her small guest bedroom, she saw dawn had come, turning the moon into a translucent crescent in a dark gray sky. It would be overcast this morning. When she rose and cracked the window, she could smell the rain coming.

She thought about the night she'd spent with her new Master. Painting with him, eating on the ledge with Niall. The soreness of her bottom after Niall's punishment. She touched her waist through her thin night rail, sliding over her rib cage, across her abdomen. Though she touched nothing improper, the firm press of her fingers against her skin made her shudder. Her whole body had become an erogenous zone.

She remembered Evan's gaze on her as she'd removed the shirt, displayed herself to him. The moment he had commanded her to undress, her body had liquefied. Then there was Niall, holding her over his knee, punishing her at the command of their Master. When he'd spanked her, only his hand snarled in her hair kept her from sinking her teeth into the seam of his pants leg. She'd craved ruthless male hands, the pierce of sharp fangs, the thrust of their cocks, pounding into her body, using her, needing her. Wanting her.

The ache in her throat was going to choke her. She'd ruined it. As the climax came upon her, something had invaded her mind, the same thing that invaded her dreams now. Failure. Hopelessness . . . Fear.

Evan hadn't taken her body yet, had barely touched her. But it made sense. He had a servant for his sexual needs. Her Master had committed crimes against the Council, but that changed nothing about her own status in the vampire world. She wasn't clean. She was a traitor. For Evan, she was simply an assignment, an intriguing diversion until her fate was determined.

It shouldn't matter. But she'd woken from Stephen's torment with the memory of Niall's and Evan's hands haunting her. She didn't know if that one kindness among the nightmares had inflated their importance, but she no longer knew herself. Pleasure on demand was a switch she'd learned to flip on and off, compartmentalized when her Master didn't need it. It didn't come unbidden, until now. In this early dawn hour, she was overwhelmed by it.

She remembered Niall pressed against her back, Evan's damp brush sliding over her flesh. She imagined that brush, coated with paint, following the curves of her body, adding her into the landscape, making her a permanent part of the forest, the mountains.

"Lass? You're all right?"

Straightening, she looked toward the door where Niall stood, his tall form cloaked in shadows so she couldn't really see him. But she could feel his heat, even from here. His voice stroked her like soft fur.

"Yes. I'm fine." Even if she had to stake herself, she wasn't going to fall apart again like she'd done earlier tonight. "Did I wake you?"

"In a manner of speaking."

She closed her eyes. She'd woken Evan. There seemed to be no way to avoid being shamed by her weaknesses. At least in her little room in Berlin, she'd been ignored.

Evan could close the connection whenever he wished, so her thoughts wouldn't disturb him. Why would he care about them anyway, this temporary servant who didn't really fit in his household? But of course he had to monitor her status in case Stephen came for her.

"I deeply apologize to your Master." She was already kneeling on the floor, her failsafe response. Even though Evan was not physically present or speaking in her mind, if he'd sent his servant, he was participating in this conversation. "I can't control the dreams, but Lord Brian gave me some medicine so I can sleep more deeply. I will start taking it."

"Why aren't you taking it now?"

When she hesitated, lifted her gaze, she saw Niall's tawny eyes glitter in the dim light, not without sympathy. "No sense lying. Ye know that."

"Of course. I . . . it's hard to wake up. I don't dream with the pills, but . . ." Yet that darkness became the nightmare. A coffin, endless death. When it became too much and she wanted to scream, she couldn't, as if her lungs had stopped functioning. She was a corpse, unable to react, or make a sound. The pills also made her groggy, an unacceptable state if she was to perform her duties.

She deserved to be up here in the woods in this totally unorthodox situation, because she was obviously coming apart at the seams, something no InhServ would ever do.

"Come up here." He'd moved, was standing over her. All he wore was a pair of worn flannel boxers, the elastic shot so they hung low on his hips. When she started to rise, he squatted down, bringing a wall of chest muscle into her field of vision, as well as the faintly sweaty but welcome male scent of him. "Put your arms around my neck, *muirnín*. We're going on a little trip."

He lifted her the way he might lift a child, fitting her to the front of his body, guiding her legs around his hips, his palms cradling her bottom and the small of her back. It was natural to slide her arms all the way around his shoulders, her face pressed into his neck. She was tired.

He rubbed her back as he maneuvered out of the room and down the hallway toward the back bedroom. She remembered he'd said this back room was suitable for Evan, at least for early morning. Since it was overcast, she wondered if he'd be there, but when she didn't sense him, she realized he was probably still in the cellar, working on the day's pictures.

It was a large bed, the headboard a crisscross of tied branches, interwoven with a string of small white lights that cast a dim light in the room. Niall sat down with her straddling his lap, her knees pressed into the mussed covers.

Stroking her hair away to massage her nape, he continued to hold her that way, her head resting on his shoulder, face pressed into his neck. She remembered her thoughts and dreams, the yearning, and felt an unsolicited contraction between her legs at the position. His cock was firm and promising beneath her, making her want to rub. Knowing she would die of mortification if she did such a thing, she tensed, determined to lock down even the most innocuous twitch. Niall's arms tightened around her, a brief warning before he shifted her. Now they were lying down, her body spooned inside the shelter of his.

"Why don't ye sleep here with me for a bit? Maybe having someone warm and breathing next to ye will help with the sleep. Imagine I'm a big, smelly bear."

Her lips quivered against that near smile she kept experiencing around him. With the only thing between them being her thin nightgown and his flannel shorts, there was a great deal of long thigh against the back of hers, his hard furred chest against her shoulders. It was natural to shift her hips closer, pressing her backside to the heat of his groin.

"You keep wiggling like that, *muirnín*, you'll get us both in trouble. Easy now. Just sleep."

Bit by bit, she relaxed. When he put an arm around her waist, cinching her in closer despite his warning, he nuzzled her hair. Settling his head deeper into the pillow, he blew through the loose strands as if they were in her way. It made her squirm, and he tightened his arm, blew on her some more, tickling her neck.

"Stop it," she told him. Warmth settled in her lower belly when his chuckle rumbled against her back.

He had that smell of forest and earth, like Evan. Beneath whatever shampoos, colognes or body washes they used, most vampires smelled of dry, cool . . . nothing. Another reason they were called the undead in lore and legend. Of course, having to dispose of Stephen's annual kill for him for ten consecutive years, she could say for an unpleasant fact the dead did not smell like nothing.

The Council allowed every vampire to take thirteen human lives per year without consequences, as long as they observed the protocols for remaining undetected by the human world, but only one of those deaths was necessary. The annual kill. A vampire needed to completely drain a human once a year to rejuvenate his mind and body, keep them in peak condition.

Niall had been with Evan three hundred years. Unbidden, she imagined a stack of bodies, like a wall of sandbags, and it speared straight into those nightmares Stephen had given her. A wave of blood, washing over the bodies . . .

"*Wheest.*" The shushing noise made his breath a soft stroke on her skin. "I'll sing you a song if you keep doing that."

Evan was still in her head, letting Niall hear her thoughts. She squeezed her lids tighter, trying to dispel such images. "You're not smelly," she whispered.

"Yes I am. Go to sleep." Niall's gruffness helped that warmth to return. "God knows what Picasso will want when he gets up tonight. Probably have me scaling the highest peak to strap a camera on a mountain goat's arse."

He trailed off at the end of the sentence, punctuating it with a half snore. At first, she thought he was teasing her, then she realized he'd truly fallen asleep in midsentence. She envied him the effortlessness of it. His unconscious state eased her somewhat, though. She was glad to be sharing the bed with him, but she wasn't sure what she'd do with the intimacy if he stayed awake. In Stephen's house, she hadn't had any difficulty avoiding unmandated physical contact with other servants, but here was an entirely different matter.

Evan had left her wanting, but that was her fault. No matter how shamefully poor her impulse control had become, she wasn't going to shame herself further by acting on her impulses with his servant.

As she worked through a calming meditation, her body relaxed further into Niall's. Servants never slept together. She was glad Niall and Evan didn't know that, and hoped she could sleep here every night, no matter how weak a thought that was. He'd been right—she felt sheltered here, safe from the nightmares.

Eventually she dozed, but when she woke, she didn't think she'd been out long. She was still firmly held in Niall's arms, his breath on her neck and shoulder. The bedroom door was open, but she didn't see daylight in the forward part of the house. The rumble of thunder told her it was storming, explaining the darkness. She became aware of the patter of rain, falling on the tin roof. A moment later, she realized Evan was in the room.

Niall had taken the center of the large bed, putting her on the right side. Behind them, she heard Evan shedding clothes, the metallic clink as he removed his watch. When she turned her head, the lights woven through the headboard allowed her to see him, down near Niall's feet. He was shirtless, the top of the pants open so they fell low on his lean hips as he dug out whatever he was carrying in the pockets. Some change, possibly some keys. Very normal things, things she wasn't used to vampires carrying.

When his gaze lifted, she didn't immediately think to look away. Instead she lingered on his brow, the way his hair fell over it, the straight shape of his nose and mouth, the sculpted cheekbones. His upper body, while lacking Niall's bulk, was strong and lean, with pleasing curves and ridges of muscle.

Niall tended to let his clothes stay where they fell, because he'd kicked them aside when he'd brought her into the room. Evan folded his, laying them over a chair. She should do that for him. It wasn't proper for him to be doing the task while his servants lay there.

It is if I enjoy watching them twined together, waiting for me. Well, you're waiting. I could be falling off the mountain toward a ravine of sharp tree branches and Niall wouldn't rouse. Unless I give him proper incentive.

The mattress shifted as Evan slid into the bed. Reaching over Niall's body, he touched her arm, let his long fingers slide over her elbow, her hip. Though the blanket was covering her, it was thin, and the night rail even thinner.

Take the gown off, Alanna. You may keep the blanket. Keep your back against Niall when you're naked, but you can turn your head to watch if you desire.

When she obeyed, lifting her upper body to free the garment, such that the blanket fell to her waist, Evan's fingertips traced her spine, the tender skin between her shoulder blades, making her tremble under his caress. When she lay back down, she left the blanket where it was, riding the edge of her hip.

His hands were back on his servant, his knuckles brushing her hair as he moved down Niall's chest. When he paused, fingers shifting, she expected he was toying with a flat nipple. Turning her head, she saw the vampire propped on one elbow, leaning over Niall's shoulder. As he scraped his nails over the man's nipple, Evan nudged the Scot's loose dark brown hair out of his way. He put his other hand on Niall's throat, collaring him as he pierced the artery.

It was mesmerizing, since Evan had been so . . . not *unvampirelike*, that wasn't the right word. But this display of power, of dominance, the glow in his eyes, the flash of fangs, reminded her that he had a side she could understand. This part of things she knew. His free hand pushed beneath Niall's arm, lingering on his hip bone. Then Evan tunneled beneath the cloth, found and gripped the cock that was fast coming to life, pushing against her soft buttocks. She started to shift to make more room for her Master.

"Stay where you are, Alanna," Evan breathed against his servant's skin. Niall's eyes had opened to half slits, as if he was caught between dream and wake, but she suspected he was quite aware, or getting there very quickly. "He likes pushing himself against a soft female ass while I'm fucking him."

She'd been in the room when a vampire was coupling with another male, but she'd never been this close and intimate with it, in this dark room where Niall's breath was quickening against her shoulders. Her own breath was escalating, Evan's energy cloaking them both, holding them under his dominion. Niall jerked against the hold on his throat, but Evan's grip only tightened.

"Going to fight me tonight, my servant?" His fingers constricted elsewhere as well, and Niall let out a groan, his lips drawing back from his teeth in a near snarl as Alanna felt Evan skillfully stroking up and down the hard cock, cupping his balls, squeezing them. Evan's arm flexed, the muscles smoothly rippling as he handled the big Scot. "You won't fight me too hard. Not with a beautiful, fragile girl pressed up against you."

"Cheat."

"Yes. Like you cheated earlier. You owe me for that."

She wasn't sure what that meant, but she understood what Evan wanted now. She undulated her hips, rubbing herself against Niall's engorged member. He let out a muttered curse as Evan pinched her in approval, stroked the curve of her buttocks. Though he shifted his attention back to Niall, the approbation warmed her. If she could focus on serving his needs, she wouldn't fall apart. Not like earlier. She didn't know what had happened then, but she knew this type of situation much better. At least she thought she did.

"Fuck . . ." Niall rumbled again. The hand he'd had on Alanna's waist had flattened on her stomach as his arm coiled over her. Now his fingers flexed, quivering as if they wanted to turn, cup a breast. She wanted that, too, her nipples tight and eager.

"No. You don't have my leave to touch her. She's mine, just as you are mine. You keep your hands right where they are, or I'll have her bind your arms to the rails of this bed."

"You'd try."

"Not me. Her." Evan's lip curled back, showing a bloodied fang. "He will fight me tooth and nail, Alanna, but in your hands he's a tamed beast. Law of the Innocents. He's peculiar about women and children, my old-fashioned servant."

"Before my time. I'm not that old."

"That's like saying you don't follow the Bible because you weren't around when it was written."

"Ye want to debate theology, *now*?" Niall's breath huffed out on a half laugh, half groan again as Evan's fingers did something else to him. "Jesus."

As far as Niall not being willing to raise a hand to a woman, her ass begged to differ. Flashing her a feral grin, Evan bent to his meal again.

There's hurting a woman, then there's using pain to arouse her. My servant has more than a touch of sexual Dominant in him, and it's my pleasure to exploit it. He loved spanking your lovely ass.

Air whistled out between Niall's teeth as Evan's hand left his cock, sliding over his hip and out of view, where the vampire put those same fingers to a more in-depth purpose. Niall thrust his hips against Alanna. As she made several more provocative circles against him, she stroked the seam of her buttocks up his length and back down. Pressing her damp cunt against the solid mass of his testicles, she could feel the wet spot against her ass where his seed had dampened his shorts.

She was wet now herself, wanting to feel flesh against flesh, and Evan granted her wish.

"Take him out, Alanna. Put him between your thighs. No penetration. I just want you to get him slick using your cunt."

Turning to her knees, she moved down the bed to get the shorts off Niall's hips. The job was already half done, since Evan had his hand and wrist well below the waistband in the back. Niall's jaw was tight, his eyes glittering on hers in the darkness. It made her look back down at her task. Yes, he was another servant, but his expression was fierce . . . overpowering. Sliding his boxers off, she left him naked for his Master. She wanted to touch the thick organ she'd freed. He had a handsome cock, clear fluid at the tip tempting taste. Her pussy throbbed as she imagined taking its width and breadth in her mouth, between her legs.

Sexual service was a part of a servant's duties. With the flow of visitors in Stephen's household, that service had often been creative. Seeing servants lose control, be pushed far beyond where they thought they could go and climax, was a vampire specialty. It was entertainment, politics, and the primitive expression of the vampire nature. Predator, dominant, top of the food chain.

Yet thinking of those demanding vampire gatherings, the political machinations that had driven many of them, Stephen's watchful gaze, his distant nod or faint smile when he was pleased with her performance . . . in comparison to this, those moments felt sterile. Physically pleasurable, yes, but there was something here she hadn't experienced then.

Intimacy. This wasn't a performance before other Council members, coupling her with other servants to show off her flexibility or exotic InhServ skills. Evan's focus was on Niall, and he was bringing her into that focus, making her a partner in taking the Scot somewhere unexpected.

"Face him, Alanna. Straddle his cock."

She slid up Niall's body, bringing her bare skin against that hard, furred terrain of muscle. Just that contact made her quiver, hard, especially when the Scot put his large hand on her lower back, digging his fingers into the top of her buttock to gather her to him. He nuzzled her cheek, her temple, his eyes still half closed.

Her Master had given her an order, but she was caught staring at the strong planes of Niall's face, the intensity of his brown eyes, the set of his mouth. The strands of hair sliding over his temples. Her fingers quivered.

You may touch him as you desire, Alanna.

She lifted her fingers toward his face, but just before she made contact, she hesitated, meeting Niall's gaze.

Niall gave her a nod of permission as well, his jaw flexing. She touched his temple first, the thick strands of hair there. As her knuckles drifted down his face, Evan turned his head to press his lips against her hand. She stilled, holding her breath at the touch of the heated, damp mouth. When he put his mouth on his servant's shoulder again, she watched the fangs lengthen, puncture the flesh again. A trickle of blood escaped, sliding over the fingers she now had resting on Niall's chest. Though it was too dark to discern the details, he had a tattoo there, something that covered most of one pectoral and his upper abdomen, because she felt the faint ridges of the scarring necessary to anchor a tattoo in a third mark's flesh.

Spreading out the fingers of her other hand, she followed the bridge of Niall's broken nose, moved over his lashes. Down the cheek to the jaw, to his mouth.

It was as if time had stopped, something significant and potent happening because of her touch. He relaxed in his Master's arms, she felt it, though he drew her even closer with that powerful arm around her waist, turning them into one sensual creature, moving in a twined pattern on the quilts, inside this earthen womb.

You said you were trained to dance, Alanna. Give him a dance that will make him fight not to come.

Evan was having to remind her to do as he'd commanded, but he didn't sound impatient with her distraction. She recalled herself to the assigned task, though she regretted drawing back from whatever this moment was. Locking both arms around Niall's shoulders again, she arched her body fully against his.

"This is called a serpent dance," she whispered. She gazed at his cheekbone, that intense stare too much for her. As she imagined the provocative dance, she relaxed and dropped her shoulders, putting her upper body into a sinuous roll, forward, then lateral, so her breasts dragged in an oblong shape across his chest and back, her nipples sliding over his. The motion carried to her rib cage. She was a serpent, moving through grass, over the curves of a stone. Over the curves of a rock-hard body.

Niall's hand flexed on her lower back, his breath sharp and hot on her face. His cock grew thicker, longer, so when she brought her hips into it, he was a hard bar against her mons. The tip brushed over her navel, leaving that moisture. She wanted to gather it on her fingers, taste him.

"Do it," Evan rumbled. "And look at our faces as you do it."

Sliding her fingertips over her stomach, she collected Niall's semen and brought it to her mouth. As she did, she lifted her gaze. The tissues between her legs became even more swollen, glazed with her own honey at the twin gazes lasered on what she was doing. Two male bodies this close to her, demanding and wanting a tangled variety of things. Strangers, and yet somehow far more familiar to her than the many others she'd coupled with regularly before the Council.

Mindful of Evan's original order, she opened her thighs, shifting upward to capture Niall's cock. It brought her breasts closer to the temptation of his firm mouth before she sank again, bearing his thick cock into a horizontal position between her thighs. As she made the adjustment, he thrust forward unexpectedly.

Unexpected to her. Had Evan not anticipated it, Niall would have sunk halfway into her channel. Instead, Evan's hands locked hard on his hips, holding him fast. He bit his servant's shoulder in another place, a rough penetration that made Niall grunt, just as Evan thrust deep into his ass, turning the grunt into a growl, a groan. Niall's fingers dug into Alanna's buttocks in involuntary reaction. She felt the impact of Evan's penetration all the way to her womb, even though she merely held Niall between her thighs now.

"Bastard," Niall hissed.

"You had no leave to fuck her. You're more disobedient than usual tonight, *neshama*." Evan's voice was a croon, though, as his hand slid down Niall's chest. Alanna swallowed as he plucked at her nipple. "And you're not doing as you were instructed, Alanna."

She began to roll her body against Niall's cock once more. Since she was dripping wet, it was easy to do the sinuous lower body movements against him. Her priority was her Master's desires, not her own, but when Niall had tried to slide into her, she'd had to fight the desire to angle up, take him deep. Her lower belly had a sexual clench to it that was longing, need . . . lust. She remembered earlier on the mountain, the tears. That ache was part of what was in her lower belly now, but she was helpless to back away from it.

"Do you want Niall to touch you, Alanna?"

He was already touching her, the grip of his fingers likely leaving additional bruises on her buttocks. She wanted more, though. Wanted him to cup her breasts in his large, heated palms, pinch the nipples the way Evan had his. But it wasn't about her wants.

"If that would please you, Master."

Beyond the initial thrust that had taken him balls deep in Niall's ass, Evan hadn't moved. Now those gray eyes that became fully dark in the gloom lifted to her face. "Keep working him while you look at me," he murmured.

She sensed Niall's eyes on her face as she performed the slow, provocative glides, her hips and clit coming in contact with Niall's pelvis each time she came back up. Then back down, the ridge of the head stroking unevenly over her tissues, a delicious friction. Her pussy spasmed, making her hand slip to his chest, fingers tightening in the hair there.

"You could come just by doing this, couldn't you?"

"If it's what my Master desires me to do."

Dropping a casual kiss on Niall's shoulder, a quick lick over the area he'd punctured, Evan pulled out and rose, moving out of view. Niall let out a breath, registering the pang of loss, his mouth tightening. To make up for it, Alanna kept doing as Evan had commanded. She worked herself over Niall, all her most skillful movements called into play as she stared at the Scot's neck. He touched her jaw, drawing her face up toward those fierce eyes. He had a hunter's look, intent on pursuing his kill, running it to ground. He knew it was beyond escape. It made her shiver.

"Bring her to the edge of the bed, Niall. Your feet on the floor, her between your thighs, continuing to do what she's doing, only facing me."

She let herself be lifted, turned, and when Niall slid them to the end of the mattress, she saw Evan had taken a seat in one of the roomy chairs facing the end of the bed. She braced herself on Niall's knees, her feet on the floor between his as she recaptured his cock between her thighs, began to dance and slide upon it once more, a titillating lap dance. As she positioned herself, she had to glance down. The sight of his cock pushing out between her thighs, splitting her labia, both of them slick with her juices, made her whimper. She moved her hands so she was holding his on her hips, and he was moving with her, helping to work her on him, taking over with his strength, making it less about the dance and more about male demand, the urge to be thrusting inside her, instead of through the split between her thighs. He was rubbing against her clit, taunting her, making her lose her focus.

Look at me, Alanna.

She was no longer leading, for Niall had taken over the movement. She was bent forward, a supplicant position toward the vampire facing her.

Evan was casual about his nakedness, one leg draped over the chair leg, the other braced on the floor. The artist would make a good subject himself, and she wondered if he'd ever done a self-portrait. Not an easy thing, since vampires had no reflection. Regardless, she wanted to paint a picture of him in her head and hold it there forever.

His cock brushed his belly, testicles drawing the eye. He was a good size, in proportion with his body. Her gaze covered the pale expanse of his chest, the knotted musculature of his shoulders. She didn't know if she had leave to keep looking at him, but he didn't say not to do so.

"Do you want Niall to touch you, Alanna? Cup your breasts, stroke your clit?"

Imagining such things sent a shiver through her, another gasp. Vaguely, she realized he was asking her the same question over and over, as if she wasn't providing him the answer he was seeking. But the answer was the same. "If it pleases my Master."

Evan cocked his head. "So anything that pleases me, will please you?"

"I am your servant, to do with as you will."

He slid his hand down his body to grip himself. Stroking his length, he rubbed his thumb over the head, using that lubrication to help with the pumping motion. His hips shifted, responding to the stimulation, his head dropping back to the chair. Lips parted, eyes on the ceiling.

She licked her lips. She wanted to go to him, put her mouth on it, finish it. So she put more effort into working with Niall, though he was getting her more and more excited, rubbing her clit against his cock, pulling her against him with his fingers digging into her hips, her backside smacking against his hard lower abdomen.

Was Evan aware of what was happening within a few feet of him? She sensed Niall's eyes were on his Master as well, watching him work that long cock. Was he wishing, like her, that he was over there, having the chance to taste, touch . . . be used for their Master's pleasure? Why had he pulled out, drawn away from them?

She kept doing the long strokes on Niall's cock. Each one was torture now, a desire to bear down harder, grind herself on him. The pocket between hip and labia was damp with her fluids now, her thighs tracked with it.

Evan's hand convulsed into a fist, hips lifting up off the chair as his chest expanded in a shuddering response.

Please . . .

His gray gaze came back to her. "Please, what? Tell me what you want, Alanna. No. Don't tell me what you want. I'll tell you what I want."

That is what I want, Master. To serve your desires.

She hadn't intended to disobey, but the words just tumbled from her. His brows knitted, lips firming.

"I want your mouth on my cock, Alanna. But you have to come to earn that. And I want you over here pretty damn fast."

"Yes, Master."

When Niall put his other arm over her chest, just above her jutting nipples, so close the hairs of his arm tickled them, it gave her an anchor for her hands. She worked her hips harder on him and he pressed his thighs closer. She realized he was moving his hips in tandem with her now, thrusting between her thighs, against her wet, empty pussy. He'd overwhelmed her serpent dance with pure male aggression. As she tightened her thighs on him, the ridged head of his cock bumped against her clit with devilish knowledge.

"Oh . . ."

"Aye, there I am, *muirnín*." Niall's voice was thick and dangerous. "Think ye can play with a wild beast and not get run to ground?"

"I'm getting impatient, Alanna," Evan said silkily, his eyes pinned on her in the darkness. "Come now. I want you to gush on Niall's cock."

Her pussy spasmed again, her clit hardening, and her nails dug into Niall's arms. "Work that pretty cunt against me, girl," Niall muttered against her ears. "God, you have the finest arse. Makes me want to sink deep into it, make ye scream."

She gave a small cry when the climax took her. As she went over, Niall's grip shifted, capturing her breasts and pinching the nipples, sending sensation screaming straight between her legs, adding to the climax. She was bucking against his cock with no training at all now, just pure involuntary reaction to the climax crashing through her.

She forced herself to ride it not one second longer past the strongest waves, so she was still quivering with it when she slid down between Niall's legs, moving on all fours to cross the few feet to Evan's knees. Niall's hands steadied her on her way down, then they slipped away. Her long hair was loose so it slid from her back, the ends teasing her knuckles as she came to her vampire Master. Evan made a low noise of approval.

"Still in those aftershocks, aren't you, you lovely beauty? Hold still, right there. Not a single move. Look at me. I want to see the need on your face."

Her mouth was within inches of his erect cock, but he bade her stay still as those aftershocks rolled through, making her shudder, her thighs tighten and quiver. She whimpered, licking her lips.

"You want it badly, don't you?" Evan's eyes glowed in the darkness. "I can smell how ready you are for us."

She didn't hear him command Niall, but since he could be in either of their minds, it gave him the element of surprise. When the Scot's hands slid over her backside, slipping between her thighs to nudge them farther apart, she widened her stance at Evan's nod. Then even farther to accommodate Niall's shoulders when he lay down on the floor between her knees. Her breath came in shallow pants, her eyes on Evan's watching face.

"Like a beautiful wild animal. She's all desire and need, Niall."

Niall's fingers curled over her thighs, pulling her down onto his mouth. She arched up as her thighs flattened toward the floor, coordination lost at the first touch of his mouth. As she made tiny, involuntary jerks against his hold, Niall licked up her fluids, his thumbs parting her buttocks as he did so, teasing her rim so more aftershocks fluttered and spasmed against his tongue.

Evan leaned forward now, stroking her cheek as she made pleading noises. She could smell the musky scent of his cock on his fingers. Though he was obviously hard and ready to release himself, he was studying her every reaction, driving her out of her mind. Vampires were the epitome of patience when it came to this. Anticipation was their greatest aphrodisiac.

Sliding the chair closer, he gripped his cock, finally giving her the gift of angling it toward her mouth. She took him in deep as he propped his hips on the edge of the chair, knees splayed wide to push her down on him deep. Then he held her there, hand fisted in her hair, not allowing her to suck or pull, just feel the length and breadth of him stretching her mouth, tickling her throat, while Niall teased her pussy with his mouth, tongue flicking her clit. Then his whole mouth sealed over her to suck and nibble. Because they'd started this so soon after her climax, she was trapped in that hyperstimulated state, unable to go back or forward, imprisoned by their skill.

Her pleas became short screams as Niall began to thrust his tongue rhythmically in her, making her want to move her hips in an act of copulation against him. Evan hadn't forbidden it, but he was making her stay still on his cock, so she assumed that meant the rest of her body. But oh, it was so hard.

She'd always anticipated what her vampire wanted before he wanted it, staying a step ahead and ready to shift gears at the exact moment he desired. Staying a step ahead of Evan was impossible, because he and Niall were fully on top, their demands like rushing water, powerful rapids taking away her ability to move or think . . .

"Please . . ." Her fingers dug into the floor.

"Now, Alanna. Start sucking me. If you come before I do, you'll be in for quite a punishment."

She got to work with a fervor that had his fingers tightening in her hair in reproof. "Easy," he chuckled, a dark sensuous sound. "I'm the only one who uses fangs around here. Niall, take your pleasure."

Yes. Oh . . . God.

Niall left the floor, fingers gliding up her legs. In the next moment, the head of his cock was pushing into her cunt. He stopped when it breached the gate, and she lifted her hips involuntarily, begging to be fucked, for him to come in deeper, harder.

"She's hot for it now, Evan. Completely lost, pretty flower."

"Fuck her, Niall. Be rough about it. That's what she needs."

The Scot sank into her wetness and the clenched postclimactic tissues. He stretched her painfully, but she welcomed every inch. He let out an unintelligible oath, a reverent expletive. Those large hands gripped her buttocks, nearly covering them as he began to work himself inside of her in long, powerful strokes. She tried to do the same with Evan's cock, taking him deep, working her tongue furiously against him. Too fast. She needed to slow down, but she was ravenous, sucking and nipping at him, pulling hard as Niall fucked her. He was ruthless, making her feel the slap of his testicles against her clit with every thrust. She wanted to close her legs, reduce the sensation, but he knocked her legs farther apart, and she was lost.

She came again. Through the insanity of it, she kept trying to work Evan's cock in her mouth. He wouldn't let her use her hands. Holding her neck and hair, he pushed her down on him when she couldn't coordinate her own movements, could only scream out her climax against his cock.

That wave kept coming. Was it possible the hypersexuality that came with being a third mark—a servant's only chance of keeping up with a vampire's insatiable sex drive—had not been impacted by the blocker? The thought energized her, renewed her resolve. She'd failed to wait for him to come first, but she would finish him. When he convulsed under her tongue, his thighs pressing against her shoulders hard, a precursor to ejaculation, she felt the surge of triumph. But then he drew her off him abruptly.

"Down on the floor, Alanna." Naill withdrew as Evan spoke. "Faceup. Head between my feet, arms at your sides, legs closed."

She was confused. What could he . . .

"Now," he said sharply, and she dropped. She was looking up at his glistening erection, the heavy sack of his testicles, the spread of his thighs as he rose. As Niall moved forward, straddling her shoulders, Evan fed that beautiful cock into his servant's mouth right above her. She imagined the pressure building, saw his testicles drawing up . . .

She'd wanted to feel him jetting against the back of her throat. But he'd denied her, because she'd failed the test, hadn't she? She stared up at Niall, the ripple of muscle across his abdomen and through the long lengths of his thighs as he used his strength to increase his suction on his Master. She wanted to be part of it. She wanted . . .

By the InhServ oath, it didn't matter what she wanted, what she felt. What mattered was what the Master wanted, and she'd failed. The shame and humiliation of this was her punishment.

She refused to let those horrible tears fall, though to do it she had to go cold and dead inside once again, cutting herself off from all feeling. If she'd done that earlier, she wouldn't have come so quickly. She'd let herself get carried away by . . . by what? The close darkness of the room, the two men's desires . . . *her* desires.

Apparently sixteen years of training and discipline, thirteen years of exercising it, could be weakened and erased by one traitorous act. Or she'd always had the weakness of character, and it had never been tested. Just like this test, she'd failed.

Niall reached down and grabbed her wrist, bringing her hand up to his stomach. He wanted her touching him, and her traitorous fingers curled into his flesh, seeking the heat and hardness of him.

Now there was enough room between them to see what she'd felt on the bed. He had a tattoo on one side of his chest, a large dragon whose head and shoulders covered his pectoral, the lower body and long, spiked tail curling over his rib cage. She traced the tail, the gleaming scales of the haunch, as she heard Evan's breath rasp faster. Yearning and hungry, she saw the slick stalk of Evan's cock exposed a few inches, then taken deep by Niall's mouth again. Her gaze followed his working throat, back down to his chest.

A female dragon wound around his biceps, screaming back at the male dragon. As Niall serviced his Master, the flex of his body brought those dragons to life. She let her hand glide down his belly, toward the temptation of Niall's stiff organ. She stopped short of touching it, however. His cock was the vampire's personal property, and she wouldn't go there without a direct command.

She curled her fingers against his lower abdomen, staring at the male dragon. As she'd detected with her fingertips, the design was marked with ridges where the ink had been set into the flesh with the aid of Evan's blood. A third mark's flesh healed all wounds without scarring, unless marked with his Master's blood. Looking at the painstaking detail in the two tattoos, she wondered at how long it had taken, the pain involved. Had Evan himself done the work?

He works with paint, metal, clay . . . whatever medium strikes his fancy . . .

Evan came at last, exploding in his servant's mouth, his groans of pleasure enough to make Alanna press one hand on her empty belly, her nails digging into Niall's flesh. She turned her head, pressing her mouth to the side of Evan's bare foot. Even if that was forbidden, she needed to be a part of their connection.

She also wanted to put her hand between her legs. Not to stimulate, but just to hold herself, a small comfort. Instead, she opened her eyes, watched Niall finish the aftermath, licking Evan clean. As he did, he gave the vampire a sharp nip, earning a box of his ears, a tug of his hair, though Niall glanced down at her in a perplexing sense of conspiracy, his brown eyes glinting. She hadn't brought Evan to climax before her own pleasure. Niall had managed to retain such control, while balls deep and thrusting inside her.

Maybe it wasn't her failure that made Evan push her away before completion. He'd let his servant fuck her, but Evan himself hadn't. She was another vampire's leavings. *Unclean.* The word came back to her, hated yet undeniable. She wanted to go back to her own bed. But her wants weren't important, damn it all. Did she need to have that tattooed on her flesh? The sad irony was that she'd need Stephen's blood to make it permanent. No, maybe not. She was more human than servant now, right? She could cut the words into her own flesh, the reminder that her wants were supposed to be the furthest thing from her mind.

Niall sat back on his heels. When he did, Evan knelt over her. Before she could guess his intent, he'd grasped her chin and pulled it up. Her heartbeat stuttered as she found herself locked in the grip of gray eyes as steely and determined as any Council vampire's. "Alanna, what have you noticed about me since you've come here?"

He was angry at her. She deserved it. She had to make sure she responded appropriately. Honestly. The only way a servant could.

"You're . . . different. From the other vampires I know. You're . . ."

"How do I experience things?"

She scrambled for it, trying to think it through. "You don't like to miss any details. You take time to absorb them."

His touch eased. As he stroked those long fingers along her face, she couldn't help it. She raised her face, seeking more. It startled her enough she might have drawn back, except a pleased warmth entered his gaze. Daring, she put her lips on his hand. His gray eyes heated further, encouraging her. She kissed his fingers, traced the lines of his palm with her tongue.

If he liked to take his time, not miss any details, he would want that from his servant as well. She could do that. She was trained to be very thorough, missing no detail when it came to pleasure. She'd just never done it spontaneously like this, without specific direction.

A sweep of her lashes showed he was hardening again. Her pussy, still recovering from taking Niall's thick cock, didn't care. She wanted him now. Her Master. Some sense that she was still a servant, serving a vampire.

"I'm sorry," she whispered. "I failed. I won't fail again."

"You'll fail if that's my intent. I wanted you to lose control," he said.

"But you ordered . . ."

"Yes, I did. But who holds the control? You or me?"

She swallowed. "You, Master."

"Good." His fingers tightened on her face, his expression getting that hard look again. "You're not unclean to me, Alanna. Nor a failure, not in any way."

Rising after that surprising statement, he took a seat in the chair again. "We're going to let you ride this feeling for a while, I think. But I want you to wash my cock. Niall put bloody garlic in that stew. I think he does it just to annoy me."

"The fact that it's not kosher doesn't bother you, but the garlic does." Niall snorted.

"Your kills are humane, thanks to your excellent hunting skills. That honors the spirit of Jewish law."

"I'm thinking the drinking of human blood puts ye outside o' most religions, let alone their dietary restrictions. The Satanists might welcome ye, though."

"Particularly if I offer a big, strapping Scot as a sacrifice."

"Heathen." Niall had gone into the bathroom. When he came back out with a basin of steaming water and a washcloth, he set it on the ground next to Evan, who'd returned to his chair, his knees spread, waiting for her. His cock had returned to a somewhat softened state, but she could scent the remains of his seed on it, the earlier lubricant he'd used to fuck Niall, and, as he'd said, the faint smell of garlic from Niall's mouth.

Sliding over to him on her knees, she wrung out the washcloth.

Niall took a seat on the bed behind her. As she felt them both watching her, she wondered what they were thinking, if they were discussing her. Her hands were shaking a little, her body hot with need.

Putting her hand on Evan's knee to scoot forward a few more inches, she wrapped her hand around him. His cock stirred, interested under her touch, and she had to resist the urge to explore further, bring it back to life. She shifted, her pussy rubbing against her calves, gooseflesh rippling across her lower back from her reaction. "Yes, I did his tattoos."

When she dared a glance up at him, she saw the vampire's jaw was set as if resisting his own response to her touch. It made things coil even tighter in her lower belly. These two made her act so strangely, out here in this rustic cabin in the middle of nowhere. A pair of owls hooted at each other outside.

She liked handling him, liked the feel of him. Like most vampires, he didn't become immediately flaccid after climax, part of why she expected they recovered so quickly, capable of fucking a servant countless times in the same night. The thought made her nipples tighten, particularly when her left breast brushed against the inside of his thigh. Vampires had no hair other than what was on their heads, so his smooth marble flesh slid easily beneath her skin. Sensing his sharpened regard, she focused harder on her task. Up, down, a careful rubbing to remove all trace of Niall's saliva, his semen, though Niall had done a good job taking his Master's seed down. She envied him that honor.

Glancing back, she saw Niall was still naked. Though he hadn't come, his arousal from the tip had leaked over the head, painting small lines on the ridges of his stomach. He was still hard, making her swallow.

"After I clean our Master, I can do the same for you . . . if you like. If our Master approves."

Niall's brow lifted. He was a servant, so why would she offer such a thing? She didn't know, so she bent her head again.

"That would please me," Evan said neutrally. "You may serve us both, Alanna."

It eased the band in her stomach. She wasn't useless.

When he tugged her hair, brought her head up, she met that cool stare again. "Alanna, you and I are going to make a pact. It's a devil's bargain, because I'm fairly certain you're going to break this rule often, and Niall and I are going to reap the pleasure of you doing so."

Bargain? Pact?

"You won't think of yourself as useless, unclean, traitorous, or deprecate yourself in any way. Not while you're with me. You understand?"

"How can I be what you desire, sir, if I have no standards to strive for?"

"You follow my lead. Be who you are, Alanna, and I'll let you know if I require anything different. The real question is, do *you* know who you are?"

His hand on her face had gentled, at odds with the spear of pain that came with the question. Fortunately, he didn't require her to answer. "You break this rule," he continued, "you won't like the punishment I mete out. It will be severe, because I intend for you to remember it. Do you understand?"

"Yes sir."

"Good. Now go tend to Niall. You're trying to get me hard again, and it's far past dawn. Time for me to go below." He rose, picking up his clothes. As Alanna turned to watch him go, she was aware of Niall's attention on her. The vampire turned at the door, gave his servant a significant look, then shifted it to Alanna. "During the day, when I sleep, you obey and serve Niall as you would serve me."

Her fingers tightened on the cloth, not sure she entirely understood. "Master, do you mean . . . ?"

"Whatever he orders or desires, you obey as you obey my will."

She swallowed. "Yes sir."

7

Aᴀꜰᴛᴇʀ he left, she went to the bathroom sink, washed out the basin and retrieved a new cloth. Niall was still sitting on the edge of the bed, watching her in a way that made her skin warm.

He was an extension of her Master. It wasn't difficult to think of him that way, not when she was this stirred up. She already dropped her gaze when he spoke to her in certain ways, and the way he'd held her, spanked her . . . *My servant has more than a touch of the sexual Dominant . . .*

But had Evan meant . . . *anything*?

She thought of how it had felt, lying on her back beneath them, feeling Niall's muscles flexing beneath the dragon tattoos as he serviced Evan, the jut of his unsatisfied cock between his thighs. The way that cock had felt, penetrating her hard and deep. Her fingers trembled anew as she knelt between his legs and closed her hand over it as she had Evan's. While she washed the organ, he was still staring at her, and it was a little discomfiting. He was getting even harder. Should she offer, since Evan had said . . . whatever?

No. If she was to treat him like Evan, it was his place to tell her what he wanted. Otherwise it would be too easy to confuse her own wants with his, and she was already far too lost in that regard.

Finishing the cleaning, she patted him dry with a towel. When she was done, Niall rose, taking the basin from her to walk it into the bathroom, dump it.

"Go to bed," he said shortly, nodding to his bed. "I'll be back."

~

Niall secured the bar over the front door, then went to the cellar. When Evan had left them with that unexpected directive, she'd missed Niall's what-the-bloody-hell look, which he supposed was a good thing. It was also a good thing she didn't have third-marked senses to overhear the upcoming conversation, though of course if he yelled, she'd hear him well enough. Her and the deer on the next mountaintop.

Evan was sitting on his cot, doing something to one of his cameras, something he'd probably mess up and Niall would need to fix. The male was an outstanding photographer, but he had as much mechanical aptitude as a wizard with a wand. He'd drawn on those cotton drawstring pants he often wore to sleep. As he sat on the edge of the cot now, one leg crooked under him, the other braced, Niall could see the upper curve of his buttocks, the precise curve of his spine. He knew the vampire had a particular liking for this mountain location, because the ancient earth covering the back bedroom and surrounding this cellar allowed him to stay up longer and get up earlier than he normally could. Even so, he was pushing it. His pale skin tended to look thin, his angular features more prominent, if he didn't go under when he should.

Over the years, he'd studied the vampire a good deal, and yet Niall still couldn't quite explain what made Evan so mesmerizing. At times he seemed almost too lean, and his movements could be as graceful and refined as a woman's. But that predatory glance, the solid jawline, the broad shoulders and sheer intensity of him—all of that was purely male. That and his thought process. Deliberate, decisive, unapologetic. There wasn't an ounce of give to him. No submission in his demeanor at all. Not that all women had that, but there was a give to women, a complementary softness to men's hardness.

Centuries ago, before he met Evan, he'd convinced himself that was the way it was always meant to be, that any thoughts men had toward one another were the devil's work, condemned and unnatural. Like the desire to lie or cheat, it was a sinful, base weakness that should be resisted.

As Evan had just noted in their exchange about kosher meat, vampires were outside the realm of religious structure, not because they were damned, but because they, like gods, saw a much bigger picture, one of the gifts of immortality. During their first years together, Niall surmised that faith mattered more to those with shortened life spans. But after spending three hundred years with the vampire, he knew Evan was one of the most spiritual and least religious men he'd ever met. At other times, one of the most profane. He still had a strong grasp of the faith of his childhood. Though he'd reconciled himself to being outside its requirements, there were odd, unexpected things he did that honored it. Three centuries, and there was still too much to pin down about the male. But for all that, Niall knew Evan like no one else. Which was why he had a bone to pick right now.

"What the bloody hell are you doing?"

Evan didn't look up. "I told her to serve you as she serves me."

"I dinnae want a bloody trained poodle."

"You think that's the kind of Master I am?" Evan held the lens up to the light, frowned at it. Swore. He'd obviously found a scratch.

"Ye know what I mean. One minute you want her thinking for herself, the next you tell her to treat me like she treats you. As if the whole bloody world revolves around my farts. It's a total cock-up."

"It's a multipronged strategy. Different approaches, same goal. We're trying to get her to be who she truly is. Serving us both will help." Evan glanced at him. "Be who you've always been, Niall. That's all that's needed from your end of things."

"Oh, well, aye. Your vague and cryptic responses always solve the universe's problems, for certain."

Evan didn't use sarcasm, such that when Niall did, he felt a bit mean-spirited. At least if Evan would respond in kind, Niall could put his head through a wall. Then Evan could break a limb or two to teach him a lesson. It would relieve the frustration that came with conversations like this.

Evan sighed. "My practical Scot. You remember when we met that federal agent, the one with the dog that could sniff out explosives?"

The vampire cycled around a point like a fucking carousel. But it was the only way to get to it. "Aye. He looked appetizing to ye. The lad, not the dog."

It didn't happen often, but at times during their life together Evan had taken a blood meal from another throat, male or female. The agent looked fair interested in Evan, but Niall didn't know if he buggered the poor bastard or not. Evan had cut Niall loose to enjoy the other offerings at the hotel.

It was just an overnight stay for the two of them, the agent and his dog part of some kind of law symposium at the hotel. Fortunately, there'd also been a wedding reception. Niall had crashed it, hooking up with a pretty bridesmaid. They'd danced, and he'd taken her back to her room for a quick tumble. He hadn't even turned on the lights, her breath sweet and warm on his face as he took her against the wall, glad he was nowhere near the underground room and bed he would share later the same night with Evan.

He'd been a little rough about it, feeling somewhat out of sorts. Usually if sex was involved, Evan wanted to share his choice. Fortunately, the girl was one who liked it a bit rougher, more demanding, wanting her lover of the moment to hold all the reins.

"I enjoyed experiencing her through your mind. Her blood would have tasted better than the agent's. The dog didn't like me much." Evan shrugged. "Anyhow, to the point."

"Please God."

Now it was Evan who gave him the narrow glance. "The dog was trained with food. He only ate when he sniffed out an explosive material. Hence, even on their days off, Rudolph had to divide the dog's daily food portion into fifteen search exercises. Food is only associated with performance for the beast. If you threw a steak on the ground next to him, he wouldn't eat it."

Evan tossed the lens in the trash. "We have to figure out how to undo thirty years of training and help Alanna understand the benefit of her having a will other than ours."

Ours. Evan didn't use words casually. Rising, the vampire went to the wall where a half-finished painting was stretched on a large frame, as big as that side of the cellar. It was the moon, rising above a river. Its light made such a glowing, clear track through the water, the viewer felt beckoned into the picture. Within that light were hundreds of wee lanterns, an earthbound Milky Way. It was from a *toro nagashi* they'd attended in Japan, commemorating the dead on the last day of the Obon Festival. They'd sat on the bank together, shoulder to shoulder, watching all those lanterns head toward the moon, like gifts offered to the souls they remembered. Evan had explained the people believed that humans came from water, such that the lanterns represented their bodies returning to it.

"Humans are mostly made up of water, so the logic is sound. Vampires are creatures of blood, so I expect that's why we turn to ash, returning to the earth." Opening a jar, Evan used the pad of his index finger to dab out a bit of paint and add a swirl over one section of the water. Now it seemed the wind had touched that spot, or a fish had disturbed the surface. There were always details within details in Evan's work, but none of his pieces ever seemed cluttered. It was like looking at a natural landscape, seeing something different each time the eye passed over it, but never being overwhelmed by it. Each feature was praised and distinct, unique and yet complementary to the whole.

Evan glanced back at him. "Thank you."

Niall grunted. Shifted his feet. When Evan looked around for a cloth, Niall picked one up, stepping close enough to wrap it around the other man's hand. As he massaged the paint off Evan's finger, he realized he hadn't been doing things like that lately. Never one given to lots of impulsive, affectionate gestures, he'd nevertheless done more of them in the past. For some reason, seeing Alanna, how she perceived things about vampires, he wanted to offer one now.

Evan met his gaze. A quick brush of his knuckles against Niall's jaw suggested he was pleased, but then he took the cloth and his hand away, finishing the task himself. "You want more clarification."

"Not to put too fine a point on it, but aye. I want to know where you're heading with this."

Evan lifted a shoulder. "When she sees me, she shuts down. Everything is 'If it pleases my Master.' You're my agent, so she'll obey you, as long as she sees it's my will. That's my part to handle. You're a servant with a long history of serving me, but also a very different kind of servant from what she's been. You keep her off-balance. Show her, help her. Touch her. Help her learn how to feel again."

Niall considered that, turned toward the ladder.

"You don't like the idea."

He stopped, glanced back. "Nae much point in restraining my opinion if you're reading it."

"Not true. If you hold your tongue, I can decide which thoughts I want to deal with, and which to ignore. What's bugging you so much about this, Niall?" Evan set the cloth aside, gave him a frown.

Niall blew out a breath. "Would it not be kinder tae let the girl just be what she is? She's comfortable there. Another lass, being buggered by two total strangers would have terrified her. Instead, she's hungry for touch, to serve. It's all she knows."

"While having our own female sex slave is lovely for us, I've more interest in what's good for her."

Niall bristled. "Or perhaps she's a blank canvas, and ye want to see what kind of painting she could be. The fact that she's not long for this life makes it more intriguing. She's like a rainbow, or an eclipse. Too bloody ephemeral."

Over near three centuries, he'd learned to either accept certain things about the vampire world, or go mad. But this . . . it made him exceptionally mad.

"Ephemeral? That well-educated mind you go to such effort to hide is showing."

Niall made sure his next thought was a properly uneducated response. Evan's lips thinned, telling Niall he was pushing it, but he returned his gaze to the canvas. Studied it. "Say you've always lived inside the walls of a prison, Niall, and you discover you only have one more day to live. Wouldn't you want to step outside, see the sky, lie on the grass? Touch, taste, feel . . . everything."

"She doesn't know she's in a prison."

"Those tears earlier say her heart knows. We can be the key to open the door."

"And if we do open it? What have we done to her, Evan? She's not likely to survive this, and then she follows him into the afterlife, his slave for eternity."

"I don't believe that nonsense."

"I didnae believe in vampires, either," Niall fired back. "But how about this, then? Say by some miracle, they capture him alive and sever the link. She'll be reassigned, because they only give InhServs to made vampires who are fancy overlords or ambitious bastards willing tae trample everything in their way."

"I'm flattered you don't put me in that category, even though I think you simply chose not to call me an aimless ne'er-do-well outright."

"Since I'm using my big, impressive words, how do you feel about *dilettante*? It seems to fit."

Okay, so maybe this conversation was starting to jab to life things best left undisturbed.

When Evan closed the distance between them, Niall held his ground, even as the vampire brought all that intensity up close and personal. There was a certain line he didn't cross with Evan, not often. Unless pushed.

"If you have something poisonous in your gut, *neshama*, spit it out." Evan's gray eyes were locked on his like a hawk's.

"You take a bird who's always been in a cage and show her what it is to fly. Then ye put her back in the cage and say that's the end o' it. There's nothing crueler than that. She'd be better off dead."

"She likely is going to be dead, Niall. Very shortly."

And that was the crux of it, wasn't it? She didn't deserve that fate. One would think he was past railing about what was fair in this world. Yet something old and deep stirred in his gut, something he didn't want to rouse. The scope and depth of what a man could accept were amazing, but the ability was dependent on him burying certain things deep.

"Ah, hell with it. You're the vampire. You'll do what ye bloody want." He turned away. *It's all a prison, anyway, isn't it?*

Evan was so close, he felt the brush of the vampire's hand when he turned. Niall tensed for an attack, or even something different, but then the hand was gone.

A glance over his shoulder showed Evan in front of the painting again, staring at it. His back to Niall.

Bloody, fucking hell. He hadn't meant . . . Niall clenched his fist on the ladder. When it creaked in protest, he reined back his strength. He didn't want to spend tomorrow rebuilding it. "I hate what's been done to her. I hate how she was hurt. I hate how she thinks it's her fault."

You hate bloody vampires.

"No. Not all of them." He paused, knowing he'd been dismissed, but still waiting for . . . he wasn't sure what. Evan said nothing. After a muttered oath, Niall forced himself into motion, heading for the kitchen level.

Fuck, *that* was a bloody cock-up. After three hundred years, he fucking knew better. Maybe he wasn't so different from Alanna. Staying in the boundaries was safer, more comfortable. But whereas she'd been born in captivity, so to speak, he'd been a wild falcon, who'd willingly, for a debt of honor, let the jesses be tied onto his leg, allowed another man to become his Master. A man who could tear through his shields and knew too much about him. A man he sometimes hated almost as much as he . . . didn't hate him.

~

Serve Niall as you serve me.

She'd fallen asleep puzzling over that. When she woke in the early afternoon, once again discomfited by how long she'd slept, it was to the sound of . . . well, she wasn't sure what the sound was, until she rose and discovered Niall chopping wood on a stump in the narrow front yard. Apparently they needed more logs for the woodstove; she remembered him saying something about that on their plane ride, along with the assurance that it was a chore she wouldn't be asked to do. She was sure she could learn to wield an axe, but then she remembered the blocker. While a human woman could chop wood, a third-marked male servant would make short work of it.

Thinking of the blocker reminded her it was time to take it. She grimaced through the burn of the injection, then showered and dressed. In the bathroom, she found Niall's shaving gear, toothbrush, other toiletry items. Using a comb, she cleaned his hairbrush. The brown strands wound into the bristles looked like they'd been forming a nest there since the brush was bought. She also picked up the cloth he'd carelessly dropped on the floor and dried the water spots on the sink. After she straightened all the towels and cloths, she swept a critical eye over the bathroom and gave it a nod. Not too clean for two men, but tidy enough for a woman.

Returning to her room, she donned one of the long-sleeved shirts. Niall had opened the screened windows, letting in the cool air as well as the fresh smell of the forest. Though she suspected she might need hiking pants or jeans later, she went ahead and slipped on a thick cotton skirt that swirled around her ankles. Unless their vampire instructed them otherwise, female InhServs rarely wore pants. They were supposed to be accessible to the desires of their vampires at all times, and for women, pants were an obstacle to that. So the skirt felt more comfortable.

Serve him as you serve me . . .

As she went to the kitchen window, she saw Niall stripped down to jeans, each swing of the axe capable of making a female heart do an extra trip at the display of male strength and virility. She was accustomed to noticing sexual appeal, using it to stoke desire on command. But she was trained to notice far more details than that, and what she saw told her Niall was not in a good mood. He was chopping the wood as if he was cleaving an enemy, tossing the pieces into a pile with a bit more aggression than needed.

Given his habits, she was sure there'd be dishes in the sink if he'd had breakfast. So he hadn't eaten. Pinning up her hair, she started on afternoon breakfast, planning enough if Evan wanted to sample her cooking later tonight or Niall wanted more later. So she started the coffee, found some eggs, a slab of bacon. A biscuit mix quickly became dough and the rolled pieces were put in the oven. A few raw vegetables still surviving in the crisper were chopped up for the omelettes.

The primary job of the chefs at the Council headquarters was preparing delicacies for the vampires. The servants might get the leavings, but for their own nourishment, the InhServs had a small kitchen area to prepare their food. She'd often cooked for the others, as well as visiting Randoms. Because of that, she'd learned one universal truth about men and well-cooked food.

As the biscuits browned in the oven and the coffee percolated, the axe bit into the wood at a slower cadence. A tiny smile touched her lips when the thudding stopped at last, and she heard the well pump. He'd probably don his shirt, making her regret not snatching one last glimpse out the window. She'd also like a closer look at those tattoos in the daylight, as well as what tattoos he might have on his back.

Was it wrong to indulge her own lust that way? She frowned. Acting on it without a vampire's order was forbidden. But Evan had said . . . She suppressed a sigh. Since last night, she'd come up with so many interpretations of that one statement that all she'd done was confuse herself.

Art in every form is to be appreciated, Alanna. Ogle him as much as you wish. You might even make him blush.

Startled, she knocked the plate of bacon off the counter, barely saving it from the floor. Yesterday, she'd accepted Evan's voice in her head. But after the break provided by a few hours sleep, her brain had rebooted. The only voice she'd been used to hearing in her head was Stephen's, and for the past few months, Stephen's voice brought pain, agony.

It wasn't Stephen. She settled her heart down to a regular beat. It was Evan. *Evan.*

Yes. His voice was warm, but she caught something dangerous in his tone, unexpectedly effective. *He has no hold on you here, Alanna. We'll let no harm come to you.*

Self-preservation was supposed to be the least of a servant's concerns, but one didn't argue with a vampire. Plus, it did make her feel better. *Thank you, sir. Would you like me to bring you some breakfast?*

Not right now. Still sleeping. Your incessant inner monologue woke me.

She would have blurted out an apology, but she picked up a wry note suggesting he was . . . teasing her?

The minor downside of a female servant, I suppose. Niall's mind is exceptionally unobtrusive. Like an oak stump.

Niall came through the door then, filling the room and making the floor vibrate with his weight, underscoring Evan's point so well, she had to bite back a smile.

There you are. I'm going back to sleep. Try to be less chatty in your own head.

She blinked, not sure how she was supposed to accomplish that, but she supposed not thinking about how to accomplish it would be a start. She'd move on to breakfast.

Good girl. You're getting it. But Alanna? There's only one way to interpret my command. Niall is your Master, as much as I am.

He was right. That was crystal clear. She didn't know if it unsettled or relieved her, but the subject himself was providing a distraction. His presence considerably reduced her maneuvering room for cooking, especially when he loomed over her, peering into the skillet. "Omelette?"

"Yes. I put vegetables in it, but there's also bacon. The biscuits are about to come out."

"You cook."

"Of course." She blinked at him, surprised. "I have extensive culinary skills, to serve the various appetites of my Master and his or her guests, should they prefer not to have their own cooking staff. Or when traveling. That's one of the reasons I bought the plant book. I thought I could add some local herbs to the food. An alternative to garlic."

Since he had his arm propped by the stove, she was inside the shelter of his body. Giving him a shy glance, she ducked under his arm to retrieve the pot holder and backed him up with a gentle elbow to get the room to pull out the biscuits. "If you'd like to sit down, I've put out a setting for you. I can bring you your food as it's ready. If you'd like that," she repeated, in case she sounded like she was issuing orders.

"I'm underfoot," he guessed.

"Of course not," she lied staunchly, and now he smiled. Not as easy as his usual grin, but she took heart that she might be able to improve his mood. Saying nothing further, he went to the table and took a seat. Mindful of his reaction yesterday, she'd done nothing more than a simple fold of his napkin. She hadn't set a place for Evan, knowing he wouldn't be joining them here in daylight.

"The birds were pretty," he said gruffly. "If ye want to keep doing that, you should."

"No, you were right. My skills are better spent toward things that apply to your lifestyle." She was more than pretty place settings and decorating herself for the pleasure of a vampire. Perhaps her origami skills were useless here, but her cooking wasn't, if Niall's appreciative yet impatient glance over his shoulder was any indication.

She brought him his plate, the omelette with melted Gouda cheese emitting a fragrant steam. The rescued bacon was crisp and glistening, and she could tell the basket of fluffy biscuits won his approval when he immediately reached for one of those. As she put a glass of juice next to his plate, she noticed his gaze wandering over her torso, particularly the way her breasts looked beneath the cling of her shirt. She wished he'd reach out and touch her so she could give him pleasure, comfort for whatever was bothering him this morning. What would happen if she reached out and touched him?

Control. *Discipline.* If she was to serve Niall as she served Evan, that meant at their pleasure, not her own. The sharpness of her own mind-voice was enough to have her withdrawing, but Niall caught her wrist. "Where's yours?"

"I'll eat later, after you do." Even when she cooked for the visiting servants, she tended to stand behind the counter while they ate. An exercise to reinforce her primary directive, a different form of service.

"You've had no breakfast yet, have ye?" His grip on her wrist eased but stayed there, fingers straightening to caress her palm.

"No."

"Then fix yourself a plate."

She hesitated. When his fingers pressed firmly into her flesh, drawing her eyes back to his face, he added, "That's what I want, lass. Come eat with me."

He dropped his hold, letting her retreat to the counter. While she made up her plate, he turned to preparing his own, buttering his biscuit and adding salt to his bacon before tasting it, telling her the man liked copious amounts of salt. Good thing he was a third mark; otherwise, at three hundred, he'd have a blood pressure problem bad enough to make him a medical case study.

After she filled her plate, she returned. Sinking to her knees next to his chair, she balanced it, putting the glass of juice to the side. When she looked up to see if he'd begun eating so she could do the same, he was staring at her.

A flush climbed into her cheeks. "Have I done something wrong?"

"Why are you nae sitting in a chair, like yesterday?"

"Evan told me to serve you as I would him. I'd never sit in a chair next to a vampire."

Niall took a bite of his biscuit and chewed, his attention remaining upon her. Now she wasn't sure if she should start eating, so she waited. If she had to, she'd ask him. Because he really wasn't a vampire Master. He just had a way of looking at her like one.

"Let me have that." Taking her plate from her, he set it next to his, then held out his hand for the juice and utensils. When he dropped them on the table in a casual disarray that made her wince, he held his hand out for hers. As he brought her up, he scraped his chair away from the table.

"Why don't you come sit on my lap?"

His handclasp was warm, and she thought of his body lying behind hers on the bed. Warm and safe, protective. She couldn't understand her hesitation now, except it was new to her, having an inordinate desire to obey that seemed out of proportion with the requirement of service. It was as if Evan had merely pushed a gate wider that was already unwisely ajar.

"Do you want to sit on my lap?"

Since he wasn't her Master, "If that's what my Master desires" didn't fit. And "Yes, because Master said I should do it" sounded wrong.

"Do you want me to command you to sit on my lap?" Niall asked before she could respond.

An entirely different reaction flooded into her chest. He saw it in her face, a muscle flexing in his jaw that tempted her fingertips to trace it. "That's it, isn't it? Whether you want it or no, an order makes it your desire as well."

"Yes." She was relieved he understood. "It's how I'm trained. I have no desires until you command it."

His brow creased. "What if Stephen commanded you to sit on his lap? I know 'twould be different, because I'm a servant, but say Evan was commanding ye to do the same thing. Would it feel different?"

She didn't like all these questions, but it wasn't her place to like or dislike anything, right? "Yes, there's a difference." She hoped he wouldn't ask her to explain.

"Different because of how he betrayed the Council, or even before, when he was your Master? Don't think, just answer," he added sharply.

"It's not the same," she blurted out. Her fingers closed into a tight ball, her wrist still in his grasp. Since she had an alarming desire to pull away, she went rigid.

She was an intelligent woman. It was one of the reasons she was so good at being an InhServ. From the outside, it might appear as mindless obedience, but anticipating the needs of another, always putting those needs first, learning myriad ways to be genuinely responsive and enthusiastic, no matter what was demanded . . . it took tremendous psychological skills and an in-depth understanding of one's strengths and weaknesses. It also required a brutal understanding of who and what her Master was, what he most desired from her.

Stephen's priority was obedience; she was a service given to him by privilege. If he loaned her to another vampire, he expected her to obey that vampire no differently than she obeyed him. But Niall and Evan wanted her to obey their commands specifically. To respond to them specifically. To *want* them specifically.

Beyond that, their expectations had nothing to do with the code of being a servant. They wanted her . . . to want to please them. She'd been trained that it was one and the same, but they understood there was a difference. And they were right. Otherwise, why had she automatically responded that it *was* different, the same command issued by Stephen and Evan?

This whole line of thinking set her feet on a dangerous road, where her own desires became a separate entity from those of her Master. No, it was not a road at all, but a forest as wild and mysterious as that which surrounded their cabin. But she had no choice, for Niall was waiting for an honest answer. She thought of that first moment after Evan second-marked her, when she could hear both him and Niall in her mind. It had felt different from Stephen's second mark, too.

"I want to be commanded to sit in your lap. I want you to want me to sit in your lap."

He squeezed her wrist, an unfathomable look in his golden brown eyes. Last night, she'd given more of her heart to them than she'd offered to Stephen in all thirteen years of her service. Because her heart was the last thing he'd wanted. What's more, with Niall and Evan, it felt like what a servant should be offering. Unconditionally.

"I want you," she whispered, walking a frayed tightrope over land mines.

Evan's voice slid into her head. Teasing.

Only him?

It flustered her again. She shook her head, but Niall spoke for her. "She's nodding emphatically, Evan. Sorry, old boy."

"I am not," she exclaimed. "Master, he is making up things."

Niall grinned then, merely locking his grip when she tried to pull away. With a quick yank, he pulled her into his lap. She caught his shoulder so she didn't fall, but he already had her securely by the waist, steadying her. He nodded to her utensils, pulling her plate closer to his. "Eat."

She picked up her fork, bemused by her perch, his fingers splayed over her hip bone. His thigh muscles shifted under her, a pleasant sensation with her legs straddling his, her buttocks pushed back against his hip and abdomen. He held her with one arm and ate with the other. As she cut her egg, she watched him shovel in the breakfast. His table manners weren't bad; he just had a healthy appetite, one that made her glad that she'd cooked plenty.

Putting down her fork, she plucked several wood chips from his hair, smoothed the strands over his temple. In response, he pressed a kiss to her collarbone, his hair brushing her cheek, and left the scent of bacon and coffee on her skin. She didn't mind.

Evan had gone quiet after his teasing, so she assumed he'd returned to sleep. The earlier rain was long gone, the sun's heat penetrating the windows, despite the fall chill. "Does Evan sell his work? Is that how he makes a living?"

Evan's world was a curious one for her, since the vampires in the upper circles were already wealthy, through centuries of investment and business interests. She knew vampires who worked regular jobs like humans existed; she'd just never met any.

Niall shrugged, sitting back with his coffee, still balancing her on his knee. "It's how he makes his living now. In the beginning, he had a sponsor, and that and portrait commissions took him through lean times. Before electricity, there were few night jobs. But when he did find one, he didnae mind doing it. The lad's not afraid of hard work." The approval in Niall's voice was clear.

"In fact, he liked doing them. Before he was turned, he wasnae a very healthy human." Niall picked up another biscuit. Since the butter was closer to her, she took it from him, added the same amount she'd seen him slather on the other and handed it back. Niall grunted his thanks.

"He said the work added to the experiences he brought to his art. Even now, he'll take the occasional job to see what it's about. He's done security, helped build a skyscraper, flew private planes, worked as an apprentice gardener at a big estate for near a year. Even joined a paving crew."

She couldn't conceal her amazement. "He's done manual labor? With humans?"

"Has some great pictures from them as well. The night shots o' the crew, the lighting over the job, the headlights of cars looking like shooting stars." Niall chewed, considering. "He never forgets the important details. The faces o' the lads, sweating, intent on their work, or their eyes wandering, distant, thinking about what they'll be doin' when the shift is over . . ."

Despite his dismissal of her origami, Niall was far more aware of aesthetic nuances than he'd first revealed. It was obvious he admired Evan's work, was intrigued and involved in it. Did he realize how Evan studied him the same way? Last night, she'd seen how the vampire responded to every movement, every gasped word from his servant. They were linked and interwoven, a tapestry three hundred years in the making. It made her heart hurt . . . and long for the same.

Niall moved onto his third helping of bacon. "Interaction with the human world is more common among working-class vampires like Evan. He has a New York art dealer who handles the sales o' his work, but Evan still stays hands-on with the managing o' his coin. He has a hell of a sense for knowing when to save, when to spend, and what's worth the price tag. Though he'll still get that price knocked down if he can manage it. He's your lad for the bazaars in Marrakesh." He winked. "Most of it he sinks into assets and costs—camera equipment, rentals like this, transportation—but he always manages a comfortable nest egg." He smiled at her. "We might not be rich, but we willnae ever starve."

He adjusted her over both his thighs then, which snugged her backside right into the heat of his groin. His fingers slipped over her thigh, a casual stroke that risked her choking on her eggs. She put down her fork. "Why did he choose you as a servant?"

While the circumstances of the choosing had seemed to be an off-limits topic, she hoped the why would be safe.

"Not real obvious, is it?" His interested cock stirred, increasing the pressure into the tender pocket between her thighs. His touch moved to her hip, the crease between it and her leg. "You're not wearing panties, are ye?"

"No, sir." Her mouth had gone dry, her heart starting to pound faster, especially when he didn't correct her address.

"Lean back against me, lass, if you're done with your breakfast."

As she did, his hand slid between her thighs. When she spread them, he brushed her sex through the skirt. Even as she shuddered in response, he continued on in that same conversational tone, though his cock was getting harder and thicker.

"Not obvious, is it? He does a lot for himself. Doesnae need someone to wipe his arse or . . ." He cut himself off before he said anything else, making her think he was about to say something about what he considered her more purposeless skill sets. It didn't matter, since she was fighting an unacceptable urge to turn around, straddle him. Curling her fingers over his arm on his waist, she dug into his flesh.

"Aye, ye like sitting spread like that for me. I can smell your sweet honey, lass." His voice had a husky note, but he kept on, making her more insane. "Even beyond blood and buggering, it seemed he mostly wanted a pack mule, like he said. Nane o' what he wanted was obvious, though. Not in the beginning." Niall took a breath.

"When I met Evan, I was married."

8

Niall had no idea why he'd said it. Maybe because she was getting more nervous. Her body was responding, but he expected she had no frame of reference for responding to a servant the way she would a vampire. The lass was all about structure. However, typical for a woman, an unexpected bit of knowledge brought her attention back to him.

"Your wife . . . she came with you?"

"No. Here, scoot this way." He put her in the chair next to him, needing the space for a couple of reasons now. She looked a little disappointed, and he hoped to make that up to her. For now, though, he finished up his breakfast. He liked how she waited on him to gather his thoughts, realizing he needed that pause. Evan was silent as a corpse, suggesting he was dead asleep. Given the sun was well up in a bright blue sky and he'd stayed up longer than he should have done, that was pretty likely.

Leaving the wife question alone, he backtracked. "When Evan and I met, he was just over a hundred. He told me having no servant was like a human not being married at a certain age. Everyone starts tae wonder what's wrong with ye."

Female vampires get a little more latitude, because they're expected to be choosy. Most males are itching to take one by the time they're fifty,

to have the feeding trough close. We tend to be lazy in food and sex. Plus,
we go through full servants more quickly in our first century or so. Ran-
dom fights and typical young man deviltry.

"I thanked him for his honesty," Niall said dryly. Alanna gave him
a polite smile, but he couldn't tell if she saw the humor in it. "At first he
wanted a scout in Scotland, to help him on his scavenger hunts for
subject matter. But he was also looking for a lad with hunting and
tracking ability, one who could pick up the lay of new terrain swift-like
and serve the same purpose in unfamiliar lands."

He shrugged. "I've no doubt there were others, better fed, more educated, who could have done for him, but that's the why he gave me.
He also said if he was going to have a servant about, he preferred the
straightforward company o' a male. At least at that time," he added
quickly, not wanting her to think Evan didn't welcome having her
here. As for Niall's thoughts on the matter, her soft arse and her biscuits made her well worth the company. He wondered if she had any
more of the latter stored in the oven.

"And your wife?" She asked it softly, obviously understanding it
might be a tender subject. Since he hadn't guarded his tongue as he
should, he'd pay the fair price for it. That was the danger of women.
They opened up things, dug into them.

"I didnae know I was one of Evan's subjects, weeks before he met
me, but I had a prickly feeling on the back o' my neck during that time.
When I told him about it, the feeling matched when he started following me about. A scout's instinct, he called it, which confirmed his
opinion of me." That initial meeting flashed through his mind, the
glen, the deep, cold creek, the touch of Evan's hard hands, holding him
pinned, but he pushed that away.

"A few weeks after we had our proper meeting, I was injured in a
battle. It was a mortal wound. Evan carried me from the field, told me
what the whole servant thing was about, which of course meant he had
to let me know what he was. Said he could try it to save me, but he
wasnae going to expend the effort if I wasn't interested, if I believed
he was condemning me to eternal damnation."

Though Niall was as devout as the next man, that issue hadn't figured into it. All he could think was Ceana and the two bairns would
be left without him. The village was already near starving. Though
others would do what they could for them, it wouldn't be enough.

They'd be turned out of the croft, unable to pay the rent. He'd already seen children starve to death in his short life, and he would sell his soul to the Devil to keep it from happening to his own.

"So we struck a bargain. If he could save my life, I'd serve him when my wife passed and the wee ones were grown up and able to care for themselves."

"I've never heard of such a thing," she murmured, the truth of it reflected by the wonder in her expression. "A servant doesn't age once they reach their thirties. How did you explain that to your family?"

"It wasnae an issue," he said shortly.

As he'd already noted, she had a fair intuition. Reaching out, she touched his hand. "I'm sorry."

Straightforward sympathy, no pity in her gaze. *It is what it is.* The vampire servant's creed. At least he understood that much about her. But something about that touch made him keep talking, like a fool.

"Starvation took a lot o' our young and old, but sickness had its way with those in-between. She was a braw lass, but she couldnae hold against it. My daughter went with her but it spared my son, Eric." He pushed his chair back. "My brother and his wife . . . they had no children. They helped me raise Eric, and when I saw him handfasted to a lovely lass, I turned over the croft and all that went with it to him. Things were getting summat better, and he had some job prospects in Jamaica with a sugar planter, so I knew he'd be fine. I told him my grief for his ma was giving me the yen tae travel, to seek my life elsewhere. His aunt and uncle were like another Da and Ma to him, so I knew he'd be all right. Back then, if your kin left Scotland, it was likely you wouldnae see him again, though I sent letters. Until there was no need to send them anymore."

He rose abruptly. "It was a guid breakfast. I'm going to finish up the wood. Next visitors will appreciate it when the snow flies."

Her fair brow creased, those bonny brown eyes seeing far too much of his heart. "I'm so sorry, Niall. I didn't mean to raise difficult memories."

"You're a guid listener, lass. It makes a man say things better left unsaid. That's not your fault," he added at her stricken look. "Anyone who remembers me died a long time ago, and I made sure they didnae suffer from my absence while they lived. That's all a man can do." Giving her a nod, he left the cabin.

After the first hundred years, he'd stopped thinking about most of it. It wasn't until recently, facing his own closing life span, that the ghosts had stirred. A man didn't fester over these things like a woman did, and probably for this very reason. It left a dull ache in his belly, made the sun seem a little less bright, the crisp breeze more cutting than cooling. Picking up the axe, he twirled it, then brought it down with such strength, he cut a good three inches into the stump itself.

~

Take the time you need. I know you'll honor your oath. You'll feel it when it's time to come find me.

Niall spent eight years with his family after making his oath to Evan. During that time, the vampire wasn't wholly absent. He'd recognized his future servant needed to get to know him. Therefore, whenever he was within range of Niall's mind, he would reach out. After his initial start at the unexpected intrusion, Niall found the vampire good company. He became accustomed to those surreal, long conversations in his head while working the field, seeking scarce game or thatching the roof.

When he was with Ceana or the children, he could sometimes feel Evan there, watching, but the vampire didn't try to distract him then. Niall even felt an occasional sense of warmth, as if Evan was enjoying a family vicariously through him.

Evan told him about wonders Niall never thought he'd see, and offered him counsel about managing his relationship with the landlord. Thanks to the advice, Niall revealed to the man that he was a good tracker, and earned some extra coin taking the gentry out on their hunts.

Evan had packages delivered to Niall, books about the places where he was, the legends of Norway or history of China. Niall's reading was rudimentary at best, but he enjoyed the pictures. Evan also sent money. At first, Niall had been reluctant to use it, but a look at the thin faces of his family, and those in worse shape in his village, and he'd gotten beyond that. Evan also chided him for it, reminding him about his oath of service, telling him he would end up earning every cent. Why shouldn't he use the coin to make things better for as many of them as he could?

To his neighbors, Niall explained he had a distant relative sending him funds from the Colonies. Ceana met Evan on his in-person visits, but she never warmed to the vampire, as if sensing the things that bound Niall to him. Evan treated her with great courtesy and kindness and, except for the circumstances of their initial meeting, he never made another inappropriate move toward Niall during her life span.

It wasn't all smooth, however. Once, Niall had felt Evan's presence while he was making love to his wife. He could feel the male's heated regard through his own eyes as he looked down on Ceana's heavy breasts and the plump pleasure of her sex, the silky curls wet with her arousal and his seed. He pulled back so abruptly, Ceana blinked at him in confusion.

"I need to take a piss," he explained. Ignoring the chamber pot, he stalked out into the frigid night in the altogether. *You're no more welcome to be ogling her than any other man. That's my wife. My wife. She's nae part of our agreement.*

I never said she was. The voice was cool, but amused enough to put Niall's teeth on edge. *I wanted to see how you touch her, how you feel with her. What pleasures you . . . and how you pleasure her. It's different than when you're rutting on a male, isn't it?*

I've never done that, and ye damn well know it. Now bugger off. I'll be up at dawn slopping pigs if you want to feel that.

She's a lovely girl, Niall. You're a lucky man.

He'd have thought it empty flattery, but by that time he knew vampires never wasted flattery on a human. Ceana looked like an average village girl with a nice figure, unless one noticed the softness of her dark hair, the generous mouth and kindly, thoughtful look to her brown eyes. In the weathered lines of her too-thin face he could see the physical appeal that more food and less difficult childbearing would have lent her.

But to him, Ceana was beautiful, and Evan had seen that through his eyes. At the time Niall hadn't thought much about it, but within the first few decades of traveling in his footsteps, he realized the vampire saw beauty in full spectrum—not just where every one else saw it, but where it actually existed, the true layers of beauty below the surface.

∽

The restraint that Evan demonstrated with Niall until Ceana's passing hadn't been the usual thing for vampires. Niall had quickly learned that in his service. It was one of many unusual traits the artist had that separated him from his own kind, but it had made a lasting impression on Niall. Coming back to the present, he thought again about Evan's decision to shelter Alanna. She was beautiful as a sunrise, no question, but like Ceana, there was something far deeper to her. Her brown eyes had the same depth and poignant understanding he'd often seen in his wife's eyes, limited as her world was.

But Alanna's world was pretty limited as well, wasn't it? Though Ceana had been bound by poverty, and Alanna by servitude, they both lived in a heavily restricted world. They'd also found a way to live in that box, and make the most of it. Ceana's last words to him had proven it.

It's been a fine life, husband. Your love and the wee ones . . . I could-nae have asked for more . . . except more time. And that's God's realm, not a woman's.

Though God took her from him first, sometimes he wondered if his decision to bind himself to Evan had somehow been a catalyst for everything that followed after. *Soon you'll be free to go your own way, and I know you were meant for that. I'm glad to have had such a bonny man . . .*

He'd wanted to die with her . . . but not enough. Her acceptance of her fate echoed Alanna's. It roiled in his gut, goading a rage he'd long ago dispelled. He was glad that Sheila had died after her mother, so Ceana hadn't had to bear that.

Ach. It is what it is. Looking up, Niall was surprised, but not displeased, to find Alanna perched on a log. She had her feet drawn up, hands linked over her knees, the skirt modestly folded over everything. He wished she was still wearing her jeans so he could see that pretty arse and the intriguing terrain between her thighs exposed by the position, but she was still a picture. She seemed quiet, not expectant. Just seeking another's company, he supposed. Or being ready to serve him . . . as Evan had required. He pushed away how good she'd felt sitting on his lap. He wasn't going to jump on the offer like an impulsive boy in short pants going after a jar of candy.

Figuring out how her mind worked was more important. She honestly didn't know what to do with herself unless a vampire had a to-do list for her. Picking up a towel, he swiped it over his face and chest and came to her, sitting down on the ground next to the log, his shoulder brushing her foot. She'd brought him a glass of ice water and offered it now, her feet sliding to the ground and her calf pressing against his shoulder. When her gaze slid over his bare chest, it gave him a pleasant idea. With the way things were pricking at him, he didn't mind giving her something for her to-do list. Or at least taking the lid off that candy jar.

He nodded to the glass. "Rub the ice on me, lass. Help cool me down."

Aye, that was going to cool him down for sure. A flicker in her eyes suggested she was wise to the irony herself, but she slipped her well-manicured nails into the glass and pulled out one of the cubes. Her cheeks pinkened in a fetching way under his close regard, her lashes fanning her cheeks. Sliding off the log, she folded her legs beneath her so she could lean over him. As she placed the ice against the base of his throat, her attention flitted to his face to make sure it was all right, before she made the ice glide down his sternum. He stayed on his elbows, watching the way she pressed her lips together, her eyes clinging to the movement of the ice. When she cut across his pectoral, following the dragon, then down to the nipple, he shuddered. She paused, but then kept at it, a few more turns there before she worked her way over his sectioned stomach muscles.

His skin was so warm, the ice began to melt almost immediately, so in addition to the cold pressure of the cube, drops of water trickled down his torso. He had a very pleasant vision of her lips making the same track, then lower. He already knew she was well-schooled in how to take a man's cock in her mouth, sucking him to a state of repletion. Last night, it had been all Evan could do to pull free of her mouth and give over to Niall.

Christ, she wasn't some whore. While the outside world might not see a distinction, he sure as hell did. Why had Evan opened this door? She didn't have a will of her own, and Niall wasn't a damn vampire who was going to assume she was his to use as he pleased, just because she called him Master. It did odd things to him, when she called Evan that, then flicked her gaze toward him, as if the two of them were an extension of each other. He wondered if she realized she did that. Evan obviously had.

She traced the male dragon, the vibrant colors of the scales. When she paused over the crest of the dragon's head, centered over his heart, he wasn't surprised she picked out the difference in texture between that area and the rest of the tattoo. If a person looked close, they could see the pattern, a symbol delineated in the design of the dragon's scales.

"My third mark," he said.

Every third-marked servant had one, a branded imprint on the skin. It appeared spontaneously after the mark was set, no control over its shape or meaning, except it always seemed to have some discernible significance, not just a random inkblot like a birthmark.

Her brow furrowed. "What is it?"

"The Hebrew symbol for *chai*. Life."

"Oh." He was glad when she changed direction. Intuitive lass. "Do you have a tattoo on your back?"

"Aye." Shifting to his hip, he showed her the one there. She drew in a breath, not surprisingly. All of the work was striking, but that one always garnered the most attention. Done in black ink, the dragon covered most of his upper back, the wings angled so one curved over the beast's head and followed the line of Niall's shoulder, the other curved low so it followed his rib cage. He was a craggy-looking creature, horned and intimidating, but with the character and mystery of an ancient wizard in his steely-eyed expression.

Her fingers slipped over it, following the upper wing. When she reached the ridge of his shoulder, she was touching his hair, loose on his shoulders. She made a tiny stroke of it, a little tug as it caught between her fingers. When he shifted his gaze to her, she removed her hand.

"They must have taken a long time, especially with injections of Evan's blood to hold the design. Was it painful?"

He gave her a short nod. Christ above, yes. He tapped the one on his chest.

"Evan did this one in front of an audience. I was performance art."

It was far more than that, Alanna.

Niall bit back a deprecation. He should have known Evan wasn't asleep as he should be.

I didn't realize I had a bedtime. Do you want to come spank me, Niall?

If you'd fight fair, I'd break a two-by-four over your narrow ass.

Alanna's eyes widened, telling Niall that Evan had let her hear that. *Keep rubbing the ice on him, Alanna. He's still rather heated. Niall, tell her more about that day.*

You're the "Master" storyteller here.

He didn't know why he was being petty about it. Hadn't Alanna made it clear that wasn't a luxury a servant had?

You are not the same as Alanna, neshama.

God, he hated how it made him feel, when Evan changed tracks like that. Niall caught Alanna's wrist as she started to rub the ice on him again. "If he told ye to do something to me, and I refused, that'd be a pickle for ye, no?"

If Evan could reach him, he'd probably be physically hurled off the mountain. Maybe. What was goaded by irritation was tempered into curiosity for them both, as they watched her struggle with the question, Evan through Niall's eyes.

"I can only serve my Master's will to the full extent of my ability to do so. If you resist his will, and push me away, then I must see if his will is for me to force you to do his bidding."

Niall gave her far slighter form a dubious look, but she shook her head. "My size is not the question. Just how far I am willing to go to do my Master's will."

How far are you willing to go to oppose it, neshama?

Evan hadn't shared that one with Alanna, because her expression didn't change. Niall answered that by answering her.

"As much as I'd enjoy a wrestling match," he noted, gaze sweeping appreciatively over her, "we'll call this a draw, lass. But I'll ask Evan to tell the tale. I'm nae much of a storyteller, and he'll include the bits you'll like best. But be warned, he's like looking for Walter Scott tae tell a true story about Scotland. Far more romance and legend than the sad reality."

She touched the male dragon, her fingers resting on the third mark within the design. "This appears to be both," she said quietly. "Legend and reality."

He made a noncommittal sound at that, but lay back fully, lacing his fingers behind his head while she plucked another piece of ice out of his glass. As it made contact with his skin, sliding with sensual purpose over the tattoo, making the dragon's scales gleam anew with the moisture, Niall tried to keep all his blood from draining into his cock. Given the story that Evan was about to tell, he didn't hold out much hope for success.

Neither do I. Evan's dry voice filled Niall's head. *Despite his disparaging analysis of my storytelling abilities, Alanna, I intend to tell it as it truly happened, and in great detail. Master Storyteller, indeed.*

⁓

It was a private fund-raising event, a carnival for well-heeled individuals who preferred the pleasures of bondage and submission. The sizeable price to attend was donated to a domestic violence cause. Evan had offered his work for a silent auction, as well as agreed to do a special performance art demonstration at the request of the host.

Tiki torches and strung lights illuminated the grounds where the carnival was being held. There was no moon that night, but the sky was full of stars, given that the host, Tyler Winterman, held the carnival on his historic plantation property in the Florida marshlands off of the Gulf, far from any of the larger cities. Evan's stage was an outdoor area set a little ways from the main carnival activities. The space had been cordoned off with black silk rope, but outside its boundary, chairs had been provided for those Masters and Mistresses who wished to watch. It was on the lawn, so there was enough soft grassy area for their slaves to kneel at their sides. At this event, the lines between Dominant and submissives were clearly drawn.

An elegant St. Andrew's cross dominated the performance area. It was a piece of art itself, a dark polished wood, the ends carved with birds and decorative scrollwork, the flat surfaces below the restraint eyelets worn even smoother by the sweat and struggles of former occupants. Evan ran his fingers over the silk of those spots, felt the contrasting shapes of the carvings.

Glancing over at Niall, he was pleased with the way his servant looked. He wore only a dark gray kilt, and his hair was tied back loosely on his shoulders. Niall had never been tattooed, not during all these years. He was a blank canvas except for Evan's third mark, the *chai* symbol on his chest that most in this crowd would take for a brand. They were not entirely wrong.

He remembered the night he'd lain in bed with his servant, his hand on that third mark, imagining the design he'd put over it. He was feeding, inhaling the scent of Niall's skin as he teased his throat, sipping his rich blood. Niall had followed the movement of the fingers on his chest, figured out the shape.

A dragon, the symbol of the bloody English?

The Scot's voice had been thick, trying for amusement, but laden with something else as Evan tasted him. Sliding his hand down Niall's stomach, Evan clasped his cock, working it slow and steady, the way he was taking his nourishment. When he was done, he wanted him hard, because he'd roll him over and make him come into the sheets while Evan released inside him.

When Edward raised the dragon banner, it meant no quarter. No rules. Total domination.

And that's what ye have over me?

He'd lifted his head, seen his servant's tawny eyes studying him, his mind rolling that over. Evan's answer had been to shift on top of him, hands on either side of his face, fingers digging into his hair as he captured his mouth. As he rubbed himself against Niall's stiff cock, the Scot groaned, kissed him back fiercely. Evan planted his knee so he couldn't roll them, pushing against his testicles as he plundered the heated mouth, the lashing tongue, biting the delectable mouth.

When he slid back down to press his lips over that spot, Niall's hand brushed his back, moved up to his nape, fingers digging into his scalp as Evan scraped a fang over him. He was done feeding, but he didn't turn him yet. He put his head on Niall's chest, listening to his heart beat. As he was doing that, his servant's mind stilled, as it often did in such moments. When he rested his large hand between Evan's shoulder blades, those fingers curved against Evan's flesh, a need unspoken.

Coming back to the present, Evan focused on the task at hand. He'd ordered Niall to remove his chest hair. He'd planned the design so it wouldn't be affected negatively when the hair returned, but he liked the unique experience of seeing that broad expanse as a tanned, firm canvas. Beneath the kilt, Niall was just as bare and firm, but Evan wanted him even firmer. He indulged a vision of pushing his servant to his knees, raking up the kilt and taking him right here, before the curious early arrivals.

Niall was leaning against the cross in a seemingly casual pose, but now his head lifted, attention shifting to the vampire.

"Maybe afterward," Evan murmured.

He was ready to begin. Even though there was a sign posted outside the silk cord, *Artist at Work—please keep voices down to help with creative process*, it wasn't necessary. His head would soon enter that space where he would create, tuning everything out. The canvas would be everything. He'd stood in the middle of a plant factory, machinery so loud the employees wore ear protection, and gotten lost in photographing and sketching the workers' faces, the mysteries they didn't recognize in themselves as they became one with the machines. He'd turned that scene into a painting where the people were overlaid with a depiction of the creation of the world, the divine machinery that put it all into motion. It had been one of his more complex works.

This was not so complex, but it would be equally absorbing. He'd already developed it in his head, and knew eventually Niall would bear three dragons on his flesh. Evan could see each clear in his mind, how they would relate to one another on his servant's skin. He wouldn't do them all at the same time, but every detail of this first, fierce male predator must be perfect. A protector for his most important treasure, the man whose heart embodied the noble tragedy of the chaotic mortal world.

Niall remained still as he circled him and the cross. He was being uncharacteristically obedient, but he understood the environment enough to respond to it appropriately, even if it wasn't his natural way. His lips tightened, though, as Evan knelt before him. Capturing his Scot's gaze, he slid his hands under the kilt, up the powerful thighs, thumbs grazing the testicles as he wrapped long fingers around Niall's hips, the curve of buttocks. The carnival was so saturated with sexual promise, it took no time for Niall to respond, his cock rising, held in place only by the heavy fabric of the utility kilt.

Evan easily read Niall's desire to see his Master take his cock in his mouth. On the occasions Evan had done that, Niall was usually at his mercy, hands tied above his head or behind his back, body hard and straining toward Evan's relentless mouth. But here, his hands were free, body held back only by Evan's command. He could thread his fingers through Evan's silken dark hair, tighten and pull, push him down harder, feel his clever mouth and tongue at his pace, all along his shaft.

Evan rose, meeting him near eye to eye. *Provocative*, neshama. *Stay still.* Fingering Niall's belt, he unbuckled it. His servant obeyed, though his tension increased. Evan removed the kilt, folded and put it aside. Niall was barefoot, so now he was fully naked, on display for the admiring—and growing—crowd. Evan didn't blame them for looking. Niall's muscles were developed through his hunting and scouting skills, his combat training and their active physical life. The fighting skills were necessary, but in watching Niall train, Evan often reminded him those skills were to be employed against servants or other humans with nefarious intents; not for Niall to step between him and another vampire.

Niall gave him a gimlet eye now, since Evan was letting him see the drift of thoughts in his mind. *The day might come when I save your arse.*

Lord Uthe's letter of patronage is sufficient to handle the vampires.

Aye. Vampires are a civilized lot. All of 'em offer you tea while their lawyers look that over. Nae a single one of them has tried to rip you to shreds for being in a territory, unmarked by the overlord. Oh, wait. A couple o' them have, aye?

Evan gave him a level look. Sliding his hand onto Niall's broad shoulder, he tangled his fingers in the man's loose hair. "Get on the cross."

Niall angled his chin, brushing Evan's knuckles and freeing his hair in a slow movement, the men's gazes staying locked. Then he inclined his head. Moving to the cross, he aligned his arms with the upper ties, spreading his legs to accommodate the lower part. The way he looked on it made Evan wish he had the ability to carry such a thing on all his travels. Now he crisscrossed the straps provided over ankle, calf and thigh, then biceps, forearms, wrists. As he cinched them, he noted his servant's cockstand became more pronounced and thick. When he was done binding him, he stroked it with a curled fist, squeezing the heavy balls. Niall's pulse leaped, the broad chest expanding. Turning his attention to the crowd, Evan saw admiring glances, even from the pretty slaves ordered to keep their gazes down. He didn't blame them for the transgression.

He raised his voice so he could be heard by the audience. "I need a female slave to keep my servant occupied while I prepare. Any volunteers?"

The redhead in the blue see-through frock has a mouthwatering rack.

Stop trying to direct, or I'll pick the biggest, ugliest male brute out there to work you like a steam engine.

Bugger off. It'd be a shame to break this cross. You couldnae afford to pay Tyler for it.

Evan pressed his lips against a smile. Ironically, the dark-haired Hispanic Master of the redhead with superior heavy breasts and lush hips had stood up, bringing her with him. "My slave, Leila, is at your service. I am Joseph."

Evan could already smell her arousal. The overload of sensual stimulation in this environment had her dripping wet. Niall, with his heightened third-mark senses, would be driven crazy by the scent. *Perfect.* It would help him manage the pain. "My thanks. I want her to work him in her mouth during my preparations. But I don't want him to come. Just get him so close to it he's hurting for it. I want to hear him beg."

Not in this lifetime.

Evan noted Niall's hands curling into clenched fists inside the restraints, and wondered if he was even aware of it. Probably not.

"As beautiful as your slave is, I doubt mine's self-control. Put this on him first." Opening the container beneath the table holding his tattoo supplies, he lifted out a heavy cock ring, one he knew was a tight fit on Niall, a torture and provocation at once. At Joseph's nod, Evan handed it to Leila.

"Go do as the Master instructed," her Dom told her. "Don't let him come."

"Yes, sir." As she moved toward Niall, the Scott fastened a glittering gaze on Evan. To lubricate the ring, Leila placed it in her mouth. Finding Niall already too tumescent for that to work, Leila proved herself a quick thinker. Kneeling where Niall could see her, she spread her knees, and the ring disappeared between her legs, along with a couple of her fingers. When she removed it, dripping with her body's natural lubricant, Niall's gaze was now pinned on her.

This time, she was able to get it to the base of his cock, though she had to work it over him carefully. Niall said something to her that made her cheeks flush, her lips part before she settled herself on her knees. Placing her short but well-manicured nails on his thighs to balance herself, she put her moist lips on the broad head of his cock and slid down the shaft, taking him almost to that ring. When she slid back up, her throat worked in a most engaging manner.

Evan closed his eyes, enjoying the first shudder through Niall's mind as much as the outward reaction of his body. "Would you lend me your assistance, Joseph?" At his nod, he handed the Dom a blindfold. "He's never docile, but he's more intriguing when he can't see."

Niall didn't fight him, but did shoot Evan a look that indicated it wouldn't have been his first choice. Then he was blind, Joseph lacing the sides snug so the blindfold molded to Niall's face, the bridge of his nose.

I want you in your head, neshama. *Feeling everything. Her mouth on your cock, my hands on you, the needle as I stitch the paint and my blood into you . . . the invisible eyes of your many admirers.*

Niall stayed quiet, likely sensing Evan getting into his own head as well. The Scot was intuitive that way. Pulling up a stool, Evan adjusted his table of inking tools, the variety of colors, the tiny cups to clean the needle and dip into new colors. He also had a scalpel and ceramic bowl handy, the most important elements for what he was about to do.

When he'd first told Niall he was going to do this, the Scot had said little about it, but since then it had drifted through his head with the constancy of clouds in the sky. The fact that he didn't think too deeply on it told Evan it intrigued him more than he was willing to admit.

Niall bore his third mark, the significance of the *chai* symbol not lost on either of them, given that Niall had come to him on the brink of death, but Evan wanted to enhance it with his art. Make Niall one of his canvases.

"Thank you, Leila. That's enough." His servant's powerful thighs were trembling with the effort not to thrust into her mouth with the little movement permitted by his bonds. Evan could smell the semen that had oozed from the slit. The ring was cutting viciously into him, barely holding back the climax boiling in his balls. Leila had a very skilled mouth.

Now his servant was aroused, alert, fiercely agitated. Good. That was where he wanted him. Evan had no concerns about Niall tensing up over the process itself, which sometimes happened with first-time tattoo subjects and could degrade the design as a result. Niall had no fear of pain at Evan's hands, could even get aroused from it, when applied correctly. But if Evan could get him into that floating state that Niall didn't embrace as readily as a natural sub, the skin would accept the ink even better. He was on the threshold of that now, whether he realized it or not.

When Evan slid his fingers over Niall's pectoral, where he would start the tattoo, the man quivered, his lips parting. "Only one focus. What I do to you here." He gave him a single prick with the needle. Niall didn't flinch, but his stomach muscles tightened like a drum. Evan could already see how he would edge out the dragon's neck, using thicker lines for the turn of the head to give it a 3-D effect. He could use more whites and yellows for a highlighting effect, because the blood— and the fact that Niall didn't spend most days in the full heat of the sun—would keep the fading to a minimum.

Evan picked up the scalpel next to the bowl, made a functional slice across his forearm. As the blood dripped into the bowl, Niall's nostrils flared. The audience might be curious about the use of Evan's blood, but the visceral and macabre easily blended with the primitive drives of Domination and submission.

Lifting a brush, Evan swished it through the blood, then applied a thin layer to Niall's skin, over the first area where he'd be working. Then he took up the machine. "When the pain intensifies, listen to my mind, *neshama*. Find your center."

He'd taught that inward focus to his servant early, a coping mechanism to handle a vampire's more extreme demands, as well as to manage Niall's personal demons. While a normal tattoo hurt, adding the blood to hold the design made it worse. Third marks had a high tolerance, but pain was pain. Being able to suffer in stillness didn't mean that it didn't hurt like hell.

Putting his hand on Niall's shoulder to steady his stance, Evan eschewed the stool for now. He'd use it eventually, when he tattooed the dragon's body along Niall's upper abdomen, but he preferred to stand before his canvases when he could. It seemed more respectful to the muse—and the subject.

It took several hours to do all of it. He'd already sketched out the pattern, painted it, so he didn't need to do a tracing. He had it locked in his mind, had inked it into Niall's skin a hundred times. He knew every inch of his servant's body as well as his own. Maybe better.

His servant had firm, healthy skin, thick and supple. Stretching it to allow the ink to flow into the skin smoothly and consistently was not difficult, but it still required concentration. Navigating the curves of bone and muscle, adapting when the layers of skin varied, adjusting the needle in the guide for deeper or more shallow lines. Pausing when his servant had to shift his body, because of the length of time it was taking. Though Evan could read that from Niall's mind, he had known the Scot long enough to anticipate the movement, such that he would lift the needle even before the thought happened. Or utter a quiet admonishment, so Niall would hold still an extra few seconds until Evan was at a better stopping point.

Later, Tyler would tell him that most of the guests who came by to watch for a period of time ended up staying, absorbed by what they were seeing, the powerful energy humming between the two men, artist and subject. Master and servant. However, from the first prick, Evan was aware of nothing but his canvas. The rise and fall of Niall's chest, the hitched breaths and quiver of muscle when things became too intense. The ribs were the worst, because the lack of adipose tissue made it particularly excruciating. Evan kept cool cloths handy, wiping the work area down frequently. Ink feathered during the tattoo process, so it was necessary to keep the area clear, but the side benefit was that it was soothing to the skin as well.

When he finished that section, Evan took a short break. Caressing his Scot's broad rib cage, his bare hip, he rose to brush his lips over his shoulder, his throat, his mouth. Niall turned into the kiss, his lips for once almost docile under Evan's, his mind caught in a deep well. His servant had stumbled into that area of his heart that embraced the possessive intimacy of what Evan was doing. It was the closest Niall came to subspace, a rare and precious gift that Evan savored. Niall didn't often surrender, no matter the odds against him.

Taking a seat on the stool, he slid his knuckles along Niall's inner thigh, grazing the testicles. "Time to keep going."

Part of that subspace condition was a hyperalertness to every point of contact. Evan had stayed in Niall's mind throughout, keeping track of his servant's well-being, how he was holding up, so he also knew the man was aware of how Evan's fingertips lay on his chest, pressing into his flesh, stretching it where needed. Or sometimes just resting, maintaining that contact as Niall was inked, a tactile reminder that he was restrained at Evan's will as he became his art. That aroused his servant as much as anything else.

Evan took the emotional response and integrated it into his own, making it part of the work. The tattoo master who had trained him for over a decade had often used music to inspire the muse as he created on skin. Evan used the feedback from Niall's heart, mind and soul to do the same now, following that orchestra to drive the fire in the dragon's eyes, the defiant tilt of the head, the lifelike gleam of the scales as he mixed colors of gleaming golds and purples, blues and silver. They merged into one another like the glittering edges of an oil spill on pavement. The work was painstaking but all consuming, the tiny caps needing to be refilled often so the ink wouldn't dry out.

If he had any doubt of Niall's reaction to the additional claim Evan was putting on his flesh, the man's aroused state spoke volumes. His cock was so turgid it brushed Evan's elbow, his side. He'd stripped off his own shirt to enjoy the breeze, and feeling the damp tip of his servant's organ sliding along his rib cage when he was leaning forward to ink him just added to the intensity of the experience. Once or twice he ran the heated side of the machine along the velvet shaft, making Niall flinch at the unexpected burn, the threat of the needle being used there. But then Evan set it aside and clasped the organ, sucking the moisture off the tip, giving him a firm lick that had Niall's hands turning into fists again in his bonds, an oath whispering through his mind.

After Evan had completed the design around the sensitive nipple area, where the dragon's precise claw overlapped the areola, he brought his bloodstained fingers to Niall's lips. Niall sucked on them, taking the nourishment and what else was offered with them. Evan noted the skin was red around the nipple, but that would fade far more quickly than it would on an unmarked human.

It was done. Evan stared at the entire design for a few moments, but felt that click in his mind that told him there was nothing more needed. Tiny drops of blood beaded up on the dragon, the skin weeping. The bleed out was the necessary endstep to ensure the tattoo stayed sharp and clear. This was Niall's blood. Evan's had absorbed into the skin, helping the ink set, the unique scientific reaction between a third mark and his Master. He put a finger over a thicker drop and brought the small, tantalizing taste to his mouth. It had been hard work. He was hungry for his servant's throat, but tonight he would feed Niall from his artery. His servant had earned the right to be nourished first, and a tattoo this complicated, integrated with a vampire's blood, was akin to sustaining a wound. He would need the type of sustenance to rejuvenate only his Master could provide.

Evan stepped back, rolling his shoulders. He needed some distance from the blood or his fangs would start to lengthen. Picking up a bottle of water, he drank. It was cold. One of the wait staff must have changed it out.

Ye need to stay more alert. You're the most unguarded vampire I know. His servant's mindvoice was slurred, lethargic. Evan's gut tightened, feeling a Master's sweet satisfaction.

Think how easy it will be to stake me when you tire of my company.

Is that an option? I didnae get the memo.

Evan removed the blindfold. As he stroked his servant's hair, Niall slowly opened his tawny eyes. The Scot might be aroused, every nerve ending alert to Evan's demands upon his body, but emotionally he'd been spiraling on a different plane for some time. It was time to bring him back to earth.

Evan brought the bottle to Niall's lips, cupping the back of his head. "Take a swallow, *neshama*."

Niall did, throat working, and Evan touched it with lingering fingers. "You did beautifully."

All servants learned that hazy place of patient endurance, where the body was malleable to almost anything. Niall had acquired it from diligent practice, not natural instinct, which made his threshold all the more amazing. Curving his fingers around his nape, Evan brought his lips to the man's mouth for a heated kiss, playing with his tongue. When Niall groaned against the bite of that cock ring, Evan gave him a prick of his fangs. Niall let out a soft curse as blood bloomed on his gum. Blood Evan teased away with his tongue.

"I'm going to have a willing sub lubricate your fine ass," Evan murmured against his mouth. "Then I'll put your kilt back on you. When I finally release you from this cross, I'm going to put you down on the ground, push your kilt up to your waist like a girl's skirt and take you hard and fast. You'll spend yourself in the grass."

You're spoiling for a fight, then.

One you know I'll win.

He would of course, but Niall would give the audience quite a show with his resistance, no matter how tired he was. After so many years, the Scot never stopped trying. It fascinated Evan.

That dragon gleaming on Niall's abraded flesh would always be there because of Evan's blood. He abandoned the banter, clasping Niall's beautiful cock hard.

You're mine, neshama. *Every beautiful inch of you.*

~

Through Niall's eyes, Evan could see Alanna staring at that dragon as he finished the story. She'd been tracing it with more ice, but at some point, her hand had stilled. The two fingers holding the cube were stationary, but her other digits were doing curious little flutters around it. An involuntary tell, a burning desire to touch without the ice's interference. Niall's hand covered hers, brought it to his mouth. Taking the nearly melted ice cube into it, as well as her two cold fingers, he warmed them in the heat, pulling her over his chest so she was lying upon him. He cupped her head, fingers tangling in her hair, thumb passing over her mouth.

Her gaze darkened. Desire radiated from her. If she'd been wearing panties, they would have been soaked. As it was, her honey had made her inner thighs slippery. Her hard nipples pressed against Niall's chest, but there was a dark gloom in the center of her mind, a place of uncertainty.

Evan held back the knowledge, not wanting to interrupt Niall's forward progress. The Scot had excellent intuition. He didn't kiss her . . . smart man. Instead he slid his other hand under her T-shirt in the back, released the clasp of the bra. She was still as a baby bird in his hands, staring at him, breath shallow.

He found her breast under the loosened undergarment, cupped the soft curve. As he let out a pleased sound, he investigated the weight and shape of her, his thumb passing over the nipple in a slow, easy stroke. Then a quick flick that made her jump, a tiny noise catching in her tight throat.

"Easy there, lass." Sliding the hand back down her waist, he palmed her ass, and maneuvered her so her thighs were straddling one of his, her hip bone pressing into his cock. "Sit up and take the bra all the way off. Show me the way you look beneath the T-shirt without it."

Good man. He'd commanded her. She complied, still moving in that trancelike way. Evan, lying in his bed beneath the earth, was tempted to order them to come below, but anticipating her reactions was worth denying himself. She was incredibly beautiful—Aphrodite-like in her perfection. The round set of her breasts, the nipples pushing against the cloth, made it impossible for them to be meant for anything other than a reverent yet demanding touch. Niall gave her that now, pushing them together, flicking both nipples through the cotton such that she arched toward him, her eyes closing. He brought her up his body, put his mouth on one over the shirt, dampening the cloth by suckling her. The noise of it, as well as the sensation itself, stimulated her more.

Yet that darkness was expanding. Evan saw the moment it took over and she switched gears. The part of her mind he most wanted engaged pulled away.

I am responding for Master's pleasure. This is not for me, or for Niall.

Straightening to a full straddle, she removed the shirt, her hair sliding over her cream skin. She was well aware of her beauty, but not in the sense of owning it. It belonged to Evan, as it had belonged to Stephen before him. She was its caretaker, softening her skin with those fragrant lotions they'd both detected and enjoyed. Her hair was brushed often and well, treated with products to keep it to a lustrous shine. Everything about her said she was a polished gem, intended to be displayed as part of the wealth of a vampire Master.

She met Niall's gaze before she swept her own down. "How may I please our Master with you, Niall?"

Niall caught both her hands. "Where did you go, lass?"

Her brow creased. "I don't understand."

"You were here, with me. And now you've taken your heart and soul away, only leaving your body."

"If it is my Master's wish for me to be more . . . emotionally engaged, then I will do so."

"You'll act like it, you mean."

"No. My emotions are my Master's to command. If he desires enthusiasm, or tears, or passion, then I provide that."

Christ, Evan. She doesnae know the difference.

Evan considered the issue. *Let her go, Niall. Tell her I have no further need of her today. Do not allow her to help you with anything. Let's see what she does with that.*

Niall's reply to that was a continuation of last night's *what's the point of all this* disagreement. But Niall hadn't liked where that argument had gone, and neither had Evan. So he was relieved when Niall suppressed it. Somewhat.

Fine.

Is that a woman's "fine"? Meaning "not fine," but you'll do it, despite the fact that you think I'm wrong and you plan to brood about it? Or is it a man's "fine"? Which, by the way, men don't often use the word in either manner. It's "okay," "right," or "piss on you."

Piss on ye, then. That works.

Evan smiled tightly. *Yes, it does.* For now.

9

ALANNA was bewildered. Niall had retrieved her T-shirt and bra, pressed them into her hands as he set her aside. He'd told her he had some other things to do up the mountain, and that she was to spend the day as she liked.

She found him putting together a backpack in the kitchen. "I don't understand. What should I do?"

Niall shrugged. "Ye have the books you bought. I'll show you some easily marked trails that'll take ye to pretty overlooks, but dinnae wander off them looking for plants or you'll be lost. There's plenty of food to make yourself something for lunch. I'll nae be returning until early dinner."

She trailed after him as he moved around the small cabin. When she would have helped him pack a sandwich or put water bottles in his pack, he firmly shouldered her aside. "I've been caring for myself for a while now," he said. "No need for a woman's help."

"I wasn't . . . I didn't intend an insult." She shouldn't be hurt that he set her aside now, or even earlier. Perhaps the vampire had decided to sample her directly. But she didn't like how this felt.

"I didnae take it as one. We do for ourselves, and when Evan has nothing for me, I pursue my own interests. You need to do the same. There's no threat to him here, so no worries about leaving him on his own. He can call us if he needs us. Go exploring, read a book, bake yourself a cake and eat the whole thing yourself." He flashed her a grin. "Soften up that pretty arse."

She narrowed her eyes. "I am soft in all the proper ways."

"A woman's arse cannae ever be too soft. Makes it much nicer when skelping it. Or other activities." Niall winked at her, shouldered the pack.

"I could help you do . . . whatever you're doing." She tried to keep the desperation from her voice.

"No. I'm checking some places Evan wants tae visit. I'll be moving fast, so I can cover them by dusk. You can't keep up. Enjoy your day, lass."

Going to the doorway, she watched him take one of the deer trails, his long strides removing him from sight in a blink. The mountain view stretched out before her, magnificently indifferent to her dilemma. There was birdsong and insect life, a breeze, but also a complete stillness, an underlying lack of noise and activity she'd never experienced in her city life.

She sat down on the log bench, crossing her arms over her breasts. The contact immediately made her think of Niall touching her, two sets of eyes on her through his vivid gaze. She'd nearly lost herself in it, until she recalled her duty to be focused on their pleasure and desire. A moment later, things had changed. Cupping her breasts as Niall had, she closed her eyes, remembering his fingers rubbing over the nipples. She almost did it herself, but pulled herself up short. Self-pleasuring was forbidden.

It didn't matter anyway. Her much smaller hands didn't feel like his. The heat and solidity of him beneath her was missing, the pressure of his aroused cock between her thighs.

She rose, surveyed the yard. "No need for a woman's help," she mimicked. Well, he hadn't turned down her breakfast, had he? She could cook up some more things, but making too much food would be wasteful. The cabin was clean and well-ordered, and of course the small outside area was well tended.

What do you want? Need? What can I do? Wandering back into the cabin, she moved to the trapdoor, squatted and laid her hand there. The vampires she knew didn't sleep with their servants, and she supposed Evan was no different. She imagined him sleeping, though, wondered if he slept on his side or stomach. Niall sprawled out like a lazy bear, unafraid of anything. The few times she had to come into Stephen's chamber during his sleep she found he kept his back to the wall, arms drawn up close as if protecting himself from attack.

She had an odd desire to simply lay down on the trapdoor, curl up there to be as close to her Master as was allowed. Like a pet shut out of the bedroom, knowing her proper place was at her Master's feet, on his bed, where she could be near if he needed her. It was pathetic, she knew it was, but they hadn't given her any boundaries, tasks, rules.

Fine. She'd meditate. That was what an InhServ did when she had no immediate responsibilities.

Taking a seat on the picnic table outside, she crossed her legs in the lotus position. Back straight, hands relaxed and open on the knees. Deep breaths in and out. Though her eyes closed, she still saw the beautiful view before her. She began to work through the chant that would cycle her brain into the right state.

Service, not self. There is no self. Desire, need, want. All for my Master. His needs, his desires, his wants. I am perfection because I am Service. Every thought, every act, every breath belongs to him. With my last breath, with the last beat of my heart, I exist only for his benefit. I am Slave, with no need for name.

She remembered the joy she'd experienced when she'd first learned the mantra. She'd gilded it with more devotionals, guided by her impulsive euphoria during the first days of her in-house training. They'd been required to recite it during the lessons that taught acceptance of pain and punishment. The trainers knew how to give out maximum doses of pain without marring pure flesh, a blank canvas intended only for the vampire's marking. The pain didn't matter. That mantra, spoken through every act of service others might consider torment, only increased her commitment. She could get lost in the words while a whip struck her naked flesh, wouldn't flinch from flame brought so close to that same flesh it felt scorched. It wasn't until after she was assigned to Stephen that she understood the true reason the training had reinforced that mantra.

Just as a child grew to adulthood, learning the difference between romance and love, she'd learned the difference between the idea of pure service and the reality of it. But there was a strength and depth to the reality the idea could never provide. So why was it she was back to that romantic yearning, as if that fantasy truly was out there, intertwined with the deeper reality to create the perfect meshing? Something she'd fallen just short of finding, because she hadn't been a good enough servant to get there.

Meditation wasn't going to work. Her throat was tight, her stomach hurting. Suppressing a sigh, she opened her eyes.

She found herself looking at a black bear, who'd apparently lumbered from the wood and was now no more than three feet away from her picnic table, wet nose stretched out to sniff the oddly still human.

She blinked. She could remain motionless before vampires like Lady Lyssa, who had reduced lesser vampires to cowering gelatin with a glance. She was not going to run shrieking into the cabin. But it was a *big* black bear. A bear that now rose on his hind legs and planted his taloned paws on the bench next to her. The rumbling noise that he made could be a harmless inquiry, or a pre-dinner growl. She knew several languages, but not one of them was bear.

The first thing a servant learned was that one didn't run from a predator. It would transform her immediately into prey.

"You're looking for food," she said quietly. "And I smell like eggs and bacon. I'd get you some, to be neighborly, but I expect it's not a good idea to encourage you to visit humans. The next one might have a gun and think you're a threat. And I'm hoping . . . you're not one?"

That rumbling noise came again. She tried not to move as he nosed her leg, snuffling, moving to her hands. If he opened his mouth, tried to eat her hand . . . The paws shifted on the table, those talons closer to her knee. This time she couldn't help it. She flinched.

"Oy there, off with ye! Ye know better, black beastie."

Niall had returned, thank the gods. She suppressed the embarrassing cry of relief as the bear turned his attention from her. He gave Niall a narrow consideration, but the man advanced steadily, calling out and gesturing his warning with calm purpose. While he wasn't presenting an imminent threat, his advance indicated he could be one if needed. As he passed the well, the Scot reached down into it, pulled out a shotgun that apparently had been sheltered under the interior lip and cocked it. The noise made the bear flinch. When Niall brandished it, now close enough for the bear to make it out, the creature let out an irritable huff and lumbered across the yard, disappearing into the bushes.

"There now. I'm away for ten minutes, and already she's entertaining strange men."

Despite his teasing, she saw Niall was out of breath, sweat staining the front of his shirt. He'd come at a full run. As he approached her, his gaze shifted toward the cabin. Turning, she saw Evan nearly in the open doorway. He was holding to the shadows, but she heard the click of another gun being uncocked, saw him give a spare nod and turn. But there was something wrong...

She was off the picnic table immediately, brushing past Niall and reaching the cabin before another breath had passed.

"Master, let me help." She didn't wait for permission this time, sliding under his arm when he staggered. Through sheer determination, she kept him from falling toward the sunlight. Fortunately, Niall was right behind her and able to steady them both.

"Came right out o' a sleep, no?"

"I realized the big furry thing nuzzling me wasn't you," Evan coughed. "And that I normally don't feel terrified of it."

"I'm sorry, Master," Alanna said. "I should have controlled my reaction. I didn't mean to disturb your sleep."

Actually, no vampire she knew would have stirred themselves. Such a matter was a servant issue, and Niall had responded capably. But of course he'd been running through the woods when the bear had his paws on the table. If he'd decided to swipe at her...

"Yes. Next time please allow yourself to be mauled more quietly."

The amusement was unmistakable, but his pallor startled her, the sweat on his face. "Are you all right, sir?"

He was four hundred years old. Yes, he'd come above ground, but he hadn't stood in sunlight. It was only vampires under a hundred years who reacted this badly to being above ground during daylight, even inside the shelter of a building.

"I'm fine," he said shortly. Squeezing her shoulder, he nodded to Niall as he opened the trapdoor. "I can get down the ladder."

"Sure you can." But she noticed his servant watched until he managed it, a certain tension to him until it was done, and then Niall replaced the trapdoor.

"Is he all right? Does he need anything?"

Niall shook his head, after that brief internal look that said he had checked on the same thing. "No. He says to leave him be." Reaching out, he tugged her braid, distracting her. "Black bears are mostly herbivores, until people start feeding them, then they become scavengers. That one's probably spent too much time picking up scraps on the trail. You're fine, then?"

When he closed his hand on hers, she realized she was shaking. "My first encounter with a bear." She tried a shrug. "It was silly of me to get alarmed. I'm sorry . . ."

"If you'd done the wrong thing, lass, he might ha' attacked. Any wild animal can get testy or aggressive if he thinks he's threatened or thwarted. Ye haven't any experience with that situation."

"No?"

"Well, nae with that kind o' beast." Niall paused. "That was almost a smile, girl. The first time I see a real one on your face, I'm going to kiss ye senseless. Do me a favor then," he continued before she could respond to that remarkable statement. "While I'm gone, it might do to stay in the cabin or close to the door. At least 'til you and I can go hiking and I can show ye a few wee precautions for being up here."

"You could show me now."

When he passed a hand over her hair, he was extraordinarily gentle about it. Even pulled her close to brush a kiss across her forehead, hold her against his body. She wondered what she'd done to cause such a response, but then he stepped away.

"No. Not today."

∼

So off he went again, once again leaving her to her own devices. She read her plant book, sat on the bench right by the front door. Went to the well to see how Niall had replaced the gun in a mounting below that lip.

If only Stephen had realized giving her nothing to do would drive her to suicide far faster than grinding pain and the twisting of her every thought into a nightmare. He could have saved himself a great deal of effort.

Closing her eyes against those memories, she let them shudder off her skin like rain. Resolutely, she went back inside, looked at the selection of books. While she should make herself study the Scottish history or one of the cookbooks, instead she picked up a tattered romance apparently left by previous renters. The virile male hero was standing on a grassy hill, a woman in a lavender dress on her knees before him. Her hands were on his thigh, his waist, her whole body longing toward him as he bent over her, his hand cupping her face. She had his total attention, his posture suggesting he was going to take her over in a devouring kiss.

The picture brought back the arousal spiked by Niall's skillful touch, but she knew how to suppress arousal not commanded by her Master. She did.

Stephen hadn't been interested in driving his servants' pleasure into extreme realms where they lost complete control. In fact, he didn't seem very interested in her responses. If it wasn't for political purpose and show, he'd rather her pleasure him. Often he left her wanting, with no permission to take care of herself, an indifferent sadism. So she dealt with it, without dealing with it. She'd channeled the energy elsewhere.

Thirteen years of such control and discipline, yet earlier she'd nearly caressed her breasts without thought.

Had Niall set her aside because of what Evan had suggested, their desire that she want what they were doing for herself as much as for her service for them? It was an alien idea to her. The tight frustration in her lower belly became a tiny ripple of rebellion. If they wouldn't give her any direction, and she wanted to pleasure herself, that was a desire, right?

She waited for Evan to correct her, then was ashamed of herself. He was trying to sleep, had risked himself to honor his charge to Lady Lyssa to protect her. She puzzled over his weakness above ground, out of proportion for his age. She might ask Niall about it.

Nowhere else to go with that, so her mind boomeranged back to her body's humming needs. Bringing herself to climax would definitely disturb Evan's rest. But if she disturbed his sleep often enough, maybe he'd learn to give her a to-do list.

It was a nasty idea, one that appalled her. Her thoughts were like children pinned up in a schoolroom too long, their energy and wildness out of control.

Shoving it all out of her head, she slipped off her shoes, plunked down on the couch, curling her feet beneath her. She'd set the romance on top of the plant book. Considering both, she lifted the romance novel. Well, she *wanted* to give the story a try. There. She was acting on one of her own wishes, small though it was. Hooray for free will, something she'd never desired but Evan seemed to be forcing upon her.

Damn it. She closed her eyes. She'd kneel on rice for an hour for that one, but Niall had made it clear Evan had to order any punishment.

Just stop thinking and read. She opened the book.

In her current state of mind, she wasn't expecting much, but after struggling through a chapter or two, she found her focus. The characters were engaging, the historical setting well drawn. As the chapters progressed, she was absorbed more deeply into their romance . . . as well as the overload of sexual tension between them.

She was a swift reader, but on certain passages, she slowed down. A lot. Her mind started returning to the moment Evan and Niall had trapped her against the ladder to give her that first mark, two sets of male hands on her. Niall, fondling her breasts as they lay on the ground together, the wind rippling her hair across his forearm.

She stroked her cheek, her chin, down her throat, like this hero was doing to the heroine. Like Evan had done to her before he gave her that mark. Stephen rarely touched her face or neck, and now she did it again, feeling with some amazement how it roused nerve endings far below the range of that touch. The intensity of Evan's gaze had captivated her, the way he watched her every reaction like it mattered. Mattered for reasons that had nothing to do with how other vampires perceived his power over her.

Sliding her hand down to her breast, she curved her fingers around it. That bare contact brought the nipple to an aching fullness, enhanced as she thought of Niall suckling it with the strong, heated pull of his mouth. Evan, holding her arms, biting into her throat as her hips rose in a plea to be filled by them both, shameless begging.

She'd been taught to masturbate to prepare her body for penetration if the vampire had no desire to arouse her himself. She'd also learned how to do it for the viewing pleasure of others. This was more than that, a desire to make Evan and Niall hard, to please them, to please herself, but not in a way that felt self-serving. It was something she'd never considered, let alone experienced. Yet it felt so familiar.

Even though she knew she should put the book away, she turned back to it. She wanted to finish it.

Whenever you think "I want," *immediately do something else.*

The number one InhServ rule snapped into her head so fast, it was as if the training Mistress was right in front of her. The book fell onto the floor, facedown, crumpling the pages. Closing her eyes and taking a deep breath to steady herself, she bent, retrieved it. Smoothing the paper, she mulled it over for several moments. She needed to follow the rules she'd followed all her life. Faced with a path back to them or toward uncertainty, the right choice was obvious. The rules couldn't be wrong.

Rising, she replaced the novel on the shelf. She stood there for a while, though, her fingers on the spine, thinking of that picture on the front. The heroine on her knees, the hero bent over her. She could imagine his hand sliding down from her face to collar her, hold her still as he sipped from her mouth, teased her tongue, bade her to be so still. Every nerve ending focused on what he was doing to her. Overwhelming her so it felt like he held her heart in his hand.

Backing away from the bookshelf, she forced herself to return to the chair and sit down. Feet flat on the floor, back straight, buttocks on the edge. Since her Master had no tasks for her to perform, and she couldn't meditate, then she'd simply sit here, waiting as if commanded to do so. Like at a vampire dinner, where she'd stood behind Stephen's chair, motionless for hours until called to perform for the entertainment of his guests.

As a result of that thought, an even better idea struck her. She rose and went to the kitchen. Positioning herself on the wall behind the chair where Niall had sat, she assumed that silent, waiting posture. To help her remain still, she imagined she was back in Berlin, in the opulent dining room with two dozen place settings and chandelier lights. The room full of Council members and their servants, ready to do and be whatever their Masters desired.

~

When Niall returned several hours later, she was still standing there. She'd left the door open to allow fresh air in the cabin, and the sounds of the mountain—birds, bugs, the wind—had been a quiet symphony playing in the white noise of her head. They couldn't suppress the anxious tendrils of feeling, but they'd helped her manage them. Even so, she felt an almost dizzying flood of relief when the screen door creaked.

Taking a step away from the wall, she found her joints were stiff. As a third mark, she hadn't had that issue with prolonged periods of immobility. In the future, she would stretch every once in a while to maintain flexibility.

Niall looked at her as he entered, then his gaze covered the rest of the cabin. His expression suggested he'd expected to see evidence of something that wasn't there. She suppressed the desire to ask him what.

"I cut up some of the meat for sandwiches. Would you like me to make you one?"

"Ye can make me two or three. I've covered twenty miles of this bloody mountain. A couple beers would be bonny as well."

The band around her chest loosened, telling her how much she'd dreaded the crushing weight of his refusal to let her do anything for him. As he put away the items he'd taken with him, she moved to put together his dinner.

By the time she had the plate ready, he was at the table with two large plastic cases he'd brought from the back bedroom. As she put his meal in front of him with the cold beer, he nodded toward the containers. "Evan keeps a lot o' slides, but these are a shambles. He wants them organized into some useful system."

"I'd be happy to do that." In fact, she would be delighted to seize them and get working on them immediately, but instead Niall gestured to the kitchen.

"You look peely-wally, lass. Make yourself a sandwich as well and come eat with me. In the chair next to me," he added. "Nice as ye feel on my lap, I'm sweaty as a winded horse. I'll shower off outside after something's between my gut and backbone."

He was right. She hadn't eaten since breakfast. After preparing a sandwich, she came and sat next to him as ordered. The kitchen table wasn't large, and his legs were long. When she would have eaten sideways in her chair, so as not to encroach on his space, he grunted and reached beneath the table. Curving his fingers around her nearer thigh, he directed her to put her feet on his boot. She was barefoot, so her toes curled into the animal hide and laces. In that state of casual intimacy, they ate their lunch.

Mindful of Evan's order to treat Niall as she treated him, she wouldn't speak until Niall asked her to do so, but she wished he would talk. She'd been in her head for too long. No matter how much she tried to keep clear of it, Stephen's torment, how much her life had altered, the fact that she could die at any moment . . . they closed in on her when things became too silent, too still.

"Tell me about your first kiss."

She looked up, startled. The Scot's brown eyes twinkled at her. "Was he a scrawny seven-year-old, besotted with your red hair?"

"Would you tell me about the first time Master kissed you?"

Niall looked surprised by the question, and she was surprised she'd asked it. But she was thinking about the book she'd been reading, the way the heroine had yearned for that very first kiss. Alanna had been kissed by servants when they were entertaining vampires, but it was usually a perfunctory stop before their mouths were put to good use elsewhere. In the romance, that amazing first kiss had taken two and a half pages to write. And it was only the first of many kisses the hero had given the heroine.

"No," Niall said. "But I'll tell you about *my* first kiss. If ye tell me yours."

He gave her one of his wicked looks, but she thought it was a distraction. Why wouldn't he want to talk about the first time Evan had kissed him? Surely almost dying on the battlefield would have been a more painful memory, yet he'd told her about that. "Will you at least tell me when he first kissed you?"

He gave her an exaggerated sigh, a mock frown. "*Women.* About two decades or so after we met."

She blinked, not sure if he was serious, but it appeared he was. It also appeared he was waiting for her answer.

"My first kiss, outside of training practice, came from Lord Stephen."

"Oh." She'd given him a handful of thick, kettle-cooked potato chips, and he pushed several onto her plate. "You practiced kissing in training?"

"Yes. Though I came to Stephen pure, we were required to have extensive training in sexual practices."

"So did you kiss a lot of other girls in training? Or only lads?"

"Both." She arched a brow. "Would you rather hear about my experiences kissing the other girls?"

"As often and in as great detail as ye wish," he assured her.

She bit back a smile, shook her head. "You said you'd tell me about your first kiss."

"Eat those potato chips first."

She gave him a look. "You're just trying to make me softer."

"You've not eaten since I left." Picking up another chip from his plate, he extended it. "Open up."

When she did, he brushed his fingers along her lips, making her think about tasting the salt and grease on his lips with her own.

"A bonny lass named Ainsley," he said. "She was eleven and I was twelve, fancying myself quite a man. Until she had me behind her croft. When she put her wee hands on my shoulders and pressed her lips against mine, I near fainted. I lost my balance, grabbed her waist, and toppled us both in the mud, which is where her two older brothers found us. They thrashed me within an inch o' my life and sent me home with my tail between my legs. But Ainsley smiled at me behind their backs. She always kept a sweet spot for me, since I was her first kiss as well."

She looked down, hiding her smile again. "I can't imagine anyone thrashing you."

"Well, I was scrawny as Evan then. Hadn't hit my growth spurt."

"Do you remember it so vividly? The things that happened long ago?"

"Aye. Of late." Her head rose at the briefness of the answer. He was staring into space. "It's odd, how that goes. The far past becomes more vivid, whereas the recent things become less remarkable, no matter how remarkable they truly were. Until Evan, I had little knowledge of anything beyond my own small world, but reading about the history you've lived, a lot of it is pure bollocks. Kings and politics. The things a man truly remembers and history forgets are home and family. That first kiss." A faint smile touched his lips.

When he was done with his meal, Niall went to wash off with the outside spigot while Alanna considered the task he'd left her. She intended to attack the slides right after doing the dishes, but the spigot was outside the window, the distraction of it slowing her task at the sink. Niall had stripped off his shirt to splash water along his chest. He dunked his head in a bucket, straightening to toss his hair out of his eyes, smooth it back with his hands. Realizing he hadn't taken a towel, she went back to his bedroom and found one. When she came outside with it, he met her at the door.

"You're a handy thing to have around," he admitted. "Or were ye just worrit I'd drip on the floor looking for one?"

As he flashed a grin at her, he took the towel and stepped back in the yard. When he covered his head with it, vigorously rubbing, she was caught by the beautiful play of muscle on his upper body. She wanted to reach out, touch, so instead she hurried back inside. How many times today was she going to be reminded how her control was slipping, how low she was sinking in the InhServ standards? Perhaps Stephen was just the catalyst for a weakness that had been there all along.

The rest of the day, she worked on the slides. Niall stacked wood, repaired a few other things around the house, settled in to read newspapers he'd bought from Henry. When the trapdoor opened right after sunset, Alanna felt a loosening in her chest, anticipation at seeing their Master.

As she turned toward the vampire, there was no sign of the earlier lethargy. In fact, he had a rather determined spark in his eye, a set to his jaw that Alanna wasn't sure how to interpret. Niall rose, so she looked to him for cues, but he had an inscrutable expression, giving her nothing.

"Good evening, Master. Can I—"

She bit back a startled noise as Evan caught her chin, jerking it up so that he brought her to her feet. "Alanna, what did I expressly tell you not to do?"

"Not to . . . devalue myself."

"What have you done today, except find yourself lacking?"

Her flesh warmed under his hand. "I apologize, Master. I will do better."

"Yes, you will. A punishment will help your memory. Niall?"

Evan didn't even glance at his servant. He strode past Niall and picked up the canvas, easel and paint supplies the Scot had set by the door. As he left the cabin, Alanna looked toward Niall, who was considering Evan's back, but then he moved across the cabin, gripped her wrist.

"Come with me, lass. Best get it over with."

Niall swung her up on his shoulder, clamping a hand on her backside as he moved toward the door with strides as purposeful as Evan's. "I can walk," she protested. "I don't plan on avoiding punishment, Niall."

"Better if ye dinnae see this one coming."

He crossed the front yard. She had a brief glimpse of Evan, setting up his canvas, his back to them both. What did he want Niall to do—

A moment later she was airborne. Though she managed not to shriek during that part, it was impossible not to do it when she landed with a resounding splash in the creek. A frigid mountain creek that drove the breath from her like a thousand daggers through the flesh, especially since she dropped below the waterline like a cannonball before she floundered up, gasping.

"Over here, lass. I'll give ye a hand out."

She paddled that way, the chill making it hard to coordinate her movements. She was desperately glad for the warmth of his hand, wished she could curl up inside it. Her hair was dripping, clothes clinging to her in a most unpleasant manner.

"You're lucky it's a first offense," Niall observed. "For a second or third, he'll make ye stay in there for about fifteen minutes. Turns your balls blue."

He hauled her out. Once he had her on her feet, he kept her wrist manacled in his, and guided her back up the hill. Evan was at the picnic table, sketchbook before him. Because she was so disoriented, Niall put out a hand to make her stop a few feet away, so she wouldn't drip on it.

"I'm s-sorry, M-master. What more can I d-do t-to p-p-please you?"

"Nothing." His tone was indifferent, almost bored. "I require nothing from someone like you."

10

THE distinction brought her head up. "Excuse me, sir?"

Though it was an effort, given he could hear her teeth chattering, Evan ignored her for several moments, continuing to study his in-process sketch. He felt Niall's gaze on him, ignored it as well.

"Did I . . . have I done something to offend you, sir?" He was surprised she dared the follow-up, but it gave him the opening he needed.

"How could you possibly offend me? You're as capable of that as this blank pad. No will, no interests. You can't even say what you want."

"I want your will."

He cut across that with a snort. "Do I look like I want a plastic doll as a servant? No thoughts or feelings of her own? One whose responses to my touch are like a trained circus poodle? Do I look like I want to fuck a dog?"

"Evan." Niall's fingers tightened on her wrist. "Stop."

Evan tossed him a look. "Holding her leash now? If I told her to sit, stay, roll over, sit up on her hind legs and bark, she'd do it. Wouldn't you, Alanna?"

She had her free hand in a tight knot at her side, her face now a hard brittle shell. "I will do whatever my Master commands."

"No, not always." He pinned her with his gaze. "For one very vital, very significant moment, you didn't do what your Master commanded. You turned him in to the Council. You crossed a line, because you *have* a line. Find it, Alanna. Where is it? What do you want? Tell me one thing you want. Salt instead of pepper, to dance instead of sleep, bread with or without butter. What the hell do you want? Say it. Tell me. Your Master is commanding you to have a will, to have a soul, to be a fucking human being."

"Evan, for God's sake." Niall released her. In another moment he would step forward, as if to shield her from the words with his body.

Stay where you are. He rarely used such a sharp tone with Niall, such that it brought him up short, but it wouldn't hold the protective Scot for long. Evan couldn't blame him.

Alanna was disintegrating. The cold water had shocked the body, and he'd delivered the same dousing to the mind, intending to knock her off-balance. Shuddering, hands clenched, she had tears dripping down her face. She had the desperation of a drowning person, trying to find an answer to save her life. To please him. But only to please him?

"It's what I am," she whispered. "What I want."

"What?" She would never know the effort it took him to sound impassive, but Niall finally picked up on it. He saw the shift to understanding in the man's eyes. A good thing, because otherwise he'd have to put the Scot on the ground to keep Niall from pummeling him. Which would definitely detract from what Evan was trying to accomplish.

"I've always . . . I just wanted to serve a vampire . . . one who . . . one who . . . would value me."

"Value you. For your origami skills? Your trained sexual skills? The way you keep your hair nice and shiny?"

She swallowed, got paler. "I didn't . . . I was taught certain things, but Stephen wanted a virgin. I learned by watching, doing, emulating. He . . ."

She didn't say it, but Evan saw it in her mind. He let Niall have the information as well, saw his lips tighten with helpless anger. Stephen had taken her virginity with careless indifference. Fucked her, pulled out, made sure of the blood, then told her to clean herself up and come down for dinner while he went to handle a phone call. A sixteen-year-old girl who'd never even been kissed. She'd been a small ball on the bed for a few moments, passing her fingers over that bloody patch. She'd thought it would matter more to him. But then the shift had happened, the training kicked in, locked into place. Her feelings weren't important. They'd never be important, and that was okay. Humans were inferior to vampires, yet also vital. Service was what was important.

Though he didn't show it on his face, Evan shared Niall's murderous thoughts toward Stephen. It also made him gentle his tone. Somewhat.

"But you felt empty. Why did you feel empty, Alanna?"

Niall picked up his cue now, keeping his voice low, neutral. "Why did that book you read today make you feel different?"

She flushed. She'd probably think Niall had made that connection from Evan's mind, but he hadn't. It was one of the ways Niall had taken him by surprise, in the beginning. The Scot might act dense as a pile of bricks, but he was a deep well, fed by a whole network of underground water sources.

"I thought . . ." She was still struggling, and Evan saw Niall fighting the desire to reach out to her. But she needed the mental thrashing room. "I wanted so much to serve a vampire, and I thought . . . Please . . . let me go back to the house. I'll work on the slides."

"You'll stay here and answer my questions," Evan said. "My will is everything, right?"

Anguish gripped her expression, so sharp and painful it was as if she'd been skewered by knives. "Please, I'm begging you. Don't."

"You expected to be valued, but you expected more than that, from your own feelings. There's another word you're seeking, Alanna."

She was so pale. Her fingers were trembling, her whole body. *Evan . . .*

"Tell me." He spoke sharply. The answer was there, but she was under siege, a hurricane happening in her head, her soul.

"Please don't make me say it. It's wrong to say it."

"You thought if you served him with everything you are, you'd love him. And he'd at least care about you. But he didn't do anything worth loving, and he never cared for you."

"If that was what I thought, it was wrong, and selfish. The point of serving is serving, giving your Master everything he needs. Your needs and wants are unimportant. It's not wrong to love your Master, but that love should never expect anything in return. That's why I failed. Why I betrayed Stephen. I did it because I thought he owed me something. And that's unforgivable."

"Your twin's death had no significance in the face of your Master's every whim. You couldn't accept that, and that's why you failed."

"Yes." But the word came out like a serrated blade from her flesh.

She still had no color in her face. The shaking was past her ability to control it. Niall had left them, disappearing into the cabin. She continued to stand there, her hands at her sides, her carriage erect and open. Accessible. She was so cold, her nipples stabbed through the T-shirt, and the skirt clung to her like a second skin. Her straight stance put all that on full display. Even when her emotions were crumbling, she was so well-trained she wouldn't cringe. There was a personal pride in that, whether she acknowledged it or not.

Niall returned with his heavy coat. Putting it on her shoulders, he threaded her arms into the sleeves that swallowed her, then rubbed them briskly to keep them warm. She kept her eyes on the ground. It would take more, perhaps one more push. Evan stood in the maelstrom of her mind, watching the conflicting emotions churn around him like the storm he'd once experienced in Darwin, Western Australia. Every flash of lightning had been like a Titan's hand striking marks against the sky. He'd wondered if they would split the firmament and show the divine face that hid behind it, pulling all the strings.

Rising from the bench, he moved toward her until the tips of his shoes were in her view. He slid his hands under the heavy mass of wet hair, used his hold on it to tilt her head up.

"Look at me, Alanna."

She had a doll's eyes. She'd retreated from the pain, the confusion. But he was inside her mind; she couldn't retreat from that. He thought about the third mark, what it would be like to stand inside this woman's soul, and felt a sudden hard desire for it. To own her completely. To ensure she knew exactly what it meant to be cared for. To be cherished by a vampire Master.

She had a wealth of sexual skills, but had never been given the opportunity to enjoy and participate, to develop her own desires and wants. Stephen was a single-minded ass.

Framing her face in his hands, he leaned down. Paused a hair's breadth from her lips. "Kiss me, Alanna. Explore my mouth the way you'd like to do it. It's your true first kiss. You can do nothing wrong, as long as I'm getting the pleasure of your mouth."

His fingers teased the corners of her eyes, took away a few tears. "Stop your crying," he added curtly. "You're tearing my heart from my chest."

Her eyes widened at that, but then she pressed her lips together. As she considered his words, the doll look started to fade. It was a hushed moment in the universe, time stretching out like the heartbeats between those Darwin lightning strikes.

Lifting onto her toes, swaying unsteadily, she put her lips on his, a light and tentative touch. She tasted him. Nibbled. The tip of her tongue darted forth to touch his mouth. It took tremendous effort to rein back his natural dominance to take over, have her beneath him, but he managed it. As much as he wanted to be inside her, he wanted to see her take this step.

It was too much for her. The storm howled, intensified, sweeping into the marrow of her shaking bones, gripping her heart so strongly she made a sound of pain. She pulled back. As her eyes filled anew, she shook her head. "I can't. I can't want anything. I wish Stephen had killed me."

At the broken declaration, she bolted, tearing herself from his grasp. She ran back into the house in the oversized coat, the fist she put against her mouth not enough to hold back sobs.

Niall stood tensely next to him. "You're a total bastard," his servant said. "But a smart one."

"There's not much difference between a smart bastard and a fucking sadist. Give her a few minutes, then go to her. Make sure she's okay."

"Think that helped?"

"Maybe. She chose to run, and she's never run from a vampire. That in itself means something. Sometimes things become clearer after a hard storm."

"Unless the storm destroys everything. They made her too fragile, Evan."

"Well, that's why she has us, right?" Evan arched a brow at him. "We protect her, help her get stronger."

Niall gave him a short nod, strode toward the house. The irritable set of the broad shoulders was easy enough to read. It was torment, trying to help her embrace a life all odds said she wouldn't be given. But though Niall might rail against it, Evan knew they had no choice but to try, because it was the right thing to do.

And Niall never turned away from that.

~

Stripping off her clothes in her room, Alanna rubbed herself hard with a towel. She was not going to curl up on the bed to cry. She'd handled all that badly, but she could pull it back together. Yanking on dry clothing, she picked up her brush, turning it over in her hand. *The way you keep your hair nice and shiny . . .*

She slapped it down, raked her hair back and fastened it with a clip. She'd let it dry snarled, if her hair being shiny meant nothing to him. Coming back into the main room, she saw a napkin on the floor. She recalled Evan had brushed it off the table when he went toward the door.

As she leaned down to pick it up, Niall came in. When he'd helped her out of the creek, he'd been braced on the bank, so now he tracked mud over the braided mat.

"Leave it," he said. "He can pick it up." The edge to Niall's voice suggested he and Evan had disagreed over what had just happened. From any other vampire–servant pairing, she'd say that was beyond the realm of possibility, but not for them.

Training. That was the only anchor she had left. The one they seemed determine to pull up.

"It's our job to pick it up."

"Why? He knocked it off."

She wasn't having this ridiculous argument. She knew her duty, even if Niall chose to ignore his. As her fingers brushed the cloth, Niall put his muddy boot square in the middle of it, where she couldn't tug it free.

"Leave it."

His order gave her that odd shiver, but something else came to the forefront as well. She'd been thrown in a creek, had failed to kiss her Master as he desired. He asked for skills she didn't have and ignored the ones she did, ones that could be used for his benefit. Of course, out here in the middle of nowhere, with no political standing, no power at all, he didn't even want or value her training. He wanted her to "do for herself" when he didn't need her. As long as she was under his ward-ship, hours and hours of horrifying free time were going to be stretch-ing before her.

This was not who she was.

"I will *not* leave it." She snapped up straight, faced Niall with a set jaw. "Just because you delight in being lazy and pretending you're your Master's equal, doesn't mean I'm going to throw away years of Council training to suit your whims. I am an InhServ. I am completely at the mercy of our Master, and *grateful* for any chance to be of service."

She decided to ignore the fact that she'd run from Evan's demands. She couldn't seem to stop her mouth, or the emotions boiling up inside her. "I will not emulate your blatant disrespect, even if he accepts such an unnatural egalitarian relationship with you."

With that, she gave him a shove to get him off that napkin. He didn't move of course, but his brows lifted nearly to his hairline. Then the corner of his mouth tugged up, and he took a step back. Snatching up the napkin, she saw him grin. It made her even angrier. Turning away, she intended to put the napkin in the trash, but instead Niall caught her about the waist, hauled her back against him. She snarled at him, astonishing herself by calling him some highly uncomplimentary names.

Niall's chuckle against her ear was sensual and dangerous. "You're asking for another spanking, lass. A much harder one."

If he tried, she swore she'd take a pound of his flesh in trade.

Under those conditions, I might enjoy watching you get spanked. Why doesn't Niall deserve a spanking?

Evan's laughter confused her. Somehow she'd pleased him. It made her angry, because everything in her responded to that approbation, even as she felt like she was being teased.

"Easy, lass." Niall kept a firm hold on her, stroking her hair off her neck, knuckles tracing her still damp temple and cheek. Then he put his warm lips against her throat.

Her nails dug into the hand holding her waist, not gently, but he scored her with his teeth, a sharp bite that made her whimper. His other hand tangled in her hair, held her immobile as he took his time with it, suckling beads of water from her skin, nuzzling her beneath her ear.

She was in no-man's-land. Though still riding a storm of emotions, she realized she'd just behaved horribly, said unforgivable things. Yet Evan was pleased with her, and Niall was kissing her as if he'd just discovered a woman's flesh. She couldn't resist pressing her head against his shoulder, tilting it away to give him better access, her nails now biting into his hand for a different reason. Her body above and below his arm were cold, needy.

She had her eyes closed, but she knew when Evan came into the cabin. Niall was the deep parts of the forest, earthy, warm and dark. Evan was the wind through the pines, swirling out over the gorges and through the folds between the mountains.

Keep your eyes closed, Alanna.

Evan's hands closed on her breasts, thin cloth alone between her taut nipples and the warmth of his palms. Slowly he squeezed, thumbs tracing down the cleft as he brought the curves together. She swayed against Niall's unbreakable hold, a cry breaking from her lips as Evan put his mouth over her nipple.

They gave her no time to change gears, to go back to docile service. Instead that storm swirled inside her, becoming something new and strange. Violent, needy. Her heart ached like someone was trying to rip it from her chest.

"Master . . ."

I'm here. We have you. You're ours.

"I need . . . you. *Both of you.*"

There was no room for anything but the free flow of thoughts. She wasn't trying to explain her training, but something far deeper. And Evan understood.

"I know, *einayim sheli, yekirati.* My *metuka.*" The language was soothing, musical, sensual, and he kept repeating the words as she surrendered to Niall's strong grasp, leaning into him. The Scot kissed her brow, her eyes, tasted her skin. Her lips felt bereft, but she wanted, needed . . . to do it better. To kiss Evan first. She wanted that chance at a first kiss again.

As his fingers brushed her chin, an acknowledgment, she made a glad sound. The vampire's mouth covered hers, fangs making a short scrape over the sensitive inside of her bottom lip. When he used his tongue to tease hers into a dance, she realized she'd put her arms around his neck, that dark silky hair at his nape threading through her fingertips. Niall adjusted them forward so she was full against Evan, his arms taking over the embrace as Niall knelt behind her, pulling her skirt down to her ankles and freeing her from it before raining kisses on her bare thighs, large hands stroking her calves and the backs of her knees.

Evan's arms were strong and sure, holding her against him as he explored her mouth. He didn't discourage her from using her hands, so she caressed his shoulders, feeling the shape of him, the strength of his upper arms. When he broke the kiss to nudge her head back and take a sharp nip at her throat, her fingers spasmed on his shoulders, nails digging in. She wanted to draw blood, wanted to be . . . fierce. Show him how much she wanted to please him.

She needed to serve, to take care of him. It was what they trained her to be.

No, yekirati. *This was part of you long before the Council groomed it. They gave you technique, skills, but you are the artist. Show your desire to serve, to surrender, in the way that fits your soul, not their requirements. That's what I want from you. I need you to feel who you are, and let that spread your wings. Be a flower feeling the sun, no thought, just reaching for the warmth and the pleasure, because that is what you are.*

Spinning on that thought, she dug her fingers into him further as Niall's mouth touched her inner thigh, his strong hands spreading her so he could use his mouth to tease the sensitive perineum. When the tip of his tongue traced her rim, his hands spreading her wider, lifting her, the stimulation had her bucking against Evan's hold. This was what she wanted. To be passionately responsive, totally mindless, at their mercy, giving them pleasure . . . simply by responding to the pleasure they were giving her.

She cried out as Niall's thick fingers slid into her pussy, his mouth still busy on her nerve-rich rear opening. Evan let her fall back against their combined hold as he bent to suckle her breasts once again. She was teetering, off-balance, with no fear she would fall. It was unusual to feel so safe, even while she was whirling through a heavy haze of desire.

The men handled her as easily as a doll between them, though not the kind of doll Evan had denigrated. Now Niall relinquished her fully to Evan, and the vampire hiked her up his body, guiding her legs around his hips as he moved toward the back of the house, toward

Niall's large bed. As he did, he recaptured her mouth. It was at least a three-page kiss, because by the time he was done with it, she was making quiet pleas in the back of her throat from his relentless plundering of her lips, mouth, tongue. When he laid her back on the bed, straddled her waist and opened his trousers, she was already parting her lips, wetting them, her eyes avid for what he was offering.

His long, thick cock was as pale and beautiful as the rest of him. She wanted to close her hands around it, but he'd adjusted his knees over her arms, holding them pinned as he slid closer. When he teased her mouth with the head, making her reach for it, she felt a curious joy at the playfulness. Then that playfulness disappeared, eyes darkening as she cried out, a guttural, yearning noise. Niall had plunged his tongue deep into her pussy, holding her thighs down and open with his powerful hands as he swirled and suckled, then teased her clit. He was going right for aggressive arousal, and she was catapulted up that ramp so quickly, she was almost afraid to take Evan into her mouth, for fear of biting down from the wave of passion that tumbled her in its grasp.

But her Master was demanding she service him, and she rejoiced in his want, his need. She took him deep, no choice, because he thrust hard, pushing into the back of her throat, taking control of the motion so she had to struggle to keep up. A true struggle, with what Niall was doing to her. Oh God, she couldn't focus. It was too much, Evan's taste, his organ stretching her lips, requiring mindless submission from her, Niall catapulting her toward orgasm.

Master . . . I can't . . . I'm going to come . . .

Yes, you are. By our will alone. Let go and feel, Alanna. I want to see it.

She redoubled her efforts on him, trying to do what she should, but it was erratic, her lower body shuddering and jerking in Niall's firm grip. The orgasm rolled over her, and she was screaming against Evan's cock, no finesse, sucking him out of crazy need, lost in the pleasure of serving their desires. The dense heat of male lust in the dark room cocooned her like Niall's coat. Something sure, solid, real.

The Scot kept licking her even after the largest wave of the orgasm had passed, keeping her struggling and moaning. Then they were turning her, lifting her onto all fours. Smoothly, the men changed places, Niall stretching out on the bed beneath her and Evan behind her, his hands firm on her hips.

Take care of him, now, my sweet. While I enjoy your wet pussy. Yours, Master. It's yours.

She made a sound of pure ecstasy as Evan filled her, stretching her. Putting a hand between her shoulder blades, he pushed her down toward Niall. She clawed at Niall's shirt, tearing buttons off so she could put her mouth on the dragon tattoo. Niall's eyes flamed with heat and he gripped her shoulders, exerting pressure. Telling her what he wanted.

Watching you suck me drove him crazy, Alanna. He demands you service him as well.

"Yes, Master." It was a whisper as she met Niall's tawny eyes and then lowered her lashes, intent on her goal and his demand.

Working her way down, Evan moving with her, she pulled open Niall's jeans, pushed the boxers out of the way. Seeing the slit of his cock pearled with fluid made her salivate. Evan was driving in deep, pulling out slow, taking his time despite how hard he was. Vampires never rushed unless it suited their purpose. He'd have her insane with arousal again in no time, not that she was far from it now.

"Show this lazy servant what you can do, eh, lass?" Niall muttered.

When she nipped at his broad head, she earned that dangerous chuckle. "You'll be under me again, InhServ. Mind those fancy manners now." He tugged her hair, in lust and reproof.

In answer, she bit him harder, but groaned as Evan sank deep again, staying there this time, rotating his hips as he held hers fast, letting her feel the rub of him against every clenching part of her channel. "Ohhh..."

I gave you a command, yekirati. Take care of my servant.

Niall's cock was thick and hard, ready for her mouth. She felt nourished by the heat and weight of him filling her mouth. He pushed into her throat as she took him just as deep as their Master. Gripping his base, she teased his testicles. He had a heavy, large sack, and she reveled in noting every difference between the men, the overwhelming sensations that came with serving her Master's cock in her body, while pursuing the sharp pleasure of caring for his servant's with hands and mouth.

All the way up and down, she used every oral skill she had on Niall's shaft, working him as relentlessly as Evan was working his cock inside her. Deep plunge, then slow drag up, tormenting all those wonderful nerve endings around the ridge of the head, sucking the precum off the tip, worrying the slit with her tongue. She wanted him to come, wanted to swallow every drop of his seed.

~

The lass had considerable talents, but it wasn't that which overwhelmed Niall. He could now clearly see what Evan had suspected was held deep within her. Enthusiastic yet trained compliance couldn't hold a candle to an uncontrolled passion for surrender. Tightening his fingers in her hair, he goaded her to new heights, even as he had a fierce response of his own.

Fuck. We're never giving her up, Evan. Never. Not to those bastards.

When their eyes met, he saw some of the same resolve in the vampire's expression. As well as Evan getting lost in a vampire's savage lust, his eyes glinting red, fangs baring as he worked himself closer to climax.

It catapulted Niall toward the same finish line. Alanna was rocking against him, her nipples brushing his thighs as Evan thrust into her. Niall's seed boiled in his balls when the lass made pleading, animal noises against his cock, her efforts becoming more frenetic, bringing them all to the same high pinnacle. God, he wanted to be where Evan was, and yet experience her mouth like this.

There is time, neshama. *She has much to learn about true pleasure, giving and receiving.*

Overlapping Niall's fingers on her shoulders, Evan leaned closer to them both, driving into her. Her mouth took Niall even deeper, her cry strangled as Evan sank his fangs into her shoulder right next to Niall's grip, perfuming the air with the metallic odor of blood mixed with arousal. Her hands scrambled for a purchase, landing on Niall's thighs to brace herself, every feminine fingertip pressing into his muscles, hard enough to leave bruises. He drove up into her mouth once, twice, and then, at Evan's nod, he let go, the same moment the vampire did. Their combined release pushed her over.

A gasp, another gasp, and then she was fair howling, scrabbling, digging her nails in, scoring him with her teeth, but in a savage, pleasurable way he embraced, making her work to get all of him. Evan had his arm around her waist, holding her snug against him as he made those last few deep plows that felt so good to a man when he was deep in a woman's climaxing cunt, spending himself. Alanna made soft kitten cries as the movement took her over another rise, and Niall held her tight as her claws bit further into his flesh. Aye, she was theirs, no doubt. All theirs.

~

There was something to be said for that training, after all. As soon as she oriented herself to it, she set that pretty tongue to cleaning him, getting every drop she'd missed off his balls and shaft, his thighs. She was still experiencing aftershocks, making those sexy little noises against him as she tried to take care of him. God, he could fuck her all night long. She wanted to give so much to a Master, it was intoxicating.

Evan was right. The Council hadn't made her anything. They'd merely polished the gem, but the true value was in the rough cut, when her real emotions took over. If only they could convince her of that without having to shock her with cruel words and cold water. He couldn't do that to her again. Not after seeing this.

Evan pressed his hand into her back, bringing her to a halt. She was breathing hard, an emotional as well as physical response. Aye, it was catching up to her, the significance of what she'd just done. Plucking her off her elbows and knees, Evan guided her to straddle Niall as he rose to a sitting position himself. Niall gathered her close so she could curl one arm under his arm, around his back. She was limp, her other arm folded against herself, but not impeding the pleasant press of her breasts against his chest.

Evan slid in behind her, his knees over Niall's, tangling all their legs. Niall stroked her hair, which had become snarled from drying wet, but he could help her work that out later. "Hope ye can sew, lass. You tore my shirt. I'll expect you to fix that."

"Yes, Master," she said groggily, nestling her face in his chest. When Niall looked at Evan, the vampire merely lifted a brow, then licked the puncture wounds on her shoulder, soothing the bites.

Then he reached out, touched Niall's face. Not sure what Evan was seeking, Niall remained still as the vampire traced his jaw over the girl's head.

What?

Just feel, Niall. Same as her. No thoughts tonight.

Niall swallowed. He kept his eyes on Evan, the pensive gray eyes, the firm mouth that was far too attractive, that mysterious charisma that could draw a man into it like a dark abyss. He thought of Alanna, her fingers threading through Evan's hair as he kissed her. Evan had once teased the Scot, telling him he had hair as soft and thick as a girl's, but that was a rock tossed in a glass house. Those silken pieces that feathered over Evan's brow and brushed his collar tempted Niall to touch, same as Alanna's red locks. So he lifted his hand to do the same, blunt fingers sliding through the strands as Evan's eyes stilled on him. They'd been part of each other's lives for so long . . .

I'm sorry. For the things I said earlier. I shouldnae have said them.

Catching Niall's wrist, Evan turned his mouth to it, scraped a fang over his palm. *It didn't make them untrue. The world is what it is. Help her sleep,* neshama.

Unsatisfied, but never one to argue with simple honesty, Niall shifted to a reclining position on the bed, taking the girl with him. Surprisingly, Evan stayed. The vampire slid down on the other side of her, but it still somehow felt as if he was curled over the two of them. Protective. When his Master laid a hand on his chest, it eased the ache there. Overlapping it, his fingers brushing Alanna's delicate jaw where she rested her head on him, Niall closed his eyes and was content.

11

ALANNA woke. For a moment, she felt an incredible ebullience, an elation like nothing she'd ever experienced before. Her body was deliciously sore, well-used, and she smelled like the men who'd possessed her. She recalled the few times she'd surfaced, staying in a half doze, but so aware of their bodies close around her, bare skin and heated muscle pressed to her flesh.

It hurt, such . . . happiness. Everything was so vivid around her. Though he wasn't speaking in her mind right now, she could feel Evan's mark there, her connection that said she wasn't alone. And yet . . . what had she done?

Sitting up slowly, she saw a note on the nightstand. It was from Niall, telling her he'd given her the evening injection while she slept, so she wasn't overdue for it. But he'd had to do it while she lay here, as lazy as she'd accused him of being.

She dressed carefully. Her hair was untangled and smooth. Niall's doing as well, she was sure. Vaguely, she remembered the brush stroking her scalp, his hand following it.

It was perhaps an hour until dawn. Evan might already be below, but when she came into the main room, she saw him through the window, sitting at the picnic table. He must be working on the sketches he'd started earlier, when Niall threw her in the creek. As she approached, she saw what appeared to be lightning across a dark sky on the paper, but a corner of the sky was being drawn back, a blinding light coming from behind it. In that blinding light was a face. Merely a sketch, but already intriguing. She'd like to see it become a painting.

But that wasn't very likely, was it? She rubbed at the sore spot on her arm, suppressing that unsettling place in her mind.

She didn't see Niall, but she didn't look for him. Instead, she went to Evan, dropped to her knees, bowed her head and waited to be acknowledged.

Niall was sitting on the log bench, repairing one of the kitchen chairs so it wouldn't rock. He'd seen the girl come out, looking so intent and serious. Evan had warned him there might be fallout from last night, but he'd hoped . . . He was a fool, of course.

It was a few moments before Evan looked up from his drawing. He'd been deep in his creative process, so he blinked as if coming out of a sleep. Niall sheathed his knife, but she didn't register the movement.

"I'm sorry, Master. I failed you. I sought pleasure for its own sake, and not yours."

"Isn't that what I told you to do?"

Her gaze lifted, confused. "But it didn't feel that way. It felt . . . different."

"Aye, it did. It felt bloody marvelous," Niall said. Now she did glance toward him, though Evan sent him a mildly quelling look.

"You did what I wanted you to do, Alanna, so you've done nothing wrong." He touched her face. "When I rise tonight, I will have a list of things for you to do."

She brightened considerably, like a false sun, and nodded. But before she could rise, he bade her stay with a firm gesture. "I'll leave you a list daily, but they come with a condition. There's one task I expect you to do every day. No matter what other things I give you, it has the highest priority."

"Yes, Master. Anything."

"Every day, you'll spend two hours doing something you choose to do. Entirely for yourself."

Her brow furrowed, considering it. "What if what I *want* to do is something that pleases you?"

The lass was a clever thing, and far more stubborn than she realized.

Evan's lips twitched against a smile, but by the time she'd glanced up, he was giving her a stern look.

"You'll be doing that with the tasks I give you. You've learned to be the kind of servant the Council requires. But I'm not a Council vampire. If you truly want to serve me according to my desires, then you'll need to expand your skill set. Those two hours will help you do that."

She mulled that over. "I will try, Master."

Honest as well. It was like when they were hiking and Evan had asked her if she could keep up. Even if she wanted to, she wouldn't lie.

"Do better than that," Evan reproved, making her flush. "You are fully capable of this task, Alanna. For now, I want you to go back to bed. You're exhausted. If Niall sees you out of bed before three in the afternoon, he'll tie you there. Your body is still recuperating."

She pressed her lips together, but bowed her head. Evan touched her hair, letting a long strand slide through his fingertips. "It's not a punishment, *yekirati*. I want you well-rested. Go."

With a nod, she rose to her feet, turned and hurried back into the cabin. As Evan watched her, Niall came to his side. "What are you thinking?"

"If a vampire had a heart, that girl would break it."

~

She reluctantly realized Evan was correct. Once she laid back down, her eyes didn't open again until three thirty, startling her. But her momentary dismay was dispelled by Evan's note on the side table.

If it's past three o'clock, you have obeyed your Master. I'm pleased with you. As a reward, you may feel free to bedevil Niall about his laziness as much as you wish, without repercussions.

Underneath that had been scrawled an additional note, in Niall's handwriting. *He can only enforce that at night, muirnín. During the day, I wouldn't push your luck.*

They made her smile. Then she remembered Evan was supposed to have left her a list.

He had, a full page on the kitchen table. Niall was gone, but he'd left a message on the counter that he'd be back in time for a nine o'clock dinner. That prompted another smile, the less-than-subtle hint in the message that he'd like for her to have something ready. He was probably scouting for Evan again.

The item at the top of Evan's list was slide reorganization. He directed her to sort out the ones that appeared extraneous or redundant. Suspecting he wanted to test her understanding of what she'd seen of his work so far, she embraced the challenge. Considering the slides carefully, she put her discard choices in one box, and the others useful for future inspiration in another.

Then there were lenses to clean and file back in their velvet-lined box, something Evan's to-do list indicated Niall was far too clumsy to handle. To underscore it, he'd sketched a picture of a bear trampling broken glass in the margins. It made her chuckle, but it also made her think about the needs of their "bear." Amusingly enough, the next item on the to-do list was to make Evan "a sugar cookie." In parentheses, he'd added, "and three dozen more." That list item was accompanied by a picture of a bear sitting with all paws curled possessively around a cookie jar.

While she was sleeping, he'd spent time on this. Vampires did not go out of their way for their servants. Any servant that expected them to do so didn't deserve the honor of being a servant. But this made her feel warm, good. And somehow her reaction seemed to feed his. It pleased Evan and Niall both to see her . . . happy.

The revelation was so far outside her milieu, she couldn't take it any further than that, so she decided it was time to work on those cookies. While she waited on them to bake, she put together a short grocery list for the next time they went down the mountain, planning a few meals ahead.

It was somewhat pleasant, being in charge of a kitchen. She wondered if Niall would let her take the Rover down and do the shopping herself. She remembered the route and felt sure she could handle the vehicle. Then she recalled the reason she was supposed to remain close to them. It startled her that she'd forgotten. Her fetal-curled subconscious never let her forget what shadow loomed over her fate. Apparently, cocooned by the memories of last night, the two men curled around her, she'd been given a respite.

Was that another reason Evan had given her such an extensive to-do list? As Niall had said, most of the time Evan did for himself. Had he realized having too much idle time could make her feel like a victim on a chopping block, waiting for the fall of the axe?

Once again, vampires didn't make such effort for servants. Except maybe one of them did. A vampire who not only provided her such a list, but illustrated it with cartoon characters of bears to make her smile.

She looked through his basket of unopened mail, tossed there by Niall when they'd brought it up from the mountain post office, which also happened to be Henry's store. Finding a case knife to use as a letter opener, she went to work on Evan's correspondence. Most were notices of automatic check deposits from a New York gallery, probably the art dealer Niall had mentioned. The surprisingly large amounts were signed in a bold hand by Marcus Stanton, a handwriting she matched to the Post-it note stuck on the latest one.

Cell phones were invented a decade ago. Heard of them? Use smoke signals, Morse Code or a damn medium, but send me info about next project. Have buyer on line, but wants to know what he's buying. Such pesky details will keep you solvent! And—much more important—keep me in fucking Gucci.

She put that on top of the pile for Evan to see first, though the tone of exasperated affection in the note suggested it was a routine nudge. At the bottom of the basket, she discovered a wedding invitation that had been opened some time ago. Since she wasn't sure if he'd responded to the RSVP, she added it to the top as well. She couldn't imagine he planned to attend, but all his correspondence suggested he had far more human interaction than vampires she knew.

Seeing it was seven o'clock, she stopped to put together dinner. While she'd slept, Niall had added a pair of rabbits to the refrigerator. She appreciated that he'd already turned them into meat, not sure if she could handle soft fur and dead staring eyes. Finding a recipe that cooked the flesh in apple cider, she coated the parts in flour and got started. The recipe included a side dressing of apples and potatoes, as well as a cornstarch and spice gravy for the meat.

It was past dark when she finished, so she was listening for Evan's footsteps, but he reached out to her with his mind first. *I'm going to join Niall at the location he's found. Pack up dinner and I'll take it to him. It's a bit remote, so I want you to stay here for now. And I want my cookie.*

She was a little disappointed not to be going, but feeling that she was part of the household, rather than something they had to make plans around, helped soothe the feeling. That, and his amusing request for the cookie. She also put a bit of the rabbit dish in a separate container for him to sample. When he came up, he was in a hurry. He hadn't even buttoned his shirt, had simply raked his fingers through his hair. Hatefully male, he merely looked sexier, reminding her of being in bed with him the previous night. He must have gotten caught up in something downstairs once he woke, and lost track of the time. Respecting his urgency, she gave him the container and managed a smile as he nodded absently, taking it from her and heading for the door.

She suppressed a sigh and turned to face the kitchen and the stack of dirty dishes there. She'd make herself a plate of the stew and eat at the counter, then start cleanup.

"Ah—" She let out a little gasp as Evan turned her toward him. She hadn't even heard him return. His expression was still distracted, so she expected he'd forgotten something, but then he had her hauled up against his body and was kissing her with heat and need. He pushed her up against the counter so her legs locked around his hips. His fingers dove into her hair, freeing the clip and filling his palms with her tresses as he rubbed himself against her, earning a gasp from her lips against his.

"Behave," he told her with a feral smile, and then he was gone. She had her feet on the ground but was holding on to the sink, the whole world tilting on its axis.

It took several heart-thumping moments to realize she had a smile on her face, her lips still tingling from the corners to the soft, fleshy center. It took her five whole minutes to pull together her distracted thoughts, during which time she gave serious thought to adding an intense masturbation session to her two-hour "task."

Keep imagining that, yekirati. I will plague Niall with that vision, so that when we return to you, he will be like a bear tormented by the scent of fresh meat. Leave the actual pleasuring of your body for us. We are in a selfish mood.

She'd never heard happier news.

～

She returned to the slides. Since there were thousands, it was not a one-day task, but she made steady progress. Around one in the morning, she heard her Master's voice in her head, a teasing, liquid sensation, much like the aftermath of that kiss.

Don't forget your highest priority, Alanna. You do not wish to disappoint me.

No, Master. She tried to dispel her automatic reluctance to it. She'd approach it like any other assigned task, considering herself a third party her Master had asked her to entertain. That would work. But how was she going to entertain herself? Sighing, she rose from the table and stretched.

Sir, I'm making a sandwich for myself. Do you or Niall require anything?

Nothing for me. He sounded distracted now. *Niall's always hungry. We're close now. Northwest, about a quarter mile. Take the trail behind the well.*

Elation filled her. Making several sandwiches for Niall, she included chips, cookies and soda in a basket. She decided to bring the romance with her, as well as the plant book. Comparing the pictures to find edible plants was something she'd enjoy, so it would be useful to her two-hour task quota as well as her cooking. Women did multitask, after all.

They also rationalize.

She jumped at Evan's reproof, but she picked up a warm chuckle. *That's fine, Alanna. As long as you are sincerely trying. I expect you to do a little better each day, though.*

Yes, sir.

He'd given her a picture of their location in relation to the cabin. They were in a secluded glade. A small creek, probably the same one that wound alongside the cabin, formed a gurgling furrow in the earth, the glossy stones beneath the water causing spouts and waterfalls. Rock outcroppings thrust through long, silver-white grass, drawing the eye toward the dark shadows of the surrounding forest. Leaves released from the fall foliage were caught in the grasses, and though it was too dark to see the color on the trees, her flashlight moved over the tinges of red and orange, the curled dried edges of fallen leaves.

Once in the glade, she snapped off the flashlight. The second mark and the moonlight filtering through the trees gave her the ability to see the glade adequately without it, and she didn't want to interfere with Evan's view.

Evan had his camera set up, but he wasn't using it now. Putting his fingers to his lips, he warned her to remain quiet, and he did so without taking his eyes off the trees on the other side of the glade. When he extended a hand, she put the basket down, came to him. Niall was stretched out on the grass to their left, his head propped on a rock. It had to be uncomfortable, but from the even rise and fall of his chest, he was asleep.

Closing his hand on hers, Evan moved her in front of him. He had his hips propped on one of those jutting rock clusters, so he could bring her back between his thighs. Sliding an arm around her waist, he brushed her ear with his lips.

Keep your gaze on the trees before you. It will take a while, but when you see something, tell me.

She nodded. The moment he touched her, everything in her became still, tranquil. Earlier, he'd taken her to a near-painful state of arousal with one kiss, but he could do this as well. She was comfortable in his arms, and she'd never applied that word to a vampire. When he was like this, he was relaxed, at all levels. It was a pervasive, unwavering calm, a dense energy like being near a warm fire, both attractive and unexpectedly vibrant, something that made her fingers curl over his on her waist. In response, he stroked her skin between the shirt and her jeans, inhaled her hair, nuzzled it with his lips. Enjoyed her as he watched and waited for her to see the world through his eyes.

She'd found it. A gray fox, sitting in the tree, studying them. She detected the gleam of his gaze, a stray bit of moonlight catching his silver pelt.

They climb trees quite well. But they're used to hikers up here. We're not why he's in a tree.

Studying the animal, she watched to see who else he was monitoring. She found the young mountain lion in another tree, closer to the creek. His tail gave him away, the thick rope of it twitching, hanging down from his branch. At last deciding they weren't close enough to be a threat, the cat leaped down, padding toward the creek. As he bent to drink from one of those shallow waterfalls, the spray made him lay back his ears and close his eyes.

Anticipating Evan, she adjusted so he could move to his camera. The mountain lion lifted his head, but then, after satisfying himself they weren't a threat, he returned to drinking.

Alanna leaned against the rock, watching. She was entranced by the animal, but even more, she was entranced by Evan. He was on one knee, the tripod lowered to get the angle he desired. His shirt stretched over his shoulders, his short hair curving over the collar, tempting touch. His mouth was set in concentration, yet his eyes . . . there was magic happening in those eyes. He was seeing some form of ever-changing perfection, something he could capture. No, *capture* was the wrong word. He was seeking something to honor, as if his work was a praise to the gods.

When she'd sorted through his slides, her wonder at their diversity had slowed her task. Though he seemed focused on wildlife and land-scapes in the mountains, he didn't limit himself to one subject matter. She'd found city scenes, people, animals, experimental uses of light that turned everything into streaks and surreal impressions, like look-ing at an alternative world, layered over this one.

He combined subject matter in a disturbing way. She'd used a small, battery-operated projector to examine the slides on a larger scale, and found one of Niall, asleep in a field like this. However, the field had been overlaid with another picture, lifeless bodies, broken and bloody, the aftermath of a battle. The overlay had been arranged so the bodies cut a wide, noticeable circle around Niall, underscoring the contrast of his peaceful sleep with their not-so-peaceful death, a permanent sleep.

The mountain lion moved off. Evan straightened. When he began making notes on the tattered pad he propped on his thigh, she re-turned to her picnic basket. She brought it to Niall, but he didn't stir, so she retrieved her book and sat on the grass next to him. It was a good position to watch Evan, and she wondered if Niall had chosen it for that reason. No matter their occasional friction, there was an obvious, unbreakable tether between them.

Even in sleep, no one would mistake Niall for anything but what he was, a powerful man, sure of himself, alpha in every respect. It made sense that vampires didn't pick unappealing or ordinary servants; a human had to be extraordinary to desire three centuries of service to a vampire. But even for all that, the link between these two was unusual.

Covering a yawn, she set the book aside. She shouldn't be tired, but the blocker she'd taken right before coming up here gave her that ir-ritating burst of fatigue. Today, a nap would have to count toward her two hours.

She had no desire to pillow her head on a rock, though. She considered Niall. He'd worn those serviceable cargos that clung to his thighs, creasing around his groin. His T-shirt marked out the breadth of chest well, and her fingers wanted to touch.

She wanted to lie next to him. Wanted to be close to his heat. She thought of Evan coming to lie with them, as they had done in the bed, her in between them. Vampires didn't cuddle, not to her experience. It was an unthinkable, nonpermissible thought, on so many levels, but with Niall, it might be acceptable.

Shifting closer, then to one hip, she moved as carefully as she had to avoid startling the mountain lion. A part of her was afraid if Niall woke up she'd be in transgression of something unforgiveable. She'd never reached out to anyone for affection, closeness.

She eased down next to him. His arm was over his head, making it easy to lay her head on his shoulder, inch her body closer. Putting a hand on his chest like a butterfly landing, she pressed her cheek to his shirt and inhaled his scent.

If only our Master were here with us, she thought. *It would be perfect.*

What makes you think I'm not, yekirati? The response made her jump, but Niall, muttering in his sleep, put his arm around her.

What does that mean . . . yekirati? And what you said the other night . . . *einayim sheli . . .* My *metuka.*

You have a good ear for languages. Your pronunciation was almost flawless. Yekirati *is "dear one." The rest . . .* einayim sheli *is "my eyes," meaning very precious to me, and* metuka *is "sweet."*

Very precious to me. It was a simple endearment of course, but it still warmed her to hear it. She glanced down the pleasurable terrain of Niall's body. Evan wasn't looking at her, was in fact still working on his notebook, but there was a light curve to his mouth.

Do you still want to know about the first time Niall and I met?

Yes. I would like that. If it wouldn't upset Niall. She usually only thought in terms of what would offend her Master, but it felt right to qualify it, given Niall's earlier avoidance of the subject. *Can I ask something else first? About your first kiss?*

Possibly. Ask, and we shall see.

You were with him awhile before that. Why . . .

Why did I wait so long? It was a monumental test of my restraint, one he has never appreciated.

Glancing up, she saw wry amusement in his gray eyes. *I wanted certain things to evolve in our relationship first. Create the proper setting, lighting. I was waiting for the muse to strike.*

There's a muse for that?

There's a muse for everything. That's what you learn over time. Every moment is rich with art and possibility, every interaction. But patience is key. And sometimes a tough skin, especially when dealing with an irascible Scot.

Alanna smiled. When Evan lifted his head, met her gaze briefly, her lips tingled under his regard, her smile replaced by more intent, heated things.

It wasn't until she felt a provocative flush across every inch of the skin his gaze covered that he lowered his attention to his work again. But he didn't break the connection between them. Instead, he began to paint in her mind as well, creating the picture of his first meeting with Niall and bringing it to vivid life for her.

12

THE Scot was looking for a campsite, too far away from home to get back tonight. Evan followed his human scent to a rocky glen, a deep creek running through it. There were a few soft spots near the bank to roll up in his plaid and sleep. Evan didn't detect a fresh kill, so it seemed the man hadn't had any hunting luck, despite ranging so far afield. If he had caught something, he'd be on the way back home with it, no matter the distance or time of night. His family was starving, like so many others in his village, the result of failed harvests, illness and the indifference of the few who held rents over the heads of the many.

Though it was dark, Niall—Evan had learned his name during these past few weeks of watching him—wasn't willing to give up yet. He'd apparently been trying to get a fish interested in biting, despite the cold. Evan maneuvered up into the cradle of a tree overlooking the glen, a good perch to watch the desperation mount on his face. Niall was a big man, even though he was barely past twenty.

"Well, piss on ye, then," the Scot snarled, leaping up from the bank and throwing his fishing gear away from him. "If ye cannae provide me any help, maybe the Devil is listening." He shouted out a few more things in Gaelic. It was probably a good thing Evan was here, because no telling when English dragoons might be on a patrol. They'd cut down a strapping male like this no questions asked, assuming right off he was a Jacobite.

Unlike many of his fellow villagers, Niall was no Jacobite. But he didn't support the current English rule, either. Evan had been in the village shadows the night of a community bonfire, when talk had led to politics and hunger, matters closely linked for men trying to care for their families. Pushed a little too hard for his viewpoint, Niall had tartly remarked that not all Scottish problems were to be laid at English feet. "Our landlords can take their fair share of the blame. Ye dinnae need tae English to starve and beat us down, when the sons of the auld clan chiefs will do it."

Like most of them, Niall and his family worked their rocky land and scraped together what living they could to barely cover the rents on their crofts. But unlike most, he had a keener grasp of where to lay the blame. It wasn't the first time Evan had been impressed by the man's intelligence.

Though most didn't see the appeal of the rocky Scottish terrain, Evan saw a harsh beauty in the unforgiving land. He saw the same in the grooves of the young Scot's face. In the privacy of this glen where Niall didn't have to put on a brave face for kin or stranger, Evan watched the rage and frustration build into sorrow, helpless incomprehension . . . Every emotion strong men experienced when they confronted a terrible possibility: that scraping on the edge of survival was likely the most they would ever be able to do, for themselves or their families.

Many in his village had already accepted that. Evan had seen the hopeless resignation in their faces. Niall didn't know what that was. No matter what the morrow brought, he wouldn't come home to his family empty-handed, even if he had to cut up a dragoon and call his edible parts venison. Evan would lay money on it.

Ripping off his plaid and ragged shirt with another oath, Niall discarded his worn boots and plunged into water that Evan knew had to be frigid. The man disappeared beneath the surface. With his vampire hearing, Evan could hear him screaming his rage. Perhaps he'd become mindful of an English threat. Or, in the slim hope that a higher power *might* help him, he'd tried to at least muffle his invective toward it.

He shot back up, water sluicing off the broad chest and wide shoulders, his hair whipping back like an angry lash as he tossed it out of his flashing eyes. When Niall slogged back to the water's edge, his jaw showed granite resolve.

"Bollocks on all of it," he spat. Then he froze, his gaze snapping up to pin Evan where he perched in the crotch of the tree.

Remarkable. He hadn't given away his position with even a twitch. Dropping to the ground from the ten-foot height, light as a cat, he moved toward the water. Niall's attention went to whatever he could use as a weapon, but they both knew it was too late if Evan had a pistol or sword and was any good with either. Evan could have told him he meant him no harm, but he had other priorities. Making them clear, he stopped and gave the Scot a thorough perusal.

Skin of pale marble, bluish from cold. Though he needed feeding, his knotted muscles were ropes along his arms and thighs, his chest powerful and deep, the stomach a hard plane that arrowed down to his pubic region. The water lapped at the snarl of dark silky hair, revealing a hint of thick cock. He was half turned, so the slice of taut backside gave Evan all sorts of inspiration. But the young man's reaction was the real gem.

His initial wariness gave way to an equally intent scrutiny, aware of how Evan was looking at him. What he was thinking, wanting. The man's lip curled, but it wasn't derision. It was angry challenge.

Having no desire to soil good linen, Evan pulled off his shirt. It showed the Scot he carried no weapons of merit, an odd thing for a man alone, but Evan wasn't introducing the why of that into the conversation. Producing his knife from its scabbard, he tossed it aside so it lodged in the ground next to his shirt.

"I have a cow for your family, and a job offer," he said. "Impress me, and they'll both be yours."

A cow's milk would feed the Scot's children, and her calves would be a source of income or meat. The job offer would ensure he could care for the animal, as well as give his family a steady diet and keep a roof over their heads. Evan saw disbelief replaced by calculation, and then sheer determination.

Nakedness didn't hamper him. The man had pride, but it wasn't wasted on modesty. He charged out of the water like a rutting stag, and Evan was pleased to note adrenaline had already made him half hard, despite the cold water. Ready for the initial grapple, he let Niall take him to the ground, but after that it was a simple matter of breaking the grip, working the man out to his full capacity, testing his holds, his strength, his staying power. Given his physical state of near starvation, it was more than impressive. It was bloody phenomenal.

The Scot had tremendous heart, which just made the picture grow in Evan's mind as they grappled, dodged punches, broke holds. He could see the way he'd paint the stark lines of this man's body, portray the character and perseverance in his face. Noble desperation, honor without hope, the most miraculous type of honor there was. This man was all of that.

He was capable enough to land a few good blows. Evan had to focus now to avoid dislocated limbs, a crushed rib. Having his balls kneed into his throat. The bastard would pay for that one. He could feel the tide turning, though. The Scot had been given something tangible to fight, something that understood his rage . . . and with understanding came a different sort of reaction.

This time when he flipped him, Evan unleashed his vampire strength. He made Niall fight harder and harder, until his breath was sobbing in his throat. It took longer than expected, but Evan finally had him down on his knees, face to the muddy bank. Niall heaved, but couldn't buck him off. He tried a couple of times, but then he had to take a breath, and when he did, Evan slid his hand beneath him, closed it around the fully turgid cock. Holy blessings of God.

The man went utterly still. Disbelief emanated off him, a protest dying on his lips. As a vampire, Evan detected the sexual preferences of humans as easily as the rush of blood through their veins. This man had his wife regularly. He was a generous lover, giving her pleasure as well. Evan had been outside his tiny sod house, heard her bitten-back cries, inhaled the gush of her orgasm and the spill of her man's seed. The Scot had given her the side of his hand to bite down upon as he pushed her to climax, and she'd broken the skin, bringing Evan the sweet smell of passion-fired blood.

So yes, Niall enjoyed women, but there was that within him that also enjoyed males. His ass was provocatively virginal, given that there was no acceptance for sodomy in his world. Beyond that, he was the type who would be faithful to his wife, no matter the temptation provided by man, woman or fetching sheep.

He wanted that cow, though, and Evan knew if he was ruthless enough, the Scot would allow himself to be used to get it. He explored the feeling, pushing his own hard arousal against the bare, wet backside. The muscles flexed in apprehensive anticipation.

"We'll leave that alone for now, I think. I don't fuck with a man's honor unless it serves a better purpose than my cock." Tightening his hand in Niall's long hair, he enjoyed the thickness of it. "You impressed me, Scot. Get your clothes, and we'll get your cow."

As he eased off, Niall slammed his elbow back into his face, knocking him to his back and straddling him. Evan could have put him back down, but he was curious. Niall was panting, staring down at him in confusion. Blinking through the agony ricocheting from the bridge of his nose, Evan let his gaze slide down the bellows of his chest, to the shaft jutting over his bare rib cage. "Wouldn't mind a taste of that. Now that you've washed it off."

A muscle flexed in Niall's jaw. "I'm no whore."

But Evan could easily make him one. That wasn't his intent, however, so he pushed the shallow temptation aside. "No. But you're interested in how my mouth would feel. Bring it closer."

Niall swallowed, shook his head, stood and offered his hand. "Your mouth's bleeding."

He'd love to see Niall taste that blood, but he'd scrambled the poor chap's brain enough. So he licked it off himself, suppressing another surge of desire when Niall couldn't take his eyes off the movement. "I gave you the one shot, but if you take another, you'll have the broken nose. I only tolerate so much."

"You're nae English." Niall yanked his shirt over his head, rewrapped his plaid around waist and shoulder. Evan catalogued the graceful power for later replay and sketching as he retrieved his own shirt.

"Raised in Italy, with my great-grandparents coming from Spain. My home base now is in the Colonies. I have some property there. Since I've traveled most my life, most people assume I'm English when I talk. It seemed intelligent to cultivate the accent of the currently most powerful nation. You have a good ear. I'm impressed."

"If that's all I had to do to impress ye, we could have skipped the wrestling match."

Evan lifted his head from the laces of his shirt, gave him a slow smile. Niall was braced on the bank with one knee bent to manage the incline, a hand on his belt. It was a solid, thick thing, quite capable of striping those taut buttocks. "Yes. But that would have deprived me of the pleasure of handling your cock."

Niall shook his head. "I'm no sodomite."

"Only for lack of opportunity." He'd love to bind Niall over the edge of a bed and rut on that fine "arse" until the man came against his belly a dozen times, wrung out like a dishrag. He'd fight being fucked at first, but then he'd give himself to it with shameful pleasure. As Evan adjusted his erection, he was pleased to see Niall unable to look away. "But you like women too. As do I."

"What's a landowner from the Colonies doing here?"

Evan decided to let him change the subject. It wasn't his main reason for following him, anyhow. Just a pleasant fantasy. "Painting."

At Niall's perplexed look, bordering on astonishment, Evan managed not to bare his fangs in a grin. Instead, he clapped him on a tense shoulder. "I need a scout."

Not every man born into mean circumstances realized there was more and longed for it. Niall did, but his world had little room for such things. He'd pushed it down as something of no matter, knowing he'd live and die at that croft. But it would churn in his gut like a poison.

On those surreptitious nighttime visits, Evan had sometimes come inside, blending in the shadows as vampires could do. He'd seen Niall make love to his wife, taste her everywhere. They explored each other in the uninhibited way only sexual innocents could. Nothing was considered taboo, but even so, Evan sensed the Scot holding back with her. He had a savage hunger for a rougher, more demanding sexual desire. During their wrestling match, Niall had recognized a match for his true needs. He had enough sorrow and fury to take pain, respond to it with rage, and release it through passion.

As Evan let his hand linger on Niall's shoulder, slide down his back, possessive desires dug into him like thorns. He wanted this one, and it had been a while since he'd wanted one for more than food.

However, vampires observed certain inviolate rules when it came to taking servants. This man wouldn't abandon his family, and Evan would respect that, help him if he could. As for the rest, he'd channel the fantasy into his canvases and move on.

Unless Fate decided it had different plans.

~

Meeting him was like that first kiss. A delicious energy sweeps through the muscles, makes the heart leap, brings to life a special kind of hunger where the mind isn't a part of it. You wonder when you'll next get to touch him that way again, and how quickly you can make it happen. But there were things that had to heal first. We had to get to know each other. We shared women during that time, but they were a buffer between us as well as a passing pleasure. Not kissing him, not claiming his body for my own, for all those years, was hellish.

Alanna nodded against Niall's chest, hearing his steady heartbeat. She'd been stroking her hand across the muscles of his stomach for a while now, tracing that silken arrow of hair that pointed to the groin area. She felt it beneath his shirt. His arm tightened around her again, but this time the movement was more deliberate. When Niall put his other hand over hers, he slid it down, making her wet her lips as she covered a cock experiencing the hardness men carried out of dreams. He pushed against her, like a man stretching the rest of his body after a good nap.

"Aye, that's nice," he murmured. "Nothing like pressing against a pretty lass's grip when waking. Though 'tis even nicer to press against her arse. Unless of course, she puts those fingers tae guid use."

"I've a better idea."

Evan was standing above them, with a glint in his gaze that suggested her two hours of "free time" were over. "Roll over, Niall. On your knees, over her."

When Niall met his gaze, she anticipated conflict between the two. Hoping to head it off, she wriggled to give Niall room to obey, tugging on his arm, showing her desire that he follow Evan's order and prop himself over her.

"Kiss her senseless, Niall. But stay on your hands and knees, your knuckles pressed into the ground on either side of her. Alanna, you can touch him however you desire."

"Evan, what the hell—" Niall grunted as Evan leaned over him, stripped the belt out of his pants, reaching under him to open them. With the familiarity of long practice, he reached in, gripped Niall's cock, making him groan. "You were having good dreams, *neshama*."

His other hand slipped into Niall's side pocket, coming out with the lubricant oil most male servants, especially those serving male vampires, carried with them, knowing the carnal nature of their Masters.

"Alanna?"

Her view was incomparable, seeing the vampire take hold of the rigid cock at close range. But at Evan's admonishment, she snapped out of her distraction to place her hands on Niall's strong face. Bringing him down to her, she pressed her lips to his. She'd been studying his mouth for an hour, so deep pleasure thrummed through her as she kissed him deep, teasing his mouth. Triumph surged when he growled against her lips. He took over, pressing her back to the ground, his elbows bending so he could devour her lips, tangle with her tongue.

Kiss her senseless was what Evan had said. Niall surpassed the challenge. Even without him touching her body, it was lifting up toward him, nipples tingling, sex dampening, muscles quivering as he seduced and plundered, so every nerve ending was attuned to his demand, surrendering to it.

He jerked, a groan vibrating against her lips. His body rocked forward against her double-handed grip on his T-shirt, her fingers digging into his sides. Evan was kneeling behind him, and had yanked Niall's trousers down out of his way.

She couldn't see Evan's cock, but when he thrust it into Niall's ass, she felt it all the way to her womb, her need intensifying as he put his hands on the Scot's hips and drove deep, making Niall groan again. Sharing the memory of their first meeting had obviously stirred their Master, giving him an urgent need.

The intensity in the two sets of gazes that met hers was enough to take her breath away. "Kiss him, Alanna," Evan ordered.

She was trying, but Niall was so overwhelming, she was just along for the ride. She ran her hands up his solid biceps, clutching as he teased her lips, bit her, moved to her throat to bite as Evan rammed into him. Being this close to the two males fucking was as primitive and mysterious an experience as watching that mountain lion in the wood.

Finding the hem of Niall's shirt, she raked it up so she could run her nails over his chest. Evan's thrusts were plowing Niall a little farther up her body, so she could close her hands on his bare cock, the wet tip trailing her stomach. When he came, he would come on her skin.

Following her desires, she pulled open her shirt. She arched to release the bra, flushing with sexual heat under Niall's avid gaze. He knew full well why she was doing it, and that shared knowledge just aroused her further. His facial muscles were tense, flexing with Evan's movement inside him, his lips tight against the desire.

Her legs were spread to make room for his knees. It wasn't practical, but she wished she'd worn one of her skirts. In this position, it was likely he would drive into her if given that opportunity and . . .

No. I want to see you soak the crotch of your jeans just from watching us. Your scent is intoxicating, Alanna.

"Bastard," Niall muttered. Evan chuckled maliciously, giving him a harder thrust.

"Your own fault, *neshama*. You woke needing to be fucked."

Alanna reared up, took Niall's mouth again. She wanted him to know how wet they were both making her. When Niall groaned and kissed her back in his overwhelming way, she raked her fingers over his chest again, then up his rib cage, over his sides, to his back. Evan's hands overlapped hers, capturing her there, holding her tangled fingers with one hand as he braced himself against Niall's buttock with the other.

Niall was grunting with each thrust, and his cock was pushing against her belly. Yet the movement of his mouth over hers held her prisoner as much as Evan restraining her hands. Her pussy was throbbing, hungry for attention, but she put everything into the kiss, as her Master had required.

With a snarl, Niall came, jerking against Evan's hold, his heated seed spraying across her stomach, her breasts, her throat. She quivered from it, continued to kiss him long and deep as he groaned into her mouth, muttered expletives. He kept kissing her back, though, with passionate ferocity. Evan came right then as well, and she opened her eyes to see the concentration of his face, the dangerous light in his eyes, the gleam of his fangs.

She was quivering, needy. It was one of the most erotic things she'd ever experienced, despite a long list of far more elaborate sexual scenarios. Even though they hadn't fucked her, she was shaky from head to toe. When Niall put his face against her neck, breathing hard, she shuddered. It seemed natural to put an arm around his shoulders. To reach up toward Evan. He captured her hand, his chest rising and falling with deep breaths as he bent his head to her palm and kissed it.

When his lips passed over her InhServ tattoo, on the soft skin under her forearm, she quivered anew. With his second mark, the InhServs' cut had healed, leaving only the sign of her service there, caressed by his mouth.

"It's time to return to the cabin," Evan said at last, stroking his other hand down Niall's back. "You'll sleep with us, Alanna. And dream good dreams, because Niall and I are here. We'll be around you."

∼

On the way back to the cabin, she told Evan about the correspondence. "You were invited to a wedding, scheduled for next week."

"Did you RSVP?" Evan directed the question to Niall, who'd been quiet since they left the clearing.

"Aye. I kept the invitation so we'd have the details."

"You should mark the invitation," Alanna said primly. "That way there's no confusion about what's been handled."

Evan shot Niall a look. "Sounds like you've been replaced as my secretary."

"Thank the gods."

"No, I didn't mean it that way. I was just—"

She stopped when Niall bumped her hip in affectionate amusement. Evan was pleased to see she was learning. Pressing her lips together, she shook her head. "Are you attending the wedding?"

"Yes." Niall answered for them both. "So are you. If you're still . . . Unless they've resolved things and reassigned you."

Niall fell silent again. Alanna gave him a peculiar look, but little else was said. When they arrived in their cabin clearing, Evan put his pack on the picnic table. He studied his servant's brooding profile as the Scot did his usual check of the grounds to ensure the precautions, like the shotgun, were still in place.

Alanna intercepted Niall, retrieving the empty picnic basket he'd insisted on carrying down the mountain. "You don't have to spare my feelings, Niall. I know what will happen when the Council kills Stephen." Clearing her throat, she added, "Though I want them to achieve their objectives, I hope the wedding happens before then. I've never been to one."

Carrying their empty picnic basket, she disappeared inside. Niall stared after her.

"Does it even matter to her?"

"Of course it does." Evan sighed. "She's been trained to accept a vampire's will without question. Her life can be taken for no other reason than her Master desires it so, and she accepts that."

"Bollocks," Niall snapped. "She's afraid. I can feel it, every time she lets herself feel."

So could Evan. He knew it fought to take hold of her every waking moment, but she wouldn't let it. "Her training ensures that every unpleasant emotion can be controlled. She treats her fear as an insult to her submission, her total acceptance that the Council dictates whether she lives or dies."

"And ye have no problem with that?" Niall gave him an incredulous look.

"Vampires are what vampires are, Niall." Evan set his jaw. "But training alone can't make a person stand fast on a battlefield where they know they'll be cut down. Honor and courage are required. Training only works if strength and integrity are already part of the mold."

Niall met his gaze. "This isn't about that."

"The way a man—or woman—sees the world, is all about who they are, Niall."

"She expected something different from her life. You made her admit it."

"Yes, but one admission won't change a lifetime of conditioning." Evan lifted a brow at Niall's sour expression. "First you criticize me for pulling her out of that shell. Now you're full of moral outrage over the shell itself. Make up your mind, Niall."

As the vampire turned toward the cabin, Niall stared at his unyielding back. Damn him. He was at the end of his life, and aye, he had a normal man's anxiety about what happened in the hereafter, but she'd barely had a life at all. *Twenty-nine years old. Bloody, fucking vampires.*

He wasn't ready to go into the house. He'd get a drink from the well, maybe chop some more wood. Instead, he pivoted and kicked the picnic table. The force of the blow was enough to flip it, and to bring Evan to a halt. Niall clenched his fists at the cool gray gaze that was judging, assessing. Waiting.

"She was a vampire's ideal little Barbie doll. The moment she was-nae, her mind and soul were torn apart, and every day is borrowed time. She's standing on the front lines like a lad at his first fight, only there's nae telling when the horn will blow to have it done with. She has to hold that fear inside her every moment. No one even gives a shit. It's all about catching Stephen."

"Not for me."

"No. She's the same as everything else you encounter in your life. She's a blank canvas." Niall sneered at him. "When it happens, will you capture it all on film?"

～

Niall didn't even see the blow coming. One moment he was facing the vampire, the next he'd been punched soundly, sending him rolling. Niall sprang back to his feet, a red haze across his vision. Throughout their lives together, Evan had inflicted pain for pleasure, because like all vampires, Evan enjoyed that. He'd even taught Niall to understand and embrace it. But he could count on one hand the times Evan had struck him down for crossing a line.

He was still vibrating from that hard fucking in the glade, the way it felt to be subjugated while over Alanna. She'd kissed him like she couldn't get enough, pulling him in, twisting things inside of him. The unfairness of it all filled him with fury. With a bellow, he charged.

Evan could have let him crash like a bull into the cabin wall, but he met the frontal assault, and they went down together. He was sure Evan was pulling punches, else he would have knocked his sternum into his spine. It pissed him off further, but he was in the mood for a fight, dirty or fair.

He landed several hard blows, which Evan returned, driving the wind out of him with a fist to the gut. Fuck, he could fight, he'd give him that. Before Evan had been a vampire, he'd been a skinny Jewish kid, and his father had taught him to defend himself. Just as Niall's da had taught him.

Did Evan remember what it was to be human? To feel all the futile weight of mortality? Niall roared and plowed into him again, taking him off his feet, but Evan somehow brought them to the ground again, hard.

A cold blast of water hit Niall square in the face, because he was on top, but Evan got the resulting waterfall in the same place, blinding and dousing both of them.

They broke apart in reaction. Christ, the water had to have come from the creek, because it was frigid enough to freeze his lungs. As one, they saw Alanna standing several paces away, holding the empty bucket. She was deathly pale.

At Evan's regard, she fell to her knees, bowing her head. She gripped the bucket like she couldn't let it go. "I'm sorry, Master. It seemed the only way to stop it."

Evan swiped the water from his brow, considering her. Niall couldn't read his expression, such that when the vampire stepped toward her, Niall tensed. However, Evan dropped to a knee, covering her clenched hands. "Alanna, it's not your place to stop an argument between me and my servant."

She nodded, keeping her head down, her nose almost touching his knuckles. "But you were fighting about me. My fate. I don't wish to cause anger between you. It's . . . upsetting to me." Lifting her face, she gave Evan an earnest searching look, then turned that expression toward Niall.

When she'd told him so calmly that she knew her time was limited, there'd been a flat deadness to her gaze. He expected she'd looked the same when she made the decision to betray her Master. She'd known there was no going back, that her fate was set. She was standing on the cusp of Hell, and the ground would give way under her feet in short order, plunging her into an eternity of torment, and the only way she could manage it was by feeling already dead.

That was not the expression she had now. She wasn't dead at all, so full of life it made everything in him hurt. He didn't know if he believed the idea that a servant followed her Master into the afterlife, but, as he'd told Evan, at one time he hadn't believed in vampires. He could say he didn't know how she dealt with the possibility that she might spend eternity with the Master she'd betrayed, but he was watching her do it, every day. With grace and strength, as Evan had said—and nightmares that plagued her dreams.

"You've been with each other so long," she continued. "I am so honored, so grateful to have the chance to see . . . to be a part of what you have with your Master, no matter how long my time here lasts. Please don't fight about who or what I am."

Niall stared at her, unable to summon any words. Evan touched her face. "Go inside," he said quietly.

Nodding, she rose. She left the bucket. Evan straightened, watching her disappear back in the cabin. He had his back to Niall. His shirt had been torn, and there was a trickle of blood below his left ear, diluted by the water so it stained the collar. When Evan turned at last, the gray eyes swept over Niall, his own dripping hair, the tense lines of his body.

"You still look fair scunnered, *neshama*. But I don't think her nerves will take another round."

Evan knew a great many languages, and could pull off a Scottish accent passably well, as he proved now, with a faint smile that didn't reach his eyes. "I know you're frustrated about the girl's situation. But stewing about injustices that result in the astonishing conclusion that life isn't fair is pointless." He lifted a shoulder. "As for the rest, you know certain things about me, Niall. If a man doesn't accept a wheel is round, then it does no good for me to tell him it is. He must come to the obvious truth himself."

The vampire closed the gap between them once more, placed a hand on his shoulder. "But I will tell you what you need to hear. She matters to me. As do you."

A quick thread of his fingers through Niall's wet hair, then Evan was gone, likely headed for the bowels of the house. A good thing, since the sun would be showing its dawn rays over the mountain's edge far too soon.

"Fair scunnered." Niall snorted to himself, shook his head. As vampires went, Evan had more compassion than most. Niall could usually pick up the vampire's moods, but there was a different dynamic with Alanna in the mix. Harder to pin down. Of course, he was honest enough to admit that could have as much to do with where he was at this point as the vampire's own state of mind.

He didn't know what it all meant, but he only had the choice Evan had given him, to wait it out.

As always.

~

Since they'd been derailed by their argument, Alanna didn't have the opportunity to sleep between the two males as Evan had intimated would happen. Her body was aching to be used after watching Evan take his servant right over her body, and letting Niall spend his seed on her flesh. If she closed her eyes, she could feel the heat of their lust wash over her again, the short gusts of Niall's breath against her collarbone as Evan thrust into him.

She was sitting on the edge of her bed, reconciling herself to taking a short nap alone, when Niall appeared in the doorway. He had a towel and was drying his hair, a reminder of her unthinkable transgression. Yet she would have done it again. She couldn't bear them fighting about something as irrelevant as her situation, even if it brought punishment on her.

"If you're nae too tired, we're going to Asheville." At her blank look, he added, "You'll need something to wear to the wedding, aye? Evan and I keep things stored that can be shipped to us, but we have no reserves of women's clothing." He shot her a faint smile. "Evan's never tried to dress me in women's clothing, or had the urge himself, thank God. Him in a bra and heels is an image I wouldnae want burned in my brain."

She blinked. "Are there cross-dressing vampires?"

"I met one in Amsterdam. When he shaved his legs and wore fishnets, he could compete with any starlet I've seen. Decent lad. His female servant was a professional wrestler. Six feet tall and the most bonny head of red hair you'd ever see. Damn near beat me in a caber toss."

"Do I have time to get a shower?" She almost wished he'd say no, because she liked his scent on her skin. When his gaze slid down her throat, over the modest cleavage exposed by her cotton shirt, she knew he was thinking along the same lines. As a third-mark servant, he could smell himself on her even more vividly than she could.

"Aye," he said. "Take off the clothes, *muirnín*. All of them."

She swallowed at the heated command in his voice. Her body needed no awakening, but apparently his own had recovered quickly. Standing, she removed the shirt, let it fall. Unhooked the bra and watched his eyes flicker with lust over her bared breasts, the nipples already tight peaks under his gaze. When she toed off her shoes and removed the trousers and underwear, he was two steps closer. She held her breath as he closed the gap, brushing his fingers over her arm, her waist, her upper thigh, and then she caught hold of his arm for balance as he stroked her clit, her wet labia.

"You're hurting for it, aren't you, *muirnín*? Selfish bastards, we did-nae do a thing for ye. Evan says for me to take care of that."

It might be true or not, but she didn't want the risk of asking Evan herself. She wanted to be touched, to be held and filled, hard, the way Evan had filled Niall. She was already trembling when Niall opened his trousers, releasing his cock, full and thick. Catching her around the waist, he lifted her onto him with effortless strength, standing in the middle of her bedroom, one hand palming her ass, the other snarled in her hair as he lowered her onto his erect cock, filling her inch by blissful inch. She was already spasming around him when he reached the hilt. As he lowered them both to the bed, him over her, she clasped her legs around his hips, not wanting to let go of him until this scald-ing need eased.

"There you are, lass. You're such an eager wee thing." He shoved himself deeper, and she made a soft cry that pleased him, for his eyes flamed hotter, and he did it again. "Hold on tae me now. I want to take ye to climax so fast you'll feel ye stepped on a roller coaster."

Fast or slow, she wanted this. Wrapping her arms around his shoul-ders, she buried her face into his chest and bit down on his flesh as his hips pistoned between her legs. Slow then fast, then slow again, mak-ing her work her hips against him in response.

"Please . . ." She whispered it against his flesh, tasting him. He lifted up enough to push her down flat on the bed, hold her there with a hand on her throat, his other hand tracing the dried tracks of his come over her breasts, her abdomen. She kept her legs clasped tight around him, her inner muscles milking him, begging him to move again, because watching him touch her like that, idle tracings of his seed, his cock still and full inside her, broke her into pieces.

"Shhh. Be still, *muirnín*. Feel how hard you make me. I loved mark-ing you." Then his fingers brushed her hip and something cold touched her heart. No, she didn't want that to intrude on this moment. She put her hand over his, but he made a reproving noise.

"Arms above your heid. No interference with what I do to ye."

She didn't want to interfere, but Niall was studying the third mark she carried as Stephen's servant. "Please . . ." She didn't want him to say anything. At the time she'd received it, she thought it was evidence of what she would do for her vampire Master. Take her own life if needed, a mockery now. But the mark was shaped like a dagger, the universal sign of betrayal.

Niall said nothing further. He slid his arm back under her waist, moved them up the bed, which changed the angle of his penetration, making her whimper with pleasure. He'd told her to keep her arms above her head, but when she reached for his face, he didn't stop her. She traced his jaw, his brow, lingering on his nose and mouth. She didn't get to touch many of those who'd touched her. Not this way. Not with the time to consider what emotions might be passing behind his brown eyes, the words held back behind the firm lips.

"If I could save ye a moment of pain, lass, I would. We both would. We'd fight dragons for ye."

It made things hurt inside of her, so badly she couldn't speak. She was afraid of what might happen to her when Stephen died, but she hadn't anticipated having something she might regret leaving. Someone. Letting her hand drift to his shoulder, she drew close to him once more, burying her face in his neck. He could make her lie back, look at him, but instead he increased the constriction of his arms around her, cradling her like a child while he stayed deep inside her, caring for her with his compassionate silence, the demands of his body, nurturing the emotional and physical both.

"I want you to come for me, lass," he whispered in her ear. "I want tae hear you cry out. Let our Master hear your pleasure."

He started moving once more, and this time she caught on fire within only a few strokes, as if by words alone he'd brought her to that pinnacle.

Come for us, Alanna.

Evan's voice, and all she needed. The two of them around her, even if it wasn't in the same room. They were both in her mind as the cleansing fire swept through, carrying her with it. She moaned against Niall's flesh as he thrust deep. Curving his powerful back, he latched onto her nipple and suckled it, drawing out the orgasm in an excruciating roll of pleasure that kept on and on as he worked his hips against her, her body arched up into his, wanting to fuse every inch of her flesh against his.

"Sweet lass," he muttered against her. His hips pushed her legs wider, and she drummed her heels on his tight backside, in rhythm with his thrusts, her nails digging into his shoulders, drawing blood.

He rolled them then, putting her on top. He stayed in charge, controlling her descent, his gaze latched onto the quiver of her breasts with each solid downward impact. She was riding his aftershocks, but he wasn't done. She clenched on him, dropping her head back, crying out with pleasure when he reached up, caught her throat to hold her upper body straight. It made her feel owned, possessed, the mere thought sending her over another pinnacle. One that became even more intense when he released himself, jetting hot seed into her welcome heat.

～

In the aftermath, as she sprawled over him, he brushed a kiss over her forehead. "Now ye can take that shower. But we leave in the next half hour, so no lingering over female nonsense."

The teasing smugness in his voice made her think about getting onto her knees and whacking him with the pillow. Then he added, "You'd be lovely if I took you tae town just as you are. Though I'd much prefer to stay here and do this all the day."

She wanted to stay here, too, just like this, for the next decade. However, the past few minutes were gift enough. She couldn't ask for more, nor should she. As she slipped from the bed, she sensed his gaze on her. He rolled out the other side, zipping the pants only enough to hold them on his hips. "If we had a larger shower, you wouldnae be getting away from me so soon. I'll take the outside spigot."

"Oh." She bit her lip, realizing she should offer to take the colder outside water, but instead she yelped as Niall's shirt landed over her head, where he'd tossed it. By the time she removed it, he was striding down the hallway. She watched the play of the dragon on his back and the way those pants, low enough on his hips to show the upper rise of his buttocks, drew the eye to their movements. Then he disappeared out of view.

If she had three marks, she could have showed that view to Evan. She was sure he would have appreciated it as much as she did. Artistically, of course. She imagined taking that shower with Niall, her skin flushed anew. He'd pleasured her, but she was nowhere near sated. They'd unleashed a hungry monster inside her, and she wasn't sure if she should thank or curse them for that.

With her fingers digging into the soft stuff of Niall's shirt, she lifted it to her face, brushed it against her cheek. He'd let her sleep on his body in the glade, held her. Then he'd been so angry, arguing with Evan about her. That part had felt so horribly wrong, and not just because of her worry about them. All the terrible things she was having to contain, the worry and fear, the guilt and failure, could be cracked open so easily by such stress.

When she looked up, he'd returned, was studying her. She still had the shirt up to her face, making it obvious what she was doing. She lowered it, discomfited. "I'm hurrying. I was just—"

He shook his head, crooked a finger at her. She came to him, still holding the shirt against her. Putting his hand to her waist, he brought her full against him. He kissed her, long and slow. She made a noise in the back of her throat and stretched up on her toes, reaching for more of him. Sexual energy stirred, but something else, too. Her chest was tight as her arms circled his neck, fingers curling there, tangling in his long hair. His hand roamed downward, over her buttock, stroking, slow and easy. Soothing.

When he lifted his head, he was holding her weight with his solid strength. He squeezed her buttock. "*Aw richt*, then?"

The warm affection in his tone helped ease some things. She nodded. "I was fine. Am fine."

"Okay." He brushed her lips with his again. "Go get ready, then. We're behind schedule."

~

Though she hurried, he checked on her a couple of times while she was doing her hair. Apparently, Evan had also given him additional things for their "town list," and since it was obvious going into the city wasn't Niall's favorite thing, her bear became more gruff and impatient.

She expedited hair and face preparations, not wanting to cause him further delays. It was a good decision, because as soon as she emerged in the main room, he had her out the door and bundled into the Rover. When she hesitated with her foot on the runner, looking back at the house, Niall touched her shoulder.

"Don't worry, he'll be fine. He always is." That touch of acid suggested their fight was preying on his mind again. It had been frightening to watch, like savage dogs, but she understood men could be like that. Niall discouraged any conversation about it, however, maintaining an otherwise companionable silence with her until they reached the main highway.

He nodded to the console. "You can play some music if you want."

She chose a playlist titled "Niall's Theme Songs." When it started with the powerful drum and guitar notes of "Eye of the Tiger" by Survivor, Niall gave it a disgusted look, hit the button to take it to the next selection, a more general rock tune. "Wiseass vampire. Oh, Evan wants ye to choose things for your daily two-hour deal. Skateboarding, macramé, beading, cookbooks, whatever."

"I think you added the last one," she said. "You want me to cook more."

"Aye. Your cooking is far better than mine. Evan agrees."

She smiled. "Do we have time to buy groceries? No offense to Henry, but there are things I can get in a city that he might not have."

"We have time for that," Niall decided. He shot her a teasing glance. "So what else are ye going to get? More romance stories?"

"Maybe a good spy thriller," she said evenly.

"Pity," he said. "I liked how the romance stirred ye up." Reaching over, he stroked her hair away from her brow, passing his fingers through the ponytail she'd done so hastily. She leaned into the touch, quietly thrilled with such affection. When he took his hand away to adjust the music volume, she studied him. He had one knee comfortably propped against the driver's door, an attractive look in his jeans, a button-down shirt loose over them, casual clothes that accentuated a body and presence that would catch any woman's eye.

"So do you think about it?"

"What?" He changed lanes, moving smoothly around a slower car.

"When you . . . You're three hundred years old."

He cocked a brow. "You're terrible at small talk, lass. 'So, lad, have ye been thinking about your impending death?'"

She was torn between a smile at the exaggeration of his accent and her chagrin at the truth of it. "If you don't want to talk about it—"

"Hmmph. Doesnae matter much, does it? It can happen anytime after the three-hundred-year line. Somewhere between one to three years for most, but some have lived tae see three-ten." He shrugged. "Not much different from any other day with a vampire. It's not the safest way to live your life, aye? Especially with Evan. He gets through other vampires' territories on his charm and Lord Uthe's sponsor letter, but plenty places are less respectful of that. He also takes plenty of risks for his camera shots. He'll be barbecued one day, trying to get in that one extra moment, and that'll be the end of me, right alongside him."

"I've never known a vampire like him," she admitted. "Or a servant like you. Who was he, before he was turned? If it's not inappropriate to ask."

"Not inappropriate to me." He flashed teeth at her. "We're all servants here, ma'am. He was an artist then as well. Showed a remarkable aptitude for it even as a wee lad, a child prodigy. He's a Sephardic Jew, born in Italy. His da was a merchant and would ha' had no patience for it, except Evan was bedridden most his life. They called it a wasting disease back then, nothing the doctors could do with it. The family business fell to the second son, because they didnae expect Evan to live. It went into remission for a few years, giving him a chance to travel about, but it came back with a vengeance by the time he turned twenty. He was dying when Lord Uthe discovered him. He'd stumbled on a few pictures Evan had sold, and tracked him down. When he found out Evan was near the end, he offered him immortality."

She'd heard the various stories of made vampires, but she'd never heard anything as remarkable as that. She thought of how Evan could be so patient, remain so still. How he saw miracles in the most minute details. It was easy to imagine that skill being cultivated by an invalid child whose only changing landscape would have been through a bedroom window.

The Council was required to approve all turnings, but four hundred years ago, they hadn't been in existence. Lord Uthe had acted on his own desires, which she found intriguing. The formidable right-hand member of the Council was an austere born vampire who'd served as a Knight Templar, a remarkable thing itself.

"I never realized Lord Uthe was a patron of the arts."

Niall gave her a wry look. "He told Evan he wanted to see what a truly gifted artist would do with immortality. Ye know vampires are eternally curious about things like that, like little gods. He wanted to know whether mortality, the sense of the finite, gives an artist his talent, or if immortality would take it tae heretofore unknown heights."

She digested that. "Perhaps it's wrong of me to ask this, but . . . Evan. He doesn't seem as strong as most vampires his age. Regarding the sunlight, I mean. Did his childhood disease somehow cause that?"

"Aye." Niall took his time expanding on the answer, giving Alanna the sense that it was a question that preyed on the servant's mind as well. "Uthe had Brian take a look at Evan a couple decades ago, when Brian first got their attention with his research. That's how Evan knows him. They've stayed in contact, became friends. Evan respects Brian's field."

"It makes sense," she observed. "His focus is different from that of most vampires, much like Evan's."

Niall inclined his head. "Brian thinks Evan's mortal wasting disease, how close he was to death at turning, affected him. The abilities that grow with a vampire's age mature slower for him. His sensitivity to sun is like a hundred-year-old vampire's. Same with speed, agility, the whole package. Since a vampire can sense the strength of another vampire and estimates his age based on it, Evan's often taken for far younger than he is."

Alanna now fully understood Niall's concerns about the risks their Master took, but he gave her a reassuring look, a wink. "He's far stronger than us humans, of course, but in the vampire world, he's the gym class runt."

At her disparaging look, he held up a hand. "That's his description, not mine."

"And yet he travels across territories where he might run afoul of vampires far stronger than him."

"What he lacks in strength, he makes up for in intelligence, diplomacy. Sheer cleverness. He's also got a hell of a poker face. Not much rattles him. Even when things should," he added darkly.

"You worry for him, but he's brave." She considered it. "Most vampires don't have to be brave. They follow the political path, fall in line with the hierarchy, and rely on their age and strength to make their way."

"That's not his focus."

"You admire it," she realized. "Even as his motives elude your understanding at times. To a brilliant man, the complex is obvious, leaving the rest of us searching for answers."

"Didnae swell his head too much. He's aggravating enough already." Niall switched gears on her. "Is psychotherapy part of the whole InhServ training?"

"Somewhat, yes. I'm supposed to anticipate my Master's needs, understand those around him, anticipate their moves and feelings as well."

He sighed. "Can ye turn it off awhile and be a lass all aflutter about dress shopping?"

Alanna had no clue what such a person would act like, but she nodded demurely. When he reached over and squeezed her knee at the ticklish point, making her jump and pull away, he winked at her. In retaliation, she took the playlist back to "Eye of the Tiger" and fended off his attempts to change it. His pokes at her side to tickle her and get the player controls away from her had her laughing in no time.

She'd hit a few raw nerves, but seeing the grin that covered his handsome features and stayed there, the earlier shadows driven away, proved that his playing with her successfully turned his thoughts to a better place.

It gave her a sense of satisfaction, the feeling that she'd served both Master and servant well. For the moment, that was enough.

13

*O*H, *damn it.* The sudden surge of panic was an unwelcome disruption. For the last forty-five minutes they'd listened to music and enjoyed casual conversation, the city skyline of Asheville rising before them as they descended from the mountains.

However, now she remembered. Due to all the new experiences the day had brought, as well as Niall's impatience to get going, she'd forgotten to bring the blocker, and she was due for it. She cringed inwardly, recalling Lord Brian's stern admonishment. *Never forget to take it at the proscribed time.*

Damn it, damn it, damn it.

They had a full to-do list. If it was only about her dress, she might say something, but they had a list of items for Evan. She was not going to inconvenience her Master by making this a wasted trip. It would be okay. There had to be some residual effect from one blocker to another. She'd manage.

She turned her attention to the passing scenery. The garish tourist traps were of particular interest, with everything from chain saw-carved wooden black bears—similar but not as well-done as Henry's—to dream catchers fluttering in the wind, feathers dyed in bright colors.

"Okay?" Niall's hand was on her shoulder. He'd picked up on her worry. Since it was noon, Evan would be well asleep, but he'd likely deduced it on his own. The Scot was quite intuitive.

"Fine. Just . . . I like the quiet at our cabin."

Our came out without thought. Home was wherever her vampire Master was, but she realized that it felt like home to *her*. Despite her uncertainty of how best to serve Evan and Niall, the short span of her time with them, she realized she'd embraced the peace and quiet pace of their existence like a drowning swimmer reaching land. A sanctuary.

Brushing his knuckles over her cheek, Niall turned into the parking lot of a camera shop. "I do, too. I expect serious sexual compensation for the sacrifice o' taking ye to a mall, *muirnín*."

"But I didn't ask you to take me," she pointed out.

"I'll still expect payment."

When she imagined what type of payment she could give him, a warmth expanded in her lower vitals, helping to dispel the tension about the blocker. It was going to be okay.

Niall let her trail after him in the camera shop, though they weren't there long, since the shop already had the items Niall had ordered on a previous trip. The next stop was unexpected. It was a lingerie store, with a variety of fetish offerings discreetly offered in the back. Once again, Niall picked up a boxed package. He held the door for her, taking her back outside the shop before he explained.

"Evan anticipated ye going to the wedding with us, so he had me order a couple things several weeks ago for the postwedding celebration. Nope." When she reached for it, he held it over his head. "Ye cannae open it yet. I'll want to see ye in it, and then we'll be arrested for what I'll do to ye, right here."

She eyed the package as he set it in the back. "What kind of postwedding celebration requires something like that?"

"The wedding hosts are a Master and Mistress. There's a private party the night after the wedding for guests who like bondage play."

Her jaw dropped. "You and Evan . . . play with humans?"

"A vampire and servant blend in that environment, no? And dinnae worry, 'tis easy compared to vampire dinners. They believe in rules, pain thresholds, boundaries. All that silly stuff," he added with a wink.

He parked them outside the mall. When he helped her out of the car, something he insisted on doing, he retained her hand. "Your fingers are cold, *muirnín*." He tucked them under his arm. "Ye should have brought a sweater. I should have brought one for ye."

"You're not required to take care of me," she reminded him. "I'm fine."

He opened the door for an elderly woman in a wheelchair, being pushed by a friend, and nodded courteously to them. Then he gestured to the tent provided by his arm, indicating Alanna should precede him. "I'm not going through a door in front o' a woman unless a threat's waiting on her," he said when she hesitated. "And in a women's clothing store, I'm far more worried about my well-being than yours."

He was irreverent and irrepressible. She liked that about him, very much. Especially when, as she moved under his arm, a high enough arch she didn't even have to duck her head, he caught her waist to stop her, bent and kissed her throat, an incredibly intimate caress, his fingers tight on her hip.

"It *is* my job to care for ye, lass. In every way."

Her insides dissolved at the heat in his eyes, his voice. She had to stay in place for a blink of time, a little dizzy from it. She'd gripped his side without realizing it, and he gave her a brief, firm embrace before nudging her gently into the store, discreetly squeezing her backside.

"So the wedding and proper reception are an evening thing, more formal, but also outdoors, on a Southern plantation. Should be warm, even with it being fall. I'm thinking the less fabric the better." He gave her a wink.

"Of course," she said dryly. She fingered a garish, colorful muumuu. "Nothing absorbs perspiration like a serviceable cotton."

"You're killin' me, lass. Killin' my fantasies, right here."

She nudged him with her hip, and he bumped her back. "So what would my Master prefer?"

"Whatever ye like. Pick some other things as well. After the wedding, we're going tae an art colony. It's not hiking terrain, so ye can wear skirts and such. They have a lake, so I'*d* prefer a bikini."

"I don't want to hurt your feelings, but you'd look ridiculous in one." She wasn't used to teasing others, but he tended to be infectious, especially when she was rewarded with a broad grin.

"Evan can buy whatever ye like, as long as you aren't the type of lass needing five-hundred-dollar shoes. Lyssa also gave him some funds for your care, but he willnae use those."

"Why not?"

He gave her a level glance. "Because you're ours to care for, lass. Evan may not always seem like it, but he has as much of a man's sensibilities as any of those 'lord' vampires ye know."

Actually more so, to her way of thinking. She turned her attention to the rounders of clothes, all the more determined to find things Evan would enjoy seeing her wear. Niall as well.

She was an efficient shopper. In fifteen minutes, she'd found several suitable things to try on. Niall had wandered over to the nearby lingerie area, where he was studying a wall of mannequins in an array of lacy bras and panties. Despite the selection being far more tame than the fetish store, he seemed just as fascinated. With his hands tucked in his back pockets and rocking back and forth on his booted heels, he was amusing and captivating passing female shoppers and store clerks.

Coming over to him, she shot him a look of mild reproof. "It's a good thing you're handsome. Otherwise, they'd call security to remove the creepy man from the women's underwear section."

"I'm happy ye find me easy on the eyes, *muirnín*." He gave her another wink, then studied her choices. His silent inspection made her feel uncomfortable, as did the look he raised to her face.

"You're doin' it again," he said. "Evan wants ye to pick out things *you* like. Consider this your two hours, aye?"

She didn't *want* to wear things that Evan and Niall didn't like, so why couldn't she pick the things she was sure they would? Evan wanted her to express her desires, because he said it increased their pleasure with her. Why couldn't that work in the opposite direction? Even though he'd been teasing, of course Niall would prefer her to wear a string bikini. Imagining the way he'd look at her when she wore it heated her from head to toe.

That hard knot moved up under her ribs. The store seemed overly warm. She ran a hand under her hair, lifted it. She was now nervous and out of sorts, almost teary. Why couldn't they let her be who she was, instead of trying to make her into something different?

Because you aren't a true servant. You're a failure. You don't know what you are . . . lost little girl . . .

She'd moved away from Niall, was at the store's interior opening to the rest of the mall. Crowds of people moved like ocean waves, crashing into shore. She shrank to the wall, a secluded corner formed by the display mannequin. She envied the doll its mindless stoicism.

Niall was still with her. He put his hands on her arms. "It's okay, lass. Easy."

"No, it's *not* easy. I can't do this." She didn't want to sound angry or frustrated. That wasn't her. But she wanted to push away, she wanted to run, and she never ran from anything. In reaction, she sank down to the floor, a defensive, folded position, her knees under her chin, fingers linked on them. It made her smaller, more walled-up, less noticeable. She needed to breathe.

"Aye, you can. Ye can do anything." He squatted on his haunches before her, shielding her from curious eyes with his wide shoulders. She never caused public scenes. She stared at his knees.

"Help me, Niall. Help me make sense of it."

He paused. She focused on the rise and fall of his chest, tried to let the steady rhythm restore the same to her.

"If ye truly ken there's a difference between wantin' to do it because ye feel obligated, and doing it because pleasing him pleases *you*, then that's different. Don't ye think?"

She lifted her eyes to his face. "Is this what Evan called cheating?"

He lifted a broad shoulder, his lips quirking. "Not so much, because you're the more honest of the two o' us. Ye'll decide if what I say is true or not. Ye like him, no?"

"I don't . . . liking or not liking him makes no difference to a servant's actions."

"Perhaps it does in this case. Ye like him. You're thinking o' what he'd enjoy seeing ye wear, and that makes you feel guid, makes you anticipate what he might like. He'd be fine with that. Long as the feeling's true."

Maybe her reaction had alarmed him, such that he was merely soothing her, but his words did make sense. "It is. I do . . . like him. Is that how you do it . . . how you make choices? Do you dress for his pleasure?"

"Aye. My platform heels and baby-doll nightgown drive him insane with lust."

She tried to cover her startled laugh, but he took her fingers away, held both her hands.

"'Tis just shopping, lass. Picking out a frock. Let's get on with it, aye? A lad loses a pint of testosterone for every minute he's in a woman's clothing store. If we dinnae go soon, I'll be eyeing the purses and stockings."

Nodding, she let him help her to her feet. He plucked the first dress she'd chosen from her hands. "Why did ye think he'd like this one?"

"The splashes of color on the skirt are like marks from a paintbrush, so the flared hem will set them off well when I move. The pattern on the bodice is from a Monet print." She gave him a small smile. "And the neckline will show cleavage."

"Sounds bonny, but this one will show off even more of everything." He plucked a leopard-skin print tube dress off a rack. The short skirt had a hip-high slit in the side. "With these earrings." From a display on top of the rounder he unhooked a pair of large orange plastic ones, shaped like stars.

"You are teasing me." She elbowed him in the hard stomach, made him put the dress back.

"I'll go into the dressing room and watch you put it on."

She arched a brow. "What if Master commanded you to go into the dressing room with me, but you were only allowed to sit in a chair and watch, not touch me? What would you say to that?"

First she'd teased him about the bikini, now this. She wasn't sure who'd taken over her mouth, but she knew who took over her senses in the next second when his tawny gaze kindled. He leaned down, his lips nearly brushing hers, and she stopped breathing, except for the necessary pleasure of inhaling him.

"I'd say 'Master' isnae around to stop me from doing whatever I like. I'll gladly take his punishment later." His arm around her waist, he drew her to him, putting his lips back to that same spot on her throat, nose pushing aside her ponytail so he could tease her with his tongue, tracing her collarbone. He dropped his touch, taking a firm grip of her ass to press her against him. He was hardening under his jeans. Even without Evan providing the conduit, she could visualize what Niall wanted to do to her in the dressing room.

"We're in a public place," she whispered, clutching his upper arms. If it was Evan, she would provide no resistance regardless, but the few functioning brain cells she had left told her Evan might not be overly pleased to have to get them out of jail.

"I'd fuck you right here, to make it clear you're taken property."

Despite her best efforts at decorum, the weight of his desire swept her away, and not just his alone. *You're ours.* He'd said that, and she felt it now, a sense of duality that she wasn't sure he even realized was part of his personality, so closely connected to the vampire's. He'd fuck her for himself, but also for Evan, staking his claim right alongside his own. Was it because even in his dreams, Evan registered a moment like this and made his presence felt in his servant's mind, such that Niall's subconscious and Evan's were almost one and the same?

Niall's aggressiveness made her feel . . . powerful. Sexy and desirable as well, and not just because she was groomed to be that way. It was how *they* made her feel, not her endless supply of beauty products and stringent exercise regimen. Was that what Evan had been trying to tell her?

Together they were teaching her to express passion in a way she'd never experienced before. Unsettled, she extricated herself from Niall to gather up the dress and her several other choices—but not the leopard print. When she hurried toward the dressing room, Niall was sauntering after her, casual as a stalking tiger. She would have discounted it as more of his sexual teasing, except she noticed the flick of his glance between her path and those of others in the store. She disappeared into the fitting area but then, thinking about it, came back out. Niall was leaning against the wall, waiting on her.

"Problem?" he asked.

She shook her head. "Am I in any danger here? Or are you are worried about me doing something I shouldn't?"

"You're not capable of doing something you shouldnae." The corner of his mouth quirked. "Just best for me to keep ye in sight. We want to keep ye safe, *muirnín.*"

She thought of last night, of how they'd showed their understanding of the demons she fought. Niall knew he couldn't protect her from those fears, but with his steady tawny gaze and the weight he gave to the last words, he was telling her he'd protect her from everything he could.

She'd been Stephen's possession. Any protection he'd offered her had been about that, not about her. On its face, it sounded the same. But Stephen had never given thought to her safety, just her preservation for his needs. She'd understood that, accepted it. Even so, she had a perverse desire to put her arms around Niall and squeeze him as tightly as her heart was being squeezed.

Hastily, she withdrew before she embarrassed herself.

There were several women in the dressing area. She could hear the rustle of clothing being removed or adjusted. One had a friend with her, because they were comfortably chatting behind the louver doors. Sliding into an empty stall with pale pink walls and a velvet bench, she hung up the dresses and pulled off her top, toeing off her shoes to remove her jeans.

Since it was her first choice, she tried on the paint splash dress first. Though it fit, she could see where she could make it better, altering the upper body fit with her seamstress skills so the off-the-rack dress was more suited to her figure and more pleasing to her Master and Niall. When she was done, Niall wouldn't miss the leopard-print dress.

Executing a spin, she confirmed the expansive hem flowed the way she'd expected. She'd need some accessories, but department stores were always having discount sales on such items. She'd find something suitable that would minimize the time Niall had to endure female shopping. The thought gave her a small smile. She'd smiled more these past few days than she had in thirteen years.

The cramp hit her so abruptly her forehead hit the mirror when she doubled over, cracking it. Putting the heel of her hand there in reflex, she crouched, counting her way through it. Breathe, *breathe*. When she'd been in the grip of such full-blown spasms, Debra had taught her ways to manage the pain. It didn't stop them, but it gave her a focus until it passed. Only it hadn't ever passed. Not until Brian figured out those injections.

The headache exploded, a battering ram against her brain. It was the symptom that indicated Stephen was back inside her mind. He could reach down into her soul, twist it . . .

She'd never resisted his invasions, never thought about having the strength to resist his ability to scramble or plumb her mind. Her lack of resistance was her penance for betrayal. Now, though, battling to think through the pain, she thought if she could stay clear, hold the line long enough between them, Daegan would get a better grip on where he was.

Evan had forbidden her to do that. No, he'd forbidden her to not take the injections. She'd forgotten purely by accident, so this was different.

Women rationalize . . . She choked on a despairing sob. She was remembering his voice, not hearing it, because he would not be strong enough to override Stephen's roar.

Think about shopping, the to-do list . . . But that would tell Stephen exactly where she was. She couldn't endanger Evan and Niall. He would kill them for sheltering her.

She was his possession. Not to keep safe, but to destroy.

She should have told Niall to take her back. She'd made a fatal error. The next cramp knocked her to the floor. She was gripping her head, certain her skull was about to split.

"Help . . . Niall."

He was already there. She'd woken Evan, she was certain. The wave of shame came with nausea. Niall held her as she jacked up from the floor, threw up into her own lap, into the beautiful silk skirt of the dress.

The thunder in her head drowned everything else out, but she was vaguely aware of Niall speaking to a half-dressed woman in bra and skirt, a matronly woman with steady eyes who knelt by Alanna when he rose. The press of his hand on her shoulder was gone too quickly.

She must have called his name, for the woman's response penetrated the fog. "It's all right, honey. He just went to get your medicine. I'm a nurse. It's all right."

He was going to drive to the cabin and back? *Lost little girl* . . . *Adam dead and gone* . . . *You should just kill yourself now. Save your Master the trouble.*

She froze. The idea that Evan would think such a thing hurt her deeply. But she wasn't supposed to feel emotional pain, unless that was what her Master wanted.

You said it yourself. You wished I'd killed you . . .

It wasn't Evan. She clung to that thought. If she concentrated hard enough, she could almost imagine she was hearing the artist, even as a far distant voice.

Kill yourself, kill yourself . . . *you know you deserve death. I command it.*

"Help . . ." She was gasping, back down on the floor, holding on to it as the world spun. She heard the woman saying they needed to call an ambulance, but Niall was telling her in a remarkably calm voice it would be all right, that she just needed this shot. He had the silver box of syringes. He'd brought a dose with him, planning for any eventuality. That was what a good servant did. She, on the other hand, had forgotten to take it.

The searing burn in her thigh was welcome, despite the pain. Usually she bit down on her tongue, rocked until the scalding fire subsided. Now she cried out, unable to contain it. The cramps and headache increased exponentially. The effect would last only seconds, but was intense enough to feel like an hour.

Stephen howled, then he was yanked out of her mind and sent away, like a cartoon character kicked and sent sailing over distant hills. Over those beautiful blue and gray mountains she saw out the front door of the cabin.

"She's fine. She just needs a few minutes. Water's splendid, aye. Chocolate if ye have some."

Niall had her cradled against his chest, was stroking her hair. As coherence returned, she looked down at the lovely colors, splashed with blood and her breakfast.

"Niall . . ." She couldn't believe how plaintive she sounded. Like a lost little girl, just as Stephen said.

"It's all right, *muirnín*. Why didnae ye say anything? Never mind, Evan told me. You didnae want to be a bother. Because *this* is so much more convenient. When you're back on your feet, I'm going to skelp your arse."

She made a noise of regret, and he muttered a curse, held her tighter. "'Tis all right. Not your fault. None of it."

Of course it was her fault. But she didn't have the strength to argue with him about it. As the pain ebbed, the shame intensified. He wouldn't let her dress herself. He buttoned her shirt, got her jeans started and had her hold on to him as she stood and he brought them all the way up, even managing the zipper and button.

"I'm all right," she said hoarsely. "It's okay. I can finish."

"You're the color of a snowbank, lass, and your hands are shaking. Let me help ye."

He couldn't imagine how much she hated those four words, but she was leaning against him, so she fell silent, stood in stolid misery while he finished. When he touched her face, she wouldn't lift it. He didn't push it, simply folding her into his body and holding her.

"It's all right, *muirnín*. You dinnae have to be fucking invincible."

She shook her head against his chest, but to deny or accept it as truth, she didn't know. "Please don't carry me. I want to walk out of the store."

"All right." He pushed her down on the velvet chair. "But only if ye stay right there. I'll go pay for things and come back for ye."

He pressed the chocolate bar and water the store manager had brought into her hands. As she gazed at them, he picked up the dresses. The damaged one had been tucked into a plastic store bag.

"I haven't tried on the others," she said. "So they should be put back. I'm sorry about the first one."

Niall had made it clear that Evan didn't waste money, and she herself had always been prudent with her Master's funds. It made her all the more ashamed.

"The leopard print is one-size-fits-all, if ye'd like to reconsider that one. Spandex 'tis God's miracle."

She grimaced wanly. "I'd go to the wedding in a bedsheet first."

"Ach, see? You thought you'd never be able to tell us what ye want for yourself." His eyes remained serious, though. "You in a bedsheet would be prettier than the prettiest bride, lass."

He held up one of the dresses, a silver gray fabric with a beaded diamond bodice and a fitted satin skirt that had a tight grouping of rosettes at the hem. "I'm buying this one. I like it, and I know Evan will. If it fits wrong, we'll return it on the way to the wedding."

"I can alter it."

"Aye? Guid. Because my dress slacks have a hole in the side seam. I held it together with duct tape on the inside last time I wore them."

Despite her condition, the thought of him attending a formal event with his pants held together with tape horrified her. He ran a finger down her cheek.

"Stay in that chair," he ordered again, and then disappeared.

Typical man. She had no shoes to wear with the gray. She doubted he or Evan had a pair of stilettos or strappy sandals lying about. The one helpful thing about being in a large household with other women was they could borrow from each other. The thought wasn't enough to make her miss them, though. Stephen's domestic servants would have turned on her, same as the InhServs had.

As was appropriate, she reminded herself. She didn't blame them, but it had hurt. The InhServs were a tightly knit corps, and she'd counted on that bond, even if she couldn't call her relationships within it friendships.

Nibbling on the chocolate helped, but the shaking in her hands and quaver in the pit of her stomach were going to take more than the blocker and the chocolate to dispel. They weren't related to the physical effects of Stephen's attack.

This is it. The thought had exploded in her mind with that first cramp. Stephen had been found, Daegan had staked him, and only a few minutes of her life remained.

Then she'd felt Stephen's presence and heard his voice. For the millisecond before the agony began, she'd been swamped by relief she wasn't about to die.

Though she did fear being chained to Stephen eternally, she'd accepted that as her sentence for what she'd done. But now, after being with Evan and Niall, she feared other things. She didn't want to leave them. As ludicrous as that sounded after a mere handful of days, it was the truth. Niall had even stated it baldly. From the first time both touched her in her delirium, Evan painting on her skin, Niall speaking those soothing words to her, she'd become theirs, taken into their care.

She'd picked up on enough of what the fight between Niall and Evan had been about that she knew Niall wanted the vampire to let her be whatever she wanted to be, since her time was so limited. Even so, the Scot exhorted her to choose the dress *she* wanted, following his Master's direction. That meant some part of him believed Evan was right, because Niall wasn't the type of man who did anything against his principles, whether vampire's servant or no.

Who are you, Alanna? She remembered Evan's question. Betraying Stephen had ripped her heart from her chest. She'd been paying for that choice ever since, but Evan had understood the deepest, most shameful truth about it. No one had asked her to say she was sorry for it and no one would. But if they did . . .

She wasn't sorry. Not now, not ever. Not through all eternity, chained to Stephen's soul.

Niall had returned. Setting the shopping bag down, he squatted in front of her, placing his hand on her knee. His touch was warm, strong. She was still disoriented, so she responded as trained. She parted her quivering knees for him, a female servant's instinctive response to a Master. His gaze heated, registering why she'd done it. *Serve Niall as you serve me.* It was as easy as breathing to her.

"Why did you ask for the chocolate?" she said, trying for a normal voice.

He ran his finger along the jagged line of the chocolate bar, the place where she'd bitten it. It transferred some of the sweet to his finger and he stroked it on her bottom lip. When she licked it off, she caught the pad of his finger at the same time. She sucked the rest off his skin. His other fingers settled on her throat as he watched her. "Your pulse is still rabbiting," he observed in a low rumble. "It's okay, lass. You're all right."

For now. "If something does happen, I want to say . . thank you. To you and our Master. I don't know if he was compelled by Lady Lyssa to take me into his service, or if it was his choice, but you've both been . . . I'm glad I've had this experience."

"He approached her, lass. The moment ye calmed under our hands. The way you're calming now."

He was right. His other hand had been stroking her arm, her hip, caressing her thigh, and she'd stilled beneath that possessive, soothing stroke.

"As far as the chocolate, Brian said there's something in it that would help if you missed an injection and had a bad reaction. It makes sense. Just like my clever hands, it calms most women down."

He was teasing her, but she couldn't smile yet. When she looked down, his hand slid along the length of her thigh. She parted her legs farther, caught her bottom lip in her teeth as he stroked between them, a methodical caress of her pussy beneath the denim.

"That can calm a woman down as well," he noted in that throaty growl. "As well as stir a man up." Taking his hand away, he brought it back to rest on her knee, but kept his weight forward, his grasp firm, telling her he liked her legs spread for him. His attention swept over her burning cheeks, the moistness of her lips. "Time to finish our shopping. Much as I'd like tae pursue that dressing room fantasy, we've caused enough drama for now."

Relief swept through her. "You're not taking me back?"

"You'd have an aneurysm if Evan's list wasnae finished," he noted. "If you're up to the groceries, we'll do that as well. But ye get more color in your face in the next thirty minutes, or we're headed back, no matter what. You can rest in the car at the shops where I can see you from the storefront. Plus, there's no reason to drag ye into the hardware store for the ropes and clips he's wanting."

"Ropes?"

Niall grinned. "No wild ideas, *muirnín*. He has a couple cliffs he's wanting to scale. Even a vampire doesnae relish falling off a mountain." He cocked a brow, glancing down at her open thighs. "However, I like the idea of tying ye on our bed and tasting ye until you're writhing like a captured soft rabbit. Or"—his gaze came back to her, a little more ominous—"tying some knots in it and applying it to your ripe arse. I'm going to do my best to put it in his head, since ye nearly scared the rest o' my life off me."

"And because you'd like doing it."

"Some vampire preferences tend to be contagious." Giving her a wicked look, he helped her to her feet. Despite his teasing, she noticed he kept a strong arm around her. "Let's go finish our chores."

～

Finishing Evan's list left her with a false sense of satisfaction, because Niall had to do a lot of it. Her color had improved, but it took time for her strength to return. She requested a brief stop at a shoe store, however, where she found a suitable pair for the gray dress, as well as some pretty matching baubles for her ears and throat. Niall frowned at her choices, but he paid for them, shaking his head when she asked him if there was a problem.

As they pulled into the grocery, their last stop, her curiosity motivated her to ask again. "Did I offend my Master or you with the jewelry? Were they too excessive?"

"Hardly. They were three for fifteen dollars. Evan isn't as wealthy as Council vampires, lass, but he does have enough money to buy you decent jewelry."

When he put the Rover in park, she shook her head. "It doesn't matter if the Council assigns me to the most wealthy and powerful, or to the poorest. I am still only a servant, Niall. Our Master's money is not mine, and I would never act as if it was. From what I know of your lifestyle and the infrequency of formal events, the costume jewelry I bought is sufficient." *As well as how long I have to wear them.*

He reached out, touched her mouth. "Do you have anything that's yours? That ye brought from your life before bein' an InhServ?"

The question was unexpected, but she took it in stride. "I was promised to the InhServ ranks at birth, Niall. I had no life before that."

"Your parents never gave ye a doll, or a toy?"

"Of course. When I was little, I was given toys to stimulate my mental growth, and they did everything necessary to ensure I was a happy, well-adjusted child. And Adam . . . whatever toys Adam had, we also shared, because we were twins, and it was just natural to us."

She looked toward the grocery store. "We should go in. It will be dark in a few hours, and Evan will want us at home."

"So you've no personal possessions? A memento or trinket?"

She continued to gaze at the storefront, aware of his eyes upon her. "I have no possessions, Niall. Every piece of clothing or jewelry, every book I read . . . everything is to serve my Master. It all belongs to him. I know you don't understand that."

In his room, there was a carved wooden chest, no bigger than a music box. She'd peered inside it, not to invade privacy, but just to familiarize herself with the things that she might be required to know about the household. There was a carefully preserved sketch, a couple of letters, an antique pocket watch. A tattered Bible. There was also a heavy pewter ring with a Scottish thistle design that she suspected Evan had given to him as a gift. The sketch appeared to be of Niall's children, a boy and a girl.

His experience was different than hers. That wasn't something that ruffled her, but for some reason his persistence did. "Did you ever see Adam after he was assigned?"

"Yes. A few times, when we were at the same events."

"They didn't make you . . ." His brow creased in affront at the idea.

"No." She gave him a sharp look. "Even vampires have their limits. Adam's Mistress wanted the pleasure of taking both of us to her bed, because we were twins. We resembled each other quite closely.

Stephen allowed it, but our focus was on her, serving her desires. She didn't order us to interact with each other. We merely focused on her pleasure."

She could tell he wanted to ask, *What if she had?* Something in her expression must have warned him she wasn't up for that topic, because he shifted focus.

"What was she like?"

"Beautiful. Kind, as vampires go. She seemed fond of Adam and he seemed . . ." She shook her head, stared at the grocery store marquis again. "He cared a great deal for her. He . . . loved her. When he died in her service, I'm sure he was glad to follow her into the afterlife. It's what every servant desires, right? That ultimate act of devotion."

She remembered the night they'd pleasured his Mistress. How, as dawn's light came, they lay on either side of her sleeping form, staring at each other. Adam had laid his hand on his Mistress's hip and Alanna had overlapped it, holding hands. The last physical contact she'd had with him.

She'd felt his death, even though they hadn't been at the Council Gathering. Stephen, not yet serving on the Council, had planned to attend, but he'd had other business that delayed him. She'd been on a plane with him, headed into a landing in Mexico City because Stephen would stay there overnight to discuss business opportunities with other vampires.

The severing of that twin connection had been brutal, Adam suddenly not there. Just a blast of fear and pain. Even her severing from Stephen had not felt like that. Physically, it had been worse, but emotionally . . . Her twin gone, forever. And then that night, Stephen had made her service twelve other servants in front of a dozen watching vampires. Testing her loyalty to him.

That had worked out well for him, hadn't it? She curled a lip in derision, then quickly erased it, appalled at herself.

Niall's hand had covered hers, but she drew away. "We need to get groceries," she said. Shoving open the car door, she didn't wait to see if he was following. She found a cart, pushed it into the brightly lit environment of the store, populated with everything from harried mothers with cranky children to aimlessly wandering tourists. Before she'd rolled to a stop before a display of cantaloupes, Niall's hands slid onto the cart handle on either side of hers, his body pressed up behind her, caging her against it. "I'll drive, you shop," he said against her ear, his lips brushing it, capturing a strand of her hair to tug.

As she closed her eyes, he put his head down in the curve of her shoulder and neck, a gesture of comfort. "It's all right, *muirnín*," he murmured. "I know how much ye loved him. I had a family, too. I ask too many questions."

She shook her head, but was glad he let it be. She'd loved Adam, yes. But she remembered her stabbing envy, seeing the connection between him and his Mistress. She'd been so pleased by their service to her that night, she'd told Adam if he wanted his sister to become part of her household, she would do what she could to make that happen.

Alanna had known it was impossible. A lower-placed vampire having two InhServs, and Stephen giving up the only one he had? But that didn't matter. It wasn't her choice. When Adam asked her if she would like that, she'd given him the only answer she could.

"I serve my Master. I follow his will, not yours or my own."

Adam's face had darkened with disappointment, though she knew he understood. Maybe. He'd never comprehended what being an InhServ was about as completely as she had, and yet he'd ended up with what she'd dreamed being a vampire's servant would be about.

She ducked out from under Niall's arms, afraid of how much she wanted the feeling he was offering her. She selected fresh fruit, some herbs, and moved briskly through the aisles, choosing what both men might like.

When she was steady enough to tune back in to her shopping companion, she found Niall had made his own additions to the cart. Lifting a bag of candy, a Chef Boyardee pizza mix and a party-sized bag of cheese puffs, she gave Niall a look.

"The pizza is like comfort food from the gods, believe me. It will put more meat on your bones. And ye might need more o' the chocolate."

"We should have given you a bigger lunch before taking you grocery shopping."

A woman passing them with a pair of active toddlers in her cart chuckled. "Never take them shopping on an empty stomach. You learn early, darling." She gave Niall an appraising look that said junk food wasn't causing him any problems. In return, Niall offered her a grin that made the mother blush and trip over her feet like a girl.

"Stop it," Alanna said sternly.

Niall cocked a brow at her. "Orderin' me about, lass?"

His lazy look made her flush as well. Not dignifying that with an answer, she turned back to her shopping. By the time they reached the checkout, they had items that suited both their tastes, and Niall had offered some useful suggestions for the meals she planned for the two of them. She admitted his teasing and companionship had balanced her once more, as if the episode earlier hadn't happened. She was even looking forward to trying on the silver-gray dress, seeing how it would fit.

"I'm glad you're smiling, more, lass," he told her when they left the store. "It lights up the whole world when ye do that." Which just made her smile again.

On the way back up the mountain, he used the same strategy that he'd employed to get her to choose dresses to choose music. He played country music, singing along gustily in his abysmal baritone until she snatched the controls from him. Since she'd never considered her music preferences, she spent most of the trip listening to different selections and deciding what she liked. He of course teased her for the romantic ballads she chose. However, once she listened to a few of those, the charged emotions in the lyrics, she returned to Niall's safer theme song playlist, where the music didn't make her feel quite so . . . wistful.

Placing her temple on the window glass, she closed her eyes. That was a mistake, because she instantly recalled that cold terror when she thought it was all going to be over . . . or Hell just beginning. She counted down, a mind-wiping meditation to calm herself, dispel the thoughts. She could only embrace each moment.

"Then catch the moments as they fly, And use them as ye ought, an: Believe me, happiness is shy, And comes not aye when sought, man."

She'd spoken the words softly, but now turned her gaze to a surprised and touched Niall. "Robert Burns," he said.

She nodded. Forcing her mind to blankness, she let herself drift, imagining the mountains turning to silent guardians in the descending darkness, watching over them.

"Do ye have a picture of him?" Niall asked after quite a few miles had passed. "Your brother."

They were beyond the city lights, so now only the headlights provided any illumination of his features. From the steep grade and winding path of the road, they were close to the turnoff toward their cabin. "Ye draw so well," he added, "I thought if ye didn't have a photograph, ye would have sketched him."

"Anything you own can be taken by your Master, Niall," she said wearily, hoping she wouldn't have to keep saying it over and over. It made her feel oddly bleak. "That's the InhServ oath. He's in my heart, but my Master owns that as well."

"No, *muirnín*." Niall looked toward her, his brown eyes boring into hers with a sudden intensity that held her still. "That's the one thing they dinnae own outright. That one, they have to earn."

14

IT left her with a mix of emotions when they pulled back into the cabin site. Evan was on a fairly precarious perch, along the northern rocky slope above the cabin. Niall muttered something about how nice it would have been if he waited until he had the ropes to start scaling cliffs. "Impatient bugger."

To Alanna, it looked like the vampire was evaluating the sky, which still held various dark streaks, residue from the long-past sunset. Since he didn't acknowledge their arrival, Niall nodded to Alanna, indicating they would unload the car and leave him be.

However, after she put things away, she couldn't shake a sense of foreboding. When Niall was occupied, she slipped out to figure a way up that slope. Before she could set her foot to a likely path, though, Evan's voice came into her head, clipped and short.

I have no need of you right now, Alanna.

Yes, Master. I apologize. Chagrined, she turned back.

Of course, if he'd be consistently one thing or another, maybe she could keep up with how she was supposed to act. She immediately chastised herself for making her Master responsible for her proper behavior, but confusion was an acceptable reaction. He'd given her what couldn't be called anything but what it was—affection, attention, approval—none of which he was required to do. She'd been acclimated to doing without those things from her Master. But getting even a taste of it was like a drug.

She remembered her resentment toward Adam, the brusque answer she'd given him. Two months later he was dead. She was mature enough to know that one moment didn't destroy their love for each other, but she regretted it was the last face-to-face conversation they had. And not just because she loved him. It was as if that simmering regret held a wealth of other messages for her, important things she couldn't decipher.

She sat down on the path. Evan wanted her out of his field of vision, and here, sitting among the silent trees, she accomplished that. She should cook something for Niall's dinner, for Evan's later sampling. She also hadn't completed her two hours of "me time" yet. Maybe she'd draw a picture of Adam. She'd tear it up of course, because it was one of the InhServ's top rules, not to have any possessions. But why would anyone other than her want a picture of a servant's face? A servant who was gone.

Putting her head down on her knees, she freed her hair, letting the wind blow it over her shoulders and forward so it hid her face. Her shields against the terrifying reality she was facing were thin, but since she'd been taking the blockers, she'd been managing them better. However, today's error had cracked them back open, such that the fear kept coming back at her like a boomerang, refusing to let her be, especially with no current occupation for her thoughts.

The waiting was the worst part, wasn't it? Everyone feared the unknown, but she feared certainty. She would be with Stephen for all eternity.

"I'm afraid," she whispered to her knees. "I don't want to be, but I'm so afraid."

If she sat here a moment longer it would overtake her, paralyze her. So she jumped up, hurried down to the cabin. When she reached it, she came up short, because Evan was there. How long had she been sitting on the slope, and how had he passed her without her knowledge?

Niall was putting his camera equipment away. As the vampire turned toward her, she didn't need any exceptional intuition to know he was not in a good mood. In fact, he looked angry. Shifting her glance to Niall, she didn't get any clues. In fact, he was watching the vampire as warily as she was.

"Master? May I do something for you?"

Evan studied her, his mouth a harsh line. "Strip. I want it all off."

She lifted her hands, began to slip the top button. "*Now*," he snapped.

She yanked open the rest, her fingers trembling a little, and pulled the shirt off her shoulders. Unhooked the bra as she was toeing off the shoes, pushed the jeans and panties off her hips. Niall had made her indulge a second pair of earrings at the shoe store to wear with her current outfit, and she deposited those on the pile of clothes, heedless of whether they'd tumble off into the grass and be lost. She could feel Evan's eyes on her like two brands.

Closing the distance between them, he clamped his hand on the back of her neck, turning her toward the picnic table. A brief arm around her waist and he'd put her knees on the bench, pushing her facedown to the table. "I said everything." He yanked the clip from her hair and tossed it away.

"I'm sorry, Master."

"No talking. Grip the other side of the table, arms spread as wide as they'll reach."

She did it. Her cheek pressed against the rough wood.

"Spread your knees and lift your ass. Hold that position."

She obeyed. Her breath was shallow. With Stephen, punishment had been performance. He'd never punished her in private. Ironically, except for that one unforgivable betrayal, she'd never done anything to merit punishment, though of course with vampires it wasn't necessary to do anything, if they enjoyed dispensing it. Stephen hadn't.

From what Niall had said, she knew Evan enjoyed the pleasures of dispensing punishment, but it was obvious this was not that. She wasn't frightened; her heart was pounding and tears were close to the surface because she'd done something to displease him, and she couldn't bear that thought. She wanted him to punish her, to make it okay, so that he would go back to his thoughtful discussions with her, the half smile, the unexpected yet entirely welcome caresses . . .

Like now. She let out a tiny noise of hope as he spread her hair over her shoulders, stroked it so he was also stroking her skin beneath. When he swept it off to the side, it pooled on the table by her right shoulder. She closed her eyes, shuddering again as his fingers trailed down her spine.

"Niall, give me your belt."

She swallowed, fingers spasming on the table. She'd never been struck by a belt, and Niall's was a thick leather strap.

"Count them off, Alanna."

"Yes, Master." Her voice was quavering, but she made up for it by lifting her ass higher, spreading her legs another inch, increasing the strain on her hips, because she wanted to make it clear she would take whatever punishment he desired.

The first stroke was a hard, stinging burn. She bit back the cry, but strangled out the count. "One."

Each one was worse, because he stayed in the same target area, hitting no more than an inch above or below the last stroke, so he was overlaying them in no time. By the time she reached ten, she was sobbing, fingers digging into the wood. But she bit down on her lip so hard she drew blood and kept raising her ass, anticipating by his rhythm when the next one would fall. She would prove her devotion to him, her acceptance of his Mastery. She would win his forgiveness by showing she submitted to his will in all things.

Though she was in pain and heartbroken that she'd disappointed him, he'd also taken away the fear she'd felt, sitting on the mountain path. She'd whispered *I'm so afraid* because she felt so alone with all of it, but this . . . She'd affected Evan enough to make him angry. Maybe it wasn't his intent, but with every strike, it felt like a part of her was being bound more firmly to him and Niall. Perhaps firmly enough that her entire soul wouldn't go to Stephen when he was killed. Maybe a vital splinter would be left here, with them, and that would make the rest bearable.

"Twenty-five." She barely got the words out, and when he stopped, she wasn't aware of it immediately, holding the pose and ready to count out another.

"Stand up, Alanna."

It wasn't easy, but this time he didn't snap at her. His voice was stern, but not angry. Her body was stiff, aching, and the edge of the bench had left furrows in her knees. Turning to face him, she kept her head bowed, her hair curtaining her face, teasing her breasts and stomach, her smooth mound.

Evan didn't speak, just stared at her long moments. She kept her hands at her sides, waiting, wondering if she should kneel, but he'd said to stand. Her ass was still throbbing, and she knew there'd be bruising, blood vessels exploded under the skin. With Evan's second mark, she would heal faster than a human, but she would still see and feel those marks tomorrow.

"When I am done with you," he said, "you will go inside and sit in the straight chair at the living room desk. I want it turned around to face the room, so Niall and I can see you. You will keep your back straight, your ass pressed down fully on the seat, and your knees parted, ankles hooked around the legs. I want you to feel your punishment."

"Yes, Master." That ache in her throat made her words thick. Strands of her hair close to her face were damp from tears. *I'm sorry, I'm sorry. Please let me make it right.*

He muttered a curse. Plunging a hand in her hair, he yanked her head to the side, so her chin was pressed against her left shoulder. She cried out as he sank his fangs into her throat, a ruthless penetration where pain was obviously intended to be part of the experience. He had her waist in an iron grip, and she needed the support. As he drank deep, she had to grip his rigid biceps because the dizzying rush of blood made her knees buckle. While his long fingers spread out to press into her sore buttock, his other hand continued to grip the opposite side of her neck and her hair, holding her fast to him.

He was demanding, passionate about his feeding. His hand slid around her body, leaving her buttocks to push between her thighs. As he rubbed her in a knowledgeable way that had her arching up against him, it pressed her breasts into his chest. She was already wet, had become aroused while he punished her, because that was in her nature as well, so she made a grateful mewl as he sank his fingers into her, scissored against that slickness.

It wasn't the first time she'd been lost in pleasure to the point of physical disorientation, but this had started on the emotional end and then incorporated the physical. *Longing.* The word stuck in her mind as he hiked her up his body and sat them both down on the picnic table, her straddling him as he continued to feed, now holding her backside with both hands, kneading her against his stiff cock beneath his jeans. He wasn't gentle, mixing the pain with the desire, but that wasn't why it was excruciating.

He controlled the pace, working her against him, even as her response built, and she wanted to rub against him more fiercely. He had his arms over hers, so she could only cling to his shirt along his rib cage, wish that she could get her arms around his shoulders. She still had her face pressed to one. Even after his hand had left her neck, she'd obeyed the indication that he wanted her to stay in that position.

Then he moved a hand back between her legs, furrowing in to find her wet folds and manipulate her clit with a demand that went along with the aggressive feeding. She thrust herself against his touch in a coital rhythm, no thought, just desire taking over. She hadn't been able to spare a thought to what Niall had been doing during her punishment, but when Evan pushed her upper body back, her shoulders were caught in Niall's sure hands.

Evan's steel gaze was tinged in red, pure predator as his eyes coursed down her body. If she'd had any clothes on, she was sure he would have laid his hands on her shirt and simply ripped it, tearing the bra open beneath it so her breasts would spill into his waiting hands. Niall held her still as their Master leaned forward and licked away the blood he'd allowed to drip down her collarbone onto her breast. His fingers were still scissoring inside her when his fangs sank into the ample curve. She cried out, her body shuddering from the overload of feeling, but then he pulled his fingers from her cunt.

"Please, Master . . ."

She'd never begged without it being commanded. But the loss of his touch, her heart so open, her soul so afraid, her mind whirling at this sensual assault, seemed to make it essential.

Niall's arm banded across her shoulders as he moved closer, his body pressed up behind hers. As his hand slid over her hip bone, a noise broke from her throat, anticipating. She arched up violently, her breasts and jutting nipples on bold display for her Master as the Scot's thick fingers thrust into her, his thumb working across her clit. Where Evan was relentless, breathtaking skill, Niall was strength and power, overwhelming. She was helpless in their hands.

A growl startled her, because it wasn't human. Evan's head lifted, and she followed his gaze to the edge of the clearing where a pair of wolves, attracted by the scent of blood, had appeared. Seeing humans, they were uncertain, but Evan made up their minds. Baring his fangs, he snarled at them with the clear message that they'd stumbled onto a much bigger, scarier predator. They were gone, their gray pelts melting into the brush.

Yes, Evan might be a less arrogant, less ego-driven vampire. But in that moment, she knew it didn't make him one less bit savage predator than any other vampire.

As if nothing had disturbed his concentration, he returned his attention to her, a thrilling and terrifying thing. Cupping her breasts, he suckled the nipples, then bit down around one again, making her moan with the pain, but he wasn't as ruthless this time, and it was mixed with all the other sensations. She was hurtling toward orgasm. "Master . . ."

Wait. Evan's command was as daunting as his snarl at the wolves. But Niall's fingers were diabolical, as if the servant was determined to make her break. She panted, she wailed, she shuddered, she fought it with all she had, until tears were coming from her eyes and her nails dug into Evan's sides through the shirt. He watched her with those still vampire eyes even as his mouth teased and nipped, made her nipples aching and full. Leaning back from her, he opened his trousers, adjusting to free his cock, thick and ready, the flesh a pale marble in the dim light of the clearing.

As he straightened, Niall's fingers pulled out, and he returned his grip to her arms. As Evan took hold of her hips, the Scot lifted her as well, the two men taking her up to mount the vampire's erect cock. Evan pushed her down in a slow, indescribable descent, her body stretching to take him, even as it convulsed in that state of near climax. Niall's fingers flexed on her upper arms, his mouth pressing against the tender flesh below her ear.

"Hold here," Evan said, his voice remaining in that growl, fangs still showing. He pulled her hips in close, so that her throbbing clit was pressed to their joining point, his fingers tightening on her bare ass as she quivered. "Don't you move."

Niall had withdrawn, was doing something behind her, but she held her Master's gaze as he coiled his hands in her thick hair, making her be still as he caressed her. She couldn't help it, her internal muscles were making little clenches on his cock, and he gave her an admonishing look.

"Behave."

"Trying, Master. Hard . . . not to move."

He looked down her body, where another trickle of blood had

crossed her navel. Now he dipped his fingers there, smearing the blood in a wide slash across her abdomen, then lower, over her bare mound, teasing her clit as she gasped and shuddered, continuing to hold his gaze, since that was what he seemed to desire.

It was what she wanted, too.

He wasn't angry anymore. His order was driven by lust, the truth of it in his eyes, in the deep invasion of his cock. So she needed, had to say it.

"I'm sorry, Master. I'm so sorry."

"You should be." He squeezed her ass, making her whimper. "Be quiet. Feel."

He spread her buttocks as Niall's well-lubricated fingers dipped into her rear entry, oiling her up for penetration. Her shuddering increased. Having the two of them inside her . . . she wanted to devour Evan's mouth, wanted to press her breasts against his chest, but she had to settle for staying still in his grasp, holding her captive to his desires as he registered her every reaction.

Niall set his hands alongside Evan's. He'd removed his shirt, but she could feel the scratch of his open zipper on her buttocks, suggesting that, like Evan, he'd simply opened his jeans to ready himself for her. She was naked and vulnerable, underlining her full submission, her surrender to them.

She couldn't remember ever feeling so much of her heart involved in a coupling with her Master or anyone he commanded to take her.

"You've done this before, *muirnín?*"

No. She'd never done it like this before. Never felt this way. But then she realized what Niall was asking. Anal penetration. He was making sure he wasn't going to hurt her, determining how slow he needed to go. When the tears spilled out, Evan caught them with his mouth, cupping her face. She couldn't help it, she rubbed her lips against his jaw, wherever she could reach, and then he turned his mouth to hers. She licked his fangs, cleaning off the blood, and then moaned as he sealed his mouth over hers, sweeping her away in the kiss.

She's done it before, Niall. Just never like this. Join us, neshama. Close the circle.

Niall pressed a kiss to the tender bone at the top of her spine. She marshaled enough brain cells to push against him properly, to allow him to break through those muscles. But she had to fight with everything she had not to come, because the dual stimulation, this sudden claiming by both men, pushed her right over.

Once Niall was in balls deep, she was panting like a dog, trying not to move. Her only lifeline was the hold she had on Evan's sides, the stuff of his shirt balled in her fingers. But Evan kept her still, stroked her hair off her neck, making it tumble over the arm Niall had secure around her waist.

"You will never forget that blocker again, Alanna. Not now, not ever." The vampire's gray eyes bored into hers.

"No." She couldn't manage anything more coherent than that. "No, Master."

"I don't care if we're in the middle of a meeting of the whole damn Vampire Council, if it's time for you to take it, you'll tell me and it will be done, you understand?"

Niall drew back, and then thrust in, hard. Since he was a well-endowed male, the effect was immediate and intense, particularly when Evan exacerbated it by thrusting up higher inside her. She was filled, crazed with sensation and discomfort both. From Evan's uncompromising expression, she knew he could make it worse, would make her climax in the midst of excruciating pain and devastating pleasure both.

"Yes, Master. I understand. I'm sorry." She was spinning like a top in her own head. The anger and passion she'd sensed from Evan now came from Niall as well, in his punishing thrusts, the grip of his hands over the vampire's. She'd assumed Evan's anger was about the risk to which she'd exposed them by opening her mind to Stephen, or the inconvenience of her having such an episode in a public place, but his words and his actions told her differently. They were angry that she'd harmed herself. They were punishing her for being careless with her own well-being.

That perverse sense she'd had, that Evan's punishment was binding her even closer to them, now made sense.

The thought was a quick, jumbled flash, too many distractions competing for her attention, the largest one being the climax threatening to crash over her. Evan changed his angle, rubbing his head inside her, making her gasp, and then pushed in deep once more.

"You don't go until I say so."

She cried out, as close to climax as she'd ever been as he began to pump himself into her, using her to sate his lust, commanding her to hold back. Niall was moving as well. Their complementary rhythm built into harder and harder thrusts, until she was crying and begging, but her discipline and their will held her on that knife edge, just short of the release she wanted more now than she'd ever wanted anything.

When Evan started to come, he pulled out, despite her involuntary cry of protest, the clench of her muscles on emptiness. He spurted some of it across her belly, the underside of her breasts. When he gathered the cream on his fingers, brought it to her mouth, she sucked on him, stared at his taut face with hungry eyes.

Then he thrust back inside her, making her scream at the pleasure of it. He kept fucking her until she was whimpering in distress, because even as he was ejaculating he was changing his angle and rhythm so that every time she was close to coming, he pulled her back from the edge. Niall came then, his hand flexing on her shoulder, pelvis slapping hard against her ass as he thrust, holding nothing back. Evan had her braced against his body, sandwiched between them.

No . . . please . . . She was throbbing, head to toe, so needy for a climax . . . for something. As good as her control was, she knew she wouldn't have been able to stop herself. The two men had worked together to keep her balanced precariously on that cliff as they enjoyed their own release. It was terrifying evidence of their own control and self-discipline, the power they held over her.

When Niall pulled out, Evan lifted her off him, ignoring her soft pleas. He pushed her down to her knees. *Clean your Master with your mouth, Alanna. No hands. Only your mouth touches me.*

She was shaking so hard, even harder than she'd been in the store. Those tiny whimpers came from her while her pussy throbbed. Still she obeyed, her heart about to explode, swamped by a feeling that echoed what she'd experienced when listening to those romantic ballads. Something terrible was happening, and yet it was something she wanted as well. She was wild, out of control, cleaning him on pure instinct, licking and suckling the still hard flesh, tasting his seed, wanting to keep tasting him, touching him, staying in contact with him. She wanted to curl between his feet and stay there always.

He stopped her at last, taking a grip on her hair again. "I'm sorry, Master. Please let me know what I can do to earn your forgiveness."

"Tell me what you want, Alanna."

"You, inside of me, while I come. Niall, touching me . . . together. Close . . ."

She stopped, startled, her eyes snapping up to his. But Evan merely nodded and lifted her from the ground, bringing her back onto his lap once more. She thanked God for vampire virility, as he sank his hard cock back into her sensitive, tight tissues. Niall's strong hands helped until she was fully, blissfully impaled on the vampire once again.

While Evan started a slow flex, thrust, retreat motion, sliding inside her in a way destined to rip her apart, Niall took a seat on the bench next to their Master. His brown eyes were intent on hers as he cupped her jaw. She was lost, Niall's expert kissing ability taking her into another plane of existence while Evan kept her grounded, guided her movements. The men both held her around the waist, arms overlapping. Evan's other hand steadied her hip while Niall's cradled her face.

As she pleaded into Niall's mouth, one of her hands was on Evan's chest, gripping him, the other on Niall, holding on to them both, a triangle as she rose and fell. The pleasure was thundering toward her like the end of the world. An end she could embrace.

Evan broke her kiss with Niall then, turning his servant's face toward him to capture his lips with his own. As he did, she reached up with one shaky hand, tracing their jaws, the way they dueled, lips wet, Evan's tongue plunging in to tangle with Niall's. Niall nipped at her fingers as she dipped into the joining point between them, then they were back to her again. Evan devouring her mouth, pushing his cock in deep once more while Niall started kissing her throat, licking the place Evan had bitten her, suckling her tender flesh. Evan was working her on him hard enough her breasts quivered with each downward impact. It made her nipples ache.

Come for me, Alanna.

She broke on the last syllable, her eyes wide and lips stretched like a wild animal's, a flush running the length of her body. She ground herself down on Evan's cock as their strong hands held her fast.

"Master . . . God . . . help . . . me . . ."

Evan went preternaturally still, watching her, absorbing all of it. Niall paused, lifting his head to do the same, both of them so close, their intent regard increasing the power of the orgasm. Her heart was literally going to explode. Then Evan's expression became more intent, facial muscles tightening, and she knew the spasming of her pussy would bring him to climax again.

"Please, yes . . ."

As he pistoned up inside of her, letting the second climax go, Niall turned to his Master. Threading his hand through Evan's hair, he set his mouth to the vampire's neck and bit. He bit hard, such that Evan growled, clamped a hand down on Niall's thigh with bruising force. Finding the opening of Niall's jeans, he gripped his cock in a pumping fist. Niall bit even harder, his hand skating across Evan's chest, pulling open his shirt to scrape strong fingers across his chest, the flat nipple. She gasped as Evan released, his seed a hot stream bathing her channel. When Niall came in his Master's grip, the milky fluid fountained, bathing Evan's fingers, Niall's bare abdomen, splattering across her spread thighs. Her aftershocks intensified.

With trembling fingers, she collected some of the seed and brought it to her pussy, smearing it over the base of Evan's cock, her still sensitive clit, and then brought those same fingers to her mouth. Both men watched her with hot, demanding expressions that made her want to start it all over again, even the punishment.

Especially the punishment. It had made her feel more . . . at peace, than she'd felt in quite a while.

Evan's gaze softened, and he cupped her face, running a thumb over her lips. "*Motek*," he murmured. "Such sweetness. You're a treasure."

Alanna shuddered under his touch. They were all done, staring at one another, breathing hard. Niall had eased his bite, given Evan a nuzzle, then a lick to deal with the mark he'd left. Evan didn't appear ready to let her go, and Alanna wasn't sure what to do. This was when she'd normally climb off Stephen, attend to cleaning him. Instead, Evan eased her forward, guiding her to put her head on his shoulder. Niall stretched his arm behind Evan, so she was cradled between them. Particularly when Evan shifted her so she straddled his thigh and Niall's adjacent one, her knees pressed between the splay of each man's legs. Evan's arm was back around her waist, Niall's overlapping it again, both keeping her close.

She never wanted to disappoint him, wanted to make them both happy. She wanted to say she was sorry again, but she understood she'd done that, and been punished. Then her Master's words rendered her speechless.

"I've never cared that I'm not the biggest dog in the yard, Alanna. That wasn't what being a vampire was about to me. But feeling him in your mind, hurting you, knowing my mark wasn't strong enough to override his . . . I've never in my life wanted power the way I wanted it then, to crush him for causing you a moment's pain."

For hurting what's mine.

Niall was obviously startled by the thought his Master had shared with them both. Evan touched his knuckles to Niall's jaw, linking the three of them. Alanna felt a desire to reach up and touch Niall there herself, increasing the bond. However, before she could, the Scot gave Evan a short nod. Adjusting Alanna so Evan had her cradled in his lap, Niall rose and left them. She watched him stride toward the cabin, refastening his jeans as he went, the muscles across his wide shoulders tense.

"Why does he do that, Master?" she whispered. "Why does he draw away from you when it's obvious how much he loves you?"

Evan stilled against her. When she glanced up, she caught a brief tightness in his expression. Had she acknowledged something about the men's relationship that Niall never did?

Evan brought her face back down to his shoulder. She was content to be there, just listening to the sounds of the night, his fingers stroking the bare curve of her spine, the other hand idly kneading her sore buttock, but at length, she thought she could ask another question.

"What was he like . . . back then?"

Evan toyed with her hair, following the line of it over her breast, down her abdomen. She loosened her thighs and he slipped between, playing with her pussy. The tissues there were still very sensitive, so she quivered under his touch, but she loved the feel of his long, sensitive fingers stroking her.

When Evan let her into his mind, he took her back to that first meeting, giving her a longer, more thorough look at Niall this time as he emerged from that loch, dripping wet, naked. Though the Scot appeared about a dozen years younger than he did now, he was tall and proud, then. Strong, yes, but so thin, his cheeks gaunt. Rage and determination burned in his eyes. She wondered how many times he'd given his family his portion, telling his wife he'd eaten part of the kill while out hunting?

"You see the physical beauty, but you immediately seek what's below the surface. It's an admirable quality." Evan's lips curved in a poignant expression. "I told him to impress me, and from the first day, he never disappointed. After that first meeting, I left Scotland for another project. I told him I'd be back in six months to check on the results of his scouting for me, but I came back five weeks later. I wanted to see him again, to see if the money I was sending him had improved things for his family. At times, Fate shows her hand quite clearly in our lives."

Her fingers tightened on Evan's chest as he gave her another image of Niall, this one of him bleeding to death on a dark battlefield.

"His landlord forced him to fight for the Jacobites, threatening to turn out his family if he didn't join his army."

~

Evan drove away the midnight looters, making it clear they'd pay with their lives if they lingered, but he had no desire to stay on this desolate battlefield under a cloudy nighttime sky, either. He hiked the Scot over his shoulders, a narrower span than Niall's, but he held him with sure hands and used vampire speed to leave the bloody scene behind. Taking him deep into the wood, he laid him down in a secluded glade whose cushion of grass had provided safe slumber to more than one deer family.

Eyes darkening, he squatted by the man. A gut wound was a horrible way to die. Niall should have been moaning, but he was suffering it in silence, his expression caught between anger, anguish and desperation. Not for himself. Evan already knew enough about this man to know what would make him afraid. And make him fight for his life beyond all reasonable expectations.

He was groping for his dagger. Evan pulled it free and tossed it out of range, before he pushed him to his back again. "It's me. It's your wrestling mate, man. Not a bloody enemy."

He pressed a cloth to the gut wound, trying to staunch the blood flow as those lion's eyes focused on him. "My family, I cannae die. They need me . . . Ceana, she nae . . ."

The path to what Evan wanted was clear as a paved street to Hell. Fate wouldn't have lined things up like this if it wasn't meant to be. Right? His sire would have given him an ironic look through cool eyes, calling the rationalization the horseshit it was, but fortunately Lord Uthe wasn't here at the moment. "I can help you live. But you'll owe me something."

The Scot gazed at the bloody mess under Evan's hands. "You're a devil, then."

"You're not making a pact with Satan. Though I expect you have enough of a brain to figure that out. Eventually."

"Will what I owe you . . . hurt my family?"

"No. But it will hurt you. No help for that."

Vampires didn't apologize to humans. Evan had once been human enough to understand how arrogant that was, but a vampire was too superior in strength and other skills to ever see a human as an equal. He'd give him the choice to live or die, but that was the only choice he'd offer. Yeah, he was a bloody bastard, wasn't he? But he wouldn't see this man die. Even now, with his hand pressed on the gut wound, as if the insistence in his touch would keep the life in him longer, Evan was tempted to commit one of the few vampire sins. Take that one vital choice away.

"Hurt . . . as in pain worse than this?" Niall's lips drew back in a ghastly smile, telling Evan he cared little about pain to himself, even though he was near convulsing with it.

"The marking will hurt like a son of a bitch, but I'm talking about this kind of pain." He put his other hand on Niall's heart. "Choose fast. Better to do this sooner than later."

"My family . . . I'll be able to care for them."

"Better than ever." Niall would belong to him. He didn't have a lot of excess funds, but he had far more than Niall, such that no landlord could blackmail him again. "Choose, Niall."

"Death and leave my family tae starve . . . or you."

"I make few promises, but I guarantee I'm a better choice than option one."

Niall stared up at him, then offered his hand. The effort was such that his fingers, the entire arm, were shaking badly, but Evan lifted his own blood-soaked hand, clasped palms. "If it doesnae work, you'll take care of my family."

"No, I won't. You have to fight to live, to honor your promise. I won't give you that escape route. I get what I want, or you get nothing." The wound was severe. Even a vampire couldn't win a one-on-one with the Grim Reaper. Much would depend on Niall's strength, his desperate will to live.

"Bastard. All right then. Aye. I owe ye a debt. Give me my life so I may care for my family."

First your family, then me, Evan thought. "Close your eyes. This will feel like dying, but then you'll feel better than you ever felt in your life. If it works." Giving all three marks at once could kill the Scot in his current state, but there was no time to do it any other way. Hopefully, the first two would provide enough vitality to give the irrevocable third mark the chance to latch on to his soul.

Bending, he laid his hand on Niall's jaw, pressing his cheek to the earth, and unsheathed his fangs. The brown eyes flashed in shock, as Evan bit down on the first sweet, sweet taste of his servant's blood.

～

"What happened to his son?" He'd shared the images in his head, but it was obvious Evan had gotten as lost in them as she had, so she brought him back to the present with the quiet question. He blinked.

"A few years after Niall left, Eric booked passage on a ship to take his family to Jamaica, to join a sugar enterprise there. The ship went down, no survivors. Niall broke off all contact with his other relatives then. He's never been back to Scotland. I've honored his request not to return for all three hundred of our years together."

Evan's face was shadowed. There were lights inside the cottage, and she saw Niall foraging in the kitchen.

"You sent money to help his son, didn't you?"

"I did." A smile touched his lips, but it didn't reach his eyes. "When Niall came into my service, he told me whatever salary he was paid should be sent to his family, minus any small pittance he might need for his upkeep. By the time he realized there is no salary associated with being a vampire's servant, I'd ensured his family had been cared for. His service was more than enough compensation. It's only taken him three centuries to believe that. Stubborn Scot."

She nodded. "Niall said . . . you visited him while he was still married."

"You want to know what his wife was like."

At her dismayed look, he tugged her hair. "Female curiosity is one of the very few predictable things about you creatures."

He had forgiven her enough to tease her, his gentle touch sending warm tendrils through her stomach. When she pressed her lips against his hand, his gaze stilled upon her. She reached up, touched his mouth, fingertip grazing a fang. He nipped her enough to draw some blood, sipped it away while her body stirred at the attention.

"Insatiable creature," he murmured. "I think your desire is greater than your curiosity."

She couldn't block the thought, and was glad she hadn't when he laughed. "Yes, I expect you would like both satisfied. But I'll tend your curiosity first. Ceana was courteous but reserved with me. Typical of a country girl, but I think it was more than that. They were childhood friends, pushed together by their families as a practical matter, but they had a real fondness for one another, if not a huge passion. She was protective of him, which I think is the real reason she was never over-friendly to me." His lips twisted in a wry expression.

"Niall had no sense of his reputation in the eyes of other men. He'd grown up poor, struggled through difficult times, but he'd proven himself. He was a better hunter, warrior and scout than a crofter, but he worked hard at whatever was necessary to care for his family and community. Despite his refusal to take a political stand in a very political time, people respected him. In short, he had stature, despite the meanness of his lot. It told me a great deal about him."

"I think you don't want to let him go now, any more than you did then. I think you love him, too, Master."

She stiffened, appalled at herself. Lulled by Evan's images and story, she hadn't thought to censor her tongue. Vampires didn't love their servants. They might value them, have affection for them, but love was never a possibility. Servants might whisper about it, crave the impossible dream, but it was dismissed as a fanciful side effect of giving one's heart fully to a Master or Mistress. In the vampire world, such an unlikely love would be condemned. If the vampire was female, it could even endanger her life and freedom. Lady Lyssa was the only exception, and that exception existed only because she was at the top of their food chain. The queen was likely keenly aware of that.

Love for a vampire, if it existed, was always one-sided. All servants accepted that truth, because if there was any one thing forbidden in the vampire world, it was a vampire being in love with a servant.

"My apologies, Master. I shouldn't have said that."

Evan merely tightened his arms around her, dropped a kiss on her head. "Go to him. He's probably eating something out of a can with a spoon, looking pitiful."

She smiled against him, relieved. "Should I make something for you?"

"No. I've fed well from your lovely throat. I'm going to spend some time on my own tonight, up in the mountains." Lifting her off him, he rose to his feet, but recaptured her attention with a firm hand on her chin. "But after you feed him, I expect you in that chair, as I ordered. I'll let you know when you can get up. I don't want you to forget the lesson you learned tonight."

"Yes, sir." She never would, but she'd do anything he asked of her.

Giving her a searching look, he ran his hands down over her hips, dropping one last kiss on her shoulder, a prick of fang against her throat. Despite the protection of his second mark and her attempt to mask it, she had started to shiver from the cold night air. Removing his own shirt, he slid it over her shoulders, buttoned a couple of buttons down the front, then teased the cleft between her breasts with a brush of his knuckle. "You're lucky it's not summer. I would have made you sit out here and let the mosquitoes and gnats chew on your pretty pale flesh. It's not a good place to be bare-arsed, as Niall might say. Keep that in mind."

Then he was gone, leaving her standing alone in the night. Yet she wasn't alone. She felt a thread, a connection between the vampire artist traveling through the night with his own thoughts, and the servant brooding inside the cabin. Even after three centuries together, there was obviously a final step to be made between them. That they were bound to each other was beyond question; one responded to the movements of the other like a mirror image. Recalling their sensual expertise was knee-weakening vivid proof of it. They were brothers-in-arms, but also adversaries. Would they reconcile it before Niall was gone forever?

Death was a part of life. Every living being knew that, even vampires. Most didn't live to the great age of Lady Lyssa, who was reputedly over a thousand. Various factors could bring their lives to an end, though at an age much greater than humans. Despite Niall's three centuries of life, the thought of his death made her throat ache. As the warm light of the kitchen spilled out into the yard, she compared the strong, powerfully built male against the thin, fierce fighter Evan had shown her in his mind.

We all grow up, sister, but few of us learn to be adults. Not until we know what love truly means. Duty and honor are part of it, but when duty and honor transcend, become devotion and unconditional commitment, it is an entirely different realm of possibilities.

Adam had told her that, in a letter he wrote to her. A letter she now wished she'd kept, though that line had stayed in her head.

Since her betrayal of Stephen, she wasn't sure who or what she was from day to day. But tonight, thinking how she'd lost herself in Evan and Niall's desires, their passion, she wondered if she was at last going to discover the answer, only to lose it with her life, in a matter of weeks, days . . . hours?

No. If there was an afterlife, and even if she was stuck with Stephen, she'd hold on to that knowledge. Once discovered, it couldn't be taken from her. If it could, then there really was such a thing as Hell.

15

S HE'D started toward the house when Niall came back out. She'd intended to ask him what he wanted for dinner, but at his pensive expression, she changed tactics.

"Are you in there eating SpaghettiOs?"

Brooding turned to surprise at her obvious attempt to tease him, but he recovered quickly. "I'm making dinner for you tonight. You're goin' to eat half o' the pizza with me."

"I will not."

He grinned then, that wicked smile that could actually curl her toes, because they dug into the earth the minute he did it. "We'll argue about it after."

"After what?"

His gaze roamed over her body. She'd served at vampire dinners involving elaborate servant orgies. Stephen regularly called her to his room to service his needs, requiring her to pad barefoot from her quarters, completely naked. The staff and other servants she passed found it unremarkable, unconcerned about her appearance.

The way he looked at her now, clad only in Evan's shirt, was not unconcerned at all. He took his time with it, not answering her right away. "Christ, we should make ye stay like this all the time."

Even after a demanding session like she'd just experienced, she was trained to be sexually prepared at the merest hint of vampire interest, her pussy automatically lubricating itself, her nipples tightening. Niall, being a third mark, would have no problem responding in kind. His nostrils flared, eyes registering her reaction.

"Christ, lass. You're going to kill me."

Her pulse leaped in her throat as he took a step closer. "You need dinner," she said, but her voice was unsteady to her own ears. The expression on his face became more intent, male senses recognizing female compliance, and becoming even more concentrated on his desires as a result. "But not pizza."

"Aye, pizza." His brown eyes glinted. "There'll be no arguin' that. But first, we have to deal with the other matter. Ye were tearing yourself down in your mind today. At the store. Evan told me. Ye recall what happens when ye insult his property."

Oh no. Evan's shirt had warmed her, though the gesture itself, his touch, his possession, had kindled the small furnace in her vitals even more. Niall's look now only increased it. She didn't want to lose all that delicious heat in the cold creek. She shook her head, backing away. "No. I'm sure he misunderstood."

"I'm entirely sure he didnae, lass. All-powerful vampire and all that."

When he lunged at her, she dashed behind the picnic table, sending the tails of Evan's shirt flying away from her bare backside. When she spun to face him, her hair swirling around her face, Niall eyed her appreciatively. He began to stalk her. "I'll probably need to hold ye under the water a minute or two. Get ye nice and cold so you'll want to cling to me after."

"I think you're taking undue liberties with Master's instructions." She circled the table as he followed her from the other side. The moment he started around the far corner, she dashed for the cabin door. She'd lock him out, entice him with dinner smells so he'd forget all about throwing her into that creek. When he caught her at the door, she was laughing, which morphed into a squeal as he banded his arm across her chest. She lunged forward, offsetting his balance, allowing her to duck out from under his grip and make it back to the picnic table.

Sparring with other servants was a regular activity, given that there might be reason to defend the Master's home or belongings. Or prove oneself against the power games that other servants sometimes played. But the last time she'd wrestled for fun and sport was with Adam when they were young.

Niall was like a cougar, not stalking dinner, but playing with his mate. Had Evan given Niall the parting command to throw her in the creek because it might result in this, lightening his heart and drawing it from the dark place it had gone? Had the vampire also known she would figure it out, giving her a service she could do for them both? The confidence that she was right gave her a bolstering warmth, something she was reluctantly certain she would need in the next few moments.

With a bellow, Niall charged, coming over the picnic table, effectively chasing her out from behind it. Around the yard and cabin they went. He always managed to block her so she couldn't get into the cabin and lock him out, but she was nimble enough to keep out of his clutches.

"Quick and small have their uses," she noted when she was behind the temporary protection of the well. "Bears are fierce, but they're big and lumbering, too."

"Hmm." He lunged again, and she relocated to a rock outcropping almost taller than herself, but she could still see over it. Since the creek was gurgling behind her, she'd taken a risk, getting so close to where he'd intended to throw her, but he hadn't left her much choice. She'd been herded. Wily Scot.

"Bears can sprint, Alanna," Niall said, giving her a portentous look. "Especially when we're hungry."

She shrieked and bolted as he came around the rocks, moving faster than he'd yet moved. Though he had to put three hundred years of agility and speed into it, her satisfaction was short-lived. He caught her about the waist, flipped her in the air and slung her over his shoulder, clamping his large hand over her ass, Evan's shirt sliding up her spine.

He hadn't anticipated the tactics a sister had learned against a twin brother. Reaching down the loose waistband of his jeans, Alanna grabbed the edge of his boxers and yanked. It wasn't as effective as briefs, but the wedgie would put an uncomfortable pressure on the sizeable package she knew the man had.

"Should have worn a kilt," she suggested when he snarled at her. She squealed as he gave her still very sore ass a smart pop.

"I wasna planning to enjoy this, but now—" As he shifted, preparing to heft her, she grappled his body like a cat digging in her claws.

"I'll never bake you cookies again."

"Aye, ye will, because you'll make them for Evan and I'll eat the rest."

"I'm . . . not . . . going . . . in . . . alone," she gritted, clamping onto that muscular torso with arms and legs, bringing them face-to-face. He caught his hands in her hair, tilting her head back so he could eye her with malevolent, amused intent. He looked about to kiss her, her lips parting in involuntary anticipation, but he started tickling her instead, making her squirm and squeal, loosening her hold.

"You bastard," she pronounced, right before she hit the cold water with a resounding splash.

He was on his ass on the bank, roaring with mirth, when she surfaced. Though she was freezing, the sight caught her, him laughing like a boy. She was glad to give that back to him. He'd been too serious since the mall episode, and his reaction to Evan's statement about wanting to protect them both gave her a remarkable realization, one too remarkable for her to acknowledge on her own.

You are not alone in your fear of your fate, yekirati. *It's a shadow over his heart, just as it is mine. Please him, make him laugh. It will help dispel the shadows for you both.*

Maybe not just the two of them, she thought. She slid through the water, teeth chattering, but the warm weight of her heart, pounding in her chest at such a miraculous admission, balanced it. She was cared about. How much or how little was inconsequential—she'd never had the sense of any degree of it before. That shouldn't matter to her, but it did, and Evan made it seem like that was okay.

But her Master had also given her a charge, and she was more than willing to carry it out.

The bucket was on the bank, right there by the stump. And Niall was not the only one who could move quickly.

He'd thought the fight would go out of her with her dunking. By the time he realized otherwise, she was upon him, full bucket in hand. A startled exclamation and she'd doused him full in the face and chest. Then she dropped the bucket and ran.

He caught her right before the cabin door. He took her down to the ground, his body covering hers, and though she struggled to flip him, to break the hold, he had an attack strategy she hadn't expected. Evan's shirt was glued to her body. When he lifted off of her enough to bring her up onto her hands and elbows, his body still covering hers, he skimmed his hand beneath her, over the stiff, cold points of her breasts, down along her abdomen.

"Stay on your elbows, lass. Pull your hair over your right shoulder."

She was breathing hard, shivering, but that heat against her back spread between her legs. When she obeyed, he cupped her breasts again, fondling them, enjoying the tight tips as he pressed his lips to the small of her back where he peeled Evan's shirt away from her damp flesh.

"When he had ye bent on the picnic table I wanted ye tied there, your pale arse in the air, your quim slick and pink, ready." The accent got stronger, its effect devastating. She imagined him walking right out of the eighteenth century, a Highland Scot as wild and untamed as the land itself. She closed her eyes, her body rippling in response. "Would ye like that, lass?" he rumbled.

"Yes."

That dual level of approval coursed through her, increasing the heat in her core. Once again, admitting her own desires made these two men even harder. Her own needs and wants were something this vampire and his servant *demanded* to know.

Good girl.

Won't you come join us again, Master? Evan's voice made her push her luck.

You are a shameless wanton, but no. I will enjoy this through Niall's mind and yours. Give me that gift, Alanna. Let me feel everything you want to feel under his touch. He is an incomparable lover.

She breathed out a low hum of pleasure as Niall opened his jeans. He paused, making an adjustment with a huff of sound. "Have to get my drawers out of my arse, thanks to you, *muirnín*. And just for that . . ."

He put a firm hand on the back of her neck, holding her there, and gave her several firm smacks across her abused buttocks, making her yelp.

"Lucky I didn't use this." On their last dash past the table, he'd retrieved the belt Evan had used. Now he looped it around her thighs, cinching them tight just above her knees. "No more running from me tonight."

"No, sir." She moaned as he captured her breasts again in his large hands, fondling and kneading, brushing his fingers over the nipples, rubbing them until she was squirming from the sensations shooting through her body from those sensitive zones. When his cock probed her wet folds, she was eager, ready. With her thighs held together like that, it made the entry even tighter, more excruciating, and would give her a slow build to climax. Niall had some of the same pleasurably sadistic tendencies as their Master, when it came down to it. And she didn't mind.

He was in the mood to pleasure himself. She wondered if he knew how hot it made her, being so obviously used for his own desires. He started thrusting in, good and deep, grunting his enjoyment of it.

"So hot and wet . . . so fucking tight."

His strokes became stronger, his testicles slapping against her clit, but not enough, not enough friction. She pressed back against him, ground against him, wanting more, needing more. He gave her backside another sharp slap, making her behave, but then he reached beneath her to capture a nipple and flick and tweak it, increasing the sensation.

"Oh . . . Niall . . . God . . ."

"Fuck, you have gorgeous hair." He wrapped his hands in it, pulling her head back, his knuckles pressed into a mass of silken strands between her shoulder blades as he straightened to make his thrusts faster, more intense. She dug her fingers into the ground, holding on, because he was powerful enough to drive her into the earth itself. She could feel his strength, restrained to protect her far-too-human frailty, even as he was letting enough of his third-mark strength loose to make her feel totally taken.

He released, hot seed spurting through her, making her groan with the shooting pleasure of it, her body quivering, cunt squeezing him, so close to that pinnacle, but needing his help to get her there. She wanted it with a fierce intensity that could turn her into a snarling cat. She scrabbled at the earth, raked her nails over it, meeting him thrust for thrust, the earth becoming mud against her forearms, her knees dug into it, because they'd both dripped water into the ground they were plowing.

As he finished, he pulled out, making her cry out in angry need. He gave her a sharp pinch for that which made her bite back any more protests. Sliding his hands under her thighs, he lifted her hips up to his mouth, keeping only her elbows in contact with the ground.

She moaned as he put his hot mouth on her still spasming pussy, began to work her, sucking her clit, eating her out with lashing tongue, sucking lips, nipping teeth.

She came with a gush of fluids that he lapped and suckled like mother's milk, making noises of hunger and approval as she screamed, echoing out across the mountains. When she was shuddering through the last spasms, he put her back on all fours and plunged into her once more, letting her feel that fullness, that possessive branding, the aftershocks exploding into another orgasm.

As he wound down, he fell over her body, hands planted into the mud on either side of hers, cock still buried deep, pelvis flush against her backside, knees on either side of her bound thighs.

"You're a treasure, lass," he muttered. "An absolute fucking treasure. Anyone makes you feel different, me and Evan will take his fucking heid."

~

Amazing words. A powerful experience that woke her several times during her early morning sleep, shivering with the need for their hands on her again. Her punishment after dinner, sitting in that chair, seeing Niall's gaze course over her naked body, lingering on her exposed cunt, had left her feverish. Especially when Evan released her two hours later, only to order her to go to bed without further relief. They really had unleashed something in her, a need to touch and be touched that seemed to be growing, sweeping over her in heavier waves, until she put her hand between her legs and held it there as she slept, a pressure that couldn't replace them, but comforted and soothed . . . somewhat. It was never-ending, this feeling of being wanted . . . desired . . . cared for.

She'd had such a malady before, in the days before she was assigned to Stephen. A girl's romantic imaginings, wanting to be everything to

262 Joey W. Hill

her Master. After he'd taken her virginity, then ordered her to assume her household duties, she learned the most critical InhServ lesson. She'd imagined herself becoming the center of his universe, a reward for her making him the center of hers. She was not a girl in love, however, able to moon about, wanting to be touched and loved. He was the center of her universe always, while she was merely a star that shone for his benefit.

For a month, she'd punished herself daily with a steel-tipped cat for the unforgivable emotional faux pas. Just as it had kept the monks' minds away from temptation during medieval times, the bite of the whip served a useful purpose. It tore the flesh from her back in the morning, but she was healed by the time her Master rose at dusk. Nothing unsightly about her appearance to inconvenience him, and her emotions were channeled only to his needs.

She understood her human reaction to certain stimuli. Such emotions couldn't be prevented, but an InhServ learned to suppress them so they didn't interfere with one's responsibilities. However, instead of suppressing them, Evan wanted her to feel such things. Was it possible she could channel the energy into service, and still obey the InhServ code?

She had an immediate chance to test it. As she lay there with her hand between her thighs, Niall came into their bedroom and kissed her even more awake, until she was clinging to his neck and he was holding her hard against his body.

"No time for that, *muirnín*," he muttered against her mouth. "Much as I hate to say it. We have to travel today. Time to pack."

Anticipation is part of the pleasure. Evan's voice stroked her. *While we travel, you'll put your hand between your legs again, Alanna. You will pleasure yourself for us. Well, for me. Niall will be driving, and we wouldn't want to encourage unsafe driving practices.*

"Bastard," Niall snorted, but his mouth was busy across her cheekbone, the corner of her mouth.

Evan's mind-voice changed, became more intent. *I want to see her get lost in it.*

She was lost in it now. Niall groaned against her lips as she deepened the kiss, using her tongue to tease as she slid a leg up over his hip, pressing herself against his groin.

"Needy wee thing," he muttered. "Fuck. Evan . . ."

Alanna. The sharpness in her Master's voice recalled her instantly. What was she doing? Startled, she pushed away from Niall, moving to the edge of the bed, trying to get her breath.

"I'm sorry. I apologize, Master. I don't know . . . it won't happen again." She hurried to the bathroom, not looking back as she closed the door, put her hands to her heated cheeks. Was it possible she didn't have the strength to manage *or* suppress it? It seemed to be taking her over.

In the bedroom, Niall pressed his forehead to the quilts. He realized his mistake as the warmth of her body, the smell of her, filled his senses. Straightening, he willed his aching cock to ease off so the fit of his trousers wouldn't be this damn uncomfortable. *Was it necessary to be that harsh? 'Tis new to her, the wanting. And a pure pleasure to watch, even if it's pure hell to resist.*

She's learning to be a different kind of servant, but she's still a servant, Niall. She needs the boundaries, the reminders. For someone with her training, it's critical.

Ye just wanted to deprive me.

There was that added benefit.

Niall had a creative response to that, to which Evan responded in kind. The Scot heaved out a sigh, shoved off the bed. "Join me in the kitchen," he called out to Alanna. "We'll make a quick breakfast, then start packing."

Evan, down in the cellar, gazed at the final prints drying, but his mind wasn't on them. Niall wasn't the only one aching. He'd wanted to join them both last night, as well as this morning. Alanna had slept in the back bedroom with Niall last night, not just because she wanted to be near his servant. She'd already made the connection that Evan could remain in that bedroom, at least during the early dawn hours, and she wanted to be accessible to both her Master and his servant. She was chastising herself for letting her passion override his command, but he himself had never managed the heady experience of a servant so committed to pleasing him. If it had been the rote response of her training, he could have contained his own response, but she was right. They'd opened something inside of her, something he was fairly sure Stephen had never discovered, the true gem of what she wanted.

A Master who would let her love as well as serve him.

He'd proven to her that, when her will and desire were added into the mix, it increased the pleasure for her Master, but in his self-appointed position as mentor for that sensual treasure trove, he hadn't expected what it would do to him and Niall. His servant was getting as captured as his Master by the intriguing contradiction of Alanna. Since becoming Evan's servant, Niall had enjoyed many women and some men as part of their travels. But he hadn't truly wanted a female heart since the death of his wife. The circumstances of her death, his guilt about not loving her as much as he felt he should, had kept a wall in place.

Alanna was breaking that wall down, in more ways than one, and she didn't even realize it. *It's obvious how much he loves you . . .*

Evan shook his head, made himself focus on the photos again. Soon he'd have to sleep, and he needed to pack these up now, so that when he rose at dusk they'd be ready to get on the road.

The rest would figure itself out. Or not. *Small fish in a big pond*, he reminded himself. He was valued among the vampires because of Lord Uthe's sponsorship. Like Alanna recognizing it didn't matter who she served, she was still a servant, he had no illusions as to how much influence that sponsorship gave him.

Some of his original humanity remained, but Evan thought it was more his isolated circumstances than humanity that gave him latitude to exercise things that most vampires didn't. Compassion, interest in the minds of their servants, what they were thinking, feeling, wanting . . . Niall wasn't all wrong about the blank canvas. Sometimes Evan did have to remind himself there was a value separate from his artistic impulses. A separate soul.

But a soul that was his. It was hard to resist the vampire compulsion that told him his servant was all his, to do with as he would. And now he had two of them.

But that compulsion also helped him do what he'd done earlier, keeping Alanna mindful of her service. Raised from birth to be an InhServ, mandated to come to that service a virgin, untouched except for the clinically in-depth sexual training they were required to have, she'd never experienced the glow of first love, that overwhelming rush of emotions that attended it, except in her early naive fantasies of what a servant was. As she herself had recognized, her fervor was like that of a Catholic schoolgirl, her strict upbringing creating a rhapsodic relationship with Christ, confusing it with mortal passion and desire.

As pleasurable as it was to see her explore her real feelings, he wouldn't let her completely lose her compass. Despite what Niall thought, Evan wasn't ignorant of the consequences of that. He was in charge of protecting her, and he didn't see that as limited to the time she was under her direct protection. The blank canvas wasn't blank. There were obstacles already painted onto it. No matter how much the artist wanted to step back and watch her discover the woman beneath the InhServ—the true reason she was such a remarkable servant—he wouldn't let her drop all her defenses.

~

Over the years, Niall had become skilled at packing up quickly. Thanks to Alanna, the job became even more efficient. He'd anticipated having everything transported down the mountain to the waiting RV by dusk. Instead, they finished by midafternoon, so he enjoyed playing cards with Alanna and watching her prepare him dinner from the few provisions they'd left for that purpose.

She stayed quiet most of the day. Whenever they brushed hands in the course of their duties, she would still, like a bird deciding whether to take flight, then resume moving as if nothing had happened. When he met her eyes, hers would often skitter away as she smiled at something he said. He wanted to kiss her about twenty times, but held himself back, mindful of Evan's words. Not so much because he was obeying, but because he did understand the other man's logic.

Whatever it helps to tell yourself, my ever-obedient servant.

That made him snort, in a way that won a curious look from Alanna. It was almost midday at that point, so it was the last time he'd heard from Evan. His words had been slurred even then, telling him the idiot had pushed his waking hours longer than he should, probably finishing up his last film roll.

Since they had some spare time, Niall took her on a quick hike to a waterfall surrounded by jewel-toned autumn trees. The magical place won him the pleasure of seeing a rare, wide smile on her face. She leaned out on slippery rocks to put her hand under the water and feel its flow. It was the most natural thing in the world to hold her about the waist to keep her steady. When she looked up at him, eyes shining, he was lost in her brown eyes like a starstruck lad. It was absurd, and yet he couldn't help smiling down at her.

Once they were back on level ground, they stayed by the falls for a while. He whittled at a knot he found, and when she came to sit by him, she studied it. "It's a bear," she exclaimed.

He nodded, handed it to her. "Rough work, but bears are rough creatures. Best not make them too refined."

She turned it over in her hand. "It would be an impossible task, anyway."

"Hmmph." He bumped her with his shoulder, and she smiled at him again.

"Why . . ." She paused. "May I ask you a question?"

"Depends on the question. Have tae ask it, no?"

"Evan said you've never wanted to go back to Scotland. Would you tell me why?"

He could tell she was worried she'd bring on a dour mood, so he made an effort to appear casual about it. "People tend to romanticize things. We were hungry to the point o' starving, cold in the winter. What we had as roads were as likely to kill ye, if you didnae turn into an old man trying to get anywhere on them. Nothing could change your lot in life, nothing that wasnae against God's law or man's. By the time I was born, the clans were long gone, that community and solidarity my grandda got all misty-eyed about. A lot of folks went to America, Canada, Jamaica . . . if they could figure out how to afford it."

His lip curled. "Walter Scott wrote his Rob Roy tale and reinvented Scotland, making it seem this place of romantic, undaunted heroes . . . For my time, that was an imaginary place. Scotland was strong enough to become its mythology later but I . . . couldnae reconcile myself to the lie and return. Evan has never made me go back. I'm . . . grateful to him for that."

"I saw the drawing of your children. In the box in the bedroom. I wasn't prying," she added hastily. "Just checking . . ."

He shook his head. "You're welcome to look through my life, lass. There's not much to it. Evan sketched that on one of his visits to my home, watching the wee ones play by the fire. He won a smile out of Ceana, for no one but wealthy folk had pictures of their bairns."

Alanna sensed it wasn't a moment for contact, but she drew close enough she was folded on her knees next to his elbow, where he sat on a rock by the creek. "In fact, Evan's picture, for all it was just a pencil drawing, was much better. Those fancy portraits in the homes of noble folk were mostly poor, stiff things. There was even an artist traveling about Scotland around that time who had a stack of preset poses. He'd put the likeness of your head on top of whichever one you wanted." He gave her a wry grin. "'Twas one o' many reasons I was suspicious of Evan. No one drew pictures of trees, rocks, hills. What was the purpose o' that? He was a crazy heidbanger, was all, and somehow had enough money to support the nonsense. But the day he drew that picture, the wee ones were playing, and . . ."

He stopped, staring at the waterfall. "For a long time, I carried it in a pouch to protect it, but things happened to damage it. Couldnae bring myself to throw it away, even when the lines all faded away. Then one day, Evan happens tae see it. A couple days later there's a new one in my box, redrawn, just as he had done that day. Only . . ."

A smile touched Niall's face, twisting Alanna's heart. "He'd added a dimple to Eric's face. Said he'd forgotten it that day, having sketched it out so quickly. 'Your son had a dimple,' he says, 'Just like you do.' Then he touches it." Niall brushed the corner of his mouth. Alanna, unable to restrain herself any longer, did the same. Niall's gaze turned to her.

"I couldnae give my children and wife smiles and plenty that often. Not until Evan came. I worked hard for him, I did, but yet, he was the one who gave them that. That hurts a man's pride hard, no?"

"You never gave up on your family. You never stopped trying to take care of them." She touched his knee. "Food, warmth, safety, those might be vital, but I think love is the only thing that makes their lack bearable."

"It's poor comfort, when all's said and done," he said shortly. "If you've never known the lack of the vital things, you'll not say otherwise to me."

"No," she agreed. "But I know what the lack of love feels like. You never had that, Niall. Your wife and children loved you, and it's obvious you loved them."

"Not enough," he said. "Never enough. I guess America is where Ceana thought I'd go after she died, but she knew Evan was the key to it, even then." He swallowed, looked down at the stone between his splayed feet. "'You tell Mr. Evan to take guid care of my man.' That's what she said. 'For he's a guid lad.'"

Alanna linked her fingers with his. "Did you tell Evan that?" she asked after a long silence.

"No." Niall shook his head. "But I guess he knew, because he did, aye?"

"You've taken care of each other." Alanna could tell Niall didn't want to talk about it anymore, though, so she simply laid her head on his shoulder and they sat together, watching the sun descend over the trees.

"Why do you sometimes whittle stakes when you're with Evan?"

"Oh, that." He snorted. "It started as a bit o' a joke. Ye might have noticed he sometimes stomps on my nerves?"

"No. I didn't notice at all."

He pinched her. She fended him off, linking fingers with him during the short tussle, and won a true smile from him. He pulled her up onto the rock between his thighs, holding her there with his jaw pressed to her temple, his hands linked around her waist.

"One day I said I was goin' to get a stake and put us both out of our misery. We were in some godforsaken corner o' the world, a swamp where the mosquitoes could drain ye faster than a vampire, but he wanted to take pictures of it during a bloody fog, which took about two weeks to happen. Long as I stayed near him, the mosquitoes did-nae bother me, since vampires are bug repellents. Have ye noticed?"

She shook her head. "We weren't in outdoor situations much."

"Aye, Stephen's not really the outdoorsy type, is he? Anyhow, having to stick that close or be sucked dry brought my temper to a boil. Coming back tae camp one day, I found he'd collected a fair pile of cypress knees. Evan told me to make as many stakes as I'd like, and that he'd let me stake him with all of them, but for the love o' God to please leave off my carping and complaining until he got this one shot done."

"So whenever you're mulling on something about him that irritates you . . ."

"I carve a stake. 'Tis therapy." He grinned at her. "'Tis also a useful thing to have. We've several occasions where we've had to use them."

"You've killed a vampire?" Alanna's eyes widened at the thought.

"That's an executable offense for a servant, aye? Unless I'm aiding my Master in a fight." Niall inclined his head. "The vampire had him down, and I'd cut his servant's throat. Bastard wasna expecting that.

While he was recovering from the shock to his system, I took my shot, right between the shoulder blades."

Niall recalled it, that moment of squeezing panic when he thought he was going to be too late. As Evan had met his gaze, recognized the possibility of it, Niall had seen regret in the vampire's gaze, as well as felt it in his mind. Regret that he wasn't strong enough to preserve his own life, and thereby protect Niall's. Niall had staked the attacker with a savage vengeance, pulled his body off Evan's before it stopped twitching.

"If anyone's goin' to stake him," he said, forcing himself to sound casual again, "it's going to be me."

She touched his arm. "You didn't even think of your own life, did you? Just his."

"Aye." But that hadn't surprised him. What had surprised him was that Evan had done the same.

"You two are like brothers . . . but not."

"Thank God. While I'm hoping He's a bit more flexible than I was taught, He's pretty clear on incest. Plus . . . Evan as my brother . . ." He shuddered as if touched with a slimy worm, making her chuckle. She covered it with her hand, though he saw the dancing light in her serious brown eyes. "He didnae tell ye what I told him when I first found out he was a vampire, did he?"

She shook her head.

"He'd already marked me, so the deed was done. But after he explained what he was, I thought it over, then told him I was relieved. I was far more worried about being indentured to a Jew than a vampire."

She couldn't bring her hand up fast enough this time and he caught it, grinning at her as she laughed. He'd been right. Her laughter could turn a man's heart over in his chest.

At length, though, she sobered. "Do you think there's a Hell?"

He knew where her thoughts had gone. Reversing their grips, he held her firmly. "I dinnae care what the vampire world says. It may be that ye follow your Master into an afterlife. But if there's the kind of God there should be, He willnae be tying you to that bastard for eternity, Alanna."

"I wish . . ." She looked down at the bear he'd given her.

"Tell me, *muirnín.*"

"I wish Evan would give me the third mark. I don't care what it might do to me. Even if it tore me apart, even if it's not strong enough to hold me here, maybe it would hold me . . . somewhere, until he came. I'd wait forever. I wouldn't mind."

"I know you wouldnae." He slid his knuckles along her face. "Though you're not thinking this through properly. You've known Evan only a short while, and Stephen suffers in comparison to cow manure, let alone an obsessive-compulsive artist who has no clue what a proper vampire is supposed to do."

Her lips curved. She turned in his arms, putting her own around his shoulders and staying that way. He could feel her holding the bear against his neck. Pulling gently on her arm, he brought it back to her lap and closed her fingers more firmly over the small carving.

"I want ye to keep this."

When her expression got that look he was beginning to anticipate, he wanted to snap at her. What did it matter if she kept something for herself now? But he'd try to respect what she held so sacred.

"Hold on to it for me," he said, and her tension eased. She nodded.

If she was taken from them, he'd remember he gave her something for her own, even if only for a little while. Then he would be gone as well. What would Evan do with it, as well as his mementoes? After three hundred years, what retained value wasn't physical, any items kept usually symbols of the intangible. Able to fit in that one wee box. When he died, someone who cared might keep something from it, but it would be a struggle to know what to do with the rest. The world was an ever-changing landscape, and only memory kept it the same.

My memory is quite sharp, Niall. And long. Come back to the cabin. The obsessive artist is up and it's time to go.

Well, thank the saints. We could have been on our way three hours past, if ye weren't such a wean about the sunlight.

Grinning at Evan's response, he pulled Alanna to her feet. "He's ready," he told her. He bent, kissed her soft mouth. When she leaned into him, he held her against his body, felt her tension and worry. He'd find ways to distract her. She was proving herself adept at doing that for him, and he was determined to do as proper a job.

16

S HE was attending a human wedding.

From Niall and his correspondence, she knew Evan was comfortable with humans, but finding he had relationships with them made the whole situation even more remarkable. Tyler and Marguerite Winterman, the couple providing their graceful plantation home for the wedding couple, obviously considered Evan a friend, and his decision to attend the nighttime event seemed to reciprocate the feeling.

Tyler and Marguerite were both Dominants, in the human sense of the word. She recalled Niall's amusing recap of *rules, pain thresholds, boundaries—all that silly stuff.* Marguerite, a reputedly formidable Mistress, was submissive to her husband. Brendan and Chloe, the young engaged couple, also had a unique dynamic. Brendan was a dedicated submissive, but his bride-to-be wasn't a Domme, just a sexually adventurous young woman who was somehow compatible.

In the vampire world, all vampires were Dominants. It was part of the physical makeup of the species, whether born or made. Vampires only capitulated to greater political or physical strength. As interested as Alanna was in the wedding, she was equally curious about the "private party" planned for the following night, where she'd observe human Dominant and submissive practices. *Safe words* and *consensual* were not in the vampire dictionary.

Niall had told her they would participate in the private party like any of the human guests, though Evan would restrain himself from any extremes, including blooddrinking. The political pressure that attended vampire gatherings would also be absent, though she could behave as the servant she was. Among a group so immersed in the Dominant/submissive mind-set, the three of them would "blend." Well, she and Niall would blend. She wasn't sure a vampire ever fully blended, particularly one like Evan, who didn't even mesh with the expectations of his own species.

Tyler had given them accommodations in a one-bedroom guesthouse, but Niall's insistence on what appeared to be the smaller of Tyler's annex guest accommodations became clear when he told her there was an overflow wine cellar there. They'd arrived well past midnight, traveling in the luxurious RV outfitted like a home on wheels. The vehicle had specially treated windows for Evan, though Niall explained it was for emergencies only. "He willnae turn to ash, but he'll still cook above ground at the height of noon. All in all, 'tis a nice way to travel, though. Unless he has me drive this behemoth through Atlanta traffic. That's when he really proves he's a sadist."

Upon their late-night arrival at the Winterman estate, which was on the Gulf side of Florida, they went straight to the guesthouse. Tyler had left the door unlocked for them. Her opinion of their host increased when she found he'd already had the cellar rearranged to create a comfortable bedroom for Evan. Niall indicated Evan had visited before, and his preference for underground sleeping quarters was explained away as artistic temperament. Niall's snicker over that won him a slap on the back of his head before the vampire disappeared into the cellar. Niall was still grinning, though.

She fell asleep in Niall's arms in the upstairs bed, a situation that was more than acceptable to her, though she wished the bed downstairs could accommodate three. Since she took her injection right after arriving, she was asleep almost before her head hit the pillow.

The sound of hammering woke her. Rubbing her eyes and looking out the window, Alanna saw it was midmorning. The grounds appeared to be overrun with workers erecting pavilions and people dashing about with flowers, ribbons and other decorations. The guesthouse had a pleasant view, angled to see down the lawn toward a stretch of green and blue marsh, framed by an array of old live oaks.

Donning Niall's discarded T-shirt, she wandered out into the small sitting room and kitchenette to see what the day would bring. The interior décor had a strong Japanese influence. A rice paper screen divided the kitchen from the sitting area, and a polished dark wood table sat in the center of that room, surrounded with sea green cushions. A jasmine scent told her tea had been prepared and laid out on the table, along with a tray of fruit, bread and cheese options.

There were bay windows on three sides, and the one nearest her showed a small outdoor area intended for the private pleasure of the cottage occupants, complete with rock garden, rake and a stone Buddha serenely overlooking a birdbath and feeder, well-attended by the feathered public. Seeing the birds puffed up on the edge of the bath, preening and chirping, the screened windows open to allow their song, she realized the cottage did not fall short in the least. Did Evan have a gift for this, finding places that one never wanted to leave, except for the chance of finding another enchanted nook even more lovely than the last one?

Well, it might fall short in one regard. She gave Niall's tall form an amused look. He was on his knees on one of the green cushions, his elbows on the low table as he perused what appeared to be a local paper. She nodded to two wicker chairs with silk green cushions. "Wouldn't you be more comfortable in one of those?"

"Wicker makes me summat nervous. It's like straw when ye sit in it. From what I ken o' Marguerite, she buys things for their artistic value, not their practicality." He grimaced. "Cannae imagine why she and Evan get along."

Thinking about Evan's well-appointed room, Alanna expected their hosts had kept in mind the needs of all their guests. Going to the larger of the two wicker chairs, she sat in it, then brought her feet up into the chair, standing and shifting her weight. Niall lifted a brow, his lips curving as she jumped down, exposing a great deal of thigh and a flash of more intimate areas. "I think they're here for you. See?" She gestured at the room's arrangement. "Japanese decorating emphasizes central placement of key pieces, not putting things along the walls, like the chairs. They've been added."

"Is there anything ye dinnae know, lass?" Giving her a wink, he pushed himself up off the cushion, letting out a grunt at the effort.

"Do you need help getting up?" she asked solicitously.

He gave her a narrow glance. "My knees are strong enough tae give you a sound thrashing over them, young lady."

When Alanna smiled at him, he levered to his feet. "Come here." Snagging her arm, he cupped her bottom beneath the T-shirt and took his fill of her mouth. The flood of pleasure left her leaning into him, heart pounding and body even more restless. He touched her face, thumb tracing her mouth. "You're in a guid mood today, lass."

"I think it's the energy." She waved a hand at the window. "There's this feeling . . ."

"A *ceilidh*'s in the air." He gave her a wink. "A celebration, a visit of guid friends. And 'tis a wedding, which affects you lasses in peculiar ways, no matter you've ever been to one or no. And while I'd enjoy taking advantage of some of that energy"—he let her go with a look of regret—"once you're up, you're supposed to take all your wedding clothes up to the main house. The bride wants to spend the day with the female guests, and then get ready all together."

"Oh. Well, surely she meant her friends and—"

"No." Niall shook his head. "Marguerite was clear. Chloe has peculiar ideas about things, and today is her day. The bride's slightest whim commands us all."

Alanna's brow creased. "Don't you and Master need . . ."

"Noooo." Exaggerating the Scottish sound of the vowel, he pushed her toward the bedroom. "I drove through the night. I plan to get in another hour or two o' sleep. Once my head hits the pillow, all that hammering will nae be an issue. When we wake, we'll slap on our pretty clothes, and be all set."

"Don't forget to brush your teeth," she admonished, scowling at being dismissed.

"I'll eat an onion just for you, *muirnín*."

She wasn't sure why she felt nervous. She'd interacted with many strangers, but they'd always been vampires and servants, with rules she understood. But what if something happened with Stephen . . .

She couldn't live her life like that. She also wouldn't shame herself by being timid, too dependent for Evan and Niall to count on her to conduct herself as she should. Putting together the items she would need and donning dark jeans and a tunic top, clothes versatile enough for whatever would be required at the main house, she returned to the main room, finding Niall now comfortably ensconced in the wicker chair.

By the light of the window, she realized he looked tired, not a usual thing for a servant. Then he looked up from his paper. The chair did creak rather alarmingly at his shift in attention.

"You took your injection?"

"Yes. When we arrived. I won't forget again." She patted her shoulder bag. "The evening one is in here."

"You should have called me to help." His mouth firmed. "I know it hurts."

She shook her head. "You were already asleep." Niall, for all that he had the energy of a grizzly when he was awake, slept deep and long.

I plan to get in another hour or two o' sleep . . .

Her breath caught in her throat as it hit her. How could she have been so caught up in her own circumstances that it had escaped her? She thought of his frequent, impromptu naps on the mountain, how Evan would occasionally glance toward his servant, a pensive look on his face. He knew. She'd rarely been around servants past three hundred, but now she remembered what a visiting servant had said about the one she'd replaced for her Mistress. *The old servants sleep more often, and then one day, they just don't wake up . . .*

She moved to him, crawling in his lap and crushing his paper. He began to protest, but she put her mouth on his, her need immediate and sharp enough he closed his arms around her, taking over the kiss, teasing her tongue and lips, stroking her hair, which she'd left loose on her shoulders.

"Fuck, if ye were still in that T-shirt, we could really test this chair."

She put her forehead against his, holding on to the collar of his shirt. "I think that might be beyond its tolerance. But we could go back into the bedroom . . ." She didn't care about joining the other women. Her what-ifs until this moment had been focused on her own well-being. But what if she came back and Niall . . .

"Ye tempt me to damnation, lass, or worse. Upsetting the bride on her day. Get on with ye now, and leave an old lad alone. I have to put some salve on my knees."

He was teasing her, but she didn't smile. Touching her face, his brown eyes searching her face, he incorrectly guessed what was bothering her. "We'll be close, *muirnín*. There's nae to worry about. I promise."

She nipped at his bottom lip, daring herself to tease him. "Come to bed."

"Dinnae order me about, woman." He gave her a hard kiss, but she locked her arms around his neck, pressing her upper body against him, letting him feel every soft curve.

"Please . . ." she murmured.

He groaned as she shifted so she was straddling him, bringing her heat against his growing arousal. "You're trying to top, lass," he muttered.

"No." She would never do such a thing. She just needed to be with him right now.

He rose, the paper falling to the ground, and hitched her up so her legs were wrapped around him. He narrowly missed hitting the low table, below his field of vision, but Alanna reminded him of it with a whisper that averted their tumble. He chuckled against her lips, and then they were in the bedroom. He had her down on her back and was pulling off her clothes, taking over in a way she welcomed eagerly.

He was right. After a certain point, the hammering all disappeared.

She didn't want to upset the bride, but she slept with Niall another several hours, her hand on his heart, her head on his shoulder, eyes occasionally fluttering open to look at him. As anticipated, after giving them both pleasure, he'd fallen asleep. Now she noticed, with heart-stopping awareness, how deep that sleep actually was. His heart rate slowed to the point she wanted to keep waking him up. But instead she kept her arms around him, holding him, dozing in and out, inhaling his forest and male smell, until late afternoon came.

It's time to go, Alanna.

She closed her eyes, her fingers tightening on Niall's broad, bare shoulder. He'd kicked off the covers, so she was gazing at the beauty of his naked body, the dragon tattoos. Evan's mark was beneath her fingers as she traced the scales. His thick cock rested on his thigh, and she wished her Master was able to see through her eyes.

On very rare occasions, you'll get away with topping behavior with

Niall. You won't with me. Don't make me come up there and get you out of the bed.

Where she would have been mortified by the reproof a few days before, she heard the tenderness in Evan's voice. But it was still an order.

She took a quick shower, donned her clothes again, and paused at the bedroom door. He didn't stir, even when she brushed a soft kiss on his mouth. Despite the fact that she knew she was being remiss in her duties, she was unable to make her feet move. It felt like her priority was here.

I'm always watching over him, Alanna. As much as he watches over me. Go take care of the bride. That's your task for the rest of today.

For all their bickering, she wondered if Evan's calm presence in his mind steadied Niall the same way it did her. She hoped so. Nodding, she left the room.

When she stepped out on the porch, she took a deep breath. For various reasons, it was difficult to go down the stairs, but she did it, reminding herself of the same thing she'd told herself earlier. She couldn't live her life on what-ifs. Niall and Evan expected more of her than that.

Making her way across the grounds, she saw the results of the morning preparations. A wooden altar was down by the waterway bulkhead, framed by a pair of sprawling oaks. She saw florists considering different color choices, while others embellished the altar with sheer, sparkling fabric and greenery. Even though it was a life she'd never entertained for herself, she understood the desire to bond, to commit oneself to another. Enough that she indulged her desire to watch for a few moments.

Continuing, she passed pavilions with tables of elegant china and glassware, the floral centerpieces and dance floor for the reception. As she approached the house, she saw a breathtaking garland of pure red roses hung between the large, graceful columns from the upper verandah. The red of the roses was remarkably vivid and deep, suggesting the velvet silk of the petals even without touch.

"Gorgeous," she breathed.

"Thank you."

Turning, she saw a tall man standing just behind her. His eyes were somewhat like Niall's, but with more amber than gold. Perhaps in his late forties, he had a steady attention in his gaze, an alert quality to his body language. That, plus the fit, combat-ready form displayed in tailored gray slacks and white dress shirt open at the throat, told her he was ex-military, since she'd seen those qualities in servants who'd come from military service. Only this man was no servant. The authority he naturally carried on his shoulders, the way he held her gaze, making her want to drop hers, told her what he was.

She knew they weren't in a Master–servant situation, but since her conversations with humans not part of the vampire world had been short, functional interactions related to errands, groceries, et cetera, it seemed safer to go with what she knew. "You grew these, sir?" she asked.

"I did, though I had a great deal of help and guidance from my gardener, Robert. Tyler Winterman."

Before he extended a hand, she almost knelt in instinctive subservience, as she would when a vampire made himself known to her. Flustered, she managed to stop midmotion and extend her hand. Rather than shaking it, though, he closed his hand over it, pressing her fingers in warm reassurance. "It's all right. You've done nothing wrong."

"This is a new situation for me."

"You'll do fine. You must be Evan and Niall's Alanna."

She liked the sound of that, far too much. So she lied and said what she wanted. "Yes, sir." *I'm theirs.*

"Hmm. From what I heard from Evan, I have a feeling that ownership goes both ways. I can see why." Before she could think how to reply to that amazing statement, he glanced up. A tidy, attractive woman probably a decade older than Tyler had emerged on the veranda.

"Mr. Winterman, don't delay your guests. We have to make sure all the ladies are ready on time."

"Sara, my housekeeper. She's a tyrant." The amber eyes twinkled, again reminding her of Niall, with some of Evan's dry humor thrown in. "You better go, or I'll be in a great deal of trouble."

"It was very nice meeting you, sir."

"You as well." He released her hand. "I'll look forward to seeing you in the company of your Master later."

She'd heard similar words from vampires before, if they deigned to speak to her at all, but this was the first time she'd be serving Evan and

Niall in front of others. The thought brought butterflies, not at all unpleasant.

He held the door open for her. Niall had helped her understand the notion of male courtesy, and the underlying sense of protectiveness that attended it, not as inconsistent with a Master–sub relationship as she might have initially thought. However, what had been learned over so many years was hard to forget. Tyler helped her past that hitch, ushering her in with a solicitous but firm hand on her lower back.

She had a brief impression of an open sitting room with white furniture enhanced with pale pink Japanese cherry trees before Sara took her up a dual curving staircase. She led her to a large room that had been cleared of everything but what would be useful to women changing for a formal event. Well-lighted, multiple vanities, floor-length mirrors scattered about the room and a half bath as large as a master, complete with several sinks. The room had the overwhelming female scents of lotions, hairsprays and light perfumes, dizzy and pleasant at once. Many had apparently stayed for the night, hence the need to prepare on premises.

Sara was everywhere, prepared to assist the women with any unexpected needs related to hair, fittings, a jammed zipper or lost button. The roomful of nearly twenty women, in various stages of dress and preparation, engaged Alanna pleasantly enough, but not at length. They obviously knew one another, and not her, and of course had already spent most of the day together. The bride was being prepared in another room with her immediate attendants.

Seeing that Sara was being inundated with requests for help, Alanna quickly donned her shimmering gray thigh-high stockings, silver dress and heels, adding the silver braid necklace and earrings she'd bought to accentuate them, and put the final touches on her makeup. Then she stepped in to assist Sara where needed.

The housekeeper was grateful for the help, especially when a harassed woman with bright green eyes and her hair scraped back from her face with a plastic band called her away to deal with a situation in the adjoining room.

Alanna fixed a torn hem and freed a zipper from the organza it had snagged. When she managed it without the smallest tear in the delicate fabric, she was hugged for her trouble. Before she could react to that shock, Sara was back.

"Alanna? You know how to do hair, right?"

She straightened as all eyes turned to her. "Yes." She had trimmed and shaped both Evan's and Niall's hair, Evan taking over at the wheel of the RV to navigate the nighttime traffic while she did Niall's, but she wasn't sure how that was general knowledge.

"Great." The green-eyed woman with the frazzled look pressed up urgently behind Sara. "Chloe—our bride-to-be—just got back from the hairdresser. It being Chloe, something went wrong between here and there, and not only is she forty-five minutes late, we need something to happen fast. Come with me. I'm Gen."

Her hand was seized. Alanna hurried to keep from being dragged down the hallway. It opened up into a carpeted catwalk that crossed to the other side of the house. The tall windows of the grand foyer provided a breathtaking—and brief—view of the river. Now she was in the bride's preparation area, an area similar to the room she'd just left. From the panic in Gen's face, and what she'd heard secondhand of brides, she expected to find Chloe in tears. However, while her russet hair was in shocking disarray, the bride wasn't. Chloe was a lush pixie with cheerful brown eyes. At their arrival, she hopped off her stool to take Alanna's hands in her own.

"Thanks so much. Gen is freaking out, but Marguerite said she saw Niall earlier this morning, and had never seen his hair cut so well. That queue and the feathered layers on the side . . . she says he looks positively edible. Of course, he always does. When he said you'd done it, and had done Evan's hair besides, I knew you could fix this."

She pointed at her brow, where it appeared a sizeable spot had been hacked out of her bangs. At Chloe's encouraging nod, Alanna lifted the poor shorn pieces on either side of it. "What happened?"

"Chloe happened," Gen interrupted. "Tyler said he'd bring Monica here to do your hair, but you had to do it your way. Had to leave in the middle of the day and drive an hour to go get your hair done. And wouldn't take anyone with you."

"You all have been wonderful today, but it's been a whirlwind. I wanted to get my energy straight. I do that best when I'm driving. Plus, Monica had another wedding to do. She couldn't drive all the way out here and leave the other bride in a lurch. You would have done the same thing."

Still holding her hands as if they were close friends, Chloe turned her attention back to Alanna. "On my way back, there was this puppy in a ditch. Some total asshole had obviously thrown him out of a car. One of those idiots who believes if you release an animal in the country, it's kinder than taking him to a shelter. Poor thing, he was starving and tangled up in trash and cut barbwire. I got into the ditch to get him out, up to my knees in muck, stumbled and went down head first. When I hit the opposite bank, someone had thrown gum out of their car, and it got stuck in my hair. This farmer working in his cornfield saw me. He came over and was trying to help. I guess he figured the best way to remove it was with his pocketknife."

Alanna glanced at Gen. The woman nodded, pursing her lips. "Yes, believe it or not, these are the types of things that actually happen to Chloe." She gave the bride-to-be a severe look. "Having unbalanced energy would have been far better than being shaved bald for your wedding."

"You only say that because you're not a very balanced person."

Gen had a muttered expletive for that. Chloe merely shook her head at Alanna. "When I saw it in the car mirror, I cried about it. Wasn't that stupid? That poor farmer. I'm going to bake him cookies, because I know I freaked him out. It's a good thing Gen hadn't done my makeup yet. It was so dumb, because Brendan wouldn't care if I *did* show up bald." She gave Gen a censorious glance.

"The most important thing is the puppy's safe now. Robert, that's Tyler's gardener and Sara's husband—and oh my God, he's almost sixty but he's the sexiest gardener in the world—said he could stay with him and Sara until after the wedding. I was thinking he'd be the perfect dog for me and Brendan, because he's a rottweiler mix, which is just the best sign for how great this marriage is going to be, because the first gift Brendan ever gave me was a stuffed rottweiler puppy—"

"Chloe."

Alanna doubted anything could stop the rush of words, but the simple utterance of her name was enough to bring her to a halt. Possibly because the two syllables were infused with the power of a warm, sultry wind, reminding her vividly of Lady Lyssa. A tall woman with moonlight-colored hair now stepped away from the wall, putting a hand on the girl's shoulder. "It's all right for you to talk, but we have an hour to get you ready. Let's see if Alanna can fix it."

This had to be Marguerite Winterman. *Reputably an exceptional*

Mistress was an additional comment Niall had made about her, and it fit this woman to a *T*. Obviously in command of her surroundings, aware of every nuance in the room, she was practically a feminine mirror of her husband. When her gaze turned to Alanna, she lowered her own on instinct, barely suppressing the same compulsion to kneel.

"Yes, ma'am. It would be my pleasure to help."

"It doesn't have to be anything elaborate," Chloe assured her. "I mean, look at me. I'm a flower child throwback. My dress is way fancier than I am, but a girl's got to dress up sometime. Look at you, you'd be gorgeous in a sack. Tyler went running with Evan before dawn— yeah, they're complete freaks, but Tyler is so hot, how can you argue with that workout schedule? Anyhow, Marguerite said Evan and Niall are so into you, but it's not just because you're pretty. They're not that simple. You have that 'other' quality that makes Evan's gears jam. With the way his brain is, that can happen, but what's funny is she sees it in Niall the way Tyler saw it in Evan. They're over the moon about you."

While Chloe chattered, Marguerite guided her back to the stool and directed Gen to bring scissors, comb, brush and other hair accessories. From Gen's significant glance, Alanna understood that, though Chloe was normally quite talkative, wedding nerves were taking it to excess. Fortunately, erratic hand movements and head bobbing from animated conversation were no deterrent to Alanna's hairdressing skills.

She'd handled preparations for vampires in the middle of heated political discussions, including scenarios that had ended in bloodshed. As a servant, she had no right to request stillness, so she'd learned how to make the most of brief pauses of motion and anticipate unpredictable movement where she might otherwise stab her subject in the eye or worse, hack off a piece of hair. A vampire female knew the eye would heal immediately, but the hair would take several days to grow back. In such a situation, a servant paid a higher price for injured vanity.

Since Chloe was unlikely to backhand her in the face and knock her into the wall, this would be easy. She had to quell the inappropriate desire to ask her to elaborate on what Niall or Evan had said, though. Of course, humans engaged in extraneous talk, social niceties to make things flow. But Chloe didn't seem the type to do that. *Over the moon* . . . The unexpected heat in her cheeks wasn't unwelcome. Just confusing.

The girl had beautiful, unruly hair, but Alanna had a lot of experience in dressing hair, as well as a knack for it. Thinning the girl's bangs so she had a pretty spiked fringe framed by her lustrous curls, Alanna used a silk ribbon for a hairband. It gave her hair an artful wildness. The ends of the ribbon trailed down her bare, soft-skinned shoulder since she was dressed only in lacy white bra and slip right now.

Delighted with it, Chloe hugged her, then was towed off by an impatient Gen and other attendants to put her strapless dress on, since they were in a thirty-minute countdown to the wedding itself. Alanna could see the dark rose and gold streaks of impending sunset out the room's window. Evan would be up soon, and she'd be able to see both of her males in tuxedos. Her heart beat a little faster, even as she wondered at her possessive thoughts.

Last to leave, Marguerite paused and examined Alanna with pale blue eyes. "Well done. Thank you, Alanna."

"It's my pleasure to serve, ma'am."

"That's quite obvious." Another few moments of scrutiny, then Marguerite stepped closer. Placed a precise hand on Alanna's shoulder. That Mistress quality thrummed through Alanna's skin, keeping her still beneath Marguerite's touch, her eyes down. She had an elegant French manicure. "Evan is an unusual friend, but a good one," the woman said. "Tyler said you are only in his care for a short period of time. I suspect Evan wishes it could be much longer."

"So do I." She was getting bad about blurting things out. The two men were ruining her training. The fact that she was blaming them for it, rather than her lack of discipline, underscored it. But she didn't regret the words.

"Sometimes the deepest wish comes true, even when it seems the most unlikely one to ever be granted." Marguerite nodded. "I'll hope that for you. I'm also glad you'll be joining in our festivities tomorrow night."

"Thank you, ma'am. I hope I'll be a credit to my Master, and an asset to the celebration."

"I expect you never accept anything less than that from yourself, Alanna."

Another squeeze and direct look—Marguerite really did remind her of Lady Lyssa, minus the sense that she could rip her throat out—and the woman was gone, following the trail of female laughter . . .

giggles, even. Women bonding over a rite as old as time itself. It gave her an unexpected wistful twinge.

When she lifted her gaze, she saw Marguerite hadn't gone after all, merely stopped in the doorway. "If your Master doesn't require your attendance, Alanna, why don't you join us? She's been chirping like a nervous bird since seven this morning, and you can listen to her, keep her centered, while we're getting her ready."

Marguerite's voice was full of affection for the young bride, but Alanna wondered what had motivated the invitation. She paused. *Master?*

When she sent a quick thought to relay the request, she received a wave of warm humor from Evan. *Consider yourself at Marguerite's disposal until she sends you back to me. Niall said he would appreciate any flashes of mostly naked bridesmaids, but I will try to curb his barbaric behavior. You can send those images to me, though.*

She pressed her lips against a smile. *I will do no such thing for either of you, Master, and you know it. That would be entirely dishonorable.*

I didn't think a servant's job was to protect her Master's moral character.

Perhaps she's simply trying to make sure he has one.

She was teasing him. Her daring made her wonder at herself, but then she heard his laughter, the echo of Niall's snort behind it.

I'll deal with your disobedience later. Marguerite is waiting for your response.

In the vampire world, she was used to others waiting for a mental conference with her Master. At the reminder that this was not that world, she snapped out of it quickly. "My Master says that's—I mean, I'm sure my Master is fine with that. He holds you in high esteem, ma'am."

Marguerite arched a brow, cocked an ear toward the hallway. "You better follow me, then. They sound like a flock of disturbed pigeons. We've probably experienced another unthinkable horror, like a missing earring, or a run in Chloe's stockings. They don't realize we were lucky just to get her to wear shoes today . . . "

∽

For the next thirty minutes, she held Chloe's hand, blotting the occasional tears carefully with a handkerchief so Gen wouldn't murder her best friend for destroying her makeup work. She was told countless times how Brendan was the most wonderful man ever created.

She was barely older than Chloe, yet the girl acted as if Alanna was much older, and she expected in many ways she was. Still, she hoped Chloe wouldn't ask a question about the nature of human marriage she couldn't answer. Fortunately, there were others present who could help with that if she did.

Chloe's mother and sister helped with the dress, snapped pictures, cried as well. When Chloe at last asked them to go check on some other wedding preparations, she leaned forward to speak to Alanna in a conspiratorial voice. "Okay, now it's just those of us who are going to be at tomorrow night's thing. We can't talk about that in front of my mom. I mean, who could?"

When Alanna was ten, her mother told her why she must keep herself pure and untouched. At thirteen, there'd been a detailed discussion of what would be required of her sexually as a vampire's servant. Being shared with other vampires and their servants, men or women, whatever her Master commanded. If she failed in maintaining the sanctity of her flesh for the InhServ training, the whole family would be dishonored and suffer.

She'd hungered and imagined what that training would be like, blowing it up in her mind the way only a hormonal teenager could. It had in fact been very physical, but that was all. There'd been no bond with the trainers or other servants with whom she learned foreplay, sexual positions and other practices she wouldn't actually do until her virginity was taken by her assigned Master.

On the day of their departure for the InhServ program, her mother had sent Alanna into the plush interior of the limo with a brief straightening of her collar, a brush at her hair, and the firm admonishment to make them proud. Then she'd hung onto Adam and cried.

You were promised to someone else before you were even born, so she's like you. She not only has to act a certain way, she has to be that way, feel it. You were never hers. You were hers to train, to guide, to teach, to prepare. If she doesn't do it right, it could go badly for you, be harder for you. Your dedication, your ability to compartmentalize and focus on one goal utterly . . . you got it from her. Adam had told her that.

Chloe was looking at her expectantly. "Yes," she agreed. "I'm sure it would be difficult for most mothers."

Chloe nodded. "Brendan is blood and bone on the submissive side of things, like you, if it doesn't offend you for me to say it that way." When Alanna shook her head, thinking it was the greatest compliment anyone could give her, Chloe forged onward.

"He has this desire to serve, to please, but he's a guy as well. So protective, always thinking about what's best for me. It took me a while to agree to marry him, because I wanted to wait, to be sure he'd be happy with me. He was such a dedicated sub at Tyler's club. So many Mistresses wanted him, I was afraid I wouldn't be enough for him. I can play at it and have a good time, but I'll always be just Chloe. Never 'Mistress' Chloe."

She straightened, doing a credible imitation of an imperious Mistress, an obvious emulation of Marguerite. "But even when you decide you're sure, you're not really sure, right? You have to take the leap of faith that it's going to work out, that you've done everything that you can."

When she stopped and looked expectantly at Alanna, Alanna thought it through before answering. From what she'd learned about Brendan—and she was fairly sure Chloe had crammed everything about the purportedly most wonderful man on the planet in those twenty minutes—she could see why he'd fallen for her. Chloe had qualities that would attract a certain type of submissive male. The kind who was ultimately more interested in service and care, in making a woman happy, than in having a Mistress wield her power over him. Alanna had seen a few of them in the InhServ program. If her evaluation of her soon-to-be husband was accurate, Chloe had been his unlikely and unexpected deepest wish.

"I think you're right," she said, and received a grateful look from Chloe, another impulsive hug that warmed her. She really was a genuine spirit, her optimism infectious. Even the stressed-out Gen bent to kiss the top of Chloe's head.

Alanna thought of Evan, his decision to make Niall a third-mark servant. She was fairly certain that, unlike Chloe, Evan did nothing impulsively. Niall might have been on death's doorstep, but Evan had weighed the choice, determined if Niall would truly be able to accept the life of a vampire's servant and find value in it. Though she'd seen friction between the two men, she also saw the synchronicity that existed in vampire–servant pairings. Niall had told her Evan taught him to read; Evan had told her he'd merely improved Niall's literacy.

As she imagined the two men sitting side by side by candlelight, Evan watching Niall's profile as he worked through a page of words, she realized every experience they'd shared had integrated their personalities to create that synchronicity. But it wasn't an automatic result of such a pairing, as Stephen had proven.

There were times early on, when he was frustrated with our arrangement, that I might have released him from his oath. It was before the Council's restrictions on such an act. But I didn't. It was the first time I realized I'd truly become more vampire than human.

She hadn't expected Evan to be listening in. But she thought her Master might be wrong. If a human had the power to hold on to something they wanted, the way a vampire could, she expected they would . . . and did.

Therein lies the issue of moral character.

She didn't think about morality when it came to vampires. There was what they wanted, and that was it. Mortals were absorbed in issues of right and wrong. In the vampire world, there was no room for it.

That's not true, Alanna. When Stephen became a traitor to the Council, you embraced your moral character, rejecting his lack of one.

Where was he that he could conduct this involved conversation with her? Of course, vampires could multitask. He might be doing a tango with a wedding guest.

If I knew how to tango. She's waiting for another response from you.

Case in point. She snapped her attention back to Chloe, but the pause had become too protracted. The girl didn't seem offended by her apparent lack of attention; in fact, the inquisitive brown eyes were riveted on her face. "Is Evan telepathic? The reason I ask is Niall does that, too. It's a lot more subtle, but they've been together longer, right? You catch it, here and there. It's like he's tuning in to something in his head, and then all of a sudden he answers the question you've asked him on Evan's behalf, and it's always what Evan wants."

Alanna blinked, but Chloe shrugged, relieving her of having to answer. "Gen says I'm nuts, that I believe in aliens and magic, but why not? If we only use 10 percent of our brains, and some of us way less than that, then there's 90 percent we don't know and understand.

Everyone who meets Evan can tell there's something very different about him. There's this deep river thing happening, as if he's filing and comparing everything with this vast well of knowledge in his head. I think he's carrying around the Alexandria Library in there."

She waved a dismissive hand. "You don't have to answer. I've been around enough subs of über-Doms to know it puts you on the spot if I ask anything too personal. Have you been with him and Niall at the same time? Because, oh my God, what woman wouldn't die for the chance at that? Niall is just sheer Chris Hemsworth sexy, and Evan has that Adrien Brody intense artist thing happening, sans cheesy goatee . . . I think you'd just die from pleasure, having them both inside you."

"Chloe." Gen cast Alanna an apologetic look. "I'd smack you in the head, but it would muss your hair. Do you have *any* kind of filter?"

"No." Chloe shot Alanna a mischievous grin. "C'mon, give me a couple details. Brendan and I've been apart three days, with nothing to think about but being with him forever and ever. At the rehearsal dinner, he smelled so good I wanted to bite him. When I get him alone, I swear I'm going to eat him alive." She winked. "Here come Mom and Cherry, but I'm not letting you off the hook. I'll pester you later on for deets."

Alanna couldn't refuse her. Leaning forward, she clasped Chloe's hand, brought her lips to her ear. The girl, her eyes alive with pleasure and happiness, grinned even wider as Alanna murmured into the delicate shell.

"When they are both inside of me, it's what I imagine Heaven is. A Heaven I never want to leave."

As Chloe gripped her shoulder, holding the private, intimate pose, Alanna felt an unexpected but overwhelming desire to linger in the embrace of a girl who knew what it was to fall in love, who lived so exuberantly. Chloe picked up on the desire immediately, her arms encircling Alanna's shoulders in a gesture overflowing with care and friendship.

"I hope you never do, then."

~

Out under the night sky, Evan sat in a folding chair at the back row of the assembling wedding guests. He was gazing out toward the marsh when her words hit him in the chest. And not just him. He'd kept his mind open to Niall, so that he could also track her whereabouts. If she needed anything, it was best to have Niall handle it, because though he could move among humans, Evan knew he had to maintain a certain reserve.

At the moment, his servant was having a discussion with Thomas about proper tires for the RV. Though Thomas was a celebrated artist specializing in male–male erotic paintings, he was an adept mechanic as well, like Niall. The shy yet down-to-earth North Carolinian was also the spouse and submissive of Evan's current art broker, Marcus Stanton, who was New York to the bone, neither shy nor down-to-earth. Yet the two men were an obvious fit. Marcus was across the room, comfortably talking to a trio of elderly women who looked like they were old Southern money. Every once in a while Evan would see Marcus's or Thomas's attention shift, touching base with each other, holding that connection. The two men were so closely bonded it often seemed they could read each other's minds like vampires and servants.

If the third mark were taken away tomorrow, would he and Niall know each other that well, or did the mark allow an illusion of what Marcus and Thomas had?

Hearing Alanna's words, the Scot now looked toward Evan, his tawny eyes reflecting the same strong emotions her feelings stirred in the vampire.

We cannae let Daegan kill him, Evan. She's nae dying with that bastard.

I know. He just didn't know how to stop it. He'd already been back in touch with Lord Uthe, exhorting him to protect her as much as he could, but for a human servant, only so much could be asked.

Niall shot him a look, but then his face became bland, pleasant, as he turned back to Thomas. His thought came through as sharp as a knife drawn across a major artery. *Yet the bloody lot of you dinnae hesitate to ask everything of us.*

~

A human wedding was a fairy tale. Caught up in it, Alanna sat between Niall and Evan. The men had tried to give her the aisle seat so she could see even better, but Niall needed it for his long legs and she insisted. Being on the back row, her view of the bride's entry would be unimpeded regardless. Plus, she didn't mind being between the two most handsome men at the event. Evan wore a yarmulke, which surprised her, but Niall explained that Evan still observed certain tenets of his faith, like wearing the small skullcap for sacred occasions. In his well-tailored tuxedo, his hair styled in rakish disarray across his brow, the vampire looked like he'd stepped out of a black-and-white 1920s film. All that was lacking was the cigarette in his elegant fingers.

His eyes gave her a start. He was wearing colored contacts, a vivid green. Niall quietly reminded her that close proximity to large numbers of humans could trigger his bloodlust. "He can control it, but he cannae control his eyes. The gray starts turnin' red. So he wears the contacts."

Whereas Evan had the elegant polish and dangerous style of an early film star, Niall carried himself with the self-assurance and raw power she'd expect of a clan chief, no matter how romanticized he claimed her notion of that was. He wore the dress shirt and silk black tie of a tuxedo, but his jacket was what he called a Welsh Charlie, with gold buttons and a fly plaid pinned over the shoulder. Instead of slacks, he wore a kilt and rabbit fur sporran gilded with silver, his feet clad in the long socks and ghillie brogues.

She saw more than one woman give the two men a lingering look. Given that Tyler Winterman and a variety of other handsome men were in attendance, including the groom himself, that was saying something. Brendan was every bit as handsome as Chloe believed, with his swimmer's physique, silky dark hair and jewel-toned hazel eyes, but Alanna only had eyes for her own escorts. She had an irrational desire to clasp both their hands, to make it clear they were with her.

Then the bride arrived, saving her from that embarrassing impropriety. As she turned for that vital moment, Niall's arm was on the back of her chair, so she gripped his solid biceps. Chloe was a perfect match for her groom. The upper part of her dress was a glimmering corset the color of old ivory, highlighted by an antique garnet necklace that looked like it had belonged to an Egyptian queen. Alanna suspected it was a "borrowed" item from Marguerite. Her silk ribbon in Chloe's hair was the color of taupe, and the way the ends trailed over her bare shoulder worked well with it, softening the severe look of the necklace. It also fit Chloe's softness, the glow in her eyes, the smile on her lips. The skirt had an overlay of lace embroidery that split at the thighs to cut over the hips, etching their shape, before rejoining at the point of the buttocks and tapering down to the train.

Looking back toward the altar, Alanna saw Brendan was overcome by his bride as she came toward him, ready to join together as man and wife. Chloe was no different, her happy eyes glistening with tears by the time she reached him. It made Alanna's throat thicken, her own eyes sting.

While he'd been waiting for the ceremony to begin, Brendan had been talking to some of the guests, and she'd noted how deferential he was toward obvious Dominants like Tyler. He was clearly in love with a woman who was not a Mistress, so Alanna hoped her first impression was right, that Chloe would be the type of person who could allow Brendan to serve her with his whole heart.

She'd embraced being an InhServ, seeking what this couple hoped to find when they clasped hands. A yearning that became something full and complete, a knowledge that the need would forever be satisfied in that bond.

Finding a handkerchief pressed in her hand, she looked toward her Master. Evan brushed her cheek, revealing the tear there. His touch, the kindness of the handkerchief, made her want to do all sorts of unlikely things. Sink down to the grass at his feet, stay on her knees, showing her devotion and desire, her need to at last be everything to a Master. A Master who *wanted* what she had to offer.

She closed her eyes as he stroked her hair in response. That tightness in her chest increased as Niall removed his arm to give Evan more access, but he closed his hand over hers in her lap. When Evan stopped stroking, she tentatively turned her other hand palm up, not daring to look down and witness her own presumption.

Barely a blink, and Evan's hand closed over hers. She gripped them both, that three-way link, and then she brought both hands together in her lap, such that her hand ended up beneath both of theirs, their fingers loosely entwined over them. Two men, and she submitted to both, wanted to belong to both.

Evan had encouraged her to think of them that way. Having that reassurance, having them touch her now, she didn't question it.

As the young couple made the sacred vows that would carry them through a lifetime, she noted Brendan had no best man. Marguerite stood in that place, a Mistress giving him into Chloe's keeping. Gen stood behind Chloe as her maid of honor.

She recalled the oath of an InhServ, the words they were required to say first thing upon rising, and when lying down for rest. It was their only sanctioned prayer, their only approved faith.

I will serve my assigned Master with everything I am. Mind, heart, body and soul. No reservations, nothing withheld. My life belongs to the vampire who owns me, and I will never hesitate to give him whatever he desires, be it my last drop of blood or my last breath of life.

The oath didn't include love. It was the service, the honor of living up to that oath, that had become her identity, not love for her Master.

Her glance flitted to Niall. Was that how he viewed it, his oath to Evan? *A debt of honor,* he'd said. Maybe that was what rankled between them now, the fact that it had become far more, and yet it was about to end. If she'd found with Evan what Niall had, no amount of time would ever be enough. Was the friction between them as simple as coping with the impending grief of separation? Did seeing her serve Evan remind Niall another would be taking his place before long, such that he was dredging up old angers and resentments to manage his emotions about that?

Evan's fingers stilled on her nape. When she looked toward him, there was pain in his expression. Had he been listening, and she'd struck a nerve too close to home? If so, she suspected he wouldn't share the thoughts with Niall, for which she was grateful, since she sensed Niall was dealing with his own private demons. His gaze had shifted from the bride and groom to the river beyond, and his eyes were distant, his mouth tight. Did Ceana's ghost haunt him here, reminding him of promises he felt he hadn't honored properly?

Putting her other hand on top of his, she stroked the Scot's knuckles, a pressure that said she was here. Whether a crofter who'd had to bury his wife and daughter, or an InhServ who'd expected to be everything her Master had ever needed, they both understood losing the right to have expectations. As if they were the dreams of children, embarrassing and painful to recall now.

When he looked at her, it seemed perfectly natural to touch his face, stretch upward to kiss him. Evan's fingers slipped to her shoulder, caressing her there, keeping the three of them still linked.

"It's all right, *muirnín*," she whispered, adopting Niall's endearment for her. "She understood. And she loved you."

She wasn't sure if it was the right thing to say, for Niall's expression gave nothing away. She'd swept some of her hair up, the excess a thick, silk tail, and now his hand came under it as he leaned in and kissed her. Not just a brush of lips, either. He deepened it, a slow, lazy exploration of her lips and tongue that made the back row a good decision.

A heavy tide of emotion came with that kiss. Evan's fingers twined in her hair, taking a firmer hold to keep her head tilted upward as Niall's fingers overlapped his on her neck, the two of them holding her that way until Niall at last lifted his head. He nodded to her. His tawny eyes were quiet and dark, his expression reminding her of a lone bear, heading for winter hibernation.

Clasping his hand again with both her own, she refused to let him go for the rest of the ceremony. Evan laid his hand over theirs, reinforcing the bond.

17

ALANNA decided a wedding and reception were aphrodisiacs. Niall and Evan both danced with her at different times during the reception. Holding her close, the two men took turns stroking her sensitive neck, shoulder blades and lower, the curve of spine revealed by the low back of her dress, hands lingering low on her hips. Niall played a game with her, seeing if she could guess the Dominants and submissives on the guest list through body language, nuances of conversation, significant pauses. It made her think about the following night and what type of participation Evan would prefer. The anticipation gave her some very vivid fantasies.

But there was a strong emotional draw to the festivities as well. Watching her handsome males interact with other guests, smile and laugh, hearing the rumble of their voices near her, noticing how they both glanced her way often, maintaining the connection with her, she felt like she was being woven into the fabric of their relationship, a permanent and accepted part of it. Since it was clear she was involved with both men, she was the recipient of a few speculative and envious glances from attendees who were unaware of the orientation of the groom and the many other guests, but she had no desire to discourage Niall or Evan from their obvious physical possessiveness.

When the bride and groom were escorted to a garden house prepared especially for their first night as a married couple, and the reception concluded, she and Niall returned to the guesthouse hand-in-hand. Evan indicated he would join them after a brief discussion with Tyler. Shrugging out of his coat and pulling off the tie first thing, Niall draped them over the wicker chair, then tugged her to him.

"Ye can put that up later. Come here."

"What happened to 'If he knocked it off, he can pick it up'?"

"That was before I realized how nice it is tae have a lass doing all the chores." He fended off her punch, and tucked her in close, running his hand over her backside, thumb pressing into the crease with brazen intent as he gripped her hard. "Christ, I've wanted to do that for hours."

"I wish we could all three share the cellar bed." She breathed against his mouth. "I want to be with both of you."

"So I heard." His brown eyes warmed as he lifted his head. "Heaven in both our arms . . ."

She flushed. "I exaggerated for the bride. I didn't want to remind her of the more tiresome and boorish habits males can have."

"Tiresome and boorish? 'Tis a lucky lass who gets to be with the likes of us."

Did he know what thickening the accent while he still wore the Highland garb did to her? She had a feeling he did.

"So you say." She managed a credible sniff, but it was no contest when he pulled her closer, brushed her hair to the side and put his lips to her neck, her jaw pressed to his, feeling the working of his throat as he gently teased that sensitive vein. Her breath left her, fingers coiling in his hair, trying not to mess up how she'd arranged it. With an impatient noise, he pulled the queue loose, letting her know he wanted her fingers buried in it.

"Being pretty is done for the day. I'd rather look well-used by an eager wench."

She bit his jaw, earning a chuckle as he returned the favor. She willingly dug her fingers into his scalp, enjoying the thick tangle of his hair, her body starting to pulse in fervent need. She thought of what Chloe had said about wanting to devour Brendan, and knew exactly how she felt.

Niall banded his arms around her waist to lift her. He didn't take her to their room, but instead surprised her by taking her below, to the cellar. In Evan's bedroom, he put his mouth on hers, holding the embrace until he laid her on the bed facedown. He moved the pillows so her cheek was against the mattress. "Arms and legs spread, *muirnín*," he ordered.

She obeyed instantly, her body amping up its responses when he produced silken rope from a drawer next to the bed. The type of amenities available when one stayed on the property of a sexual Dominant. Not much different from being in the guesthouse of a vampire, after all.

Niall skillfully knotted the ropes around her wrists and ankles, drawing out the spread position until her body was pressed even deeper into the mattress, her mound and breasts tingling with the pressure. When he was done, he slid his knuckles down her spine, swept her hair off her back, so there was a clear expanse of flesh for him to see. "Fucking gorgeous," he muttered. She tried to look toward him, but he made a quiet noise of command.

"Nane of your temptations tonight. Ye led me by my cock to get me to sleep, but ye only get away with that on rare occasion. Evan wants to peel ye out of everything but those flimsy stockings and heels himself."

He slid a blindfold over her eyes, one with a snug Velcro closure on the back to ensure that it wouldn't loosen. She was beginning to tremble. Though it was certainly not the first time she'd been bound this way, everything with them felt like the first time.

When he put his knee on the bed between her legs, her heart was beating high in her throat, her pussy weeping. True to his Master's desires, he'd kept her in her wedding attire, the silver dress, thigh-high lace stockings. She wasn't wearing any panties since it would have ruined the snug line of the skirt. He hadn't even removed her heels, looping the rope over the tops of her feet so it kept the shoes bound to her soles.

Sliding down the side zipper of the dress, he slid his fingers into the opening, stroking her body from below her breast to her hip bone. At her noise of pleasure, he made an approving rumble.

"Aye, you're hot for it. We could tell, those hungry eyes at the reception. Fair killed us, not taking ye then and there. But 'tis a drug to us, lass, drawing out your desire. Particularly to a vampire. I'm to leave you like this, let ye think about what Evan might have planned for you."

She didn't want him to leave. It wasn't a demand—never that—but a plea. She wanted to give them both pleasure, let them take their fill of her, of each other. She could vividly imagine Niall buried inside of her from behind like this, while Evan fucked him, held them both under his power.

"I serve our Master," she responded. She wouldn't let her own desires eclipse theirs. "Whatever he wants. Whatever either of you want."

His fingers paused in their long stroke, then he pressed a kiss to her spine, just above the back of the dress. "You, *muirnín*. We both want you."

Then he was gone. Being a wine cellar, the room was cool, but it wasn't uncomfortable to her, not with the heat of Niall's touch still affecting her. She was vulnerable, facedown, blindfolded, but an InhServ had no defenses against her Master's desires. She submitted, surrendered. Heart, mind, soul, body . . . utterly his . . .

She used it as a meditation exercise, weaving arousal with acceptance, patience. She'd never had difficulty waiting on Stephen's desires. Perhaps patience and indifference could look very much the same.

Now, however, there was no mistaking one for the other. Her pussy was wet, needy. As she squirmed, rotated her hips, the mattress gave her clit the pressure it craved. She thought of Evan watching her, perhaps allowing Niall to do the same, and made the movement as provocative as possible, lifting her hips like an animal in heat, tempting a male . . . or males . . . closer. She licked her lips at the resulting wave of sensation, did it again.

Her continuing dance brought the short skirt high enough to expose the slick pink lips of her sex when she lifted her hips, begging to be fucked, to be tongued there. She thought of Niall's thick fingers pushing into that opening, the clever way he had of rubbing her, making her come apart. Her fingers flexed in her bonds. He'd used a knot that wouldn't tighten on her wrists, keeping her bound but not restricted in circulation. No pain or discomfort. He and Evan cared for her, watched over her, and it made her long for them even more.

Tomorrow night, she would perform with any other submissive they required, but the end goal would be the same. Them touching her, taking her . . . She didn't want anyone else, she wanted them. She needed them. Longed for them.

She wasn't being deliberate now. Her body moved of its own accord against the mattress, rubbing her clit in a faster motion, building the orgasm in her lower belly. She couldn't go over, wouldn't without her Master's consent, but she wanted to show him how hot she could get for him, making her pussy cream to the point the scent would reach his enhanced vampire senses.

"You teased your Master into coming to you."

He was here. She came to a shuddering halt, almost moaning at the sound of his voice. It held a sternness that made her doubt herself, though. She'd misbehaved, earned his disapproval.

"No, Alanna. You have not earned my disapproval. Only my punishment."

Thin strips slid down her exposed buttock, the dress bunched at the small of her back. "So courteous of you to lift your skirt for me. There are craftspeople here who make things for Masters to inflict punishment. I got a tawse for Niall, which might be powerful enough to pull a grunt out of him. I look forward to the attempt. But this slapper of treated wood strips is perfect for you. Lift that beautiful ass of yours, like when you were begging for my cock. You hold it there until I say otherwise. I don't want to hear a sound out of you."

She complied, trembling, and when the first blow landed, she bit down hard to obey. Thin and flexible, the slapper stung like bees, and it smacked against her ass with a sound like a shot, increasing the reaction. The last time he'd punished her, it had been to chastise her only. He intended to goad her arousal with the pain this time, and with her current level of stimulation, she was simply swept away.

Thwack, thwack! He covered all the territory she'd exposed, and her muscles were trembling with the effort to hold her ass in the air, to hold completely still. She dug her fingers into her bonds, bit the mattress, tried not to scream into it, but before he was done, she was, trying to muffle the noise as best she could.

She was panting. When a few moments passed without further blows, she thought he was studying his handiwork, the marks on her buttocks. Was he hard? She imagined him opening the dark slacks he'd worn with his tuxedo, stroking himself over her, coming so that his seed splashed against her abused ass. She kept her hips lifted as he required, hoping for it.

He didn't give her that, but something just as blissful. The heat of his breath, so close to her soaking wet folds. He didn't touch her with his mouth. She just felt its proximity when he blew gently on her. A soft, continuous air flow moving over her clit and labia, a ripple of sensation that made her sob. "Please . . . Master . . ."

"Shhh. Be quiet." He kept doing it, that tiny little current of air across her engorged clit until she would have given him anything to come. There was nothing in her mind but those sensations. Then he touched his lips to her clit, one solid pressure, and she was lost.

Stay still, but come for me, Alanna. Do it.

He pulled away, leaving her bereft, yet she would obey him no matter what. All it took was the thought, the echoes of those sensations still vibrating through her. Her empty pussy spasmed, taking her over the edge. She was unable to quell the involuntary, short pumps of her hips, but he was suddenly there, hands now on her hips, holding them up higher. She shrieked as he slammed his cock in deep, working inside her.

"Oh God . . . Master . . ."

"That's my sweet, sweet servant," he muttered, the strain in his voice sending a surge of triumph through her. She clenched her muscles over him, reveling in the slick, excruciating glide of his shaft inside her. That strained note became a groan of release, and she cried out with him, sharing that ecstasy as aftershocks shot through her with his seed.

She couldn't ever imagine wanting anything more . . . but then she was proven wrong.

When he finished, he slid from her, slow and easy. She made a noise of loss and yearning that seemed to please him, for he tugged her hair, a partial caress. Her bonds were released, but only so the vampire could turn her over, restraining her spread eagle once again. It was decadent, her clothes in disarray but still on her body, as if he hadn't the patience to rid her of them. His fingers caressed her thighs, teasing the lace tops of the stockings.

Then she made another noise of pure ecstasy as she smelled Niall, the scent of his aroused cock, a moment before it was pushing into her eager mouth. As he straddled her, testicles brushing her sternum, bare thighs around her shoulders, equally bare buttocks pressing against her breasts, she realized he was blissfully naked. The mattress shifted beneath her as Niall caught hold of the headboard.

"Yes . . ." She breathed it against his rigid flesh, sucking and working him as deep as she could, while Evan straddled her waist. Both men were over her body, and she loved it. She wished she could see them, but that wasn't her job. She was here to keep Niall hard, to take him down her throat when Evan fucked him to climax.

The Scot gave a grunt as his Master took him, thrusting deep into his ass, such that their knees pressed harder into the bed on either side of her. *Oh God . . . yes. Yes.*

Your ass is as sweet to me as hers, neshama. *Tighten against me. Come in her mouth. Let me feel what I can do to you. To both of you.*

Tonight the Scot was in full accord with the vampire. With a deep, guttural sound, Niall came, the headboard rocking ominously. They might have to compensate Tyler and Marguerite for damage to the furniture after all. Both men had found release quickly, telling her their need had built the way hers had, until it was pushing inexorably against whatever control they had. She loved the thought, as well as the idea they might do it again and again tonight, their need stoked that high.

Her throat worked, taking down the jet of Niall's semen. It filled her mouth, forcing her to seal her lips firmly over him, holding it all in as she managed it in several swallows. She kept sucking on him, tongue sliding over the sensitive underside, pulling hard on the ridged head as he became progressively more sensitive. When he grasped her hair in a quelling motion, he let out a half chuckle, half curse as she nipped at him.

"Payback'll be hell, lass. I can eat your cunt all day while ye wiggle and scream and plead for me to stop."

She wouldn't ever want him to stop, no matter how oversensitized the area became. Just the idea of his mouth on her pussy had her shuddering anew. It must have stimulated Evan as well, for as she predicted, he made the decision to start all over again, working himself deeper and harder in Niall's ass, winning strained grunts from the big male as the vampire reached back with those long, clever fingers to tease her clit to that high pinnacle again as well.

She'd never felt so . . . purposed. A true servant at last.

◇

The full-sized bed might be too small for two sizeable men and one woman on a normal night, but not when they were tangled together like vines. They'd fallen asleep for a short nap, her coiled in between them. When Niall roused later, she would have gone with him, but Evan cinched her closer, and Niall put a kiss on her shoulder. "Sleep with our Master, *muirnín*," he said. "You'll need your strength tonight. I'll take care of the things that need doing."

Evan kept her in the curve of his body, one hand on her waist, the other resting on her throat, fingers along her pulse, elbow in between her breasts. It was an effective and sensual body lock that made her aware of every inch of her skin pressed to his, for not only had they stripped her fully following their thorough lovemaking, Evan had shed his clothes as well. She enjoyed the rare pleasure of their completely bare, hard bodies pressed against her.

They'd left her tied and blindfolded for a while, forbidding her to speak. They'd spoken to each other, though, casual conversations as they took their fill of fondling her body. It had aroused her to an excruciating level again, and she knew that was what Evan wanted. It was what a vampire enjoyed most, that sadistic infliction of pleasure, and the fact that Evan was unleashing it with her as well as Niall kept her in a lust-filled euphoria.

Now, still dozing, Evan pressed his erection against her. When she parted her thighs, he pushed inside, making her draw in a deep, shuddering, peaceful breath as he stopped there, simply staying inside her as he slept on. Wherever his dreams were taking him, he wanted to be buried in her cunt, joined to her.

Most vampires she knew would react to the idea of postcoital cuddling like having windows thrown open over their beds in broad daylight. But Evan and Niall . . . they'd done it several times, now. Well, Niall had. Usually Evan had to leave them to it, because they were above ground and the sun came up. But now she was in the arms of a vampire who obviously intended for her to stay in his company until it was time to rise for the evening festivities, where she would be presented as his devoted slave.

If she was to make a list of the most wonderful experiences she'd ever had in her life, she had a feeling all top ten would be counted among these few weeks. Closing her eyes, she slept.

∾

In their skill for presentation, Tyler and Marguerite could compete with vampires. It being another nice night, they'd turned the elaborate back gardens into a dungeon play area. Expensive pieces of BDSM equipment were integrated into the landscaping as if they'd always been there. Staff from the club where Tyler shared part ownership moved around with hors d'oeuvres and drinks, taking requests for particular toys or accessories, if they weren't readily at hand.

Beside a fountain pool graced with a center statue of Aphrodite, Alanna saw a male submissive kneeling. He was pressed down over the fountain wall, his hands flat on the pool's bottom, arms immersed to the biceps in the water. Koi slowly swam around them, nibbling, as his Mistress worked herself inside his flexing ass with a sizeable strap-on. At her order, he would periodically lower his face in the water, keep it there for a few seconds as she fucked him, until she put her fingers on the head harness he wore to draw him back up, gasping.

Niall, strolling along arm-and-arm with her, discreetly pointed out staff members in black shirts whose job it was to watch over the play, make sure nothing got out of hand, since there were obviously a lot of edge players in the ranks. As such, one was carefully monitoring the sub when he was underwater, but she noted the Mistress was just as alert to any signs of distress or choking.

"'Tis pretty tame, compared tae a vampire gathering, but for humans, this is as extreme as it gets, within the boundaries of mortal frailty and common sense, of course. Speaking of which . . ." He passed a hand over her backside, giving her a fond squeeze. "Any soreness left? You wouldnae know it to look at the skinny runt, but Evan can get . . . enthusiastic."

She'd found one thing she liked about the blocker. The marks inflicted by her Master lingered, allowing her to touch them, see them. With the outfit Evan had ordered her to wear, they were also on display to everyone who passed. And she was overjoyed by it.

The upper garment was an arrangement of black velvet-coated straps that passed under and over her breasts, constricting them in a mild breast bondage to make them even more full and eye catching. The buckled strap beneath had an edging of silver chains tipped with tiny stars that pricked her skin as she moved. The bottom was a thong accentuated by thigh-high latex stockings, as well as teetering stilettos that arched her back and put her buttocks on high display, along with the marks of her punishment. Slim chains encircled her ankles and passed underneath the soles of the shoes, locking there.

Evan had sat in a chair, watching Niall dress her, his gaze passing over the curve of the Scot's back as he knelt to lock the shoes onto her feet. For this event Niall wore only a utility kilt and Goth-style heavy boots with a series of buckles. She loved the look on him, had wanted to trail her fingers up his bare back, press her mouth to the dragon on his chest when he rose, but since Evan had told her to keep her fingers locked behind her head until he was done outfitting her the way he desired, she'd obeyed her Master. Tonight, she wanted nothing more than to serve his every desire, no matter if it left her in a mindless frenzy, caught up in her own arousal.

She loved the idea of wearing something that pleased them both, going as their servant, ready to perform for their pleasure. Stephen had rated her performance in terms of political advantage, but with Evan and Niall, she would be acting purely on their desires, their interests, and that gave her a swirl of anxious anticipation that was new and exciting.

Evan had left the last piece of the outfit for himself. When her Master rose from the chair, Niall stepping aside, her breath had caught, seeing that Evan was holding a collar. His eyes on her reaction, he put the wide strap around her throat. It fastened in the back, secured with a padlock. When he showed her the key, brushed his knuckles along her cheek, she pressed her lips fervently to the fingers that held it.

"If I had time, I would have had a tag made for it," he'd said, his gray eyes caressing her face. "So they would know who your Master is."

She'd closed her eyes as he tightened the collar, one step beyond restricting her breathing, just how she wanted it. Actually, she would have been fine with him stealing her breath away entirely. She knew who her Master was. It was stamped on her every reaction. The intensity of his expression had told her he heard her thought.

Niall brought her back to the present. "The rosy color of your nipples is driving everyone to distraction. If ye had a third mark, he'd have told me to pierce them tonight, put a pretty silver bar through each one."

"We can still—"

"No." Niall gave her that steady, brook-no-argument look that, unlike his teasing, could stop her words in a heartbeat. "He kens ye can bear the pain, but they wouldnae heal right away. He wants your breasts accessible to him. And so do I." As they walked, he brought a hand up along her side to boldly cup one, heedless of the passersby. She made a needy sound as he caressed and squeezed it. "You'll tell me if the straps get too restrictive, lass. We're goin' to loosen them in the half hour regardless."

She could bear any discomfort for their pleasure, but Niall had made a good point. Without the regenerative power of a third mark, too much pain or discomfort would impair her ability to serve them. Of course, the healing of a nipple piercing, the loss of circulation to her breasts, were only problems if her agony was an issue to the vampire. But it was to this particular vampire and his servant, far more than it would have been to Stephen. Which perversely made her want to have Niall do it, prove she'd endure any pain for Evan.

Niall's fingers tightened on hers. "Behave," he murmured. "Submitting to your Master means submitting to his will in all things. Ye didnae get to pick and choose. Ye know that, lass."

So Evan was close, and sharing her thoughts with Niall. It was a direct reproof. A few days ago, any rebuke had diminished her, emphasizing her failure and inadequacy. Now she absorbed it into this new fragile sense of herself, a servant eager to serve a Master who cared enough to protect her.

Him and his servant. Niall might appreciate her appearance, but she couldn't take her eyes off him. The hard muscles of his bare upper body shifted against her side and back where he walked close beside her. The way he moved in the dark utility kilt, his sheer size and presence, was mesmerizing, and not just to her. The other women might speculate, but she knew there was nothing under the kilt. She wanted to go to her knees in her provocative outfit, push the fabric up his strong thighs and put her mouth on him. Lubricate his cock from the arousal between her thighs and then rub him between her tender breasts until he came . . .

Niall gave her a rough, impatient kiss. "We should have kept ye in the cellar and fucked ye a hundred times. Stop thinking thoughts like that."

"If my Master wants to torment you with my thoughts, it's not for me to deprive him of that pleasure," she observed demurely.

His pinch made her jump. "Remember what I said about 'Master' not being around to protect you. I'll put ye over a bench and strap you within an inch of your life. Evan'll join us after his meeting, but Marcus Stanton isnae known for being short-winded when harassing his artists. I have a guid hour at least tae impress upon ye the wisdom of yanking a bear's chain."

She suppressed a smile, but when he rested his hand high on her buttock, long fingers wrapped around it to stroke her bare hip bone, she had to concentrate to keep her head up, to walk in a way that best presented her Master's assets.

"I was watching Evan and Tyler at the reception," she said, attempting to distract herself. "Their relationship seems to extend beyond a mutual appreciation for art. How did they meet?"

"Always the observant one." Niall nodded. "Tyler used to work for the government. One o' those mysterious agencies. He's never said which one. Our paths crossed his in the Middle East. Tyler got betrayed by a key informant, and we stumbled on him in a tough spot. He was overwhelmed in numbers and firepower. Though we didnae know a thing about him, neither Evan nor I liked the feel of it, so we got him out of there."

Niall shrugged. "The lad was beat up pretty badly, so Evan took most his weight and dragged him out of there. Guid thing he was there to shield Tyler, because Evan took several slugs in the back that would have killed a human. I took a gun away from one of the bastards and laid down cover fire while Evan used his speed to get Tyler free of it. I caught up with them later. That third mark speed is fair handy at times." He gave her a wink.

"After that, he must have realized the two of you were something . . . different. Or was he too out of it to remember what happened?" She didn't like to think of bullets hitting Evan, or Niall in the line of fire, no matter how indestructible they imagined themselves.

"Ye could beat that lad's head into a brick wall for an hour and he'd still have his wits about him," Niall said dryly. "If I didnae know for certain he was human, I'd swear Tyler had vampire or Fae blood. But aye, I think he realizes we're not exactly what we say we are. Never to this day has he said a word about it, though."

Which was good, because the Council forbade knowledge of vampires among humans not integrated into their society through at least a first- or second-marking.

"Most folk find it easier tae overlook something like that than to entertain the idea of vampires," Niall said. "But Tyler's like Evan. He sees things other people dinnae, and he's careful how he uses the information."

She thought about that as they continued to wander through the party, studying the public scenes being executed by other Masters and Mistresses with their willing subs. While Niall nodded to several submissives not currently engaged, ones he obviously knew, he also demonstrated courteous deference to the Masters and Mistresses. She saw them acknowledge he was here as Evan's, but she also caught the speculative looks, reflecting some of the same thoughts she'd had about Niall.

Evan and Niall reminded her of Tyler and Marguerite. Niall told her Tyler rarely exercised his rights as Master over Marguerite in mixed company, but she'd seen the subtle signs of her submission when Tyler touched his wife. Her gaze would briefly lower, her body gravitating toward his, her fingers docile in his grasp, seeking permission to touch. Yet when the woman looked toward a sub, she exuded a Mistress's power, the sense she had the right to touch anything she damn well pleased . . . and he'd beg for her to do so.

"Oh . . . my."

They'd reached the side lawn. Down where the wedding had occurred, a different ritual was occurring at the altar. Brendan's upright body was a demonstration of Japanese rope tying, done by Chloe herself. A rope harness ran from throat to groin, with further diamond patterns and wraps down his legs and arms. His limbs were bound to the altar, holding him upright and stretched to the limits. He'd been thoroughly oiled beforehand, so his flesh glistened. His bride was on folded knees, staring up at him in adoration. She wore a brown velvet skirt that came to her ankles and purple Ked sneakers. A lavender T-shirt hugged her lush curves. She still wore the satin ribbon Alanna had put in her hair.

Brendan had been blindfolded, much like Alanna had been earlier on the bed. Apparently, Chloe understood as well as Evan and Niall did how sensory deprivation heightened and focused response. When Chloe reached out, slid her fingers through the oil on his thighs, up to the part of the harness that pressed against his testicles, his muscles flexed in instant reaction. She'd used a smaller grade of rope to do an intricate cock harness, the head plum-colored from the restraint.

Now Chloe leaned forward and tasted, a kitten's lick on the tip, and he bucked, showing how aroused he was. Loosening the cock harness, she slid it free and massaged him, rising to her knees to put her mouth on his abdomen, his hip bone, a reverent worship of the man who'd surrendered to her.

Chloe had woven a spell around those watching, yet it was obvious the new bride wasn't aware of anything but her husband. When she stood up, she slid her arms around his bound torso. "I love you," she said. "You are so perfect."

He was unable to dip his head because she'd attached the wide collar he wore to two horizontal tethers, but the strain of his body against her gave his answer to that. Sliding under his arm, she went behind him. Her hands glided down the front of his body to curl around the ropes, tug on the ones that looped under his testicles. His cock slit glistened with fluid.

Alanna was at a side angle to the stage, so she could see the harness in back had a line of knots threaded between his buttocks. When Chloe worked them against his rim, he pumped against her hold, fucking the air.

"Do you want to please me?" she whispered.

"More than anything," he said hoarsely. "Let me please you."

Niall had his arm around Alanna's waist. She gripped his forearm hard, aware of his heartbeat behind her back, the press of his heavy kilt against her bare buttocks. He cupped her breast, thumb brushing idly over her nipple, making her whimper softly.

"Do ye want to please me, lass?" Niall's voice was in her ear.

Yes. God yes. She was so wet she felt the sucking dampness when he moved the thong aside. His probing touch made her catch her lip in her teeth. She wanted him to lift his kilt, bend his knees and drive into her with third-mark strength. With Niall's strength.

Despite the oil on Brendan's skin, Chloe pressed fully against her husband's back, wrapping both hands around his cock. "Come for me. Here. In front of all of them, so they know you're mine. Okay?"

Her soft voice wasn't a Mistress's demand, but a sweet desire, a need expressed, and Brendan thrust into her fingers. "Please . . ." he said. "Yes. Anything."

She began to work him, slow, long strokes. The gathered audience was absorbed in it, Alanna no exception. Niall brought her closer to a bench in front of them. The Mistress who sat there looked nearly six feet tall, black skinned and red-haired, intimidating even without the coiled single tail next to her. She wore a buckled corset over tight leggings and thigh-high boots.

When she looked back at them, her dark brown eyes coursed over Alanna's features, measuring her aroused state, as well as Niall's hot male intent.

"She's welcome to put her hands here, Niall." She nodded at the back of the bench, her voice a husky purr. "I've seen what meat you bring to the table. She'll need something to hang on to."

"Do it," Niall ordered, breath bathing her neck. Alanna clamped down on the smooth wood. As Niall adjusted his kilt, the Mistress tilted her head to watch, her tongue touching her top lip at what he revealed. Her gaze shifted to Alanna's face as Niall drove into her wet cunt.

Alanna shuddered, internalizing the incredible energy, because she wouldn't distract from Chloe's beautiful display, any more than she would deny Niall. The Mistress was right, however. She needed the brace of the bench, especially when the Scot lifted her off her feet enough that she hooked her stilettos around his calves for further support.

The Mistress turned her attention back to the stage, but a feral smile curved her lips, showing her pleasure in the rhythmic vibration going through her seat as Niall mirrored Chloe's pace, thrusting in slow, pulling out slow, making Alanna come apart.

At this angle, she realized Brendan had a brand on his lower back, a fleur de lis like her InhServ mark, with two decorative elements around it. The mark of a willing slave.

The air was so dense with lust, it didn't surprise Alanna when the Mistress put her hand between her own legs, began to play with her pussy through the latex. She threaded her other arm beneath Alanna's grip, so that Alanna's exposed nipples were brushing her forearm, increasing the friction. That female–female contact galvanized Niall as well, and Alanna clutched the bench harder, biting back an involuntary grunt at the power he used to drive into her.

"Showing ye about like this brings out the animal in us, *muirnín*," he muttered in her ear. "Evan wants me to take ye hard, remind ye and everyone else you're ours. And so do I."

So did she. Oh God, she did.

The Mistress was still masturbating, her fingertips sliding along the bench edge as if she was caressing flesh.

"Now, baby," Chloe said. Brendan began to release, ropes of come spurting through Chloe's fingers and over the platform. He groaned loudly, all the swimmer's muscles flowing under her touch. Chloe had her face pressed into his back, but as she turned her cheek so it was pressed against his heart, Alanna could see she was whispering to him, words of utter devotion as she held herself against his flexing ass.

"Niall . . ." She was gasping herself. There were other similar interactions happening on the lawn, helping to cover the noise, but then the Mistress began to idly tug on the buckle beneath Alanna's breasts, teasing her compressed cleavage with scarlet nails.

"Come quietly, *muirnín*." Niall put his large hand up to Alanna's mouth, and she sank her teeth into the two fingers he pushed against it like a bit gag. She shrieked, unable to control herself. The stimulus was overwhelming, Brendan coming before her eyes, the Mistress's contact with her breasts, Niall and Evan's not-so-casual decision to possess her in public to validate their claim. Most of all Niall, releasing in her spasming pussy.

He kept thrusting well after the major crash, so that she was still bleating against his hand, small aftershocks. She wanted nothing more than to go to her knees and clean him with her mouth, finish her duty.

"Nae right now, lass. We owe Mistress Regina a debt."

As he eased her back to her feet and her mind steadied under the Mistress's close regard, Alanna understood what he meant.

"Is your servant practiced at giving a woman pleasure?" the Mistress asked, looking past Alanna, treating Niall as her Master-by-proxy. "I thought you might sit with me while she licks my pussy."

Niall pressed a kiss to Alanna's sweaty neck, pulling his kilt down. "She's not my servant, as ye well know, but Evan demands I be courteous to all ladies." He gave Regina a wicked grin. "A hot poker in my eyes is the only thing that will keep me from looking, though, so I might still be in your debt when she's done for you."

The woman chuckled. "If I was Evan, I'd put your cock in a sharp-pronged chastity device to keep your mind where it should be, Niall."

"What fun would that have been, just now? You'd have missed the chance to ogle it."

Niall guided Alanna around the bench, fingers on her elbow to steady her wobbly knees. "Do as the lady desires, Alanna."

She was still vibrating, could smell the woman's desire strong and sharp. Going down on her knees in the grass exposed her bare backside to those whose attention turned to their activities. She could handle the physical demand; it was no different from much more strenuous things she'd done at vampire dinners. But wrapping her mind around what had just happened—her reaction to Chloe and Brendan, Niall's claim spoken hotly into her ear, how she herself reacted to his touch, to the way he and Evan were—gave her a lot of emotions to manage.

As such, it was good to have Niall's reassuring presence. He slid onto the bench next to Regina, stretching out a leg so Alanna could grip his thigh to steady herself. She positioned herself between the woman's legs.

"I can order my boy to do whatever you desire to her exposed parts." Mistress Regina nodded to a pretty, slender man in a submissive posture a few yards away. When he thought he could get away with it, he was casting her brooding looks. "He's being punished for insolence, so he gets to watch his Mistress be pleasured rather than doing it himself. I'm certain he'd be able to give her a most enthusiastic whipping with the object of your choice."

I'll break him like the twig he is if he puts a finger on her. He's looking a little too angry for my tastes.

That came from Niall, but Evan had let her hear it. Throughout their evening, Niall had purposefully steered her away from any interaction with males. Was that Evan's desire or his own? Or both? Stephen hadn't cared one way or another, but then Evan never fit the mold of what she expected.

Of course, she herself had unexpectedly tensed at the Mistress's suggestion, that feeling easing when Niall stroked her hair.

"It's not necessary." He drew Regina's attention to the marks on Alanna's backside, gently sliding the toe of his large boot along the curve of her buttock. "Her Master already attended to her discipline today. Alanna, proceed at the Mistress's order."

∼

She completed the task to Mistress Regina's satisfaction, though the woman had formidable control and drew out the torment of her male servant until the young man was fair quivering with vitriol. When she finally came, her fingers locked on the back of Alanna's neck, she left the imprint of her nails there, though she stopped short of drawing blood.

Once done with that, Niall took them strolling again. He must have realized she was a little drained, at least emotionally, so he set a relaxed pace, and made it clear they were just observing. Evan had been silent since letting her hear Niall's thought, obviously now too deeply into his meeting to interact with them. She was starting to miss him quite keenly, seeing so many Masters and Mistresses interacting with their committed submissives. Though he didn't say so, she had a feeling Niall shared her restiveness about it.

While some groups were still using equipment, others were merely socializing, sitting in chair groupings, sipping drinks refilled by the circulating staff. Others were in the indoor pool, whose windows and doors were thrown open to allow viewing of the naked, wet bodies.

She studied the Dominant and submissive pairings, guessing which ones were in more intense, permanent relationships versus those still in "dating" or play mode, perhaps together for this event only. Niall played along, confirming or denying, but she was warmed by his surprise at how many she guessed accurately.

About an hour later they ran into Chloe and Brendan again. Now they were both dressed, Brendan in a pair of faded jeans, Chloe on his lap, the couple sitting on a large blanket on the lawn. Chloe hadn't changed her shirt, and it had an interesting, artistic stain pattern, transferred to the fabric from the oil on Brendan's body. The couple was surrounded by a chatting group of friends, but when Chloe saw them, she waved them over, jumping to her feet. "*Niall.* I didn't get to say hello to you earlier. The whole wedding thing and all."

Alanna blinked as Chloe took two steps and leaped upon the Scot. He'd anticipated the reaction, adjusting as she wrapped legs and arms around him and squeezed. "Hey, what happened to the other dragon? You used to have two of them, here." Chloe thumped his broad chest.

"Evan drew a few on me until he decided what he wanted—fighting dragons, mating dragons—but I told him I'd prefer not having beast pornography on my chest for the rest of my life."

Chloe grinned. "I was so happy you were able to make it. Tyler was sure you guys would be in an Antarctic cave. It blew me away to find you were so close by. It was fate."

"How could ye doubt it, little sprite?" Niall kissed her soundly on the mouth, then let her slip back to her feet. "Brendan, ye've walked right into a fairy ring with this one."

Seizing Alanna's hands, Chloe turned her toward her husband. "Brendan, this is Alanna. She belongs to Niall and Evan."

Brendan might have gotten to his feet in courtesy, but Chloe flung herself back into his lap, so he caught her with one arm, grinning as he and Alanna maintained precarious balance through a handshake. "My pleasure, Alanna." His voice had a sexy, firm timbre.

Chloe shook her head, already on to another topic. "Niall, go rescue Evan from Marcus. Josh and Thomas haven't come back, either. Lauren couldn't make it, because of a pediatric emergency, so Josh has no one to rescue him, and of course Thomas is Marcus's, so he's stuck with his bullying. Don't send Alanna. She's much too sweet. Marcus will do the Dom thing to scare her away, and I'll have to punch him in the face. You'll tell him to piss off and drag Evan out of there."

"Dinnae underestimate Alanna. She's handled Masters far scarier than Marcus." Niall shot Alanna a droll look.

Chloe sighed. "Knowing Marcus, he's trying to make them create his next hefty commission check right out of their backsides, here and now. I want to see Evan, and I'm getting sleepy. I know how you guys are. You disappear in the middle of the night, and I won't see you again until forever."

Niall gave Alanna's hip a caress. "I cannae refuse the bride. Stay with Chloe until I get back. Understand?"

"Yes, sir."

"Guid lass." He gave her backside a firm squeeze, a reminder. As he strode away, she watched the graceful power of his movements until he disappeared past the pool house.

"See, even she does it."

Chloe spoke to Brendan, drawing Alanna down to sit on his feet on the blanket. Brendan courteously adjusted so Alanna could prop her back on his calf while Chloe leaned against his hip, a casually intimate pose. "Does what?" Alanna asked.

"You don't treat Niall like another sub. No one does, except Evan, and even with him it's hit or miss. I thought Niall was a Dom when I met him, until I saw him with Evan, and then you can definitely see it.

Niall's an über-alpha sub. He can flip the Dom switch when he wants, but I bet Evan's the only one who gets the awesome benefit of the sub side." Chloe gave her an impish wink. "Both the artists I know, Josh and Thomas, they're subs to the bone, but with Evan, you're around him two seconds and you know that's not him."

Brendan nuzzled Chloe's ear, his fingers slipping along her side, thumb caressing the underside of her breast. The gaze Chloe turned upon him, the press of her lips to his jaw, suggested it might not be sleepiness that would have them retiring soon. On the altar stage, they'd given and received pleasure for the audience as well as themselves. Now it was obvious they wanted to indulge the quiet intimacy of a married couple.

"Evan has a different kind of Dom vibe though," Chloe mused, a little more breathless. She offered another cheeky grin. "Marcus and Tyler, they broadcast theirs like a moose's mating call. They can't hide it. But Evan's sneaks up on you, surrounds you. You sense it like a pittosporum bush in bloom. Have you ever smelled one?"

When Alanna shook her head, Chloe inhaled deeply, stretching out her arms as if she was about to embrace the referenced foliage. "The flowers have a light, barely there scent, but after the first or second whiff, suddenly it's all inside you. If that makes sense. Evan probably doesn't want to be compared to girly flowers though."

"I think Niall worries more about that kind of thing than Evan does." It was new to Alanna, speculating on the type of Master she had, but it seemed all right in this context, as long as she chose her words carefully. "Evan's focus is different. Being a Master is part of his blood, almost an afterthought. So he doesn't pay much attention to it. It just is. The art . . . that's what drives him first and foremost."

Chloe nodded. "Yes, that's exactly it." Slipping her hand around Brendan's calf, she slid down farther against his body so she could lean her head against his knee. He stroked her head, his expression absorbed, quiet. Familiar with the state of mind, she could tell he was taking in not only their conversation, but everything else happening. He was tuned in, ready to anticipate Chloe's needs, but also easy, content with it. It was how she'd felt earlier in the evening, sated by both men, dozing in between them. She wondered if Evan or Niall experienced a contentment like that. She'd like to give that to them, but sometimes it was difficult to know what would bring a Master ease.

"If you'd rather follow Niall, go be with him and Evan, that's fine." Chloe touched her arm. "I can tell you want to."

"Niall said I should wait here."

"I don't think they mind if you disobey a little. That's part of the fun, right?"

Perhaps in the human world. But Niall had particular reasons for wanting to keep her where he knew where she was. But there was no danger here, and Evan knew where she was at all times. Still, she waffled. She listened to the conversations, participating when invited to do so, but she had an increasing sense of needing to go to Evan, needing to go *now*.

When she rose at last, her mind made up, Brendan squeezed Chloe's shoulder, rose as well. "I'll go with you, make sure you find them."

Safely hung in the air. It seemed absurd, since Tyler's staff were everywhere, and they were in a rural environment well off the main roads, but her uneasy feeling was growing. Perhaps Brendan had picked up on it. She thought about speaking directly to Evan in her mind, but he was in a meeting. There was no concrete evidence that she should disrupt him.

"Thank you. I'm sure that's unnecessary, but . . ."

"Not at all." Exchanging a look with Chloe that showed the couple were in agreement on it, he offered his arm to Alanna. As he guided her away from their group, he put a warm hand over hers in the crook of his elbow. "I recognize when a Master has a specific concern with respect to his property. Niall had that concern."

Niall had said he wasn't her Master, but her mind wasn't concerned with correcting semantics. As Brendan skirted past the pool house, and took the winding path by the river that led up to the west gardens, her heart started to beat more rapidly, her pulse rate increasing.

She stopped, scanning the darkness. "We need to go back toward the pool house, Brendan," she said, low. "Please. Right now. But . . . don't look like you're hurrying."

Nodding, he took a more secure hold of her hand, his other one moving to her waist, altering their direction but maintaining a casual pace, taking them toward where the swimmers were. "Who is it?" he murmured.

"I'm not sure, but . . . it's best to be where more people are."

"I'll let Tyler know once we get—"

"No." She caught hold of his arm, squeezed hard enough to earn a startled glance from those vivid hazel eyes. "It doesn't concern Tyler or . . . any of you. I'm seeing shadows. I'm on some medication that makes me a little more . . . nervous. It's nothing. I just need to find Evan."

Sub or not, this male had a broad protective streak, just as Chloe had intimated. It was obvious from his expression he didn't believe her. He was going to let Tyler know, putting all the human guests, including himself, at risk.

Evan? Master, forgive my interruption, but there is a vampire close by. It's not Stephen. He's detected your presence and is investigating. I don't know how bold he will become.

Most vampires avoided human gatherings like this, but the very fact that a vampire not normally part of this territory had been detected had brought him closer. He also might call a few other vampires to help him investigate. Like Niall, she knew there were vampires far less civilized about Council directives on territory crossings.

Understood. Stay where you are. I'm coming.

She realized then Brendan had slipped away from her. He was a few yards away, talking to Tyler, who'd come out of the pool house. *Damn it.* Though the men's backs were to her, Tyler's posture changed to one she recognized very well, a male preparing to defend his territory and what was his within it. Why couldn't she have acted less concerned, so as not to tip Brendan off? She was so rarely around humans uninitiated into this world, she had no skills in that regard.

Tyler might be a dangerous human to cross, but he'd have no chance against a vampire. Chloe would be widowed before she finished her honeymoon, Tyler torn apart. She imagined Marguerite standing over his body, that austere demeanor forever shattered. No matter her strength as a Mistress, the unique submission Marguerite gave Tyler suggested he was her foundation, the strength that helped her with everything else.

InhServ training had always been that for Alanna. Her fail-safe. She realized it was also what could save their lives now.

Master, the men are thinking of confronting the vampire. I will stall him, but they must be dissuaded or they will come to harm.

Alanna, no. Stay with Tyler and Brendan. That's a command.

Please protect them, Master. I know I will be all right.

18

S HE slipped away into the darkness, hoping Tyler and Brendan would assume she'd gone to find Evan. She had to walk carefully in the stilettos toward the forest edge. She wished she could remove them, but even without the locks on them, she knew it was better to remain in the full trappings of a submissive. When the feeling was too strong to be anything else but close proximity to the vampire, she made a formal curtsy that became a full kneel.

"Sir, are you here to speak to my Master?"

She waited, head bowed. Even though she heard nothing, she knew when he was there, standing before her. His hiking shoes were crusted with marsh mud. Did he live in one of the secluded cabins out in the marshlands, taking his blood from boating tourists?

Alanna.

Evan's tense voice in her head was welcome, even as she registered his vast displeasure with her decision.

"Who is your Master, fair one?"

The voice was even and reasonable, but she wasn't fooled. She kept her eyes lowered, her posture open in all ways. "Evan Miller, sir. He travels throughout all territories freely with the sponsorship of Lord Uthe of the Vampire Council."

"That does not excuse him from coming to the overlord for a token marking before traveling through his territory. I don't scent Lord Richard's marking on him."

"Yes, sir. Lord Richard was appointed by Lady Lyssa. Lady Lyssa has sanctioned my Master's travel as well."

A hand with long, sharp nails closed over her throat, lifting her to her feet. Raising her gaze, she saw the vampire holding her had snarled dark hair and a red bloodlust coloring his eyes. He was hunting, had not yet fed. That meant he had no servant. That, combined with his remote location and rough, feral appearance, told her he was a Traditionalist. Her blood ran cold.

The Trads were a more radical splinter of the vampire world, though there was a certain romanticized regard for them, like the human view of pirates or Jesse James. Many vampires, while enjoying the comforts the human world provided, respected the Trads' purity of intent, their commitment to viewing humans only as prey, no more willing to live in their world than humans were to dwell in a field of cows.

Considering they were a sect of the vampire world who kept human kills only to the level that would escape Council attention, she'd been correct to draw him away from the humans. Killing Brendan or Tyler would be no more to him than snapping off a branch. If called to task for it by Council, he would assert he was protecting the secret of vampire existence from the unmarked human world. Easy to substantiate, since he made no attempt to disguise what he was.

"Why does your Master insult me, sending a servant to explain his presence? He needs a reminder that powerful friends do not excuse him from courtesy to his superiors."

"I can assure you, sir, my Master meant you no insult. He has to excuse himself from the humans' presence without causing curiosity. He was protecting your privacy. He says"—she kept her voice steady while telling the lie—"you may sate your hunger upon me, to appease any unintended offense. You may do with me as you wish."

"That is true, regardless of his will." His grip eased, though he didn't release her. Stroking a long-nailed hand over her breast, he sniffed her throat. His breath smelled of stale blood, for Trads shunned what they considered human hygiene. She thought of Niall making out a grocery list that first day, patiently explaining to Evan that *"Henry's out of Aquafresh. You'll have tae put on your big-boy knickers and make do with Colgate."*

The comfort of the memory vanished as the vampire's touch dropped. His jagged nail caught the edge of the thong, dipped beneath to scrape her clit roughly. When she stole a quick glance at him from beneath her lashes, he was emotionless. It sent a chill up her spine.

"You are lovely. Quite . . . cultured. Why are you with a Master below your station, InhServ?"

Damn it, he'd recognized the InhServ tattoo. "I serve at the Council's choosing, sir. Rank is unimportant. Only service matters."

"I've no patience for a servant. I couldn't tolerate even that much of a human around me. But one trained from birth to serve is . . . intriguing. Taking you from your Master will teach him a needed lesson."

When he closed his hand on her shoulder, his grip made her collarbone protest. He could break it, but he was giving her a direction, pressing her knees deeper into the ground. "You'll suck me off with those pretty cultured lips while I feed from your wrist. Once your Master arrives, we'll settle the issue. You might last a few hours in my service, but it will be memorable. A true test of your training."

As he opened his trousers, she closed her eyes, keeping her head bowed. She told herself it was no different than Niall ordering her to go down on the Mistress earlier. She was trained to do whatever a vampire, or even his higher-ranking servant, told her to do.

Leaning forward, she moistened her lips to lubricate his entry. With a satisfied growl, he clamped down on her skull and shoved himself into the back of her throat. Even with her training, the abruptness took her by surprise. He smelled terrible, and she fought her gag reflex. *Focus.* Pushing past it, she used her tongue and lips, all her knowledge of giving oral pleasure, to settle him down, help him realize how much more enjoyable it would be if he worked with her.

Wrapping his hand around her wrist, he pulled it toward his mouth. She couldn't worry about Evan and Niall right now. Evan would be talking Tyler and Brendan down, addressing the same primary concern she had, of a human bloodbath. Her best service to her Master was to put her mind in a state of silence, of open service, doing whatever was required.

You are not doing what your Master *requires, Alanna.*

She stilled, as did the vampire, sensing Evan's approach. The male drew his fetid cock from her mouth, thankfully, but he didn't move away, or drop her wrist. After he fastened his trousers, he stroked her hair, fingertips whispering down to the heavy beat of her neck pulse. Smelling metal, she identified razor tips under his nails, explaining their length. Cutting her throat would be easy.

"Alanna, come to me."

The vampire tightened his hold. Blood trickled over her collarbone, a shallow cut, but the threat was clear. "You gave her to me to enjoy until you could deign to speak to me. She will take my dick, feed me. And then we'll see if you have the balls to take her from me."

"The blessing and curse of an InhServ is her anticipation of a Master's needs." Evan's voice was reasonable. Controlled. Could the Trad hear what she heard beneath it? It reminded her of when she'd first seen Evan feed off Niall, the dangerous glint in his gaze proving he was as much a predator as any other vampire.

"Sometimes they anticipate . . . and offer, too much," Evan continued. "She will be punished for it. Severely. My letters of sponsorship from Lord Uthe and the Lady Lyssa prove I have clear passage across this territory, with no requirement that I petition the overlord. If you take advantage of my servant, or cause me harm, you answer to them."

"That may be so, but they care little what I do to your servant."

"You will take nothing further from her without killing me, and then she'll be dead as well." She realized he was hedging his bets that the Trad couldn't tell she wasn't third-marked by Evan, not with the mixed stew of blocker, Stephen and Evan all in her blood. "You answer to the Council for the death of another vampire. Lord Uthe is not known for his tolerance. InhServs have a particular value to the Council as well."

The vampire stared over her head. Alanna could feel Evan's presence at her back, a deadly stillness. Niall was there as well. The charged testosterone was like ozone, a prelude to an explosion.

The vampire's nails dug into her flesh, deeper this time. The artery started to bleed freely under his touch. "I can sense your strength, vampire. You are no match for me. Your other servant, though obviously far more of a warrior than his Master, will not stop me, either."

"This isn't a pissing match," Evan said patiently. "I'm simply telling you how things are. You kill me, harm my servant—either of them—you will answer for it."

"And that's supposed to make me quake in fear?" the Trad scoffed.

"No. But this might."

At the sound of a fourth male voice, Alanna lifted her gaze in time to see the lethal silver blade of a katana slide along the Trad's collarbone, notch against the side of his throat in the same way his razor-tipped nails were against hers. A long-fingered hand wrapped over his opposite shoulder, holding him firm. "I've no problem removing your head from your body, Colin. Remove those razor tips from her throat. Very slowly. I might shift my weight and cut through your spine."

She knew that ice-cool voice, despite the fact that she'd only heard it several times. "Alanna, return to your Master's side."

The Trad released her. As she rose on shaky knees and stepped back, she came up against Evan. In the blink since Lord Daegan's appearance, he'd closed the distance between them. Her Master handed her off to Niall without a word, the Scot pressing her down to her knees just behind him, so that she saw the wooden stakes thrust into the back of the kilt, as well as a wicked knife scabbarded on his calf. Evan didn't appear armed, but she wouldn't trust her eyes on that, not with the menace emanating from him.

Though she had her hand pressed to her neck, blood ran over her knuckles. The Trad had cut too deep. It wouldn't kill her, but she could pass out. She increased the pressure, willing herself to stay upright. If an opportunity presented itself to help Evan or Niall, she wanted to be ready to take it. The memory of Adam, here one moment, gone the next, gripped her with terror now.

"You know me, but I do not know you." Colin's gaze narrowed, but he was prevented from turning around by that hand locked on his shoulder. "You, too, are traveling where you shouldn't be. I will have your name."

"Most of those who know it are dead. Are you ready to pay that price? You've broken no laws. Yet. Leave without looking back, and the matter is concluded. Turn around to see who or what I am, and it will be the last thing you do. Evan and his servants are under the Council's direct protection, as he said. I am his proof." Daegan adjusted his grip, and blood started to seep out from beneath the blade.

Colin bared his fangs in a hiss but, true to vampire nature, he accepted he was outmatched. In a brief flash of movement he was gone, the trees whispering of his passing. All three men, the two vampires and one hunter, listened in alert silence, making sure he was taking a path away from the house. Alanna felt the Trad's presence dissipate like an acrid smoke blown away by a clean wind.

Daegan's blade disappeared back inside his coat. Though there was moonlight in the clearing, he stayed where the shadows still claimed him. "It's a good thing I came looking for you, Evan."

"Yes." Evan's response was short, tight. "My thanks, my lord. Is there a problem?"

"Stephen is within a hundred miles of his InhServ. That can't be a coincidence. He was never fond of the North American continent."

Alanna's heart leaped in her throat as she thought once again of the unprotected humans here. But Lord Daegan was already ahead of her. "You need a more protected location."

"We planned to go to the art colony after this," Evan said.

Daegan lifted a brow. "With Nerida and Miah?"

"Yes."

The Council's assassin nodded. "A defensible position. Head that way as soon as you can travel and plan on staying there unless I indicate otherwise to you. I'll maintain a perimeter of a few miles and watch for signs of him. He'll likely bide his time. He has nothing else at this point."

"She gains him nothing." Niall spoke now, the frustration obvious in his voice. "It only makes him vulnerable to capture."

"Stephen isn't linked to a stronger vampire, Niall. Even his original overlord, the one who took Stephen's blood before he started rising in the vampire ranks, died of Ennui some time ago. She's the only living link to his whereabouts. He knows that's why she's being kept alive. She's bait, yes, but once she's gone, he can disappear, go to unpopulated areas like that Trad. Wait for the times to change and vampires to forget." Daegan paused. "That's the practical side. But at heart, Stephen is a vampire, and an excessively arrogant and unforgiving one. He wants her head."

It was what she herself had thought, but hearing it said out loud chilled her skin. She pushed that aside. "Master, is there any way I can help? If not taking the blocker will draw him closer—"

Niall's hand landed on her shoulder, a warning. When Evan didn't respond to her, she looked toward Daegan. "If it will help, my lord—"

Pivoting, Evan caught her by the hair, yanking her up onto her knees. A twist of his wrist arched her throat, her neck at an agonizing angle. "Did I give you leave to speak?" His cruel tone stabbed her heart.

"No, Master."

"Then you will shut your mouth unless I do. You proved tonight why you shamed your InhServ training. Serving your own will is far more important than serving your Master's."

If he'd struck her in the face with a closed fist, he couldn't have delivered a more lethal blow. She was so stunned she just stared at him.

"Eyes down," he barked at her, reminding her of the first rule a servant ever learned. Dropping to her palms, she pressed her forehead to the ground, the InhServ's most submissive posture. When he turned back to Daegan, his feet were planted on either side of her shoulders. "If you'll give me leave to make my excuses to the Wintermans, my lord, I'll meet you at a rendezvous point of your choosing, to discuss further matters before we part."

～

Evan was so angry every muscle in his shoulders were tight, his eyes cold steel. During their three hundred years together, Niall had incurred that level of wrath perhaps twice. Though he felt very protective toward her as a result, it was clear Evan would put him on the ground if he tried to interfere. Not that it would stop Niall from trying, but it likely wouldn't result in any help for her.

Though he didn't agree with what Evan said to shut her down, he understood Evan's fury with her, because he shared some of it himself. As she'd anticipated, they'd had to deal with Tyler, and convincing a trained operative nothing was amiss, while she was approaching an unknown vampire head-on, had been ten levels of bollocks. It was bad enough her lips had been wrapped around that bastard's cock. He'd almost had his fangs in her, and that was the least thing the Trad had intended to inflict upon her.

Evan and Daegan had set a place to meet. Daegan disappeared back into the woods, once again a silent, deadly shadow. Despite Evan's amazing luck with most vampires—tonight notwithstanding—if he ever ran afoul of that one, Niall knew they could share a final drink and toast their asses good-bye.

Evan sent Niall a look brimming with anger, which caused the Scot's brow to crease. It was merely the truth, but Evan was obviously pissed at everyone at the moment. The vampire jerked his head at Alanna, still in the silent, subservient posture.

"Take her back to the RV. Get it packed up. But before you do that, I want her stripped and chained to the bunk in the back sleeper. If she wants anything . . . food, water, bathroom, she has to ask for it. If she can't obey me, she'll be treated like she can't be trusted."

He strode away. Looking down, Niall saw Alanna was quivering. A tiny sob escaped her, quickly swallowed. It made his jaw tighten, but when he reached down to pick her up, she shook him off and rose, albeit on legs as shaky as thin branches. The incredibly provocative outfit seemed too exposed for her now, her defeated eyes too vulnerable, no matter her straight posture. He wished he had a shirt he could put over her trembling shoulders. "I can walk, Niall. Unless it is my Master's will otherwise."

"No." He shook his head, not trusting himself to say anything else, because what he wanted to do was pull her against him, hold her fiercely. Then beat her arse for scaring them, right after he threw her down on a bed and buried himself between her legs. He expected Evan had a similar plan in mind, given that he wanted her tied to the bed. "Follow me."

She did, dutifully, silently. He skirted the party, knowing Evan would handle the apologies. If they ran into the vivacious Chloe now, Alanna would shatter. Their InhServ looked like brittle porcelain.

When they came to the RV, he opened the door, guided her up the steps. She moved away from him, toward the back sleeper. With wooden efficiency, she stripped, leaving the garment of mostly straps and chains in a neat pile on another bunk. Then she knelt, pulling out the box beneath it, because she'd of course familiarized herself with her surroundings, so they wouldn't have to tell her where anything was.

It held things that could be used for play or punishment, depending on Evan's mood. No question on which mood held sway right now, so she showed her courage as she laid out a switch, hot stick and scalpel, the items that could deliver the most pain in close quarters. No, not courage. Her shaking had stopped, such that now he didn't even detect a tremor in her hands. Seeing the dead resignation in her eyes, Niall realized no physical agony would surpass that inflicted by Evan's words.

She removed four steel manacles. After putting them on her ankles and wrists, she moved to the back bunk and knelt on the thin mattress pad. The manacles had been fitted with clips that could be attached to holes bored into the metal frame. Christ, that brought back some over-the-top memories, when Evan had been of a mind to stop for an hour between destinations and slake his Dominant tendencies with Niall's body.

She used the heel of each hand to press the wrist clips into the ones at the head of the bed. Sliding onto her stomach, she turned her face to the wall, but spread her legs, waiting for him to do the same to her ankles. Niall's ankles could reach the holes at the foot, but her legs weren't that long. They'd have to be fastened on the sides, spreading her so her feet would hang over the sides, making her look more helpless and small.

Aye, the vampire was in a murderous rage, and not just because her foolish bravery could give even an immortal Master heart failure. She'd done it to protect Tyler and the rest, but she'd also done it to keep Evan and Niall safe. Evan had let him hear that much and, as such, Niall understood some of their Master's anger—better than Alanna in this instance. Thinking about it now, Niall also realized why his comment about Daegan had incensed Evan further.

Regardless, he refused to let her keep on like this. He squatted by the bed. "Look at me, lass."

She didn't obey. "It doesn't matter, Niall. Master is right. Leave me like this until Daegan kills Stephen. It's the only function I have. I won't take the blockers anymore, so gag me when the nightmares start."

"I'll give ye the injections."

"He will find me quicker without them," she responded tonelessly.

Putting his hand on her bare back, he found she was cold. He let his fingers glide over her buttock, but he could have been touching a statue. Over their short time together, she'd begun to tailor her responses to them, as well as explore the heated realm of her own pleasure. Now it was as if she wasn't inhabiting her body.

"Alanna, stop this." When she didn't move, he tightened his fingers on her hip. "Damn it, look at me."

"Please just leave me alone, Niall. I'm tired."

"He was angry, Alanna. It was more than the fact that you didn't obey him; you didn't trust him to handle the situation."

"Tyler and Brendan are your friends. I had to stop the vampire from coming onto their property."

"By offering your blood, your body. Things that belong to your Master, that are only his to give."

"I knew Evan would want to protect his human friends. That was a sacrifice I could make. It doesn't matter. It's all a lie, really. None of it matters."

"Yes, it does, damn it." Fuck Evan's temper, as well as her lifeless compliance. Unlatching the manacles from the bedframe, he turned her onto her back, one hand gripping her forearm. She resisted, stiff, but when he forced the issue, the wall she'd put up between them crumbled. She swung at him with the other arm, but he pulled her to her feet, almost getting his ear taken off by one of the steel cuffs as she struggled, spitting at him like an angry cat. Catching her wrists, he put her back down on the bed, this time on her back, himself on top of her. She nearly emasculated him with her knee.

"That's enough," he snarled, giving her a good shake. As she stared up at him, panting, he realized that, in their struggles, she'd raked up the kilt, so that his cock was pressed against her bare mound. Given how close they'd come to losing her, he was the size of a dock piling. "No." She shook her head. "No."

His determined thrust pinned her to the bed. Her legs kicked and thrashed, then locked over his buttocks as her body betrayed her, wanting to hold on to him. Pressing her deeper into the mattress, he framed her face with both hands. "You're not hiding from us, lass. We willnae let you."

"No." Tears spilled over his fingers. "Don't do this to me. It's better not to feel . . . not to care, or love, or want anything. They told us that. It wasn't our job to want . . . to . . ."

"To live? To love? To fucking feel? Why do you think he's so angry, Alanna? Think with that incredibly intelligent mind of yours. *Think*, damn it." He thrust fast and hard, until she was clasping his shoulders, nails biting as she hung on. Her whimpers told him he was giving her a rough ride, but he was taking out some of his own anger, his fear that they wouldn't reach her in time. He also wanted to scald away the filth of that vampire's touch from her soft flesh. She wanted it too, her hips lifting to his, as if trying to scrub it away with the friction.

He was ruthless enough to exploit that, pushing her back down, holding her to the mattress with a hand on her throat as he attacked her breasts, suckling and nipping, tasting her flesh as he slammed against her clit with every stroke. He hiked her knees up higher on his rib cage so he could go deeper, stronger.

"We're here, inside ye, *muirnín*. Ye cannae get free of us. You belong to us. Feel it. Feel me."

She cried out, the orgasm detonating throughout her body before she could stop it. He spurted inside her savagely, wanting her to have him there always, his scent, his mark. The rough texture of Stephen's dagger mark rubbed against his pelvis, and he wanted it gone. Wanted it replaced by Evan's, making it clear she no longer belonged to that life. That she could let it go.

"He hates me." Now the tears came like a storm. She tried to turn her face away, but he cradled her slim jaw. "He said I shamed him. Just like Stephen."

"Oh God, no, lass. Not at all." He wasn't sure who he wanted to smack more, her or Evan, but in all fairness, Evan lost his temper rarely, and he'd had just cause this time, for certain.

"Colin was going to kill you, *muirnín*. He would have done it in front of Evan, tae prove he had the upper hand. As important as ye are to the Council . . ."

"They wouldn't retaliate against a vampire killing a servant." She closed her eyes. "Evan promised Lady Lyssa he'd keep me safe. He would have failed in his task."

"Damn it, that wouldnae have mattered. He would have lost you. *We* would have lost you." Stroking her tears away with his thumbs, he felt her thigh muscles quivering against his hips where she still held him inside her. He settled down even farther, nudging her very womb. God, he could stay inside her cunt for days, the clasp of those brown eyes, her trembling arms. All they needed was Evan to make it balanced.

He and Evan had made an agreement, early on in their unique arrangement. If Niall occasionally wanted to enjoy a casual fuck with a

woman and Evan wasn't around to share, that was well and good. It
had been fine for Niall, but he'd never been with a female and had the
thought he had now. The active wish that Evan was here, a closed
circle.

Though he was certain his decision to take Alanna now didn't have
Evan's approval, meaning he'd likely pay for it with blood, it didn't
make the feeling about the vampire's absence any less strong.

Evan and he had another agreement as well. No male touched Niall
without Evan's say so and participation. The vampire was unapolo-
getically possessive on that score, and Niall had accepted the condition
so easily. He'd told himself it was because he preferred women most
times anyhow, but the passing of years, and how long he'd adhered to
the restriction, had proven that a lie a long time ago.

"You're important to him, lass," he murmured. "Why is that so
hard for you to ken?"

"Why do you ask me questions you should be asking yourself?" He
should have remembered how intuitive she could be, even in a torn-up
emotional state. Opening her eyes, she stared up at him. "I'm going to
die, Niall. I know Evan wants me to be something else, but perhaps it's
better for me to be what I've always been. Just like you told him in the
beginning. Because when Stephen dies, and I wake on the other side
and find myself . . . bound to him . . ."

Her voice started to shake, betraying the fear, the dread. She'd let
it loose on the mountain that one time, when a stressful situation had
pushed her to breaking, and he saw it again now. She was like that
little lad with his finger in the dike, always aware of the great wall of
water waiting to overcome her on the other side.

"What will help me endure it for all eternity?" she whispered. "The
training that says anything he does to me, I deserve, or Evan's world,
where I have no idea what I am? Who I am?"

Closing her eyes, she turned her face away. "Please leave me alone.
I just . . . let me be alone. I'm afraid . . . and so tired . . ."

Tears spilled anew over his fingers, but now the sobs were held inside, with such effort her ribs might break from it.

When he slid off of her, giving her the ability to breathe, she turned
toward the wall. He didn't leave her, though. Instead, he wrapped his
arms around her, bent his thighs under hers to cradle her, keep her
together.

As she made a plaintive noise of pain, he merely held her closer. "I'm nae going to leave you. Cry, be afraid, whatever ye need to let it out."

The sobs burst forth, though she turned her face to the pillow to muffle them. She couldn't muffle the shudders, though, the jerking of her muscles. She was so reserved, so self-possessed, he'd overlooked how truly young she was. Not even out of her twenties. Her upbringing had forced great maturity on her, but she'd brought great maturity to it. A young woman facing the certainty of her death, and the terrible uncertainty of what came after.

Age didn't offer much in the way of comfort, though. Here he was, nearly three hundred, helpless to do anything to make it better other than holding her like this and wishing like hell something could be done.

Male fingers caressed him, sliding down the bare curve of his back to rest on his arse. Glancing up into Evan's somber eyes, Niall wasn't surprised to see his anger was gone. Like him, the vampire'd had time to recover from the fright she'd given them both. Evan tilted his head, indicating he intended to take his place. Reluctantly, Niall slid off the bunk. Alanna, oblivious to them, caught in her own misery, remained hunched in a ball, quivering.

Go pack up the cottage. I'll deal with things here.

Niall nodded, but as he slid past Evan in the narrow space, he gripped the male's hip, still uncertain about leaving the lass. Evan touched Niall's face.

All will be well, neshama.

Absurdly enough, the vampire's words brought him comfort. It was a reminder that, even when such a reassurance was all that could be offered for an impossible situation, sometimes it was enough.

～

Alanna was lost in an exhausted haze, body twitching with stress. A part of her was desperately glad Niall hadn't left her alone, but then he shifted away. She stilled as a body she well recognized slid behind her, hand settling on her hip.

"Alanna. Turn over and look at me."

In her entire life, she'd never considered ignoring a vampire's command, but this time, she wanted to. When his long fingers tightened on her, a warning, she let out a shaky sigh, turned over on her back. She had enough vanity to swipe at the strands of hair plastered to her cheeks by her crying, but he pushed her fingers away, did it himself. His gray eyes were so close, the sculpted mouth and jawline. He had such an interesting face, she thought tiredly. Not classically handsome, but an ironically artistic appeal, a charisma that had told her from the beginning he was a resourceful and exceptionally intelligent male.

"Yes, I am exceptionally resourceful. I wish you'd believed that an hour ago."

Her mind was clear enough to recall Niall's words. *You didn't trust him enough.* Looking at the tightness around Evan's mouth, the lingering disappointment and frustration in the vampire's gaze, it clicked, what Niall had been trying to tell her. The realization horrified her enough she would have scrambled off the bed and knelt in penitence, but Evan was in front of her. Instead she tried to genuflect as much as the narrow bed allowed, even with his grip on her upper arm. "Master, I'm so sorry. The last thing I ever intended was to make you feel . . . Of course I trust you to care for me. *Always.*"

At least as much of "always" as fate would give her. "I just wanted to care for you, and Evan, and the guests . . . it never occurred to me that you would think . . ."

"I know it didn't." Those gray eyes were quiet, accepting. If anything, that hurt her heart worse. Putting his fingers on her mouth, he stopped the rush of words. "I am in your mind, if not in your soul, Alanna. Now that my heart isn't racing like a train, certain Colin was going to drop your bloody corpse at my feet, I know what you were thinking. I expected you to respond to me the way Niall does. It was unrealistic to expect the intuitive understanding he and I developed over centuries."

He stroked through her hair, caressed her ear. She wanted to lean into that touch, needed to do so, but she didn't deserve that. She forced herself to stay still, to simply listen and ache, wishing she could do so many things differently.

"Ah, *yekirati.* Your political and sexual skills, your incredible beauty and training; you base your decisions on those things. You've never had a Master value you for more than that. When one does, it introduces a whole different set of decision-making variables."

Her brow creased, but he touched her chin, guiding her tearstained face back to his. "I've been trying to help you know what that means. Remarkable student that you are, I think you've just about figured it out, despite the short time we've been together. Perhaps what confused you is that I intended my participation to be as a teacher, a guide. I didn't realize I was going to become a living example of what I was trying to show you."

Her heart fluttered uncertainly when his lips curved, a faint smile. "Though I regret the events of this night, if it helps you make the connection, it was worth it. Do you understand it yet, Alanna?"

She couldn't breathe, not with the way he was looking at her now. He slid his knuckles to her cheek, waiting for her response.

She'd never been much of a movie watcher, but she remembered one she'd seen, a long time ago in her mother's kitchen. She'd been sitting in the corner, practicing her patience and waiting skills, and the small TV on the counter, left on by her sisters, had been showing the black-and-white version of *The Miracle Worker*. Annie Sullivan's struggle to help a blind and deaf child communicate had caught her attention.

By the time they reached the climactic scene at the well pump, Alanna had been captured by the story line. Helen finally made that connection, learning something everyone had expected to be beyond her reach. The simple link between a finger sign made in her palm and its actual meaning. Words. Connection. It had opened up the entire universe to her.

Now Alanna truly understood it, the momentous shift when Helen spelled *water* in her teacher's hand. She swallowed. Evan had forced her to face the fact that she'd wanted to love Stephen and had wanted him to care about her. Not for her skills or the political prestige she'd brought to him. Not even for her unconditional service to him. She had wanted him to see past all that, see *her*. Value *her*. Her unconditional service was more than training—it was key to every need, desire and vulnerability she had. Everything she truly was. She thought of her brother kissing his Mistress's foot, the look his vampire had given him. Devotion, caring . . . love. Perhaps vampires didn't feel it the same as humans, but she'd seen it in the Mistress's face, and the desire to find that, to earn it, had burned in Alanna's heart like acid.

But there were two parts to it. It wasn't only about finding someone who would value her, who would let her serve them as she desired. It was also about finding the Master who captured her heart, who she *wanted* to serve with everything she was.

Evan was still holding her wrist. Slowly, she put pressure on his grip, reaching for his hand with straining fingers. When he loosened his grasp, she let out a tremulous breath, closed her fingers over his wrist, reversing their positions. Then, shifting her hold, she brought her face down to his hand, pressing her cheek into his palm, her lips. He allowed it. Allowed her to show her affection, her regret, and accepted it. Accepted *her*.

He cared about her. Not like a passing thought, a favorite toy. She, Alanna, had emotional value to him. Enough that putting herself in danger had enraged him, because she hadn't been where he could protect her.

She had no words for how she was feeling, only that she was feeling so much, she had to press herself as hard as she could against that contact point. He gathered her in closer to him, so her face was between his palm and chest, her ear pressed over his heart when she heard him say something so remarkable—for a vampire—she thought she'd misheard it.

"I am sorry, Alanna. I shouldn't have said what I said. It was cruel. I said it because I was furious, not because it was true. Brian said you were the best of your InhServ class, the example all others wished to follow. No, let me finish. I think that happened because you exceeded the program, representing the true spirit of it. InhServs should be assigned to vampires *worth* serving. Which is part of why you told the Council what Stephen had done. You served the well-being of all of us. You thought like a Council member, not a servant. Just the same way you did today."

"It wasn't that noble. My brother—"

"Was the catalyst," he inserted. "Stephen was betraying his own people. When he showed such disregard for your brother's death, and you knew he was planning Lord Daegan's death, it helped you make the right decision, no matter the circumstances."

She thought about that, her cheek still pressed to his chest. "You're worth serving, Master."

"Thank you for that, but I think you've always been meant for far bigger things than sorting slides and cutting our hair. Any vampire would be lucky to have you, Alanna."

She liked sorting slides and cutting hair. She liked being with the two of them. But she was too drained to say that. Instead, she stayed silent. Content to just be here, in this moment.

He stroked her hair. "I will take you to your brother's grave, let you put flowers on it. You can visit your family as well if you wish."

She choked on another unexpected, overwhelming sob, and he tightened his arms around her. "It's all right, *motek*. It's all right."

"I'm so sorry, Master. I didn't intend to hurt you, or do the wrong thing. It tears my heart out, thinking I made you feel for one moment I thought any less of you. You're the most wonderful vampire I've ever met."

She flushed, realizing how simple she sounded, but he chuckled warmly, held her closer. "I think you should remember what Niall said, about even a pile of manure looking better than Stephen. But you're forgiven, sweet girl. Totally forgiven, if you stop crying. You've made Niall a mess. Your bear is beside himself. He's supposed to be packing up, but instead he's lurking outside, sure I'm going to murder you."

When he tipped her chin up, she saw his wry, tender look. It undid her. Though she'd sounded like a starstruck teenager, she'd meant it. And with or without the third mark, he was in her soul. They both were.

A muscle flexed in his jaw. *Now you're trying to do it to me. Jewish men are notoriously emotional, even the vampire ones.*

It made her smile, even through the tears. "I'm glad you took off the contacts," she said shyly.

Evan's lips quirked. "The first time I used them at an event like this, Mistress Regina was quite taken with them. She tried to tie me up. Niall teased me tonight, said I wore them just to impress her. He knows that woman scares me to death."

Alanna couldn't imagine anyone wanting to cover up Evan's gray eyes, the way they changed from storm clouds to a dove's breast, to the hazy predawn sky when rain was promised. Realizing she was gazing up at them now, she blushed again, but Evan touched her face.

"You paint words in your mind beautifully, *yekirati*." He kissed the salty tracks of her tears, stroking the hair at her temples, then rested his hands on her shoulders.

"As much as I'd like to hold you well through the morning, Daegan can't wait indefinitely. I want you in my sight while I meet with him.

In fact, you may be chained to my bed every dawn until I stop having waking nightmares about you in the hands of that unwashed, *mishugina* zealot."

She was chagrined anew, but he turned her so her feet were on the floor, her sitting next to him on the bed. The look he cast at her manacles and bare body heated her skin. "You still have that severe punishment coming. I'll just wait until I can enjoy it more. Can you put yourself together in five minutes?"

"Three, Master."

"Get to it, then."

19

SHE was as good as her word. She and Niall had the RV packed and ready when Evan returned from talking to Tyler. Less than fifteen minutes after that, they were pulling into a protected birdwatching area frequented by naturalists during daylight hours. From the picnic shelter, Evan watched Niall and Alanna, sitting in the wooden observation tower overlooking the marsh. He'd sent both servants there, primarily because Niall's emotions were still quite . . . Scottish. If he shot his mouth off during the more problematic discussion points, Evan might have to prevent the loss of another servant.

Niall hadn't liked being excluded, especially when he saw Gideon, Daegan's servant, would be staying in the shelter to attend the conversation, but Evan had nodded to Alanna.

She's still in a fairly fragile state. I want her reassured that her place among us is restored. And there's no need for her to hear this.

While Niall rightly suspected Evan had reasons for wanting him specifically out of earshot, the reasons to remove Alanna were equally truthful. So the Scot reluctantly took her off to the tower, though Evan expected he'd be thoroughly interrogated later about his discussion with the Council's assassin.

Of course, now that his and Daegan's conversation had extended longer than expected, his servant was stretched out in the bird watch while Alanna moved around below, studying the foliage with her plant book. Every once in a while, he saw her go back up into the tower and check on Niall.

Even though all the lore said he would feel Niall's loss like a ton of bricks falling on his chest, these days Evan often left camera or canvas to lean over his servant just as Alanna was doing, making sure the man's eyes were closed in sleep, not staring at an eternity he'd not yet experienced. His hand closed into a fist on the table.

"You're distracted. More than usual, I suspect, according to Lord Uthe's description of you."

Lord Daegan had been leaning against one of the shelter posts, but now resumed his seat across from Evan, demonstrating that lithe warrior's grace that said he could slice an unfortunate gnat out of the air. Niall was a fair hand with a blade, but Daegan's every movement underscored he had one primary purpose, and he did it well.

Thinking of the last time he'd seen Niall pick up a claymore, Evan wondered if Daegan had ever watched the movie *Highlander*. One night, a long, long time ago, due to his own poor planning, his need to use up that one last roll of film, Evan had taken daylight refuge in the basement of what turned out to be a sorority house. He was discovered by two of the girls doing their laundry, but Niall's charm had quickly overcome any concerns. In fact, several other girls had joined them for a day-long party, complete with beer, junk food and parlor games, most of which Evan missed because he was sleeping on the cot they brought him.

However, he'd been awake enough to hear them ask Niall to say the infamous Highlander hook-up line: "I am Connor McLeod of the Clan McLeod, et cetera, et cetera . . . and I can never die." Surprisingly, it did work outside the movies. Thank God Niall had a third mark, or he might not have survived the pleasurable demands of that day.

Enough of this. Realizing he was proving the vampire's point, Evan straightened, gave Daegan his full attention. Gideon was propped on the brick fire pit, arms crossed over his broad chest. While his gaze strayed periodically toward Alanna and Niall, the alert set of his lean, warrior's body said he was as focused on the task at hand as Daegan himself.

"I'm in agreement on everything we've discussed, my lord," Evan said. "But I have one more thing to add. If you find Stephen, you can't kill him."

"On the contrary, I'm quite capable of it." Daegan picked a shiny red apple out of the wooden fruit bowl, examined it. Alanna had brought it out from the RV stores for the vampire assassin and his servant. "But I expect that wasn't what you meant. You've already discussed this with Uthe. Why talk to me about it?"

"Because you will be the one wielding the sword, not Uthe." Evan spoke carefully. The assassin's eyes were so dark that it was difficult to see the whites at times. It made him all the more intimidating, but Evan didn't intimidate. He didn't consider himself particularly brave; it just wasn't in his nature to be dissuaded from his goal by power discrepancies. Niall had once likened it to the way a small terrier went after a wolfhound, certain he could take him if he could get the right grip.

"Lord Brian has an experimental treatment that might break a bond as old as the one Alanna carries from Stephen," Evan explained. "But the treatment is a three-week process, requiring live samples from the vampire throughout. I understand the Council has its priorities, and those priorities are greater than the consideration of the life of one servant . . ."

"Far greater," Daegan said. However, his tone was neutral, flat, such that Evan wasn't certain if Daegan agreed with that perspective or was regurgitating the expected party line.

"You saw her tonight. She's impressive. Brave and clever. And she's done nothing but serve the Council's interests in this matter. I believe her preservation merits consideration."

"It does. But if the choice is to let him get away or take him out, I have only one choice."

"I understand that." Evan saw Alanna tilt her head back. She was staring up at the star-strewn sky. When her hair fluttered over her shoulder, she captured it with one hand so it didn't impede her view. Always such a quiet, pensive thing, so hard to surprise a smile or laugh out of her. But he remembered the day in the kitchen, when she'd gotten so angry at Niall, his boot on that napkin. He almost smiled at the memory. Then he remembered the past hour, which didn't make him smile at all. Her fear, revealed so clearly.

"With all due respect, I am asking you to please . . . do what you can to bring him in alive."

Daegan met his gaze. "She is more than an assignment to you. More than a chance to curry favor with Lady Lyssa."

It was the elephant in the room, the one so many vampires squeezed past, no matter how close the creature pressed against the walls of their existence. The fine line of what was appropriate or inappropriate to feel for a servant. Evan had never had much patience for what was so obvious, but he curbed his irritation now, chose diplomacy. And insight. He'd watched the way Daegan and Gideon moved together, reacted to each other.

"She's impressed me with who and what she is," he said quietly. "If you know me through Uthe as it seems you do, you know I study people carefully, and I judge character well. Courage and integrity are not exclusive vampire traits." Taking the risk, he glanced meaningfully toward Gideon. "I expect with your greater age and wisdom, you already know that."

"Don't exert yourself on flattery, Evan. You want her." The assassin stated it bluntly. "But there are a lot of ifs between that goal and the reality. If Stephen can be captured alive, if Brian can find a way to break the link safely, if a higher-ranking vampire doesn't come forward, wanting her. A lot of time and cost went into training her to serve a vampire with stature, political aspirations. Does understanding that change your interest in preserving her life? Because I can assure you there isn't a single Council member who will care overly much if I deliver his corpse."

Evan remembered that spontaneous, terrible thought Alanna had, the first time he'd pushed her to want something for herself. *I wish Stephen had killed me.* Underneath the new feelings and desires, there was still so much of the InhServ, forbidden to have wants and desires. Death was acceptable, if it was what the Council ordered.

Yet he also remembered that nearly audible click in her mind when she understood she wasn't merely a status symbol or a tool to him. That he valued her for who she was, a remarkable, brave, unexpectedly stubborn woman, her weaknesses and strengths both part of her appeal. He thought of how she'd gripped his hand, pressed her face into his palm, overwhelmed by the discovery. Seeing that change, feeling her flood of emotions not only from her mind but through that one contact on his palm, he knew the truth. If this woman was loved the way she should be, she would embrace her full potential. She was already amazing; with love, she would evolve into the realm of the extraordinary, a living work of art like nothing the world had ever seen.

He met the vampire assassin's gaze squarely, forced himself to say words that could slice his heart in two like Daegan's sword. "Whether or not she would stay in my care is irrelevant. She deserves to live for her own merits, not my whim."

"But in the vampire world, it's only a vampire's whim that will give her any consideration at all." Daegan sat back, studying him. From the faint flicker of Gideon's expression, Evan sensed a conversation happening between the two men. Abruptly, Daegan rose, extending his hand.

"I'll do what I can, Evan. You have my word."

The band around his chest eased a few notches. He might not know much about Lord Daegan, but he suspected the male said nothing he didn't mean. As he rose and clasped the assassin's hand, Daegan tilted his head toward Gideon.

"Despite this poor excuse of a servant, you are correct. I do understand the value of a good one."

Gideon raised a brow, but didn't comment on that. Instead, he said, "If we're done here, I'll go kick Niall onto his feet for a short sparring match. Make sure his skills are still sharp."

"No," Evan said. When both men looked toward him, he softened the brusqueness of his reply. "Let him sleep. He needs it . . . more often now."

He thought of Niall in a pillow fight with the sorority girls, roaring with laughter, yet so gentle while wrestling with them . . . Niall had been the subject or part of the scenery of so many of his works, but there were millions more in Evan's head, a gallery that pressed in on him now, making him short of breath in a way that didn't happen to vampires.

Realizing the conversation was best concluded, he nodded to Daegan courteously, then left the shelter, striding across the field toward his servants.

≈

As Evan moved away from them, Gideon glanced at Daegan. "He's that close? Niall?"

"The increased sleep patterns are the only real indication we have, other than the number of years. A few have lived up to a decade beyond the three-century mark, but if he's already sleeping more, he will not be one of those." Daegan came to stand shoulder to shoulder with his servant, both males watching the three. Alanna had straightened. Whatever Evan said to her caused her to come to him swiftly, take his hand. He swung her around, catching the herbs from her hand to examine them as she tried to take them back. He was obviously teasing her. With their enhanced senses, Daegan and Gideon heard him suggest throwing rocks at Niall to wake him, though they knew he had no intention of doing so.

"Do you think Lyssa will take that in to account, if they can break Stephen's mark?" Gideon asked. "The fact that Evan will be alone soon?"

"You know her better than I do. What do you think?"

Gideon pursed his lips. "If she can manage it politically, I think she'd do it. She's pretty much Head Bitch in Charge now. Don't think anyone will mess with her on it. But Brian's had piss-poor luck breaking any mark over five years old. The Council made him put it on the back burner. It seemed pretty pointless, anyhow. How many vampires would break from a servant after that length of time? Stephen's kind of a onetime freak issue. Not worth the cost of the research, to their way of thinking."

"Should I ask why you were asking Brian about such a thing?"

Gideon tilted his head as Daegan shifted closer, an intent look in his dark eyes that Gideon took for the sensual warning it was. One he couldn't resist poking at. "Just keeping my options open," he said lightly.

Daegan's hand was on his chest before he could block him, using that electrifying speed to move into his personal space, crowding him against the pillar. He had his hand under Gideon's T-shirt, bypassing the nine millimeter holster and dagger sheath to find the three teardrop servant's mark high on his chest. "You have no options when it comes to our ownership of you, vampire hunter," Daegan murmured, brushing his nose across Gideon's cheek, baring fangs so he felt the scrape on his jaw. "We resolved that long ago."

"You're already in my mind, asshole." Gideon fought to keep his mind unscrambled as Daegan's mouth touched his throat, sending a shot of adrenaline straight to his groin. He suppressed a groan as Daegan cupped his balls, a threatening squeeze. "I told him you wanted to determine what kind of chance you could give the girl, if it suited the Council's purpose."

Daegan arched a brow. "Lying to the Council's scientist. I'm sure there's a severe punishment for that."

When his fangs pierced Gideon's artery, he gripped the vampire's waist beneath the long coat, the steel of the sword's scabbard brushing his thigh. "Not lying. Anticipating. You know you wanted to know. You're not as blackhearted as your reputation. 'Those who know my name are mostly dead'? Really?"

"Not mostly dead." Daegan lifted his head, licking a smear of blood off his lip. "*Most* of those who know it are *dead*. Ass."

"Yeah, yeah. I was thinking about what was going to be on cable tonight. Wasn't really paying attention." Gideon tempted fate, tasting the blood on Daegan's lips. His hand slid past the sword to another weapon, one that was nearly as hard as the steel.

Daegan's eyes glinted as he caught Gideon's wrist, twisted it up against the column above his head. Holding his body pinned, the vampire spoke against Gideon's ear. "Your Mistress is not here to protect you. You will be beneath me at dawn, and I will prove just how ruthless and blackhearted I can be."

Fuck that. Anwyn's way scarier than you are. Gideon took another nip at his mouth, and Daegan chuckled.

He slipped away like a shadow, back to sitting at the picnic table before Gideon could blink. Though his pose was casual, his glance wasn't, the way it swept Gideon's body. Daegan being Daegan, the bastard would run him half to death tonight, then fuck him into the ground to prove who had the upper hand. But that struggle was the pleasure they shared.

The vampire picked up the apple again. "Warrior to warrior. Tell me what you're thinking, rather than making me pick it out of that caveman brain of yours."

"She stood up to that piece of shit tonight. And she gave up everything to do what was right. I'll say what Evan won't to the big, bad Council assassin. We should do everything we can to save someone like that."

"Agreed. You know me too well. I'm spending far too much time in your company."

"You have no other options. Anwyn and I are the only ones who can stand you."

"Says the kettle." Daegan fended off Gideon's punch at his chest as he came to sit on the table next to him. "Careful. Show some respect to the big, bad assassin."

"In your dreams." Gideon sobered. "Stephen won't want us to take him alive. That's our biggest challenge."

Daegan propped his elbow on Gideon's thigh, took a bite of the apple. As he chewed, he offered the rest to Gideon. "He knows his fate at the hands of the Council. He will want a quick death." Daegan flashed his fangs. "Which is why I am motivated to deprive him of it."

Gideon looked back toward Alanna and Evan. She'd hopped onto Evan's back, and he was carrying her farther into the marsh. Knowing Evan, he was probably showing her some kind of luminescent water bug. Above them, Niall sat up. When he swung down to join them, the bond between the three, the way they drew together like a gravitational pull, was as obvious as the bond between the two males watching. Not that Gideon dwelled on such things often.

Daegan stood, bumping Gideon's shoulder. "Liar. You can't keep your thoughts off my ass."

"Only how much I'd like to kick it, stuff a grenade up it . . . the fantasies are endless."

"Keep telling yourself that, vampire hunter." Daegan checked the placement of the sword in his coat, adjusted the gun at the small of his back. "Let's go. The challenge of a capture instead of a kill is a rare pleasure, a refining of existing skills. I might actually enjoy this."

"Well, just so you're a happy vampire." Gideon tossed the apple core into the grass outside the picnic shelter and flashed him a dangerous smile.

As elusive as the shadows themselves, the two warriors melted into the night.

∼

Niall waded into the marsh. Evan was holding Alanna piggyback as he showed her a sleeping heron. The ghostly white bird had his head tucked into his chest feathers, his body hidden among the weeds. Niall had woken in a curious mood, so he followed his inclination. He slid an arm around Alanna's waist, and leaned against Evan's body in simple affection. The vampire brushed his temple with a dip of his head.

"What will be will be," Evan said quietly. "But we have this."

"We're a long time deid," Niall agreed. At Alanna's look, he gave her a squeeze. "It means enjoy life now, lass."

She nodded. Putting her hand over Niall's on her hip, she settled her other one into Evan's grasp when he reached up, drew it down to hold it over his heart. "Thank you both for your care," she added after a pause. "Whatever happens . . . I expected to be alone for all this, and I don't feel alone."

Evan was right. She could break a man's heart. Niall hooked a finger in Evan's belt loop, tightening there as he held Alanna closer to his side.

Any luck with Daegan?

He understands the situation and will do his best. I believe he understands my feelings on the matter. Our feelings on it. Evan shot him a humorous glance. *I am not the only vampire fond of a surly human male, Niall.*

Leaning closer, he put his mouth over Niall's, a quick press of fang. Then he turned his head and drew Alanna over his shoulder, giving her a taste of them both. "We're taking you to one of my favorite places in the world," he told her. "Niall likes it, too. A wealth of voluptuous women cook him food there."

When her gaze narrowed, her lips thinning, Evan tossed Niall an amused look. "Be careful, *neshama*. Nothing more dangerous in this world than a jealous woman."

∼

As they traveled to their next destination, Alanna dozed on the sleeper. She'd stayed up front with the men for a while, but she'd been tired and

Evan had sent her to bed. However, even in her somnolent state, she held on to her connection with them like a child holding a stuffed animal. They talked about Evan's next project, the mundane events of the past few days. Overhearing their mention of the wedding reception, her mind returned to it as well.

She'd spent some time with Chloe and her family, but at a certain point, she'd gone looking for her Master and Niall. Evan was sitting under a live oak, almost lost in its shadows. Earlier, when she'd seen him by the dim light provided by the Chinese lanterns, she'd realized he was hungry, but he'd told her he'd be fine until dawn.

Niall stood casual guard, keeping those who approached engaged in conversation so that Evan would be unnoticed. The Scot was about ten yards away, yet she could see it, the connection between them. It wasn't just the vampire–servant, mind-to-mind physical connection. They had a chemistry she suspected had existed from the beginning. Was it that way for vampire–servant pairings that were fated, instead of arranged? Perhaps not, because many vampires didn't have the kind of bond with their servants that Evan obviously had with Niall . . . that Lady Lyssa had with Jacob.

Dangerous thoughts she couldn't help but have. The slight tilt of Niall's head, his body language, told her how aware he was of his Master at all levels. Whether Niall admitted it or not, he'd be as lost without that connection as he would when his heart stopped beating. She wondered if that was the real reason a servant died when his vampire did.

Going to the waitstaff, she asked for half a glass of red wine. Moving into a convenient screen of oleander at the corner of the pool house, she drew the small blade a servant routinely carried for such things. A syringe would be more efficient, but a small pocketknife was easier to explain. She was well-practiced at it, such that the cup was filled in no time.

When she approached the tree, Niall's nostrils flared as he caught the scent. Giving her an imperceptible nod, he caught her arm and said something that made her smile before he resumed his conversation with the two men. Slipping under the oak's canopy, she dropped to her knees between Evan's feet.

"Mother hens, the both of you," he said, but his lips curved. He bade her stay, so she shifted at his direction, resting her head on his knee, her body pressed against his calf as he idly stroked her hair, sipped the blood.

"Niall said it was necessary. He didn't want you trying to eat the guests. Tyler won't invite you back, and Niall likes the food here."

"It would be a braver man than myself that stood between Niall and a feast." Evan brushed her cheek with his knuckles. "You're learning to tease and be teased."

She nodded, returned her head to his knee. She fingered the hand he had dangling loosely over it, touching the pewter ring on his middle finger. *Time heals all things.* "Was this a gift?"

"Yes, from Niall. He gave it to me the year I turned three hundred, on Yom Kippur. Day of Atonement." Evan studied the ring. "It's a solemn day, a fast from sunset to sunset, during which a Jew reviews the past year and seeks atonement for his sins against God. He's also supposed to make amends for any sins against others before the day itself." He looked up at her. "Niall says I get gloomy as a cloud on Yom Kippur. He gave me the ring because he thought a shiny bauble might perk me up, like it would a lass."

She smiled. "He likes teasing you. But I expect you teased him back."

"Several times, the next night. It would have been forbidden on that day." The heat that went through his gaze told her exactly what he meant. "With his bad influence, he'll teach you the way of it in no time."

"I like teasing you," she admitted. "As long as I don't offend or anger you. You seem to enjoy it when Niall does it."

"Yet you're developing your own inimitable style."

That made her glow a little, especially when his eyes warmed on her. "May I ask . . . What about Yom Kippur makes you sad?"

"After Yom Kippur, you start the new year with a clean slate. But after so many years, you learn there really is no such thing as a clean slate." He lifted a shoulder, giving her a wry smile. "I'm a blood drinker and a sodomite. Rather hypocritical to atone for something I won't stop doing. But by its very nature, Yom Kippur is a day of remembrance. After hundreds of years, so many things are forgotten or devalued. So many moments can be like water drops, slipping away from you as the years progress. But I remember my parents vividly, as well as the lives I've taken for my annual kill. I've made amends for those in the ways that are possible, and I always say prayers for them.

"As far as my parents . . . I was dying when Uthe came to me. There was no way to make them understand the decision I made or reconcile it. I wanted a chance to live . . . to experience life without illness, to pursue this burning drive I had inside me to create, to . . . illuminate. It felt like a mistake, like I was meant to *live*, and fate had sent me this chance." He shook his head. "The delusions of ego, but the decision was made. I left in the middle of the night, leaving nothing behind but a note saying that I wished to spare them the pain of my death and would see as much of the world as I could before God claimed me. Honest, in part. But now that I've left behind a young man's self-absorbed view of life, I know that decision caused my mother unimaginable pain. Not just going away from her, but the idea that my body might not have been cared for properly in death, according to our ways."

She considered that. Despite her mother's aloofness, once she left home, Alanna still cried herself to sleep for quite some time, knowing she'd never see her again. That first year, the feelings had sometimes been unbearable. To be bonded to someone for three hundred years, sharing emotions, intimacy, everything . . . When Niall was gone, only Evan would hold those memories. It sounded very lonely.

"How will you bear it?"

"The same way we bear anything in life. One moment at a time."

~

When she woke, she knew it was daylight, because she was in pitch-black darkness. The rumble of the RV moving over the highway was now matched by the sounds of heavier traffic. Because of yesterday's events, they had to move during daylight, so Niall had shut all the window coverings. There was a small anteroom between the driver's area and the living quarters to prevent any sunlight.

She heard Evan shift off the sleeper across from her. Grunt in pain.

"Master?"

"Moving to the floor," he muttered. "Cooler."

Before they started on their trip, she'd helped Niall unroll a cool mat, filled with chilled water that plugged into the electrical, and slid it under the camper sleeper. The rough sound of canvas scraping the floor, the slosh of water, Evan's thud as he flopped down on it, told her he was making use of it.

In pitch black, she had very little vision, but she knew the layout of the RV. Even artificial light would be too much for him right now. Finding the kitchenette, she created an ice pack out of a wet cloth and ice and brought it back to him. Going by sense and light touches, she stepped around his feet, knelt and lay down on her side, propping herself on her elbow.

He'd stripped off his shirt, so she put the ice pack there first, sliding it over his hot skin.

"It's always an aggravation, traveling during daylight." The strain in his voice concerned her, though his irritable tone helped ease it. Somewhat. "No matter how well protected I am, nothing less than underground results in this. It's like when I had fevers as a child, enhanced ten times." His hand found hers, glided up her forearm. "That feels good. Keep doing that."

She shifted so she was closer, but didn't touch his skin with hers, not wanting to add to his heat. It emanated off him like steam. "Master?"

"I'm fine, Alanna. I've done this before. My fucked-up anatomy may think I'm a hundred, but I'm not going to act like a fledgling, always going underground before daylight."

"Do vampires acknowledge any sins, Master?"

"Pride is a virtue to vampires, Alanna. You know that. Coveting is our favorite sport. Gluttony . . ." Capturing her forearm, he lifted her wrist to his mouth, ran his tongue lightly over her InhServ mark. "We never get enough of certain things."

When he bit down, the ripple of pleasure, right on the heels of the pain, made her tighten her fingers over his knuckles. Blood would help him, keep him strong, and she'd willingly give it all to him. But despite the pleasurable euphoria his feeding caused, she kept bathing him with the ice pack, enjoying his chest, the muscles of his abdomen, his upper thighs. When his other hand came up, cupped her neck, he brought her down to the taste of her blood and his hot mouth. She savored both as he shifted her closer.

"*Unh.*" He grunted a laugh against her mouth, hand dropping to seize her wrist. She'd let the hand with the ice pack press against his genitals, covered by thin cotton boxers.

She sputtered an apology, reflexively jerking back. The back of her head met his palm, saving her from the metal edge of the sleeper, though the momentum of her reaction had rapped his knuckles. He hadn't had to do that. It was just a bump to her head. But he had.

He was still chuckling, and it was infectious, foolishly so. Deliberately this time, she slid the ice pack right under the loose waistband of the boxers, freeing the ends of the cloth so the ice tumbled over his privates.

His roar of indignation would have sent her scampering, but he could see far better in the dark than she could. So she found herself wrestling with a vampire. He restrained himself enough to make it somewhat even, at least for a moment or two, but then she was giggling and squealing as he rolled over, pinning her to the camper floor.

He put ice down her soft tank top and into her panties, making her squirm and thrash until he put a cube directly against her clit and labia.

"Master," she panted. His hand closed on her throat, his elbow pinning her arm to the floor of the camper.

Put the other one over your head.

She obeyed immediately. When he put his mouth on the damp curve of her breast, swelling above the neckline of the tank, the mood shifted back to Master and servant in an instant. She went still and quivering beneath him. Oh, but the ice was excruciating . . .

"Stay still," he murmured. "Not even a twitch, my servant. Bear it, for me."

As she shuddered hard, he nuzzled her throat, inhaled the scent of her hair. The ice began to make her flesh ache, an icy burn. The heat from her cunt was melting it. "Master," she begged again. "Master."

Just to say it was enough to make all of it bearable. His head lifted. Now that her second-mark eyes were more accustomed to it, she could see a bare silhouette of his face. Lifting her free hand despite his order, knowing it was okay, she feathered it through his hair, that silken layering at the temples. "You're so handsome," she whispered. "So unexpected."

"All vampires are handsome. We're tediously beautiful."

"No. I see you . . . differently."

She sensed him studying her face. When he put his hand back into her damp underwear, he had more ice. She jerked, whimpered. "Spread your legs wider for me, Alanna."

The ice went inside her, his fingers guiding it deep, and staying with it, exploring her, manipulating the smooth cubes. "How am I different?"

She struggled to think. Oh, God, it was unbearable . . . and yet she never wanted it to stop, either.

"I . . . *feel* when I look at you. It makes you look different. Like the difference in painting a stranger, and painting . . . someone you know. Isn't there a difference?"

She needed to stop blathering. But his fingers were doing a gentle thrust and retreat, and her hips were coming up to meet his touch. She wanted him inside her. Wished for his cock with a fervency he could hear, but would deny her as long as it pleased him to do so, for that was the sorcery of being a vampire. Of being a Master.

"Yes. Like the difference between any willing woman's pussy, and the wet heat of yours, just for me. For my pleasure. Your heart and soul open to me like this."

Her lips parted, head tilting back, throat offered as the waves started to hit. "Master . . ."

Come for me. His mouth settled on the pounding artery. At the moment the climax hit, he bit, sinking his fangs into her during that rush of pleasure, his fingers still working inside her.

Though he took his time on the feeding, she was still moving rhythmically against his touch, riding the aftershocks as his fingers played beneath her panties. He licked her throat, closing the wounds, but then took her hand, bringing it under his boxers.

Work me with those lovely fingers, Alanna. I want to gush over them, smell my come on your flesh.

Lost in the glorious darkness, she obeyed.

20

They wouldn't reach their destination until midevening, so once full dark came, Evan told her to go up front with Niall so he could do some work in solitude. As a result, she enjoyed the winding roads up into the Tennessee hills. Niall eventually turned off on a more narrow access. It wasn't quite as primitive as the deer paths to reach the mountain cabin, but it twisted enough to keep his attention firmly on managing the hairpin turns and grumbling about the steep grades that slowed the heavy vehicle considerably. Finally, he turned off at a parkway entrance. A carved wooden sign indicated they'd arrived at Farida Sanctuary, a private artist colony.

A half mile down the road, Niall slowed for a guard booth. The woman who stepped out of its shelter was easily six feet tall. In boots, crisp jeans and a dark golf shirt embroidered with the sanctuary name, she looked like a cross between an Amazon warrior and Native American princess. Her beautifully sculpted arm muscles and long, dark braided hair, as well as the fact that she was armed with a combat knife in a beaded and fringed scabbard, added to the dual impression. She also had a nine-millimeter in a shoulder holster.

Despite her daunting appearance and watchful expression, the moment she shined her flashlight on the driver's side, she smiled broadly.

"Niall. Right on time." She tucked her tongue in her cheek. "Evan must be dead."

The Scot snorted. "No such luck. I do occasionally keep him on schedule. Guid to see ye, Mel."

Her gaze shifted then, sharpening on Alanna. "It's all right," Niall said. "She can be trusted. She's a friend in need."

Mel nevertheless shone the flashlight over Alanna, covering her from head to toe. "Any trouble following her I need to know about?"

"Aye," Niall said, surprising Alanna. "Nothing that'll risk a straight-on attack, but Evan'll brief the girls so they know what tae expect."

"Brief them fast, so they can bring me into the loop on what I need to know." Snapping off the flashlight, she shot him a disgruntled look. "You're supposed to let me know when you're bringing a guest. But since Nerida and Miah gave Evan an unconditional pass on whatever he drags in here, including you, I'll let you get away with it."

"Guid. I'd hate to get out of this thing and kick your arse. I'm creaky as an old man from driving all the day."

She harrumphed. "Big words, paleface. We have the usual bunga-low ready. There's still quite a few folks up, so you might get mobbed."

"I'll warn Evan. See you when you get off shift."

She gave him an appraising look, frankly sexual. "If I'm in a giving mood, I might help you work the creak out of those old bones."

Chuckling, he lifted a hand in acknowledgment. When he put the RV back in gear, Mel opened a well-reinforced security gate, but Alanna watched the way the woman's eyes lingered on Niall's profile as they drove past. Of course Niall enjoyed the pleasures of other women. That had been clear from the first, and it wasn't entirely unusual, particularly for male servants in the service of male vampires. Many vampires who had a more utilitarian relationship with their servants cared little if they had extracurricular liaisons, as long as it didn't interfere with their loyalty and service to the vampire.

Stephen had been less tolerant of such things with his female servants, but it wouldn't have mattered if he had been. An InhServ didn't indulge that option. Performing with another servant at the vampire's behest was a different matter, an extension of their will. While she'd enjoyed those other female and male bodies, united in their purpose and trained to give one another pleasure, Stephen's will had remained the driving factor.

She didn't like thinking about Evan allowing such liaisons, though she had no justifiable reason for feeling that way. But when he or Niall merely looked at her, she was so overwhelmed. She couldn't imagine participating in an empty sexual encounter with a human outside their world. It could only be a pale shadow of that connection. She should leave it alone, but . . .

"So, Evan doesn't mind you having sex with others?"

Niall turned onto a paved single-lane road, cloistered by thick forest growth. A rabbit bounded out in front of the RV and stayed there, guiding the vehicle for a hundred feet. Given that they were on an incline, the RV trundled along, accommodating the creature's pace until the rabbit jumped back into the foliage. "Not with other women. As long as it doesnae interfere with what he wants from me. It's a pleasurable way to pass the time. 'Tis not like we can pursue a career, cultivate an absorbing hobby. The vampire's the center o' our universe, aye?" He shot her a droll look, but she couldn't summon up a return smile. In fact, she felt an urge to scowl. "Our diversions have to orbit him, not cross the path and crash into the planet."

"Very visual. Evan is rubbing off on you." She bit her lip at her catty tone. Raising a shoulder, she tried to sound more casual. "So if an attractive male here wants to have sex with me while Evan is sleeping or otherwise engaged, I have the freedom to—"

Fortunately, there was no one following them, because Niall braked sharply. "No. *You* don't."

She arched a brow. "It shouldn't affect the blocker. Why should it matter to you who touches me when—"

His hand landed on her leg, possible in the roomy RV only because of the long reach of his arm. "As far as you're concerned, whatever comes from my mouth on this topic, comes from us both." That tawny gaze had gone gold, his expression and tone not one whit less compromising than one of Evan's orders in truth.

"Why?" She never questioned an obvious order from either male, but her mind was snared by the woman's blatant appraisal of Niall. It was obvious she'd enjoyed his body, and was looking forward to doing so again.

"I told you to take care in dealing with a jealous woman, Niall. You're out of practice." Evan slid through the opening between the main camper and the driving area, taking the backseat centered between them. As he stretched out his legs behind Alanna's seat, he propped his other hand on the back of Niall's.

Alanna pressed her lips together, cheeks reddening. She was being irrational. It was a reality of a servant's life, she knew that. With Evan here as a vivid reminder of that, she forced herself to behave properly. "I simply want to be sure I'm following the correct etiquette for the situation here, Master."

"Would you like the option of sex with another man, Alanna?"

No. It was such a vehement declaration, the recoil of it sent a pain through her chest. Leaning forward, Evan tangled his fingers in her hair. "Then the correct etiquette isn't really an issue, is it?" His tone was neutral, reasonable, though something in his gaze wasn't. "You'll let me know if that changes."

But what were Evan's thoughts on it? Niall's were obvious, and flattering, though in a backhanded way, since the Scot didn't seem to think there was any problem with thrusting his cock into some tall Amazon woman who probably didn't shave her armpits and used skunk spray for deodorant. She ignored Evan's muffled chuckle, staring out the window, her face averted from their driver.

Of course, Niall's thoughts could be more sexist than emotional. Being three hundred years old, he couldn't hide the fact that he found women fragile and in need of protection from male advances. She was pretty good at hand-to-hand. She could show "Mel" a thing or two, maybe put her on the ground to safeguard Niall's virtue. Not that he seemed to desire its protection.

The forbidding darkness to Niall's expression discouraged further poking at him. Though she felt a perverse desire to do just that, Evan tightened his fingers on her nape.

Do not goad him, Alanna. The old friends he sees here, he may not see again.

Shame flooded her. Why had she not thought of that? Evan shook his head, telling her not to speak of it, and she didn't, but she could do something else. As Niall brought the vehicle to a halt in front of their lodgings, she touched his hand on the wheel.

"I have no desire to be with anyone other than you and my Master, Niall. I am here for the two of you only, no matter what other engagements you desire."

The words stuck in her throat, but she was here to serve. Never to make demands, never to have anything of her own. No possessions didn't mean material items only, after all.

Though Niall put his other hand over hers, acknowledging the words, he said nothing himself. In fact, he immediately took his touch away, shutting down the RV.

The bungalow was a neat, small cottage. A wealth of flowers spilled off the porch rails from wooden boxes, while lush groupings of black-eyed Susans and various colorful flowers she didn't yet know screened the foundation. Instead of balustrades supporting the porch rails, there were carved panels in between the main posts. A bear guiding her two cubs, a deer leaping over a stream, a hawk in flight. She expected they'd been done by colony residents.

"Is the art they have here very valuable?" she asked Evan. "Mel seemed well armed."

"This is more than an art colony. It's a sanctuary for women and children," Evan said.

As Niall left the vehicle, Alanna watched him stride up the stairs to unlock the door, scope the interior. From the tense set of his shoulders, it was clear he wouldn't welcome her assistance right now. Evan's expression reminded her to let it be, so she focused on his explanation.

"Many of them are victims of domestic violence. Others have escaped countries where women don't have basic freedoms, access to education, and this is a place of transition for them. It was a sanctuary before it was an art colony. Forty years ago, one of the women who came was a very gifted painter and sculptor. Initially, she developed art programs to help women and children deal with what had happened to them, or to express what they were becoming." Warmth touched Evan's serious gray eyes. "Some of the residents had the talents and desire to achieve commercial success. Out of those, a few returned to be permanent staff, to use this as their main studio while continuing to teach others the way she did."

Alanna absorbed that. "Are there any men here, other than the two of you?"

"Yes. Else your suggestion wouldn't have gotten under Niall's skin." Evan gave her a tight smile. "The colony's population is about two hundred people. Twenty-eight are resident artists. They're all women, ones who originally came here for sanctuary. Forty are maintenance, administrative and security staff, like Mel, with about fifteen of them being men. The founder of the sanctuary realized early on it was important to have men present who could be role models of how men should act toward women and children. Many of them serve under Mel as security, which proves there are men who take their well-being and protection very seriously."

"Does the founder live here?"

"No. I'm sworn not to reveal his identity." Evan squeezed her hand. "What he's doing is not against the rules of our kind, but it's a vulnerability to know too much about a vampire."

The founder was a *vampire*? She looked toward the lit cottage. Niall was standing inside, studying something on the floor. Or perhaps he was staring into space, working through his thoughts. Glancing back at Evan, she saw he had his wrist resting comfortably along the top of her seat, his posture relaxed. It appeared he was giving his servant time to do just that.

"Master, may I ask you something?"

His gray eyes shifted to her. He could of course see the question in her mind, but seeing and responding to it were two distinct acts.

"You've asked me often what I want, but I wonder . . . what it is you want from me."

The answer had been simple before she met them. A vampire wanted obedience, unquestioned loyalty. Immediate compliance to anything he demanded.

"Those are all good things. And you need to work on them."

She flushed, knowing he was referring to the Trad, but on other things, he had to assume some fault, because he was asking her to break out of her mold, walk in territory she wasn't used to treading.

She'd tried to squelch that, but when his gaze sparked with amusement, she knew she was all right. Though her working on a less vocal mind was probably starting to be on his list of desires.

"Most likely," he responded dryly. Then he leaned forward, gazing into her face with such intensity she was tempted to look down, but she knew now when he wanted her meeting his eyes.

"I want you to live to be three hundred, Alanna," he said. "I want you to have as full a life as Niall has had. And I want to do whatever is necessary to make that happen. But should that be beyond my abilities"—a muscle ticked in his jaw—"I want you to take what pleasure and happiness you can from what you're given."

She swallowed. It was the most generous thing anyone had ever said to her. But it wasn't what she was seeking. Her real question was one she had no right to ask at all. Ironically, she'd never worried about the answer to it, until now. "You want me to embrace my feelings, my desires, my wants. You've demanded I act on them, instead of my training. I never thought I'd meet a vampire who . . . would make me want to demand the same from him."

His brow arched, the gray eyes sharpening. "Demand?"

"I need to know what I have no right to know, Master. For me to make the most of that pleasure and happiness, I need to know how you feel."

He shook his head. "The devil blesses a woman's tongue to confound male senses. Niall used to say that, early in my service. I told him it was superstitious nonsense, but you've just rendered him speechless, and trapped me in my own clever and magnanimous verbiage."

She suspected she was going to have a permanent blush, but still she persisted. "I've never wanted to be with a human not of our world, Master. I've always wanted this world, and to serve a vampire. What you are, what you feel, what you need. That's my purpose . . . my desire. So I need the answer of the vampire, not the civilized man."

He nodded. Considered. The veneer she'd sensed when he asked her if she wanted to have sex with another man dropped, the gray eyes steeling in a way that sent desire arrowing straight through her. He gave her a clear and ruthless answer.

"If you let another male touch you, other than Niall, I will take a belt to you in a way that will get me thrown out of here in a heartbeat, banned forever. And I won't regret it a bit. Now, go make amends with Niall, because he feels exactly the same way."

Something bloomed in her heart, an explosion of flowers like those in front of the cottage, a variety of shapes and colors, but all wondrous to experience. "Is Niall . . . all right with you touching me?"

A trace of humor cut through Evan's hard look. "Reluctantly, I'm sure. But there's nothing he can do about that, or I'll take a belt to him as well. Or maybe a two-by-four. He's a little more stubborn than you are. Or so I thought."

With a grunt, he stood, pulling her out the opening between the front seats to direct her through the side door. Catching her waist, he skipped the steps, landing on the ground with her held against him. As he let her feet touch, he ran his hand down her back with not-so-casual ownership. "Enough of that, now. I'll leave you two to set up house. My privilege, as lord of the manor, to avoid manual labor. We'll be here awhile, so make it home. I liked the touches you put on the mountain cabin."

As she glowed at the compliment, he gave her a fond pinch. "I'll go speak to Miah and Nerida before Mel puts herself into a froth. She's probably already called them twice to see if I've met with them."

"Are they part of the security team?"

"Yes and no. They're permanent residents here, and help in whatever way is needed." He checked the tuck of his shirt, began to unroll his cuffs, but Alanna shook her head.

"They'll be wrinkled, Master. I can prepare another shirt for you."

"No, this will be fine." As he raked his fingers through his hair, she feathered his bangs so he looked well tended. He gave her a smile. "You're a treasure, *yekirati*. Now, so you won't get alarmed when you sense them, Nerida and Miah are vampires. Except for those who serve their blood needs, we are the only ones here who know that." He paused. "They were turned as children, Alanna. They're in their seventies, but they're physically trapped at those ages. Nerida looks six, Miah about twelve or thirteen."

The idea horrified her. "What vampire—"

"Long dead, as he full deserved." His jaw firmed. "The founder took the two of them under his wing, and they found a permanent place here. In our world, they would never be safe." A grim smile touched his lips. "They're like me, only their comparable lack of strength is much more obvious. However, the fact that they're still far more powerful than humans makes them an excellent backup to the security detail. An abusive husband or a team sent from one of those oppressive countries to reclaim their women won't expect a six-year-old to disembowel them. Another reason for the deep forest location. Easier to dispose of bodies."

He flashed his fangs. "Mel is one of their two marked servants. Her grandparents, Kohana and Chumani, served the vampire who helped Miah and Nerida acclimate to the vampire world, as much as they could. And of course, this territory, while ostensibly under Lord Richard, is also still considered very much Lady Lyssa's as well. They exist in the shadow of her protection as well."

He lifted a shoulder. "Because Miah and Nerida clearly have the mannerisms of adults, residents have been told they have a rare aging and sun disorder where they will always look like children, and can't go out in daylight. They stay here so they aren't turned into freaks and exploited by the outside world. Some may wonder at the truth of that, but science is more easily believed than the supernatural. Those who came here for safety and secrecy also tend to respect that need for others. So far, Miah and Nerida have always been safe here."

The vampire world was turning out to be so much more than she knew. Though she wanted to hear more, she understood his responsibility to bring them into the loop about Stephen. "We'll get the household set up to your liking, Master."

"I've no doubt." He gave her an appraising look, then he was gone, turning and disappearing into the night. But her body heated at that look, remembering his threat in the vehicle, a threat that she took in a way perhaps most women wouldn't. But most women weren't raised in the vampire world. Other than her brother, it was the closest to an emotional declaration she'd received from a male.

Well, perhaps not the only one. Mounting the stairs, she found Niall now in the kitchen. A plate of cookies had been left next to a vase of daisies on the counter. He'd turned back the cellophane and was finishing what appeared to be his third or fourth helping. He nodded to the plate. "Nerida left us cookies. Better eat them now, because there won't be any later."

"Apparently," she noted, trying to smile at him, reclaim their easy earlier state. He straightened.

"We'll pull in his equipment first. I can get most of it if you're tired. Or if you want tae rest up for whatever 'extracurricular activities' ye have planned."

She narrowed her gaze. "*You're* the one with extracurricular plans. Perhaps you should refuel with cookies while *I* unpack. I wouldn't want her disappointed by your performance."

Yes, she knew what Evan had said about old friends, but she hadn't expected Niall to be nasty. Though his expression became more hostile, she bumped toes with him, glaring back. "I asked because I wanted to know what was expected. Not because I intended to go out and jump the first available male. I don't want that."

"But you'll condemn me for it? Like I'm some sort of *hoormaister*? It's only supposed to be about the vampire? His wants and needs?"

"To an InhServ, yes. You and Evan have your own ways. I expect he would prefer to have your full devotion, but—"

"Excuse me?" His brows knitted together, clouds drawing together before the storm. Crossing her arms, she took a step back, not in retreat, but to avoid a crick in her neck.

"It's not an insult, Niall. Knowing you hold yourself only for his will, whether it's to watch us with another, or for another purpose, but always to serve him—it says something." She took a breath, trying to give him an earnest explanation. "It builds the bond, deepens it. Most vampires . . . when you give them your full devotion, there's an energy to it. Like the slow anticipation of a climax, when Master is teasing you, keeping it out of reach until you think you'll explode from it."

"Aye, ye know so much about it. Your mindless devotion to Stephen was bloody perfection."

She slapped him. When he caught her wrist, dragging her to him, she didn't try to yank free, but stayed stiff and angry, her face close to his enraged one. They'd taught her expressing her emotions was acceptable, so she'd embrace the lesson.

"What Stephen was or wasn't to me wasn't relevant to my oath. I served him fully, no matter what. There was honor in that, purpose. Your debt of honor to Evan was the excuse for something you wanted but couldn't give yourself." Her voice had lifted to a near shout. She'd never shouted in her life.

Okay, maybe she was embracing the lesson a little too much. She pulled back. She wasn't showing proper control, but beyond that, her anger would accomplish nothing in the face of his own temper. So she took it down a notch, speaking calmly despite the fact that she was hurt, a dull throb beneath her heart.

"You fear the risk I took with Stephen, but it's nonsense. However wrong it was for me to wish for it, you have within your grasp what I hoped to have. You have it because you *aren't* an InhServ."

His gaze flickered with surprise, some of the anger chased away by it. Her lips quivered, then she firmed them, lifting her chin. "The irony of that isn't lost on me. What I truly wanted may have been lost to me from the beginning. But I think if you had only a touch of what I am, you could let yourself love Evan the way you've always wanted. With everything you are. You think you betrayed your wife because you didn't love her the way you love Evan now. So you withhold it, to punish you both."

The flush in his cheeks drained away. As Niall stared at her, speechless, she realized she'd gone too far, said too much. Had she smashed a wall behind which he hadn't even sensed the truth? Or had she simply hurt him to no purpose other than to assuage her own anger?

"Niall."

He shook his head, a sharp slice of his hand silencing her. A hundred thoughts were moving behind his eyes. Perhaps he was right about the devil blessing a woman's tongue. First she'd offended Evan by not trusting his judgment with the Trad, and now this. She wished they'd let her do self-flagellation, because she was sorely in need of it. Her emotions were so uncontained, the two she least wanted to offend kept getting caught in the maelstrom.

Reaching out, she caught that hand. He didn't pull away, but he was rigid, stiff. Even so, she lifted his hand to her mouth, pressing her lips to his rough, large knuckles. She held her cheek there, just as she had with Evan.

"You were right. I was jealous." She could swallow pride, an unusual indulgence for her anyhow. Her cheeks were burning, though. "I meant what I said. I'm here to serve you and Evan, however you need me. No matter what."

"Both of us?" His voice was wooden, but she took heart from the question.

"Yes. I serve you both."

"You slapped me."

"Well . . ." She cleared her throat, keeping her eyes on his thick fingers. "Sometimes that's a necessary service."

Hearing a low rumble, she dared a glance up. He was chuckling. The anger dissipated, but it left the pain. She touched his mouth before he could tell her no. "I shouldn't have said those things."

"Do you think they're true?" He met her gaze, his jaw tight.

"Does it matter what I think?"

"Aye, it does, lass." He sighed, a resigned, weary sound she didn't like. "You ken how to read people. There's summat to what ye said, even if I dinnae want to hear it. Though it matters little now."

"Maybe it matters more than you realize." His accent had thickened, and she was starting to realize what that meant.

Putting her arms around him, she hugged as much of him as she could, a man of his bulk. They both faced death, and no matter how brave he was, it had to be unsettling to come to terms with the loss of all he knew. To lose Evan, the one continuous presence in his life. His family.

After only these few days, she had an understanding of what it meant to truly belong to another, to love and have a family. It was a far more precious thing than a functional, one-sided and mostly emotionless relationship. Burying her face in his chest, in the heat and solidity of him, her precarious world steadied as she tried to do the same for him.

She was glad he hadn't pressed her for an answer to his question. She'd said she was sorry, not because she didn't believe what she said, but because she was afraid she'd tear apart the fragile thing she'd been enjoying with them. That wasn't very noble, but it was honest.

"Did Evan tell ye what he thought of ye and other men?" The rumble in his voice made her smile.

"You know he did. You just want to hear me say it. He said he'd take a belt to me."

"Mmph. That'd make two of us." He had a fondness for those hard squeezes of her backside, the ones that made her squirm against him, which she expected was his intent. When she punched him in the side, he chuckled again.

"You're getting a feisty side, lass. 'Tis a guid thing, even when I want to strangle ye for it. Leave off, now. Let a man be a man and maintain his demons as he pleases. Women always want to turn us inside out, put that nonsense on the outside, make us soft. I'll take care of the unloading; you go find Evan. He wants to make sure I didnae murder ye. I'll leave all the nesting to you, so you willnae feel ye shirked your duty."

"You just want me to do all the unpacking."

"There is that. Go to him. Nerida and Miah want to meet ye."

"All right." Evan wanted her, and that required an immediate response, but she did pause to put both hands on his firm jaw. "Can you say 'murder' again? You're so Scottish when you get mad."

"I'm always Scottish, *muirnín*. No matter how far I get from the bloody place. Murder, murder, murrrdurrr. Here's another you'll like. Houghmagandie. That's sex for pleasure, not for procreation, a right sinful thing, ye ken."

She smiled, then sobered, curling her fingers against his face. "Whatever the truth is, Niall, I didn't intend to hurt you."

He closed his hands on her wrists, holding her there. "Ah, lass. I guess I started it, didn't I? I wouldnae have reacted the way I did to ye talking about other men if you didnae matter to me far more than you should. Three hundred years since a woman captured my heart, and ye did it in less than a week."

When her eyes stilled on his, he continued, "I do hope guid things for you, but maybe, once things are resolved and they reassign ye, which they will, 'tis fine my time's coming tae an end. Knowing I'd lose you, on top of Evan . . ." He shrugged, gave her a smile that wrenched her heart. "To my way of thinking, Heaven only exists if my heart stays here with you two."

Turning her toward the door, he gave her a pat on the bottom and a gentle shove. "Go to your Master. For all he pretends to be different, ye know vampires get in a high do if they have to wait."

～

The last thing she'd wanted was to leave him after that astounding declaration, but she wanted Evan, too. So she went, because her Master had ordered her to his side.

Her mind was spinning over the other things Niall had said. Up until now, she hadn't allowed herself to think about it. It was easier to accept her inevitable death. But if she did miraculously survive, and was somehow released from Stephen's mark to be reassigned? She imagined her return to the austere, regimented world of the vampire aristocracy, after experiencing Evan and Niall. She'd be leaving not just them, but the relationship they were developing with her.

The choice would not be hers, not any of it. But would she learn what it felt like to lose her heart entirely, the way Niall suggested? Stephen had fallen short of her expectations, but she'd accepted responsibility for that, knowing she'd assumed something that wasn't in the typical vampire–servant relationship. She thought she'd evolved in her training. Instead, she'd simply buried what she wanted, and Evan and Niall had unearthed it in less than a week.

No matter the long penance sessions and doing everything to be the most obedient, most useful InhServ ever to Stephen, she'd watched vampire–servant pairings like that of Lady Lyssa and Jacob and fed that fuel to the tiny fire that had stayed alive deep in her heart.

Her training said nothing was about her wants or desires, but was it possible she would be a *better* servant if those wants and desires were taken into consideration? The InhServ program had always been about gifting an InhServ to a vampire showing political promise. Since they were all trained the same way, to be adaptable to whatever the vampire required, only the vampire's preferences were considered. What if the program went more in-depth, considered variables in both InhServ and vampire, to make the relationship a more compatible one, beyond the services the servant was trained to offer?

She was turning into a radical. Though wryly amused, she was also a bit shaken by her thoughts. As she followed a path lit with solar lights toward where she felt Evan waiting for her, she did some calming mind exercises.

The colony's layout added to that steadying influence. Cottages like theirs formed a loose, irregular circle around the main compound, which had a variety of functional buildings and open-air pavilions. Three of the former were obviously laid out for studio work, since she could see a variety of projects in process through the plethora of tall windows. One artist was still at work, her blowtorch throwing off a festive shower of sparks as she bent to her metal sculpting, her protective headgear in place.

The pavilions appeared to serve as communal areas as well as additional outdoor studio space. Groups of residents were playing cards at the assembled tables, others holding sleeping children on their laps as they chatted together. A group of staff members, wearing the dark embroidered shirt like Mel, were sharing a late dinner. They noticed Alanna, but she merely gave them a polite nod and continued onward. Unless they stopped her, it wasn't appropriate to seek introductions until she determined what her Master required.

Her steps slowed despite herself when she passed the children's playground. All the swings, mazes and climbing equipment were wooden carvings designed to look like mythical creatures, dinosaurs, trains. There were painted stone statues of fairies, comical gnomes and woodland animals, all of a size to encourage the children to touch or climb upon them. She let her hand slide along the arch of a unicorn's neck before she recalled herself.

Among the trees bordering her paved path she was surprised by the occasional face, wooden pieces pinned to the trunks to create remarkably human expressions. Shrubs had been pruned into the shapes of fauns, unicorns, a car. These artistic touches were blended into the natural thick forest border around the compound, such that locating them became a treasure hunt.

At the crest of the path the forest opened up before her. A mowed, grassy field sloped down to a large pond, where the docks were stocked with paddleboats and canoes. The moon hung low over it, creating a silver lake, and the light pointed her to her destination.

Cutting off the path, she headed across the tended field. He waited for her inside a large gazebo, meeting her on the steps with a half smile. When he reached out a hand to help her up those stairs, she hesitated as she always did from the unexpected offer of assistance, but it was barely a pause, since she was eager for his touch. His eyes warmed on her.

"Nerida and Miah will join us shortly, but I figured you'd need a few minutes to get across the compound. Even with your eye for detail, in daylight you'll find you missed half of it. The children call the perimeter paths The Enchanted Forest."

"I can't imagine how you ever bring yourself to leave." Of course, she could say that for every place he'd taken her thus far.

He winked. "Mel kicks me out when I overstay my welcome."

She suspected his art drove him ever onward to see new things, but he likely returned to this place when the ideas were overflowing, so he could execute them in familiar surroundings.

Always insightful, beautiful InhServ. This is a place of refuge, in many ways.

As he guided her into the gazebo, she saw art mounted on the interior walls, the piece directly before her catching her eye. It had been protected in a glass box, the lighting positioned around it making it clear to the viewer at night.

"This is your work." Alanna drew closer. "But it's different, and not just because it's paint. What did you do?"

"Highlighted what was already there." Evan moved to stand just behind her, his hip brushing her buttock. When she turned her head to look up at him, her hair fluttered across his shoulder, moved by the wind coming from across the lake. She made a move to draw it back, but he captured her hand, held it against his chest, though his eyes were on the canvas.

"You're familiar with the saying, 'we don't see the forest for the trees'?" When she nodded, he added, "It works the opposite way as well. You look at a forest, but do you see the trees? Do you really see them?"

He pointed. "Each has a different shape, different leaves, even if they're the same species. Some have been scarred by lightning or a bear's claws during their lives, and that causes them to grow differently. They even respond differently to the touch of the wind, based on the shape of the trunks, the weight of the limbs. We don't notice because we lack time, patience. Yet sit in one spot and watch, listen, notice, and you see it, how incredibly individual every single thing in life is. And yet"—he stepped back, taking her with him—"in key ways, very much the same. They all reach toward the light, though of course in this picture it's moonlight."

When she glanced at him, his gray eyes were intent on the work, studying what he'd done, what he could do better, though he kept speaking. "They all drive their roots into the ground to hold on to their space, to draw strength and nourishment. However, some go deeper than the others. As they grow up, their roots overlap. For some, it's like fingers tangling together. Others tie knots."

He drew her attention to a separate canvas, directly below that one. Whereas the upper one showed the forest above ground, the lower one showed what was happening beneath the earth. How the roots did become like fingers or, in the case of thicker tubers, like bodies. Bodies twined in passion or in a fetal waiting position, the nest of roots around them becoming the womb. Another shape was bound up in the more ropelike roots as if bound by a Master, waiting for whatever he desired. And then . . .

She bent to examine it more closely. At the very bottom of the lower canvas, near his signature, was a tiny, whiskered mole, working blindly on his small tunnel, oblivious to all of it.

"As long as you've lived, you could have painted historic events, but you seem to paint . . . everything else." She didn't mean it as an insult, and fortunately, he didn't seem to take it as such. He shrugged.

"I've seen some amazing work. I've been to the Louvre, I've been to Rome . . . What I saw there was amazing, but it was intended for display, much of it commissioned. That doesn't make it less remarkable, but what always interested me was the type of art created when it was simply what called to the artist. In a little, out-of-the-way church in the mountains of North Carolina, there's a painting done by a nineteen-year-old, of Jesus laughing. When I looked at that, I thought, this is how it must be done, a direct conduit of the muse, no middleman of priest or art patron to interfere with that flow of pure energy."

He nodded at the paintings. "As life grows short, it's the small moments remembered, not what war was fought, or when the rocket went to the moon. It was the day you went to the beach with your mother, or a lover's touch in a predawn light. The true history of the individual life. That's what interests me."

"Niall said almost the same thing." *Reading about the history you've lived, a lot of it is pure bollocks. Kings and politics. The things a man remembers and history forgets are home and family. That first kiss.*

She straightened, still gazing at the picture. "You two are the most remarkable men I've ever met."

Looking back, she found him staring at her oddly. Before she could open her mouth to apologize, he lifted her hand to his lips, kissed her palm. Her heart beat in her throat as he kept those mesmerizing eyes on her.

"I'm simply an eccentric vampire, Alanna. You are the remarkable one. Any artist would be lucky to have you as a muse."

"You already have a muse." Her fingers trembled under his touch. Her body had been used in every imaginable way, but whenever he did things like this, unmistakably romantic, she was as new to it as an innocent schoolgirl.

"I do?" He cocked a brow. "Is there another woman I'm overlooking?"

"Muses can be male, Master." She paused. "His humanity, his sense of honor, his complex idea of love yet simple embrace of life . . . I see Niall in almost everything you've created."

Her attention shifted to another work. It was a photograph, blown up to the size of the tree pictures, showing people standing on a busy nighttime street corner. Some smoked and talked, caught in dramatic gestures. One leaned on a lamppost next to a couple making out, wrapped up in each other. A tight knot of others focused on the light changing, all of them bathed in the city lights. Her gaze slid to the tree canvas, then back across. They weren't identical, but the postures were so similar, it was impossible not to draw the connection.

"How did you . . . Did you pose them?"

"No. I took thousands of street corner shots for nearly a month. Niall helped me sift through all of them. Don't get me started on his grumbling, because I had to clout him on the head to get him to shut up about it—but eventually I found one that was similar yet different enough to work."

"I could look at your work all my life and never get tired of it," she said honestly. Then, realizing that could be insulting, given that she didn't have much life left, she added, "I wish I had a much longer life to do so."

Evan knew why Niall reacted the way he did when she said things like that. Though he'd rarely responded as openly about it as Niall did, now his fingers tightened on hers, conveying his fierce reaction, his recurring wish that he had more power to change her destiny.

Shyly, showing how new it was to her to seek contact, Alanna reached up with trembling fingers, caressed his jaw. It was rare he'd felt held in place by a human's touch, but Evan was now, moved by the deep, powerful feeling he saw in her eyes. She claimed to see something amazing and unexpected in his art. One-of-a-kind. All he had to do was look at her to see a living example of that.

He'd heard Niall's words to her about losing his heart. At the time, he'd been glad to be elsewhere, so he had time to school his reaction to it. Yet now, when Niall's declaration gripped his heart anew, he looked up and saw him there.

He'd been caught up in her emotions, hadn't sensed his approach. As he met his servant's gaze, he reached out a hand. At least in this moment, there was nothing between them except her.

Niall proved it, coming to him without hesitation, so that they held Alanna between them. It was as if with the wall of their bodies, they could keep her from harm. Evan put his arms around both of them, while Niall gripped Evan's side, strong fingers stroking his hip. It was a painful yet precious peace, holding his two servants to him.

Whether you wish to hear it or not, Niall, I feel very much as you do about her. Pressing his head against Niall's jaw, he put his temple against Alanna's silken hair. *And losing you will tear the heart out of me. The curse of being a vampire is that we absorb the blows we wish would kill us.*

His servant's grip tightened. Niall might actually crack his pelvic bone, but Evan would bear any pain to absorb the emotion behind the gesture.

You need to make sure she stays yours, Evan. You need each other.

Evan lifted his head. The Scot's tawny gaze was full of things Evan wanted to capture, and not only in a painting. If he could internalize every gesture, emotion and thought, Niall could never leave him. His muse would be part of his mind forever. His soul.

I need you, Niall. I always have.

The Scot looked as if he was going to respond to that, then his attention shifted, as did Alanna's. In a heartbeat, both servants stepped away and turned toward the entrance of the gazebo, an automatic united front.

It's Miah and Nerida. But even if they were enemies, the proper response is to step behind me, both of you.

Niall gave him his patented look that said he was wasting his breath. Though Alanna lowered her gaze and stepped into a proper position behind him, Evan wasn't fooled. Not after what she'd pulled with the Trad. Servants. A blessed pain in his ass.

Niall shifted to his left, not as far behind him as Alanna, but enough to pass for proper etiquette, given that the vampires coming out of the shadows knew what kind of servant he was.

Oh, and Niall? As far as houghmagandie, it's only Christians who think sex for pleasure is sinful. Jews think it's just fine.

Aye? Well, ye also think eating a pig is wrong, and bacon is a God-given treasure.

Alanna choked on a snicker, looking mortified with herself, but sharing their conversation had achieved Evan's desired result. Niall was grinning, and the seriousness of the moment had been eased. He turned his attention to the approaching vampires.

Miah and Nerida were mixed-blood, white and Aborigine. People often thought they were sisters, but the trauma of their making had made them kin, not blood. As he'd warned Alanna, Miah appeared to be an adolescent, Nerida no more than six, but their body language, the mature wisdom in their eyes, reflected their seventy-plus years. However, when needed for deception and survival, both could emulate children flawlessly.

Lord Mason had chosen a good place. Farida Sanctuary was a stimulating and stable environment for them. Nerida was a successful author, published under a pseudonym, and Miah was working on her second Masters in literature. With their shared love of stories, they were the bards of the sanctuary. They regularly offered bedtime stories in the communal pavilion to a rapt crowd. When needed, they made house calls to the cottages, soothing an anxious new arrival to sleep, whether woman or child, with their enchanting tales.

Nerida skipped up the stairs and jumped so Niall caught her in his arms and swung her around. "What's this?" the Scot demanded. "A kitten with fangs and big brown eyes who can entice a lad to do anything."

As she hugged him, Evan saw her check her fangs with her tongue, making sure Niall hadn't remarked on them because they were showing. They weren't able to retract them like mature vampires, but Lord Brian had taught them how to file them back.

She punched Niall's shoulder, seeing from his dancing gaze he'd intended to make her self-conscious. "Not you. Head harder than rock."

"In the Highlands, there are rocks that could knock some sense into me, sure enough. That's why I left and never went back. A man with too much sense willnae get into trouble with the lasses, and what fun is that?"

Miah gave him and Evan both a hug. "Do you like where we put your paintings? Quite a few of our visiting artists use this space as a studio. Your work inspires their own creations. '*Nature never hurries. Atom by atom, little by little, she achieves her work.*'"

"Emerson is one of my personal favorites," Evan approved. "As always, coming here is like coming home. '*Discovering this idyllic place, we find ourselves filled with a yearning to linger here, where time stands still and beauty overwhelms.*' Anonymous, but a good friend to Emerson. As you are a good friend to me, and not just because you stroke my vanity by displaying my work."

"Actually," Niall drawled, "there were a couple ugly paint-stripped spots in here. They thought 'well, now, that's what we can do with Evan's eyesores.'"

Though he ducked Evan's head slap with the smoothness of long practice, Alanna tag-teamed with her Master, jabbing him in the ribs. The Scot gave her a heated look. "Hit me once more tonight, lass, and I'll hit back, on the spot o' my choosing."

When Miah and Nerida turned their attention to her, Alanna knelt. "Mistresses, thank you for your hospitality to my Master. In accordance with his will, I am at your service."

Miah snorted. "What did this poor child do to deserve you two? She's obviously way above your station, Evan."

Evan laughed. "She had an overdose of courage and integrity. We were her punishment."

Alanna was appalled by Miah's comment, but Evan's good humor eased her mind. However, when he began to summarize her situation, the vampire females sobered and her tension returned. A quick glance at their faces told her nothing. When Evan finished, there was a harrowing moment of silence in the gazebo. Alanna twisted her fingers together in her lap.

"It's not too far off the path of what we already do here," Miah said at last. "Protect a female from the violent advances of male relatives or spouse. Sometimes, shamefully, even the female relatives try to extricate them. We've been fortunate, though. The only time we've lost one was when the resident is so damaged, she goes back to the situation on her own. I assume Alanna has no intentions of assisting Stephen in locating her?"

She didn't look at Alanna, making it clear this was a vampire conversation. It didn't stop Niall from interjecting, however.

"Only if she gets the misguided idea it will protect us," he snorted. "In which case, I'll strangle her before Stephen can do it."

Alanna bit her lip, but said nothing. The unavoidable truth was that there was no command that would force her to endanger anyone further to protect her own life.

Evan shot her a sharp look. "Then I expect we'll need to ensure that scenario doesn't occur." Though it appeared he was responding to Niall, she knew differently, especially when Niall sent her a censorious look, indicating Evan had shared her thought.

"Well, our gates aren't for us to hide behind," Nerida said. "They're to better defend and protect what's here."

When the female vampire glanced at her, Alanna bowed her head anew. It was difficult not to stare when a mature woman's speech came from the bow-shaped mouth of a six-year-old child. Miah at least had some of the angular features of an adolescent about to step across the threshold to womanhood.

"We'll advise Mel and increase our own security measures," Nerida continued. "It sounds like we have reinforcements on standby."

"Yes. The Council vampire will be patrolling the perimeter. It's our hope he'll apprehend Stephen before the situation crosses our path."

"Regardless, consider yourself welcome, Evan. You and those you protect." Miah gave him a nod. "Niall of course is always welcome. A to-do list is already waiting for him."

"For the usual compensation I suppose?" When Niall arched a brow, the two female vampires grinned, showing fangs this time.

"They started cooking a week ago. You'll be so fat Evan will leave you behind. Then you'll never be out of our clutches."

"Promises, promises, ladies."

Miah rubbed against him like an affectionate cat. "Mel just went off shift. She has that list ready if you want to get an early look at it." Affecting a passable Scottish accent, she added, "Though we willnae be needing ye 'til the morrow."

The Scot got a nod of assent from Evan. When Niall looked toward Alanna, she made sure she was looking at the floor. *I serve them. They do not serve me.*

Niall touched her hair. Alanna put all her effort into brushing her lips across his palm with the proper devotion and full submission. "I'll take care of the things at the cabin," she managed. "And be there if you need anything."

She pushed away the thought of his flesh carrying the musk of another woman's body. *I am a servant. I serve. That is my pleasure, my only desire . . .*

Hearing him leave the gazebo, the boards vibrating as he descended the steps, made things hurt inside of her. Fortunately, his departure gave her an excuse for her own. "Master, do you need me further, or should I attend to the cottage?"

"You're excused, Alanna." The gentle understanding made it more unbearable, but she bowed to the vampire females and left the gazebo before her reaction could choke her. How far she'd fallen, that her emotions could command her in such an irrational way. Evan, being a vampire, would thankfully leave her alone to manage the reality of being a servant.

Because who understood that reality better than her?

21

S HE threw herself into unpacking. After that, she set out some pho-
tographs Evan carried as trip mementoes. Cutting a handful of
black-eyed Susans from the front stoop, she arranged them in water
glasses. The refrigerator was well-stocked with stews, casseroles, meats
and vegetables that only needed heating. Two apple pies had appeared
on the counter, so she ate a slice that fairly melted in her mouth. She
tried not to resent it. Caring for Niall and Evan was her job.

She imagined the Scot in a cottage bedroom with Mel, her arms
and legs twined around him, Niall plowing into her willing, slick folds,
her throat arched to him, ample breasts pressed into his chest . . .

Stop it. Despite Evan's proscription on penance, she knew her duty.
She had to get her emotions under control. At the gazebo, the desire to
create had been humming off his skin. He'd be lost in his painting, so
she could handle it without disrupting him.

Fortunately, the well-stocked kitchen had uncooked rice. She
scattered a thick covering over a bath towel and knelt facing the wall.
As the sharp pieces bit into her knees, she began the meditation, letting the building discomfort pull her into that mindless zone.

She kept at it until her knees felt as if they were on knife blades,
then she rose, stifling the short cry with vicious purpose. She didn't
feel better about Niall's whereabouts, but she was less wound up about

it. Evan's second mark helped the cuts heal over quickly. Rechecking the vampire's cellar room, she confirmed it was ready for him. She'd added a quilt and a glass of flowers, placing out a couple of books he was reading, along with a bottle of wine. She added a covered sampling of the cookies and apple pie.

She would go to bed. Alone. Putting on the shirt Niall had discarded earlier, she considered the bed he would share with her, if ever he deigned return to it. Turning away from it, she went back down to the cellar.

Merely a week ago, she'd never have dreamed of insinuating herself in her Master's room without his direct invitation, but tonight she would risk his punishment. Niall felt too far away, though she wrapped the excess of the shirt closer around her body, inhaling his scent, taking that into her fitful sleep.

Sometime close to dawn, she was aware of Evan joining her. She was so exhausted she didn't come out of sleep quickly enough to verify if he wanted her there. However, he put her at ease, sliding into the bed behind her, caressing her hip. When his lips touched her throat, she lifted her chin, offering. A dream-laden sigh left her as he bit into her flesh, tugged the quilt away and turned her onto her back. She wore nothing under the T-shirt so her legs spread for him, surrendering to his demand. As he pushed his cock inside her, stroked, he took her into a drifting, liquid, swirling climax where she moaned into his shoulder, held on to him through their mutual release. Then she was curved back into his body, his quiet reproof in her drifting mind.

You will not harm yourself again, Alanna. Chaos is the precursor to creation. Let your emotions spin as they wish. I will have Niall punish you for your disobedience.

She'd welcome any attention the Scot would offer her, even punitive. But at the same time, she wanted him to choke on apple pie. She fell back asleep with Evan's tender amusement in her mind.

∾

When she woke, she was in the upper bedroom. Niall had returned to change clothes, for what he'd worn yesterday was draped over the corner hamper. Light streaming through the window offered her a brilliant sunrise as she dressed. Evan had left her a note on the dresser, telling her to report to the commune coordinator to help with the tasks that kept the little community self-sufficient.

She arrived there with a group of people, apparently used to a similar routine. When introductions were made, she wasn't surprised to find some of the residents wary. Given their circumstances, she knew trust would have to be earned, but this morning that was fine. The staff embraced her eagerness to work, not talk.

A vegetable garden and orchard needed weeding and pruning. After breakfast, there was dish duty in the communal eating area. Once they found out about her cooking skills, she was invited to help the lunch crew. Later she went to the infirmary, where she helped as orderly and nurse assistant. A few residents had arrived with broken limbs, one with a wired jaw. The infirmary monitored them, kept them under observation and gave them medications as needed. They also provided walk-in assistance for minor injuries. Alanna watched a nurse talk to a new resident about proper nutrition for her children, something the haggard, poorly educated woman had never had the chance to learn.

As she proved herself a willing and capable asset throughout the day, many residents became friendlier toward her. The few male staff were courteous and not flirtatious, keeping that pressure away from the residents, many of those having experienced only the ugliest side of sexual interest. Alanna found it especially heartbreaking to watch the children. Though instinctively desiring the balance male energy could provide, they watched the men with uncertain eyes. The male staff treated them with calm affection, helping them take those first steps toward trust again.

The environment was designed to be safe, nurturing. It was the self-contained comfort of a mother's womb, occasionally punctuated by the expected squabbles, reminding her of the women's hall of the InhServ training institute. The conflicts here were resolved with mostly good humor, everyone sensitive to the more nervous temperaments of newer arrivals, women who kept their children close, still unsure of their welcome.

She thought of Stephen invading this environment, bringing all the terror and darkness a vampire could command. Reminding herself she had to trust her Master's judgment, she recalled Nerida's words.

Our gates aren't for us to hide behind. They're to better defend and protect what's here. From the dangerous flash in the female vampire's eyes, she'd enforced the words when necessary.

It was midafternoon when she saw Niall. He was repairing one of the cottage roofs with another man, a stocky redhead whose upper body was covered in freckles and muscles. The two of them had already stripped the shingles and were putting down tar paper.

Putting aside the festering issues she had from his night with Mel, she enjoyed the casual grace and virile strength Niall exuded doing the demanding physical task. He wore a faded pair of jeans and rubber-soled work shoes, his T-shirt hanging on a bush. When he saw her below, he sent her a warm smile that lit up her heart, foolish creature that she was.

"There she is. *Muirnín*, could ye bring me and Frank some o' that fresh-squeezed lemonade over at the canteen? Get yourself a glass as well. 'Tis the best thing you'll ever taste."

She nodded, went to do his bidding. Mel was there, having a late lunch with some others. The Native American woman noticed her arrival, however. She gave Alanna a short nod that, while not unfriendly, was a clear assessment. Alanna was likely the top security risk in the compound right now. She was determined not to cause Mel a problem, though. She didn't want the compound's resources channeled toward her protection, when they had far more important priorities.

Was the woman carrying Niall's scent between her legs this morning? Did she have a faint abrasion on her smooth, high cheekbone, left by the friction of Niall's jaw as he thrust into her body?

So what if she did? That was Niall's right. If Stephen had come to her, his cock dripping from another woman's orgasm, and bade her suck him clean, her job was to respond with enthusiasm, making it as stimulating for him as he desired and more.

She'd damn well exceeded expectations in that department.

"All right this morning?"

Mel was at her shoulder, but when the woman reached out to touch her, Alanna shifted out of range. She covered it with a courteous nod. "Yes, ma'am. Thank you. Is there anything you require?"

"Just wanted to be sure everything's right in your world. You looked a little . . . intense. If there's anything that's worrying you, you can feel as comfortable coming to me for help as you do your Mas—Evan. Especially if it's daylight or Niall isn't readily at hand. Keeping this place safe is my number one priority, and you're part of that until you leave. I'm here for you as much as anyone, Alanna. All right?"

"Thank you. That's very kind." Surprised at the woman's sincerity, Alanna still took a deeper inhale, under the guise of a relieved sigh. She didn't detect Niall's scent on the woman. Of course, Mel would have showered, and Alanna's third-mark senses were muted by the damn injection.

"Niall and I shared a bottle of Jack last night. You've got him tied up in knots. He's even a little goofy, teenaged-boy stupid." Mel flashed a grin. "We've been fuck buddies in the past, because he's just a pure pleasure in that department, but his mind was all about you. I got a kiss or two and a squeeze of his fine ass, but I didn't ask for more. His heart wasn't in it. He mainly needed a drinking companion."

Alanna blinked. "I . . . I have no hold on him. He is free to . . ."

"Save it, sister." Mel nudged her, picked up one of the lemonades Alanna had just poured. "You were ready to throw down just now. I wouldn't mind seeing your capabilities in that department, because you look like a lightweight to me, all that pretty hair and long lashes." She flicked the former with a casual finger. "So, you want a wrestling match? I have a bet with the girls over at the table about how long you'd last."

"I . . . No. I'm fine."

"You can't hurt me. I'm a third mark." Her gaze swept over Alanna. "Not that I think that really matters."

"I've been trained to fight."

"Training and doing are two different things. I teach women self-defense here, but I also give them an outlet. They get surly with one another, I bring them to the sparring mats, let them work it out. Makes things move a lot smoother. An out-and-out fistfight works better than a catfight any day. Want to get rid of what's griping your gut, like me putting hands on your man?"

He wasn't her man, though she liked the way it sounded so much she turned away to pour Frank's glass. "The one you're drinking is Niall's."

"His loss." Mel took several more healthy swallows. "Besides, he owes me. Despite his sighing over you, I did give him some relief. There's something to be said for being all female, but having the grip of a man, if you get my meaning."

Alanna narrowed her eyes as the woman sauntered away. Was Mel deliberately picking a fight? Mel confirmed it, glancing over her shoulder and rolling her eyes.

"You need a written invitation, girl?" she muttered. "Show him what you got."

Niall knew her combat abilities. Still . . . As Alanna waffled, Mel put down the now-empty glass and looked across the compound where the men were working on the roof. "He'll be ready for a break soon. I might just saunter over, take some of that sweat off with my tongue. He's real sensitive around his throat. Can't imagine why. You know, there's a nice, shady spot behind that building, right up against the wall . . ."

Alanna hit her midbody. Mel was standing on the edge of the shelter, such that the difference in grade was enough to make her stumble. She recovered fast, catching Alanna around the body as she turned, tumbling them both into the grass. They rolled, pulled apart, but before Mel could recover her feet, Alanna followed up with a blow to the midriff, a sharp punch that hit where that lemonade had gone. Of course, Mel was a full servant, and things like that wouldn't slow her down as much. She tackled Alanna with the advantage of sheer mass, and they rolled across the grass again.

When they regained their feet and danced apart, Alanna stripped off her overshirt, revealing the dark tank beneath. Mel got in a face punch, but Alanna swept her leg, landing on top of her again.

In some strange way, Mel was her ally, but Alanna was seeing red. *A kiss or two* . . . She visualized Niall kissing this woman the way he kissed her, Mel's hands touching him where Alanna's had. At a vampire gathering, she and Niall would touch other servants at the whim of their Master, but he'd *chosen* to touch this woman. Or to let her touch him. Pounding on Mel was a different approach from the rice, but one Alanna found she immensely preferred.

She managed a few more solid punches before she was plucked off the woman like a toddler.

"Here now, enough o' that," Niall scolded her, inserting his body between the two women when Mel sprang to her feet, blood in her gaze. "What's got into ye?"

"It's more like what got into me," Mel scoffed. Alanna lunged past Niall, her fist whizzing so close to Mel's nose the woman had to jerk her head back. The dark eyes laughed at her. Gave her a wink. "Pretty effective moves, Barbie. I'm impressed."

"You're testing her fighting skills?" Niall, keeping a firm hold on Alanna, gave her a glare.

"Yeah. And no. It's a girl thing." She nodded to Alanna. "You'll need to make some more of that lemonade. You used up the last of it." Picking up the other glass Alanna had poured for Frank, the security woman strolled off, offering a friendly smile to the table of staff members.

"What's all this about, lass?" Niall gave her a shake. "I sent ye for lemonade, and you're causing a row."

"She started it. I'll get you some more. Since she drank all of it, it will take a few minutes." Tossing him a glare, Alanna stomped toward the canteen kitchen. At the swinging door, she spun on her toe. "I'll bring it when it's ready. Mel says there's a nice shady spot behind the cottage you're roofing."

When she disappeared behind the door, she heard him speak to Frank, who'd come to investigate as well. At the sound of the two of them moving away, her shoulders eased. She shook her head at herself, then for some inexplicable reason, a smile crossed her face. Despite his irritation, Niall had looked impressed. She was a servant, not a doormat.

She'd also give Mel credit. The "bringing it to the mat" idea worked wonders. She felt much lighter than she had after she'd woken.

She found the men behind the cottage, lounging on the grass beneath leafy red maples. Colors had started changing for the fall, but the leaves weren't yet dropping, except for a few that added to the comfort of their mattress. More self-conscious now, she handed Frank the lemonade, nodding at his courteous thanks. She was aware of the muscular redhead's appraisal as she turned, but nothing that would be considered inappropriate or rude. When she went to Niall, her lowered gaze traveled over the big feet, the long denim-clad legs, the curve of groin below his belt and impressive bare terrain of muscle above it that mapped his upper body.

Yes, he was easy on the eyes, as Mel had made irritatingly clear. He had the overshirt she'd discarded, was idly rubbing the fabric between his fingers. "You have dirt on your cheek, and your hair is mussed," he noted. "As particular as ye are about a napkin on the floor, I expected you'd tidy up after a scuffle."

"You can drink this or wear it," she responded. When he grinned, the sheer sensual impact of it proved to be too much. Heedless of Frank's presence, she straddled him, sitting down on his lower abdomen. His hands landed on her calves, following her legs up to slip his thumbs beneath the hemmed cuffs of her shorts as she settled. When she put the cold glass against his chest, his skin shuddered like a horse's flank.

Collecting some of the condensation dripping from the side, she painted it along his flesh like Evan might. As she followed the flat curve of his nipple, she watched it respond, draw up at her touch. In the end, the jealousy had only been a mask for the real issue. She'd missed his scent in the bed, his heat and strength. His closeness. She was far too aware of how short a time she was likely to have that pleasure. She wished he was in her mind so he could hear the thought, but she put it in her touch, her eyes. She wanted him to see it. She wanted him, period.

"Frank," he said casually, "think you could take your lemonade elsewhere for a bit?"

"Sure." The man's amusement was obvious. "Ma'am."

As soon as he was around the corner of the house, Niall's hand closed around her wrist. His mouth was a firm, sensual curve. "You're being very forward, lass."

"You didn't come to bed last night."

"I thought I might be skewered." His smile became rueful. "I drank too much, *muirnín*. For a third mark, that's saying something. I wasnae much company for anyone. Mel left me sleeping in the field above the lake. Woke up with ants crawling in my arse."

"You could have come home." She touched his face with the other hand. "I'm here. Evan and I are here. I need you to . . ."

He took the lemonade away from her, sat it on a flat rock. "What do you need from me, Alanna?"

"For whatever time I have, I want . . . I'm not trying to demand things. But I need you . . . to treat me as yours. The only thing I've ever wanted is to belong to a vampire." Only now she understood how much more that word *belong* meant. It was a specific, targeted need. "I'm yours and Evan's. *Yours*," she emphasized, because she liked how it sounded. She curled her fingers in the sleek arrow of hair on his upper abdomen as his hand covered hers.

"I'm not a vampire."

"The two of you are the same, even if you're different. Treat me as yours. Please. Like Evan said, but . . . I want that, too."

He studied her for another few pounding heartbeats, then he lifted his hand. She sat still, though her breath caught as he slid his fingers along her throat. When she lifted her chin, he curved them around, holding her collared. Another trio of heartbeats, more rapid this time, and he constricted that grip, letting her feel the hold. The heat of it swept over her, tightening her nipples, making her bear down so her body pressed closer to his, her dampening pussy against the hard muscles of his stomach.

"Aye. Ye might belong tae both of us at that."

In one quick move, he'd turned them so she was under him, her legs finding a place along his hips and thighs, his body seated firm against the core of hers. She gasped when she realized how hard his cock was, hard and thick, throbbing against her. Rubbing herself against him earned a quiet noise of reproof.

"You'll be still. You're mine, are ye?"

"Yes," she whispered. She tried to put her hand on his face again, but he caught both wrists, pulled her arms over her head.

"Ye leave them there, *muirnín*. If you're mine, I'm going to have full pleasure of what's mine. I woke up with a huge cockstand and no snug, wet cunt to take it. Then there ye are, coming across the compound, a beautiful angel I want to profane with every lustful thought I have. Next I know, you're fighting Mel like a wee demon. Nothing stiffens a lad's cock like seeing two women fighting over it."

He gave her an arrogant grin then, one she should have answered with a proper cut down to tease him, but she honestly couldn't think beyond the fire burning inside of her. *I'm going to take full pleasure of what's mine.*

"Please," she whispered, showing that fire to him. "I need you inside me."

Evan and Niall had taught her to wear her desire on the outside like this, but hadn't warned her how it could consume the insides. Fortunately, seeing her need in her face ignited the same in Niall. He was done talking, but not done teasing her.

He pushed up the tank to find her naked beneath it, something he registered with a sound between conservative disapproval and full male approbation. She bowed up into his mouth as he covered a nipple, began to suckle, while his hands wandered down her body, opening the shorts. When his fingers quested under the waistband of her panties, finding her cunt swollen and wet, she breathed into his mouth, a wordless plea. With a quiet oath, he shifted off her enough to rid her of the garments, then he was moving down her body.

They weren't in the vampire world, where being taken in the open like this was beyond remark. When that penetrated, she made a reluctant movement, a reminder, but his grip held her fast. "If you're mine, lass, then you'll be mine whenever I desire. In the end, I'm just a rough and crude lad who wants my way with ye."

A rough and crude lad whose tongue was capable of wringing a poetic symphony from a woman's body. He immersed himself in eating her pussy, licking her clit, nipping at the labia, suckling her juices, plunging his tongue deep to swirl and taste and sample, while she writhed under his touch, bit down on the cries that kept building until she had to risk his displeasure to lower one of her arms and press her mouth against it. Instead, he pushed her arm back up, gagged her with his discarded T-shirt. He could have used the one she'd been wearing, but now she had the taste of him, his scent filling her nose. She bit down on it as he pushed her higher and higher, her legs now up on his bare shoulders, heels striking his back as she writhed. When he took one finger, lubricated from sliding into her wet folds, and slowly inserted it in her anus as he continued to tongue her cunt, pushing and withdrawing, she started screaming into the fabric.

He couldn't speak in her mind, and his mouth was otherwise occupied, but she didn't know if she could have waited for permission to come, regardless. The orgasm gushed from her, no time to beg or ask for anything.

When she was still shuddering from it, he braced himself over her body, keeping her ankles at his neck. He ripped open the jeans and slid into her to the root, her spasming tissues invaded by his engorged cock. He hadn't been jesting—he was so thick and hard, and the orgasm had made her so tight, it was almost uncomfortable, but she reveled in it, still making small cries as his sweat-coated upper body slid along hers, an erotic sensation. Keeping her arms above her head, her mouth gagged by his shirt while he looked down at her with pure, feral possession in his eyes, had her body convulsing against him even more. She added to it, squeezing down, ankles locked over his shoulders.

I'm yours. But you're mine, too. Whether or not Evan was awake to convey such a thought, she put all of it in her eyes, the strength of her body, and told him with all those things she wasn't letting him go. That she'd defy even death to keep him, no matter how empty a promise that was.

It was easy to get pulled into the daily routine of the commune. There was the sense of being cut off from the world, of there being time for healing, for laughter, for quiet reflection. For creation, for whatever the mind and soul needed to explore. It made Farida Sanctuary one of the most remarkable places she'd ever been. There were short times she even forgot the scythe hanging over her own head, of Stephen lurking somewhere in her future. Perhaps he'd given up and would simply disappear. She was supposed to hope he was apprehended for the well-being of the Council, but Evan and Niall were teaching her how to have some of her own dreams. She knew they were futile, but it didn't make them less of a stolen pleasure. In some ways, it made them even more bitterly sweet.

She helped in the kitchen, trading cooking skills with others. Working alongside the gardeners, she learned more of their craft, finding she had an intense interest in learning about plants, how they grew, how to tend them. Looking up throughout the day, she could always see a panorama of a harmonious community. Artists at work at various projects, children at play or being schooled in the pavilion. Sometimes it was their mothers being schooled, learning about the basics of home finances, or the more complicated world of legal proceedings, appropriate to their specific situations. Clay, paint, oils and chemicals mixed with the forest and lake smells, an unexpected complementary aroma that always pervaded the atmosphere.

Niall was far more than the rough and crude lad he claimed to be.

He was an accomplished carpenter and handyman, a jack-of-all-trades, such that he was in demand for any type of repair or renovation put on the back burner until this visit. Yet despite his busy schedule, her Scot still found time to check on her throughout the daylight hours.

Near mealtimes he'd come through the kitchen to sample until he was chased off, though none interfered when what he came to sample was her. Pressing her up against a counter with unmistakable erotic intent, he'd steal a mind-numbing, knee-weakening kiss before he'd take off again, leaving her with a warming slap on the ass. He'd usually snatch a cookie or piece of meat as well. She'd try, unsuccessfully, to glare at him instead of smile. His charm and raw sexuality exonerated him from reproof. The other women were almost as captivated as she was by how he left her vibrating from his sensual assaults.

He'd taken her plea to heart, with a single-mindedness that was overwhelming. No less than twice a day, he'd surprise her on her way between tasks, making her aware of how closely he was keeping an eye on her while Evan slept. He might pull her back behind that cottage, or take her into the forest off the paved path. There he'd reaffirm her surrender to him, claiming her on all fours like a woodland animal, or putting her on her back and tying her hands with whatever bonds he'd tucked in his pockets. Then he'd work his mouth over her cunt until she was completely lost and helpless, open to the fierce thrusts of his cock, his own release.

As a result, her need only grew. Sometimes he stood up and started to put his clothes on, leaving her tied and naked so he could enjoy the pleasure of seeing her at his mercy. She'd rise on her knees, brace her bound hands against his thigh and pull him into her mouth, servicing him there in the wood. Then he might put her on her elbows and order her to spread her thighs, giving her a firm spanking for her wanton behavior. His flat palm would sting against her buttocks and labia, still so damp from his juices and her own that it made a wet sound. Often, he'd take her again, with the harsh grunts of a male animal and an appeal to any gods listening to save him from her insatiable demands. Yet by the end of it she was exhausted, proving he was more than her match.

Nighttimes were the best, for then she had the opportunity to enjoy both her Masters. Evan often painted down at the lake through the darkest hours of night. She could sit and watch him for hours, her body and heart humming in frequency with his graceful movements, his intense concentration. He could surprise her with his keen awareness of her presence. One night, he bade her remove her shirt, then put a pair of cuffs on her, hooking them to eyehooks on the gazebo walls she suspected Niall had installed earlier in the day. While she sat there, spread and helpless, he painted a field of flowers across her breasts with the soft, damp tip of his brush, using his fingers to apply the proper swirls and smudging. Then he kissed her, long and deep, and made her stand like that for the next couple of hours while he finished his painting. When he freed her, she was so intensely aroused she was trembling. Lifting her up against the wall, he sank deep into her, letting her cling to his shoulders, her face pressed to his shoulder as he brought both of them to release.

At dawn, Niall would take her to Evan's bed so they could both have her as they desired, one working himself into her mouth while the other thrust into her from behind or front, depending on how they had her positioned. Or they'd both be inside her at once. Her face pressed against Niall's chest, arms clinging to his waist as he hammered into her pussy, while Evan pushed into her backside, sending her into a near-blackout state from the pleasure.

She was used, pleasured, teased . . . sated. For the first time in her life, she felt she was fully serving a Master, the way she'd always desired. On top of that, she was now part of a community with people she cautiously called friends. Niall pointed out that the sanctuary members gravitated toward her because of her intuitive ability to determine what a person needed at any given moment. In less than a few days, she was considered as useful as any staff member. She would play with a child while his mother took a nap after an intense therapy session. Or strategically sit as a buffer at the lunch table between the others and one of the newer arrivals who was feeling shy. She'd use her steady calm to integrate them in the conversation, help them feel safe, yet included.

Most of the motivations and needs, worries and priorities, were fairly simple to her, compared to the complex mechanics of anticipating vampire needs. As such, only Miah and Nerida remained an enigma to her. She'd learned Mel and Frank were third-marked servants to both female vampires, though, and when she started seeing them together, the bond was obvious.

During one late supper, while the artists and residents chatted and women rocked children to sleep, she'd seen Mel with Nerida. The vampire was sitting on the woman's lap, brushing and then braiding her thick, dark hair. When she was done with that, Nerida put her hands on Mel's face, raining affectionate kisses on her mouth and cheeks, her temple.

Another night, close to the 3 a.m. hour, Alanna was bringing Evan some wine at the gazebo when her eye was caught by people on the dock. Mel, Nerida and Miah had been swimming, a unique thing to see because vampires had no buoyancy. However, all three were still wet, their dark hair sleek and dripping. Mel was stretched out on her back, her head in Miah's lap. The woman was pointing out something in the stars while Miah played with her dark hair, tracing the thick braid across Mel's breast. Nerida lay between their servant's thighs, head pillowed on the Indian woman's stomach, her arms curled over her hip, small fingers hooked in the belt loop of her wet cutoffs, listening to whatever story she was telling. Pausing to hear better, Alanna caught the singsong quality, as if Mel was chanting a poem.

After their wrestling match, Alanna had found herself meeting up with Mel more often. The growing bond was spurred in part because of their shared status as servants, but they also sparred once a day. Sometimes Mel used her to help demonstrate techniques to other women, but on one day when it was just the two of them, Alanna took the opportunity to find out more about her unique relationship with the two female vampires.

"Nerida and Miah . . . did you learn to fight from them?"

"No. My grandfather." Taking a swig from a water bottle, Mel swiped at her sweaty forehead with her arm. They'd been working out in the open area behind the playground, and now she propped on a wooden snail. It was schooltime for the children, so they had the area to themselves. "He had one leg, but with that and a crutch, he could put me on my back in a heartbeat. Wily old goat. I taught Nerida and Miah, as did the founder of this place and his servant. They're sponges. There's nothing they won't learn if it catches their interest. Pretty much anything that needs repair around here, they can jerry rig, but of course we all have other tasks, so unless it's an emergency, it waits for its permanent fix until Niall gets here." Mel grinned. "Where is he today?"

"He slept in this morning. I told Frank he'd catch up with him later to work on the plumbing at the admin cottage." Alanna, looking toward the forest, took a sip from her own bottle. When Mel's hand covered hers, she wasn't easy enough with it yet to turn her hand and grip, but she did say what was in her head. "I don't want to leave him when he's like that. Evan has to order me to do it. I was afraid . . . but Evan told me he'd watch over him."

Mel's fingers tightened. "For all that they're only here a few weeks a year, Niall's presence is so large. I'm not sure what we'll do without him. I worry about Evan without him, too."

Alanna discovered her fingers had tangled with the woman's, were squeezing them tightly. They sat in silence for a few minutes, listening to the birds in the forest, the wind moving through the trees.

"I just figured you'd finally worn him out for a change." Nudging her with her hip, Mel pushed back the somber look Alanna knew reflected her own. "I've seen the mornings where you can barely walk, because the two of them have used you so hard."

"They are very . . . attentive," Alanna admitted.

Mel snorted. "The prissy ladylike way of saying they fuck you blind, girl. And who needs sight that badly?"

"So," Alanna said, clearing her throat. "Do you spar with them? Nerida and Miah?"

"Yeah. Like wrestling a pair of ferrets. They keep me on my toes. And regularly kick my ass, of course." She lowered her voice, despite the fact they were well away from any listening ears. Human ones, that is. "Though with vampires, that can be more win than loss, right?"

Alanna blinked, not sure how to respond. Mel shrugged, obviously uncomfortable. "Sorry. Forget it."

"No, it's all right. You don't get to talk about your relationship with them, do you?"

How vampires and non-InhServs worked out their relationships with one another had become a topic of intense interest to Alanna, as if she'd find the key to her own evolving one with Evan and Niall, no matter how pointless it seemed to analyze it. She wanted to hear more, and her obvious interest seemed to relax Mel.

The woman nodded. "Other than Frank and Niall, it's pretty much only the founder's servant, when they visit, and Elisa. She's the servant of the vampire who taught Miah and Nerida to adapt as best they could." All humor disappeared, her expression becoming dangerous, the Amazon warrior. "I sometimes wish we could resurrect that bastard who made them and kill him all over again. When he turned them, even though they were kids, they got some of the amped-up hormones that drive vampire adults. They crave sexual release for themselves and from their servants when they take blood, same as most vampires."

"Oh dear," Alanna murmured.

"Yeah. Frank tried like hell, but he's never been comfortable with it, so they mostly use him just for blood. That's not really the worst of it, though. They may have the bodies of children, but they have the hearts of women. They want relationships . . . love, and they won't ever have that. Not for however many hundreds of years they live." Mel took another swallow from the water bottle. "Not only do they have to stay hidden from the vampire world, no vampire *or* servant can get past the fact they look like kids. The ones who can aren't anything they want near them."

"You love them, though."

"I can't imagine life without them," Mel said seriously, meeting her gaze. "And I love them as women. But even me . . . there are things they know I have a hard time with, no matter how I try. I guess there's something in our chemical makeup, when we're decent human beings, not fucked-up twisted pervs, that won't let us get past it. I mean Nerida . . . she fucking smells like a little girl. I play with the kids here, and then I'm holding her and . . ." She shook her head, sighed.

"I learned more about their early years from the founder's servant. She told me it got really bad once or twice, such that they were considering a suicide pact. The founder made them a promise. He said if it ever became too much, whether today, tomorrow or decades from now, he would help them with that, make it merciful." Mel's face tightened, showing her pain about that, but her acceptance as well. "When they decided to take me and Frank as third marks, they'd made a semi-permanent peace with it. At least for the next three hundred years, according to Nerida," she added wryly.

"They have this place, and most importantly, they have each other. And that was the solution, wasn't it? What none of us can comfortably give, they give each other. It's a weird thing to talk about. I should really stop."

"No, I'm curious," Alanna assured her. "I've seen you with them, and it's an unusual . . . dynamic."

"Yeah. No kidding." Mel smiled fondly. "Nerida is the odd one. She can have sexual impulses, but it's like the six-year-old's in there, too, because nine times out of ten, those impulses have to do with affection. Closeness. She's like an Olympic postcoital cuddler, without the actual coital part."

Alanna's return smile seemed to relieve the woman's tension, her worry that the conversation was too much. Thinking how young she'd been when educated about her sexual requirements, Alanna realized she was probably more prepared for this conversation than most.

"The two of them are the only two vampires I know who like to swim. They hang onto a float and paddle around like beavers." Mel chuckled. "Or they have me or Frank cart them around, hanging onto our necks. They felt your presence the other night, and appreciated your respect of our privacy." Mel gave her a knowing look. "But what you saw, that's the way it is. It's probably the most difficult thing they have to cope with. Getting killed or preyed upon by a much stronger vampire, yeah, that's rough, but finding someone to love, to whom we can give our soul, that's the end of the rainbow for all of us, even vampires."

Mel tilted her head up, closed her eyes so the sun could touch her face. Alanna saw her sadness, suffering for the two vampires she loved. "Nerida says it's enough to have each other, because it has to be. She's pragmatist and spiritualist both, and I think that helps Miah when she gets too bogged down in her emotions over it, over what will never be. Guess we all have to live with things like that, don't we?"

"Yes." Alanna felt the bite of that truth. *Finding someone to love, to whom we can give our soul, that's the end of the rainbow.* "The more I discover about vampires, the more I realize how little I really knew about them, if that makes sense."

"Truer words, Barbie." Mel tugged her hair, which she'd braided for their sparring. "Hey, I'll arm wrestle you. If I win, you take dish duty tonight. And don't be a subby and volunteer to do them for me. I want to win the right to dump my least favorite chore on you, fair and square."

"You'll only cheat," Alanna said archly. "Using your third-mark strength against me. Let me do them. You're on the midnight shift, and your vampires will want to spend time with you. Evan will likely be painting and not need me right away. Plus Niall will be up by that time"—she hoped—"and can handle any immediate needs he has. Though he'll likely demand something in trade."

"You hope. Careful, girl. Keep it up and that funny walk will become permanent." Mel cleared her throat. "Not sure I intended that entendre, but . . ."

Alanna rolled her eyes, bumped shoulders with her again. "I'll do the dishes."

Mel gave her a fond look, a stroke to her hair. Then she surprised Alanna by giving her a swift, fierce hug. "I'm glad Niall fell in love again, before the end."

The woman strode away without looking back, probably knowing the tears her words would evoke. Yesterday, Alanna had played tag with the children. When a little girl tackled her, Alanna wrapped her arms around her and took them both to the ground, holding her gently as the child giggled. The child was picking grass out of her long hair, and she was doing the same to her silken curls. Looking up, she'd seen Niall staring at her the way Evan did a subject for his painting. As if he was seeing something remarkable, something that kept him in that one spot, enjoying it as long as it wanted to be before him.

Forgive me, Master . . . but I really want to come and see him.

That's fine, Alanna. I haven't been able to sleep anyway. It would help, if you came and stayed with him.

It was rare that she picked up emotion in Evan's mind-voice so clearly. It made her hurry to their bungalow. Once inside, she headed for the cellar. All three of them had been sleeping below these past few nights, the intensity of their couplings such that Evan had kept them both there in the aftermath, until daylight and his servants' responsibilities above called them away.

It was dark downstairs, though Evan had a lantern on a low setting as a night-light. The vampire was propped on an elbow, stroking Niall's hair off his forehead as he slept, just as heavily as when she'd left hours before. She could tell Evan was fighting sleep hard himself, for the sun was well past when his body would force him to unconsciousness. She chastised herself for spending so much time with Mel and not anticipating this need. Evan shook his head, hearing it. As she shed her shorts and overshirt, she crawled over the mattress in her panties and thin tank to the both of them.

She'd decided this cottage was used for the founder when he came, because it had more of a finished basement than a cellar, with painted walls, a king-sized bed, electric hookups and a full bath with a shower comfortable for a man—and his servant—to use. There was even a sitting area with a spacious desk where Evan could consider slides or handle paperwork Alanna brought to him.

Now she curled up on the other side of Niall. Panic seized her. He was cool, not emanating heat as he usually did. Her gaze snapped up to Evan, but he was already in her mind, reassuring her.

He's fine. I've heard other vampires call it death practice, *the deep sleeps, the coolness of the body. His system is preparing . . .*

No. *No.* She'd just found him, just found them both. But with Evan within touching distance, she couldn't put her own feelings first, no matter how strong they were. Niall had been his for so much longer.

It took me only an instant to know he was mine. Perhaps it's the same for all of us, Alanna. Time may deepen it, enrich it, teach us so many lessons, but that first moment, that spark—that's what sets the fire burning forever.

She laid her hand over his, resting on Niall's chest. The vampire nodded, acknowledging the touch, but didn't take his eyes off his sleeping servant.

"Is he dreaming?"

"Yes. A dog . . . a collie. It belonged to him as a boy. You . . ." A faint smile touched his mouth. "He's holding you in his sleep."

She was lying on Niall's outstretched arm, and now she reached behind her, drawing his hand to her hip. The arm muscles constricted, bringing her closer. Without prompting, she laid her head down on Niall's broad shoulder. "You can sleep, Master," she whispered. "I'll listen to his heartbeat."

The anguish that crossed Evan's face was so strong and immediate she didn't have to think. Reaching out, she cupped his jaw, caressed him. When he lifted those tormented gray eyes to her, she let her fingers slide to his nape, tangling in the silken strands there. With gentle pressure, she helped him do what he wanted to do. She adjusted so Evan laid his head directly on Niall's chest, over his heart. The moment he rested it there, she could see the involuntary sleep that would pull him under starting to do so, but she eased his frustration with it, stroking his hair away from his brow, saying soft, unintelligible things. She held both of them, hoping to give them the strength they needed. Niall, to live as long as possible, and Evan, to let him go when the time came.

As for her, she'd found her strength. It was in the love she wasn't afraid of acknowledging anymore, for them both. She would take care of them however she could, as long as she could.

When Niall's other arm came up, sliding over Evan's back, hand coming to rest on his side so he was holding her Master as well as her, she pressed her face harder against his firm flesh and let her silent tears give heat to its coolness.

22

They'd had lasagna and salad for dinner tonight, but the dishes were manageable. She wouldn't be able to tease Mel about leaving her too much responsibility. Not that she would anyway. As she washed, Alanna watched the sanctuary members playing volleyball by the lake, a family canoeing out against the night sky, a full moon shining on the water. Mel, Frank, Miah and Nerida were by the communal bonfire. The purpose of the nightly ritual was to share stories, everyone encouraged to contribute a positive anecdote, whether it was the birth of a baby, a school accomplishment, the witnessing of a lovely sunset. Or the moment a woman decided to take control of her life and stop allowing another to harm her or her children. Though she couldn't hear the stories over the splash of the water and clank of the dishes, she enjoyed seeing the looks on the participants' faces, their reactions.

When arms slipped around her waist, she smiled, pleased by Niall's mouth on her throat. He'd gotten up around late afternoon. True to her word, she hadn't slept, but she pretended she'd been napping, invited to come back by Evan because her sparring match with Mel had tired her out. She wasn't sure he'd believed her, but he'd gotten dressed, said he was overdue to help Frank with that plumbing job. He'd left her with a warm kiss that made her try to pull him back into the bed.

He evaded her with a chuckle, then bent to Evan, brushing his lips over the oblivious male, still deep in sleep. "You worry too much, vampire," he murmured. Then he'd straightened, given Alanna a fond look and left her.

Now he was back, freshly showered, suggesting the plumbing job had been messy. "Do you need help drying, *muirnín*? The sooner you're done, the sooner I can take you out and have my way with ye under the stars. Finish what you tried tae start, you shameless hussy."

She poked him with her elbow. "Yes, you can help. If you can keep from breaking the dishes with those big hands of yours."

He pinched her, but picked up a towel. For a few minutes, they worked in companionable silence, and then he laid his hand on hers, stopping her. Alanna glanced up at him, saw he seemed to be contemplating something, his mouth serious. Then he glanced at her. "I need tae tell you some things, lass. I know you think that your time is limited, but nothing is sure in this life. And I know you want to stay with Evan. If the stars align and that happens . . . ye need to know things about him. Like his annual kill." He gave her a poignant, wry smile, even as his eyes stayed serious, sad. "His annual kill's always a Jew who strictly follows kashrut. Sounds twisted, but 'tis as close to kosher as he can get. He has an odd way of honoring his past, his faith, even as he's had to move away from it, ye ken?"

"No." She pulled her hand away from his. "I won't talk about this. You're not going to—"

"Aye, I am," he said, catching her chin. "And we both know it's going to be sooner than later. You want to serve him, right?"

He had her on that one. She put her hand over his, clung to it tightly. Nodded.

"All right, then. We dinnae have to talk about it this moment, but I am going tae start telling you things. Though I expect you'll already know most of it, sharp as ye are. But no more sadness in your eyes."

He flicked suds at her, splattering the front of her T-shirt, startling a gasp out of her. Retaliating set off a splash war. The damn man refused to stop until she was giggling and splashing him more boisterously.

He snatched up the sprayer and aimed it at her, but before she could squeal and fend him off, he stopped abruptly, as did she, Evan's voice commanding their attention.

Come to me. Quickly. Come from the northwest.

His urgency wasn't tension, but excitement. Even so, they left the kitchen without hesitation, headed out across the grass. Niall seized her hand so they could run together across the compound. They were moving away from the lake, toward the forest where it headed deeper into the surrounding hills.

When you pass the perimeter marker, come as silently as you can. Stop at the crest of the hill, where the trees open up, so you can see it.

They exchanged a glance, but kept moving together swiftly. As they drew closer, Niall slowed them down, cutting down on their noise. When they at last topped the hill, Alanna drew in a breath. The rising moon appeared huge and yellow, dominating the sky. But what made it even more remarkable was what Evan had intended them to see. On the hill directly across from them was a family of bears. The mother bear was sitting in that peculiar humanlike way, her legs out before her. One cub leaned against her, the other exploring the grass, occasionally standing on his hind legs like a human toddler. Less than ten yards away was a doe and her fawn, the mother browsing the grass as the baby took tentative steps toward the cub, and he toward the baby.

They'd arrived downwind, explaining why Evan had told them to come from that direction. Putting his fingers to his lips, Niall lifted Alanna, then moved like the silent hunter he was, like the wind itself, until he'd reached Evan. The vampire was sitting so still amid a spray of bushes, she almost missed him. They sank down next to him, Alanna in between. Evan was studying the scene with that intensity that suggested he wasn't even aware of their approach, except that he'd called to them.

In fact, he opened his mind, showed her how he'd paint it, adding the haze of a fog, increasing the sense of suspended time, an unlikely moment where the mother deer would normally take her baby out of range of the adult bear, or the adult bear would chase the doe off as a potential threat to her cubs. Perhaps Farida Sanctuary spun magic even over the wildlife.

Unbidden, she thought again of Stephen coming here. It made her cold, a shiver running over her skin. Though she never wanted to leave, if Stephen could get to her, she'd prefer it to be far away from this place, so no harm could come to the people. To that magic.

She put her hand on top of Niall's, the other aligned with Evan's leg, just barely brushing his trouser leg, because she didn't want to disrupt the artist's flow of thought, but that connection was enough to steady her. She was done running. She would stand with them. She breathed in the moment, breathed deep.

Her heart stuttered, seized . . . and she screamed.

~

The deer bolted, her fawn right on her heels. The bear made a surprised growl, then she, too, disappeared into the darkness with her progeny. Evan and Niall never noticed, having caught her together, but Alanna saw it. She was arched up from the ground, agony jerking her head back at an unnatural angle.

Gasping, she clawed at their hands. She struggled to focus on their faces, wanting to hold on to them as long as she could. *I'm sorry, so sorry, Master.*

She hoped Evan knew she meant him. If Stephen was dying, she would go within moments of him. But maybe the blocker would give her a precious extra minute, and she could say something.

"Alanna, no. Hold on, lass." She tried to reach up to Niall. He caught her fingers, and Evan overlapped them. The vampire had his hand on them both, and she could see it, how hard he wanted to hold on to them, to defy the terrible mortality vampires had to face. Not for themselves, but for their servants.

Alanna, you will not leave us. He knew it was a futile order. She couldn't fight the biology of Stephen's bond. But the saying of it meant everything, the expression in his face, the tension of his body that proved he would fight with everything he had to keep her here. Niall was a hard rope of muscle as well, wanting an enemy to fight, but he could only hold her hands. She saw the flash of it in his mind then, him holding his wife's hands, telling her not to go, telling her he loved her.

He had, though it hadn't been the type of love he'd discovered later. That nebulous feeling of something more out there would have been plowed down in his subconscious as he plowed his fields, except Evan had brought it to glorious life. She knew how he felt. Exactly how he felt, because their minds, for this painfully blissful instant, were held together inside Evan's.

It's all right to love him, Niall. There's no shame . . . to loving. To wanting. No matter how little time there is left. Thank you . . . for letting me . . . love the both of you.

The Scot's gaze became dark, anguished. "Damn it . . ." He snarled something at Evan, and Evan's hand merely tightened on him, his gray eyes fastened on her face. He was watching for something, measuring . . . Something that suddenly gave her hope. He said something to Niall she was spinning too high in her mind to catch, but Niall lifted her. The two males were moving swiftly through the grasses, back toward the compound, so fast everything was a blur. Or perhaps that was her physical state, everything hazed by disorienting pain.

The agony was incredible, frightening, as she'd expected. How bad would it get before she actually died? At a certain point the soul finally leaped into the dreaded chasm of death because the pain afflicting the body drove it to leap. But her Master had forbidden her to go.

Her heart had to be exploding. She couldn't breathe. Perhaps she'd passed out for a while, because when she became aware again, she was in the bedroom in the cottage. Evan and Niall were . . . they were outside, talking to someone. She felt disoriented, and had the strange sensation that she'd become disconnected from her body for a while, everything in a bright light, a peculiar drifting. Coming back to her body was like a wall meeting an oncoming car. The pain was back, in full force, radiating out from her stuttering heart.

Shadows were collecting around her vision. She sensed him there, the presence she dreaded more than any other. She tried to open her mouth, call out, but then there was one very large shadow, falling down over her now like a cloak. Pain exploded in her head, struck through that covering. She was plunged into darkness, the terror following her like maniacal laughter.

~

It *had* been a cloak, not death. Opening her eyes, she looked at the close stone walls of a narrow cave. She could breathe a little better, but her chest still hurt badly. It was an effort, but she turned her head to see Stephen sitting against the wall, staring at her as if he could hate nothing in the world the way he hated her. And being hated by a vampire was a terrifying thing.

Being on the run had marred even his vampire beauty. The smooth black hair was shorn close to his head, his green eyes burning with anger in a gaunt face. His unkempt state reminded her of the Trad.

"Your chest hurts because I drove a stake into my own heart and then ripped it out," he said in a monotone, those flat eyes staying on her. "You died, InhServ. As did I. Just for a moment, just long enough to make them leave your side. A calculated risk, but I have nothing to lose anymore, do I? Thanks to you."

"You . . . betrayed them," she managed.

He surged from the wall, moving so fast she couldn't follow him, But she felt the single, precise kick that broke ribs, punctured a lung. As she sputtered, blood frothing her lips, he loomed over her. "Your loyalty was to me," he snarled.

It was a squeezing, drowning sensation, but he could do much worse. Despite the madness and desperation driving him now, she saw the calculation in his burning gaze, lingering evidence of the intelligence that had driven his ascent in the vampire ranks.

"You deserve far worse, but you'll have to wait on that in the afterlife. I intend for you to have centuries to dread my arrival. But before I kill you, InhServ, you'll feed me one more time."

He spat *InhServ* like a curse, yanked her upper body off the floor and stabbed his fangs into her neck, as excruciating as a knife blade. The stress to her system had overridden the blocker, which meant Stephen could scramble Evan's radar, his ability to find her. A lot would rest on how good a tracker Daegan was. Not just Daegan. Niall.

He was a better hunter, warrior and scout than a crofter . . . But if Niall and Evan found her first . . . oh God. She knew just how powerful Stephen was.

If I had time, I'd fuck your traitorous cunt, bludgeon you to take away your beauty.

He wasn't listening to her mind. He never had, had he?

"You . . . betrayed . . . me," she rasped.

Stephen pulled back. The shock of hearing words an InhServ would never speak had snagged his attention. By doing what she'd always done—tell the truth to her Master—she'd make sure he killed her fast, before Evan or Niall were in danger. Licking her lips, she met his gaze. Deliberately. And since she could barely breathe, she spoke in his mind.

A servant serves for one reason. Because we love our Master or Mistress. I wanted to love you, and I couldn't. I based my devotion on my love of service, not of you. That was my greatest mistake.

"I'm not your whore," she coughed. "Or your maid service. I'm your servant." *A soul-deep oath, a commitment to the vampire, to be loyal and protect his soul with all that I am.* Pushing herself up on weak elbows, she put her face right up into his, showing no fear. He wouldn't get that from her.

"My brother died," she whispered. "And you let twelve servants fuck me until I bled. To prove my loyalty to you. I owe you nothing."

Blood was trickling out of the corner of his mouth and she used a trembling hand to collect it, placing it on his tongue as he stared at her. His fang pressed against her knuckle and she increased that pressure, letting it cut her. "I may wake in the afterlife chained to you forever," she rasped, "but you will be chained to me as well. Do what you feel you must, my lord."

"If you value your fucking head, you'll step away from her."

Stephen let go of her, leaping to his feet. The jolt made her groan, cough up more blood, but through the wracking pain she was able to see Evan arrive in the cave entrance, Niall at his shoulder.

Let him have me. Don't . . . I can't bear for either of you to be hurt. Please. Don't let me take that to my grave.

"Daegan too far away?" Stephen passed a contemptuous gaze over Evan. "The weakling of the litter. This InhServ belongs to me, her fate mine to decide. You interfere with that, I'll kill you with her. I'll kill you anyway, for daring to mark what was mine."

"She was never yours," Evan answered, the gray eyes fired steel. "You never deserved her."

Niall drew a wooden stake from his belt, flipped it in his hand. "How fast are ye, *Lord Stephen*?"

Stephen bared his fangs in a hiss. "Faster than you can throw."

Niall threw in the middle of the sentence, and Stephen was gone. But he didn't reach Niall. Evan met him in between, the two of them crashing into the stone side of the cave so hard dust billowed from the ceiling. Heart in her throat, Alanna saw Stephen had the immediate advantage, his hand locked on Evan's throat, fist striking him midbody, hard enough she could almost see the organs rupturing beneath the skin. Then Evan was airborne, only not alone, for her Master had seized Stephen's body. Both males spun out of balance, hitting the ground with a sound of cracking rock.

Another stake sliced through the air, as precise as a thrown knife. It caught Stephen in the lower back. He howled, pivoting. As he did, Evan shoved him back to the ground, driving it in farther.

Pain exploded in the same location, but Alanna bit through her lip, containing the cry. Niall leaped on Stephen as Evan grappled him from behind, holding on with an expression of grim, fierce determination. Stephen flailed, knocking Niall back, but the Scot returned in a blink, plunging his hunting knife hilt deep into Stephen's chest.

Stephen screamed, and Alanna did as well, the pain far too much to bear. She writhed, fireworks exploding in her vision. The darkness of the cave became silver green, and she was dying, she had to be dying, because no one could hurt this much and live. She couldn't even move, because there was no way to escape the pain.

Help . . . help . . .

Alanna, I'm here. I'm here. Evan's voice, her Master, in her mind, and then Niall, too, the two of them holding on to her. There was the smell of blood and metal, a howling rage in her head breaking through, drowning them out

There was no practical purpose to his invasion now. Stephen was caught. This was pure, malicious vengeance. He cracked open her subconscious, the nightmares flooding in. The agony twisted her, choked her, yet she was screaming.

A hard thudding, and she had a moment's respite. Someone was hitting Stephen, trying to knock him insensible, probably Niall, or maybe Evan, she couldn't tell. All she knew was her soul was clutched in his hand, a vise grip intended to destroy her.

Fire sizzled from her throat, down into that place deep inside the body that ached from emotional pains too great to bear. Blood on her lips, fingers working on her throat, making her swallow. Adam, a skeleton with skin dripping off him like water, reached out to her, wanting to pull her into a swamp of nothingness, of despair. So real, she could smell the mud, bony fingers around her wrist.

Alanna, don't listen. Don't look. Don't let him win.

Such a faint noise. Someone speaking . . . it was like being in a pitch-black room, a haunted afterlife, everyone moving, no one aware of one another, yet each person able to see all the insensible ones. She could hear that voice, would move toward it if she could find it.

I'm here. In your heart, in your soul. It's a choice, Alanna. Choose.

No, it wasn't a choice. It was about power and strength . . .

You're stronger than any of us. Forest for the trees . . . trees for the forest . . .

No. Stephen was her Master. She had to be true to her training.

Be true to your heart. I am your Master, Alanna. Niall and I both. You serve us, and us alone. Not Stephen. You love us. You will obey us, no matter the pain, no matter your fear. I forbid you to fail us. Be the extraordinary servant I know you are.

She struggled like a child pulling against an adult hand as Stephen dragged her toward that abyss. She couldn't find Evan or Niall. There was nothing in the chasm but utter madness. She wasn't strong enough. She couldn't override her Master . . .

He was never your Master, Alanna. Your heart has tae be earned, remember? Ye gave us your heart and soul. Now get your arse back to us, where ye belong. Dinnae make me come after you.

Need . . . you . . . to do that. Help. Trying . . .

Try harder.

Arteries exploded, her heart galloping. She'd give anything for one touch from each of their hands. When she went to that abyss, they'd be lost to her forever.

Choice . . . she thought she'd given up choice, but Evan had proven that a lie. In a world where they gave up all other choices, servants retained a single significant decision.

Who they served.

She wanted to make that choice, but it was too late. *I'm so sorry.* She threw herself against that steel wall, again and again, bloodying herself, breaking bones. She'd lost, but they'd know she'd tried to obey. The walls closed in on all sides, a permanent, fearful coffin.

Evan . . . Niall . . . Masters . . . She went down screaming, fighting. Then her grip slipped, and the fall happened, plunging her into permanent oblivion.

~

It was utterly horrifying, what the spirit could bear. Hellfire, terror, pain, darkness, suffocation. As she spun through that endless morass of familiar nightmares, she discovered a known nightmare was far worse than a new one. Faced with the unfamiliar, hope could exist for a blink. She had died. This was the Hell Stephen had designed for her to share in their eternal afterlife, for she could feel his howling presence throughout all of it.

She was used to letting go, submitting, so she didn't fight any longer. There was nothing left to fight for. She existed in that macabre world, in jerky motion under strobe lights. Screams and tears. A soul, cut apart from everything else and plunged into this, had no sense of death or life, Heaven or Hell.

"It may save her . . . she knows how to be empty . . ."

A voice she knew, here then gone. She marched with an army of stumbling, headless children, whose arms fell off and geysered black blood if she touched one of them. They became charred toys.

In a world of horrors, she saw everyone she knew. Adam was the worst, his corpse, his twisted spirit, his screams in the night as she lay wrapped in sharp barbs, unable to help him. But there was someone missing from the never-ending morbid show. She didn't want to long for them, because the worst nightmare of all would be to have them here. But she couldn't help it. She was a child in need of the only source of comfort she trusted. As the river of blood eddied and spun, taking her on and on, she needed them there, no matter in what terrible form they'd come. She struggled for anything about them. A scent . . . a touch . . . any memory at all. She needed one single scrap of memory. She couldn't remember their names. Stephen had taken that from her.

After what seemed like centuries in the place of the eternally damned, she received the miracle of a single moment. Large hands on her face, a Scottish brogue soothing her, another long-fingered hand touching her arm, both holding her . . .

It was a memory, the past, yes, but she clung to it, made it hers, defended it with a futile savagery. She spun a cocoon around it and herself, letting the nightmares do everything else they wished, as long as they didn't try to touch that cocoon. She could put faces with those hands. Brown eyes, gray eyes. Wanting something from her, demanding something from her.

Her world of fire, of death and decay, despair and pain, started to turn gray. Fiery color leached away, taking all substance and form with it. Before she was aware anything had changed, she was drifting in a storm, where there were lightning flashes and thunder, but she was in the colorless current, oscillating in the eddies. The nightmares boiled onward in the sky above, indifferent. Then everything became gray and still.

She lay there, blinking at the uniform solidity of it. She hadn't been aware of herself as a body for some time, so it felt like working a puppet when she lifted her own hand. She pushed at the gray. It swirled around her hand, odorless smoke, its coolness clinging to her fingers. Her arm was bloody and thin. Bloody thin, someone might say. It gave her heart a twist, the memory of that voice.

Not just thin. Bone. She was a skeleton herself, her soul a monarch butterfly fluttering against her rib cage. Veins traced their way over the bone and then muscle surrounded them, like clay settling around straw, forming something solid, enduring.

It was odd to watch oneself be created. Skin adhered to the muscle. In the hollowness of her torso, a mass of organs started to fill her. Heart, lungs, all those things a doctor knew about. Brian would know what they all were, she was sure, and then she wondered who Brian was.

Her toenails and fingernails, her hair, came last. It was brittle, but it would perhaps get stronger. Because Evan liked her hair so much. Niall was fond of wrapping his hands in it . . .

She cried out at the painful joy of it. The return of their names was the greatest gift she could imagine Heaven bestowing upon a wretched, lost soul. Evan, Niall. *Evan Niall Evan Niall . . .*

"We're here, *muirnín*."

Evan Niall Evan Niall Evan Niall . . .

"It will take her a while to be coherent. Perhaps never. There was significant trauma to her brain."

"Bollocks. You said she'd die. She'd never wake up. She'd never speak. She's doing all that."

"I said it wasn't likely. The odds have been against her throughout. She continues to defy them."

"Of course she does." A hand closed over hers, those artist's fingers stroking her. "She's a constant discipline problem."

"Always mouthing off, telling everyone tae truth about themselves. 'Tis damn irritating."

She twitched, frowning, and those hands tightened on her. She wanted to say something, but she couldn't. Something was missing. The emptiness . . . truly empty. There was no connection, no mind inside hers. Nothingness. It alarmed her, scared her in a way even the nightmares hadn't.

"Gone. Marks . . . gone." She was straining for something, but then she felt lips brush her face, her hands, and things eased.

"*Wheest*. It's fine. We'll fix it. But now ye have to rest, grow strong again."

"You are the most perfect servant," Evan said. His breath touched her still-numb face, but yet she felt it. "You'll get better now, return to us. Niall has been a rabid bear. He stormed into Council chambers, demanding that Lady Lyssa—'High Heid Yin of the whole bloody Council'—get off her 'arse' and help you. I've promised to have him severely flogged, but with you occupying my nights, I can't get any work done. Marcus has sent me dire messages about the death of my career. I'll have no money to feed Niall."

The words were flowing water, gurgling beneath the surface, then coming clear again. She was a leaf spinning in the eddies, trying desperately to follow the current, to hold on to their voices.

"An artist who cannae do his art is like living with a fully stocked pincushion up your arse all day." Niall was speaking now, his fingers tightening on her, helping her focus. Tears were running over her gaunt cheeks. Tears of joy. "I'd stake him, swear to God, except I'd follow him, aye? So I'm fucked unless ye come back."

The gray was closing in again, but the touch of their hands wasn't going away. She drew in a sigh, so very tired, but it was all right. She could sleep now. Somehow, they'd rescued her from Hell. How or why wasn't important. They were her Masters, and she expected nothing less than miracles from them.

~

As she sank back into oblivion, but for the first time in weeks with a look of peace on her face, Niall's and Evan's gazes met over her body. When his usually stoic Scot reached across and gripped Evan's wrist, hard, Evan put his other hand over Niall's. They were both shaking.

"Fucking hell. She made it through. The lass did it."

Evan wanted to agree, but he couldn't trust it yet. Over the past several weeks, he'd endured every dismal daily report on her condition. Brian had frowned, scrubbed his hair to spikes in frustration, retooled his treatment formula. The next day, he'd prepare the same report. No obvious progress on removing the marks.

She'd just said they were gone, but they had no idea how clear she was in her own head. It would need to be verified. Stephen might have figured out a way to make her believe they were gone so they'd kill him and he'd get the last victory. He'd figured out the only reason he was being kept alive was to preserve a servant's life, an ignominy that was small vengeance compared to the agony he'd inflicted on her.

In sync, both men's attention went to Lord Brian. Daegan stood behind him. The Council's assassin had his arms crossed and was leaning against one of the lab's stainless steel counters. Out of the way, but awaiting the verdict. Earlier in the evening, when she'd first started saying Evan and Niall's names with such determined purpose, Daegan had reappeared. Gideon sat on one of the rolling chairs at the other end of the lab, pushing it back and forth over the same yard of ground.

Brian ignored the wall of male impatience, checking the readings from her blood draw. He handed them over to Debra for a second verification. Her brow furrowed as she read the screen. Evan always watched her more closely than her Master, because it was impossible to read anything from Brian's face. The scientist took a blood smear to a microscope, adjusted the lens, then scribbled into one of his many notebooks. He used a form of shorthand that only he and Debra knew. Evan and Niall had both shamelessly tried to translate it when he wasn't around.

Clearing throats wouldn't increase the scientist's pace, nor death threats. During these twenty-two days, they'd tried all of those things, and everything in between. So Niall settled back onto his stool at Alanna's head. As he lowered his hand to stroke her hair, there was a hesitation, a brief glance at Evan before he made contact. When she didn't react with convulsions or terror, a sigh eased the great shoulders. Only in the last few hours had they been able to touch her without making things worse.

They'd both gone mad from her screaming, the pitiful whimpers and cries, the thrashing of her body to get away from an enemy they couldn't see or fight for her. To make it worse, Brian hadn't been able to use anything to sedate her. It would interfere with the experimental treatment. He'd had to put her in a soundproof room, monitoring her through machines and a window. Otherwise, she would have driven everyone but Evan and Niall out of the Savannah estate that was temporary Council headquarters. Of course Lyssa would have ordered her to be put down before that, and then Evan and Niall wouldn't be here, because they would have had to be dead to allow that.

Well, at first. Within three days of witnessing her in such obvious agony, it was like having a preview of Hell, piped straight into the speaker system. He and Niall took turns standing outside that window, one of them always watching over her. More than once, fingers digging into the sill of the viewing window, Niall had fought the overwhelming compulsion to break into that room, to end her suffering. Evan hadn't blamed him, for he'd fought the same feeling. Even Lady Lyssa, who'd come down to view Alanna's condition, had compassion in her jade green eyes. The tightening of her mouth reflected Evan's own uncertainty about this course of action, yet she'd told Brian to do whatever he could for her, to spare no expense, a high honor for the Council to bestow upon a human servant.

Evan would never forget that hasty drive to Savannah in the RV. Niall had driven the heavy vehicle like a bat out of hell, with her making those horrible hoarse, continuous screams every time Stephen regained consciousness. Daegan had used restraints that a vampire couldn't break, put him in one of the storage lockers. Each time the captured vampire roused, Gideon would open the lid and use a pipe to knock him out again, but it was only a temporary effect. Unfortunately, once they arrived at Council headquarters and the treatment began, Stephen couldn't be sedated for the same reasons Alanna couldn't, and the vampire seemed determined to exercise the one power he had left, to punish her for his fallen state.

The treatment put on the back burner by Council, that Brian had been tweaking in his spare time, was the only possibility to break the mark between a servant and Master who'd been bonded beyond five years. From the first, Brian made it clear that it was untested, volatile.

"It has a slim chance of working, and even then depends a great deal on her own strength." He'd made the case to Lady Lyssa in his lab. Evan had turned away from the window to Alanna's soundproof room to hear his report, though Niall kept his attention on the girl. Instinctively, the men had fallen into a pattern. Evan focused on the things that would require a vampire's approval, whereas Niall kept his attention on her. On whatever front necessary, her needs would be met.

"It's administered over a twenty-one-day period," Brian continued. "Two treatments a day, and it's essentially a poison."

Lady Lyssa nodded. "Will there be any effect upon Evan, since he's marked her?"

"If it works, he'll feel the break when it happens, because it will obliterate any marking in her blood. However, it should be no worse than the physical sense of severing that occurs when a servant dies."

An experience he hadn't had. *Yet.* He was keenly aware of Niall, the man's heat and presence within a yard of him.

Lyssa looked toward him then. Though she was a slim woman and barely over five feet tall, her presence filled a room, riveting all attention upon her. Except for one. Her gaze shifted to Niall. On a normal day, Evan would have sent Niall a sharp command to show respect and attention to the vampires in the room, but she gave him a slight shake of her head before he could do it. His servant had put his hands on the window, as if he could somehow draw the evil plaguing Alanna to himself. Evan gripped his shoulder, then gave Lyssa full attention for both of them.

"You are her Master, Evan. This decision is yours."

It was an unexpected privilege, since his guardianship was temporary. But all that mattered was Alanna. If it worked, her mind would be out of his reach, but it would also be out of reach of Stephen's.

He couldn't make an obvious overture to his servant, especially not in this company, but he would do it. *Niall?*

The man bowed his head, pressing his fingers harder against the glass. *If there's any chance she can be free of this bastard, we need to do it.*

Evan met Lyssa's gaze. "I've never met a servant as strong as Alanna. Given the strength of my own servant, that's saying something. Let's give her the chance to fight."

If the treatment had not involved Stephen, they could have transported him outside of the range of her mind, taken him to the North Pole. But Brian needed daily samples, comparisons, brain activity readings on them both.

Though Evan knew Stephen had to remain untouched for the treatment to have any chance of success, watching her continued torment made Evan appreciate Daegan's and Gideon's wisdom. Throughout the three weeks, neither male told him where on the estate the vampire traitor was being held.

~

When day twenty-one had passed with no obvious change, Evan felt like his soul had been torn in two. Even Lord Brian and Debra, who'd given so much to this effort, looked affected by it. On day twenty-two, he would have to confront other options. No. The *only* other option. Near midnight, he left Niall watching over her, and went to find Daegan. The assassin was in the garden, doing graceful, lethal exercises with his katana while Gideon straddled a bench, cleaning and sharpening an array of knives. Given his reason for seeking Daegan out, the sight brought Evan up short.

The vampire's awareness was as finely tuned as that of any predator Evan had witnessed. So he wasn't surprised when Daegan's attention turned to him the moment he stepped on the path toward them.

They didn't offer small talk, empty chatter. Things were well past that. Since Evan had second marks on Alanna, he could hear what was happening in her mind, pulling him into the hell with her whenever he lowered the shield between them. At first, he'd felt he was abandoning her by keeping that wall up. Finding his way through the maze of her nightmares had been futile, though. It had made it far worse for her as well, Stephen punishing her for Evan's competing presence, the fucking hell spawn. When Evan had tried harder to break through, it had affected Niall as well. Evan had passed out in front of Alanna's window one night, suffering a gushing nosebleed. Debra went to get Niall and found him almost impossible to rouse, in a sleep so deep, his body so cold, she'd struggled to find his pulse.

Lyssa has forbidden you to lower the shield between your minds again. Lord Uthe had delivered the stern admonition to him in his room, while he was cleaning up. His gentle fingers on Evan's face, the rough threading through his hair, had belied the reproof. *I know you will not heed her words if you think it will help the girl, but think of Niall's well-being. Your own sanity.*

His sire was right. He hated it, though. There'd been no way to help her. Not until now.

"If this goes on much longer . . ." He cleared his throat, met Daegan's gaze. "If we can't sever their link, I'm going to ask the Council to spare Stephen's life. I'll take over any care and expense associated with that." He'd devote his life to being the vampire's jailer. "I want to free her the only way we can, for as long as we can."

The second part was much harder to say. "If the Council agrees . . . you know how to take a life without pain? Any pain at all?"

Daegan's dark eyes were fathomless, but in them, Evan sensed the poignant understanding. Gideon rose, coming to his Master's side.

"Yeah, he can." The servant's midnight blue eyes revealed an empathy with Evan's plight that almost cracked him open, then and there. "He'll make it as gentle as a mother laying a baby down for a nap."

Evan couldn't speak, so he nodded, turned away. He'd never believed in that nonsense about the servant following the Master into the afterlife, but he wasn't going to take a chance. It might be the only thing he could do for her.

Fifteen minutes later, on his way back to the lab, he felt a stabbing pain through his chest, a disorienting dizziness that drove him to his knees in the hallway. A castle servant stopped, called for help, asked him what he needed. He bent forward, fingers tented on the wall to steady himself. *No. Niall. No. Not now.*

Then he felt his servant, the thread there as strong as ever. It wasn't Niall. Alanna. The connection had broken. His marks had been erased.

∼

When he was steady enough to regain his feet, he'd run for the lab, despite the fact he had to stop and throw up into what he was sure was a very expensive vase. He wiped his mouth, kept going. Debra met him at the lab doorway, eyes alive with tentative hope. "I was just coming to get you. There's been a change. She's saying your names."

He saw the welcome sign of an open door to Alanna's soundproof room. As he came to her side, her eyes were still closed, but that mantra was a whispered song coming straight from her embattled soul.

Dear God, thank you. When he met Niall's gaze, there were too many things that couldn't be said in his Scot's face. "Try touching her,"

Brian said quietly. He and Debra were watching the monitors on her vitals.

Niall's hands quivered, but Evan nodded to him. "Try it, *neshama*."

Niall slowly laid his hands on her brow. It creased beneath his touch, but then she murmured their names again. The wrenching in Evan's heart nearly drove him to his knees again. Forcing himself to take his time, he closed his fingers over her pale, thin ones. When she didn't react by screaming or flinching, it overwhelmed him. He didn't care that Brian and Debra saw the tears fill his eyes. As he put his hand on Niall's head, his servant was openly weeping.

~

Coming back to the present, Evan realized they'd come full circle, from that absurdly short time ago when they'd first met Alanna in a lab like this one, touching her, soothing her. The thought made it bearable, barely, waiting for Lord Brian to announce the results. Had Stephen's marks been removed? His second-marking wasn't as strong a bond as Stephen's third mark, so the former's removal hadn't been a guarantee of the treatment's success. But it showed the treatment *had* had an effect, which meant they could give her more time. If she was plunged back into the nightmares again, though, would that make him any better than Stephen, tormenting her with no sure end in sight?

Brian lifted his gaze from the microscope, met Evan's. He kept his grip on Alanna, his other holding Niall's shoulder.

"The marks are gone," the scientist said. "All of them."

Niall choked on another sob, and Evan tightened his fingers on the man. He had to swallow the ache in his own throat. Over three weeks of watching her writhe and cry, enduring horrors they couldn't see. It was over.

"Until she truly wakes, we won't know what neurological damage she's suffered," Brian said. "Her vitals are dangerously low. She's fully human again, no protection or added strength from vampire marks."

Evan understood Brian's warning. They'd watched her turn into a ravaged skeleton over the past three weeks.

"Would a new third mark help her chances of survival?"

The question was on Evan's lips almost instantly, but it was Lyssa who asked it. The queen had arrived without Evan noticing. Her sharp attention was on Brian, though, not their failure to rise as she entered the room. She made a curt gesture, dismissing etiquette.

"Yes," Lord Brian responded. "But not for seventy-two hours. The treatment has to cycle fully out of her system first. Her body might give out before then."

But she was at peace. She was free. Evan told himself that was the most important thing, even as he burned for that seventy-two hours to vanish, so they could do whatever was needed to help her.

"So, three days to choose the appropriate vampire to re-mark her." Lyssa nodded.

Niall started to surge off the stool. Evan had the presence of mind to clamp down on him, keeping him still. *Peace, Niall. Remember your place.*

Despite Lyssa's leniency for Niall's earlier behavior, the crisis had passed. Niall had no voice here, and she expected Evan to control his servant accordingly.

Fortunately, Evan did have a voice, albeit he was considerably outranked in the room. He was rising, even as he compelled Niall to stay seated. At the Scot's jerk of motion, Lady Lyssa's jade eyes had strayed to him, one brow rising in subtle, deadly challenge. She was likely well aware of what kind of exchange had just occurred between him and his servant.

Evan bowed to the queen, drawing her attention. "I know Alanna's training was intended to serve a far higher purpose than a vampire with my lack of ambition, but is it possible her circumstances would allow my petition, my lady?"

"Prettily said. You may have more capacity for politics than you purport."

"With due credit to your intelligence, my lady, I expect it's a rare fluke, caused by how important the issue is to me."

"Very well." She nodded. "Speak plainly. Do you want her or not?"

"With all my heart. I don't believe I've ever wanted anything quite as much. Not since three hundred years ago."

He didn't look toward Niall, but he felt him acknowledge his meaning with a numb surprise. He'd also reminded Lyssa he was on the cusp of losing his own servant. Though he wasn't above using the sentiment if it would help, he hoped Niall realized it wasn't meaningless manipulation.

"I will take it under consideration. Will the girl be coherent any-time soon?" She directed that to Brian.

"Unfortunately, we can't predict that, my lady."

"But you are certain the marks are removed."

"Within a 99.9876 percent certainty."

"Despite that wide margin of doubt . . ." She sent a look toward Daegan. "Stephen's existence is no longer necessary. The Council sentenced him when he betrayed us. Please attend to it. Have the staff burn his filth to ash and thoroughly sweep it from the grounds."

"With pleasure, my lady." Daegan's eyes gleamed. Gideon rose from the desk chair, clearing his throat.

"I'll go along with you. Hold your purse while you take care of that."

Over these past several weeks, and even before then, Evan knew he and Niall would have fought for the satisfaction of taking the bastard's life. But now, seeing Alanna in peaceful slumber for the first time in so many days, neither of them could be compelled to leave this room for something as unimportant as revenge. In the end, love was a far stronger emotion than hate. It was a comforting thought.

"She'll need to stay in a hospital bed and be monitored, but we can move her to a more comfortable environment." Brian looked around the soundproofed room. "We'll put her in the infirmary quarters for staff."

"It's on the first floor level," Debra supplied. "Where she'll get sunlight and a lovely view of the garden."

Lady Lyssa had disappeared, indicating she'd take no further appeals from Evan on the matter. He and Niall would simply have to wait, and hope. As difficult as that seemed, compared to an hour ago, it was like seeing the sun rise over land after the forty days and nights of the biblical Flood.

"Thank you, my lord."

23

THE Savannah headquarters had an aesthetic appeal the intimidating Berlin fortress had lacked. There was ample underground housing for vampire guests, with grounds and amenities suitable to the stature of the Council members who met and stayed there while conducting business. Brian had even relocated a section of his research facilities there, taking up one full wing of the estate.

Beyond being the queen's preference, the new location was Lyssa's pointed way of showing her firm grip on the Council leadership didn't require the smoke and mirrors of ghoulish surroundings. The thought gave Evan grim amusement, and a grateful heart, given the queen's support of Alanna's preservation.

True to Debra's information, the staff infirmary had a large picture window overlooking a section of the vast gardens. The hospital bed was far more comfortable than the necessary gurney cot they'd used in the soundproofed room. Debra had tucked a comforter with a sea green pattern of ocean waves over Alanna, so she was no longer swathed in institutional-style bedding. Niall brought in a flower arrangement Evan knew he'd pilfered from one of the opulently appointed Council bedrooms, but he decided to ignore its origins.

The Scot sank into one of the guest chairs, one that Debra had made sure could accommodate Niall's considerable bulk. The lab tech missed nothing. Evan wondered if she ever slept, since he'd never come into the lab during the past three weeks when she wasn't here, or at least close by, running an errand for her Master. He expected Brian would be lost without her. He knew the feeling.

Niall put his hand over Alanna's pale, slim one on the covers. "What do ye think?" he asked gruffly.

"I think she didn't fight this long and hard to leave us now. She's just exhausted." He shifted his gaze to Niall's haggard face. "She's not the only one that needs sleep. Go to bed, Niall. I'll watch over her."

"You first. Ye look far worse than me. 'Tis three hours to dawn."

"It wasn't a request."

Niall gave him a nasty look, but Evan reached out, gripped his neck in one hand. "Go to sleep, man," he murmured. "She'll think she's gazing at a corpse, she wakes up and sees your face right now."

Niall nodded to a nearby cot. "I'll sleep there."

"You'd be better off in the quarters they provided for us." The quarters both of them had barely seen except to change clothes. "I'll be with her, Niall. I promise. I won't leave her side."

Niall looked down at his hands. Evan could tell the man was struggling with something. He could have looked in his mind, but Niall was right; he was as exhausted as his servant. He waited for him to say it.

"I cannae leave, Evan. I'm not trying to be an arse about things. I'm afraid she might wake up, and say something, and that will be it. I'll have missed it. Ceana . . . she died when I was outside taking a piss. Twenty seconds, maybe, and she was gone. I didnae ken . . . maybe she said something. Maybe she would have cursed me."

"For being a good husband, a loving father, a man who stood by her?"

Niall lifted his head. When the Scot leaned forward, touched Evan's face over Alanna's thin legs, hidden in the quilt, Evan stayed still. During the past twenty-two days, there'd been no Master or servant, just two men enduring something unbearable. It was a hell he never wanted to experience again, but he had a feeling it would replay itself on a nightmarish series of works. Marcus would call it his Dark Period and try to force him to wear Goth clothing at gallery openings.

The Scot's mouth curved in a tired, grim smile. "You'd look like shite with a safety pin through your eyebrow."

"I should hope so." Evan closed his eyes despite himself as Niall's fingers slid to his jaw. The Scot had such remarkably gentle hands. They could also be rough, passionate, demanding. Evan always countered the demand with demand of his own, forcing submission in their pleasure, for that was a vampire's nature, and Niall relished the fight, but this was simply a moment to savor. There was no energy to do anything else, but the quietness of it felt right.

Niall rose. "I'll go, then. Aye, I'm being foolish. You'll wake me if she . . ."

"Count on it."

Niall nodded, then turned. Evan watched his servant move to the doorway, but once there, he stopped. He didn't turn, but his unsteady voice came clearly over his shoulder to Evan.

"These past few weeks," he said, "waiting on her, praying, hoping for her, wishing I could tear that bastard apart, I could see the same thing happening to you. Yet until today, until she woke . . . I reached out tae you because I needed your strength." The Scot straightened, faced him. "You're nae the biggest of this lot, Evan, but there's a core to you I've relied on to bear all my pain and regrets. You've cared for me, no matter all that."

He'd told Alanna that Jewish men were more susceptible to emotional displays, but they were never acceptable in the vampire world. However, even if every vampire Evan knew was crowded into this room, he'd still do what he did now.

Rising, he went to his servant. "You're not being foolish," he said, putting a hand on his jaw. Niall's eyes closed, and he turned his face into Evan's palm, the wide shoulders dropping, body fairly crumpling, but Evan caught his weight, held him close. It wasn't just Alanna the past few weeks had nearly killed. He could feel Niall's utter exhaustion, so deep. If this had shortened his life further . . . Panic at the thought squeezed him. He shared some of Niall's same fears, after all.

"I've changed my mind," he said, low, gripping the man's hair. "You'll sleep on the cot here. I want both my servants where I can see them, touch them."

He didn't care that the mark was gone. Alanna was his servant. He'd imprinted on her soul, no matter the lack of physical binding, and he'd do whatever he could to keep both of them as long as possible. Even if he had to make a deal with the devil to do it.

≈

Alanna swam in that gray mist, too tired to think, but content, easy. She heard men's voices, men she knew. Trusted. Sometimes one of them laid next to her, spinning in that world with her, one hand on her stomach or hip, the other stroking her bare scalp. Was her hair gone? She was like a babe in truth, curled up and drifting in a quiet, womb-like world.

Soft rays of sunlight penetrated her gray dawn. As she rode those beams, passing her hands through them, she felt warmth on her face. The light brush of flower petals, their fragrance.

"Wake up, *muirnín*. Our Master needs you."

She responded to that as she responded to nothing else, trying to push toward where the light was brightest.

"Easy. Take your time." Her Master's voice. "Don't rush. Come to us like a butterfly. Just float in this direction."

The words were spoken in a warm voice, but they were an order nonetheless. She floated, even putting out her arms like wings, entranced by the way it felt to let them glide up and back like that. She was moving toward something, something that took shape, shadows and silhouettes. She recalled nightmares, things so horrifying she didn't dare turn around for fear they were behind her. She was moving toward safety. Toward their arms. The nightmares wouldn't outrun her.

She opened her eyes, and there they were.

Her arms were out to her sides, just like in her mind, and now she let one of them float into Niall's grasp, the other already in her Master's. She wasn't sure she could breathe. Were they real? They had to be.

She spoke their names, but her voice was not her own. It was a weak, broken whisper. Evan squeezed her hand. "Lord Brian says you'll likely get your vocal cords back once you're third-marked again, though your voice quality might be different."

"A sultry rasp, like a Hollywood starlet, *muirnín*."

Third-marked *again*? The warmth she'd felt from their presence, their touch, was swept away with a renewed awareness of the cold emptiness. She had no marks at all, belonged to no vampire, was bound to no one. She clutched at their hands, panic in her grip. "Why? Can't you . . . Master. Don't want me anymore . . . ?"

Evan's face changed in a heartbeat from concern and welcome to an emotion so strong she didn't have a name to it, but it was the most reassuring thing she'd ever seen. "I will want you forever, Alanna. I've asked the Council to consider me as your permanent Master. But they must make the decision."

"One which requires more input."

Her gaze shifted to a man standing at the foot of her bed. "Cold. Cloak . . . on my shoulders. Blue eyes. Jacob."

His blue eyes warmed. "Good to see you with us again, Alanna," he said gently. With the ease of a man used to touching and pleasing women—in fact, she recalled his primary job was to do that for one of the most difficult and intimidating females she knew—he put his hand on her covered foot, a small protrusion beneath several layers of linens, and squeezed.

"The Council wants to ask Alanna some questions." He directed the comment to Lord Brian, who stood back from the bed, allowing them access to her. "When will she be up to a visit from them?"

Horror flooded her. She shook her head, finding her hand fastened on Niall's shirtfront. "No . . . Council doesn't attend me . . . like this. I . . . get dressed. Properly. Proper audience. Go to them."

"*Muirnín*, you're weak as a newborn. Ye cannae even stand yet."

Niall's hand covered hers. That touch felt so good tears welled up in her eyes, despite the fact her mind was on the Council's request. He patted them away with a handkerchief, telling her it was not the first time tears had spontaneously generated.

She looked toward Evan in mute appeal. The vampire studied her, then gave a slight nod. "Jacob, would they permit an audience with my serv—Alanna, at the midnight break? We can prepare and carry her there. She feels it isn't befitting for the Council to come to the bedside of a servant."

"The Council tends to make their own decisions about what befits them." Jacob's tone held a mild reproof, though he nodded in deference to Evan. "But I'll advise my lady that she might be more coherent and prepared for their questions if she came to them in the appropriate setting. I'll suggest tomorrow evening, the dinner hour, because they have plenty to keep them busy tonight."

He gave Alanna a pointed look, then glanced at Evan once more. "If she can't manage it then, Lady Lyssa has no problem coming to her. Don't let her overdo."

"We'll make certain o' it," Niall said. "No matter whose the Council thinks she is."

"Niall." Evan shot him a warning glance.

"We'll see you then." Giving Alanna a warm nod, Jacob turned, putting a hand on Niall's shoulder. No words were exchanged, but Alanna fathomed both compassion and warning in Jacob's face. Niall's jaw tightened, but he gave the other man a slight nod. With a cordial glance toward Brian and Evan, the queen's servant left.

Evan shook his head, touched Alanna's face. She leaned into it like the touch of sunlight, a trembling breath leaving her. More tears. It was ridiculous, but she couldn't stop them. She hoped she had better control of far more embarrassing bodily functions. His gray eyes softened on her, and his voice was thicker than usual. "For as docile as you appear, you're as stubborn as he is."

Her attention went to the Scot, who was gazing at her with such steady intensity. Her hand was still latched in his shirtfront. When he touched her head, she made another soft sound, following his touch with shaking fingers to her scalp.

"The treatment to sever your marks was a poison," Evan explained. "When your hair became so thin it was obvious you were going to lose all of it, I had them shave it off, so it would grow back more evenly when the time came."

If it had come. She was realizing how close a thing it had all been. "Stephen . . ."

"He's dead. May the devil enjoy him." Niall bent, brushed his lips over her skull. The nerve endings were so sensitive, she shivered, particularly when his fingers trailed down the back, over the occipital bone. "You're free of him."

"But not of . . . you two?" She tried for a smile, and God in heaven, even the strain of that caused tears. But this time, it wasn't a separate, merely physical reaction. Two sets of arms closed around her, the men shifting onto the bed to hold her as she cried. Her head ended up on Niall's shoulder, her hand clutching Evan's thigh, both men soothing her. It was nerves, and so many other things. As they rocked her between them, she noticed Niall gripping Evan's biceps where their arms overlapped on her back.

The Council was in charge of her fate. Though she hoped with all her heart and soul they would let her stay with Niall and Evan, she was too politically aware to think that it was likely. Unless no one more highly ranked than Evan wanted her.

No matter how wrong it was, she hoped the entire vampire world shunned her.

"Dawn's coming," Niall mentioned after a weighted moment. "You need to go to ground. Debra will help me get her bathed and ready."

Evan nodded. When he rose, she realized she'd never seen a vampire look exhausted, depleted, but he did. Even paler than he should be. Glancing toward Niall, she saw the deep shadows beneath his eyes, the grooves alongside them. How much, or, rather, how little, had they slept? Fed properly?

"Niall, go with him," she rasped. "Feed him and yourself. Take your rest."

When Niall met Evan's gaze, she saw a raw yearning in their gazes that stole her breath. They hadn't . . . "Niall, who . . ." She coughed, and the pain of it pulled a tiny, screeching noise from her throat, drawing their attention instantly. Brian had quietly departed a few moments after Jacob, but Debra had remained. Now she came forward to hold Alanna's shoulders as Niall put a large hand on her chest, giving her a needed pressure there as she strangled through the simple exercise of talking.

"Stop it, *muirnín*. Rest your voice for Council."

But she knew what that look meant. At least she thought she did. She looked up at Debra, seeking help, and fortunately, Debra understood.

"Niall hasn't been feeding Evan. They were switching shifts so that one of them was always here with you. Lady Lyssa ordered one of the new unassigned InhServs to give him blood."

Niall shot her a quelling look, but Debra gave him an even stare right back. Her fingers flexed on Alanna's shoulders as she bent to speak in her ear. "There was a concern that the stress of giving blood to his Master, and tending to you . . ."

That it would hasten the inevitable. If Evan had lost Niall during this . . .

"Lady Lyssa kens more than she lets on. That damn servant o' hers is everywhere," Niall grumbled.

Her gaze lifted back to her Master. She was sure he'd heard Debra, because his expression of reprobation was similar to Niall's, but now she understood. Tending to her had worn them both down, but on top of that, Evan had known the high likelihood of Niall being overcome during this. She expected he'd tried to order Niall to step back from it, but they were too tightly intertwined now . . . all three of them. The worn edge of his comment about their stubbornness made even more sense. When he'd tried to order Niall away from this, the Scot had likely told him to go to hell, bugger off . . . whatever Scotsmen used for such an occasion.

She could talk if she whispered. "Feed him, Niall."

If one of them had always been with her, it was likely no other needs had been met as well. She blocked the idea of what Evan might have done with the InhServ, because she had no right to want anything with respect to that, but Niall already anticipated her, catering to her petty foolishness.

"He only used her for blood, *muirnín*."

She swallowed, trying not to shame herself by showing how much that meant to her, but Evan's look of tender exasperation told her it hadn't escaped his notice.

"Our possessive servant," he observed. "No matter how docile she tries to appear."

Our servant. How she wished that could be true, now and forever. "Debra is here. She will care for me. Please, Niall . . . care for him." *Care for yourself. Care for each other.*

"I expect I have no vote in this," Evan said lightly, but he seemed to understand how much effort she was expending toward this one thing, because he pressed her hand, nodded to Niall. "I understand your heart and can tend to myself. Be easy on that, man. Stay with her if you need that."

Niall's head lifted, and he met Alanna's gaze. Since they weren't in her mind—she felt that terrible pain again—she put all of it in her expression, everything she'd ever tried to communicate to him about why being a servant was a blood-deep commitment, beyond an oath of honor. It was a bond of unconditional love, a gritty, ugly, wondrous thing.

Debra had become her ally. "She won't be left alone, Niall. I promise. She needs a bath, a full cleaning. She'd likely prefer that done by another woman. Tend to your Master."

There were so many things in his eyes, torn between past and present, she couldn't help but put her hand to his face, stroke there. *I'm here. I love you.*

The first time in her life she'd thought it, let alone said it. Her lips had formed the words, though no sound came out. His brown eyes closed, his head bowing. With the strength and aid of Debra's hands, she put her forehead to his, then tilted to brush her lips to it.

"Go care for our Master. Care for the man you love," she whispered.

He squeezed her hands, hard enough to be painful. Planting an abrupt kiss on her temple, he rose, turning toward the door, where Evan still waited for him.

When she saw their gazes meet, a painful peace spread through her chest, in all her vitals. She shouldn't delay them, not for an instant, but wasn't it Evan who taught her to accept her desires?

"Master?"

Whatever he saw in her face, she didn't need to explain. Putting his hand on Niall's chest, a brief caress, he strode back to her. She made a soft sound against his mouth when he put his lips over hers, a gentle but lingering kiss. He gripped her chin with firm fingers.

"You obey whatever Debra tells you. If you don't, I'll hear of it."

"Yes, Master." She brushed her cheek against his, her nose against his jaw, as much of him as she could touch in that brief moment.

Somehow, she would let them both go when the Council made their decision. But she would never let go of them in her heart. No one could make her do that. Even Stephen hadn't managed it.

~

The bath knocked her back out for six hours. It filled her with despair that Niall might be right, that she wasn't up for this, but she was determined. All she had to do was imagine the Council assembled around her bed, Lord Belizar staring down his hooked Russian nose at the small lumps of her feet under the covers, and the dreadfulness of the idea gave her strength.

So they did it in stages. Debra dressed her two hours before the dinner session. Once she was in underwear and a simple copper-colored dress that wouldn't wrinkle while lying down, she was back out for another hour. When she surfaced, she asked about makeup, the possibility of putting a scarf over her bare head.

"It's best not to do that," Debra said.

"May I see a mirror? Please?"

Debra glanced toward the door. Alanna's heart leaped, seeing Niall there, and not simply because of his reappearance. He was in a different version of what he'd worn for the wedding. White dress shirt with dark kilt and plaid, high white socks and ghillies laced over them. The gray rabbit fur sporran with its handsome silver ornamentation hung from his belt. With his dark brown hair loose on his shoulders, brushed to a silken sheen, she wasn't surprised when the unflappable Debra blanked on Alanna's question.

"You look . . . like you have . . . a date." She tried to speak using her voice, a practice run for Council, but slipped back to a whisper when her vocal cords protested.

Sleep had done him a great deal of good, his face far less haggard. But he also looked . . . easier. She envied him, what that meant. Evan feeding from him for the first time in three weeks, his strong hands holding his servant possessively, plunging both fang and cock deep inside him, reasserting that claim. Niall would have gotten lost on that tide as well, likely turning once the feeding was done to clash with tongue and teeth, tasting his Master, kissing him, starting it all over again.

"I wish I could have been there," she said.

"Ye'll be there soon enough. And then you'll really ken what exhaustion is." His eyes smiled at her, but his mouth was firm, serious.

"I want to see a mirror," she repeated. Debra stepped back, deferring to Niall on it. "I need to know what I look like, Niall. Please."

"Ye look like a woman who's been to hell and back," he said shortly. "You've no meat on your bones, ye have no hair, and you're as pale as . . ."

"A corpse? So putting makeup on me would make me look more like one?"

Her big Scot flinched. "Aye."

"Well, I'll eat," she said resolutely. "And get back in the sun. My hair will grow."

"I know, *muirnín*. But no mirror. Nae right now. See yourself as I see ye. Beautiful, alive, brave . . . everything a man could want."

She did see that in his eyes, warming her inside and out. Unfortunately, female vanity wasn't assuaged as easily. She looked to Debra. "Will anything help me look better?"

"The Council needs to see what your loyalty to them cost you," Debra said. "Under the proper circumstances, they are not without compassion."

Debra was usually as dutiful as an InhServ. Hearing her say anything that smacked of influencing the Council was unexpected. But Alanna recalled several slips in the reserved woman's expression during her preparations that suggested her situation had affected Debra. She knew it had affected Niall. Despite her compliment, he still wasn't 100 percent, so she decided to poke at that.

"Put makeup on him, then," she whispered. "He looks pale."

"'Tis your fault. These needy lasses can fair kill a lad." His lips tugged up in a half smile. She wanted him to come closer, kiss her, but now she was thinking about how she looked. Besides holding no sexual appeal, a skeleton wasn't capable of much in that department. It didn't stop her heart from craving the intimacy of their bare bodies against hers, being taken by her Masters . . .

Niall was close now, his fingers on her chin. She resisted. "No. I look hideous. You just said so."

"I said no such thing. I said you're beautiful." Since he merely caught her chin in a firmer grip, she was helpless when he put his lips on hers. At that first touch, her weak arms sought purchase on his shoulders. He pulled her up to her knees, letting her feel him flush against his body, which was far stronger than she'd teased him about.

"I can smell Evan on you," she murmured, loving it. Loving them both.

"Aye. I didnae think the scrappy runt had that much strength left in him. We both fell asleep like drunkards afterward."

She smiled against his mouth, then lost herself in that kiss, weakening in all the right ways, until he eased her back to the covers, touched her well-kissed lips with a thumb. "You're the most beautiful woman

I've ever seen, now and forever. And ye best not take my earlier words as an empty threat. Get your strength back, *muirnín*. Because we intend to use ye hard for all you've put us through."

Only time would tell if such desires would be fantasy or reality. He didn't voice their obvious shared worry, that things might not go their way, but she hoped. For the first time in her life, she prayed for divine influence in her fate, humbly asking for the chance to serve the type of Master she'd always wanted.

~

Niall carried her to the Council, Evan leading the way. Brian's wing was on the opposite end of the estate, but Niall had promised they'd let her down right before they reached Council's chambers. She had to settle for the fact that she was clean and dressed; she'd figure out a way to stand on her own once she was there. During the trip in Niall's arms, she enjoyed the way her Master looked as well. Evan wore a silver-gray suit that brought out his eyes. He'd chosen an open throat for the dress shirt instead of a tie, but it was a strategic move, giving him the look of a self-assured, confident member of the vampire world, not an overeager petitioner for the Council's favor.

As always, the clever diplomat. Remembering Niall's opinion on that, she clung to her hope.

When she'd come before Lady Lyssa last time, she'd been numb, beyond everything. Now she felt everything. The weakness of her body, anxiety, yearning, worry. A tearing love for the males who accompanied her. But she kept her breathing slow and steady, mindful of Debra's parting warning.

You can't get overly emotional. Don't let your heart rate increase, or you will faint. You have zero strength.

Twenty paces before the door to Council chambers, Niall let her legs slide to the ground. As Evan disappeared within to announce their arrival, he kept his arm around her waist.

"I ken you're very determined to walk these last few steps, but lean on me. Use my strength, lass."

He shortened his strides, allowing her to proceed at her own pace, but it was quickly clear it was far too slow. After five steps the remaining distance stretched out like a distant lakeshore. Niall lifted her against his hip with a subtle hitch, her feet just barely brushing the floor. He covered all but the last two paces.

"If you have a pack mule, use him, *muirnín*." He brushed his lips over her temple, not allowing her to despair. "You're doin' fine, lass. Remember, you're not on trial. You're the hero here."

Then Evan opened the tall door from within, leaving no time for a response to the unexpected statement. A chair had been placed in the center of the room, just like for her initial audience with Lady Lyssa. Only now the whole Council was present. But so was Evan. She assumed he would take the chair, with her at his knee. Instead, Niall guided her to it. She pushed at his hands. "Evan . . ."

"Sit," her Master said quietly, and she did, warring between taking the chair that should belong to a standing vampire, and not wanting to appear as if she were arguing with him before Council. Once she was seated, Niall took a stance on one side of the chair, Evan on the other.

Lady Lyssa studied her from behind the polished table that curved around half of the chamber. It was a lovely dark wood with griffin-style feet and decorative edging that had obviously been custom-made. Alanna liked it much better than the massive one in Berlin. However, when she lifted her gaze, however briefly, the pin of those intense jade eyes made everything else disappear. It was also capable of making Alanna's heart rate increase, but she breathed through it, remembering Debra's admonition.

"Our questions will be brief, Alanna. You need to recover your strength to serve a vampire Master again. That is the only priority you have. Do you understand?"

"Yes, my lady." Alanna bowed her head.

"In deliberating your fate, I have a question I want you to answer honestly."

"I would answer the Council no other way, my lady."

Jacob was standing behind his lady's chair, the only servant present other than her and Niall. When Alanna dared a quick glance upward, she noted his expression flicker in approval at her, bolstering her somewhat. She did her best to sit even straighter.

"You are a member of the InhServ corps, your destiny specifically sculpted to support the elite of our ranks. While you may think none of those are interested in you because of your situation, that is not the case."

Weeks ago, such news would have been welcome. Now her heart plummeted. She gripped the chair arm, tried to stop her head from swimming off her shoulders. But did it matter now if she fainted? Evan's request would be denied. Giving her to him in lieu of a higher-ranking vampire's request would be an unforgivable insult.

"That aside, I want you to tell me who *you* desire to be your Master."

The question startled her enough she met the queen's eyes before jerking her head back down. "My apologies, my lady . . . I don't understand. My preferences are irrelevant. I serve the Council's desires."

"That is correct." The queen's cool tone suggested she was confirming the obvious. Alanna suppressed the need to squirm. "Your training has been so thorough that, even if you had a preference, you would submit wordlessly to your fate and fully embrace the service of whomever we choose. Isn't that correct?"

"Yes, my lady."

Except her voice quavered shamefully. Perhaps she couldn't quell her emotions the way she normally might because she was in such a weakened state. The idea of leaving Niall and Evan was going to tear her apart right before the Council.

"Look at me."

Alanna lifted her head, surprised by the unexpected command. The tilted almond shape of the green eyes suggested Lyssa's Asian blood, her skin as smooth as antique ivory silk. "You promised me honesty, did you not?"

"Yes, my lady."

"So tell us your heart, child. You're clutching that chair so hard you're in danger of splinters."

She immediately released the wood, mortified by the physical evidence of resistance, but she wasn't sure how to proceed. She could speak her heart to Evan and Niall in the infirmary, but here, the weight of tradition and ritual, everything being an InhServ meant, was before her. She was lost. Struggling.

Lyssa leaned forward, perhaps no more than an inch, but the motion held Alanna's attention as effectively as a graceful, deadly spider would hold a butterfly.

"Alanna, whatever decision the Council makes, I am telling you that you may speak your heart honestly here. It does not go against you, nor does it leave these chambers."

Oh God. She understood then. Lady Lyssa was giving her the opportunity to express her true feelings toward Evan and Niall as a matter of record. Even though politics would require her to be assigned elsewhere, Alanna's feelings toward them would be documented in perpetuity.

It was an unprecedented honor, one that overwhelmed her. It was a nod to Evan as well, for his service to the Council. But had Lyssa also realized it as a necessity, bringing closure so Alanna could go forward and perform as required? While it shamed her that the queen thought she required that to be an effective InhServ, she wouldn't reject the gift. She had all she could to do to get past her amazement about the offer in enough time to accept it.

She was swamped with the significance of the next words she would speak. If she did nothing else in her life worth note, this was the task she wanted to look back upon and know she did it well. Straightening, she swept her gaze over all of them in a respectful, peripheral way, so they knew she intended to respond.

Ten vampires. Lady Carola and Lady Helga. Lords Belizar, Walton, Welles and Stewart. Lord Uthe, Evan's sire, on Lyssa's right. She'd always found him intimidating, but she was glad he'd saved Evan's life and would forever have a high regard toward him because of it. Behind him, in the shadows, she saw the Fae liaison was here, Lord Keldwyn. She didn't know him well, for he came and went like a ghost. Almost as elusive as Lord Daegan, his preferred spot in Council chambers was always in shadows, but usually somewhere between Lady Lyssa and Lord Uthe.

Lord Mason and Lady Daniela sat together at the end as the newest Council members. Though Lord Mason's age made his stature worthy of a seat closer to the queen, he preferred the end. He stated it was for his long legs, since he was as big as Niall, but she'd seen how he watched the other Council members, particularly Belizar. He was in the best position to anticipate an attack against the queen and thwart it. Lady Daniela had come from Western Australia. Since her betrayal of Stephen, Alanna hadn't attended Council meetings, but during her recuperation, before she left Berlin to join Evan and Niall, she'd run into Lady Danny's servant, Devlin, a few times while out in the garden.

The bushman had a casual, easy way about him that she'd found complementary to his Mistress. Lady Daniela wasn't a diplomat. She was straightforward and unflinching. Alanna suspected the two of them brought an unusual yet effective addition to the Council's traditional formality. She'd also sensed some of the same type of bond between the two of them as she felt between Jacob and Lyssa. In fact, thinking about it now, Lord Mason, like Lady Lyssa, was quite open about his bond with his servant, Jessica. The queen had capably changed the Council dynamic, such that 30 percent of their number acknowledged their servants' value in a historically unprecedented way.

Which was likely why she was sitting here now, being given this opportunity. She cleared her throat, refusing to whisper for this.

"When I informed the Council of Lord Stephen's betrayal, it went against everything I was trained for, as well as everything I believed a servant should be." Her voice cracked, running out of breath. She made herself slow down. "Submission is a beautiful thing in a servant, a desired thing. Surrender is a gift, a treasure, and the Master who has received that receives the highest level of service a servant can give, which was all I ever truly wanted to do when I became an InhServ."

She met Jacob's eyes. The truth of it flamed in his blue eyes. It gave her the courage to continue.

"I do not regret my actions." There, she'd said it. "I deserve no credit for my betrayal of my former Master. I did not act as a servant, but as a sister, grieving the loss of her brother."

Niall shifted. In her peripheral vision, she saw Evan press his lips together, a tacit rejection of that statement. "However, what I say now is a conscious, deliberate decision, an honor to my current Master that I hope will not be held against him. Evan took my training to a level the InhServ program, as exceptional as it is, couldn't, because what I discovered in his service cannot be produced by training."

Dizziness overcame her then, making her lock onto those chair arms again before she pitched herself to the floor. *No. Hold on. Hold on. I'm not done.* Panic that Lyssa might think she was through and end the audience made it worse. Niall's hand was on her shoulder, his thumb stroking her collarbone. The queen spoke.

"Alanna, I am well aware you would never waste this Council's time. We will not rush your answer, so don't distress yourself on that matter. Take a breath or two. Jacob, bring her some water."

The compassion in Lady Lyssa's voice was shocking enough to send her into a full blackout, but Alanna recovered enough to accept the water Jacob brought to her. He gave it to Niall, who knelt at her side, keeping his hand over hers to steady her grip as she took a few sips. Of course it went down the wrong way, producing those tearing coughs that jerked her forward in the chair. Evan's strong hands held her shoulders as Niall pressed his large hand to her chest again. When she saw blood fleck his shirt, his hand, he looked up at Evan.

No, I have to finish. I have to.

A muscle flexed in the Scot's jaw. "Aye, we know lass. Just calm down."

As she struggled to obey, she noticed the reaction of the Council. Vampires all had that impassive stillness that could turn them into furniture, but she detected an inexplicable tension as they watched her struggle. As Niall used Evan's handkerchief to blot the blood from her lips, Lord Uthe and Lady Lyssa exchanged a glance. She wasn't sure how to interpret the mood.

Keldwyn stepped away from the wall and put his hand on Uthe's shoulder. When he bent between the queen and her right-hand man, it was obvious the three were conferring on something that the other vampires could hear. At the opposite end of the table, Lord Stewart lifted a brow, pursing his lips as if he found the subject intriguing, unexpected.

When the private conversation concluded, Keldwyn briefly met Uthe's gaze. His fingers whispered off the vampire's shoulder rather than lifting away. A Fae and a vampire? Perhaps the impossible *was* possible.

The distraction, Lady Lyssa's firm assurance and Niall's touch all helped calm her. Evan had not touched her, but she understood he wouldn't, that showing any sentiment toward her right now would not be appropriate. However, when Niall glanced up at him, telling him without words she was ready, he was the one who spoke. "She is ready to continue, my lady."

At Lyssa's nod, Alanna swallowed. This time she kept her gaze fixed on Lyssa's folded hands, though in reality she turned her focus inward, speaking to that soft gray wall, the anteroom after her trip to Hell, the place that did not judge or expect, simply allowing her to be whatever she was.

"I believe most vampires *want* to engage the emotions of their servant fully. They wish to be adored, desired, needed, in a singular way not possible among vampires themselves. To be served out of love, not politics, obligation or duty, though our responsibilities can certainly entail that. In fact, I think many vampires demand that level of devotion from their servants."

She saw a tug on Jacob's mouth, a wry acknowledgment. But now she would take her courage in both hands, prove she'd learned the lesson her Master had taught her. She'd voice her own desires.

"I want to serve my Masters. My Master, I mean." She flushed, hoping the faux pas would be taken as a result of her physical state. "Evan." *And Niall.*

The Council remained silent for some minutes, but she had done what she could. She put her attention on her hands, folded in her lap. Keeping her back straight was a monumental effort, but she told her pounding head, dry mouth and wasted lungs that they needed to hold on a little longer. Just a little longer . . .

"I think it would be useful to have Alanna meet with the InhServ trainers when she is well enough to do so. I expect her ideas might intrigue them. As well as result in more valuable service from their ranks."

As Alanna blinked, unsure she'd heard Lord Uthe correctly, Lady Lyssa made a noise of agreement. "She's the most exceptional student in the program's history, which was why she was given to the made vampire believed most likely to be the first deserving appointment to the Council. His appointment to the Council was correctly predicted"—an unmistakable edge entered her tone—"even though his deserving it was not."

Lord Uthe gave her an even look. "While our Lady Lyssa has taken a not-unjustified jab at our poor judgment prior to her assumption of leadership, the assignment of Alanna as his servant was not a poor decision. Without her, we might have lost our assassin and possibly our power base in Europe. It is an exceptional situation. Which suggests our decision on her fate might require a similar exception."

Alanna's fingers were knotted together, her gaze locked on her white knuckles. She couldn't dare to hope. Couldn't breathe at all.

"Evan, it's obvious you are the Master she prefers to serve." Lyssa was addressing her Master. "Do you have anything to add to the case to claim her?"

Evan stepped forward. As he did, he extended his arm, tapped a long finger on her clasped hands. A gentle reproof that made her spread her fingers on her lap. Niall was standing directly behind her now, such that she could feel his breath on her bare head.

"Alanna would be of great value to any vampire Master. There is no politic reason for you to assign her to me." Evan swept them all in his glance. "My desire to have her as my servant has no political agenda to it, either. Yet she is a muse in human form, inspiring my work, for what value that may provide to you. She loves me, and she loves Niall. There are matters to discuss that bear weight on that." He glanced at Niall, then back at the Council. "I can tell the Council this. If she is granted to me, I will care for her as the treasure she is."

Lyssa nodded. "Thank you, Evan. Alanna may return to the infirmary, and your servant with her. Please remain, so we may discuss this further with you."

Evan nodded to Niall, who put his hand under her arm to help her from the chair. Alanna shifted forward, but instead of rising, she began to sink to her knees. Her desperate pressure on Niall's hand told him she intended it, and the Scot anticipated her enough to ease her down, rather than letting her drop like a bundle of sticks.

Once down on her knees she bent, ignoring the trembling weakness of her body, the pain rocketing through her head, but she couldn't overcome the wheezing of her lungs. Though she wanted to make it to his feet, she had to settle for pressing her lips to Evan's leg, just below his knee. The wool and silk of the slacks, his scent intertwined with it, was so overwhelming to her she had the resist the desire to rub against him like a cat.

"Whatever happens," she whispered, "thank you for being my Master."

I've always served vampires I called my lord or my lady. They were powerful, yes. But they . . . I am going to be inappropriate, Master, but please forgive me. They never taught me what love is. You and Niall did,

both by your example and by your lessons. If I die tomorrow, these few
days will be the ones I will cherish . . . and miss, the most. Thank you for
showing me what being a servant really means.

She felt the scrutiny of the Council, but the only regard that meant
anything to her now was Evan's. As she managed to lift her head, she
saw his jaw was tight, the gray eyes full of emotion he was struggling
to push back. But it didn't matter now, for either of them, did it?

Despite her noise of protest, he lifted her in his arms, putting her
into Niall's. For one blissful moment, perhaps the last, both men were
holding her, the three of them linked. Evan brushed his lips across
both of her cheeks, made sure Niall had her securely before he removed his grip.

"Take her back to her bed," he said. "I'll join you both directly."

~

Evan paused in the doorway to the infirmary. Niall sat in a chair by the
window. Alanna was curled in his lap, looking out at the white moonflowers cultivated in the gardens. With a painful tightness in his chest
that had become a constant companion, he saw Niall had dozed off,
his head resting against the back of the chair, temple pressed inside one
of the wings. Alanna slid her fingers along his chest, idle patterns as
she stared out into the night, her thoughts entirely her own for the first
time in over a decade.

He'd been simply overcome by her in Council chambers. She might
be humbled to know that, but what would stun her was that she'd
wrested a similar reaction from the Council.

Brilliant girl that she was, she'd honored her training and taken it
to a new level, marrying desire to service. Weak as a baby, showing just
how close to the Grim Reaper's blade she stood, she'd conducted herself with calm dignity and an unconditional sincerity that proved why
she should be servant of the highest and most deserving of the vampire
ranks. Lord Belizar himself had said those words. Evan was fiercely
proud of her.

Then, when she went to her knees, he wanted to tell the Council
they could go straight to hell. He and Niall were keeping her. But of
course the world didn't work that way.

For this moment, though, the world could be what he wanted it to
be. He savored the sight of the two of them together. He expected she

was the one who'd talked Niall into taking off the shirt and plaid, so he wore just the kilt, letting her lean against his bare chest, trace his dragon and the third mark beneath. Niall could wear a suit handsomely, but Evan had always preferred him in the kilt. Niall eschewed a tartan, preferring the solid black or gray. Given that he'd been one of the broken men who lived on clan land, but was not of that clan's blood, and the fact that his landlord and clan chief had sacrificed him on a battlefield, Evan understood it. Yet he wore Evan's dragon tattoos . . . and Evan's mark.

Even after all these centuries, Evan carried a great deal of his father's religious practicality. Judaism was a thinking man's religion, all said and done, and the idea of a vampire and servant being bound in the afterlife had seemed illogical to him. For the first time he understood, whether it was truth or not, that notion had probably been born from fervent wishful thinking, by vampires who felt for their servants as he did.

Straightening from the door, he went to them. Alanna's gaze immediately turned from the window. She didn't move, however. She wouldn't disturb Niall's rest, but more than that, she was braced for the news, her pale face and sad, shorn head making his heart tighten. She'd known they wouldn't choose him, that there was no possible way in the hierarchical world of the vampires that would be acceptable. But he hated that she'd hoped enough to look so crushed now by the inevitable news.

When he squatted to his heels so they were eye to eye, she swallowed. Firmed her chin and lifted it. "I love you, Master," she said quietly.

Reaching out, he traced her thin, ravaged face. Once fed and healthy, her hair grown out, she would be beautiful again, in the way that all men appreciated, but he agreed with Niall. Her bravery, resolve and sheer character would never make her anything less than mesmerizing to him.

"That's good. Because you're going to be with me a very, very long time."

Her gasped cry woke Niall, such that he almost toppled her, coming out of it ready to fight. Evan caught hold of him and Alanna to steady them both, but as he held them there in the chair, he was gripped by a sheer ebullience that was entirely unvampirelike. Fortunately, Alanna saved him from acting upon it, because she flung her arms around him. Her joyous embrace told Niall what had happened, and now the Scot's grin brought warmth and light to every corner of the room. He gripped Evan's shoulder, but Evan saw a different knowledge in the man's eyes. A tightness rose into Evan's throat as he heard Niall's private thought to himself.

He won't be alone. He'll have her.

When Alanna pulled back, Niall tugged her hair, teasing her, even as the three of them kept that connection, arms tangled, hips touching. Evan had dropped to one knee to keep Niall settled and to prevent Alanna from being dumped on the floor, so his braced foot was between Niall's splayed ones.

"So," the Scot observed. "I have a lot to do. I have tae teach ye to be more insolent, so Evan will not get spoiled by your excessive subservience. And then I'll have to teach him how to give ye a proper strapping, because he's far too soft-handed about it."

She had a response for that, one that made Niall laugh, but Evan didn't hear it. He was poised on a precipice, one where his pleasure in their reaction could easily be turned to a cold weight, given the other news he had, but he wasn't of a mind to wait on the blow, if it was going to come.

"Actually, you might be around to do those beatings yourself for a while, if you're up for it."

Alanna stopped in midsentence, her attention snapping to Evan. Niall seemed unperturbed, but lifted a brow. "What, Brian's cooked up a way to keep me around longer? Some foul potion where I have to endure ye another decade or two?"

"Worse. I requested the right to turn you, Niall. And Council agreed."

24

WHEN Niall and Alanna departed, Lady Lyssa had turned her infamous ball-shrinking gaze upon him. "Now, to the other matter. Evan has submitted a request. He wishes to turn Niall, his servant."

A ripple of response passed through the assembled Council members, none immediately positive. Lady Carola shook her head outright. "We have very firm rules about turning servants . . ."

As the Councilwoman glanced toward Lyssa, Jacob standing behind her, her voice drifted off. "Except under extraordinary circumstances . . ."

Everyone knew that Lyssa had turned Jacob to save his life, against Council decree, a situation that had made her a fugitive for a short time. That process had been miraculously reversed when she visited the Fae world, but having a Council head who'd defied the most important tenets about vampires and servants made such absolutes problematic. It was something Evan was counting upon.

"Yes, that's true," Lady Lyssa said serenely. "Given that Lord Uthe is Evan's sire, he has unique insight into this matter and would like to discuss extenuating circumstances."

That was unexpected, though definitely not unwelcome. The enigmatic born vampire who'd been a Templar Knight had always dealt fairly with Evan. He met Evan's gaze now, making Evan recall their meeting all those years ago. The vampire sitting by his deathbed in the middle of the night, the preternatural gaze studying him, the stillness of the powerful body. Evan had been so far gone then, all he'd wondered about the stranger was whether he could talk him into drawing one of his very sharp daggers and ending the agonizing pain of his existence. But he'd so fiercely wanted another option, imagining all the things he'd never get to paint.

Uthe had provided that other option. He'd told Evan what he had to offer, but he'd had very specific conditions. *You cannot accept due to fear of death. Turning a human to a vampire requires far better reasons than that. For many of us, there is a calling that supersedes everything else material about ourselves. Gaze into your soul, boy, and tell me if you have it.*

Evan gave his sire a bow. "I hold your counsel far above my own, my lord."

The eyes of the Fae Lord standing behind Uthe flickered, making Evan think he'd said something of interest to Keldwyn. Like Alanna, he'd noted the connection between him and Uthe. Later, he might take advantage of his connection with his sire to find out more. See if he couldn't presume on their relationship to get the unlikely chance to visit the Fae world, a place with limitless wonders to put on canvas.

Bloody eejit. Of all the things ye should be focusing on right now . . . Though Niall wasn't speaking in his head, Evan could well imagine the Scot sternly doing so now. But the random thought actually helped him channel the tension away from his body, keep his expression calm, intent. Ironically it also kept him more focused on the one vital priority he had at this moment.

Lord Uthe inclined his head. "As you know, the tithe we take from the proceeds of Evan's artwork has accumulated into a not-insignificant-sum over the years. Beyond that, his successes have prompted us to encourage an artistic culture among our ranks, expanding our focus beyond survival and politics."

Lord Keldwyn had moved, though Evan hadn't seen it. Remarkable, given that he'd been in Evan's direct line of sight. The Fae was now in the back corner of the room, sitting on the ledge of a fountain. The fountain was graced by a sculpture of a kelpie, the seaweed-covered horse rearing, water pouring from his nostrils to the pool below.

"Many humans have his pieces in their homes. Thanks to Lord Keldwyn's interest, recently they've even caught the interest of the Fae world. Evan's contributions have created an unexpected bond and value between three worlds."

So maybe a trip to the Fae world wasn't out of the realm of possibility. Evan shoved the thought away, imagining Niall giving him one of his patented severe looks. Yes, his art was a driving force in his life. But there was something far more important. Two somethings, in fact.

"Evan's value is noted," Lord Stewart said. "But does it bear weight on whether his servant would be an appropriate addition to our made vampires? As Stephen proved, quite tragically, we must make those decisions quite carefully, to avoid past mistakes."

"It does bear weight on the decision." Lord Uthe nodded. "Evan's talent is of great value to us, but because of the wasting disease he had as a human, his strength as a vampire not only grows slowly, it grows more slowly as he ages, suggesting it will eventually plateau. Lord Brian is fairly certain of this."

The glances at him gave him the familiar feeling of inadequacy, particularly before such a powerful assembly. Yet Evan bit back his usual rancor at the analysis of his strengths . . . or lack thereof. For the first time in his life, it might prove to his benefit.

"Niall is an exceptionally strong third mark," Uthe continued. "If you recall, one of the reasons we have had concerns about turning a fully marked servant is that, in the instances it has occurred, the fledgling has accelerated qualities in strength, speed . . . things that could put him further up the hierarchy than the usual time and maturity allow."

"He is not being turned in his youth," Helga said thoughtfully. "He has been among us three centuries, has had time to mature past such issues."

"You simply have a fondness for Scots," Lord Stewart said without rancor. Helga beamed.

"My Torrence is a fine servant. I think my bias is based on sound knowledge."

The male vampire chuckled. Lady Lyssa sat back in her chair.

"We're entrusting a valuable InhServ to Evan, and Niall would be a good companion and protector for them both. If he is willing."

Her gaze shifted back to Evan. "As you know, no human can be turned to vampire without consent. Do you think he would be amenable?"

"I have not proposed it to him, my lady. I wanted to seek Council approval first. But rest assured, the choice will be his."

Turning his attention to Lord Uthe, he executed another bow. "Long ago, you asked me a question."

∼

"If you could live forever, how far do you think you could go as an artist?" the stranger asked. "Is limited mortality necessary to achieve and maintain creative genius?"

Evan had just finished up one of his coughing fits. The stranger had calmly held his frail body, blotted away the blood on his lips, and now handed him a glass of water poured from the side table. At one time, his mother had rushed up to his attic room every time she heard one of the episodes start, but seeing her exhaustion mounting, he'd begged her to let him deal with it himself. He wanted to be as much of a man as he could manage, with whatever time he had left.

"Since I can only speak from a position of limited mortality— extremely limited mortality," Evan replied, "I can't say. But I do know I can stare at the same blue sky and find something different in it every moment. I don't think it's a matter of time; it's a man's relationship to time. The realization that there's never enough, even in immortality. Look at God Himself . . . here before the very beginning of all things, and He never gets tired of meddling with us, right?"

He supposed that bordered on blasphemous disrespect, but seeing as he was poised on the edge of meeting the deity in question, he expected God Himself would address his impertinence.

His visitor smiled. "If you're willing, I'll give you the opportunity to test the theory."

"And say you can do this unlikely thing"—Evan's brows rose— "why would you offer it to me?"

"Because I want to see what a true artist will do with forever."

∼

"I see that same potential when I look at Niall," Evan said, seeing the memory resurrected in Uthe's gaze. "It's not in every man, the where-withal to know what to do with centuries, but there is a slow steadiness to him, like the growth of an oak over hundreds of years, where his imprint becomes a more vital part to the world around him with every year that passes. I ask that he be given the same chance you gave me, for the same reason."

He paused. "Whereas you turned me so I could continue to put things to canvas, Niall *is* the canvas, the painting that I want to endure until the end of time. That way, as long as Fate permits it, he's there for all of us to enjoy." *To love.*

He didn't add it, but he supposed it hung out there in the air, no-ticed but unspoken. He thought of how Alanna had put it together so quickly. *A muse can be male, Master.*

Should Niall agree, Evan would have two muses, and they *would* carry him through eternity. As long as they could put up with him. He suppressed the smile, but it didn't dispel the tension he concealed.

"There's something else about Niall that suggests his suitability," he added. "He's a sexual Dominant. He submits to me, but in those we've shared, it quickly rises to the top. Alanna responded to it almost im-mediately."

"Explaining why she slipped and called both of you Master?"

The queen missed nothing, God's truth. Next she'd ask if he'd ca-tered to the notion, cultivated it in his servant, and that would be a can of worms. He'd defuse it by hinting at the truth. "Yes. I expect so. Being a submissive has never been a good fit for Niall. Because of that, as well as my travels, my art, we've had an unexpected relationship as vampire and servant. He has been of course in a position of service to me, but I've always suspected, in that particular regard, we are cut from the same cloth."

"Very well. We will have you step outside while we discuss and come to our decision on both matters. But should we agree on all counts, I feel it would be appropriate for both of you to third-mark Alanna, to protect and facilitate her service. Do you disagree?"

"Not at all," Evan said. He would welcome it. He was certain Alanna would as well. She was intuitive that way.

~

He'd rendered Niall speechless. Probably realizing that reaction wasn't an automatic assent, Alanna bit back any congratulatory exclamation. She was watching the Scot's face as carefully as Evan.

"Three hundred years ago, I refused to let you slip from my fingers," Evan continued steadily. "And now Alanna needs us both . . ."

Niall's gaze flickered, recognizing the manipulative tactic. But a vampire was a vampire. "I need you both," Evan admitted. "But that said, it *is* fully your choice, Niall. Neither Alanna nor I will try to force your decision. You must come to this yourself. But there's more to it. We would both mark you, Alanna. You would have two Masters."

"I think you both already are," she said simply.

"I need to think." Niall rose.

Though he'd expected that, Evan bit back a feeling of disappointment. Instead he rose as well. "It's not an easy decision."

"Aye." Niall nodded toward Alanna. "But don't wait on me. Go ahead and mark her as soon as we reach that seventy-two-hour mark, so she can regain her strength."

"No."

They both looked toward Alanna. "No," she repeated. "It feels like I should wait until the decision is made, whether yes or no. And the one choice a servant has is to be marked, right?"

Evan sat back down and grasped her wrist, drawing her attention to the pulse which was still far too thready. "Alanna, you're very weak. The audience with the Council posed an unacceptable danger to you. Your body is human right now, and very fragile. To ensure it stays on this side of the curtain, you must be marked as soon as possible."

When her lips tightened with uncharacteristic stubbornness, he sharpened his tone. "You're not being fair to Niall. You'll hasten his decision, and it's not a decision to be made without thought. Whatever he chooses, we will respect it, and care for him as we always have. Whatever happens . . . we will bear it. As two or three, but it will be borne."

It didn't matter that the idea stabbed through his chest like one of Niall's wooden stakes. He made himself look toward Niall as he said the next words. "When Niall came into my service, the choice I gave him was not a choice at all, not to a man of honor. I won't do that to him again."

Niall stared at him, his tawny eyes suddenly full of a great many reactions. Alanna relented, reaching for the Scot's hand. "I'm sorry, Niall," she whispered. "I know he's right. But I've never been allowed to want, and I didn't realize how . . . overwhelming it can be."

Niall's expression flickered with pain. Stepping close enough to press her head against his abdomen, he dropped a kiss on her smooth skull. "*Muirnín* . . ." He drifted off helplessly, but then he knelt, caught her chin, held it in thumb and forefinger, gazing at her sternly. "If ye see us both as your Master, he'll mark you the moment the clock ticks to that seventy-two-hour mark. Whatever Fate decides, you'll ease our minds, and it will give ye the strength tae serve one or both of us. Ye mind me?"

Her eyes closed tight, her hand clutched on his. "Yes, Master."

The Scot needed out of here, needed room to breathe. Evan could see it. Letting him walk out without giving his answer was as hard for him as he was sure it was for Alanna. But the vampire understood how it must be.

I'll watch over her, Niall.

Niall acknowledged the thought with a slight nod, then rose, holding on to her hand. "Remember ye only have the one job 'til you're marked. Keep your arse in this bed and save your strength."

She tilted her head, a wicked spark in her brown eyes. "You can't order me around if you're not a vampire."

"That order came direct from Lady Lyssa," he reminded her. But he brought her hand down to his belt, made her close slim fingers on it. Though he was as likely to use it on her in her current state as he would on a newborn, his severe look almost made Evan believe otherwise. Yes, the Scot would do just fine as a vampire. If he agreed to it.

"I can order you whether I'm human, servant or vampire, lass. If you think I willnae turn your skinny body over my knee and whale on ye until you mind, think again." But he caressed her face. "Care for yourself, *muirnín*. You nearly killed us with worry."

Her gaze sobered. Dipping her head, she put her lips to his knuckles. "I will. I promise."

Niall stroked her sensitive scalp, but raised an eyebrow at Evan. "Either she's promising to worry us to death or obey, I'm nae certain which."

With a wink and a smile, he stepped back. But when he turned and strode for the door, they saw the tension return to his shoulders. It was clear the smile had only been to soothe her.

"You're in his mind, Master," Alanna murmured. "What do you think he will choose?"

Evan shook his head. "Some decisions can't be predicted, even if you're in a man's mind."

"Will you go to him?"

"No. But if he desires to come to me, I will be available. It's his decision, Alanna. I must honor him enough to give him the room to make it."

"Men put such store by honor." She shook her head, frustration obvious on her features. "Women value love. Does he know how you feel?"

Evan cocked a brow at her. "A fairly insolent question for a servant to ask."

She pressed her lips together. "It may help him make his decision, Master."

"He knows how I feel. It is how *he* feels that is the question."

∾

The exertion of the conversation sent Alanna back to sleep soon after that. At Evan's request, Debra left a trusted member of the estate staff at her bedside. He was only going as far as the gardens right outside her window, could even see her, but he wanted to know immediately if she experienced any distress. He wouldn't have left her at all except he needed some air himself, a chance to evaluate the events of the day, as well as how it might end. The past three weeks had depleted him and Niall both, on many levels, and some wretchedly insecure part of him wondered if he should have waited to tell Niall when he was more rested, more optimistic.

When he could manipulate the decision. He and Alanna both had that quality, the inability to lie to themselves. She'd been trained to evaluate herself ruthlessly to prohibit any mental dissembling. He'd learned from the need to survive. A vampire "runt"—Niall's pseudo-affectionate term—who lied to himself didn't last long.

As he stood out there, studying the flowers, the dark sky and pattern of stars across it, he kept his mind intentionally blank, letting it fuel from the silence, the realization there was nothing to do now but wait and see how things unfolded.

Tracking the movement of a moth, he centered his mind, watching everything slow down. He followed the insect's passage across a solar light, the way a petal quivered as she landed on it, then took off again. Closing his eyes, he saw Alanna at the cabin. Then at the art colony... then in Stephen's hands.

Niall had leaped into that fight like an enraged grizzly. He'd be a formidable vampire in truth. However, should he decide in favor of that, Evan didn't intend the Scot to feel bound to his side. No matter the Council's preference, he would be as free as any vampire, able to choose Evan's company or not.

He should have told him that. It might have swayed his decision. Perhaps if he... *No.* Niall would come to Evan before he made his final decision, ask some more questions, because that was the type of man he was. Right now, Evan owed him space.

"I was angry at you, when you asked Daegan if he could take her life."

Opening his eyes, Evan saw the Scot sitting on one of the garden benches, knees splayed, large hands loosely linked between them as he leaned forward. Evan wondered how long he'd been there. He could have walked up and staked him. Perhaps Niall was right about his need to be more alert.

"Aye, ye do. You're not closing your mind to me right now."

"No, I'm not. I did know you were angry about Daegan."

Niall inclined his head. "I understood it, though. If she'd had enough of a mind to know we were caring for her, year after year, being a burden—no matter that she couldnae ever be a burden to us—that would have been the worst kind of Hell for the lass."

Evan nodded, but Niall wasn't yet done. "You had to make that call, because you knew I couldnae do it. While I might enjoy warming her arse, the idea of truly harming her..."

"You're a gentle man, for all your ferocity, Niall. I know that."

"Am I too gentle to be a vampire?"

Despite the intensity of feeling that held him so very still, only a few yards from the man he cared for more than any other man he'd ever met, Evan smiled. "You know the answer to that as well as I. Your kind of gentleness fortunately does not lie in that direction."

"No. I guess not. I've helped you with your annual kill for three hundred years," Niall said thoughtfully. "I resolved it for myself, the way a hunter does. The purpose is to eat, to survive, so ye respect the sacrifice. You think about the life taken. Doesnae matter if 'tis a deer enjoying the warmth of a meadow sun, or a bloke thinking about meeting the lass of his dreams when he goes off to a club. When you keep company with vampires, life becomes both more sacred and more temporal. No." Niall corrected himself. "When keeping company with a vampire like you."

The bed of moonflowers was between them. Evan noticed a pair of squirrel statuary hidden in their foliage. "What are you thinking, Niall?"

"That day at the stream. Do you think of it?"

"Often." Evan met his gaze. "I wanted you then and there. Especially when you got hard as a tree branch, despite that fucking freezing water."

Niall grunted. His gaze fell on the squirrels.

Damn it. The things that needed to be said might as well be popping up on cue card signs, held up by the lawn ornamentation. Glancing across the garden to the infirmary window, Evan saw the staff woman reading by Alanna's bed, the girl still sleeping peacefully. He wished he'd already marked her, so he could let her hear this. Women took particular joy in being right, and their deceptively compliant InhServ was no exception.

"It's not in our nature to feel regret, particularly in our dealings with humans. But I do feel that, toward how you came into my service."

Niall lifted his head. "I was wondering about that. What ye said, about manipulating me. Didnae ken how to bring it up, though."

"It wasn't your responsibility to bring it up." Sighing, Evan spread out his hands in an empty gesture. "You watched Ceana sicken, knowing the disease would never touch you because of the mark I gave you. You watched her die, watched your daughter die, knowing whether it had happened then or forty years later, you wouldn't be able to follow them for centuries. You were denied the hope of being reunited with them in a mortal life span. There's a comfort to that aspect of mortality that those of us who are immortal will never comprehend."

Evan shifted. "And while you were going through that, all I knew was that I wanted you as my servant. I thought myself so magnanimous; waiting for your family to not need you anymore, but in reality I was as much a bastard as the clansman who used your love of your family to put you in that battle that nearly took your life. He knew how easy it was to manipulate your fate, because you had no power against him."

Niall's brow creased, his mouth tight. Though Evan could plumb his mind if he chose, he didn't now. He wanted it to be clear he spoke to Niall as an equal. It might not hold beyond this moment, but he owed the man that regard.

"I was once human, but it was so long ago, and things change when you become a vampire. You forget those inclinations, the emotions. So I can't say I understand your feelings enough, even now, to claim empathy, or even a great deal of sympathy, because I've never stopped wanting you. I might be sorry for what it did to you, but I'm not honorable enough to regret it."

Those handsome lips, the ones he'd tasted countless times, twisted in a wry expression. He'd felt their demand, felt them on his cock and other parts of his body, but now they held power over him with their simple silence.

Evan rose, paced over to a stand of dogwoods. A birdbath hung on a chain from it, and someone had put a silver quarter in it, like a wishing fountain. He wondered what had inspired the attempt to use it that way, but it underscored the point. Vampires could have wishes as much as humans. And just like humans, they often found wishes didn't come true.

"You've always held a part of your heart away from me. I have your regard, affection, your lust . . . but I don't have your love, because I've never earned it. I have your mind and soul, but I don't have your heart. Just like you told Alanna."

Saying it aloud was more difficult than he'd expected. For women, speaking painful truths aloud might be a purging, but for a male it was like engraving it in stone, making it an immutable truth. It made him realize how much he'd truly wanted that from Niall, but he couldn't blame the man for not offering it. It was his own fault.

Niall rose, coming over to the birdbath. As he trailed his fingers over the glistening quarter, he made the shallow water ripple. They'd known each other for so long. From the look in his eyes, Evan knew he was turning things over in his mind, slow and steady. To give him that time, he backed off a few steps, taking Niall's bench, feeling the boards warmed by the Scot's fine backside, those powerful thighs.

"You made me want ye when I wanted to hate ye," Niall said at last. "When I did hate you. Yet ye took me so many places. Before Ceana died, she said 'Once our bairns are grown, go with Evan. Have the life you've always wanted.' She knew, no matter how I tried to deny it. So I've never thanked ye for it. You never asked for my thanks"—a grim smile touched his lips—"only my service, and the pleasure my body could offer ye, but still. You gave me quite a life. And now, here at the end of it, like the blooming of a first flower in spring, ye gave me her."

Lifting his head then, he turned and met Evan's gaze. "So you're right. Ye didnae have my love, not that way. Not 'til her. Ye would have gone after Stephen, no matter who she was, as a matter of honor. But that's nae how ye fought him. I felt your rage. Saw the way you held her afterward, the way you looked at both of us. It was like a key in a lock. So rusty I thought it wouldnae turn, but it did, and I found it wasn't a matter of you not having my love. Ye always had it, and the seed for it was planted that first day, just as Alanna suspected. I held it locked inside myself, afraid to give it to you. Then I thought maybe you didnae want it. Ye always seemed more interested in my soul and mind. But I watched you with her, and that's when I saw your heart."

"Alanna told me that men value honor," Evan said, his mouth absurdly dry. "And that women value love."

"I've often thought ye think more like a woman." Niall's gaze gleamed, but then he sobered. "I knew how humans love, understood it from that perspective. But through her, through how she served ye, how she viewed herself, I could finally ken how a vampire loves, what it looks like. How you love. Fierce, deep and quiet, like a predator. That key . . . everything else opened up, a book flipping backward through all the pages we've written, and I put it together."

He dropped to his heels then, comfortable in the pose as he braced his elbows on his knees and templed his fingers. "That night on the battlefield. You drove the looters off of me, took me to safety. Through the pain of the marking, because ye had to do it all at once, you kept gripping my hand. I broke several of your bones, but you never let go. When I had fever after, ye brushed the hair from my forehead, gentle as Ceana might have done."

"Niall . . ."

"I'm going to finish it, so best not try and stop me."

Evan pressed his lips together. "Already acting like a vampire."

"No. Just myself. I expect you'll take your pound of flesh for it, but that's something I've learned to anticipate."

"You keep on that road, I won't let you finish."

"Aye, ye will. Because I need to say it." Niall held his gaze. "Over the years, you've had your pleasure of me, taken my pain as part of it." His lip curled. "That's your way. I've seen you . . . watch me, study me, as if ye were trying to figure something out. I finally understand, Evan. I had to step out of what I am and into what you are, but then it all made sense."

Rising, he came to Evan, dropped to one knee in front of the bench where he sat. Though his palms burned with the desire to take, to touch, Evan forced himself to remain still, curious as to where his servant was going with it. Reaching out, Niall touched his face, startling him with the gentle possessiveness and authority in the touch.

"It's not about wanting someone to love you the way you love them. It's about knowing in your soul when they're loving ye with all their ability to love and more, pushing themselves further than they thought they could go, whatever shape or form that is, and realizing what a gift that is. Though it's a guid long life, it's never long enough for any of us to refuse love when offered. Sic as ye gie, sic wull ye get."

You'll get out of life as much as you put in. Evan was at a loss for words, such that those brown eyes were suddenly dancing, the hard mouth easing. "Not much ye can say, is it? I'm still your servant. If ye tell me you'd be happy to die for me, all that means is you'd be happy to murder me."

"Ass." Evan shoved at his shoulder. Niall fended him off, though he caught Evan's forearm and held on to it, large fingers curling into Evan's flesh. They stayed that way a moment, Evan staring at the point of contact, feeling every inch of pressure tingling through his nerves. Niall hadn't put on a shirt, so his hand was on that first dragon, fingertips on the third mark. The *chai* symbol, the sign of life.

"Set me as a seal upon thy heart . . . for love is as strong as death; jealousy is as cruel as the grave: the coals of it are coals of fire, which hath a most vehement flame."

He lifted his gaze to Niall's face, and the power of the man's glance burned like that flame. "King Solomon."

"I ken my Bible," Niall said, a mild reproof.

"Yes. I've loved you, no matter all of it," Evan said quietly. "Uthe wanted to know if immortality could steal inspiration. It didn't. But to lose both of you, to lose the stubborn, rockheaded Scot who's been my constant companion, my friend, my servant, for three hundred years, and to lose the woman who brought the wall down between us, at the same time? My art wouldn't survive that, Niall. I'm not supposed to influence your decision, but I will tell you the truth. Your loss will do what nothing else can. It will take away my desire to live."

Niall swallowed hard, his hand coming up to clasp Evan's wrist. "I gave ye a hard time about forcing Alanna outside her comfort zone. Making her become more than she was, despite the short time she had left. I was wrong about that. But it did make me wonder. I know why you're with me now. But why, all those years ago, did you follow me? Care for my family? Give me the time with them?"

"Lord Uthe told me I see things others can't see, and I try to put it in a language the rest understand better." Evan shrugged. "I'm not sure about that, but there are things I see, feel, in your soul. I can't articulate them, but I follow them, the same way I follow the muse, not really understanding, but hoping, thinking, believing, that if I follow a certain path, things will unfold as they should."

"And you determine what that 'should' is?"

"No." Evan shook his head. "Not like you're thinking. I don't even know the outcome. I just know that way lies the masterpiece. If I'm wrong, then it's a discarded film or canvas. Or the loss of a lost soul. But it's better to fight for a lost soul than to leave it lost. That's one thing I'm sure of."

Hesitating almost like Niall had, that first time he'd touched Alanna after she woke, Evan at last curved his fingers into Niall's hair, needing to stroke, to touch, to hold. Niall tilted his head enough to show he welcomed the caress, and Evan knew he wouldn't restrain himself much longer. If Niall had given him the answer he thought he had, he wanted his mouth on his.

Like Alanna had done to him, Niall slid his grip to Evan's hand, brought it to his mouth, pressing his lips hard against his knuckles.

"Niall . . ." He was going to lose control, crush the fragrant flower beds with the weight of Niall's body, his own on top of it. Lyssa might have given him the two things he most wanted, but she'd end up eviscerating him over her mangled pansies.

The Scot lifted his head. "Outside of the times when we were with other vampires, and it was required, I never called you Master. I guess you understood that."

Yes. He'd never demanded from Niall what came so naturally to Alanna's lips, and soon it wouldn't apply. Not that it had ever been an easy fit.

"You encouraged her to see us both as her Master. You've been planning this awhile."

"Well, not her part of it, but I wrote the first letter to Uthe about turning you six months ago, when I noticed you sleeping more." Evan ran his knuckles along Niall's jaw, paused there, just holding that touch, pressing against his jaw with the sudden surge of feeling.

Niall put his hand over his. "Evan."

Evan shook his head. "Let me get this part out. If you choose to become vampire, your will is your own. You're free to be with me or leave, as you desire. You served the oath I imposed, but I will never impose another on you."

"Like you could. Skinny Jewish kid."

Evan smiled, but there was a pain in his heart. "You owe me an answer."

Niall nodded. "What's that name you call me?" he asked.

"*Neshama.*"

"Aye. *Neshama.* Your soul. Well, your soul never leaves ye, does it? It is what ye are." Niall's jaw tightened. "I've picked up a bit of Hebrew myself over the years. *Moreh* . . . teacher. Or *adon* . . . Master."

Niall beat him to it. Before Evan could initiate anything, he was tasting his Master's mouth, demanding, delving in, giving him everything he wanted for this moment . . . almost.

Digging his fingers into the Scot's long, thick hair, Evan gave as good as he got, but at a certain point, he let Niall take the lead, because he was savoring the feel of it, Niall *wanting* him. When the man lifted his head, his mouth was cut where his passion had brought Evan's fangs into it. Evan licked off the blood, sucking on the lip enough to cause a rumble in Niall's throat.

"*Adon* technically means 'lord'." He spoke against Niall's mouth. "I'm not one of those."

"Depends on who ye ask." Niall closed his hand on Evan's wrist, and the two men held there, Evan tilting his head so they were eye to eye. "I'm here, Evan. My body, my soul . . . and my heart. They're yours. I give them to you freely, and ye'll never have to ask for them again."

Evan swallowed twice, vowing he'd knock himself unconscious before allowing tears to fill his eyes. Niall's tawny gaze narrowed, his fingers brushing Evan's face. "I didnae . . . I didnae think it mattered to you. Not that much."

"Very few things matter more," Evan said tightly.

"Aye." Niall let his fingers slide down Evan's sternum, dipping into the open collar of his shirt and slipping several buttons to caress his bare flesh. "I'm hard and ready here . . . Master. I want ye. All of ye. And I want to take."

His gaze was suddenly fierce and burning, his meaning clear. Evan felt his testicles draw up at the thought of it. So many years, and it was something he'd never offered his servant. Despite Niall calling him Master, it didn't feel like he was asking. Instead it was somewhere between harsh begging and adamant demand, Niall's constant ability to straddle the line between servant and something entirely not-servant.

Evan dipped his head, barely a shift of motion. Niall slipped the other buttons, pushed the shirt off Evan's shoulders, but left it there as he traced the pale lines of Evan's collarbone, down his chest, over a nipple. Evan's fangs unsheathed, his bloodlust rising as his instincts perceived the challenge, the emotional intensity of it. Niall leaned in, putting his mouth to Evan's throat. As he did, Evan banded an arm around his shoulders, holding him fast. He let out a growl of his own as Niall bit down hard enough to draw blood, to taste him.

He stroked over Evan's ribs, down to his waistband, working at the belt, sliding it through, opening the slacks. Male impatience took over, such that when his grip closed over him, Evan caught his hair, pulling his head to the side so he could sink his fangs into that delectable throat, drink deep. His servant. His lover. His friend.

He wanted Niall as well, wanted him with that fierceness the Scot understood now, with his heart just as open. Rising, he drew them both up, and when Evan retracted his fangs, licking the blood off his lips, Niall tugged him over to a patch of soft grass. He worked his way around Evan, tasting his throat, trailing his mouth over his shoulders, his hands sliding into the loose waistband of the slacks to caress his hips. As he pulled Evan back against his broad chest with an arm banded around his chest, he reached into the slacks and underwear to scrape his upper thigh with his nails, close to Evan's rising cock.

"Fuck, Niall." Restraining his natural desire to dominate gave the moment an edge sharp as a knife blade, but Evan held back. He wanted to experience his servant unleashing a passion he'd kept pent up for far too long.

Niall took them both down to their knees, pressing himself up behind Evan, then shifted away to nip down his spine, tracing it with his tongue as he tugged the slacks off Evan's hips. He didn't waste time, immediately cupping Evan's ass in rough squeezing hands, thumbs teasing the seam. When he pushed Evan forward, wanting him on his hands, Evan might have resisted, except Niall's heated, moist mouth was suddenly on his rim, licking and working into him, an indescribable sensation that sent his cock jacking up hard against his belly.

Evan dug his fingers into the grass. He'd turn the tables eventually, roll the Scot over and thrust into him hard, savoring that muscular ass that could squeeze down on his cock in an excruciating, perfect way.

"Ah . . ." Niall's tongue was devil-inspired. Then Evan detected the scent of lubricant, knew his servant was working it over his thick cock. He pushed up and turned, capturing Niall's wrist. When he took over the task, he watched the Scot's breath shorten, his eyes get more dangerous and determined with every pumping, slick stroke. Evan could make him come in his hand, and Niall knew it. He could turn it into a wrestling match, but of course Evan would win. So the Scot went for a more devastating tactic.

"Master . . ." He breathed it, his face harsh, intent. "I want to fuck you. I need to fuck you."

Evan caressed Niall's bare chest, fingers slipping over the dragon, the *chai* mark. His servant had spent centuries embracing a life he wasn't sure he deserved, or should want as much as he did, but in the end they'd come to this, to celebrate what they'd been given. It filled his heart, such that he knew he'd give Niall what he desired.

With a feral smile, Niall took Evan's wrist, began to twist it slowly, an armlock that would turn his body around, ending up with that arm up against his back as Niall pressed him to the ground. Evan allowed it, the slow motion an excruciating buildup as Niall at last let him go, pushing Evan down beneath him so he could brace his arms on either side of Evan's waist, tease his spine once again with his heated mouth.

"Have ye ever done this, *moreh*?"

Evan shook his head. "You will be the first, *neshama*."

He could give him that as well, but his servant gave him back something even better, words that sent heat jamming straight into Evan's balls.

"I'll be the only."

Niall slid an arm around his chest, fingers stroking Evan's nipple, his sensitive flesh, as he pushed against that virgin opening. Evan pushed back, not insensible to how it was done, and felt the stretch of his servant's substantial cock. He didn't fear pain, especially not in the face of the emotional pleasure it was to take him inside, but he let out a groan as Niall broke through those two sets of muscles, coming to rest deep inside of him, filling something Evan hadn't even realized had been an empty part of his soul.

Balance. Niall drew back, slid in deep again, and Evan let out another low grunt of deep need. Niall's lips were on the back of his neck. "All right, Master? I dinnae want to hurt ye. Not that way."

His protective Scot. It made his cock harder, his body crave Niall's possession even more. "It's a good pain, *neshama*. Don't stop. Take what you desire. I want to feel your demand."

Some orders Niall would never have difficulty following. The Scot responded instantly, withdrawing to thrust in again, harder. Evan pushed back against him, encouraging, that moment of impact a starburst of pleasure inside. "Blessed Christ," Niall muttered, and did it again. "You . . . feel . . . so . . . fucking . . . guid."

His fingers dug into Evan's hip, the other pressed against his heart. Evan worked himself back against him, his cock leaking pre-cum into the grass, then Niall's hand shifted to it. He was greedy, his servant. He wanted it all, wanted them to come together. He worked Evan with three centuries of knowledge of his body, even as his body instinctively kept hammering, seeking its own pleasures.

"Fuck . . . yes." Evan gasped it out, fingers digging into the ground. "Niall . . . come for me."

"You . . . too. Now."

They managed it together, bodies bucking together in the moonlight, Niall holding on tight, never flagging in his stroke of Evan's cock, no matter that his own pleasure came crashing down on him. As they both released with primal groans, Niall's face was pressed into Evan's shoulder blades, his teeth sinking into flesh.

They took their time working down to a slow, even rhythm again, both panting. Niall stayed within him, and Evan allowed it, only pressuring them gently so they were on their sides on the soft ground. Niall pressed up inside him, his hand still massaging Evan's cock. He could do this all night with him.

"If only the lass were here with us," Niall rumbled. "Think of what we could do with her. She could have her mouth on ye right now, her wee nipples so tight and cunt so wet, wanting the both of us. How long would we keep her waiting?"

"Until she begs, of course." Evan pushed into his hand. "Harder, *neshama*. I want to feel that grip."

As he obliged, Evan felt the blood coursing back into the organ, readying itself. He'd take his ass hard and rough, giving them both pleasure . . . again. Like Niall, though, he felt her absence.

"If I was in her mind, I could let her feel this. See it."

"She'd want us to do it right in front o' her hospital bed. She'd spread her legs and stroke herself, driving us mad. You've created a monster, Evan." But Niall's lazy tone was amused. "Ye get much harder, I'm going to feel like I'm taking a pile driver."

"Your pain, my pleasure, *neshama*. The vampire way."

Niall grunted. "Guid thing we'll both be vampires. No indulging that female nonsense, telling her we love her all the time. Otherwise, she'll think she can make me do anything she wants."

"She already knows she can do that. Her soft bear."

Evan laughed as Niall shifted his grip to a headlock, putting pressure on his throat. Turning the tables, he slipped the hold and pinned the Scot on his back, putting his whole body down against Niall's, his mouth on his.

He'd better savor it. His dominant strength wouldn't last forever. Niall's power would surpass his eventually. Things might change.

But Evan wasn't a vampire who feared change. Change was what unfolded new, more amazing landscapes for him to capture, whether those landscapes were a mountain range, or a man's soul.

25

THE glen was a fairy world, the tree branches and leaf tips touched with a silver gleam, the deep creek emitting the occasional diamond flash when the moon caught sight of it through the canopy. They'd made camp there, knowing they couldn't stay all night, because Evan would need a more sheltered place in daylight, but they had an isolated cottage with a root cellar they could reach in an hour. Which was good, because by then, Niall would need that cellar as well.

The landscape had changed considerably from three hundred years ago, but it was still a beautiful glen, an out-of-the-way spot. Alanna stood at the edge of the water, letting it lap at her bare toes, breathing in the air. She had her arms wrapped around herself, a relaxed embrace that allowed her to lay her hand discreetly over the third mark she now bore in place of Stephen's over her hip bone. The hated dagger had vanished when the link was broken, and, increasing her joy, Evan's third mark had seated itself in the same spot.

She hadn't been quite sure of its significance, a mark shaped like a tree, the branches almost elegant in the way they spread across her skin, the longest branch touching the curve of her breast. Lord Brian said he'd never seen one so elaborate. So artistic.

Evan had taken a look at it and smiled, his eyes warming on her. "It's a tree of life, Alanna. Very fitting for your having a Jewish Master."

Would Niall miss his third mark when it was gone? Would it be gone?

He's nervous, Alanna.

She came back to the present at Evan's voice in her head. Turning, she studied Niall. He was sitting on a nearby rock, his eyes closed. Evan was on the opposite bank, sketching, waiting patiently, or perhaps not so patiently, but covering it well. Nodding to acknowledge Evan's comment, she moved toward the Scot. Coming up on the rock, she knelt behind him, sliding her arms over his chest. Since Evan had marked her fully again, her hair had begun to grow rapidly, so she now had a fine layer of down that Niall likened to a newborn bird's. He reached back, rumpled it now.

"I've seen a human go through the process of becoming a vampire," she said.

"Aye? Did he drool and try to drain anything with blood that came near him? No dog or wean safe?"

"No." She pressed a smile against his neck. "When the sire is with the fledgling, the bloodlust is managed with daily doses of the sire's blood. He does have to stay pretty close to the sire through the transition period, because fluctuations of temper or other factors can make him dangerous, but we have that all planned out, remember? Lord Daegan told us about that place in Ireland, the abandoned monastery with the catacombs. He owns the property, so we can be there for a while. Evan can draw all sorts of dusty bones and pale skulls."

"Aye."

She slid under his arm, into his lap. "I'm glad you decided to do it here. To come back to Scotland after all this time. Maybe sometime we can come back for a longer visit."

"Maybe." He lifted a shoulder." 'Tis enough to come here for this. The air is still filled with memories, *muirnín*. The voices get too loud at times."

She nodded, understanding. "Are you ready? Master will wait as long as you need, but it's been hard on him these few weeks, afraid of what might happen."

"I wanted ye strong again, *muirnín*, so you could travel, be with us. We both wanted that. 'Tis not right, otherwise."

"You're both too stubborn," she chided gently. "Is it still what you want to do?"

"I'm not sure anyone's ever ready for something like this. Like going into battle. You just charge and hope for the best." He looked down at her then, and she was relieved to see it in his eyes. "Yes, *muirnín*. My wame's just got that feeling . . . when ye step across a line and ken there'll be no backing up."

"Do you want me to leave you alone, give you more time to think about it?"

"No. I like ye fine right here."

You're not a young man, Niall. Think about it much longer and Fate will take you right on that rock.

Alanna giggled as Niall gave her a mock frown. "Nag, nag, nag. He's like an old woman nippin' over there. He's just crabbit because we're holding up his schedule in Nairobi."

"Well, as valuable as you are to me, the scenery in the Ngong changes a great deal in the dry season. I'm not sure you're worth missing that."

Evan rose, setting aside his sketchpad. Leaping easily to the other side of the creek that bifurcated the glen, he came to stand before the two of them.

"I'll see you through, Niall. I promise."

The Scot rose, clasping his forearm so that they were toe to toe. "I trust you, Evan. In all things."

A muscle flexed in the vampire's jaw, his emotional reaction to that schooled to a quick nod, but Alanna caught it. She loved watching it, the small, subtle nuances of male communication that had become far more intimate and easy between them since the decision had been made. "What may I do, Master . . . s?" She drew out the *s* deliberately, inciting amusement in them both.

"He'll need human blood immediately, Alanna. As a third mark, you can handle the first attack of blood hunger, but it can be savage. Your strength has returned, but offer your wrist, instead of your throat."

"My thigh would be better, Master. It's a better distraction, changing his hunger to something else."

Niall raised a brow. "Ye said ye watched it. That sounds like ye participated."

"Stephen turned at least two sanctioned humans during my time in his household. I helped feed both of them. Blood and sexual hunger are close during the transition. One helps to balance the other."

"Maybe the lass should take the lead," Niall said, deadpan. "Given she's the most experienced of the three of us in this."

"Nonsense," Evan said. "Alanna has the 'Turning a Vampire for Dummies' manual on standby for me."

He ducked Niall's punch with a grin, but caught the man by the nape, held him still. "All right, then," he said. "Let's do this."

At Niall's quick nod, he turned, and the Scot followed, the two of them going to the large flat rock along the bank where Evan had taken him to the ground all those years ago. As Alanna watched, Evan sat against the rock, then gestured to Niall, directing him to lie back between his thighs, his head resting on Evan's shoulder, long legs stretched out before him.

Yes, Niall *was* ready for this, but he was tense about it as well. She sank to her knees on Niall's other side, her hand closing over his.

"Look at her, Niall," Evan said. "Imagine what it will be like, her being yours for nearly three centuries."

"And you," the Scot said, putting his other large hand on Evan's knee. "You're both mine."

"Spoken like a true vampire." Evan met Alanna's gaze. *I expect he will handle himself well,* yekirati, *but animal instinct may take over. Remember, follow my lead.*

Always, Master.

Lowering his head, he placed his lips on Niall's throat, nuzzled. When he bit, it was gentle, not yet a full penetration. He made it an erotic tease, his hand wandering into the collar of Niall's shirt, stroking his chest as Alanna unbuttoned the garment, both men shifting so it fell off his shoulders, crumpled between his body and Evan's. Niall's hand briefly covered Evan's, caressing his fingers as Evan pressed against the *chai* mark. Then Niall lifted his knuckles to Alanna's face, stroking. "I love you, *muirnín.*"

Her breath caught as Evan lifted his brilliant gaze to her, held it in a lock as he bit down fully. Niall stiffened, then made a conscious effort to relax, though his hand remained tight on hers as Evan began to drink.

With a non-servant human, a vampire would pierce the major

artery, let it gush until the blood loss was mortal, but it was different with a servant. Lady Lyssa herself had instructed Evan on it, indicating that several quarts were sufficient. It left the third mark's body in a receptive condition for the silver serum necessary for the turning. Once that was flowing through Niall's veins, the transition would be completed by drinking a certain amount of the sire's blood.

The alarm Evan had anticipated started to kick in as the vampire took more and more. Niall's breath came faster, heart beating like a frantic bird's. His hand constricted on hers painfully. She bore it, putting her other hand on his brow as Evan spoke in both their minds, soothing the man.

Easy, neshama. *Everything's fine and as it should be. Don't fight me. You said you trust me. For once in your life, let surrender be part of that trust. Give your life to me.*

I did. I do. As Niall gripped Evan's thigh, holding on, Alanna felt the surge of emotion from her vampire master. The declaration was the male equivalent of what Niall had just told her. *I love you.*

For the vampire's side of things, it was a lot to drink at once, but like the old wives' lore about consuming the placenta of an afterbirth, there was an ancient wisdom that said ingesting all of a human's blood in a turning would increase the bond between sire and fledgling. She knew Evan would embrace that. As he continued to swallow, she inched closer until her knees were pressed against Niall's hip, both her hands on them, one on Niall's chest over Evan's, the other on Niall's opposite shoulder. His arm came up around her, fingers digging into her back, a sudden convulsion.

The serum has gone in. In a moment, you'll start to feel very different . . .

She knew the moment that Niall could smell her blood as a vampire could, for his eyes opened, and she saw the reddish tint.

"Almost, *neshama.* Almost." Evan's arm was now fully over his chest, holding him firmly. *Move back for a moment, Alanna. You're too close.*

Of course. She knew that. She had to give Evan time to complete the final step. A fledgling that drank of human blood before the process was complete would get sick on whatever they gorged themselves on. She was embarrassed she'd forgotten, so intent on being near.

There's no shame in forgetting yourself because of your love for him, Alanna.

Then Niall tried to surge up toward her, and Evan had no time to spare for reassuring thoughts. The vampire shifted their positions, tackling him, bearing him back down to the ground. As he straddled the male, keeping him pinned, she sensed the strain in it. Evan was trying to hold the big Scot down and make one of his own veins available to him. Sliding around them quickly, she pulled out her small knife, caught Evan's sleeve and pulled it back, cutting the vein in his wrist.

Niall's head whipped toward her hands of course, a growl in his throat, but the gush of Evan's blood drew his eye. Evan got it to his mouth, and Niall drank, holding on to his wrist with both large hands. Evan stroked the side of his head. "There you go, *neshama*. Final step." *Get ready, Alanna.*

She was. She waited until she knew Niall had swallowed enough, and then lay back on the ground behind them. She drew up her skirt, slid the panties down and off, getting them out of the way. Taking up the knife once more, she found the femoral, poised over it and waited. *Now.*

She made the quick puncture as Evan deftly levered Niall up, directing his energy and hunger immediately to where she lay. Niall, his mind nothing more than blood hunger at the moment, was a fearsome sight, lunging toward her, but Evan caught him by the chest. Despite the difference in height and weight, Evan did have the strength, barely, to hold Niall from coming down on her too roughly. Because of his advantage as a third-mark servant, Niall was likely to have at least a hundred years' worth of strength and speed out of the starting gate, but she saw no worries in Evan about that. For her own part, she expected she'd have the pleasure of seeing some intriguing wrestling matches between her two Masters.

Evan shoved Niall to his knees between her spread ones. "Here, Master," she purred, sliding her fingers over her labia, teasing herself to wetness so the two aromas came together. "Everything you see is yours."

The Scot's hands clamped down on her legs, and she let out an anxious, yet exhilarated breath as he shoved her wider, put his mouth on her thigh. He bit into it, despite the cut already there, and she made a little cry at the size of his new fangs, thick and sharp.

Easy, neshama. *She's your servant. Do not harm her. Let her serve you.*

Niall's fingers flexed as he took the blood in large gulps. It would be a hefty amount, sure to make her light-headed, but she felt no fear. She gazed up at the night sky through the trees, heard the lap of the water and thought of how her two Masters had met here, so many centuries ago. She served them, and they cared for her. The moment was everything she could want.

Sliding her other hand down, she touched her pussy again, stroked it, arousing herself further. Even without being marked by him, she knew just when it started to penetrate Niall's senses, the scent of her honey competing with the blood. She slid a finger inside herself, and then made a little noise of surprise and pleasure as Niall shifted, putting his mouth over her knuckles, her wet folds, his tongue sliding in to join her finger, stroking it and her cunt at the same time, likely bringing the flavor of her blood to mingle with her arousal.

Use your coagulants, Niall. Glands under your tongue. You need to stop her bleeding before you turn yourself to other pleasures.

Evan had to repeat it twice, but then Niall shifted, doing just that. When he came back to her cunt, he caught her wrist, drew her fingers from herself, licked them clean. Rising on his knees above her, the sight of him, aroused, powerful, fangs revealed, made her stop breathing. He would be a formidable vampire for certain, as much a bear among smaller predators as he was as a human male.

Do not build him up too much, yekirati. *As his sire, I still have to keep some type of leash on him.*

Evan's mind-voice was amused, however, and she couldn't help smiling. Niall guided her hand to the ground over her head. Obeying, she stretched both arms out there, surrendering herself to them utterly. Evan stood behind Niall, who was on his knees, and now the vampire pulled the Scot's shirt all the way off his arms. When Evan knelt behind him, he slid his arm across Niall's chest to hold and stroke. The chest hair was still there, but she knew by the following dawn it would be gone. She'd miss it, so she'd enjoy it now, once more. As Niall bent to taste her, Evan slid his hands to his hips and then lower, reaching beneath the kilt. She knew he'd gripped Niall's cock when she saw him working it against the fabric in front.

He's as big as I've ever felt him, Alanna. He's going to give you a rough ride.

Oh, she hoped so. When Niall moved up her body, her hips were already arching up, wanting to take him. Niall impatiently tore off the kilt, Evan helping, and then he sheathed himself in her, slamming home hard enough to tear her, but she would heal.

Want to mark her now.

She heard it in Evan's mind, as well as Evan's response.

Soon, neshama. *But not now. There's control you need to learn, to protect her mind, her soul. So you don't delve too deeply.*

But she knew how to be an empty vessel so well. She'd survived Stephen's assault on her soul. Surely she could handle the passionate demand and love of her new vampire Master. She feared nothing from these two particular Masters. They could never delve too deeply, because her soul was all theirs.

Though she wouldn't argue with Evan, she wanted it, too, wanted what Niall wanted. But her pleading eyes must have told him her desires, for Evan muttered a resigned curse.

Go easy. There needs to be a significant pause between each mark. If you can't exercise that control, now isn't the time.

Alanna arched her throat for the first bite, the geographical locator. Her body shuddered, clasping hard around Niall, overwhelmed by what, to a servant, was the most erotic act of all, the act by which a vampire bound her to him forever. It had been like that when Evan had given her the three marks, out in the gardens of the Savannah estate. Niall had held her against his body, the two of them taking her right afterward as Evan opened his mind and let all three sets of emotions intertwine. She knew it would be the same way now, even better, for now she truly would serve them both, in all ways.

The locator mark swirled through her blood, bringing no pain. On the contrary; it was as if each mark either man gave her enriched her blood, energized it, making it the best source of nourishment for her Masters.

In return, they offered her a flood of pleasure. Niall was thrusting, spending his time between marks in the most desirable way she could imagine. The tawny eyes had turned red of course, but she saw he was conscious of her amid the bloodlust, his attention on her aroused face, her every moan. Evan sat back on his heels, watching them, monitoring, but she could tell he was aroused, hungry, and she wanted him with them.

"Niall," she gasped it. "Turn. Let me . . . so Evan can be with us. Please."

With a growl, he rolled to his back, bringing her on top as he continued to thrust hard into her. Evan gripped her hips, then pulled the skirt over her head, divesting her of the rest of her clothes. The other advantage to being a third mark—between that and the sexual heat the three of them were generating, the chill Scottish night had no claim on her flesh. Unlike her Masters.

Evan shed his own clothes, then knelt behind her. He cupped her jaw, bringing her head back to meet his demanding kiss as Niall's fangs found her throat again, tongue swirling over her flesh as he released the second mark. Paradise became the promise of Heaven.

You're ours, lass.

Joy speared through her, hearing Niall speak directly in her mind for the first time. And he couldn't have chosen more appropriate first words. She would cherish the memory of it as long as life was given to her.

Ours forever.

And of course, Evan would add to it, making it perfect, a closed circle. They not only gave her the words, they branded them on her heart and soul, like another kind of third mark.

Yes. She swept her glance over them both, then laid her head on Evan's shoulder, looking up at him. *"Ani le odi ve dodi li . . . "*

Evan's eyes became unexpectedly moist as he translated for her, the words a Jewish bride might offer her groom. "I am my beloved's . . . "

"And my beloved is mine," she finished in English. She put the challenge in her voice, and both her males responded to it, with lust and pleasure flickering dangerously in their eyes. "But I like the other way of saying it, too. 'I am for my beloved—for both of my beloveds' . . . "

"Precious *metuka*," Evan murmured, bringing his mouth down on hers once more. Niall's hands closed over her hips, and he thrust upward, his cock impaling her deep, so she moaned against Evan's mouth. He growled approvingly against her lips, his grip dropping to her breasts, kneading the curves and teasing the nipples, making her writhe against his hold in a way that only increased Niall's strokes. When Evan released her mouth, she saw Niall's eyes had gone fully red, but she could see her bear in his rapturous gaze. He was caught up in it, the savagery and euphoria both. She knew how he felt.

Proving it, she gripped him hard with her internal muscles, rose and fell, asserting her own desires in a way she knew would provoke him further, particularly when she let her hands fall onto his chest and dug her nails into the dragon tattoo, his flesh.

Evan took over then, a hand to the back of her neck to press her down onto Niall's chest, adjusting her forward so he could slide a lubricated cock into her backside, both of them penetrating her as deep as they could reach, and their reach was considerable. She groaned with the effort of taking them both, and felt their male satisfaction crash over her. The hot wave of testosterone that rippled over her whole body was a precursor of the climax to come. But as intense as that was, nothing could match the next moment as Niall overlapped Evan's hand on the back of her neck and bit her throat once more.

It burned some, because he should have waited longer between marks, but she thought Evan's perhaps meliorated that effect. It was no worse than the heat of a brand, leaving a searing pleasure behind, the emotional impact of being fully claimed by her second Master. Alanna gasped, rocking in their grip as the serum coursed through her blood, intertwining with Evan's claim upon her, weaving a bond around her soul, holding her to them. She rejoiced in it.

She was overwhelmed emotionally, but they were also driving her past her physical limits now, taking her higher and higher. That primal need took over everything. Like an animal who knew by instinct what she most needed, she smelled the blood coursing through Niall's throat and didn't hold back, biting down hard to break the skin and finding the warm flow of his blood waiting, to make the marking complete.

Stephen's third mark had almost been like a girl's first sex—built up into so much in her mind, yet the actuality of it had been like getting off the roller coaster before the best part of the ride happened. A sense that there was much, much more, just beyond her grasp. Learning through Evan's third mark that there was a thrilling drop and rushing ascent into a state of pure euphoria didn't make her any less greedy for the same sensation with Niall.

She's an insatiable lass, Evan. 'Tis a guid thing there'll be two of us to tend to her.

Niall could follow her thoughts like Evan. The delight of it coursed through her as well. But as she swallowed the richness of his blood, she closed her eyes, felt the differences of the two males' marks, the same intriguing contrasts she'd noted in so many other things about them. Niall, the solid earth . . . Evan, the wind swirling through the pines . . . Her, the element that connected them both.

Evan pressed against her back, hands gripping her hips. Niall's hand slid over her buttock, gripped Evan's fingers. The Scot's strength steadied them all as Evan thrust, Niall pushed deeper, and she tightened on both of them, each trying to give as much as they were taking.

The climax rolled up like that roller coaster on a straight line to the sky. "Masters . . . "she gasped, and they gave her permission in one voice.

Come for us, Alanna.

As she catapulted over that edge, she dug her fingers into Niall's shoulders, pressed her body up into the curve of Evan's, reveled in the way Evan locked his arm around her waist, hand cupping her breast, Niall with his hand tangled in her hair, his other hand holding onto Evan, his strength pushing Evan and himself farther into her.

She screamed, shoved into another intense orgasm, as Evan bit back into her shoulder. The flow of marks swirled through her blood like a sacred text. She reveled in the press of both fangs, their heated mouths on her flesh, the scent of blood given and taken. When both men climaxed inside her at last, she cried out her pleasure to the night, showing them her desire, her yearning, to give and give and give.

A desire that would never end.

~

It took them all a long while to come down. When at last they were sprawled together on the soft earth, she couldn't imagine being more content. Evan sheltered her body, coiled around her back and hips, while she lay, exhausted, on Niall's chest. When her fingers slipped over the dragon tattoo, she felt a little pang of sadness. It was smooth, only the tattoo there now, the *chai* mark gone.

'Tis in my heart, lass. It will always be there.

"Will the tattoos go away?" she asked, clearing her throat. Evan's third mark had helped heal her vocal cords, but she was still getting accustomed to that "sultry rasp," as Niall called it.

"Not if I mark them with his own blood. But that's his decision," Evan said against her hair.

Niall reached over her, gripping Evan's thigh before his fingers slipped back to her. "Aye. I want to keep them. You have a new mark of your own, lass."

She raised her head to look down her body. In the shade of the tree of life, a new symbol had appeared. This one she knew, and the significance of it filled her, thickened her throat. She slipped her fingers over Niall's where he was caressing it.

"A triquetra. A Gaelic symbol for trinity," Evan said quietly. "Very fitting."

"Master . . . " She smiled, glad she didn't have to tell them which one she meant, though, since their minds were open to her at the moment, she saw the brief sorting as they figured out she was talking to Evan. He grunted in acknowledgment, giving her a light squeeze.

"I was thinking about what you said, that night in the gazebo, about your art." She looked up at the stars, comfortably held between the two men. "About doing something because something in you says that's how it must be done . . . a flow of pure energy."

She lifted her head, looked down at Niall. "I didn't know how to explain it to you, but you can see it, feel it, inside me now, can't you?"

The Scot held her gaze. She could see a lot shifting behind his tawny eyes. He was adjusting to the increased sharpness of his senses, the shape of his blood hunger, temporarily sated. It changed him dramatically, but in another way, it didn't change him at all. It was just another part of the same remarkable man.

In sifting through all those slides, she'd seen so many pictures of Niall, or ideas inspired by Evan's love for him. In a sense, each slide had given her a glimpse of both men, their many different facets, their interests and needs, intertwined so closely. Niall picked up on that thought. His mouth tightened, and she slid her fingers over his lips, caressing them. She closed her eyes as Evan laid a kiss on the back of her shoulder.

From the beginning, when I thought about serving a vampire, there was this feeling that, if I did it right, I would be lost in it. Like swimming in a sea I never wanted to leave, because I would be immersed in this one true, perfect thing. But the truth, and the perfection, is that nothing is one thing.

She turned her attention to Evan now, a tilt of her head that won her an additional brush of his lips over her temple.

"You showed me that. We're as many things as we desire to be. And I've never really seen myself that way. Or realized how much better a servant I could be if I embraced that."

"Ye have a whole lifetime ahead tae be all that ye desire, *a ghrá*," Niall murmured, stroking her hair back from her face.

"So do you," she whispered. "I like that. *A ghrá*. What does it mean?"

"Love," Evan said, his mouth continuing to tease her flesh. He'd pushed her hair over her shoulder, was laying more tender kisses along the exposed track, and Niall was wrapping his fingers in the loose tendrils, the two of them weaving an erotic spell around her anew.

She gave herself to it, to the pleasure of their hands wandering over her, their breath touching her skin, their love surrounding her. Before dawn, they'd head for the cottage. After that, on to Ireland and almost three hundred years of memories. She'd follow her vampires wherever they'd take her.

As a servant, she'd never wanted anything more than that.